PRAISE FOR LISEY'S STORY

'King is the greatest popular novelist of our day, comparable to Dickens – A consummate and compassionate novel – one of King's very best' – Toby Litt, *Guardian*

'Thrilling, genuinely terrifying, beautifully textured and full of wonderful invention' – *Daily Mail*

'A love story steeped in strength and tenderness, and cast with the most vivid, touching and believable characters in recent literature . . . a dazzling novel that you'll thank yourself for reading long after the final page is turned' – Nicholas Sparks

'It's being on this familiar territory that makes his fiction so addictive. It's so good you just want more . . . *Lisey's Story* is up there with his finest' – *Evening Standard*

PRAISE FOR LISEY'S STORY

'A psychological thriller of extraordinary sensitivity that takes the reader deep into the dark places in us all'
– Matt Thorne, *Independent on Sunday*

'Popular novelist Dickens is an apt comparison – both in stylistic terms and in terms of copia, popularity and place in culture *Lisey's Story* stands among the best things that this formidable writer has done'
– Sam Leith, *Saturday Telegraph*

'Stephen King makes bold, brilliant use of his satanic story-telling gift, his angelic ear for language, and above all his incomparable ability to find the epic in the ordinary'
– Michael Chabon

'Contains some of the most powerful and affecting passages that King has ever written' – Barry Forshaw, *Daily Express*

ABOUT THE AUTHOR

Stephen King was born in Portland, Maine, in 1947. He won a scholarship award to the University of Maine and later taught English, while his wife, Tabitha, got her degree.

It was the publication of his first novel *Carrie* and its subsequent adaptation that set him on his way to his present position as perhaps the bestselling author in the world.

Carrie was followed by a string of bestsellers including *'Salem's Lot*, *Misery*, *Different Seasons* (the collection which inspired the films *The Shawshank Redemption* and *Stand by Me*) and *On Writing: A Memoir of the Craft*.

Stephen King is the 2003 recipient of *The National Book Foundation Medal for Distinguished Contribution to American Letters*.

He lives in Bangor, Maine, with his wife, novelist Tabitha King.

By Stephen King and published by
Hodder & Stoughton

FICTION:

Carrie
'Salem's Lot
The Shining
Night Shift
The Stand
The Dead Zone
Firestarter
Cujo
Different Seasons
Cycle of the Werewolf
Christine
The Talisman (with Peter Straub)
Pet Sematary
It
Skeleton Crew
The Eyes of the Dragon
Misery
The Tommyknockers
The Dark Half
Four Past Midnight
Needful Things
Gerald's Game
Dolores Claiborne
Nightmares and Dreamscapes
Insomnia
Rose Madder
Desperation
Bag of Bones
The Girl Who Loved Tom Gordon
Hearts in Atlantis
Dreamcatcher
Everything's Eventual
From a Buick 8
Cell
The Dark Tower I: The Gunslinger
The Dark Tower II: The Drawing of the Three
The Dark Tower III: The Waste Lands
The Dark Tower IV: Wizard and Glass
The Dark Tower V: Wolves of the Calla
The Dark Tower VI: Song of Susannah
The Dark Tower VII: The Dark Tower

By Stephen King as Richard Bachman
Thinner
The Running Man
The Bachman Books
The Regulators
Blaze

NON-FICTION:

Danse Macabre
On Writing (A Memoir of the Craft)

STEPHEN KING

LISEY'S STORY

A novel

HODDER

First published in Great Britain in 2006 by Hodder & Stoughton
A division of Hodder Headline

This paperback edition published in 2007

A Hodder paperback

1

A CIP catalogue record for this title is available from the British Library

ISBN 978-1-4447-0561-4

Typeset in Bembo by Palimpsest Book Production Limited,
Grangemouth, Stirlingshire

Printed and bound by Clays Ltd, St Ives plc

Hodder Headline's policy is to use papers that are natural,
renewable and recyclable products and made from wood grown
in sustainable forests. The logging and manufacturing processes
are expected to conform to the environmental regulations
of the country of origin.

Hodder & Stoughton
A division of Hodder Headline
338 Euston Road
London NW1 3BH

For Tabby

Where do you go when you're lonely?
Where do you go when you're blue?
Where do you go when you're lonely?
I'll follow you
When the stars go blue.

—RYAN ADAMS

baby

babyluv

PART 1
BOOL HUNT

'If I were the moon, I know where I would fall down.'
—D. H. Lawrence, The Rainbow

CHAPTER ONE

LISEY AND AMANDA
(EVERYTHING THE SAME)

1

To the public eye, the spouses of well-known writers are all but invisible, and no one knew it better than Lisey Landon. Her husband had won the Pulitzer and the National Book Award, but Lisey had given only one interview in her life. This was for the well-known women's magazine that publishes the column 'Yes, I'm Married to *Him*!' She spent roughly half of its five-hundred-word length explaining that her nickname rhymed with 'CeeCee'. Most of the other half had to do with her recipe for slow-cooked roast beef. Lisey's sister Amanda said that the picture accompanying the interview made Lisey look fat.

None of Lisey's sisters was immune to the pleasures of setting the cat among the pigeons ('stirring up a stink' had been their father's phrase for it), or having a good natter about someone else's dirty laundry, but the only one Lisey had a hard time liking was this same Amanda. Eldest (and oddest) of the onetime Debusher girls of Lisbon Falls, Amanda currently lived alone, in a house which Lisey had provided, a small, weather-tight place not too far from Castle View where Lisey, Darla and Cantata could keep an eye on her. Lisey had bought it for her seven years ago, five before Scott died. Died Young. Died Before His Time, as the saying was. Lisey still had trouble believing he'd been gone for two years. It seemed both longer and the blink of an eye.

When Lisey finally got around to making a start at cleaning out his office suite, a long and beautifully lit series of rooms that had once been no more than the loft above a country barn, Amanda had shown up on the third day, after Lisey had finished her inventory of all the foreign editions (there were hundreds) but before she could do more than start listing the furniture, with little stars next to the pieces she thought she ought to keep. She waited for Amanda to ask her why she wasn't moving *faster*, for heaven's sake, but Amanda asked no questions.

While Lisey moved to a listless consideration of the cardboard boxes of correspondence stacked in the main closet, Amanda's focus seemed to remain on the impressive stacks and piles of memorabilia which ran the length of the study's south wall. She worked her way along this snakelike accretion, jotting frequently in a little notebook she kept near to hand.

What Lisey didn't say was *What are you looking for?* As Scott had pointed out on more than one occasion, Lisey had what was surely among the rarest of human talents: she was a business-minder who did not mind too much if you didn't mind yours. As long as you weren't making explosives to throw at someone, that was, and in Amanda's case, explosives were always a possibility. She was the sort of woman who couldn't help prying, the sort of woman who *would* open her mouth sooner or later.

Her husband had headed south from Rumford, where they had been living ('like a couple of wolverines caught in a drainpipe,' Scott said after an afternoon visit he vowed never to repeat) in 1985. Her one child, named Intermezzo and called Metzie for short, had gone north to Canada (with a long-haul trucker for a beau) in 1989. 'One flew north, one flew south, one couldn't shut her everlasting mouth.' That had been their father's rhyme when they were kids, and the one of Dandy Dave Debusher's girls who could never shut her everlasting mouth was surely Manda, dumped first by her husband and then by her own daughter.

Hard to like as Amanda sometimes was, Lisey hadn't wanted her down there in Rumford on her own; didn't trust her on her own, if it came to that, and although they'd never said so aloud, Lisey was sure Darla and Cantata felt the same. So she'd had a talk with Scott, and found the little Cape Cod, which could be had for ninety-seven thousand dollars, cash on the nail. Amanda had moved up within easy checking range soon after.

Now Scott was dead and Lisey had finally gotten around to the business of cleaning out his writing quarters. Halfway through the fourth day, the foreign editions were boxed up, the correspondence was marked and in some sort of order, and she had a good idea of what furniture was going and what was staying. So why did it feel that she had done so little? She'd known from the outset that this was a job which couldn't be hurried. Never mind all the importuning letters and phone calls she'd gotten since Scott's death (and more than a few visits, too). She supposed that in the end, the people who were interested in Scott's unpublished writing would get what they wanted,

3

but not until she was ready to give it to them. They hadn't been clear on that at first; they weren't *down with it*, as the saying was. Now she thought most of them were.

There were lots of words for the stuff Scott had left behind. The only one she completely understood was *memorabilia*, but there was another one, a funny one, that sounded like *incuncabilla*. That was what the impatient people wanted, the wheedlers, and the angry ones – Scott's *incuncabilla*. Lisey began to think of them as Incunks.

2

What she felt most of all, especially after Amanda showed up, was discouraged, as if she'd either underestimated the task itself or overestimated (wildly) her ability to see it through to its inevitable conclusion – the saved furniture stored in the barn below, the rugs rolled up and taped shut, the yellow Ryder van in the driveway, throwing its shadow on the board fence between her yard and the Galloways' next door.

Oh, and don't forget the sad heart of this place, the three desktop computers (there had been four, but the one in the 'memory nook' was now gone, thanks to Lisey herself). Each was newer and lighter than the last, but even the newest was a big desktop model and all of them still worked. They were password-protected, too, and she didn't know what the passwords were. She'd never asked, and had no idea what kind of electro-litter might be sleeping on the computers' hard drives. Grocery lists? Poems? Erotica? She was sure he'd been connected to the internet, but had no idea where he visited when he was there. Amazon?

Drudge? Hank Williams Lives? Madam Cruella's Golden Showers & Tower of Power? She tended to think not anything like that last, to think she would have seen the bills (or at least divots in the monthly house-money account), except of course that was really bullshit. If Scott had wanted to hide a thousand a month from her, he could have done so. And the passwords? The joke was, he might have told her. She forgot stuff like that, that was all. She reminded herself to try her own name. Maybe after Amanda had taken herself home for the day. Which didn't look like happening anytime soon.

Lisey sat back and blew hair off her forehead. *I won't get to the manuscripts until July, at this rate*, she thought. *The Incunks would go nuts if they saw the way I'm crawling along. Especially that last one.*

The last one – five months ago, this had been – had managed not to blow up, had managed to keep a very civil tongue about him until she'd begun to think he might be different. Lisey told him that Scott's writing suite had been sitting empty for almost a year and a half at that time, but she'd almost mustered the energy and resolve to go up there and start the work of cleaning the rooms and setting the place to rights.

Her visitor's name had been Professor Joseph Woodbody, of the University of Pittsburgh English Department. Pitt was Scott's alma mater, and Woodbody's Scott Landon and the American Myth lecture class was extremely popular and extremely large. He also had four graduate students doing Scott Landon theses this year, and so it was probably inevitable that the Incunk warrior should come to the fore when Lisey spoke in such vague terms as *sooner rather than later* and *almost certainly sometime this summer.* But it wasn't until she assured him that she would give him a call 'when the dust settles' that Woodbody really began to give way.

He said the fact that she had shared a great American writer's bed did not qualify her to serve as his literary executor. That, he said, was a job for an expert, and he understood that Mrs Landon had no college degree at all. He reminded her of the time already gone since Scott Landon's death, and of the rumors that continued to grow. Supposedly there were piles of unpublished Landon fiction – short stories, even novels. Could she not let him into the study for even a little while? Let him prospect a bit in the file cabinets and desk drawers, if only to set the most outrageous rumors to rest? She could stay with him the whole time, of course – that went without saying.

'No,' she'd said, showing Professor Woodbody to the door. 'I'm not ready just yet.' Overlooking the man's lower blows – trying to, at least – because he was obviously as crazy as the rest of them. He'd just hidden it better, and for a little longer. 'And when I am, I'll want to look at everything, not just the manuscripts.'

'But—'

She had nodded seriously to him. 'Everything the same.'

'I don't understand what you mean by that.'

Of course he didn't. It had been a part of her marriage's inner language. How many times had Scott come breezing in, calling 'Hey, Lisey, I'm home – everything the same?' Meaning *is everything all right, is everything cool.* But like most phrases of power (Scott had explained this once to her,

6

but Lisey had already known it), it had an inside meaning. A man like Woodbody could never grasp the inside meaning of *everything the same*. Lisey could explain it all day and he still wouldn't get it. Why? Because he was an Incunk, and when it came to Scott Landon only one thing interested the Incunks.

'It doesn't matter,' was what she'd said to Professor Woodbody on that day five months ago. '*Scott* would have understood.'

3

If Amanda had asked Lisey where Scott's 'memory nook' things had been stored – the awards and plaques, stuff like that – Lisey would have lied (a thing she did tolerably well for one who did it seldom) and said 'a U-Store-It in Mechanic Falls'. Amanda did not ask, however. She just paged ever more ostentatiously through her little note-book, surely trying to get her younger sister to broach the subject with the proper question, but Lisey did not ask. She was thinking of how empty this corner was, how empty and *uninteresting*, with so many of Scott's mementos gone. Either destroyed (like the computer monitor) or too badly scratched and dented to be shown; such an exhibit would raise more questions than it could ever answer.

At last Amanda gave in and opened her notebook. 'Look at this,' she said. 'Just look.'

Manda was holding out the first page. Written on the blue lines, crammed in from the little wire loops on the left to the edge of the sheet on the right (*like a coded message from one of those street-crazies you're always running into in New*

York because there's not enough money for the publicly funded mental institutions anymore, Lisey thought wearily), were numbers. Most had been circled. A very few had been enclosed in squares. Manda turned the page and now here were *two* pages filled with more of the same. On the following page, the numbers stopped halfway down. The final one appeared to be 846.

Amanda gave her the sidelong, red-cheeked, and somehow hilarious expression of hauteur that had meant, when she was twelve and little Lisey only two, that Manda had gone and Taken Something On Herself; tears for someone would follow. Amanda herself, more often than not. Lisey found herself waiting with some interest (and a touch of dread) to see what that expression might mean this time. Amanda had been acting nutty ever since turning up. Maybe it was just the sullen, sultry weather. More likely it had to do with the sudden absence of her longtime boyfriend. If Manda was headed for another spell of stormy emotional weather because Charlie Corriveau had jilted her, then Lisey supposed she had better buckle up herself. She had never liked or trusted Corriveau, banker or not. How could you trust a man after overhearing, at the spring library bake sale, that the guys down at The Mellow Tiger called him Shootin' Beans? What kind of nickname was that for a banker? What did it even *mean*? And surely he had to know that Manda had had mental problems in the past—

'Lisey?' Amanda asked. Her brow was deeply furrowed.

'I'm sorry,' Lisey said, 'I just kind of . . . went off there for a second.'

'You often do,' Amanda said. 'I think you got it from

8

Scott. Pay attention, Lisey. I made a little number on each of his magazines and journals and scholarly *things*. The ones piled over there against the wall.'

Lisey nodded as if she understood where this was going.

'I made the numbers in pencil, just light,' Amanda went on. 'Always when your back was turned or you were somewhere else, because I thought if you saw, you might have told me to stop.'

'I wouldn't've.' She took the little notebook, which was limp with its owner's sweat. 'Eight hundred and forty-six! That many!' And she knew the publications running along the wall weren't the sort she herself might read and have in the house, ones like *O* and *Good Housekeeping* and *Ms*, but rather *Sewanee Review* and *Glimmer Train* and *Open City* and things with incomprehensible names like *Piskya*.

'Quite a few more than that,' Amanda said, and cocked a thumb at the piles of books and journals. When Lisey really looked at them, she saw that her sister was right. Many more than eight hundred and forty-some. Had to be. 'Almost three thousand in all, and where you'll put them or who'd want them I'm sure I can't say. No, eight hundred and forty-six is just the number that have pictures of you.'

This was so awkwardly stated that Lisey at first didn't understand it. When she did, she was delighted. The idea that there might be such an unexpected photo-resource – such a hidden record of her time with Scott – had never crossed her mind. But when she thought about it, it made perfect sense. They had been married over twenty-five years at the time of his death, and Scott had been an inveterate, restless traveler during those years, reading, lecturing, criss-crossing the country with hardly a pause when he was between books, visiting as many as ninety campuses a year and never losing a beat in his seemingly endless stream of short stories. And on most of those rambles she was with him. In how many motels had she taken the little Swedish steamer to one of his suits while the TV muttered talk-show psalms on her side of the room and on his the portable typewriter clacked (early in the marriage) or the laptop clicked quietly (late) as he sat looking down at it with a comma of hair falling on his brow?

Manda was looking at her sourly, clearly not liking her reaction so far. 'The ones that are circled – over six hundred of them – are ones where you've been treated discourteously in the photo caption.'

'Is that so?' Lisey was mystified.

'I'll show you.' Amanda studied the notebook, went over to the slumbering, wall-length stack, consulted again, and selected two items. One was an expensive-looking hard-cover biannual from the University of Kentucky at Bowling Green. The other, a digest-sized magazine that looked like a student effort, was called *Push-Pelt*: one of those names designed by English majors to be charming and mean absolutely nothing.

'Open them, open them!' Amanda commanded, and as she shoved them into her hands, Lisey smelled the wild and acrid bouquet of her sister's sweat. 'The pages are marked with little scrids of paper, see?'

Scrids. Their mother's word for scraps. Lisey opened the biannual first, turning to the marked page. The picture of her and Scott in that one was very good, very smoothly printed. Scott was approaching a podium while she stood behind him, clapping. The audience stood below, also clapping. The picture of them in *Push-Pelt* was nowhere near as smooth; the dots in the dot-matrix looked as big as the points of pencils with mooshed leads and there were hunks of wood floating in the pulp paper, but she looked at it and felt like crying. Scott was entering some dark cellarful of noise. There was a big old Scott grin on his face that said oh yeah, this be the place. She was a step or two behind him, her own smile visible in the back-kick of what must have been a mighty flash. She could even make out the blouse she was wearing, that blue Anne Klein with the funny single red stripe down the left side. What she had on below was lost in shadow, and she couldn't remember this particular evening at all, but she knew it had been jeans. When she went out late, she always put on a pair of faded jeans. The caption read: *Living Legend Scott Landon (Accompanied By Gal Pal) Makes An Appearance At The University Of Vermont Stalag 17 Club Last Month. Landon Stayed Until Last Call, Reading, Dancing, Partying. Man Knows How To Get Down.*

Yes. Man had known how to get down. She could testify.

She looked at all the other periodicals, was suddenly overwhelmed by the riches she might find in them, and realized Amanda had hurt her after all, had gored her a wound that might bleed a long time. Was he the only one who had known about the dark places? The dirty dark ones where you were so alone and wretchedly voiceless? Maybe she didn't know all that he had, but she knew enough. Certainly she knew he had been haunted, and

STEPHEN KING

would never look into a mirror – any reflective surface, if
he could help it – after the sun went down. And she had
loved him in spite of all that. Because the man had known
how to get down.

But no more. Now the man *was* down. The man had
passed on, as the saying was; her life had moved on to a
new phase, a solo phase, and it was too late to turn back
now.

The phrase gave her a shudder and made her think
of things

(the purple, the thing with the piebald side)

best not thought of, and so she turned her mind away
from them.

'I'm glad you found these pictures,' she told Amanda
warmly. 'You're a pretty good big sister, you know it?'

And, as Lisey had hoped (but not really dared expect),
Manda was startled right out of her haughty, skittish little
dance. She looked uncertainly at Lisey, seeming to hunt
for insincerity and finding none. Little by little, she relaxed
into a biddable, easier-to-cope-with Amanda. She took
back the notebook and looked at it with a frown, as if not
entirely sure where it had come from. Lisey thought, considering the obsessive nature of the numbers, that this might
be a big step in a good direction.

Then Manda nodded as people do when they recall
something that should not have been lost to mind in the
first place. 'In the ones not circled, you're at least *named* –
Lisa Landon, an actual person. Last of all, but hardly least
– considering what we've always called you, that's almost
a pun, isn't it? – you'll see that a few of the numbers have
squares around them. Those are pictures of you *alone!*' She

12

gave Lisey an impressive, almost forbidding look. 'You'll want to have a look at *them*.'

'I'm sure.' Trying to sound thrilled out of her under-pants when she was unable to think why she'd have any slightest interest in pictures of herself alone during those all-too-brief years when she'd had a man – a good man, a non-Incunk who knew how to *strap it on* – with whom to share her days and nights. She raised her eyes to the untidy heaps and foothills of periodicals, which came in every size and shape, imagining what it would be like to go through them stack by stack and one by one, sitting cross-legged on the floor of the memory nook (where else), hunting out those images of her and Scott. And in the ones that had made Amanda so angry she would always find herself walking a little behind him, looking up at him. If others were applauding, she would be applauding, too. Her face would be smooth, giving away little, showing nothing but polite attention. Her face said *He does not bore me*. Her face said *He does not exalt me*. Her face said *I do not set myself on fire for him, nor he for me* (the lie, the lie, the lie). Her face said *Everything the same*.

Amanda hated these pictures. She looked and saw her sister playing salt for the sirloin, setting for the stone. She saw her sister sometimes identified as *Mrs. Landon*, some-times as *Mrs Scott Landon*, and sometimes – oh, this was bitter – not identified at all. Demoted all the way to *Gal Pal*. To Amanda it must seem like a kind of murder.

'Mandy-oh?'

Amanda looked at her. The light was cruel, and Lisey remembered with a real and total sense of shock that Manda would be sixty in the fall. Sixty! In that moment

Lisey found herself thinking about the thing that had haunted her husband on so many sleepless nights – the thing the Woodbodys of the world would never know about, not if she had her way. Something with an endless mottled side, something seen best by cancer patients looking into tumblers from which all the painkiller had been emptied; there will be no more until morning.

It's very close, honey. I can't see it, but I hear it taking its meal.

Shut up, Scott, I don't know what you're talking about.

'Lisey?' Amanda asked. 'Did you say something?'

'Just muttering under my breath.' She tried to smile.

'Were you talking to Scott?'

Lisey gave up trying to smile. 'Yes, I guess I was. Sometimes I still do. Crazy, huh?'

'I don't think so. Not if it works. I think crazy is what doesn't work. And I ought to know. I've had some experience. Right?'

'Manda—'

But Amanda had turned to look at the heaps of journals and annuals and student magazines. When she returned her gaze to Lisey, she was smiling uncertainly. 'Did I do right, Lisey? I only wanted to do my part . . .'

Lisey took one of Amanda's hands and squeezed it lightly. 'You did. What do you say we get out of here? I'll flip you for the first shower.'

4

I was lost in the dark and you found me. I was hot – so hot – and you gave me ice.

Scott's voice.

Lisey opened her eyes, thinking she had drifted away from some daytime task or moment and had had a brief but amazingly detailed dream in which Scott was dead and she was engaged in the Herculean job of cleaning out his writing stables. With them open she immediately understood that Scott indeed *was* dead; she was asleep in her own bed after delivering Manda home, and this was her dream.

She seemed to be floating in moonlight. She could smell exotic flowers. A fine-grained summer wind combed her hair back from her temples, the kind of wind that blows long after midnight in some secret place far from home. Yet it *was* home, *had* to be home, because ahead of her was the barn which housed Scott's writing suite, object of so much Incunk interest. And now, thanks to Amanda, she knew it held all those pictures of her and her late husband. All that buried treasure, that emotional loot.

It might be better not to look at those pictures, the wind whispered in her ears.

Oh, of that she had no doubt. But she *would* look. Was helpless not to, now that she knew they were there.

She was delighted to see she was floating on a vast, moon-gilded piece of cloth with the words PILLSBURY'S BEST FLOUR printed across it again and again; the corners had been knotted like hankies. She was charmed by the whimsy of it; it was like floating on a cloud.

Scott. She tried to say his name aloud and could not. The dream wouldn't let her. The driveway leading to the barn was gone, she saw. So was the yard between it and the house. Where they had been was a vast field of purple

15

flowers, dreaming in haunted moonlight. *Scott, I loved you, I saved you, I*

5

Then she was awake and could hear herself in the dark, saying it over and over like a mantra: 'I loved you, I saved you, I got you ice. I loved you, I saved you, I got you ice. I loved you, I saved you, I got you ice.'

She lay there a long time, remembering a hot August day in Nashville and thinking – not for the first time – that being single after being double so long was strange shite, indeed. She would have thought two years was enough time for the strangeness to rub off, but it wasn't; time apparently did nothing but blunt grief's sharpest edge so that it hacked rather than sliced. Because everything was *not* the same. Not outside, not inside, not for her. Lying in the bed that had once held two, Lisey thought alone never felt more lonely than when you woke up and discovered you still had the house to yourself. That you and the mice in the walls were the only ones still breathing.

CHAPTER TWO

LISEY AND THE MADMAN (DARKNESS LOVES HIM)

1

The next morning Lisey sat tailor-fashion on the floor of Scott's memory nook, looking across at the heaps and stacks and piles of magazines, alumni reports, English Department bulletins, and University 'journals' that ran along the study's south wall. It had occurred to her that maybe looking would be enough to dispel the stealthy hold all those as-yet-unseen pictures had taken on her imagination. Now that she was actually here, she knew that had been a vain hope. Nor would she need Manda's limp little notebook with all the numbers in it. That was lying discarded on the floor nearby, and Lisey put it in the back pocket of her jeans. She didn't like the look of it, the treasured artifact of a not-quite-right mind.

She once again measured that long stack of books and magazines against the south wall, a dusty booksnake four feet high and easily thirty feet long. If not for Amanda, she probably would have packed every last one of them away in liquor-store boxes without ever looking at them or wondering what Scott meant by keeping so many of them.

My mind just doesn't run that way, she told herself. *I'm really not much of a thinker at all.*

Maybe not, but you always remembered *like a champ.*

That was Scott at his most teasing, charming, and hard to resist, but the truth was she'd been better at forgetting. As had he, and both of them had had their reasons. And yet, as if to prove his point, she heard a ghostly snatch of conversation. One speaker – Scott – was familiar. The other voice had a little southern glide to it. A *pretentious* little southern glide, maybe.

—*Tony here will be writing it up for the* [thingummy, rum-tum-tummy, whatever]. *Would you like to see a copy, Mr Landon?*

—*Hmmmm? Sure, you bet!*

Muttering voices all around them. Scott barely hearing the thing about Tony writing it up, he'd had what was almost a politician's knack for turning himself outward to those who'd come to see him when he was in public, Scott was listening to the voices of the swelling crowd and already thinking about finding the plug-in point, that pleasurable moment when the electricity flowed from him to them and then back to him again doubled or even tripled, he loved the current but Lisey was convinced he had loved that instant of plugging in even more. Still, he'd taken time to respond.

—*You can send photos, campus newspaper articles or reviews, departmental write-ups, anything like that. Please. I like to see everything. The Study, RFD #2, Sugar Top Hill Road, Castle Rock, Maine. Lisey knows the zip. I always forget.*

Nothing else about her, just *Lisey knows the zip.* How Manda would have howled to hear it! But she had *wanted* to be forgotten on those trips, both there and not there. She liked to watch.

Like the fellow in the porno movie? Scott had asked her once, and she'd returned the thin moon-smile that told him he was treading near the edge. *If you say so, dear,* she had replied.

He always introduced her when they arrived and again here and there, to other people, when it became necessary, but it rarely did. Outside of their own fields, academics were oddly lacking in curiosity. Most of them were just delighted to have the author of *The Coaster's Daughter* (National Book Award) and *Relics* (the Pulitzer) among them. Also, there had been a period of about ten years when Scott had somehow gotten larger than life – to others, and sometimes to himself. (Not to Lisey; she was the one who had to fetch him a fresh roll of toilet paper if he ran out while he was on the john.) Nobody exactly charged the stage when he stood there with the microphone in his hand, but even Lisey felt the connection he made with his audience. Those volts. It was hardwired, and it had little to do with his work as a writer. Maybe nothing. It had to do with the *Scottness* of him, somehow. That sounded crazy, but it was true. And it never seemed to change him much, or hurt him, at least until—

Her eyes stopped moving, fixed on a hardcover spine and gold leaf letters reading *U-Tenn Nashville 1988 Review*.

1988, the year of the rockabilly novel. The one he'd never written.

1988, the year of the madman.

—Tony here will be writing it up

'No,' Lisey said. 'Wrong. He didn't say Tony, he said—'

—*Toneh*

Yes, that was right, he said *Toneh*, he said

—*Toneh heah well be rahtin it up*

'—writin it up for the *U-Tenn '88 Year in Review*,' Lisey said. 'He said . . .'

—*Ah could Express Mail it*

Only she was damned if the little Tennessee Williams wannabe hadn't almost said *Spress* Mail it. That was the voice, all right, that was the southern-fried chickenshit. Dashmore? Dashman? The man had *dashed*, all right, had dashed like a smucking track-star, but that wasn't it. It had been—

'Dashmiel!' Lisey murmured to the empty rooms, and clenched her fists. She stared at the book with the gold-stamped spine as if it might disappear the second she took her eyes away. 'Little prig-southerner's name was Dashmiel, and *HE RAN LIKE A RABBIT!*'

Scott would have turned down the offer of Express Mail or Federal Express; believed such things to be a need-less expense. About correspondence there was never any hurry – when it came floating downstream, he plucked it out. When it came to reviews of his novels he had been a lot less Come Back To De Raft, Huck Honey and a lot more What Makes Scotty Run, but for write-ups following public appearances, regular mail did him just fine. Since The Study had its own address, Lisey realized she would have been very unlikely to see these things when they came in. And once they were here . . . well, these airy, well-lighted rooms had been Scott's creative playground, not hers, a mostly benign one-boy clubhouse where he'd written his stories and listened to his music as loud as he wanted in the soundproofed area he called My Padded Cell. There'd never been a KEEP OUT sign on the door, she'd been up here lots of times when he was alive and Scott was always glad to see her, but it had taken Amanda to see what was in the belly of the booksnake sleeping against the south wall. Quick-to-offense Amanda, suspicious Amanda, OCD Amanda who had somehow become convinced that her house would burn flat if she didn't load the kitchen stove with exactly three maple chunks at a time, no more or less: Amanda whose unalterable habit was to turn around three times on her stoop if she had to go back into the house for something she'd forgotten. Look at stuff like that (or listen to her counting strokes as she brushed her teeth) and you could easily write Manda off as just another gonzo-bonkie old maid, somebody write that lady a prescription for Zoloft or Prozac. But without Manda, does little Lisey ever realize there are hundreds of pictures of her dead husband up here, just waiting for her to look at them? Hundreds of memories waiting to be called forth? And most of them surely more pleasant than the memory of Dashmiel, that southern-fried chickenshit coward . . .

'Stop it,' she murmured. 'Just stop it now. Lisa Debusher Landon, you open your hand and let that go.'

But she was apparently not ready to do that, because she got up, crossed the room, and knelt before the books. Her right hand floated out ahead of her like a magician's trick and grasped the volume marked *U-Tenn Nashville 1988 Review*. Her heart was pounding hard, not with excitement but with fear. The head could tell the heart all that was eighteen years over, but in matters of emotion the heart had its own brilliant vocabulary. The madman's hair had been so blond it was almost white. He had been a *graduate student* madman, spouting what was not quite gibberish. A day after the shooting – when Scott's condition was upgraded from critical to fair – she had asked Scott if the madman grad student had had it *strapped on*, and Scott had whispered that he didn't know if a crazy person could strap *anything* on. *Strapping it on* was a heroic act, an act of will, and crazy people didn't have much in the way of will . . . or did she think otherwise?

—*I don't know, Scott. I'll think about it.*

Not meaning to. Wanting to never think about it again, if she could help it. As far as Lisey was concerned, the smucking looneytune with the little gun could join the other things she'd successfully forgotten since meeting Scott.

—*Hot, wasn't it?*

Lying in bed. Still pale, far *too* pale, but starting to get a little of his color back. Casual, no special look, just making conversation. And Lisey Now, Lisey Alone, the widow Landon, shivered.

'He didn't remember,' she murmured.

She was almost positive he didn't. Nothing about when he'd been down on the pavement and they'd both been sure he would never get back up. That he was dying and whatever passed between them then was all there would ever be, they who had found so much to say to each other. The neurologist she plucked up courage enough to speak to said that forgetting around the time of a traumatic event was par for the course, that people recovering from such events often discovered that a spot had been burned black in the film of their memories. That spot might stretch over five minutes, five hours, or five days. Sometimes disconnected fragments and images would surface years or even decades later. The neurologist called it a defense mechanism.

It made sense to Lisey.

From the hospital she'd gone back to the motel where she was staying. It wasn't a very good room – in back, with nothing to look at but a board fence and nothing to listen to except a hundred or so barking dogs – but she was far past caring about such things. Certainly she wanted nothing to do with the campus where her husband had been shot. And as she kicked off her shoes and lay down on the hard double bed, she thought: *Darkness loves him.*

Was that true?

How could she say, when she didn't even know what it meant?

You know. Daddy's prize was a kiss.

Lisey had turned her head so swiftly on the pillow she might have been slapped by an invisible hand. *Shut up about that!*

No answer . . . no answer . . . and then, slyly: *Darkness loves him. He dances with it like a lover and the moon comes up over the purple hill and what was sweet smells sour. Smells like poison.*

She had turned her head back the other way. And outside the motel room the dogs – every smucking dog in Nashville, it had sounded like – had barked as the sun went down in orange August smoke, making a hole for the night. As a child she had been told by her mother there was nothing to fear in the dark, and she had believed it to be true. She had been downright gleeful in the dark, even

23

when it was lit by lightning and ripped by thunder. While her years-older sister Manda cowered under her covers, little Lisey sat atop her own bed, sucking her thumb and demanding that someone bring the flashlight and read her a story. She had told this to Scott once and he had taken her hands and said, 'You be *my* light, then. Be *my* light, Lisey.' And she had tried, but—

'I was in a dark place,' Lisey murmured as she sat in his deserted study with the *U-Tenn Nashville Review* in her hands. 'Did you say that, Scott? You did, didn't you?'

—*I was in a dark place and you found me. You saved me.*

Maybe in Nashville that had been true. Not in the end.

—*You were always saving me, Lisey. Do you remember the first night I stayed at your apartment?*

Sitting here now with the book in her lap, Lisey smiled. Of course she did. Her strongest memory was of too much peppermint *schnapps*, it had given her an acidy stomach. And he'd had trouble first getting and then maintaining an erection, although in the end everything went all right. She'd assumed then it was the booze. It wasn't until later that he'd told her he'd *never* been successful until her: she'd been his first, she'd been his only, and every story he'd ever told her or anyone else about his crazy life of adolescent sex, both gay and straight, had been a lie. And Lisey? Lisey had seen him as an unfinished project, a thing to do before going to sleep. Coax the dishwasher through the noisy part of her cycle; set the Pyrex casserole dish to soak; blow the hotshot young writer until he gets some decent wood.

—*When it was done and you went to sleep, I lay awake and listened to the clock on your nightstand and the wind outside and understood that I was really home, that in bed with you was home, and something that had been getting close in the dark was suddenly gone. It could not stay. It had been banished. It knew how to come back, I was sure of that, but it could not stay, and I could really go to sleep. My heart cracked with gratitude. I think it was the first gratitude I've ever really known. I lay there beside you and the tears rolled down the sides of my face and onto the pillow. I loved you then and I love you now and I have loved you every second in between. I don't care if you understand me. Understanding is vastly overrated, but nobody ever gets enough safety. I've never forgotten how safe I felt with that thing gone out of the darkness.*

'Daddy's prize was a kiss.'

Lisey said it out loud this time, and although it was warm in the empty study, she shivered. She still didn't know what it meant, but she was pretty sure she remembered when Scott had told her that Daddy's prize was a kiss, that she had been his first, and nobody ever got enough safety: just before they were married. She had given him all the safety she knew how to give, but it hadn't been enough. In the end Scott's thing had come back for him, anyway – that thing he had sometimes glimpsed in mirrors and waterglasses, the thing with the vast piebald side. The long boy.

Lisey looked around the study fearfully for just a moment, and wondered if it was watching her now.

2

She opened the *U-Tenn Nashville 1988 Review*. The spine's crack was like a pistol-shot. It made her cry out in surprise and drop the book. Then she laughed (a little shakily, it was true). 'Lisey, you nit.'

This time a folded piece of newsprint fell out, yellowing and brittle to the touch. What she unfolded was a grainy photograph, caption included, starring a fellow of perhaps twenty-three who looked much younger thanks to his expression of dazed shock. In his right hand he held a short-handled shovel with a silver scoop. Said scoop had been engraved with words that were unreadable in the photo, but Lisey remembered what they were: *COMMENCE-MENT, SHIPMAN LIBRARY*.

The young man was sort of . . . well . . . *peering* at this shovel, and Lisey knew not just by his face but by the whole awkward this-way-n-that jut of his lanky body that he didn't have any idea what he was seeing. It could have been an artillery shell, a bonsai tree, a radiation detector, or a china pig with a slot in its back for spare silver; it could have been a whang-dang-doodle, a phylactery testifying to the pompetus of love, or a cloche hat made out of coyote skin. It could have been the penis of the poet Pindar. This guy was too far gone to know. Nor, she was willing to bet, was he aware that grasping his left hand, also frozen forever in swarms of black photodots, was a man in what looked like a costume-ball Motor Highway Patrolman's uniform: no gun, but a Sam Browne belt running across the chest and what Scott, laughing and making big eyes, might have called 'a pufficky *huh-yooge* batch of orifice'. He also had a pufficky huh-yooge grin on his face, the kind of relieved oh-thank-you-God grin that said *Son, you'll never have to buy yourself another drink in another bar where I happen to be, as long as I've got one dollar to rub against another 'un.* In the background she could see Dashmiel, the little prig-southerner who had run away. Roger *C.* Dashmiel, it came to her, the big C stands for chickenshit.

Had she, little Lisey Landon, seen the happy campus security cop shaking the dazed young man's hand? No, but . . . say . . .

Saa-aaaay, chillums . . . looky-here . . . do you want a true-life image to equal such fairy-tale visions as Alice falling down her rabbit-hole or a toad in a top-hat driving a motor-car? Then check *this* out, over on the right side of the picture.

Lisey bent down until her nose was almost touching the yellowed photo from the Nashville *American.* There was a magnifying glass in the wide center drawer of Scott's main desk. She had seen it on many occasions, its place preserved between the world's oldest unopened package of Herbert Tareyton cigarettes and the world's oldest book of unredeemed S&H Green Stamps. She could have gotten it but didn't bother. Didn't need any magnification to confirm what she was seeing: half a brown loafer. Half a *cordovan* loafer, actually, with a slightly built-up heel. She remembered those loafers very well. How comfortable they'd been. And she'd certainly moved in them that day, hadn't she? She hadn't seen the happy cop, or the dazed young man (Tony, she was sure, of *Toneh heah well be rahtin it up* fame), nor had she noticed Dashmiel, the southern-fried chickenshit, once the cheese hit the grater. All of them had ceased to matter to her, the whole smucking bunch of them. By then she had only one thing on her mind, and that had been Scott. He was surely no more

27

than ten feet away, but she had known that if she didn't get to him at once, the crowd around him would keep her out . . . and if she were kept out, the crowd might kill him. Kill him with its dangerous love and voracious concern. And what the smuck, Violet, he might have been dying, anyway. If he was, she'd meant to be there when he stepped out. When he Went, as the folks of her mother and father's generation would have said.

'I was *sure* he'd die,' Lisey said to the silent sunwashed room, to the dusty winding bulk of the booksnake.

So she'd run to her fallen husband, and the news photographer – who'd been there only to snap the obligatory picture of college dignitaries and a famous visiting author gathered for the groundbreaking with the silver spade, the ritual First Shovelful of Earth where the new library would eventually stand – had ended up snapping a much more dynamic photograph, hadn't he? This was a *front-page* photo, maybe even a *hall of fame* photo, the kind that made you pause with a spoonful of breakfast cereal halfway between the bowl and your mouth, dripping on the classifieds, like the photo of Oswald with his hands to his belly and his mouth open in a final dying yawp, the kind of frozen image you never forgot. Only Lisey herself would ever realize that the writer's wife was also in the photo. Exactly one built-up heel of her.

The caption running along the bottom of the photo read:

Captain **S. Heffernan** of U-Tenn Campus Security congratulates **Tony Eddington**, who saved the life of famous visiting author **Scott Landon** only seconds before this photo was taken. 'He's an authentic hero,' said **Capt. Heffernan**. 'No one else was close enough to take a hand.' (Additional coverage p. 4, p. 9)

Running up the lefthand side was a fairly lengthy message in handwriting she didn't recognize. Running up the righthand side were two lines of Scott's sprawly hand-writing, the first line slightly larger than the second . . . and a little arrow, by God, pointing to the shoe! She knew what the arrow meant; he had recognized it for what it was. Coupled with his wife's story – call it Lisey and the Madman, a thrilling tale of true adventure – he had under-stood everything. And was he furious? No. Because he had known his wife would not be furious. He had known she'd think it was funny, and it *was* funny, a smucking riot, so why was she on the verge of crying? Never in her whole *life* had she been so surprised, tricked, and overtrumped by her emotions as in these last few days.

Lisey dropped the news clipping on top of the book, afraid a sudden flood of tears might actually dissolve it the way saliva dissolves a mouthful of cotton candy. She cupped her palms over her eyes and waited. When she was sure the tears weren't going to overflow, she picked up the clip-ping and read what Scott had written:

Must show to Lisey! How she will LAUGH 〇
But will she understand? (Our survey says YES) ☺

He had turned the big exclamation point into a

sunny seventies-style smiley-face, as if telling her to have a nice day. And Lisey did understand. Eighteen years late, but so what? Memory was relative.

Very zen, grasshoppah, Scott might have said.

'Zen, schmen. I wonder how Tony's doing these days, that's what *I* wonder. Savior of the famous Scott Landon.' She laughed, and the tears that had still been standing in her eyes spilled down her cheeks.

Now she turned the photo widdershins and read the other, longer note.

8-18-88

Dear Scott (If I may): I thought you would want this photograph of C. Anthony ("Tony") Eddington III, the young grad student who saved your life. U-Tenn will be honoring him, of course; we felt you might also want to be in touch. His address is 748 Coldview Avenue, Nashville North, Nashville, Tennessee 37235. Mr. Eddington, "Poor but Proud," comes from a fine Southern Tennessee family and is an excellent student poet. You will of course want to thank (and perhaps reward) him in your own way.
Respectfully, sir, I remain, Roger C. Dashmiel
Assoc. Prof., English Dept.
University of Tennessee, Nashville

Lisey read this over once, twice ('three times a laaaady,' Scott would have sung at this point), still smiling, but now with a sour combination of amazement and final comprehension. Roger Dashmiel was probably as ignorant of what had actually happened as the campus cop. Which meant there were only two people in the whole round world who knew the truth about that afternoon: Lisey Landon and Tony Eddington, the fellow who would be *rahtin it up* for the year-end review. It was possible that even 'Toneh' himself didn't realize what had happened after the ceremonial first spadeful of earth had been turned. Maybe he'd been in a fear-injected blackout. Dig it: *he might really believe he had saved Scott Landon from death.*

No. She didn't think so. What she thought was that this clipping and the jotted, fulsome note were Dashmiel's petty revenge on Scott for . . . for what?

For just being polite?

For looking at *Monsieur de Litérature* Dashmiel and not seeing him?

For being a rich creative snotbucket who was going to make a fifteen-thousand-dollar payday for saying a few uplifting words and turning a single spadeful of earth? *Pre-loosened* earth at that?

All those things. And more. Lisey thought Dashmiel had somehow believed their positions would have been reversed in a truer, fairer world; that he, Roger Dashmiel, would have been the focus of the intellectual interest and student adulation, while Scott Landon – not to mention his mousy little wouldn't-fart-if-her-life-depended-on-it wife – would be the ones toiling in the campus vineyards, always currying favor, testing the winds of departmental politics, and scurrying to make that next pay-grade.

'Whatever it was, he didn't like Scott and this was his revenge,' she marveled to the empty, sunny rooms above the long barn. 'This . . . poison-pen clipping.'

She considered the idea for a moment, then burst

out into gales of merry laughter, clapping her hands on the flat part of her chest above her breasts.

When she recovered a little, she paged through the *Review* until she found the article she was looking for: **AMERICA'S MOST FAMOUS NOVELIST INAUGURATES LONG-HELD LIBRARY DREAM.** The byline was **Anthony Eddington**, sometimes known as Toneh. And, as Lisey skimmed it, she found she was capable of anger, after all. Even rage. For there was no mention of how that day's festivities had ended, or the *Review* author's own putative heroism, for that matter. The only suggestion that something had gone crazily wrong was in the concluding lines: 'Mr Landon's speech following the groundbreaking and his reading in the student lounge that evening were cancelled due to unexpected developments, but we hope to see this giant of American literature back on our campus soon. Perhaps for the ceremonial ribbon-cutting when the Shipman opens its doors in 1991!'

Reminding herself this was the school *Review*, for God's sake, a glossy, expensive hardcover book mailed out to presumably loaded alumni, went some distance toward defusing her anger; did she really think the *U-Tenn Review* was going to let their hired hack rehash that day's bloody bit of slapstick? How many alumni dollars would *that* add to the coffers? Reminding herself that Scott would also have found this amusing helped . . . but not all that much. Scott, after all, wasn't here to put his arm around her, to kiss her cheek, to distract her by gently tweaking the tip of one breast and telling her that to everything there was a season – a time to sow, a time to reap, a time to strap and likewise one to unstrap, yea, verily.

Scott, damn him, was gone. And—

'And he *bled* for you people,' she murmured in a resentful voice that sounded spookily like Manda's. 'He almost *died* for you people. It's sort of a blue-eyed miracle he didn't.'

And Scott spoke to her again, as he had a way of doing. She knew it was only the ventriloquist inside her, making his voice – who had loved it more or remembered it better? – but it didn't *feel* that way. It felt like *him*.

You were my miracle, Scott said. *You were my blue-eyed miracle. Not just that day, but always. You were the one who kept the dark away, Lisey. You shone.*

'I suppose there were times when you thought so,' she said absently.

—Hot, wasn't it?

Yes. It had been hot. But not *just* hot. It was—

'Humid,' Lisey said. '*Muggy*. And I had a bad feeling about it from the get-go.'

Sitting in front of the booksnake, with the *U-Tenn Nashville 1988 Review* lying open in her lap, Lisey had a momentary but brilliant glimpse of Granny D, feeding the chickens way back when, on the home place. 'It was in the bathroom that I started to feel really bad. Because I broke

3

She keeps thinking about the glass, that smucking broken glass. When, that is, she's not thinking of how much she'd like to get out of this heat.

Lisey stands behind and slightly to Scott's right with

her hands clasped demurely before her, watching him balance on one foot, the other on the shoulder of the silly little shovel half-buried in loose earth that has clearly been brought in for the occasion. The day is maddeningly hot, maddeningly humid, maddeningly muggy, and the considerable crowd that has gathered only makes it worse. Unlike the dignitaries, the lookie-loos aren't dressed in anything approaching their best, and while their jeans and shorts and pedal-pushers may not exactly make them comfortable in the wet-blanket air, Lisey envies them just the same as she stands here at the crowd's forefront, basting in the suck-oven heat of the Tennessee afternoon. Just standing pat, dressed up in her hot-weather best, is stressful, worrying that she'll soon be sweating dark circles in the light brown linen top she's wearing over the blue rayon shell beneath. She's got on a great bra for hot weather, and still it's biting into the undersides of her boobs like nobody's business. Happy days, babyluv.

Scott, meanwhile, continues balancing on one foot while his hair, too long in back – he needs it cut badly, she knows he looks in the mirror and sees a rock star but she looks at him and sees a smucking hobo out of a Woody Guthrie song – blows in the occasional puff of hot breeze. He's being a good sport while the photographer circles. *Damn* good sport. He's flanked on the left by a guy named Tony Eddington, who's going to write up all this happy crappy for some campus outlet or another, and on the right by their stand-in host, an English Department stalwart named Roger Dashmiel. Dashmiel is one of those men who seem older than they are not only because they have lost so much hair and gained so much belly but because they insist upon drawing an almost stifling gravitas around themselves. Even their witticisms felt to Lisey like oral readings of insurance policy clauses. Making matters worse is the fact that Dashmiel doesn't like her husband. Lisey has sensed this at once (it's easy, because most men *do* like him), and it has given her something upon which to focus her unease. For she *is* uneasy, profoundly so. She has tried to tell herself that it's no more than the humidity and the gathering clouds in the west presaging strong afternoon thunder-storms or maybe even tornadoes: a low-barometer kind of thing. But the barometer wasn't low in Maine when she got out of bed this morning at quarter to seven; it had been a beautiful summer morning already, with the newly risen sun sparkling on a trillion points of dew in the grass between the house and Scott's study. Not a cloud in the sky, what old Dandy Dave Debusher would have called 'a real ham-n-egger of a day'. Yet the instant her feet touched the oak boards of the bedroom floor and her thoughts turned to the trip to Nashville – leave for the Portland Jetport at eight, fly out on Delta at nine-forty – her heart dipped with dread and her morning-empty stomach, usually sweet, foamed with unmotivated fear. She had greeted these sensations with surprised dismay, because she ordinarily *liked* to travel, especially with Scott: the two of them sitting companionably side by side, he with his book open, she with hers. Sometimes he'd read her a bit of his and sometimes she'd vice him a little versa. Sometimes she'd feel him and look up and find his eyes. His solemn regard. As though she were a mystery to him still. Yes, and sometimes there would be turbulence, and she liked that, too. It was like the rides at the Topsham Fair when she and her sisters had been young, the Krazy Kups and the Wild Mouse. Scott never minded the turbulent interludes, either. She remembered one particularly mad approach into Denver – strong winds, thunderheads, little prop-job commuter plane from Death's Head Airlines all over the smucking sky – and how she'd seen him actually pogo-ing in his seat like a little kid who needs to go to the bathroom, this crazy grin on his face. No, the rides that scared Scott were the smooth downbound ones he sometimes took in the middle of the night. Once in a while he talked – lucidly; smiling, even – about the things you could see in the screen of a dead TV set. Or a shot-glass, if you held it tilted just the right way. It scared her badly to hear him talk like that. Because it was crazy, and because she sort of knew what he meant, even if she didn't want to.

So it isn't low barometer that's bothering her and it certainly hadn't been the prospect of getting on one more airplane. But in the bathroom, reaching for the light over the sink, something she had done without incident or accident day in and day out for the entire eight years they'd lived on Sugar Top Hill – which came to approximately three thousand days, less time spent on the road – the back of her hand whacked the waterglass with their toothbrushes in it and sent it tumbling to the tiles where it shattered into approximately three thousand stupid pieces.

'Shit fire, save the smuckin *matches*!' she cried, frightened and irritated to find herself so . . . for she did not believe in omens, not Lisey Landon the writer's wife, not little Lisey Debusher from the Sabbatus Road in Lisbon Falls, either. Omens were for the shanty Irish.

Scott, who had just come back into the bedroom

with two cups of coffee and a plate of buttered toast, stopped dead. 'Whadja break, babyluv?'

'Nothing that came out of the dog's ass,' Lisey said savagely, and was then sort of astonished. That was one of Granny Debusher's sayings, and Granny D certainly *had* believed in omens, but that old colleen had been on the cooling board when Lisey was barely four. Was it possible Lisey could even remember her? It seemed so, for as she stood there, looking down at the shards of toothglass, the actual *articulation* of that omen came to her, came in Granny D's tobacco-broken voice . . . and returns now, as she stands watching her husband be a good sport in his lightest-weight summer sportcoat (which he'll soon be sweating through under the arms nevertheless).

—*Broken glass in the morning, broken hearts at night.*

That was Granny D's scripture, all right, remembered by at least one little girl, stored up before the day Granny D pitched over dying in the chickenyard with a snarl in her throat, an apron filled with Blue Bird feed tied around her waist, and a sack of Beechnut scrap slid up her sleeve.

So.

Not the heat, the trip, or that fellow Dashmiel, who only ended up doing the meet-and-greet because the head of the English Department is in the hospital following an emergency gall-bladder removal the day before. It's a broken . . . smucking . . . *toothglass* combined with the saying of a long-dead Irish granny. And the joke of it is (as Scott will later point out), that is just enough to put her on edge. Just enough to get her at least semi-strapped.

Sometimes, he will tell her not long hence, speaking from a hospital bed (ah, but he could so easily have been on a cooling board himself, all his wakeful, thoughtful nights over), speaking in his new whispering, effortful voice, *sometimes just enough is just enough. As the saying is.*

And she will know exactly what he's talking about.

4

Roger Dashmiel has his share of headaches today, Lisey knows that, though it doesn't make her like him any better. If there was ever an actual script for the ceremony, Professor Hegstrom (he of the emergency gall-bladder attack) was too post-op muddled to tell Dashmiel or anyone else what or where it is. Dashmiel has consequently been left with little more than a time of day and a cast of characters featuring a writer to whom he has taken an instant dislike. When the little party of dignitaries left Inman Hall for the short but exceedingly warm walk to the site of the forth-coming Shipman Library, Dashmiel told Scott they'd have to more or less play it by ear. Scott had shrugged good-naturedly. He was absolutely comfortable with that. For Scott Landon, ear was a way of life.

'Ah'll introduce you,' said the man Lisey would in later years come to think of as the southern-fried chick-enshit. This as they walked toward the baked and shim-mering plot of land where the new library would stand (the word is pronounced *LAH-bree* in Dashmiel-ese). The photographer in charge of immortalizing all this danced restlessly back and forth, snapping and snapping, busy as a gnat. Lisey could see a rectangle of fresh brown earth not far ahead, about nine by five, she judged, and trucked in that morning, by the just-starting-to-fade look of it. No one had thought to put up an awning, and already the surface of the fresh dirt had acquired a grayish glaze.

'*Somebody* better do it,' Scott said.

He spoke cheerfully, but Dashmiel had frowned as if wounded by some undeserved canard. Then, with a meaty sigh, he'd pressed on. 'Applause follows introduction—'

'As day follows night,' Scott murmured.

'—and yew'll say a woid or tieu,' Dashmiel finished. Beyond the baked wasteland awaiting the library, a freshly paved parking lot shimmered in the sunlight, all smooth tar and staring yellow lines. Lisey saw fantastic ripples of nonexistent water on its far side.

'It will be my pleasure,' Scott said.

The unvarying good nature of his responses seemed to worry Dashmiel. 'Ah hope you won't want to say *tieu* much at the groun'breakin,' he told Scott as they approached the roped-off area. This had been kept clear, but there was a crowd big enough to stretch almost to the parking lot waiting beyond it. An even larger one had trailed Dashmiel and the Landons from Inman Hall. Soon the two would merge, and Lisey – who ordinarily didn't mind crowds any more than she minded turbulence at twenty thousand feet – didn't like this, either. It occurred to her that so many people on a day this hot might suck all the air out of the air. Stupid idea, but—

'It's mighty hot, even fo' Nashville in August, wouldn't you say so, Toneh?'

Tony Eddington nodded obligingly but said nothing. His only comment so far had been to identify the tirelessly dancing photographer as Stefan Queensland of the Nashville *American*—also of U-Tenn Nashville, class of '85.

'Hope y'all will help him out if y'can,' Tony Eddington had said to Scott as they began their walk over here.

'Yew'll finish yoah remarks,' Dashmiel said, 'and there'll be anothuh round of applause. *Then*, Mistuh Landon—'

'Scott.'

Dashmiel had flashed a rictus grin, there for just a moment. 'Then, *Scott*, yew'll go on and toin that all impawtant foist shovelful of oith.' *Toin? Foist? Oith?* Lisey mused, and it came to her that Dashmiel was very likely saying *turn that all-important first shovelful of earth* in his only semi-believable Louisiana drawl.

'All that sounds fine to me,' Scott replied, and that was all he had time for, because they had arrived.

5

Perhaps it's a holdover from the broken toothglass – that *omenish* feeling – but the plot of trucked-in dirt looks like a grave to Lisey: XL size, as if for a giant. The two crowds collapse into one around it and create that breathless suck-oven feel at the center. A campus security guard now stands at each corner of the ornamental velvet-rope barrier, beneath which Dashmiel, Scott, and 'Toneh' Eddington have ducked. Queensland, the photographer, dances relentlessly with his big Nikon held up in front of his face. *Paging Weegee*, Lisey thinks, and realizes she envies him. He is so free, flitting gnatlike in the heat; he is twenty-five and all his shit still works. Dashmiel, however, is looking at him with growing impatience which Queensland affects not to see until he has exactly the shot he wants. Lisey has an idea it's the one of Scott alone, his foot on the silly silver spade, his hair blowing back in the breeze. In any case, Weegee Junior at last lowers his big camera and steps back to the edge of the crowd. And it's while following Queensland's progress with her somewhat wistful regard that Lisey first sees the madman. He has the look, one local reporter will later write, 'of John Lennon in the last days of his romance with heroin – hollow, watchful eyes at odd and disquieting contrast to his otherwise childishly wistful face.'

At the moment, Lisey notes little more than the guy's tumbled blond hair. She has little interest in people-watching today. She just wants this to be over so she can find a bathroom in the English Department over there across the parking lot and pull her rebellious underwear out of the crack of her ass. She has to make water, too, but right now that's pretty much secondary.

'Ladies and gentlemen!' Dashmiel says in a carrying voice. 'It is mah distinct pleasure to introduce Mr Scott Landon, author of the Pulitzer Prize-winnin *Relics* and the National Book Award-winnin *The Coster's Daughter*. He's come all the way from Maine with his lovely wife Lisa to inaugurate construction – that's right, it's finally happ'nin – on our very own Shipman LAH-bree. Scott Landon, folks, let's hear y'all give him a good Nashveel welcome!'

The crowd applauds at once, *con brio*. The lovely wife joins in, patting her palms together, looking at Dashmiel and thinking. *He won the NBA for* The Coaster's Daughter. *That's* Coaster, *not* Coster. *And I think you know it. I think you smucked it up on purpose. Why don't you like him, you petty man?*

Then she happens to glance beyond him and this

time she really *does* notice Gerd Allen Cole, just standing there with all that fabulous blond hair tumbled down to his eyebrows and the sleeves of a white shirt far too big for him rolled up to his substandard biceps. The tail of his shirt is out and dangles almost to the whitened knees of his jeans. On his feet are engineer boots with side-buckles. To Lisey they look dreadfully hot. Instead of applauding, Blondie has clasped his hands rather prissily and there's a spooky-sweet smile on his lips, which are moving slightly, as if in silent prayer. His eyes are fixed on Scott and they never waver. Lisey pegs Blondie at once. There are guys – they are almost always guys – she thinks of as Scott's Deep Space Cowboys. Deep Space Cowboys have a lot to say. They want to grab Scott by the arm and tell him they understand the secret messages in his books; they understand that the books are really guides to God, Satan, or possibly the Gnostic Gospels. Deep Space Cowboys might be on about Scientology or numerology or (in one case) The Cosmic Lies of Brigham Young. Sometimes they want to talk about other worlds. Two years ago a Deep Space Cowboy hitchhiked all the way from Texas to Maine in order to talk to Scott about what he called *leavings*. These were most commonly found, he said, on uninhabited islands in the southern hemisphere. He knew they were what Scott had been writing about in *Relics*. He showed Scott the underlined words that proved it. The guy made Lisey very nervous – there was a certain wall-eyed look of *absence* about him – but Scott talked to him, gave him a beer, discussed the Easter Island monoliths with him for a bit, took a couple of his pamphlets, signed the kid a fresh copy of *Relics*, and sent him on his way, happy. Happy? Dancing

42

on the smucking atmosphere. When Scott's got it strapped on tight, he's amazing. No other word will do.

The thought of actual violence — that Blondie means to pull a Mark David Chapman on her husband — does not occur to Lisey. *My mind doesn't run that way*, she might have said. *I just didn't like the way his lips were moving.*

Scott acknowledges the applause — and a few raucous rebel yells — with the Scott Landon grin that has appeared on millions of book-jackets, all the time resting one foot on the shoulder of the silly shovel while the blade sinks slowly into the imported earth. He lets the applause run for ten or fifteen seconds, guided by his intuition (and his intuition is rarely wrong), then waves it off. And it goes. At once. *Foom*. Pretty cool, in a slightly scary way.

When he speaks, his voice seems nowhere near as loud as Dashmiel's, but Lisey knows that even with no mike or battery-powered bullhorn (the lack of either here this afternoon is probably someone's oversight), it will carry all the way to the back of the crowd. And the crowd is straining to hear every word. A Famous Man has come among them. A Thinker and a Writer. He will now scatter pearls of wisdom.

Pearls before swine, Lisey thinks. *Sweaty swine, at that.* But didn't her father tell her once that pigs don't sweat?

Across from her, Blondie carefully pushes his tumbled hair back from his fine white brow. His hands are as white as his forehead and Lisey thinks, *There's one piggy who keeps to the house a lot. A stay-at-home swine, and why not? He's got all sorts of strange ideas to catch up on.*

She shifts from one foot to the other, and the silk of her underwear all but *squeaks* in the crack of her ass. Oh, maddening! She forgets Blondie again in trying to calculate if she might not . . . while Scott's making his remarks . . . very surreptitiously, mind you . . .

Good Ma speaks up. Dour. Three words. Brooking no argument. *No, Lisey. Wait.*

'Ain't gonna sermonize, me,' Scott says, and she recognizes the patois of Gully Foyle, the main character of Alfred Bester's *The Stars My Destination.* His favorite novel. 'Too hot for sermons.'

'*Beam us up, Scotty!*' someone in the fifth or sixth row on the parking-lot side of the crowd yells exuberantly. The crowd laughs and cheers.

'Can't do it, brother,' Scott says. 'Transporters are broken and we're all out of lithium crystals.'

The crowd, being new to the riposte as well as the sally (Lisey has heard both at least fifty times), roars its approval and applauds. Across the way Blondie smiles thinly, sweatlessly, and grips his delicate left wrist with his long-fingered right hand. Scott takes his foot off the spade, not as if he's grown impatient with it but as if he has – for the moment, at least – found another use for it. And it seems he has. She watches, not without fascination, for this is Scott at his best, just winging it.

'It's nineteen-eighty-eight and the world has grown dark,' he says. He slips the ceremonial spade's short wooden handle easily through his loosely curled fist. The scoop winks sun in Lisey's eyes once, then is mostly hidden by the sleeve of Scott's lightweight jacket. With the scoop and blade hidden, he uses the slim wooden handle as a pointer, ticking off trouble and tragedy in the air in front of him.

'In March, Oliver North and Vice Admiral John

Poindexter are indicted on conspiracy charges — it's the wonderful world of Iran-Contra, where guns rule politics and money rules the world.

'On Gibraltar, members of Britain's Special Air Service kill three unarmed IRA members. Maybe they should change the SAS motto from "Who dares, wins" to "Shoot first, ask questions later".'

There's a ripple of laughter from the crowd. Roger Dashmiel looks hot and put out with this unexpected current-events lesson, but Tony Eddington is finally taking notes.

'Or make it ours. In July we goof and shoot down an Iranian airliner with two-hundred and ninety civilians on board. Sixty-six of them are children.

'The AIDS epidemic kills thousands, sickens . . . well, we don't know, do we? Hundreds of thousands? Millions?

'The world grows dark. Mr Yeats's blood-tide is at the flood. It rises. It rises.'

He looks down at nil but graying earth, and Lisey is suddenly terrified that he's seeing it, the thing with the endless patchy piebald side, that he is going to go off, perhaps even come to the break she knows he is afraid of (in truth she's as afraid of it as he is). Before her heart can do more than begin to speed up, he raises his head, grins like a kid at a county fair, and shoots the handle of the spade through his fist to the halfway point. It's a showy poolshark move, and the folks at the front of the crowd go *oooh*. But Scott's not done. Holding the spade out before him, he rotates the handle nimbly between his fingers, accelerating it into an unlikely spin. It's as dazzling as a baton-twirler's maneuver — because of the silver scoop swinging in the sun – and sweetly unexpected. She's been married to him since 1979 and had no *idea* he had such a sublimely cool move in his repertoire. (How many years does it take, she'll wonder two nights later, lying in bed alone in her substandard motel room and listening to dogs bark beneath a hot orange moon, before the simple stupid weight of accumulating days finally sucks all the wow out of a marriage? How lucky do you have to be for your love to outrace your time?) The silver bowl of the rapidly swinging spade sends a *Wake up! Wake up!* sunflash across the heat-dazed, sweat-sticky surface of the crowd. Lisey's husband is suddenly Scott the Pitchman, and she has never been so relieved to see that totally untrustworthy *honey, I'm hip* huckster's grin on his face. He has bummed them out; now he will try to sell them a throatful of dubious get-well medicine, the stuff with which he hopes to send them home. And she thinks they will buy, hot August afternoon or not. When he's like this, Scott could sell Frigidaires to Inuits, as the saying is . . . and God bless the language pool where we all go down to drink, as Scott himself would no doubt add (and has).

'But if every book is a little light in that darkness – and so I believe, so I must believe, corny or not, for I write the damned things, don't I? – then every library is a grand old ever-burning bonfire around which ten thousand people come to stand and warm themselves every day and night. Fahrenheit four-fifty-one ain't in it. Try Fahrenheit four *thousand*, folks, because we're not talking kitchen ovens here, we're talking big old blast-furnaces of the brain, red-hot smelters of the intellect. We celebrate the laying of such a grand fire this afternoon, and I'm honored to be a

part of it. Here is where we spit in the eye of forgetful-
ness and kick ignorance in his wrinkled old *cojones*. *Hey
photographer!*'

Stefan Queensland snaps to, smiling.

Scott, also smiling, says: 'Get one of this. The top brass
may not want to use it, but you'll like it in your portfolio,
I'll bet.'

Scott holds the ornamental tool out as if he intends
to twirl it again. The crowd gives a hopeful little gasp, but
this time he's only teasing. He slides his left hand down to
the spade's collar, digs in, and drives the spade-blade deep,
dousing its hot glitter in earth. He tosses its load of dirt
aside and cries: *'I declare the Shipman Library construction site
OPEN FOR BUSINESS!'*

The applause that greets this makes the previous
bursts sound like the sort of polite patter you might hear
at a prep-school tennis match. Lisey doesn't know if young
Mr Queensland caught the ceremonial first scoop, but
when Scott pumps the silly little silver spade at the sky
like an Olympic hero, Queensland documents that one for
sure, laughing behind his camera as he snaps it. Scott holds
the pose for a moment (Lisey happens to glance at Dashmiel
and catches that gentleman in the act of rolling his eyes at
Mr Eddington – Toneh). Then he lowers the spade to port
arms and holds it that way, grinning. Sweat has popped on
his cheeks and forehead in fine beads. The applause begins
to taper off. The crowd thinks he's done. Lisey thinks he's
only hit second gear.

When he knows they can hear him again, Scott digs
in for an encore scoop. 'This one's for Wild Bill Yeats!' he
calls. 'The bull-goose loony! And this one's for Poe, also

known as Baltimore Eddie! This one's for Alfie Bester, and if you haven't read him, you ought to be ashamed!' He's sounding out of breath, and Lisey is starting to feel a bit alarmed. It's so *hot*. She's trying to remember what he had for lunch – was it something heavy or light?

'And this one . . .' He dives the spade into what's now a respectable little divot and holds up the final dip of earth. The front of his shirt has darkened with sweat. 'Tell you what, why don't you think of whoever wrote your first good book? I'm talking about the one that got under you like a magic carpet and lifted you right off the ground. Do you know what I'm talking about?'

They know. It's on every face that faces his.

'The one that, in a perfect world, you'd check out first when the Shipman Library finally opens its doors. This one's for the one who wrote that.' He gives the spade a final valedictory shake, then turns to Dashmiel, who should be pleased with Scott's showmanship – asked to play by ear, Scott has played brilliantly – and who instead only looks hot and pissed off. 'I think we're done here,' he says, and tries to hand Dashmiel the spade.

'No, that's yoahs,' Dashmiel says. 'As a keepsake, and a token of ouah thanks. Along with yoah check, of co'se.' His rictus smile comes and goes in a fitful cramp. 'Shall we go and grab ourse'fs a little air-conditionin?'

'By all means,' Scott says, looking bemused, and then hands the spade to Lisey, as he has handed her so many unwanted mementos over the past twelve years of his celebrity: everything from ceremonial oars and Boston Red Sox hats encased in Lucite cubes to the masks of Comedy and Tragedy . . . but mostly pen-and-pencil sets. So many pen-and-pencil sets. Waterman, Scripto, Schaeffer, Mont Blanc, you name it. She looks at the spade's glittering silver scoop, as bemused as her beloved (he is still her beloved). There are a few flecks of dirt in the incised letters reading *COMMENCEMENT, SHIPMAN LIBRARY*, and Lisey blows them off. Where will such an unlikely artifact end up? In this summer of 1988 Scott's study is still under construction, although the address works and he's already begun storing stuff in the stalls and cubbies of the barn below. Across many of the cardboard boxes he's scrawled **SCOTT! THE EARLY YEARS!** in big strokes of a black felt-tip pen. Most likely the silver spade will wind up with this stuff, wasting its gleams in the gloom. Maybe she'll put it there herself, then tag it **SCOTT! THE MIDDLE YEARS!** as a kind of joke ... or a prize. The kind of goofy, unexpected gift Scott calls a—

But Dashmiel is on the move. Without another word – as if he's disgusted with this whole business and determined to put paid to it as soon as possible – he tromps across the rectangle of fresh earth, detouring around the divot which Scott's last big shovelful of earth has almost succeeded in promoting to a hole. The heels of Dashmiel's shiny black I'm-an-assistant-professor-on-my-way-up-and-don't-you-forget-it shoes sink deep into the earth with each heavy step. Dashmiel has to fight for balance, and Lisey guesses this does nothing to improve his mood. Tony Eddington falls in beside him, looking thoughtful. Scott pauses a moment, as if not quite sure what's up, then also starts to move, slipping between his host and his temporary biographer. Lisey follows, as is her wont. He delighted her into forgetting her *omenish* feeling

49

(broken glass in the morning)
for a little while, but now it's back
(broken hearts at night)
and *hard*. She thinks it must be why all these details look so big to her. She's sure the world will come back into more normal focus once she reaches the air-conditioning. And once she's gotten that pesty swatch of cloth out of her butt.

This is almost over, she reminds herself, and – how funny life can be – it is at this precise moment when the day begins to derail.

A campus security cop who is older than the others on this detail (eighteen years later she'll identify him from Queensland's news photo as Captain S. Heffernan) holds up the rope barrier on the far side of the ceremonial rectangle of earth. All she notices about him is that he's wearing what her husband might have called *a puffickly huh-yooge batch of orifice* on his khaki shirt. Her husband and his flanking escorts duck beneath the rope in a move so synchronized it could have been choreographed.

The crowd is moving toward the parking lot with the principals . . . with one exception. *Blondie* isn't moving toward the parking lot. Blondie is standing still on the parking lot side of the commencement patch. A few people bump him and he's *forced* backward after all, back onto the baked dead earth where the Shipman Library will stand come 1991 (if the chief contractor's promises can be believed, that is). Then he's actually moving forward against the tide, his hands coming unclasped so he can push a girl out of his way to his left and then a guy out of his way on the right. His mouth is still moving. At first Lisey again thinks he's mouthing a silent prayer, and then she hears the broken gibberish – like something a bad James Joyce imitator might write – and for the first time she becomes actively alarmed. Blondie's somehow weird blue eyes are fixed on her husband, there and nowhere else, but Lisey understands that he doesn't want to discuss *leavings* or the hidden religious subtexts of Scott's novels. This is no mere Deep Space Cowboy.

'The churchbells came down Angel Street,' says Blondie – says Gerd Allen Cole – who, it will turn out, spent most of his seventeenth year in an expensive Virginia mental institution and was released as cured and good to go. Lisey gets every word. They cut through the rising chatter of the crowd, that hum of conversation, like a knife through some light, sweet cake. 'That rungut sound, like rain on a tin roof! Dirty flowers, dirty and sweet, that's how the churchbells sound in my basement *as if you didn't know!*'

A hand that seems all long pale fingers goes to the tails of the white shirt and Lisey understands exactly what's going on here. It comes to her in shorthand TV images

(George Wallace Arthur Bremmer)

from her childhood. She looks toward Scott but Scott is talking to Dashmiel. Dashmiel is looking at Stefan Queensland, the irritated frown on Dashmiel's face saying he's had *Quite! Enough! Photographs! For One Day! Thank You!* Queensland is looking down at his camera, making some adjustment, and Anthony 'Toneh' Eddington is making a note on his pad. She spies the older campus security cop, he of the khaki uniform and the puffickly *huh-yooge* batch of orifice; he is looking at the crowd, but it's *the wrong smucking part*. It's impossible that she can see all these folks and Blondie too, but she can, she does, she can even see Scott's lips forming the words *think that went pretty well*, which is a testing comment he often makes after events like this, and oh God, oh Jesus Mary and JoJo the Carpenter, she tries to scream out Scott's name and warn him but her throat *locks up*, becomes a spitless dry socket, she can't say anything, and Blondie's got the bottom of his great big white shirt hoicked all the way up, and underneath are empty belt-loops and a flat hairless belly, a trout belly, and lying against that white skin is the butt of a gun which he now lays hold of and she hears him say, closing in on Scott from the right, 'If it closes the lips of the bells, it will have done the job. I'm sorry, Papa.'

She's running forward, or trying to, but she's got such a puffickly *huh-yooge* case of gluefoot and someone shoulders in front of her, a strapping coed with her hair tied up in a wide white silk ribbon with NASHVILLE printed on it in blue letters outlined in red (see how she sees everything?), and Lisey pushes her with the hand holding the silver spade, and the coed caws *'Hey!'* except it sounds slower and draggier than that, like *Hey* recorded at 45 rpm and then played back at $33^1/_3$ or maybe even 16. The whole world has gone to hot tar and for an eternity the strapping coed with NASHVILLE in her hair blocks Scott from her view; all she can see is Dashmiel's shoulder. And Tony Eddington, leafing back through the pages of his damn notebook.

Then the coed finally clears Lisey's field of vision, and as Dashmiel and her husband come into full view again, Lisey sees the English teacher's head snap up and his body go on red alert. It happens in an instant. Lisey sees what Dashmiel sees. She sees Blondie with the gun (it will prove to be a Ladysmith .22 made in Korea and bought at a garage sale in South Nashville for thirty-seven dollars) pointed at her husband, who has at last seen the danger and stopped. In Lisey-time, all this happens very, very slowly. She does not actually see the bullet fly out of the .22's muzzle – not quite – but she hears Scott say, very mildly, seeming to drawl the words over the course of ten or even fifteen seconds: 'Let's talk about it, son, right?' And then she sees fire bloom from the gun's nickel-plated muzzle in an uneven yellow-white corsage. She hears a pop – stupid, insignificant, the sound of someone breaking a paper lunchsack with the palm of his hand. She sees Dashmiel, that southern-fried chickenshit, go jackrabbiting off to his immediate left. She sees Scott buck backward on his heels. At the same time his chin thrusts forward. The combination is weird and graceful, like a dance-floor move. A black hole blinks open on the right side of his summer sportcoat. 'Son, you honest-to-God don't want to do that,' he says in his drawling Lisey-time voice, and even in Lisey-time she can hear how his voice grows thinner on every word until he sounds like a test pilot in a high-altitude chamber. Yet Lisey thinks he still doesn't know he's been shot. She's almost positive. His sportcoat swings open like a gate as he puts his hand out in a commanding *stop-this* gesture, and she realizes two things simultaneously. The first is that the shirt inside his coat is turning red. The second is that she has at last broken into some semblance of a run.

'I got to end all this ding-dong,' says Gerd Allen Cole

with perfect fretful clarity. 'I got to end all this ding-dong for the freesias.' And Lisey is suddenly sure that once Scott is dead, once the damage is done, Blondie will either kill himself or pretend to try. For the time being, however, he has this business to finish. The business of the writer. Blondie turns his wrist slightly so that the smoking barrel of the Ladysmith .22 points at the left side of Scott's chest; in Lisey-time the move is smooth and slow. He has done the lung; now he'll do the heart. Lisey knows she can't allow that to happen. If her husband is to have any chance at all, this lethal goofball mustn't be allowed to put any more lead into him.

As if repudiating her, Gerd Allen Cole says, 'It never ends until you go down. You're responsible for all these repetitions, old boy. You are hell, you are a monkey, and now you are *my* monkey!'

This speech is the closest he comes to making sense, and making it gives Lisey just enough time to first wind up with the silver spade – the body knows its business and her hands have already found their position near the top of the thing's forty-inch handle – and then swing it. Still, it's close. If it had been a horse race, the tote-board would undoubtedly have flashed the HOLD TICKETS WAIT FOR PHOTO message. But when the race is between a man with a gun and a woman with a shovel, you don't need a photo. In slowed-down Lisey-time she sees the silver scoop strike the gun, driving it upward just as that corsage of fire blooms again (she can see only part of it this time, and the muzzle is completely hidden by the blade of the spade). She sees the business-end of the ceremonial shovel carry on forward and upward as the second shot goes harmlessly into the hot August sky. She sees the gun fly loose, and there's time to think *Holy smuck! I really put a charge into this one!* before the spade connects with Blondie's face. His hand is still in there (three of those long slim fingers will be broken), but the spade's silver bowl connects solidly just the same, breaking Cole's nose, shattering his right cheekbone and the bony orbit around his staring right eye, shattering nine teeth as well. A Mafia goon with a set of brass knuckles couldn't have done better.

And now – still slow, still in Lisey-time – the elements of Stefan Queensland's award-winning photograph are assembling themselves.

Captain S. Heffernan has seen what's happening only a second or two after Lisey, but he also has to deal with the bystander problem – in his case a fat bepimpled fella wearing baggy Bermuda shorts and a tee-shirt with Scott Landon's smiling face on it. Captain Heffernan shunts this young fella aside with one muscular shoulder.

By then Blondie is sinking to the ground (and out of the forthcoming photo's field) with a dazed expression in one eye and blood pouring from the other. Blood is also gushing from the hole which at some future date may again serve as his mouth. Heffernan completely misses the actual hit.

Roger Dashmiel, maybe remembering that he's supposed to be the master of ceremonies and not a big old bunny-rabbit, turns back toward Eddington, his protégé, and Landon, his troublesome guest of honor, just in time to take his place as a staring, slightly blurred face in the forthcoming photo's background.

Scott Landon, meanwhile, shock-walks right out of

STEPHEN KING

the award-winning photo. He walks as though unmindful
of the heat, striding toward the parking lot and Nelson
Hall beyond, which is home of the English Department
and mercifully air-conditioned. He walks with surprising
briskness, at least to begin with, and a goodly part of the
crowd moves with him, unaware for the most part that
anything has happened. Lisey is both infuriated and unsur-
prised. After all, how many of them saw Blondie with
that cuntish little pistol in his hand? How many of them
recognized the burst-paper-bag sounds as gunshots? The
hole in Scott's coat could be a smudge of dirt from his
shoveling chore, and the blood that has soaked his shirt
is as yet invisible to the outside world. He's now making
a strange whistling noise each time he inhales, but how
many of them hear that? No, it's *her* they're looking at –
some of them, anyway – the crazy chick who just inex-
plicably hauled off and whacked some guy in the face
with the ceremonial silver spade. A lot of them are actually *grinning*, as if they believe it's all part of a show being
put on for their benefit, the Scott Landon Roadshow.
Well, fuck them, and fuck Dashmiel, and fuck the day-
late and dollar-short campus cop with his puffickly *huh-
yooge* batch of orifice. All she cares about now is Scott.
She thrusts the shovel out not quite blindly to her right
and Eddington, their rent-a-Boswell, takes it. It's either
that or get hit in the nose with it. Then, still in that
horrible slo-mo, Lisey runs after her husband, whose briskness evaporates as soon as he reaches the suck-oven heat
of the parking lot. Behind her, Tony Eddington is peering
at the silver spade as if it might be an artillery shell, a
radiation detector, or the *leaving* of some great departed

56

race, and to him comes Captain S. Heffernan with his mistaken assumption of who today's hero must be. Lisey is unaware of this part, will know none of it until she sees Queensland's photograph eighteen years later, would care about none of it even if she *did* know; all her attention is fixed on her husband, who has just gone down on his hands and knees in the parking lot. She tries to repudiate Lisey-time, to run faster. And that is when Queensland snaps his picture, catching just one half of one shoe on the far righthand side of the frame, something he will not realize then, or ever.

6

The Pulitzer Prize winner, the *enfant terrible* who published his first novel at the tender age of twenty-two, goes down. Scott Landon *hits the deck*, as the saying is.

Lisey makes a supreme effort to pull out of the maddening time-glue in which she seems to be trapped. She must get free because if she doesn't reach him before the crowd surrounds him and shuts her out, they will very likely kill him with their concern. With smotherlove.

—*Heeeeee's hurrrrrt*, someone shouts.

She screams at herself in her own head

(strap it on STRAP IT ON RIGHT NOW)

and that finally does it. The glue in which she has been packed is gone. Suddenly she is *knifing* forward; all the world is noise and heat and sweat and jostling bodies. She blesses the speedy reality of it even as she uses her left hand to grab the left cheek of her ass and *pull*, raking the goddam underwear out of the crack of her goddam ass, there, at least one thing about this wrong and broken day is now mended.

A coed in the kind of shell top where the straps tie at the shoulders in big floppy bows threatens to block her narrowing path to Scott, but Lisey ducks beneath her and hits the hottop. She won't be aware of her scraped and blistered knees until much later – until the hospital, in fact, where a kindly paramedic will notice and put lotion on them, something so cool and soothing it will make her cry with relief. But that is for later. Now it might as well be just her and Scott alone on the edge of this hot parking lot, this terrible black-and-yellow ballroom floor which must be a hundred and thirty degrees at least, maybe a hundred and fifty. Her mind tries to present her with the image of an egg frying sunnyside up in Good Ma's old black iron spider and Lisey blocks it out.

Scott is looking at her.

He gazes up and now his face is waxy pale except for the sooty smudges forming beneath his hazel eyes and the fat string of blood which has begun to flow from the right side of his mouth and down along his jaw. 'Lisey!' That thin, whooping high-altitude-chamber voice. 'Did that guy really shoot me?'

'Don't try to talk.' She puts a hand on his chest. His shirt, oh dear God, is *soaked* with blood, and beneath it she can feel his heart running along so fast and light; it is not the heartbeat of a human being but of a bird. *Pigeon-pulse*, she thinks, and that's when the girl with the floppy bows tied on her shoulders falls on top of her. She would land on Scott but Lisey instinctively shields him, taking the brunt of the girl's weight (*'Hey! Shit! FUCK!'* the startled

58

girl cries out) with her back; that weight is there for only a second, and then gone. Lisey sees the girl shoot her hands out to break her fall – *oh, the divine reflexes of the young*, she thinks, as though she herself were ancient instead of just thirty-one – and the girl is successful, but then she is yipping 'Ow, *ow, OW!*' as the asphalt heats her skin.

'Lisey,' Scott whispers, and oh Christ how his breath screams when he pulls it in, like wind in a chimney.

'Who pushed me?' the girl with the bows on her shoulders is demanding. She's a-hunker, hair from a busted ponytail in her eyes, crying in shock, pain and embarrassment.

Lisey leans close to Scott. The heat of him terrifies her and fills her with pity deeper than any she thought it was possible to feel. He is actually *shivering* in the heat. Awkwardly, using only one arm, she strips off her jacket. 'Yes, you've been shot. So just be quiet and don't try to—'

'I'm so hot,' he says, and begins to shiver harder. What comes next, convulsions? His hazel eyes stare up into her blue ones. Blood runs from the corner of his mouth. She can smell it. Even the collar of his shirt is soaking in red. *His tea-cure wouldn't be any good here*, she thinks, not even sure what it is she's thinking about. *Too much blood this time. Too smucking much.* 'I'm so hot, Lisey, please give me ice.'

'I will,' she says, and puts her jacket under his head. 'I will, Scott.' *Thank God he's wearing his sportcoat*, she thinks, and then has an idea. She grabs the hunkering, crying girl by the arm. 'What's your name?'

The girl stares as if she were mad, but answers the question. 'Lisa Lemke.'

Another Lisa, small world, Lisey thinks but does not say. What she says is, 'My husband's been shot, Lisa. Can you go over there to . . .' She cannot remember the name of the building, only its function. '. . . to the English Department and call an ambulance? Dial 911—'

'Ma'am? Mrs Landon?' This is the campus security cop with the puffickly *huh-yooge* batch, making his way through the crowd with a lot of help from his meaty elbows. He squats beside her and his knees pop. *Louder than Blondie's pistol*, Lisey thinks. He's got a walkie-talkie in one hand. He speaks slowly and carefully, as though to a distressed child. 'I've called the campus infirmary, Mrs Landon. They are rolling their ambulance, which will take your husband to Nashville Memorial. Do you understand me?'

She does, and her gratitude (the cop has made up the dollar short he owed and a few more, in Lisey's opinion) is almost as deep as the pity she feels for her husband, lying on the simmering pavement and trembling like a distempered dog. She nods, weeping the first of what will be many tears before she gets Scott back to Maine – not on a Delta flight but in a private plane and with a private nurse on board, and with another ambulance and another private nurse to meet them at the Portland Jetport's Civil Aviation terminal. Now she turns back to the Lemke girl and says, 'He's burning up – is there ice, honey? Can you think of anywhere that there might be ice? Anywhere at all?'

She says this without much hope, and is therefore amazed when Lisa Lemke nods at once. 'There's a snack center with a Coke machine right over there.' She points in the direction of Nelson Hall, which Lisey can't see. All she can see is a crowding forest of bare legs, some hairy, some smooth, some tanned, some sunburned. She realizes they're completely hemmed in, that she's tending her fallen husband in a slot the shape of a large vitamin pill or cold capsule, and feels a touch of crowd-panic. Is the word for that agoraphobia? Scott would know.

'If you can get him some ice, please do,' Lisey says. 'And hurry.' She turns to the campus security cop, who appears to be taking Scott's pulse – a completely useless activity, in Lisey's opinion. Right now it's down to either alive or dead. 'Can you make them move back?' she asks. Almost pleads. 'It's so *hot*, and—'

Before she can finish he's up like Jack from his box, yelling 'Move it back! Let this girl through! Move it back and let this girl through! Let him breathe, folks, what do you say?'

The crowd shuffles back . . . very reluctantly, it seems to Lisey. They don't want to miss any of the blood, it seems to her.

The heat bakes up from the pavement. She has half-expected to get used to it, the way you get used to a hot shower, but that isn't happening. She listens for the howl of the approaching ambulance and hears nothing. Then she does. She hears Scott, saying her name. *Croaking* her name. At the same time he twitches at the side of the sweat-soaked shell top she's wearing (her bra now stands out against the silk as stark as a swollen tattoo). She looks down and sees something she doesn't like at all. Scott is smiling. The blood has coated his lips a rich candy red, top to bottom, side to side, and the smile actually looks more like the grin of a clown. *No one loves a clown at midnight*, she thinks, and wonders where *that* came from. It will only be at some point during the long and mostly sleepless night ahead of her, listening to what will seem like every dog in Nashville bark at the hot August moon, that she'll remember it was the epigram of Scott's third novel, the only one both she and the critics hated, the one that made them rich. *Empty Devils*.

Scott continues to twitch at her blue silk top, his eyes still so brilliant and fevery in their blackening sockets. He has something to say, and – reluctantly – she leans down to hear it. He pulls air in a little at a time, in half-gasps. It is a noisy, frightening process. The smell of blood is even stronger up close. Nasty. A mineral smell.

It's death. It's the smell of death.

As if to ratify this, Scott says: 'It's very close, honey. I can't see it, but I . . .' Another long, screaming intake of breath. 'I hear it taking its meal. And grunting.' Smiling that bloody clown-smile as he says it.

'Scott, I don't know what you're talk—'

The hand that has been tugging at her top has some strength left in it, after all. It pinches her side, and cruelly – when she takes the top off much later, in the motel room, she'll see a bruise, a true lover's knot.

'You . . .' Screamy breath. 'Know . . .' Another screamy breath, deeper. And still grinning, as if they share some horrible secret. A *purple* secret, the color of bruises. The color of certain flowers that grow on certain

(hush Lisey oh hush)

yes, on certain hillsides. 'You . . . know . . . so don't . . . insult my . . . intelligence.' Another whistling, screaming breath. 'Or your own.'

And she supposes she *does* know some of it. The long boy, he calls it. Or the thing with the endless piebald side. Once she meant to look up *piebald* in the dictionary, but she forgot – forgetting is a skill she has had reason to polish during the years she and Scott have been together. But she knows what he's talking about, yes.

He lets go, or maybe just loses the strength to hold on. Lisey pulls back a little – not far. His eyes regard her from their deep and blackening sockets. They are as brilliant as ever, but she sees they are also full of terror and (this is what frightens her most) some wretched, inexplicable amusement. Still speaking low – perhaps so only she can hear, maybe because it's the best he can manage – Scott says, 'Listen, little Lisey. I'll make how it sounds when it looks around.'

'Scott, no – you have to stop.'

He pays no attention. He draws in another of those screaming breaths, purses his wet red lips in a tight O, and makes a low, incredibly nasty *chuffing* noise. It drives a fine spray of blood up his clenched throat and into the sweltering air. A girl sees it and screams. This time the crowd doesn't need the campus cop to ask them to move back; they do it on their own, leaving Lisey, Scott, and Captain Heffernan a perimeter of at least four feet all the way around.

The sound – dear God, it really *is* a kind of grunting – is mercifully short. Scott coughs, his chest heaving, the wound spilling more blood in rhythmic pulses, then beckons her back down with one finger. She comes, leaning on her simmering hands. His socketed eyes compel her; so does his mortal grin.

He turns his head to the side, spits a wad of half-congealed blood onto the hot tar, then turns back to her. 'I could . . . call it that way,' he whispers. 'It would come. You'd be . . . rid of my . . . everlasting . . . quack.'

She understands that he means it, and for a moment (surely it is the power of his eyes) she believes it's true. He will make the sound again, only a little louder, and in some other world the long boy, that lord of sleepless nights, will turn its unspeakable hungry head. A moment later in this world, Scott Landon will simply shiver on the pavement and die. The death certificate will say something sane, but she'll know: his dark thing finally saw him and came for him and ate him alive.

So now come the things they will never speak of later, not to others or between themselves. Too awful. Each marriage has two hearts, one light and one dark. This is the dark heart of theirs, the one mad true secret. She leans close to him on the baking pavement, sure he is dying, nevertheless determined to hold onto him if she can. If it means fighting the long boy for him – with nothing but her fingernails, if it comes to that – she will.

'Well . . . Lisey?' Smiling that repulsive, knowing, terrible smile. 'What . . . do . . . you . . . say?'

Leaning even closer. Into the shivering sweat-and-blood stink of him. Leaning in until she can smell the last palest ghost of the Prell he shampooed with that morning and the Foamy he shaved with. Leaning in until her lips touch his ear. She whispers, 'Be quiet, Scott. For once in your life, just be quiet.'

When she looks at him again, his eyes are different. The fierceness is gone. He's fading, but maybe that's all right, because he looks sane again. 'Lisey . . . ?'

Still whispering. Looking directly into his eyes. '*Leave that smucking thing alone and it will go away.*' For a moment she almost adds, *You can take care of the rest of this mess later,* but the idea is senseless — for awhile, the only thing Scott can do for himself is not die. What she says is, 'Don't you ever make that noise again.'

He licks at his lips. She sees the blood on his tongue and it turns her stomach, but she doesn't pull away from him. She supposes she's in this now until the ambulance hauls him away or he quits breathing right here on this hot pavement a hundred yards or so from his latest triumph; if she can stick through that last, she guesses she can stick through anything.

'I'm so hot,' he says. 'If only I had a piece of ice to suck . . .'

'Soon,' Lisey says, not knowing if she's promising rashly and not caring. 'I'm getting it for you.' At least she can hear the ambulance howling its way toward them. That's something.

And then, a kind of miracle. The girl with the bows on her shoulders and the new scrapes on her palms fights her way to the front of the crowd. She's gasping like someone who has just run a race and sweat is running down her cheeks and neck, but she's holding two big waxed paper cups in her hands. 'I spilled half the fucking Coke getting back here,' she says, throwing a brief, baleful glance over her shoulder at the crowd, 'but I got the ice okay. Ice is ni—' Then her eyes roll up almost to the whites and she reels backward, all loosey-goosey in her sneakers. The campus cop — oh bless him with many blessings, huh-yooge batch of orifice and all — grabs her, steadies her, and takes one of the cups. He hands it to Lisey, then urges the other Lisa to drink from the remaining cup. Lisey Landon pays no attention. Later, replaying all this, she'll be a little in awe of her own single-mindedness. Now she only thinks *Just keep her from falling on top of me again if she faints, Officer Friendly*, and turns back to Scott.

He's shivering worse than ever and his eyes are dulling out, losing their grasp on her. And still, he tries. 'Lisey . . . so hot . . . ice . . .'

'I have it, Scott. Now will you for once just shut your everlasting mouth?'

'One went north, one went south,' he croaks, and then, for a wonder, he does what she asks. Maybe he's all talked out, which would be a Scott Landon first.

Lisey drives her hand deep into the cup, sending Coke all the way to the top and splooshing over the edge. The cold is shocking and utterly wonderful. She clutches a good handful of ice-chips, thinking how ironic this is: whenever she and Scott stop at a turnpike rest area and she uses a machine that dispenses cups of soda instead of cans or bottles, she always hammers on the NO ICE button, feeling righteous – others may allow the evil soft drink companies to shortchange them by dispensing half a cup of soda and half a cup of ice, but not Dave Debusher's baby girl Lisa. What was old Dandy's saying? *I didn't fall off a hayrick yesterday!* And now here she is, wishing for even more ice and less Coke . . . not that she thinks it will make much difference. But on that one she's in for a surprise.

'Scott, here. Ice.'

His eyes are half-closed now, but he opens his mouth and when she first rubs his lips with her handful of ice and then pops one of the melting shards onto his bloody tongue, his shivering suddenly stops. God, it's magic. Emboldened, she rubs her freezing, leaking hand along his right cheek, his left cheek, and then across his forehead, where drops of Coke-colored water drip into his eyebrows and then run down the sides of his nose.

'Oh Lisey, that's heaven,' he says, and although still screamy, his voice sounds more with-it to her ... more *there*. The ambulance has pulled up on the left side of the crowd with a dying growl of its siren and a few seconds later she can hear an impatient male voice shouting, *'Paramedics! Let us through! Paramedics, c'mon, people, let us through so we can do our jobs, whaddaya say?'*

Dashmiel, the southern-fried asshole, chooses this moment to speak in Lisey's ear. The solicitude in his voice, given the speed with which he jackrabbited, makes her want to grind her teeth. 'How is he, darlin?'

Without looking around, she replies: 'Trying to live.'

7

'Trying to live,' she murmured, running her palm over the glossy page in the *U-Tenn Nashville Review*. Over the picture of Scott with his foot poised on that dopey silver shovel. She closed the book with a snap and tossed it onto the dusty back of the booksnake. Her appetite for pictures – for *memories* – was more than sated for one day. There was a nasty throb starting up behind her right eye. She wanted to take something for it, not that pussy Tylenol but what her late husband had called head-bonkers. A couple of his Excedrin would be just the ticket, if they weren't too far off the shelf-date. Then a little lie-down in their bedroom until the incipient headache passed. She might even sleep awhile.

I'm still thinking of it as our bedroom, she mused, going to the stairs that led down to the barn, which was now not really a barn at all but just a series of storage cubbies . . . though still redolent of hay and rope and tractor-oil, the old sweet-stubborn farm smells. *Still as ours, even after two years.*

And so what? What of that?

She shrugged. 'Nothing, I suppose.'

She was a little shocked at the mumbly, half-drunk sound of the words. She supposed all that vivid remembering had worn her out. All that relived stress. There was one thing to be grateful for: no other picture of Scott in the belly of the booksnake could call up such violent memories, he'd only been shot once and none of those colleges would have sent him photos of his fa—

(shut up about that just hush)

'That's right,' she agreed as she reached the bottom of the stairs, and with no real idea of what she'd been on the edge

(Scoot you old Scoot)

of thinking about. Her head was hanging and she felt sweaty all over, like someone who has just missed being in an accident. 'Shutupsky, enough is enough.'

And, as if her voice had activated it, a telephone began to ring behind the closed wooden door on her right. Lisey came to a stop in the barn's main downstairs passage. Once that door had opened upon a stabling area large enough for three horses. Now the sign on it simply said **HIGH VOLTAGE!** This had been Lisey's idea of a joke. She had intended to put a small office in there, a place where she could keep records and pay the monthly bills (they had – and she still had – a full-time money-manager, but he was in New York and could not be expected to see to such minutia as her monthly tab at Hilltop Grocery). She'd gotten as far as putting in the desk, the phone, the fax, and a few filing cabinets . . . and then Scott died. Had she even been in there since then? Once, she remembered. Early this spring. Late March, a few stale stoles of snow still on the ground, her mission just to empty the answering machine attached to the phone. The number 21 had been in the gadget's window. Messages one through seventeen and nineteen through twenty-one had been from the sort of hucksters Scott had called 'phone-lice'. The eighteenth (this didn't surprise Lisey at all) had been from Amanda. 'Just wanted to know if you ever hooked this damn thing up,' she'd said. 'You gave me and Darla and Canty the number before Scott died.' Pause. 'I guess you did.' Pause. 'Hook it up, I mean.' Pause. Then, in a rush: 'But there was a *very* long time between the message and the bleep, sheesh, you must have a lot of messages on there, little Lisey, you ought to check the damn things in case somebody wants to give you a set of Spode or something.' Pause. 'Well . . . g'bye.'

Now, standing outside the closed office door, feeling pain pulse in sync with her heartbeat behind her right eye, she listened to the telephone ring a third time, and a fourth. Halfway through the fifth ring there was a click and then her own voice, telling whoever was on the other end that he or she had reached 727–5932. There was no false promise of a callback, not even an invitation to leave a message at the sound of what Amanda called the bleep. Anyway, what would be the point? Who would call *here* to talk to *her*? With Scott dead, the motor was out of this place. The one left was really just little Lisey Debusher from Lisbon Falls, now the widow Landon. Little Lisey lived alone in a house far too big for her and wrote grocery lists, not novels.

The pause between the message and the beep was so long that she thought the tape for replies had to be full. Even if it wasn't, the caller would get tired and hang up, all she'd hear through the closed office door would be that most annoying of recorded phone voices, the woman who tells you (*scolds* you), 'If you'd like to make a call . . . please hang up and dial your *operator!*' She doesn't add *smuckhead* or *shit-for-brains*, but Lisey always sensed it as what Scott would have called 'a subtext'.

Instead she heard a male voice speak three words. There was no reason for them to chill her, but they did. 'I'll try again,' it said.

There was a click.

Then there was silence.

8

This is a much nicer present, she thinks, but knows it's neither past *nor* present; it's just a dream. She was lying on the big double bed in the

(our our our our our)

bedroom, under the slowly paddling fan; in spite of the one hundred and thirty milligrams of caffeine in the two Excedrin (expiration date: OCT 07) she took from

70

the dwindling supply of Scott-meds in the bathroom cabinet, she had fallen asleep. If she has any doubt of it, she only has to look at where she is – the third-floor ICU wing of the Nashville Memorial Hospital – and her unique means of travel: she's once more locomoting upon a large piece of cloth with the words PILLSBURY'S BEST FLOUR printed on it. Once more she's delighted to see that the corners of this homely magic carpet, where she sits with her arms regally folded beneath her bosom, are knotted like hankies. She's floating so close to the ceiling that when PILLSBURY'S BEST FLOUR slips beneath one of the slowly paddling overhead fans (in her dream they look just like the one in their bedroom), she has to lie flat to avoid being whacked and cracked by the blades. These varnished wooden oars say *shoop, shoop, shoop* over and over as they make their slow and somehow stately revolutions. Below her, nurses come and go on squeak-soled shoes. Some are wearing the colorful smocks that will come to dominate the profession, but most of these still wear white dresses, white hose, and those caps that always make Lisey think of stuffed doves. Two doctors – she supposes they must be doctors, although one doesn't look old enough to shave – chat by the drinking fountain. The tile walls are cool green. The heat of the day cannot seem to take hold in here. She supposes there is air-conditioning as well as the fans, but she can't hear it.

Not in my dream, of course not, she tells herself, and this seems reasonable. Up ahead is room 319, which is where Scott went to recuperate after they took the bullet out of him. She has no trouble reaching the door, but discovers she's too high to get through once she arrives. And she wants to get in there. She never got around to telling him *You can take care of the rest of this mess later*, but was that even necessary? Scott Landon did not, after all, *fall off a hayrick yesterday*. The real question, it seems to her, is what's the correct magic word to make a magic PILLSBURY'S BEST carpet go down?

It comes to her. It's not a word she wants to hear emerging from her own mouth (it's a Blondie word), but needs must when the devil drives – as Dandy *also* said – and so . . .

'Freesias,' Lisey says, and the faded cloth with the knotted corners obediently drops three feet from its hover-point below the hospital ceiling. She looks in the open door and sees Scott, now maybe five hours post-op, lying in a narrow but surprisingly pretty bed with a gracefully curved head and foot. Monitors that sound like answering machines queep and bleep. Two bags of something trans-parent hang on a pole between him and the wall. He appears to be asleep. Across the bed from him, 1988-Lisey sits in a straight-backed chair with her husband's hand folded into one of her own. In 1988-Lisey's other hand is the paperback novel she brought to Tennessee with her – she never expected to get through so much of it. Scott reads people like Borges, Pynchon, Tyler, and Atwood; Lisey reads Maeve Binchy, Colleen McCullough, Jean Auel (although she is growing a bit impatient with Ms Auel's randy cave people), Joyce Carol Oates, and, just lately, Shirley Conran. What she has in room 319 is *Savages*, the newest novel by the latter, and Lisey likes it a lot. She has come to the part where the women stranded in the jungle learn to use their bras as slingshots. All that Lycra. Lisey doesn't know if the romance-readers of America are ready for this latest from Ms Conran, but she herself thinks it's brave and rather beautiful, in its way. Isn't bravery always sort of beautiful?

The last light of day pours through the room's window in a flood of red and gold. It's ominous and lovely. 1988-Lisey is very tired: emotionally, physically, and of being in the South. She thinks if one more person calls her y'all she'll scream. The good part? She doesn't think she's going to be here as long as *they* do, because . . . well . . . she has reason to know Scott's a fast healer, leave it at that.

Soon she'll go back to the motel and try to rent the same room they had earlier in the day (Scott almost always rents them a hideout, even if the gig is just what he calls 'the old in-out'). She has an idea she won't be able to do it – they treat you a lot different when you're with a man, whether he's famous or not – but the place is fairly handy to the hospital as well as to the college, and as long as she gets *something* there, she doesn't give a smuck. Dr Sattherwaite, who's in charge of Scott's case, has promised her she can dodge reporters by going out the back tonight and for the next few days. He says Mrs McKinney in Reception will have a cab waiting back by the cafeteria loading dock 'as soon as you give her the high sign.' She would have gone already, but Scott has been restless for the last hour. Sattherwaite said he'd be out at least until midnight, but Sattherwaite doesn't know Scott the way she does, and Lisey isn't much surprised when he begins surfacing for brief intervals as sunset approaches. Twice he has recognized her, twice he has asked her what happened, and twice she has told him that a mentally deranged person shot him. The second time he said, 'Hi-yo-smuckin-Silver'

73

before closing his eyes again, and that actually made her laugh. Now she wants him to come back one more time so she can tell him she's not going back to Maine, only to the motel, and that she'll see him in the morning.

All this 2006-Lisey knows. Remembers. Intuits. Whatever. From where she sits on her PILLSBURY'S BEST magic carpet, she thinks: *He opens his eyes. He looks at me. He says, 'I was lost in the dark and you found me. I was hot — so hot — and you gave me ice.'*

But is that really what he said? Is it really what happened? And if she's hiding things — hiding them from herself — *why* is she hiding them?

In the bed, in the red light, Scott opens his eyes. Looks at his wife as she reads her book. His breath doesn't scream now, but there's still a windy sound as he pulls air in as deeply as he can and half-whispers, half-croaks her name. 1988-Lisey puts down her book and looks at him.

'Hey, you're awake again,' she says. 'So here's your pop quiz. Do you remember what happened to you?'

'Shot,' he whispers. 'Kid. Tube. Back. Hurts.'

'You can have something for the pain in a little while,' she says. 'For now, would you like—'

He squeezes her hand, telling her she can stop. *Now he'll tell me he was lost in the dark and I gave him ice*, 2006-Lisey thinks.

But what he says to his wife — who earlier that day saved his life by braining a madman with a silver shovel — is only this: 'Hot, wasn't it?' His tone casual. No special look; just making conversation. Just passing the time while the red light deepens and the machines queep and bleep, and from her hoverpoint in the doorway, 2006-Lisey sees the shudder — subtle but there — run through her younger self; sees the first finger of her younger self's left hand lose its place in her paperback copy of *Savages*.

I'm thinking 'Either he doesn't remember or he's pretending not to remember what he said when he was down — about how he could call it if he wanted to, how he could call the long boy if I wanted to be done with him — and what I said back, about how he should shut up and leave it alone . . . that if he just shut the smuck up it would go away. I'm wondering if this is a real case of forgetting — the way he forgot that he'd been shot — or if it's more of our special forgetting, which is more like sweeping the bad shit into a box and then locking it up tight. I'm wondering if it even matters, as long as he remembers how to get better.'

As she lay on her bed (and as she rides the magic carpet in the eternal present of her dream), Lisey stirred and tried to cry out to her younger self, tried to yell that it *did* matter, it *did*. *Don't let him get away with it!* she tried to yell. *You can't forget forever!* But another saying from the past occurred to her, this one from their endless games of Hearts and Whist at Sabbath Day Lake in the summertime, always yelled out when some player wanted to look at discards more than a single trick deep: *Leave that alone! You can't unbury the dead!*

You can't unbury the dead.

Still, she tries one more time. With all her considerable force of mind and will, 2006-Lisey leans forward on her magic carpet and sends *He's faking! SCOTT REMEMBERS EVERYTHING!* at her younger self.

And for a wild moment she thinks she's getting through . . . *knows* she's getting through. 1988-Lisey twitches in her chair and her book actually slides out of her hand

75

and hits the floor with a flat clap. But before that version of herself can look around, Scott Landon stares directly at the woman hovering in the doorway, the version of his wife who will live to be his widow. He purses his lips again, but instead of making the nasty chuffing sound, he *blows*. It's not much of a puff; how could it be, considering what he's been through? But it's enough to send the PILLS-BURY'S BEST magic carpet flying backward, dipping and diving like a milkweed pod in a hurricane. Lisey hangs on for dear life as the hospital walls rock past, but the damned thing tilts and she's falling and

9

Lisey awoke sitting bolt-upright on the bed with sweat drying on her forehead and underneath her arms. It was relatively cool in here, thanks to the overhead fan, but still she was as hot as a . . .

Well, as hot as a suck-oven.

'Whatever *that* is,' she said, and laughed shakily.

The dream was already fading to rags and tatters – the only thing she could recall with any clarity was the otherworldly red light of some setting sun – but she had awakened with a crazy certainty planted in the forefront of her mind, a crazy imperative: she had to find that smucking shovel. That silver spade.

'Why?' she asked the empty room. She picked the clock off the nightstand and held it close to her face, sure it would tell her an hour had gone by, maybe even two. She was astounded to see she had been asleep for exactly twelve minutes. She put the clock back on the nightstand

and wiped her hands on the front of her blouse as if she had picked up something dirty and crawling with germs. 'Why *that* thing?'

Never mind. It was Scott's voice, not her own. She rarely heard it with such clarity these days, but oboy, was she ever hearing it now. Loud and clear. *That's none of your business. Just find it and put it where . . . well, you know.*

Of course she did.

'Where I can strap it on,' she murmured, and rubbed her face with her hands, and gave a little laugh.

That's right, babyluv, her dead husband agreed. *Whenever it seems appropriate.*

CHAPTER THREE

LISEY AND THE SILVER SPADE (WAIT FOR THE WIND TO CHANGE)

1

Her vivid dream did nothing at all to free Lisey from her memories of Nashville, and from one memory in particular: Gerd Allen Cole turning the gun from the lung-shot, which Scott might be able to survive, to the heart-shot, which he most certainly would not. By then the whole world had slowed down, and what she kept returning to – as the tongue keeps returning to the surface of a badly chipped tooth – was how utterly *smooth* that movement had been, as if the gun had been mounted on a gimbal.

Lisey vacuumed the parlor, which didn't need vacuuming, then did a wash that didn't half-fill the machine; the laundry basket filled so *slowly* now that it was just her. Two years and she still couldn't get used to it. Finally she pulled on her old tank suit and did laps in the pool out back: five, then ten, then fifteen, then seventeen and winded. She clung to the lip at the shallow end with her legs trailing out behind her, panting, her dark hair clinging to her cheeks, brow, and neck like a shiny helmet, and still she saw the pale, long-fingered hand swiveling, saw the Ladysmith (it was impossible to think of it as just a gun once you knew its lethal cuntish name) swiveling, saw the little black hole with Scott's death tucked inside it moving left, and the silver shovel was so *heavy*. It seemed impossible that she could be in time, that she could outrace Cole's insanity.

She kicked her feet slowly, making little splashes. Scott had loved the pool, but actually swam in it only on rare occasions; he had been a book, beer, and inner-tube sort of guy. When he wasn't on the road, that was. Or in his study, writing with the music cranked. Or sitting up in the guest-room rocker in the broken heart of a winter night, bundled to the chin in one of Good Ma Debusher's afghans, two in the morning and his eyes wide-wide-wide as a terrible wind, one all the way down from Yellowknife, boomed outside – that was the other Scott; one went north, one went south, and oh dear, she had loved them both the same, *everything* the same.

'Stop it,' Lisey said fretfully. 'I was in time, I *was*, so let it go. The lung-shot was all that crazy baby ever got.' Yet in her mind's eye (where the past is always present), she saw the Ladysmith again start its swivel, and Lisey shoved herself out of the pool in an effort to physically drive the image away. It worked, but Blondie was back again as she stood in the changing room, toweling off after a quick rinsing shower, Gerd Allen Cole was back, *is* back, saying *I got to end all this ding-dong for the freesias,* and 1988-Lisey is swinging the silver spade, but this time the smucking air in smucking Lisey-time is too smucking thick, she's going to be just an instant too late, she will see *all* of the second flame-corsage instead of just a portion, and a black hole will also open on Scott's left lapel as his sportcoat becomes his deathcoat—

'*Quit* it!' Lisey growled, and slung her towel in the basket. 'Give it a *rest!*'

She marched back to the house nude, with her clothes under her arm – that's what the high board fence all the way around the backyard was for.

2

She was hungry after her swim – famished, actually – and although it was not quite five o'clock, she decided on a big skillet meal. What Darla, second-oldest of the Debusher girls, would have called comfort-food, and what Scott – with great relish – would have called *eatin nasty*. There was a pound of ground beef in the fridge and, lurking on a back shelf in the pantry, a wonderfully nasty selection: the Cheeseburger Pie version of Hamburger Helper. Lisey threw it together in a skillet with the ground beef. While it was simmering, she mixed herself a pitcher of lime Kool-Aid with double sugar. By five-twenty, the smells from the skillet had filled the kitchen, and all thoughts of Gerd Allen Cole had left her head, at least for the time being. She could think of nothing but food. She had two large helpings of the Hamburger Helper casserole, and two big glasses of Kool-Aid. When the second helping and the second glass were gone (all except for the white dregs of sugar in the bottom of the glass), she burped resoundingly and said: 'I wish I had a goddam smucking cigarette.'

It was true; she had rarely wanted one so badly. A

Salem Light. Scott had been a smoker when they had met at the University of Maine, where he had been both a grad student and what he called *The World's Youngest Writer in Residence*. She was a part-time student (*that* didn't last long) and a full-time waitress at Pat's Café downtown, slinging pizzas and burgers. She'd picked up the smoking habit from Scott, who'd been strictly a Herbert Tareyton man. They'd given up the butts together, rallying each other along. That had been in '87, the year before Gerd Allen Cole had resoundingly demonstrated that cigarettes weren't the only problem a person could have with his lungs. In the years since, Lisey went for days without thinking of them, then would fall into horrible pits of craving. Yet in a way, thinking about cigarettes was an improvement. It beat thinking about

(I got to end all this ding-dong for the freesias, *says Gerd Allen Cole with perfect fretful clarity and turns his wrist slightly*)

Blondie

(smoothly)

and Nashville

(so that the smoking barrel of the Ladysmith points at the left side of Scott's chest)

and smuck, here she went, doing it again.

There was store-bought poundcake for dessert, and Cool Whip – perhaps the apex of *eatin nasty* – to put on top of it, but Lisey was too full to consider it yet. And she was distressed to find these rotten old memories returning even after she'd taken on a gutful of hot, high-calorie food. She supposed that now she had an idea of what war veterans had to deal with. That had been her only battle, but

(no, Lisey)

'Quit it,' she whispered, and pushed her plate

(no, babyluv)

violently away from her. *Christ*, but she wanted

(you know better) a cigarette. And even more than a

ciggy, she wanted all these old memories to go aw—

Lisey!

That was Scott's voice, on top of her mind for a change and so clear she answered out loud over the kitchen table and with no self-consciousness at all: 'What, hon?'

Find the silver shovel and all this crap will blow away . . . like the smell of the mill when the wind swung around and blew from the south. Remember?

Of course she did. Her apartment had been in the little town of Cleaves Mills, just one town east of Orono. There weren't any actual mills in Cleaves by the time Lisey lived there, but there had still been plenty in Oldtown, and when the wind blew from the north – especially if the day happened to be overcast and damp – the stench was atrocious. Then, if the wind changed . . . God! You could smell the ocean, and it was like being born again. For awhile *wait for the wind to change* had become part of their marriage's interior language, like *strap it on* and *SOWISA* and *smuck* for *fuck*. Then it had fallen out of favor somewhere along the way, and she hadn't thought of it for years: *wait for the wind to change*, meaning hang on in there, baby. Meaning don't give up yet. Maybe it had been the sort of sweetly optimistic attitude only a young marriage can sustain. She didn't know. Scott might have been able to offer an informed opinion; he'd kept a journal even back then, in their

(EARLY YEARS!)

scuffling days, writing in it for fifteen minutes each evening while she watched sitcoms or did the household accounts. And sometimes instead of watching TV or writing checks, she watched him. She liked the way the lamplight shone in his hair and made deep triangular shadows on his cheeks as he sat there with his head bent over his loose-leaf notebook. His hair had been both longer and darker in those days, unmarked by the gray that had begun to show up toward the end of his life. She liked his stories, but she liked how his hair looked in the spill of the lamplight just as much. She thought his hair in the lamplight was its own story, he just didn't know it. She liked how his skin felt under her hand, too. Forehead or foreskin, both were good. She would not have traded one for the other. What worked for her was the whole package.

Lisey! Find the shovel!

She cleared the table, then stored the remaining Cheeseburger Pie in a Tupperware dish. She was certain she'd never eat it now that her madness had passed, but there was too much to scrape down the sink-pig; how the Good Ma Debusher who still kept house in her head would scream at waste like that! Better by far to hide it in the fridge behind the asparagus and the yogurt, where it would age quietly. And as she did these simple chores, she wondered how in the name of Jesus, Mary, and JoJo the Carpenter finding that silly ceremonial shovel could do anything for her peace of mind. Something about the magical properties of silver, maybe? She remembered watching some movie on the *Late Show* with Darla and Cantata, some supposedly scary thing about a werewolf . . . only Lisey hadn't

83

been much frightened, if at all. She'd thought the were-wolf more sad than scary, and besides – you could tell the movie-making people were changing his face by stopping the camera every now and then to put on more makeup and then running it again. You had to give them high marks for effort, but the finished product wasn't all that believable, at least in her humble opinion. The *story* was sort of interesting, though. The first part took place in an English pub, and one of the old geezers drinking there said you could only kill a werewolf with a silver bullet. And had not Gerd Allen Cole been a kind of werewolf?

'Come on, kid,' she said, rinsing off her plate and sticking it in the almost empty dishwasher, 'maybe Scott could float that downriver in one of his books, but tall stories were never your department. Were they?' She closed the dishwasher with a thump. At the rate it was filling, she'd be ready to run the current load around July Fourth. 'If you want to look for that shovel, just go do it! *Do* you?'

Before she could answer this completely rhetorical question, Scott's voice came again – the clear one at the top of her mind.

I left you a note, babyluv.

Lisey froze in the act of reaching for a dishtowel to dry her hands. She knew that voice, of course she did. She still heard it three and four times a week, her voice mimicking his, a little bit of harmless company in a big empty house. Only coming so soon after all this shite about the shovel . . .

What note?

What note?

Lisey wiped her hands and put the towel back to air-dry on its rod. Then she turned around so her back was to the sink and her kitchen lay before her. It was full of lovely summerlight (and the aroma of Hamburger Helper, a lot less yummy now that her low appetite for the stuff had been satisfied). She closed her eyes, counted to ten, then sprang them open again. Late-day summerlight *boomed* around her. Into her.

'Scott?' she said, feeling absurdly like her big sister Amanda. Half-nuts, in other words. 'You haven't gone ghost on me, have you?'

She expected no answer – not little Lisey Debusher, who had cheered on the thunderstorms and sneered at the *Late Show* werewolf, dismissing him as just bad time-lapse photography. But the sudden rush of wind that poured in through the open window over the sink – belling the curtains, lifting the ends of her still-damp hair, and bringing the heartbreaking aroma of flowers – could almost have been taken for an answer. She closed her eyes again and seemed to hear faint music, not that of the spheres but just an old Hank Williams country tune: *Goodbye Joe, me gotta go, me-oh-my-oh* . . .

Her arms prickled up in goosebumps.

Then the breeze died away and she was just Lisey again. Not Mandy, not Canty, not Darla; certainly not

(one went south)

run-off-to-Miami Jodi. She was Thoroughly Modern Lisey, 2006-Lisey, the Widow Landon. There were no ghosts. She was Lisey Alone.

But she *did* want to find that silver spade, the one that had saved her husband for another sixteen years and seven novels. Not to mention for the *Newsweek* cover in

'92 that had featured a psychedelic Scott with MAGICAL REALISM AND THE CULT OF LANDON in Peter Max lettering. She wondered how Roger 'The Jackrabbit' Dashmiel had liked *them* apples.

Lisey decided she'd look for the spade right away, while the long light of the early-summer evening still held. Ghosts or no ghosts, she didn't want to be out in the barn – or the study above it – once night had fallen.

3

The stalls opposite her never-quite-completed office were dark and musty affairs that had once held tools, tack, and spare parts for farm vehicles and machinery back when the Landon home had been Sugar Top Farm. The largest bay had held chickens, and although it had been swamped out by a professional cleaning company and then whitewashed (by Scott, who did it with many references to *Tom Sawyer*), it still held the faint, ammoniac reek of long-gone fowl. It was a smell Lisey remembered from her youngest childhood and hated . . . probably because her Granny D had keeled over and died while feeding the chickens.

Two of the cubbies were stacked high with boxes – liquor-store cartons, for the most part – but there were no digging implements, silver or otherwise. There was a sheeted double bed in the erstwhile chicken pen, the single leftover from their brief nine-month Germany experiment. They had bought the bed in Bremen and had it shipped back at paralyzing expense – Scott had insisted. She had forgotten all about the Bremen bed until now.

Talk about what fell out of the dog's ass! Lisey thought

with a kind of miserable exultation, and then said aloud, 'If you think I'd ever sleep in a bed after it sat twenty-some years out in a goddam chicken pen, Scott—'

—*then you're crazy!* was how she meant to finish, and couldn't. She burst out laughing instead. Christ, the curse of money! The smucking *curse* of it! How much had that bed cost? A thousand bucks American? Say a thousand. And how much to ship it back? Another thou? Maybe. And here it sat, rah-cheer, Scott might have said, in the chickenshit shadows. And rah-cheer it could continue to sit until the world ended in fire or ice, as far as she was concerned. The whole Germany thing had been *such* a bust, no book for Scott, an argument with the landlord that had come within a hair of degenerating into a fist-fight, even Scott's lectures had gone badly, the audiences either had no sense of humor or didn't get his, and—

And behind the door across the way, the one wearing the **HIGH VOLTAGE!** sign, the telephone began to shout again. Lisey froze where she was, feeling more goosebumps. And yet there was also a sense of inevitability, as if this was what she'd come out here for, not the silver spade at all but to take a call.

She turned as the phone rang a second time, and crossed the barn's dim center aisle. She reached the door as the third ring began. She thumbed the old-fashioned latch and the door opened easily, just screaming a little on its unused hinges, welcome to the crypt, little Lisey, we've been *dying* to meet you, heh-heh-heh. A draft whooshed in around her, flapping her blouse against the small of her back. She felt for the light-switch and flicked it, not sure what to expect, but the overhead went on. Of course it

87

did. As far as Central Maine Power was concerned, all of this was The Study, RFD #2, Sugar Top Hill Road. Upstairs or downstairs, to CMP it was a clear-cut case of everything the same.

The telephone on the desk rang a fourth time. Before Ring #5 could wake up the answering machine, Lisey snagged the receiver. 'Hello?'

There was a moment of silence. She was about to say hello again when the voice at the other end did it for her. The tone was perplexed, but Lisey recognized who it was, just the same. That one word had been enough. You knew your own.

'Darla?'

'Lisey – it *is* you!'

'Sure it's me.'

'Where are you?'

'Scott's old study.'

'No, you're not. I already tried there.'

Lisey only had to consider this briefly. Scott had liked his music loud – in truth he'd liked it at levels normal people would have considered ridiculous – and the telephone up there was located in the soundproofed area he had been amused to call My Padded Cell. It wasn't surprising she hadn't heard it down here. None of this seemed worth explaining to her sister.

'Darla, where did you get this number, and why are you calling?'

There was another pause. Then Darla said, 'I'm at Amanda's. I got the number from her book. She's got four for you. I just ran through all of them. This was the last.'

Lisey felt a sinking sensation in her chest and stomach.

As children, Amanda and Darla had been bitter rivals. They'd gotten into any number of scratching matches – over dolls, library books, clothes. The last and gaudiest confrontation had been over a boy named Richie Stanchfield, and had been serious enough to land Darla in the Central Maine General ER, where six stitches had been needed to close the deep scratch over her left eye. She still wore the scar, a thin white dash. They got on better as adults only to this extent: there had been plenty of arguments but no more spilled blood. They stayed out of each other's way as much as possible. The once- or twice-monthly Sunday dinners (with spouses) or sister-lunches at Olive Garden or Outback could be difficult, even with Manda and Darla sitting apart and Lisey and Canty mediating. For Darla to be calling from Amanda's house was not a good thing.

'Is something wrong with her, Darl?' Dumb question. The only real question was *how* wrong.

'Mrs Jones heard her screaming and carrying on and breaking stuff. Doing one of her Big Ts.'

One of her Big Tantrums. Check.

'She tried Canty first, but Canty and Rich are in Boston. When Mrs Jones got that message on their answering machine she called me.'

That made sense. Canty and Rich lived a mile or so north of Amanda on Route 19; Darla lived roughly two miles south. In a way, it was like their father's old rhyme: one went north, one went south, one couldn't shut her everlasting mouth. Lisey herself was about five miles away. Mrs Jones, who lived across the road from Mandy's weather-tight little Cape Cod, would have known well enough to call Canty first, and not just because Canty was closer in terms of distance, either.

Screaming and carrying on and breaking stuff.

'How bad is it this time?' Lisey heard herself asking in a flat, strangely businesslike tone of voice. 'Should I come?' Meaning, of course, *How fast should I come?*

'She's . . . I think she's okay for now,' Darla said. 'But she's been doing it again. On her arms, also a couple of places high up on her thighs. The . . . you know.'

Lisey knew, all right. On three previous occasions, Amanda had lapsed into what Jane Whitlow, her shrink, called 'passive semi-catatonia'. It was different from what had happened

(hush about that)

(I won't)

from what had happened to Scott in 1996, but pretty damned scary, all the same. And each time, the state had been preceded by bouts of excitability – the sort of excitability Manda had been exhibiting up in Scott's study, Lisey realized – followed by hysteria, then brief spasms of self-mutilation. During one of these, Manda had apparently tried to excise her navel. She had been left with a ghostly fairy-ring of scar-tissue around it. Lisey had once broached the possibility of cosmetic surgery, not knowing if it would be possible but wanting Manda to know she, Lisey, would be willing to pay if Amanda wanted at least to explore the possibility. Amanda had declined with a harsh caw of amusement. 'I like that ring,' she'd said. 'If I'm ever tempted to start cutting myself again, maybe I'll look at that and stop.'

Maybe, it seemed, had been the operant word.

'How bad is it, Darl? Really?'

'Lisey . . . hon . . .'

Lisey realized with alarm (and a further sinking in her vital parts) that her older sister was struggling with tears. '*Darla!* Take a deep breath and tell me.'

'I'm okay. I just . . . it's been a long day.'

'When does Matt get back from Montreal?'

'Week after next. Don't even think about asking me to call him, either – he's earning our trip to St Bart's next winter, and he's not to be disturbed. We can handle this ourselves.'

'Can we?'

'Definitely.'

'Then tell me what it is we're supposed to be handling.'

'Okay. Right.' Lisey heard Darla take a breath. 'The cuts on her upper arms were shallow. Band-Aid stuff. The ones on her thighs were deeper and they'll scar, but they clotted over, thank God. No arterial shit. Uh, Lisey?'

'What? Just str . . . just spit it out.'

She'd almost told Darla to just strap it on, which would have meant zip to her big sister. Whatever Darla had to tell her next, it was going to be something rotten. She could tell that by Darla's voice, which had been in and out of Lisey's ears from the cradle on. She tried to brace herself for it. She leaned back against the desk, her gaze shifted . . . and holy Mother of God, there it was in the corner, leaning nonchalantly next to another stack of liquor-store boxes (which were indeed labeled **SCOTT! THE EARLY YEARS!**). In the angle where the north wall met the east one was the silver spade from Nashville, big as Billy-be-damned. It was a blue-eyed wonder she hadn't seen it when she came in, surely would have if she hadn't been in a lather to grab the phone before the answering machine kicked in. She could read the words incised into the silver bowl from here: *COMMENCEMENT, SHIPMAN LIBRARY.* She could almost hear the southern-fried chickenshit telling her husband that Toneh would be rahtin it up for the year-end review, and would he like a *copeh.* And Scott replying—

'Lisey?' Darla sounding really distressed for the first time, and Lisey returned to the present in a hurry. Of *course* Darla sounded distressed. Canty was in Boston for a week or maybe more, shopping while her husband took care of his wholesale auto business – buying program cars, auction cars, and off-lease rental cars in places like Malden and Lynn, Lynn, the City of Sin. Darla's Matt, meanwhile, was in Canada, earning money for their next vacation by lecturing on the migration patterns of various North American Indian tribes. This, Darla had once told Lisey, was a surprisingly profitable venture. Not that money would help them now. Now it was down to just the two of them. To sister-power. 'Lise, did you hear me? Are you still th—'

'I'm here,' Lisey said. 'I just lost you for a few seconds, sorry. Maybe it's the phone – no one's used this one for a long time. It's downstairs in the barn. What was going to be my office, before Scott died?'

'Oh, yeah. Sure.' Darla sounded completely mystified. *Has no smucking idea what I'm talking about,* Lisey thought. 'Can you hear me now?'

'Clear as a bell.' Looking at the silver spade as she spoke. Thinking of Gerd Allen Cole. Thinking *I got to end all this ding-dong for the freesias.*

Darla took a deep breath. Lisey heard it, like a wind blowing down the telephone line. 'She won't exactly admit it, but I think she . . . well . . . drank her own blood this time, Lise – her lips and chin were all bloody when I got here, but nothing inside her mouth's cut. She looked the way we used to when Good Ma'd give us one of her lipsticks to play with.'

What Lisey flashed on wasn't those old dress-up and makeup days, those clunk-around-in-Good-Ma's-high-heels days, but that hot afternoon in Nashville, Scott lying on the pavement shivering, his lips smeared with candy-colored blood. *Nobody loves a clown at midnight.*

Listen, little Lisey. I'll make how it sounds when it looks around.

But in the corner the silver spade gleamed . . . and was it *dented*? She believed it was. If she ever doubted that she'd been in time . . . if she ever woke in the dark, sweating, sure she'd been just a second too late and the remaining years of her marriage had consequently been lost . . .

'Lisey, will you come? When she's in the clear, she's asking for you.'

Alarm bells went off in Lisey's head. 'What do you mean, when she's in the clear? I thought you said she was okay.'

'She is . . . I *think* she is.' A pause. 'She asked for you, and she asked for tea. I made her some, and she drank it. That was good, wasn't it?'

'Yes,' Lisey said. 'Darl, do you know what brought this on?'

'Oh, you bet. I guess it's common chat around town, although I didn't know until Mrs Jones told me over the phone.'

'What?' But Lisey had a pretty good idea.

'Charlie Corriveau's back in town,' Darla said. Then, lowering her voice: 'Good old Shootin' Beans. Everyone's favorite banker. He brought a girl with him. A little French postcard from up in the St John Valley.' She gave this the Maine pronunciation, so it came out slurry-lyrical, almost *Senjun*.

Lisey stood looking at the silver spade, waiting for the other shoe to drop. That there *was* another she had no doubt.

'They're married, Lisey,' Darla said, and through the phone came a series of choked gurgles Lisey at first took for smothered sobs. A moment later she realized her sister was trying to laugh without being overheard by Amanda, who was God knew where in the house.

'I'll be there as quick as I can,' she said. 'And Darl?'

No answer, just more of those choking noises – *whig, whig, whig* was what they sounded like over the phone.

'If she hears you laughing, the next one she takes the knife to is apt to be you.'

At that the laughing sounds stopped. Lisey heard Darla take a long, steadying breath. 'Her shrink isn't around anymore, you know,' Darla said at last. 'The Whitlow woman? The one who always wore the beads? She moved to Alaska, I think it was.'

Lisey thought Montana, but it hardly mattered. 'Well, we'll see how bad she is. There's the place Scott looked into . . . Greenlawn, up in the Twin Cities—'

'Oh, *Lisey!*' The voice of Good Ma, the very voice.

'Lisey-*what?*' she asked sharply. 'Lisey-*what?* Are *you* going to move in with her and keep her from carving

94

Charlie Corriveau's initials on her boobs the next time she goes Freak City? Or maybe you've got Canty tapped for the job.'

'Lisey, I didn't mean—'

'Or maybe Billy can come home from Tufts and take care of her. What's one more Dean's List student, more or less?'

'Lisey—'

'Well what *are* you proposing?' She heard the hectoring tone in her voice and hated it. This was another thing money did to you after ten or twenty years – made you think you had the right to kick your way out of any tight corner you found yourself in. She remembered Scott saying that people shouldn't be allowed houses with more than two toilets to shit in, it gave them delusions of grandeur. She glanced at the shovel again. It gleamed at her. Calmed her. *You saved him*, it said. *Not on your watch*, it said. Was that true? She couldn't remember. Was it another of the things she'd forgotten on purpose? She couldn't remember that, either. What a hoot. What a bitter hoot.

'Lisey, I'm sorry . . . I just—'

'I know.' What she knew was that she was tired and confused and ashamed of her outburst. 'We'll work it out. I'll come right now. Okay?'

'Yes.' Relief in Darla's voice. 'Okay.'

'That Frenchman,' Lisey said. 'What a jerk. Good riddance to bad trash.'

'Get here as soon as you can.'

'I will. G'bye.'

Lisey hung up. She walked over to the northeast corner of the room and grasped the shaft of the silver spade. It was as if she were doing it for the first time, and was that so strange? When Scott passed it to her, she'd only been interested in the glittering silver scoop with its engraved message, and by the time she got ready to swing the darn thing, her hands had been moving on their own . . . or so it had seemed; she supposed some primitive, survival-oriented part of her brain had actually been moving them for the rest of her, for Thoroughly Modern Lisey.

She slid one palm down the smooth wood, relishing the smooth slide, and as she bent, her eyes once more fell on the three stacked boxes with their exuberant message slashed across the side of each one in black Magic Marker: **SCOTT! THE EARLY YEARS!** The box on top had once contained Gilbey's Gin, and the flaps had been folded together rather than taped. Lisey brushed away the dust, marveling at how thick it was, marveling at the realization that the last hands to touch this box – to fill it and fold the flaps and place it atop the others – now lay folded themselves, and under the ground.

The box was full of paper. Manuscripts, she presumed. The slightly yellowed title sheet on top was capitalized, underlined, and centered. Scott's name neatly typed beneath, also centered. All this she recognized as she would have recognized his smile – it had been his style of presentation when she met him as a young man, and had never changed. What she didn't recognize was the title of this one:

IKE COMES HOME
By Scott Landon

Was it a novel? A short story? Just looking into the box, it was impossible to tell. But there had to be a thousand or more pages in there, most of them in a single high stack under that title-page but still more crammed in sideways in two directions, like packing. If it was a novel, and this box contained all of it, it had to be longer than *Gone With the Wind*. Was that possible? Lisey supposed it might be. Scott always showed her his work when it was done, and he was happy to show her work in progress if she asked about it (a privilege he accorded no one else, not even his longtime editor, Carson Foray), but if she didn't ask, he usually kept it to himself. And he'd been prolific right up until the day he died. On the road or at home, Scott Landon *wrote*.

But a thousand-pager? Surely he would have mentioned that. I bet it's only a short story, and one he didn't like, at that. And the rest of the stuff in this box, the stuff underneath and crammed in at the side? Copies of his first couple of novels, probably. Or galley-pages. What he used to call 'foul matter'.

But hadn't he shipped all the foul matter back to Pitt when he was done with it, for the Scott Landon Collection in their library? For the Incunks to drool over, in other words? And if there were copies of his early manuscripts in these boxes, how come there were more copies (carbons from the dark ages, mostly) in the closets marked STORAGE upstairs? And now that she thought about it, what about the cubbies on either side of the erstwhile chicken pen? What was stored in those?

She looked upward, almost as if she were Supergirl and could see the answer with her X-ray vision, and that was when the telephone on her desk once more began to ring.

4

She crossed to the desk and snared the handset with a mixture of dread and irritation . . . but quite a bit heavier on the irritation. It was possible – just – that Amanda had decided to whack off an ear à la Van Gogh or maybe slit her throat instead of just a thigh or a forearm, but Lisey doubted it. All her life Darla had been the sister most apt to call back three minutes later, starting off with *I just remembered* or *I forgot to tell you*.

'What is it, Darl?'

There was a moment or two of silence, and then a male voice – one she thought she knew – said: 'Mrs Landon?'

It was Lisey's turn to pause as she ran through a list of male names. Pretty short list these days; it was amazing how your husband's death pruned your catalogue of acquaintances. There was Jacob Montano, their lawyer in Portland; Arthur Williams, the accountant in New York who wouldn't let go of a dollar until the eagle shrieked for mercy (or died of asphyxiation); Deke Williams – no relation to Arthur – the contractor from Bridgton who'd turned the empty haylofts over the barn into Scott's study and who'd also remodeled the second floor of their house, transforming previously dim rooms into wonderlands of light; Smiley Flanders, the plumber from over in Motton with the endless supply of jokes both clean and dirty; Charlie Haddonfield, Scott's agent, who called on business from time to time (foreign rights and short-story anthologies, mostly); plus the handful of Scott's friends who still kept in touch. But none of those people would call on this number, surely, even if it were listed. *Was* it? She couldn't remember. In any case, none of the names seemed to fit how she knew (or thought she knew) the voice. But, damn it—

'Mrs Landon?'

'Who is this?' she asked.

'My name doesn't matter, Missus,' the voice replied, and Lisey had a sudden vivid image of Gerd Allen Cole, lips moving in what might have been a prayer. Except for the gun in his long-fingered poet's hand. *Dear God, don't let this be another one of those*, she thought. *Don't let it be another Blondie.* Yet she saw she once more had the silver spade in her hand – she'd grasped its wooden shaft without thinking when she picked up the phone – and that seemed to promise her that it was, it was.

'It matters to me,' she said, and was astounded at her businesslike tone of voice. How could such a brisk, no-nonsense sentence emerge from such a suddenly dry mouth? And then, whoomp, just like that, where she'd heard the voice before came to her: that very afternoon, on the answering machine attached to this very phone. And it was really no wonder she hadn't been able to make the connection right away, because then the voice had only spoken three words: *I'll try again.* 'You identify yourself this minute or I'm going to hang up.'

There was a sigh from the other end. It sounded both tired and good-natured. 'Don't make this hard on me, Missus; I'm tryin-a help you. I really am.'

Lisey thought of the dusty voices from Scott's favorite movie, *The Last Picture Show*; she thought again of Hank Williams singing 'Jambalaya'. *Dress in style, go hog-wile, me-*

oh-my-oh. She said, 'I'm hanging up now, goodbye, have a nice life.' Although she did not so much as stir the phone from her ear. Not yet.

'You can call me Zack, Missus. That's as good a name as any. All right?'

'Zack what?'

'Zack McCool.'

'Uh-huh, and I'm Liz Taylor.'

'You wanted a name, I gave you one.'

He had her there. 'And how did you get this number, Zack?'

'Directory Assistance.' So it *was* listed – that explained that. Maybe. 'Now will you listen a minute?'

'I'm listening.' Listening . . . and gripping the silver spade . . . and waiting for the wind to change. Maybe that most of all. Because a change was coming. Every nerve in her body said so.

'Missus, there was a man came see you a little while ago to have a look through your late husband's papers, and may I say I'm sorry for your loss.'

Lisey ignored this last. 'Lots of people have asked me to let them look through Scott's papers since he died.' She hoped the man on the other end of the line wouldn't be able to guess or intuit how hard her heart was now beating. 'I've told them all the same thing: eventually I'll get around to sharing them with—'

'This fella's from your late husband's old college, Missus. He says he is the logical choice, since these papers're apt to wind up there, anyway.'

For a moment Lisey said nothing. She reflected on how her caller had pronounced *husband* – almost *husbun*, as though Scott had been some exotic breakfast treat, now consumed. How he called her *Missus*. Not a Maine man, not a Yankee, and probably not an educated man, at least in the sense Scott would have used the word; she guessed that 'Zack McCool' had never been to college. She also reflected that the wind had indeed changed. She was no longer scared. What she was, at least for the time being, was angry. *More* than angry. Pissed like a bear.

In a low, choked voice she hardly recognized, she said: 'Woodbody. That's who you're talking about, isn't it? Joseph Woodbody. That Incunk son of a bitch.'

There was a pause on the other end. Then her new friend said: 'I'm not following you, Missus.'

Lisey felt her rage come all the way up and welcomed it. 'I think you're following me fine. Professor Joseph Woodbody, King of the Incunks, hired you to call and try to scare me into . . . what? Just turning over the keys to my husband's study, so he can go through Scott's manuscripts and take what he wants? Is that what . . . does he really think . . .' She pulled herself down. It wasn't easy. The anger was bitter but it was sweet, too, and she wanted to trip on it. 'Just tell me, Zack. Yes or no. Are you working for Professor Joseph Woodbody?'

'That's none of your bi'ness, Missus.'

Lisey couldn't reply to this. She was struck dumb, at least temporarily, by the sheer effrontery of it. What Scott might have called the puffickly huh-*yooge*

(none of your bi'ness) ludicrosity of it.

'And nobody hired me to *try* and do nothing.' A pause. 'Anything, I mean. Now Missus. You want to close your mouth and listen. Are you listen to me?'

She stood with the telephone's receiver curled against her ear, considering that – *Are you listen to me?* – and said nothing.

'I can hear you breathing, so I know you are. That's good. When I'm hired, Missus, this mother's son don't *try*, he *does*. I know you don't know me, but that's your disadvantage, not mine. This ain't . . . iddn't just brag. I don't *try*, I *do*. You are going to give this man what he wants, all right? He is going to call me on the telephone or e-mail me in this special way we have and say, "Everything's okay, I got what I want." If that don't . . . if it dutn't happen in a certain run of time, I'm going to come to where you are and I'm going to hurt you. *I am going to hurt you places you didn't let the boys to touch at the junior high dances.*'

Lisey had closed her eyes at some point during this lengthy speech, which had the feel of a memorized set-piece. She could feel hot tears trickling down her cheeks, and didn't know if they were tears of rage or . . .

Shame? Could they actually be tears of shame? Yes, there was something shameful in being talked to like this by a stranger. It was like being in a new school and getting scolded by the teacher on your first day.

Smuck that, babyluv, Scott said. *You know what to do.*

Sure she did. In a situation like this you either strapped it on or you didn't. She'd never actually *been* in a situation like this, but it was still pretty obvious.

'Missus? Do you understand what I just told you?'

She knew what she wanted to say to him, but he might not understand. So Lisey decided to settle for the more common usage.

'Zack?' Speaking very low.

'Yes, Missus.' He immediately fell into the same low tone. What he perhaps took for one of mutual conspiracy.

'Can you hear me?'

'You're a bit low-pitch, but . . . yes, Missus.'

She pulled air deep into her lungs. Held it for a moment, imagining this man who said *Missus* and *husbun* and *dutn't* for *doesn't*. Imagined him with the telephone screwed tightly against his ear, straining toward the sound of her voice. When she had the picture clearly in the forefront of her mind, she screamed into that ear with all her force. *'THEN GO FUCK YOURSELF!'*

Lisey slammed the phone back into the cradle hard enough to make dust fly up from the handset.

5

The telephone began to ring again almost immediately, but Lisey had no interest in further conversation with 'Zack McCool'. She suspected that any chance of having what the TV talking heads called *a dialogue* was gone. Not that she wanted one. Nor did she want to listen to him on the answering machine and find out if he'd lost that tone of weary good nature and now wanted to call her a bitch, a cunt, or a cooze. She traced the telephone cord back to the wall – the plate was close to that stack of liquor-store boxes – and yanked the jack. The phone fell silent halfway through the third ring. So much for 'Zack McCool', at least for the time being. She might have doings with him later, she supposed – or *about* him – but right now there was Manda to deal with. Not to mention Darla, waiting for her and counting on her. She'd just go back to the kitchen, grab her car-keys off the peg . . . and she'd take two minutes to lock the house up, as well, a thing she didn't always bother with in the daytime.

The house *and* the barn *and* the study.

Yes, especially the study, although she was damned if she'd capitalize it the way Scott had done, like it was some extra-special big deal. But speaking of extra-special big deals . . .

She found herself looking into the top box again. She hadn't closed the flaps, so looking in was easy to do.

IKE COMES HOME
By Scott Landon

Curious – and this would, after all, take only a second – Lisey leaned the silver spade against the wall, lifted the title-page, and looked beneath. On the second sheet was this:

Ike came home with a boom,
and everything was fine.
BOOL! THE END!

Nothing else.

Lisey looked at it for nearly a minute, although God knew she had things to do and places to go. Her skin was prickling again, but this time the feeling was almost pleasant . . . and hell, there was really no *almost* about it, was there? A small, bemused smile was playing around her mouth. Ever since she'd begun the work of cleaning out his study – ever since she'd lost it and trashed what Scott had been pleased to call his 'memory nook', if you wanted to be exact – she had felt his presence . . . but never as close as this. Never as *actual*. She reached into the box and thumbed through a deep thickness of the pages stacked there, pretty sure of what she would find. And did. All the pages were blank. She riffled a bunch of the ones crammed in side-ways, and they were, too. In Scott's childhood lexicon, a boom had been a short trip and a bool . . . well, that was a little more complicated, but in this context it almost certainly meant a joke or harmless prank. This giant bogus novel was Scott Landon's idea of a knee-slapper.

Were the other two boxes in the stack also bools? And the ones in the bins and cubbies across the way? Was the joke that elaborate? And if so, whom was it supposed to be on? Her? Incunks like Woodbody? That made a certain amount of sense, Scott liked to poke fun at the folks he'd called 'text-crazies', but that idea pointed toward a rather terrible possibility: that he might have intuited his own

(Died Young)

coming collapse

(Before His Time)

and said nothing to her. And it led to a question: would she have believed him if he'd told her? Her first impulse was to say no – to say, if only to herself, *I was the practical one, the one who checked his luggage to see if he had enough underwear and called ahead to make sure the flights were running on time*. But she remembered the way the blood on his lips had turned his smile into a clown's grin; she remembered how he had once explained to her – with what had seemed like perfect lucidity – that it was unsafe to eat any kind of fresh fruit after sunset, and that food of all kinds should be avoided between midnight and six. According to Scott, 'night-food' was often poisonous, and when he said it, it sounded logical. Because—

(hush)

'I would have believed him, leave it at that,' she whispered, and put her head down, and closed her eyes against tears that did not come. Eyes that had wept at 'Zack McCool's' set speech were now dry as stones. Silly smucking eyes!

The manuscripts in the crammed drawers of his desks and the main filing cabinet upstairs were most certainly not bools; this Lisey knew. Some were copies of published short stories, some were alternate versions of those stories. In the desk Scott had called Dumbo's Big Jumbo she had marked at least three unfinished novels and what appeared to be a finished novella – and wouldn't Woodbody just drool. There were also half a dozen finished short stories Scott had apparently never cared enough to send out for publication, most of them years old from the look of the typefaces. She wasn't qualified to say what was trash and what was treasure, although she was sure it would all be of interest to Landon scholars. This, however . . . this *bool*, to use Scott's word . . .

She was gripping the handle of the silver spade, and hard. It was a real thing in what suddenly felt like a very cobwebby world. She opened her eyes again and said, 'Scott, was this just a goof, or are you still messing with me?'

No answer. Of course. And she had a couple of sisters that needed seeing to. Surely Scott would have understood her shoving all this on the back burner for the time being.

In any case, she decided to take the spade along. She liked the way it felt in her hand.

6

Lisey plugged in the phone and then left in a hurry, before the damned thing could start ringing again. Outside the sun was setting and a strong westerly wind had gotten up, explaining the draft that had whooshed past her when she had opened the door to take the first of her two upsetting telephone calls: no ghosts there, babyluv. This day seemed at least a month long, but that wind, lovely and somehow fine-grained, like the one in her dream the night before, soothed and refreshed her. She crossed from the barn to the kitchen without fearing 'Zack McCool' was lurking somewhere nearby. She knew how calls from cell phones sounded way out here: crackly and barely there. According to Scott, it was the power-lines (which he liked to call 'UFO refueling stations'). Her buddy 'Zack' had been coming in clear as a bell. That particular Deep Space Cowboy had been on a landline, and she doubted like hell if her next-door neighbor had loaned him their phone so he could threaten her.

She got her car-keys and slipped them into the side pocket of her jeans (unaware that she was still carrying Amanda's Little Notebook of Compulsions in the back pocket – although she would *become* aware, in the fullness of time); she also got the bulkier ring with all the keys to the Landon kingdom domestic on it, each still labeled in Scott Landon's neat hand. She locked the house, then trudged back to lock the barn's sliding doors together and the door to Scott's study at the top of the outside stairs. Once that was done, she went to her car with the spade on her shoulder and her shadow trailing out long beside her on the door-yard dirt in the last of that day's fading red Junelight.

CHAPTER FOUR

LISEY AND THE BLOOD-BOOL (ALL THE BAD-GUNKY)

1

Driving to Amanda's along the recently widened and repaved Route 17 was a matter of fifteen minutes, even slowing for the blinker where 17 crossed the Deep Cut Road to Harlow. Lisey spent more of it than she wanted to thinking about bools in general and one bool in particular: the first. That one had been no joke.

'But the little idiot from Lisbon Falls went ahead and married him anyway,' she said, laughing, then took her foot off the gas. Here was Patel's Market on the left – Texaco self-serve pumps on clean black asphalt under blinding white lights – and she felt an amazingly strong urge to pull in and grab a pack of cigarettes. Good old Salem Lights. And while she was there, she could get some of those Nissen doughnuts Manda liked, the squash ones, and maybe some HoHos for herself.

'You numbah one crazy baby,' she said, smiling, and stepped smartly down on the gas again. Patel's receded. She was running with her dims on now, although there was still plenty of twilight. She glanced in her rearview mirror, saw the silly silver shovel lying on the back seat, and said it again, this time laughing: 'You numbah one crazy baby, ah so!'

And what if she was? Ah so *what*?

2

Lisey parked behind Darla's Prius and was only halfway to the door of Amanda's trim little Cape Cod when Darla came out, not quite running and struggling not to cry.

'Thank God you're here,' she said, and when Lisey saw the blood on Darla's hands she thought of bools again, thought of her husband-to-be coming out of the dark and holding out *his* hand to her, only it hadn't really looked like a hand anymore.

'Darla, what—'

'She did it again! That crazy bitch went and cut herself again! All I did was go to use the bathroom . . . I left her drinking tea in the kitchen . . . "Are you okay, Manda," I said . . . and . . .'

'Hold on,' Lisey told her, forcing herself to at least sound calm. She'd *always* been the calm one, or the one who put on that face; the one who said things like *Hold on* and *Maybe it's not that bad*. Wasn't that supposed to be the oldest child's job? Well, maybe not if the oldest child turned out to be a smucking mental case.

'Oh, she's not gonna *die*, but what a *mess*,' Darla said, beginning to cry after all. *Sure, now that I'm here you let go,* Lisey thought. *Never occurs to any of you that little Lisey might have a few problems of her own, does it?*

Darla blew first one side of her nose and then the other onto Amanda's darkening lawn in a pair of unlady-like honks. 'What a freakin *mess*, maybe you're right, maybe a place like Greenlawn's the answer . . . if it's private, that is . . . and discreet . . . I just don't know . . . maybe you can do something with her, probably you can, she listens to you, she always has, I'm at my wits' end . . .'

'Come on, Darl,' Lisa said soothingly, and here was a revelation: she didn't really want cigarettes at all. Cigarettes were yesterday's bad habit. Cigarettes were as dead as her late husband, collapsed at a reading two years ago and died shortly thereafter in a Kentucky hospital, bool, the end. What she wanted to be holding wasn't a Salem Light but the handle of that silver spade.

There was comfort you didn't even have to light.

3

It's a bool, Lisey!

She heard it again as she turned on the light in Amanda's kitchen. And saw him again, walking toward her up the shadowy lawn behind her apartment in Cleaves Mills. Scott who could be crazy, Scott who could be brave, Scott who could be both at the same time, under the right circumstances.

And not just any bool, it's a blood-bool!

Behind the apartment where she taught him to fuck and he taught her to say smuck and they taught each other to wait, wait, wait for the wind to change. Scott wading through the heavy, heady smell of mixed flowers because it was almost summer and Parks Greenhouse was down there and the louvers were open to let in the night air. Scott walking out of all that perfumed exhalation, that late-spring night, and into the light of the back door where she stood waiting. Pissed off at him, but not *as* pissed; in fact almost ready to make up. She had, after all, been stood up before (although never by him), and she'd had boyfriends turn up drunk before (including him). And oh when she had *seen* him—

Her first blood-bool.

And now here was another. Amanda's kitchen was daubed and smeared and splattered with what Scott had sometimes been pleased to call – usually in a bad Howard Cosell imitation – 'the claret'. Red droplets of it ran across Manda's cheery yellow Formica counter; a smear of it bleared the glass front of the microwave; there were blips and blots and even a single foot-track on the linoleum. A dishtowel dropped in the sink was soaked with it.

Lisey looked at all this and felt her heart speed up. It was natural, she told herself; the sight of blood did that to people. Plus, she was at the end of a long and stressful day. *The thing you want to remember is that it almost certainly looks worse than it really is. You can bet she spread it around on purpose – there was never anything wrong with Amanda's sense of the dramatic. And you've seen worse, Lisey. The thing she did to her belly-button, for instance. Or Scott back in Cleaves. Okay?*

'What?' Darla asked.

'I didn't say anything,' Lisey replied. They were standing in the doorway, looking at their unfortunate older sister, who sat at the kitchen table – also surfaced in cheery

112

yellow Formica – with her head bent and her hair hanging in her face.

'You did, you said okay.'

'Okay, I said okay,' Lisey replied crossly. 'Good Ma used to say people who talk to themselves have money in the bank.' And she did. Thanks to Scott, she had just over or just under twenty million, depending on how the market in T-bills and certain stocks had done that day.

The idea of money didn't seem to draw much water when you were in a blood-smeared kitchen, however. Lisey wondered if Mandy had never used shit simply because she'd never thought of it. If so, that was genuine by-God good fortune, wasn't it?

'You took away the knives?' she asked Darla, *sotto voce*.

'Of course I did,' Darla said indignantly . . . but in the same low voice. 'She did it with pieces of her shitting *teacup*, Lisey. While I was having a pee.'

Lisey had figured that out for herself and had already made a mental note to go to Wal-Mart for new ones just as soon as she could. Fun Yellow to match the rest of the kitchen if possible, but the real requirement was that they be the plastic ones with the little stickers reading UNBREAK-ABLE on the sides.

She knelt beside Amanda and moved to take her hand. Darla said, 'That's what she cut, Lise. She did both palms.'

Doing so very gently, Lisey plucked Amanda's hands out of her lap. She turned them over and winced. The cuts were starting to clot, but they still made her stomach hurt. And of course they made her think again of Scott coming out of the summer darkness and holding out his dripping hand like a goddam love-offering, an act of atonement for the terrible sins of getting drunk and forgetting they had a date. Sheesh, and they called Cole crazy?

Amanda had cut diagonally from the base of her thumbs to the base of her pinky fingers, severing heart-lines, lovelines, and all the other lines along the way. Lisey could understand how she'd done the first one, but the second? That must have been hard cheese indeed (as the saying was). But she had managed, and then she had gone around the kitchen like a woman putting the icing on a madcake – *Hey, looka me! Looka me!* You *not numbah one crazy baby*, I *numbah one!* Manda *numbah one crazy baby, you bet!* All while Darla had been on the toilet, doing no more than whizzing a little lemonade and blotting the old bush, way to go Amanda, you also numbah one speed-devil baby.

'Darla – these are beyond Band-Aids and hydrogen peroxide, hon. She's got to go to the Emergency Room.'

'Oh, ratfuck,' Darla said dismally, and began to cry again.

Lisey looked into Amanda's face, which was still barely visible through the screening wings of her hair. 'Amanda,' she said.

Nothing. No movement.

'Manda.'

Nothing. Amanda's head dropped like a doll's. *Damned Charlie Corriveau!* Lisey thought. *Damned smucking Frenchy Corriveau!* But of course if it hadn't been 'Shootin' Beans', it would have been someone or something else. Because the Amandas of the world were just made that way. You kept expecting them to fall down and thinking it was a miracle they didn't, and finally the miracle got tired of happening and fell over and took a seizure and died.

'Manda-Bunny.'

It was the childhood name that finally got through. Amanda slowly raised her head. And what Lisey saw in her face wasn't the bloody, doped-out vacancy she'd expected (yes, Amanda's lips *were* all red, and that surely wasn't Max Factor on them) but rather the sparkling, childish, tripwire expression of hauteur and mischief, the one that meant Amanda had Taken Something On Herself, and tears would follow for someone.

'Bool,' she whispered, and Lisey Landon's interior temperature seemed to fall thirty degrees in an instant.

4

They got her into the living room, Amanda walking docilely between them, and sat her on the couch. Then Lisey and Darla went back into the kitchen doorway, where they could keep an eye on her and still consult without being overheard.

'What did she say to you, Lisey? You're as white as a damn ghost.'

Lisey wished Darla had said sheet. She didn't like hearing the word ghost, especially now that the sun had gone down. Stupid but true.

'Nothing,' she said. 'Well . . . boo. Like, "Boo on you, Lisey, I'm covered with blood, how do you like it?" Look, Darl, you're not the only one stressing out.'

'If we take her to the ER, what'll they do to her? Keep her on suicide watch, or something?'

'They might,' Lisey admitted. Her head was clearer

now. That word, that *bool*, had worked on her oddly like a slap, or a whiff of smelling salts. Of course it had also scared the hell out of her, but . . . if Amanda had something to tell her, Lisey wanted to know what it was. She had a sense that all the things that had been happening to her, maybe even 'Zack McCool's' telephone call, were somehow tied together by . . . what? Scott's ghost? Ridiculous. By Scott's blood-bool, then? How about that?

Or his long boy? The thing with the endless piebald side?

It doesn't exist, Lisey, it never did outside of his imagination . . . which was sometimes powerful enough to cast itself over people who were close to him. Powerful enough to make you uneasy about eating fruit after dark, for instance, even though you knew it was just some childhood superstition he never completely cast away. And the long boy was like that, too. You know that, right?

Did she? Then why, when she tried to consider the idea, did a kind of mist seem to creep over her thoughts, disrupting them? Why did that interior voice tell her to hush?

Darla was looking at her oddly. Lisey gathered herself and brought herself back to the present moment, the present people, the present problem. And for the first time noticed how *tired* Darl looked: the grooved lines around her mouth and the dark circles under her eyes. She took her sister by the upper arms, not liking how bony they felt, or the loose way Darl's bra-straps slid between her thumbs and the too-deep hollows of Darla's shoulders. Lisey could remember watching enviously as her big sisters went off to Lisbon High, home of the Greyhounds. Now Amanda was on the cusp of sixty and Darl wasn't far behind. They had become old dogs, indeed.

'But listen, hon,' she told Darla, 'they don't call it suicide watch – that's mean. They just call it observation.' Not sure how she knew this, but almost positive, just the same. 'They keep them for twenty-four hours, I think. Maybe forty-eight.'

'Can they do it without permission?'

'Unless the person's committed a crime and the cops have brought them in, I don't think so.'

'Maybe you ought to call your lawyer and make sure. The Montana guy.'

'His name's Montano, and he's probably at home by now. That number's unlisted. I've got it in my address book, but my book's back at the house. Listen, Darl, I think if we take her to Stephens Memorial in No Soapa, we'll be okay.'

No Soapa was how the locals referred to Norway–South Paris in neighboring Oxford County, towns which also happened to be within a day's drive of such exotic-sounding wide spots in the road as Mexico, Madrid, Gilead, China and Corinth. Unlike the city hospitals in Portland and Lewiston, Stephens Memorial was a sleepy little place.

'I think they'll bandage her hands and let us take her home without too much trouble.' Lisey paused. '*If.*'

'If?'

'If we *want* to take her home. And *if she* wants to come. I mean, we don't lie or make up some big story, okay? If they ask – and I'm sure they will – we tell the truth. Yes, she's done it before when she's depressed, but not for a long time.'

'Five years is not such a long—'

'Everything's relative,' Lisey said. 'And *she* can explain that her boyfriend of several years just showed up in town with a brand-new wife and that had her feeling rather pissy.'

'What if she won't talk?'

'If she won't talk, Darl, I think they'll probably be keeping her for at least twenty-four hours, and with permission from *both* of us. I mean, do you want her back here if she's still touring the outer planets?'

Darla thought about it, sighed, and shook her head.

'I think a lot of this depends on Amanda,' Lisey said. 'Step one is getting her cleaned up. I'll get in the shower with her myself, if that's what it takes.'

'Yeah,' Darla said, running her hand through her cropped hair. 'I guess that's the way to go.' She suddenly yawned. It was a startlingly wide gawp, one that would have put her tonsils on view if she'd had any left. Lisey took another look at the dark circles under her eyes and realized something she might have gotten much earlier if not for 'Zack's' call.

She took hold of Darla's arms again, lightly but insistently. 'Mrs Jones didn't call you today, did she?'

Darla blinked at her in owly surprise. 'No, honey,' she said. '*Yesterday*. Late yesterday afternoon. I came over, bandaged her up as well as I could, and sat up with her most of last night. Didn't I tell you that?'

'No. I was thinking it all happened today.'

'Silly Lisey,' Darla said, and smiled wanly.

'Why didn't you call me sooner?'

'Didn't want to bother you. You do so much for all of us.'

'That's not true,' Lisey said. It always hurt her when Darla or Canty (or even Jodotha, over the telephone) said crap like that. She knew it was crazy, but crazy or not, there it was. 'That's just Scott's money.'

'No, Lisey. It's you. Always you.' Darla paused a second, then shook her head. 'Never mind. Point is, I thought we could get through it, just the two of us. I was wrong.'

Lisey kissed her sister on the cheek, gave her a hug, then went to Amanda and sat down next to her on the couch.

5

'Manda.'

Nothing.

'Manda-Bunny?' What the smuck, it had worked before.

And yes, Amanda raised her head. 'What. Do you want.'

'We have to take you to the hospital, Manda-Bunny.'

'I. Don't. Want. To go there.'

Lisey was nodding halfway through this short but tortured speech, and starting to unbutton Amanda's blood-spattered blouse. 'I know, but your poor old hands need more fixing than Darl and I can give them. Now the question is whether or not you want to come back here or spend the night at the hospital over in No Soapa. If you want to come back here, you get me for a roommate.' *And maybe we'll talk about bools in general and blood-bools in particular.* 'What do you say, Manda? Do you want to come back here or do you think you need to be in St Steve's for awhile?'

'Want. To. Come back. Here.' When Lisey urged Amanda to her feet so she could get Amanda's cargo pants off, Amanda stood up willingly enough, but she appeared to be studying the room's light-fixture. If this wasn't what her shrink had called 'semi-catatonia', it was too close for Lisey's comfort, and she felt sharp relief when Amanda's next words came out sounding more like those of a human being and less like those of a robot: 'If we're going . . . somewhere . . . why are you *undressing* me?'

'Because you need a run through the shower,' Lisey said, guiding her in the direction of the bathroom. 'And you need fresh clothes. These are . . . dirty.' She glanced back and saw Darla gathering up the shed blouse and pants. Amanda, meanwhile, padded toward the bathroom docilely enough, but the sight of her going away squeezed Lisey's heart. It wasn't Amanda's scabbed and scarred body that did it, but rather the seat of her plain white Boxercraft underpants. For years Amanda had worn boy-shorts; they suited her angular body, were even sexy. Tonight the right cheek of the boxers she wore was smeared a muddy maroon.

Oh Manda, Lisey thought. *Oh my dear.*

Then she was through the bathroom door, an anti-social X-ray dressed in bra, pants, and white tube socks. Lisey turned to Darla. Darla was there. For a moment all the years and clamoring Debusher voices were, too. Then Lisey turned and went into the bathroom after the one she'd once called big sissa Manda-Bunny, who only stood there on the mat with her head bent and her hands dangling, waiting to be undressed the rest of the way.

Lisey was reaching for the hooks of Manda's bra

when Amanda suddenly turned and grabbed her by the arm. Her hands were horribly cold. For a moment Lisey was convinced big sissa Manda-Bunny was going to spill the whole thing, blood-bools and all. Instead she looked at Lisey with eyes that were perfectly clear, perfectly *there*, and said: 'My Charles has married another.' Then she put her waxy-cool forehead against Lisey's shoulder and began to cry.

6

The rest of that evening reminded Lisey of what Scott used to call Landon's Rule of Bad Weather: when you slept in, expecting the hurricane to go out to sea, it hooked inland and tore the roof off your house. When you rose early and battened down for the blizzard, you got only snow flurries.

What's the point then? Lisey had asked. They had been lying in bed together – some bed, one of the early beds – snug and spent after love, him with one of his Herbert Tareytons and an ashtray on his chest and a big wind howling outside. What bed, what wind, what storm, or what year she no longer remembered.

The point is SOWISA, he had replied – *that* she remembered, although at first thought she'd either misheard or misunderstood.

Soweeza? What's soweeza?

He'd snuffed his cigarette and put the ashtray on the table next to the bed. He had taken her face in his hands, covering her ears and shutting out the whole world for a minute with the palms of his hands. He kissed her lips.

Then he took his hands away so she could hear him. Scott Landon always wanted to be heard.

SOWISA, babyluv — *Strap On Whenever It Seems Appropriate.*

She had turned this over in her mind — she wasn't fast like he was, but she usually got there — and realized that SOWISA was what he called an agronim. *Strap On Whenever It Seems Appropriate.* She liked it. It was quite silly, which made her like it even more. She began to laugh. Scott laughed with her, and pretty soon he was as inside her as they were inside the house while the big wind boomed and shook outside.

With Scott she had always laughed a lot.

7

His saying about how the blizzard missed you when you really battened down for the storm recurred to her several times before their little excursion to the ER was over and they had once more returned to Amanda's weather-tight Cape Cod between Castle View and the Harlow Deep Cut. For one thing, Amanda helped matters by brightening up considerably. Morbid or not, Lisey kept thinking about how sometimes a dimming lightbulb will flash bright for an hour or two before burning out forever. This change for the better began in the shower. Lisey undressed and got in with her sister, who initially just stood there with her shoulders slumped and her arms dangling apishly. Then, in spite of using the hand-held attachment and being as careful as she could, Lisey managed to spray warm water directly onto Manda's slashed left palm.

'Ow! *Ow!*' Manda cried, snatching her hand away. 'That *hurts*, Lisey! Watch where you're pointin that thing, willya, okay?'

Lisey rejoined in exactly the same tone – Amanda would have expected no less, even with both of them buckass naked – but rejoiced at the sound of her sister's anger. It was *awake*. 'Well pardon me all the way to Kittery, but *I* wasn't the one who took a piece of the damn Pottery Barn to my hand.'

'Well, I couldn't get at *him*, could I?' Amanda asked, and then unleashed a flood of stunning invective aimed at Charlie Corriveau and his new wife – a mixture of adult obscenity and childish poopie-talk that filled Lisey with amazement, amusement and admiration.

When she paused for breath, Lisey said: 'Shitmouth motherfucker, huh? Wow.'

Amanda, sullen: 'Fuck you too, Lisey.'

'If you want to come back home, I wouldn't use a lot of those words on the doc who treats your hands.'

'You think I'm stupid, don't you?'

'No. I don't. It's just . . . saying you were mad at him will be enough.'

'My hands are bleeding again.'

'A lot?'

'Just a little bit. I think you better put some Vaseline on em.'

'Really? Won't it hurt?'

'*Love* hurts,' Amanda said solemnly . . . and then gave a little snort of laughter that lightened Lisey's heart.

By the time she and Darla bundled her into Lisey's BMW and got on the road to Norway, Manda was asking about Lisey's progress in the study, almost as if this were the end of a normal day. Lisey didn't mention 'Zack McCool's' call, but she told them about 'Ike Comes Home' and quoted the single line of copy: 'Ike came home with a boom, and everything was fine. BOOL! THE END!' She wanted to use that word, that *bool*, in Mandy's presence. Wanted to see how she'd respond.

Darla responded first. 'You married a very strange man, Lisa,' she said.

'Tell me something I *don't* know, darlin'.' Lisey glanced in the rearview mirror to see Amanda sitting alone in the back seat. *In solitary splendor*, Good Ma would have said. 'What do you think, Manda?'

Amanda shrugged, and at first Lisey thought that was going to be her only response. Then came the flood.

'It was just *him*, that's all. I hooked a ride with him up the city once – he needed to go to the office-supply store and I needed new shoes, you know, good walking shoes I could wear in the woods for hiking, stuff like that. And we happened to drive by Auburn Novelty. He'd never seen it before and nothing would do but he had to park and go right in. He was like a ten-year-old! I needed Eddie Bauer shitkickers so I could walk in the woods without getting poison ivy all over me and all *he* wanted to do was buy out that whole freakin store. Itchy-powder, joy buzzers, pepper gum, plastic puke, X-ray glasses, you name it, he had it piled up on the counter next to these lollipops, when you sucked em down there was a naked woman inside. He must have bought a hundred dollars' worth of that crazy made-in-Taiwan shite, Lisey. Do you remember?'

She did. Most of all she remembered how he had

looked coming home that day, his arms full of bags with laughing cartoon faces and the words LAFF RIOT printed all over them. How full of color his cheeks had been. And shite was what he'd called it, not *shit* but *shite*, that was one word he picked up from *her*, could you believe it. Well, turnabout was fair play, so Good Ma had liked to claim, although *shite* had been their Dad's word, as it had been Dandy Dave Debusher who would sometimes tell folks a thing was no good, *so I slang it forth*. How Scott had loved it, said it had a weight coming off the tongue that *I threw it away* or even *I flung it away* could never hope to match.

Scott with his catches from the word-pool, the story-pool, the myth-pool.

Scott smucking Landon.

Sometimes she'd go a whole day without thinking of him or missing him. Why not? She had quite a full life, and really, he'd often been hard to deal with and hard to live with. *A project*, the Yankee oldtimers like her very own Dad might have said. And then sometimes a day would come, a gray one (or a sunny one) when she missed him so fiercely she felt empty, not a woman at all anymore but just a dead tree filled with cold November blow. She felt like that now, felt like hollering his name and hollering him home, and her heart turned sick with the thought of the years ahead and she wondered what good love was if it came to this, to even ten seconds of feeling like this.

8

Amanda brightening up was the first good thing. Munsinger, the doctor on duty, was no grizzled vet, that was the second good thing. He didn't look as young as Jantzen, the doc Lisey met during Scott's final illness, but if he was much beyond thirty, she'd be surprised. The third good thing — although she'd never have believed it if anyone had told her in advance — was the arrival of the car-accident folks from down the road in Sweden.

They weren't there when Lisey and Darla escorted Amanda into the Stephens Memorial ER; then the waiting room was empty except for a kid of ten or so and his mother. The kid had a rash and his mother kept snapping at him not to scratch it. She was still snapping when the two of them were called back to one of the examining rooms. Five minutes later the kid reappeared with bandages on his arms and a glum look on his face. Mom had some sample tubes of ointment and was still yapping.

The nurse called Amanda's name. 'Dr Munsinger will see you now, dear.' She pronounced the last word in the Maine fashion, so that it rhymed with *Leah*.

Amanda gave first Lisey, then Darla her haughty, red-cheeked, Queen Elizabeth look. 'I prefer to see him alone,' she said.

'Of course, your Grand High Mysteriousness,' Lisey said, and stuck her tongue out at Amanda. At that moment she didn't care if they kept the scrawny, troublesome bitch a night, a week, or a year and a day. Who cared what Amanda might have whispered at the kitchen table when Lisey had been kneeling beside her? Probably it *had* been boo, as she'd told Darla. Even if it had been the other word, did she really want to go back to Amanda's house, sleep in the same room with her, and breathe her crazy vapors when she had a perfectly good bed of her own at home? *Case smucking closed, babyluv*, Scott would have said.

'Just remember what we agreed on,' Darla said. 'You got mad and you cut yourself because he wasn't there. You're better now. You're over it.'

Amanda gave Darla a look Lisey absolutely could not read. 'That's right,' she said. 'I'm over it.'

9

The car-accident folks from the little town of Sweden arrived shortly thereafter. Lisey wouldn't have counted it a good thing if any of them had been seriously hurt, but that did not appear to be the case. All of them were ambulating, and two of the men were actually laughing about something. Only one of them – a girl of about seventeen – was crying. She had blood in her hair and snot on her upper lip. There were six of them in all, almost certainly from two different vehicles, and a strong smell of beer was coming from the two laughing men, one of whom appeared to have a sprained arm. The sextet was shepherded in by two med-techs wearing East Stoneham Rescue jackets over civilian clothes, and two cops: a State Policeman and a County Mounty. All at once the little ER waiting room seemed absolutely stuffed. The nurse who had called Amanda *dear* popped her startled head out for a look, and a moment later young Dr Munsinger did the same. Not long after that the teenage girl went into a noisy fit of hysterics, announcing to all and sundry that her stepmom was gonna murdalize her. A few moments after that the nurse came to get her (she didn't call the hysterical teenager *dear*, Lisey noted), and then Amanda came out of EXAMINATION ROOM 2, clumsily carrying her own sample-sized tubes. There were also a couple of folded prescription slips poking from the left pocket of her baggy jeans.

'I think we may go,' Amanda said, still in haughty Grand Lady mode.

Lisey thought that was too good to be true even with the relative youth of the doctor on duty and the fresh influx of patients, and she was right. The nurse leaned out of EXAMINATION ROOM 1 like an engineer from the cab of a locomotive and said, 'Are you two ladies Miss Debusher's sisters?'

Lisey and Darla nodded. Guilty as charged, judge.

'Doctor would like to speak to you for a minute before you go.' With that she pulled her head back into the room, where the girl was still sobbing.

On the other side of the waiting room, the two beer-smelling men burst out laughing again, and Lisey thought: *Whatever may be wrong with them, they must not have been responsible for the accident.* And indeed, the cops seemed to be concentrating on a white-faced boy of about the same age as the girl with the blood in her hair. Another boy had commandeered the pay phone. He had a badly gashed cheek which Lisey was sure would take stitches. A third waited his turn to make a call. This boy had no visible injuries.

Amanda's palms had been coated with a whitish cream. 'He said stitches would only pull out,' she told them, almost proudly. 'And I guess bandages won't stay put. I'm supposed to keep this stuff on them – ugh, doesn't it stink? – and soak them three times a day for the next three days. I have one 'scrip for the cream and one for the soak. He said to try and not bend my hands too much. To pick things up between my fingers, like this.' She tweezed a prehistoric copy of *People* between the first two fingers of her right hand, lifted it a little way, then dropped it.

The nurse appeared. 'Dr Munsinger could see you now. One or both.' Her tone made it clear there was little time to waste. Lisey was sitting on one side of Amanda, Darla on the other. They looked at each other across her. Amanda didn't notice. She was studying the people on the other side of the room with frank interest.

'You go, Lisey,' Darla said. 'I'll stay with her.'

10

The nurse showed Lisey into EXAMINATION ROOM 2, then went back to the sobbing girl, her lips pressed together so tightly they almost disappeared. Lisey sat in the room's one chair and gazed at the room's one picture: a fluffy cocker spaniel in a field filled with daffodils. After only a few moments (she was sure she would have had to wait longer, had she not been something that needed getting rid of), Dr Munsinger hurried in. He closed the door on the sound of the teenage girl's noisy sobs and parked one skinny buttock on the examination table.

'I'm Hal Munsinger,' he said.

'Lisa Landon.' She extended her hand. Dr Hal Munsinger shook it briefly.

'I'd like to get a lot more information on your sister's situation – for the record, you know – but as I'm sure you see, I'm in a bit of a bind here. I've called for backup, but in the meantime, I'm having one of those nights.'

'I appreciate your making any time at all,' Lisey said, and what she appreciated even more was the calm voice she heard issuing from her own mouth. It was a voice that said *all this is under control*. 'I'm willing to certify that my sister Amanda isn't a danger to herself, if that's troubling you.'

'Well, you know that troubles me a little, yep, a little, but I'm going to take your word for that. And hers. She's not a minor, and in any case this was pretty clearly not a suicide attempt.' He had been looking at something on his clipboard. Now he looked up at Lisey, and his gaze was uncomfortably penetrating. 'Was it?'

'No.'

'No. On the other hand, it doesn't take Sherlock Holmes to see this isn't the first case of self-mutilation with your sister.'

Lisey sighed.

'She told me she's been in therapy, but her therapist left for Idaho.'

Idaho? Alaska? Mars? Who cares where, the bead-wearing bitch is gone. Out loud she said, 'I believe that's true.'

'She needs to get back to working on herself, Mrs Landon, okay? And soon. Self-mutilation isn't suicide any more than anorexia is, but both are *suicidal*, if you take my meaning.' He took a pad from the pocket of his white coat and began to scribble. 'I want to recommend a book to you and your sister. It's called *Cutting Behavior*, by a man named—'

'—Peter Mark Stein,' Lisey said.

Dr Munsinger looked up, surprised.

'My husband found it after Manda's last . . . after what Mr Stein calls . . .'

(her bool her last blood-bool)

Young Dr Munsinger was looking at her, waiting for her to finish.

(go on then Lisey say it say bool say blood-bool)

She grasped her flying thoughts by main force. 'After what Stein would call her last *outletting*. That's the word he uses, isn't it? Outletting?' Her voice was still calm, but she could feel little nestles of sweat in the hollows of her temples. Because that voice inside her was right. Call it an outletting or a blood-bool, both came to the same. *Everything* the same.

'I think so,' Munsinger said, 'but it's been several years since I actually read the book.'

'As I say, my husband found it and read it and then got me to read it. I'll dig it out and give it to my sister Darla. And we have another sister in the area. She's in Boston right now, but when she gets back, I'll make sure she reads it, too. And we'll keep an eye on Amanda. She can be difficult, but we love her.'

'Okay, good enough.' He slid his skinny shank off the examination table. The paper covering crackled. 'Landon. Your husband was the writer.'

'Yes.'

'I'm sorry for your loss.'

This was one of the odder things about having been married to a famous man, she was discovering; two years later, people were still condoling with her. She guessed the same would be true two years further along. Maybe ten. The idea was depressing. 'Thank you, Dr Munsinger.'

He nodded, then got back to business, which was a relief. 'Case histories having to do with this sort of thing in adult women are pretty thin on the ground. Most commonly we see self-mutilation in—'

There was just time for Lisey to imagine him finishing with—*kids like that weepy brat in the next room*, and then there was a tremendous crash from the waiting area, followed by a confusion of shouts. The door to EXAMINATION ROOM 2 was jerked open and the nurse was there. She seemed *bigger* somehow, as if trouble had caused her to swell. 'Doctor, can you come?'

Munsinger didn't excuse himself, just boogied. Lisey respected him for that: SOWISA.

She got to the door in time to see the good doctor almost knock down the teenage girl, who'd emerged from EXAMINATION ROOM 1 to check out what was going on, and then bump a gawking Amanda into her sister's arms so hard that they both almost went over. The State Cop and the County Mounty were standing around the seemingly uninjured boy who'd been waiting to make a call. He now lay on the floor either unconscious or in a faint. The boy with the gash in his cheek continued to talk on the phone as if nothing had happened. That made Lisey think of a poem Scott had once read to her – a wonderful, terrible poem about how the world just went on rolling without giving a

(shite)

good goddam how much pain you were in. Who had written it? Eliot? Auden? The man who had also written the poem about the death of the ball-turret gunner? Scott could have told her. In that moment she would have given every cent she had if she could have turned to him and asked which of them had written that poem about suffering.

11

'Are you sure you'll be all right?' Darla asked. She was standing in the open door of Amanda's little house an hour or so later, the mild June nightbreeze frisking around their ankles and leafing through the pages of a magazine on the hall table.

Lisey made a face. 'If you ask me that again, I'm gonna throw you out on your head. We'll be *fine*. Some cocoa – which I'll help her with, since cups are going to be hard for her in her current condish—'

'Good,' Darla said. 'Considering what she did with the last one.'

'Then off to bed. Just two Debusher old maids, without a single dildo between em.'

'Very funny.'

'Tomorrow, up with the sun! Coffee! Cereal! Off to fill her prescriptions! Back here to soak the hands! Then, Darla-darlin, *you're* on duty!'

'Just as long as you're sure.'

'I am. Go home and feed your cat.'

Darla gave her a final doubtful look, followed by a peck on the cheek and her patented sideways hug. Then she walked down the crazy-paving toward her little car. Lisey closed the door, locked it, and glanced at Amanda, sitting on the couch in a cotton nightie, looking serene and at peace. The title of an old gothic romance floated through her mind . . . one she might have read as a teenager. *Madam, Will You Talk?*

'Manda?' she said softly.

Amanda looked up at her, and her blue Debusher

133

eyes were so wide and trusting that Lisey didn't think she could lead Amanda toward what it was that she, Lisey, wanted to hear about: Scott and bools, Scott and blood-bools. If Amanda came to it on her own, perhaps as they lay together in the dark, that would be one thing. But to take her there, after the day Amanda had just put in?

You've had quite a day yourself, little Lisey.

That was true, but she didn't think it justified disturbing the peace she now saw in Amanda's eyes.

'What is it, Lisey?'

'*Would* you like some cocoa before bed?'

Amanda smiled. It made her years younger. 'Cocoa before bed would be lovely.'

So they had cocoa, and when Amanda had trouble with her cup, she found herself a crazily twisted plastic straw – it would have been perfectly at home on the shelves of the Auburn Novelty Shop – in one of her kitchen cupboards. Before dunking one end in her cocoa, she held it up to Lisey (tweezed between two fingers, just as the doctor had shown her) and said, 'Look, Lisey, it's my *brain*.'

For a moment Lisey could only gape, unable to believe she had actually heard Amanda making a joke. Then she cracked up. They both did.

12

They drank their cocoa, took turns brushing their teeth just as they had so long ago in the farmhouse where they'd grown up, and then went to bed. And once the bedside lamp was out and the room was dark, Amanda spoke her sister's name.

Oboy, here it comes, Lisey thought uneasily. *Another diatribe at good old Charlie. Or . . . is it the bool? Is it something about that, after all? And if it is, do I really want to hear?*

'What, Manda?'

'Thank you for helping me,' Amanda said. 'The stuff that doctor put on my hands makes them feel ever so much better.' Then she rolled over on her side.

Lisey was stunned again – was that really all? It seemed so, because a minute or two later, Amanda's breathing dropped into the slower, steeper respirations of sleep. She might be awake in the night wanting Tylenol, but right now she was gone.

Lisey did not expect to be so fortunate. She hadn't slept with anyone since the night before her husband left on his last trip, and had fallen out of the habit. Also, she had 'Zack McCool' to think about, not to mention 'Zack's' employer, the Incunk son of a bitch Woodbody. She'd talk to Woodbody soon. Tomorrow, in fact. In the meantime, she'd do well to resign herself to some wakeful hours, maybe a whole night of them, with the last two or three spent in Amanda's Boston rocker downstairs . . . if, that was, she could find something on Amanda's bookshelves worth reading . . .

Madam, Will You Talk? she thought. *Maybe Helen MacInnes wrote that book. It surely wasn't by the man who wrote the poem about the ball-turret gunner . . .*

And on that thought, she fell into a deep and profound sleep. There were no dreams of the PILLSBURY'S BEST magic carpet. Or of anything else.

13

She awoke in the deepest ditch of the night, when the moon is down and the hour is none. She was hardly aware she was awake, or that she had snuggled against Amanda's warm back as she had once snuggled against Scott's, or that she had fitted the balls of her knees to the hollows of Manda's, as she had once done with Scott – in their bed, in a hundred motel beds. Hell, in five hundred, maybe seven hundred, do I hear a thousand, come a thousand, someone gimme thousand. She was thinking of bools and blood-bools. Of SOWISA and how sometimes all you could do was hang your head and wait for the wind to change. She was thinking that if darkness had loved Scott, why then that was true love, wasn't it, for he had loved it as well; had danced with it across the ballroom of years until it had finally danced him away.

She thought: *I am going there again.*

And the Scott she kept in her head (at least she *thought* it was that Scott, but who knew for sure) said: *Where are you going, Lisey? Where now, babyluv?*

She thought: *Back to the present.*

And Scott said: *That movie was* Back to the Future. *We saw it together.*

She thought: *This was no movie, this is our life.*

And Scott said: *Baby, are you strapped?*

She thought: *Why am I in love with such a*

14

He's such a fool, she's thinking. *He's a fool and I'm another for bothering with him.*

Still she stands looking out onto the back lawn, not wanting to call him, but starting to feel nervous now because he walked out the kitchen door and down the back lawn into the eleven o'clock shadows almost ten minutes ago, and what can he be doing? There's nothing down there but hedge and—

From somewhere not too far distant come the sounds of squalling tires, breaking glass, a dog barking, a drunken war-whoop. All the sounds of a college town on a Friday night, in other words. And she's tempted to holler down to him, but if she does that, even if it's just his name she hollers, he'll know she's not pissed at him anymore. Not *as* pissed, anyway.

She isn't, in fact. But the thing is, he picked a really bad Friday night to show up lit up for the sixth or seventh time and really late for the first time. The plan had been to see a movie he was hot for by some Swedish director, and she'd only been hoping it would be dubbed in English instead of with subtitles. So she'd gobbled a quick salad when she got home from work, thinking Scott would take her to the Bear's Den for a hamburger after the show. (If he didn't, *she* would take *him*.) Then the telephone had rung and she'd expected it to be him, hoped he'd had a change of heart and wanted to take her to the Redford movie at the mall in Bangor (please God not dancing at The Anchorage after being on her feet for eight hours). And instead it was Darla, saying she 'just called to talk' and then getting down to the real business, which was bitching at her (again) for running away to Never-Never Land (Darla's term) and leaving her and Amanda and Cantata to cope with all the problems (by which she meant Good

Ma, who by 1979 was Fat Ma, Blind Ma, and – worst of all – Gaga Ma) while Lisey 'played with the college kids'. Like waitressing eight hours a day was recess. For her, Never Land was a pizza parlor three miles from the University of Maine campus and the Lost Boys were mostly Delta Taus who kept trying to put their hands up her skirt. God knew her vague dreams of taking a few courses – maybe at night – had dried up and blown away. It wasn't brains she was lacking; it was time and energy. She had listened to Darla rave and tried to keep her temper and of course she'd eventually lost it and the two of them ended up shouting at each other across a hundred and forty miles of telephone line and all the history that lay between them. It had been what her boyfriend would no doubt call a total smuckup, ending with Darla saying what she always said: 'Do what you want – you will, anyway, you always do.'

After that she hadn't wanted the slice of cheesecake she'd brought home from the restaurant for dessert, and she certainly hadn't wanted to go to any Ingmar Bergman movie . . . but she had wanted Scott. Yes. Because over the last couple of months, and especially over the last four or five weeks, she's come to depend on Scott in a funny way. Maybe it's corny – *probably* – but there's a feeling of safety when he puts his arms around her that wasn't there with any of her other guys; what she felt with and for most of them was either impatience or wariness. (Sometimes fleeting lust.) But there is kindness in Scott, and from the first she felt interest coming from him – interest in *her* – that she could hardly believe, because he's so much *smarter* and so talented. (To Lisey, the kindness means more than either.) But she *does* believe it. And he speaks a language she grasped greedily from the beginning. Not the language of the Debushers, but one she knows very well, just the same – it's as if she's been speaking it in dreams.

But what good is talk, and a special language, if there's no one to talk *to*? Someone to *cry* to, even? That's what she needed tonight. She's never told him about her crazy fucked-up family – oh, pardon me, that's crazy *smucked-up* family, in Scott-talk – but she meant to tonight. Felt she *had* to or explode from pure misery. So of course he picked tonight of all nights not to show up. As she waited she tried to tell herself that *Scott* certainly didn't know she'd just had the world's worst fight with her bitch of an older sister, but as six became seven became eight, do I hear nine, come nine, someone gimme nine, as she picked at the cheesecake a little more and then threw it away because she was just too smucking . . . no, too *fucking* mad to eat it, we got nine, anybody gimme ten, I got ten o'clock and still no '73 Ford with one flickery headlight pulling up in front of her North Main Street apartment, she became angrier still, can anybody gimme *furious*.

She was sitting in front of the TV with a barely tasted glass of wine beside her and an unwatched nature program before her by the time her anger passed over into a state of fury, and that was also when she became positive that Scott would not stand her up completely. He would *make the scene*, as the saying was. In hopes of *getting his end wet*. Another one of Scott's catches from the word-pool where we all go down to cast our nets, and how charming it was! How charming they all were! There was also *getting your ashes hauled, dipping your wick, making the beast with two backs, choogling*, and the very elegant *ripping off a piece*. How very

Never-Never Land they all were, and as she sat there listening for the sound of her particular Lost Boy's '73 Ford Fairlane – you couldn't miss that throaty burble, there was a hole in the muffler or something – she thought of Darla saying, *Do what you want, you always do.* Yes, and here she was, little Lisey, queen of the world, doing what she wanted, sitting in this cruddy little apartment, waiting for her boyfriend who'd turn up drunk as well as late – but still wanting a piece because they all wanted that, it was even a joke, *Hey waitress, bring me the Sheepherder's Special, a cup of cumoffee and a piece of ewe.* Here she was, sitting in a lumpy thrift-shop chair with her feet aching at one end and her head throbbing at the other, while on the TV – snowy, because the Kmart rabbit-ears brought in smuck-all for reception – she was watching a hyena eat a dead gopher. Lisey Debusher, queen of the world, leading the glamorous life.

And yet as the hands of the clock crept past ten, had she not also felt a kind of low, crabby happiness creeping in? Now, looking anxiously down the shadowed lawn, Lisey thinks the answer is yes. *Knows* the answer is yes. Because sitting there with her headache and a glass of harsh red wine, watching the hyena dine on the gopher while the narrator intoned, 'The predator knows he may not eat so well again for many days,' Lisey was pretty sure she loved him and knew things that could hurt him.

That he loved her too? Was that one of them?

Yes, but in this matter his love for her was secondary. What mattered here was how she saw him: dead level. His other friends saw his talent, and were dazzled by it. She saw how he sometimes struggled to meet the eyes of strangers. She understood that, underneath all his smart (and sometimes brilliant) talk, in spite of his two published novels, she could hurt him badly, if she wanted to. He was, in her Dad's words, *cruising for a bruising*. Had been his whole charmed smucking – no, check that – his whole charmed fucking life. Tonight the charm would break. And who would break it? She would.

Little Lisey.

She had turned off the TV, gone into the kitchen with her glass of wine, and poured it down the sink. She no longer wanted it. It now tasted sour in her mouth as well as harsh. *You're turning it sour*, she thought. *That's how pissed-off you are*. She didn't doubt it. There's an old radio placed precariously on the window-ledge over the sink, an old Philco with a cracked case. It had been Dandy's; he kept it out in the barn and listened to it while he was a-choring. It's the only thing of his Lisey still has, and she keeps it in the window because it's the only place where it will pick up local stations. Jodotha gave it to him one Christmas, and it was secondhand even then, but when it was unwrapped and he saw what it was, he grinned until it seemed his face would crack and how he thanked her! Over and over! It was ever Jodi who was his favorite, and it was Jodi who sat at the dinner-table one Sunday and announced to her parents – hell, announced to all of them – that she was pregnant and the boy who'd gotten her that way had run off to enlist in the Navy. She wanted to know if maybe Aunt Cynthia over in Wolleboro, New Hampshire, could take her in until the baby was *put out for adoption* – that was how Jodi said it, as though it were a thing at a yard sale. Her news had been greeted by an unaccustomed silence at the dinner-table. For one of the few times in Lisey's memory — maybe for the *only* time in Lisey's memory — the constant chattering conversation of knives and forks against plates as seven hungry Debushers raced the roast to the bone had stopped. At last Good Ma had asked, *Have you talked to God about this, Jodotha?* And Jodi — right back atcha, Good Ma: *It was Don Cloutier got me in the family way, not God.* That was when Dad left the table and his favorite daughter behind without a word or backward look. A few moments later Lisey had heard the sound of his radio coming from the barn, very faint. Three weeks later he'd had the first of his strokes. Now Jodi's gone (although not yet to Miami, that is years in the future) and it's Lisey who bears the brunt of Darla's outraged calls, little Lisey, and why? Because Canty is on Darla's side and calling Jodi does neither of them any good. Jodi is different from the other Debusher girls. Darla calls her cold, Canty calls her selfish, and they both call her uncaring, but Lisey thinks it's something else — something better and finer. Of the five girls, Jodi is the one true survivor, completely immune to the fumes of guilt rising from the old family teepee. Once Granny D generated those fumes, then their mother, but Darla and Canty stand ready to take over, already understanding that if you call that poisonous, addictive smoke 'duty', nobody tells you to put the fire out. As for Lisey, she only wishes she were more like Jodi, that when Darla calls she could laugh and say *Blow it out your ass, Darla-darlin; you made your bed, so go on and sleep in it.*

15

Standing in the kitchen doorway. Looking into the long, sloping backyard. Wanting to see him come walking back out of the darkness. Wanting to holler him back – yes, more than ever – but stubbornly holding his name behind her lips. She waited for him all evening. She will wait a little longer.

But only a little.

She is beginning to be so frightened.

16

Dandy's radio is strictly AM. WGUY's a sundowner and long off the air, but WDER was playing the oldies when she rinsed her wineglass – some fifties hero singing about young love – and went back into the living room and bingo, there he was, standing in the doorway with a can of beer in one hand and his slanted smile on his face. Probably she hadn't heard the sound of his Ford pulling up because of the music. Or the beat of her headache. Or both.

'Hey, Lisey,' he said. 'Sorry I'm late. *Really* sorry. A bunch of us from David's Honors seminar got arguing about Thomas Hardy, and—'

She turned away from him without a word and went back into the kitchen, back into the sound of the Philco. Now it was a bunch of guys singing 'Sh-Boom'. He followed her. She knew he would follow her, it was how these things went. She could feel all the things she had to say to him crowding up in her throat, acid things, poison things, and some lonely, terrified voice told her not to say them, not to this man, and she slang that voice away. In her anger she could do nothing else.

He cocked a thumb at the radio and said, stupidly proud of his useless knowledge: 'That's The Chords. The original black version.'

She turned to him and said, 'Do you think I give a rat's ass who's singing on the radio after I worked eight hours and waited for you another five? And you finally show up at quarter of eleven with a grin on your face and a beer in your hand and a story about how some dead poet ended up being more important to you than I am?'

The grin on his face was still there but it was getting smaller, fading until it was little more than a quirk and one shallow dimple. Water, meanwhile, had risen in his eyes. The lost scared voice tried to call its warning again and she ignored it. This was a cutting party now. In both the fading grin and the growing hurt in his eyes she saw how he loved her, and knew this increased her power to hurt him. Still, she would cut. And why? Because she could.

Standing in the kitchen door and waiting for him to come back, she can't remember all the things she said, only that each one was a little worse, a little more perfectly tailored to hurt. At one point she was appalled to hear how much she sounded like Darla at her worst – just one more hectoring Debusher – and by then his smile was no longer even hanging in there. He was looking at her solemnly and she was terrified by how large his eyes were, magnified by the wetness shimmering on their surfaces until they seemed to eat up his face. She stopped in the middle of something about how his fingernails were always dirty and he gnawed on them like a rat when he was reading. She stopped and at that moment there were no engine sounds from in front of The Shamrock and The Mill downtown, no screeching tires, not even the faint sound of this weekend's band playing at The Rock. The silence was enormous and she realized she wanted to go back and had no idea how to do it. The simplest thing – *I love you anyway, Scott, come to bed* – will not occur to her until later. Not until after the bool.

'Scott . . . I—'

She had no idea where to go from there, and it seemed there was no need. Scott raised the forefinger of his left hand like a teacher who means to make a particularly important point, and the smile actually resurfaced on his lips. Some sort of smile, anyway.

'Wait,' he said.

'Wait?'

He looked pleased, as if she had grasped a difficult concept. 'Wait.'

And before she could say anything else he simply walked off into the dark, back straight, walk straight (no drunk in him now), slim hips slinging in his jeans. She said his name once— 'Scott?'—but he only raised that forefinger again: *wait*. Then the shadows swallowed him.

17

Now she stands looking anxiously down the lawn. She has turned off the kitchen light, thinking that may make it easier to see him, but even with the help of the pole-light in the yard next door, the shadows take over halfway down the hill. In the next yard, a dog barks hoarsely. That dog's name is Pluto, she knows because she has heard the people over there yelling at it from time to time, fat lot of good it does. She thinks of the breaking-glass sound she heard a minute ago: like the barking, the breaking sounded close. Closer than the other sounds that populate this busy, unhappy night.

Why oh why did she have to tee off on him like that? She didn't even want to see the stupid Swedish movie in the first place! And why had she felt such joy in it? Such mean and filthy joy?

To that she has no answer. The late-spring night breathes around her, and exactly how long *has* he been down there in the dark? Only two minutes? Five, maybe? It seems longer. And that sound of breaking glass, did that have anything to do with Scott?

The greenhouse is down there. Parks.

There's no reason that should make her heart beat faster, but it does. And just as she feels that increased rhythm she sees motion beyond the place where her eyes lose their ability to see much of anything. A second later the moving thing resolves itself into a man. She feels relief, but it doesn't dissipate her fear. She keeps thinking about the sound of breaking glass. And there's something wrong with the way he's moving. His limber, straight walk is gone.

Now she *does* call his name, but what comes out is little more than a whisper: 'Scott?' At the same time her hand is scrabbling around on the wall, feeling for the switch that turns on the light over the stoop.

Her call is low, but the shadowy figure plodding up the lawn – yes, that's a plod, all right, not a walk but a

146

plod – raises its head just as Lisey's curiously numb fingers find the light-switch and flick it. *'It's a bool, Lisey!'* he shouts as the light springs on, and could he have planned it better if he had stage-managed it? She thinks not. In his voice she hears mad jubilant relief, as if he has fixed everything. *'And not just any bool, it's a blood-bool!'*

She has never heard the word before, but she doesn't mistake it for anything else, for *boo* or *book* or anything else. It's *bool*, another Scott-word, and not just any bool but a blood-bool. The kitchen light leaps down the lawn to meet him and he's holding out his left hand to her like a gift, she's sure he means it as a gift, just as she's pretty sure there's still a hand under there someplace, oh pray to Jesus Mary and JoJo the everloving carpenter there's still a hand under there someplace or he's going to be finishing the book he's working on plus any that might come later typing one-handed. Because where his left hand was there's now just a red and dripping *mass*. Blood goes slipping between spread starfish things that she supposes are his fingers, and even as she flies to meet him, her feet stuttering down the back porch steps, she's counting those spread red shapes, one two three four and oh thank God, that fifth one's the thumb. Everything's still there, but his jeans are splattered red and still he holds his bloody lacerated hand out to her, the one he plunged through a pane of thick greenhouse glass, shouldering his way through the hedge at the foot of the lawn in order to get to it. Now he's holding out his gift to her, his act of atonement for being late, his blood-bool.

'It's for you,' he says as she yanks off her blouse and drapes it around the red and dripping mass, feeling it soak through the cloth at once, feeling the crazy heat of it and knowing – of course! – why that small voice was in such terror of the things she was saying to him, what it knew all along: not only is this man in love with her, he's half in love with death and more than ready to agree with every mean and hurtful thing anyone says about him.

Anyone?

No, not quite. He's not quite that vulnerable. Just anyone he loves. And Lisey suddenly realizes she's not the only one who has said almost nothing about her past.

'It's for you. To say I'm sorry I forgot and it won't happen again. It's a bool. We—'

'Scott, hush. It's all right. I'm not—'

'We call it a blood-bool. It's special. Daddy told me and Paul—'

'I'm not mad at you. I was never mad at you.'

He stops at the foot of the splintery back steps, gawking at her. The expression makes him look about ten years old. Her blouse is wrapped clumsily around his hand like a knight's dress gauntlet; once yellow, it's now all bloom and blood. She stands there on the lawn in her Maidenform bra, feeling the grass tickling her bare ankles. The dusky yellow light which rains on them from the kitchen puts a deep curved shadow between her breasts. 'Will you take it?'

He's looking at her with such childish pleading. All the man in him is gone for now. She sees pain in his long and longing glance and knows it's not from his lacerated hand, but she doesn't know what to say. This is beyond her. She's done well to get some sort of compress on the horrible mess he's made south of his wrist, but now she's frozen. Is there a right thing to say? More important, is there a wrong one? One that will set him off again?

He helps her. 'If you take a bool – especially a blood-bool – then sorry's okay. Daddy said so. Daddy tole Paul n me over n over.' Not *told* but *tole*. He has regressed to the diction of his childhood. Oh jeez. Jeez Louise.

Lisey says, 'I guess I take it, then, because I never wanted to go see any Swedish-meatball movie with sub-titles in the first place. My feet hurt. I just wanted to go to bed with you. And now look, we have to go to the smucking Emergency Room, instead.'

He shakes his head, slowly but firmly.

'*Scott*—'

'If you weren't mad, why did you shout and call me all the bad-gunky?'

All the bad-gunky. Surely another postcard from his childhood. She notes it, puts it away for later examination.

'Because I couldn't shout at my sister anymore,' she says. This hits her funny and she begins to laugh. She laughs hard, and the sound so shocks her that she begins to cry. Then she feels light-headed. She sits down on the porch steps, thinking she may faint.

Scott sits beside her. He's twenty-four, his hair falls almost to his shoulders, his face is scruffy with two days' growth, and he's as slim as a rule. On his left hand he wears her blouse, one sleeve now unwrapped and hanging down. He kisses the throbbing hollow of her temple, then looks at her with perfect fond understanding. When he speaks, he sounds almost like himself again.

'I understand,' he says. 'Families suck.'

'*Yeah* they do,' she whispers.

He puts his arm around her – the left one, which she is already thinking of as the blood-bool arm, his gift to her, his crazy smucked-up Friday-night gift.

'They don't have to matter,' he says. His voice is weirdly serene. It's as if he hasn't just turned his left hand into so much raw and bleeding meat. 'Listen, Lisey: people can forget anything.'

She looked at him doubtfully. 'Can they?'

'Yes. This is our time now. You and me. That's what matters.'

You and me. But does she want that? Now that she sees how narrowly he's balanced? Now that she has a picture of what life with him may be like? Then she thinks of how his lips felt in the hollow of her temple, touching that special secret place, and she thinks, *Maybe I do. Doesn't every hurricane have an eye?*

'Is it?' she asks.

For several seconds he says nothing. Only holds her. From Cleaves's paltry downtown come the sounds of engines and yells and wild, whooping laughter. It's Friday night and the Lost Boys are at play. But that is not here. Here is all the smell of her long, sloping backyard sleeping toward summer, the sound of Pluto barking under the pole-light next door, and the feel of his arm around her. Even the warm damp press of his wounded hand is comforting, marking the bare skin of her midriff like a brand.

'Baby,' he says at last.

Pauses.

Then: 'Babyluv.'

For Lisey Debusher, twenty-two, weary of her family

and equally tired of being on her own, it is enough. Finally enough. He has hollered her home, and in the dark she gives in to the Scott of him. From then until the end she will never look back.

18

When they're in the kitchen again, she unwinds her blouse and sees the damage. Looking at it, she feels another wave of faintness first lift her up toward the bright overhead light and then drop her toward darkness; she has to struggle to stay conscious, and manages to do it by telling herself *He needs me. He needs me to drive him to the ER at Derry Home.*

He has somehow missed slicing into the veins which lie so close under the wrist — a blue-eyed miracle — but the palm is cut in at least four different places, some of the skin is hanging like wallpaper, and three of what her Dad called 'the fat fingers' are also cut. The *pièce de résistance* is a horrible gash on his forearm with a triangle of thick green glass sticking up from it like a sharkfin. She hears herself make a helpless *ouck!* sound as he pulls it out — almost casually — and tosses it into the trash. He holds her blood-soaked blouse under his hand and arm as he does this, considerately trying to keep blood off her kitchen floor. He *does* get a few drops on the lino, but there's surprisingly little to clean up later. There's a high counter-stool that she sometimes sits on when she's peeling veggies, or even when she's washing dishes (when you're on your feet eight hours a day, you take your sitdowns where you can get em), and Scott hooks it over with one foot so he can sit with his hand dripping into the sink. He says he's going to tell her what to do.

'You have to go to the ER,' she tells him. 'Scott, be sensible! Hands are full of tendons and things! Do you want to lose the use of it? Because you could! You really could! If you're worried about what they'll say, you can cook up some story, cooking up stories is what you *do*, and I'll back y—'

'If you still want me to go tomorrow, we'll go,' he tells her. Now he's *entirely* his normal self, rational and charming and almost hypnotically persuasive. 'I'm not going to die of this tonight, the bleeding's almost stopped already, and besides – do you know what ERs are like on Friday night? Drunks On Parade! First thing Saturday morning would be *lots* better.' He's grinning at her now, that delighted *honey, I'm hip* grin that almost demands you grin back, and she tries not to, but this is a battle she's losing. 'Besides, all the Landons are fast healers. We had to be. I'm going to show you just what to do.'

'You act like you've put your hand through a dozen greenhouse windows.'

'No,' he says, the grin faltering a little. 'Never poked a greenhouse until tonight. But I learned some stuff about being hurt. Paul and I both did.'

'He was your brother?'

'Yeah. He's dead. Draw a basin of warm water, Lisey, okay? Warm but not quite hot.'

She wants to ask him all kinds of questions about this brother

(Daddy tole Paul n me over n over)

she never knew he had, but this isn't the time. Nor

152

will she hector him anymore about going to the Emergency Room, not just now. For one thing if he agreed to go she'd just have to drive him there, and she isn't sure she could do it, she's come over all shaky inside. And he's right about the bleeding, it's slowed way down. Thank God for small favors.

Lisey gets her white plastic basin (Mammoth Mart, seventy-nine cents) from under the sink and fills it with warm water. He plops his lacerated hand into it. At first she's okay – the tendrils of blood lazing their way to the surface don't bother her too much – but when he reaches in and begins to gently rub, the water goes pink and Lisey turns away, asking him why in God's name he's making the cuts bleed all over again like that.

'I want to make sure they're clean,' he says. 'They should be clean when I go—' He pauses, then finishes: '— to bed. I can stay here, can't I? Please?'

'Yes,' she says, 'of course you can.' And thinks: *That isn't what you were going to say.*

When he's finished soaking his hand, he pours out the bloody water himself so she won't have to do it, then shows her his hand. Wet and gleaming, the cuts look less dangerous and yet somehow more awful, like crisscrossing fishgills, with pink deepening to red inside them.

'Can I use your box of tea, Lisey? I'll buy you another one, I promise. I've got a royalty check coming. Over five grand. My agent promises on his mother's honor. I told him it was news to me he had one. That's a joke, by the way.'

'I know it's a joke, I'm not *that* dumb—'

'You're not dumb at all.'

'Scott, why do you want a whole box of teabags?'

'Get it and find out.'

She gets the tea. Still sitting on her stool and working with one-handed care, Scott fills the basin with more not-quite-hot water. Then he opens the box of Lipton teabags. 'Paul thought this up,' he says excitedly. It's a kid's excitement, she thinks. *Look at the neat model airplane I made all by myself, look at the invisible ink I made with the stuff from my chemistry set.* He dumps the teabags in, all eighteen or so. They immediately begin staining the water a dull amber as they sink to the bottom of the basin. 'It stings a little but it works really really good. Watch!'

Really really good, Lisey notes.

He puts his hand in the weak tea he has made, and for just a moment his lips skin back, revealing his teeth, which are crooked and a bit discolored. 'Hurts a little,' he says, 'but it works. It really really works, Lisey.'

'Yes,' she says. It's bizarre, but she supposes it might actually do something about preventing infection, or promoting healing, or both. Chuckie Gendron, the short-order cook at the restaurant, is a big fan of the *Insider*, and she sometimes sneaks a look. Just a couple of weeks ago she read an article on one of the back pages about how tea is supposed to be good for all sorts of things. Of course it was on the same page as an article about Bigfoot bones being found in Minnesota. 'Yes, I suppose you're right.'

'Not me, Paul.' He's excited, and all his color has come back. *It's almost as if he never hurt himself at all*, she thinks.

Scott jerks his chin at his breast pocket. 'Cigarette me, babyluv.'

'Should you be smoking with your hand all—'

'Sure, sure.'

So she takes his cigarettes out of his breast pocket and puts one in his mouth and lights it for him. Fragrant smoke (she will always love that smell) rises in a blue stack toward the kitchen's sagging, water-stained ceiling. She wants to ask him more about bools, blood-bools in particular. She is starting to get a picture.

'Scott, did your Dad and Mom raise you and your brother?'

'Nope.' He's got the cigarette in the corner of his mouth and one eye's squinted shut against the smoke. 'Mumma died havin me. Daddy always said I killed her by bein a sleepyhead and gettin too big.' He laughs at this as though it's the funniest joke in the world, but it's also a nervous laugh, a kid's laugh at a dirty joke he doesn't quite understand.

She says nothing. She's afraid to.

He's looking down at the place where his hand disappears into the basin, which is now filled with bloodstained tea. He puffs rapidly on his Herbert Tareyton and the ash grows long. His eye is still squinted shut and it makes him look different, somehow. Not like a stranger, exactly, but *different*. Like . . .

Oh, say like an older brother. One who died.

'But Daddy said it wasn't my fault I stayed asleep when it was time to come out. He said she should have slap me awake and she didn't so I growed too big and she got kilt for it, bool the end.' He laughs. The ash falls off his cigarette onto the counter. He doesn't seem to notice. He looks at his hand in the murky tea but says no more.

Which leaves Lisey in a delicate dilemma. Should she ask another question or not? She's afraid he won't answer, that he'll snap at her (he *can* snap, this she knows; she has audited his Moderns seminar on occasion). She's also afraid he *will* answer. She thinks he will.

'Scott?' She says this very softly.

'Mmmm?' The cigarette is already three quarters of the way down to what looks like a filter but is, on a Herbert Tareyton, only a kind of mouthpiece.

'Did your Daddy make bools?'

'Blood-bools, sure. For when we didn't dare or to let out the bad-gunky. Paul made *good* bools. Fun bools. Like treasure hunts. Follow the clues. "Bool! The End!" and get a prize. Like candy or an RC.' The ash falls off his cigarette again. Scott's eyes are on the bloody tea in the basin. 'But Daddy gives a kiss.' He looks at her and she suddenly understands he knows everything she has been too timid to ask and is answering as well as he can. As well as he dares. 'That's Daddy's prize. A kiss when the hurting stops.'

19

She has no bandage in her medicine cabinet that will satisfy her, so Lisey ends up tearing long strips from a sheet. The sheet is old, but she mourns its passing just the same – on a waitress's salary (supplemented by niggardly tips from the Lost Boys and only slightly better ones from the faculty members who lunch at Pat's) she can ill afford to raid her linen closet. But when she thinks of the crisscrossing cuts on his hand – and the deeper, longer gill on his forearm – she doesn't hesitate.

Scott's asleep almost before his head hits the pillow on his side of her ridiculously narrow bed; Lisey thinks she will be awake for some time, mulling over the things he's told her. Instead she falls asleep almost at once.

She wakes twice during the night, the first time because she needs to pee. The bed is empty. She sleepwalks to the bathroom, hiking the oversized University of Maine tee-shirt she sleeps in to her hips as she goes; saying 'Scott, hurry up, okay, I really have to g—' But when she enters the bathroom, the night-light she always leaves burning shows her an empty room. Scott isn't there. Nor is the toilet-seat up, the way he always leaves it after he takes a whiz.

All at once Lisey no longer has to urinate. All at once she's terrified that pain has awakened him, he's remembered all the things he's told her, and has been crushed by – what do they call them in Chuckie's *Insider*? – recovered memories.

Are they recovered, or things he's just been keeping to himself? She doesn't know for sure, but she does know that childish way he spoke for awhile was very spooky . . . and suppose he's gone back down to Parks Greenhouse to finish the job? His throat this time instead of his hand?

She turns toward the dim maw of the kitchen – the apartment consists of only that and the bedroom – and catches sight of him curled up in bed. He's sleeping in his usual semi-fetal position, knees almost to his chest, forehead touching the wall (when they leave this place in the fall, there will be a faint but discernible mark there – Scott's mark). She has told him several times that he'd have more room if he slept on the outside, but he won't. Now he shifts a little, the springs squeak, and in the glow of the streetlight coming in the window, Lisey can see a dark wing of hair fall across his cheek.

He wasn't in bed.

But there he is, on the inside. If she doubts, she could put her hand under the sheaf of hair she's looking at, lift it, feel its weight.

So maybe I just dreamed he was gone?

That makes sense – sort of – but as she goes back into the bathroom and sits down on the toilet, she thinks again: *He wasn't there. When I got up, the smucking bed was empty.*

She puts the ring up after she's finished, because if *he* gets up in the night, he'll be too asleep to do it. Then she goes back to bed. She's in a doze by the time she gets there. He's beside her now, and that's what matters. Surely that's what matters.

20

The second time she doesn't wake up on her own.

'Lisey.'

It's Scott, shaking her.

'Lisey, little Lisey.'

She fights it, she put in a hard day – hell, a hard *week* – but he's persistent.

'Lisey, wake up!'

She expects morning light to lance her eyes, but it's still dark.

'Scott. Hizzit?'

She wants to ask if he's bleeding again, or if the

bandage she put on has slipped, but these ideas seem too big and complicated for her fogged-out mind. *Hizzit* will have to do.

His face is looming over hers, completely awake. He looks excited, but not dismayed or in pain. He says, 'We can't go on living like this.'

That wakes her up most of the way, because it scares her. What is he saying? That he wants to break up?

'*Scott?*' She fumbles on the floor, comes up with her Timex, squints at it. 'It's quarter past four in the morning!' Sounding put-out, sounding exasperated, and she *is* those things, but she is also frightened.

'Lisey, we should get a real house. Buy it.' He shakes his head. 'Nah, that's backwards. I think we ought to get married.'

Relief floods her and she slumps back. The watch falls from her relaxing fingers and clatters to the floor. That's all right; Timexes take a licking and keep on ticking. Relief is followed by amazement; she has just been proposed to, like a lady in a romance novel. And relief is followed by a little red caboose of terror. The guy doing the proposing (at quarter past four in the morning, mind you) is the same guy who stood her up last night, tore the shit out of his hand when she yelled at him about it (and a few other things, yeah, okay, true), then came up the lawn holding the wounded hand out to her like some kind of smucking Christmas present. This is the man with the dead brother she only found out about tonight, and the dead mother that he supposedly killed because he – how did the hotshot writer put it? – growed too big.

'Lisey?'

'Shut up, Scott, I'm thinking.' Oh but it's hard to think when the moon is down and the hour is none, no matter what your trusty Timex may say.

'I love you,' he says mildly.

'I know. I love you, too. That's not the point.'

'It might be,' he says. 'That you love me, I mean. That might be exactly the point. No one's loved me since Paul.' A long pause. 'And Daddy, I guess.'

She gets up on her elbow. 'Scott, *lots* of people love you. When you read from your last book – and the one you're writing now—' She wrinkles her nose. The new one is called *Empty Devils*, and what she's read of it and heard him read from it she doesn't like. 'When you read, nearly five hundred people showed up! They had to move you from the Maine Lounge into Hauck Auditorium! When you were done, they gave you a standing O!'

'That's not love,' he says, 'that's curiosity. And just between me and thee, it's freakshow stuff. When you publish your first novel at twenty-one, you find out all about freakshow stuff, even if the damn thing only sells to libraries and there's no paperback. But you don't care about the child-prodigy stuff, Lisey—'

'Yes I do—' Wholly awake now, or almost.

'Yes, but . . . cigarette me, babyluv.' His cigarettes are on the floor, in the turtle ashtray she keeps for him. She hands him the ashtray, puts a cigarette in his mouth, and lights it for him. He resumes. 'But you also care about whether or not I brush my teeth—'

'Well *yeah*—'

'And if the shampoo I'm using is getting rid of my dandruff or just causing more of it—'

That reminds her of something. 'I bought a bottle of that Tegrin stuff I told you about. It's in the shower. I want you to try it.'

He bursts out laughing. 'See? See? A perfect example. You take the holistic approach.'

'I don't know that word,' she says, frowning.

He stubs out the cigarette a quarter smoked. 'It means that when you look at me you see me top to bottom and side to side and to you everything weighs the same.'

She thinks about it, then nods. 'I suppose, sure.'

'You don't know what that's like. I put in a childhood when I was only . . . when I was one thing. The last six years, I've been another. It's a better thing, but still, to most people around here and back at Pitt, Scott Landon is nothing but a . . . a holy jukebox. Put in a couple of bucks and out comes a smucking story.' He doesn't sound angry, but she senses he could *become* angry. In time. If he doesn't have a place to go and be safe, be right-sized. And yes, she could be that person. She could make that place. He would help her do it. To some extent they have done it already.

'You're different, Lisey. I knew it the first time I met you, on Blues Night in the Maine Lounge – do you remember?'

Jesus, Mary and JoJo the Carpenter, does she remember. She had gone up to the University that night to look at the Hartgen art exhibition outside Hauck, heard the music coming from the lounge, and went in on what was little more than a whim. He came in a few minutes later, looked around at the mostly full house, and asked if the other end of the couch she was sitting on was taken.

She had almost skipped the music. She could have made the eight-thirty bus back to Cleaves if she'd skipped it. That was how close she had come to being in bed alone tonight. The thought makes her feel the way looking down from a high window makes her feel.

She says none of this, only nods.

'To me you're like . . .' Scott pauses, then smiles. His smile is divine, crooked teeth and all. 'You're like the pool where we all go down to drink. Have I told you about the pool?'

She nods again, smiling herself. He hasn't – not directly – but she's heard him talk about it at his readings, and during the lectures she's audited at his enthusiastic invitation, sitting way at the back of Boardman 101 or Little 112. When he talks about the pool he always reaches out, as if he'd put his hands in it if he could, or pull things – language-fishies, maybe – out of it. She finds it an endearing, boyish gesture. Sometimes he calls it the myth-pool; sometimes the word-pool. He says that every time you call someone a good egg or a bad apple you're drinking from the pool or catching tadpoles at its edge; that every time you send a child off to war and danger of death because you love the flag and have taught the child to love it, too, you are swimming in that pool . . . out deep, where the big ones with the hungry teeth also swim.

'I come to you and you see me whole,' he says. 'You love me all the way around the equator and not just for some story I wrote. When your door closes and the world's outside, we're eye to eye.'

'You're a lot taller than me, Scott.'

'You know what I'm saying.'

162

She supposes she does. And she's too moved by it to agree in the dead of night to something she might regret in the morning. 'We'll talk about it tomorrow,' she says. She takes his smoking gear and puts it on the floor again. 'Ask me then, if you still want to.'

'Oh, I'll want to,' he says with perfect confidence.

'We'll see. For now, go back to sleep.'

He turns on his side. He's lying almost straight now, but as he begins to drift he'll begin to bend. His knees will come up toward his narrow chest and his forehead, behind which all the exotic storyfish swim, will go to the wall.

I know him. Am beginning to know him, at least.

At this she feels another wave of love for him, and has to close her lips against dangerous words. The kind that are hard to take back once they have been spoken. Maybe impossible. She settles for pressing her breasts to his back and her stomach to his naked bottom. A few late crickets sing outside the window and Pluto goes on barking his way through another night shift. She begins to drift away again.

'Lisey?' His voice is almost coming from another world.

'Hmmmm?'

'I know you don't like *Devils*—'

'Haydit,' she manages, which is as close as she can come to a critical appraisal in her current state; she is drifting, drifting, drifting away.

'Yeah, and you won't be the only one. But my editor loves it. He says the folks at Sayler House have decided it's a horror novel. That's fine by me. What's the old saying?

"Call me anything you want, just don't call me late to dinner."'

Drifting. His voice coming down a long dark corridor.

'I don't need Carson Foray or my agent to tell me *Empty Devils* is gonna buy a lot of groceries. I'm done screwing around, Lisey. I'm on my way, but I don't want to go alone. I want you to come with me.'

'Shup, Ska. Go-slee.'

She doesn't know if he goes to sleep or not, but for a wonder (for a *blue*-eyed wonder), Scott Landon does indeed shut up.

21

Lisey Debusher awakens on Saturday morning at the impossibly luxurious hour of nine o'clock, and to the smell of frying bacon. Sunshine lies across the floor and the bed in a brilliant stripe. She goes out to the kitchen. He's frying bacon in his underpants, and she's horrified to see that he's removed the bandage she so carefully applied. When she remonstrates, Scott tells her simply that it itched.

'Besides,' he says, holding his hand out to her (this reminds her so much of how he came walking out of the shadows last night that she has to repress a shiver), 'it doesn't look so bad in the light of day, does it?'

She takes his hand, bends over it as if she means to read his palm, and looks until he pulls away, saying if he doesn't turn the bacon it will burn. She isn't astounded, isn't amazed; those are emotions perhaps reserved for dark nights and shadowy rooms, not for sunshiny weekend mornings with the Philco in the window playing that low-rider

164

song she's never understood but always liked. Not astounded, not amazed . . . but she *is* perplexed. All she can think is that she must have believed the cuts were a hell of a lot worse than they actually turned out to be. That she panicked. Because these wounds, while not exactly scratches, are far from as serious as she thought. They've not only clotted over; they've started *scabbing* over. If she'd taken him to the Derry Home ER, they probably would have told her to get lost.

All the Landons are fast healers. We had to be.

Meanwhile, Scott's forking crisp bacon out of the pan and onto a double fold of paper towels. As far as Lisey's concerned, he may be a good writer, but he's a *great* fry cook. At least when he really sets his mind to it. He needs new underwear, though; the seat of this pair sags rather comically, and the elastic waistband is on life-support. She'll see what she can do about getting him to buy new ones when the royalty check he's been promised comes in, and of course underwear isn't what's on her mind, not actually; her mind wants to compare what she saw last night – those deep and sickening gills, pink shading to liverish red – with what's on offer this morning. It's the difference between mere cuts and gashes, and does she really think *anyone* heals that fast, outside of a Bible story? Does she really? It wasn't a *window*-pane he stuck his hand through, after all, it was a pane of *greenhouse* glass, which reminds her, they'll have to do something about that, Scott will have to—

'Lisey.'

She's jerked out of her reverie to find herself sitting at the kitchen table, nervously knitting her tee-shirt together between her thighs. 'What?'

'One egg or two?'

She considers it. 'Two. I guess.'

'Over easy or want em lookin atcha?'

'Over,' she says.

'Will we marry?' he asks in exactly the same tone, cracking both eggs in his good right hand and dropping them into the pan, kerplunk.

She smiles a little, not at his matter-of-fact tone but at the faintly archaic turn of phrase, and realizes she's not surprised at all. She has expected this . . . this what-do-you-call-it, this resumption; must have been turning his proposal over in some deep part of her mind even as she slept.

'Are you sure?' she asks.

'Sure shot,' he says. 'What do you think, babyluv?'

'Babyluv thinks that sounds like a plan.'

'Good,' he says. 'That's good.' He pauses. Then: 'Thank you.'

For a minute or two neither of them says anything. On the windowsill, the old cracked Philco plays the sort of music Dad Debusher never listened to. In the pan, the eggs snap. She's hungry. And she's happy.

'In the fall,' she says.

He nods, reaching for a plate. 'Good. October?'

'Maybe too soon. Say right around Thanksgiving. Are there any eggs left for you?'

'There be one, and one be all I want.'

She says, 'I won't marry you if you don't buy some new underwear.'

He doesn't laugh. 'Then I'll make it a priority.'

He puts the plate in front of her. Bacon and eggs.

She is so hungry. She starts in and he cracks the last egg into the pan.

'Lisa Landon,' he says. 'What do you think?'

'I think it's a keeper. It's . . . what do you call it when all the words start with the same sound?'

'Alliteration.'

'Yeah, that.' Now she says it. 'Lisa Landon.' Like the eggs, it tastes good.

'Little Lisey Landon,' he says, and flips his egg in the air. It turns over twice and lands square in the bacon-grease, *splat*.

'Do you, Scott Landon, promise to strap it on and keep the mothersmucker strapped?' she asks.

'Strapped in sickness, strapped in health,' he agrees, and they begin laughing like mad bastards while the radio plays in the sunshine.

22

With Scott, she always laughed a lot. And a week later the cuts on his hand, even the one on his forearm, were pretty much healed.

They didn't even scar.

23

When Lisey wakes again, she no longer knew *when* she was – then or now. But enough of morning's first light had crept into the room so she can see the cool blue wall-paper and the seascape on the wall. So it was Amanda's bedroom, and that seemed right, but it also seems wrong;

167

it seems to her that this is a dream of the future she's having in her narrow apartment bed, the one she still shares with Scott on most nights, and will until the wedding in November.

What wakened her?

Amanda was turned away from her and Lisey was still fitted against her like a spoon, her breasts against Manda's back, her belly against Manda's scant bottom, and just what has wakened her? She doesn't need to pee . . . not badly, anyway, so *what . . . ?*

Amanda, did you say something? Do you want something? Drink of water, maybe? Piece of greenhouse glass to slit your wrists with?

These things passed through her mind, but Lisey didn't really want to say anything, because an odd idea has come to her. The idea is that, although she can see the rapidly graying mop of Amanda's hair and the frill around the neck of Amanda's nightgown, she was actually in bed with Scott. Yes! That at some point in the night Scott has . . . what? Crept through the lens of Lisey's memories and into Amanda's body? Something like that. It's a funny idea, all right, and yet she doesn't want to say anything, because she's afraid that if she did, Amanda might answer in Scott's voice. And what would she do then? Would she scream? Would she scream *to wake the dead*, as the saying is? Surely the idea is absurd, but—

But look at her. Look how she's sleeping, with her knees pulled up and her head bent. If there was a wall, her forehead would be touching it. No wonder you think—

And then, in that pre-dawn ditch of five o'clock, with her face turned away so Lisey cannot see it, Amanda spoke.

'*Baby,*' she says.

There is a pause.

Then: '*Babyluv.*'

If Lisey's interior temperature seemed to drop thirty degrees the evening before, now it seems to drop sixty, for although the voice which spoke the word was undeniably female, it is also Scott's. Lisey lived with him for over twenty years. She knows Scott when she hears him.

This is a dream, she told herself. *That's why I can't even tell if it's then or now. If I look around I'll see the* PILLSBURY'S BEST *magic carpet floating in the corner of the room.*

But she couldn't look around. For a long time she couldn't move at all. What finally impels her to speak is the strengthening light. Night is almost over. If Scott has come back – if she was really awake and not just dreaming this – then there must be a reason. And it wouldn't be to harm her. Never to harm her. At least . . . not on purpose. But she finds she can speak neither his name nor Amanda's. Neither seems right. Both seemed wrong. She saw herself grabbing Amanda's shoulder and rolling her over. Whose face would she see under Manda's graying bangs? Suppose it was Scott's? Oh sweet God, *suppose.*

Daylight is coming. And she was suddenly sure that if she let the sun come up without speaking, the door between the past and the present will close and any chance of getting answers will be gone.

Never mind the names, then. Never mind just who the hell is inside the nightgown.

'Why did Amanda say bool?' she asked. Her voice in the bedroom – still dim but brightening, brightening – sounds hoarse, dusty.

'I left you a bool,' remarks the other person in the bed, the person against whose bottom Lisey's belly lies.

Oh God oh God oh God this is the bad-gunky if there ever was bad-gunky, this is it—

And then: *Get hold of yourself. You strap it the fuck on. Do it right now.*

'Is it . . .' Her voice was drier and dustier than ever. And now the room seems to be brightening too fast. The sun will clear the eastern horizon any second now. 'Is it a blood-bool?'

'You have a blood-bool coming,' the voice tells her, sounding faintly regretful. And oh it sounds so much like Scott. Yet now it sounded more like Amanda, too, and this scared Lisey more than ever.

Then the voice brightened. 'The one you're on is a *good* bool, Lisey. It goes behind the purple. You've already found the first three stations. A few more and you'll get your prize.'

'What's my prize?' she asks.

'A drink.' The reply was prompt.

'A Coke? An RC?'

'Be quiet. We want to watch the hollyhocks.'

The voice spoke with strange and infinite longing, and what is familiar about that? Why does it seem like a name for something instead of just bushes? Is it another thing that's hidden behind the purple curtain which sometimes keeps her own memories away from her? There was no time to think about it, let alone ask about it, because a slant of red light fingered in through the window. Lisey felt time come back into focus, and, frightened as she had been, she felt an intense pang of regret.

'When is the blood-bool coming?' she asked. 'Tell me that.'

There was no answer. She knew there would be no answer, and still her frustration grew, filling the place where her terror and her perplexity had been before the sun peeped over the horizon, casting its dispelling rays.

'*When is it coming? Damn you, when?*' She was shouting now, and shaking the white-nightgowned shoulder hard enough to make the hair flop . . . and still no answer. Lisey's fury broke. '*Don't tease me like that, Scott, when?*'

This time she *yanked* on the nightgowned shoulder instead of just shaking, and the other body on the bed rolled limply over. It was Amanda, of course. Her eyes were open and she still breathed, there was even some dull color in her cheeks, but Lisey recognized that thousand-yard stare from big sissa Manda-Bunny's other breaks with reality. And not only hers. Lisey no longer had any idea if Scott had actually come to her or if she had only been fooling herself while in a semi-waking state, but of one thing she was quite sure: at some point during the night, Amanda had gone away again. This time maybe for good.

PART 2

SOWISA

'She turned, and saw a great white moon looking at her over the hill. And her breast opened to it, she was cleaved like a transparent jewel to its light. She stood filled with the full moon, offering herself. Her two breasts opened to make way for it, her body opened wide like a quivering anemone, a soft, dilated invitation touched by the moon.'

—D. H. Lawrence, *The Rainbow*

CHAPTER FIVE

LISEY AND THE LONG, LONG THURSDAY (STATIONS OF THE BOOL)

1

It didn't take Lisey long to realize this was far worse than Amanda's three previous breaks with reality – her periods of 'passive semi-catatonia', to use the shrink's phrase. It was as if her usually irritating and sometimes troublesome sister had become a large breathing doll. Lisey managed (with considerable effort) to tug Amanda into a sitting position and swivel her around so she was sitting on the edge of the bed, but the woman in the white cotton nightgown – who might or might not have spoken in the voice of Lisey's dead husband a few moments before dawn – would not respond to her name when it was spoken, or called, or shouted, almost desperately, into her face. She only sat with her hands in her lap, looking fixedly at her younger sister. And when Lisey stepped away, Amanda looked fixedly into the space where she had been.

Lisey went into the bathroom to wet a cloth with cold water, and when she came back, Amanda had subsided

175

into a prone position again with her upper half on the bed and her feet on the floor. Lisey began to pull her back up, then stopped when Amanda's buttocks, already close to the bed's edge, began to slide. If she persisted, Amanda would end up on the floor.

'Manda-Bunny!'

No response to the childhood nickname this time. Lisey decided to go whole hog.

'Big *sissa* Manda-Bunny!'

Nothing. Instead of being frightened (that would come shortly), Lisey was swept by the sort of rage Amanda had hardly ever been able to provoke in her younger sister when she had actually tried.

'Stop this! Stop it and scoot your ass back on the bed so you can sit up!'

Zip. Zero. She bent, wiped Amanda's expressionless face with the cold washcloth, and got more nothing. The eyes didn't blink even when the washcloth passed over them. Now Lisey *did* begin to be scared. She looked at the digital clock-radio beside the bed and saw it had just gone six. She could call Darla with no worries of waking Matt, who would be sleeping the sleep of the just up in Montreal, but she didn't want to do that. Not yet. Calling Darla would be the same as admitting defeat, and she wasn't ready to do that.

She circled the bed, grabbed Amanda under the armpits, and hauled her backward. It was harder to do than she expected, given Amanda's scrawny bod.

Because she's dead weight now, babyluv. That's why.

'Shut up,' she said, with no idea who she was talking to. 'Just shut it.'

She got on the bed herself with her knees on either side of Amanda's thighs and her hands planted on either side of Amanda's neck. In this position, that of the lover superior, she could look directly down into her sister's upturned, staring face. During Manda's previous breaks, she had been biddable ... almost the way a person under hypnosis is biddable, Lisey had thought at the time. This seemed very different. She could only hope it wasn't, because there were certain things a person had to do in the morning. If, that was, the person wanted to go on living a private life in her little Cape Cod home.

'Amanda!' she yelled down into her sister's face. Then, for good measure, and feeling only slightly ridiculous (it was only the two of them, after all): *'Big ... sissa ... Manda-Bunny! I want you ... to stand up ... stand UP! ... and go into the shithouse ... and use the TOIDY! Use the TOIDY, Manda-Bunny! On three! ONE ... and TWO! ... and THREE!'* On *THREE* Lisey again yanked Amanda to a sitting position, but Amanda still wouldn't stand.

Once, at around twenty past six, Lisey actually got her off the bed and into a kind of half-assed crouch. She felt the way she had when she'd had her first car, a 1974 Pinto, and after two endless minutes of grinding the starter the motor would finally catch and run just before the battery died. But instead of straightening up and letting Lisey lead her into the bathroom, Amanda fell back onto the bed – fell crooked, too, so that Lisey had to lunge, catch her under the arms, and shove her, cursing, to keep her from going on the floor.

'You're faking, you bitch!' she shouted at Amanda, knowing perfectly well that Amanda wasn't. *'Well, go on!*

177

Go on and—' She heard how loud she'd gotten – she'd wake up Mrs Jones across the road if she didn't look out – and made herself lower her voice. 'Go on and lie there. Yeah. But if you think I'm going to spend the whole morning dancing attendance around you, you're full of shite. I'm going downstairs to make coffee and oatmeal. If any of it smells good to Your Royal Majesty, give me a holler. Or, I don't know, send down your smucking footman for take-out.'

She didn't know if it smelled good to big sissa Manda-Bunny, but it smelled fine to Lisey, especially the coffee. She had one cup of straight black before her bowl of oatmeal, another with double cream and sugar afterward. Sipping that one, she thought: *All I need now is a ciggy and I could ride this day like a pony. A smucking Salem Light.*

Her mind tried to turn toward her dreams and memories of the night just past **(SCOTT AND LISEY THE EARLY YEARS!** *for sure*, she thought), and she wouldn't let it. Nor would she let it try to examine what had happened to her on waking. There might be time later to think about it, but not now. Now she had big sissa to deal with.

And suppose big sissa's found a nice pink disposable razor on top of the medicine cabinet and decided to slit her wrists with it? Or her throat?

Lisey got up from the table in a hurry, wondering if Darla had thought to clean the sharps out of the upstairs bathroom . . . or any of the upstairs rooms, for that matter. She took the stairs at a near-run, dreading what she might discover in the master bedroom, nerving herself to find nothing in the bed but a pair of dented pillows.

Amanda was still there, still staring up at the ceiling. She appeared not to have moved so much as an inch. Lisey's relief was replaced by foreboding. She sat on the bed and took her sister's hand in her own. It was warm but unresponsive. Lisey willed Manda's fingers to close on her own but they remained limp. Waxy.

'Amanda, what are we going to do with you?'

There was no response.

And then, because they were alone except for their reflections in the mirror, Lisey said: 'Scott didn't do this, did he, Manda? Please say Scott didn't do it by . . . I don't know . . . by coming in?'

Amanda said nothing one way or the other, and after a little while Lisey went prospecting in the bathroom for sharp objects. She guessed that Darla had indeed been here before her, because all she found was a single pair of nail-scissors at the back of the lower drawer in Manda's small, not-very-vain vanity. Of course, even those would have been enough, in a dedicated hand. Why, Scott's own father

(hush Lisey no Lisey)

'All right,' she said, alarmed by the panic that flooded her mouth with the taste of copper, the purple light that seemed to bloom behind her eyes, and the way her hand clenched on the tiny pair of scissors. 'Okay, never mind. Pass it.'

She hid the scissors behind a clutch of dusty shampoo samples high up in Amanda's towel cupboard, and then – because she could think of nothing else – took a shower herself. When she came out of the bathroom, she saw that a large wet patch had spread around Amanda's hips, and understood this was something the Debusher sisters weren't going to be able to work through on their own. She got a towel under Amanda's soaked bottom. Then she glanced at the clock on the night-table, sighed, picked up the telephone, and dialed Darla's number.

2

Lisey had heard Scott in her head the day before, loud and clear: *I left you a note, babyluv*. She'd dismissed it as her own interior voice, mimicking his. Maybe it had been – *probably* had been – but by three o'clock on that long, hot Thursday afternoon, as she sat in Pop's Café in Lewiston with Darla, she knew one thing for sure: he'd left her one hell of a posthumous gift. One hell of a bool-prize, in Scott-talk. It had been a bitch-kitty of a day, but it would have been a lot worse without Scott Landon, two years dead or not.

Darla looked every bit as tired as Lisey felt. Somewhere along the way she'd found time to put on a little makeup, but she didn't have enough ammo in her purse to hide the circles under her eyes. Certainly there was no sign of the angry thirtysomething who had in the late nineteen-seventies made it her business to call Lisey once a week and hector her about her family duties.

'Penny for em, little Lisey,' she said now.

Lisey had been reaching for the caddy containing the packets of Sweet'n Low. At the sound of Darla's voice she changed direction, reached for the old-fashioned sugar-shaker instead, and poured a hefty stream into her cup. 'I was thinking this has been Coffee Thursday,' she said. 'Mostly Coffee With Real Sugar Thursday. This must be my tenth shot.'

'You and me both,' Darla said. 'I've been to the john half a dozen times, and I plan to go again before we leave this charming establishment. Thank God for Pepcid AC.'

Lisey stirred her coffee, grimaced, then sipped again. 'Sure you want to pack up a suitcase for her?'

'Well, someone has to do it, and you look like death on a cracker.'

'Thanks a pantload.'

'If your sister won't tell you the truth, no one will.'

Lisey had heard this from her many times, along with *Duty doesn't ask permission* and, Number One on the All-Time Darla Hit Parade, *Life isn't fair.* Today it didn't sting. It even raised the ghost of a smile. 'If you want to do it, Darl, I won't arm-rassle you for the privilege.'

'Didn't say I wanted to, just said I would. You stayed with her last night and got up with her this morning. I'd say you did your share. Excuse me, I've got to spend a penny.'

Lisey watched her go, thinking *There's another one.* In the Debusher family, where there was a saying for everything, urinating was *spending a penny* and moving one's bowels was – odd but true – *burying a Quaker.* Scott had loved that, said it was probably an old Scots derivation. Lisey supposed it was possible; most of the Debushers came from Ireland and all the Andersons from England, or so Good Ma said, but there were a few stray dogs in every family, weren't there? And that hardly interested her. What interested her was that *spending a penny* and *burying a Quaker* were catches from the pool, Scott's pool, and ever since yesterday he seemed so smucking close to her . . .

That was a dream this morning, Lisey . . . you know that, don't you?

She wasn't sure what she knew or didn't know about what had happened in Amanda's bedroom this morning – it all seemed like a dream, even trying to get Amanda to stand up and go into the bathroom – but one thing she could be sure of: Amanda was now booked into Greenlawn Recovery and Rehabilitation for at least a week, it had all been easier than she and Darla could have hoped, and they had Scott to thank. Right now and

(rah-cheer)

right here, that seemed like enough.

3

Darla had gotten to Manda's cozy little Cape Cod before seven A.M., her usually stylish hair barely combed, one button of her blouse unbuttoned so that the pink of her bra peeked cheekily through. By then Lisey had confirmed that Amanda wouldn't eat, either. She allowed Lisey to insert a spoonful of scrambled eggs into her mouth after being tugged into a sitting position and propped against the head of the bed, and that gave Lisey some hope – Amanda was swallowing, after all, so maybe she'd swallow the eggs – but it was hope in vain. After simply sitting there for perhaps thirty seconds with the eggs peeping out from between her lips (to Lisey that peep of yellow had a rather gruesome look, as if her sister had tried to eat a canary), Amanda simply ejected the eggs with her tongue. A few bits stuck to her chin. The rest tumbled down the front of her nightgown. Amanda's eyes continued to stare serenely off into the distance. Or into the mystic, if you were a Van Morrison fan. Scott certainly had been, although his pash for Van the Man had tapered off quite a bit in the early nineties. That was when Scott had begun drifting back to Hank Williams and Loretta Lynn.

Darla had refused to believe Amanda wouldn't eat until she tried the egg experiment for herself. She had to scramble fresh ones to do it; Lisey had scraped the remains of the first pair down the garbage disposal. Amanda's thousand-yard stare had robbed her of any appetite she might have had for big sissa's leftovers.

By the time Darla marched into the room, Amanda had slid back down from her propped-up position – *oozed* back down – and Darla helped Lisey get her back up again. Lisey was grateful for the help. Her back already hurt. She could barely imagine the mounting cost of caring for a person like this day in and day out, for an unlimited run.

'Amanda, I want you to eat these,' Darla said in the forbidding, I-will-not-take-no-for-an-answer tone Lisey remembered from a great many telephone conversations in her younger years. The tone, combined with the jut of Darla's jaw and the set of Darla's body, made it clear she thought Amanda was shamming. *Fakin like a brakeman*, Dandy would have said; just one of his hundred or so cheerful, colorful, nonsensical phrases. But (Lisey mused) hadn't that almost always been Darla's judgment when you weren't doing what Darla wanted? That you were *fakin like a brakeman*?

'I want you to eat these eggs, Amanda – *right now!*'

Lisey opened her mouth to say something, then changed her mind. They would get to where they were going more quickly if Darla saw for herself. And where were they going? Greenlawn, very likely. Greenlawn Recovery and Rehab in Auburn. The place she and Scott had looked into briefly after Amanda's last outletting, in the spring of 2001. Only it turned out that Scott's dealings with Greenlawn had gone a little further than his wife had suspected, and thank God for that.

Darla got the eggs into Amanda's mouth and turned to Lisey with the beginnings of a triumphant smile. 'There! I think she just needed a firm h—'

At this point Amanda's tongue appeared between her slack lips, once more pushing canary-colored eggs before it, and *plop*. Onto the front of her nightgown, still damp from its last sponging-off.

'You were saying?' Lisey asked mildly.

Darla took a long, long look at her older sister. When she turned her eyes back to Lisey, the jut-jawed determination was gone. She looked like what she was: a middle-aged woman who'd been harried out of bed too early by a family emergency. She wasn't crying, but she was close; her eyes, the bright blue all the Debusher girls shared, swam with tears. 'This isn't like before, is it?'

'No.'

'Did anything happen last night?'

'No.' Lisey didn't hesitate.

'No crying fits or tantrums?'

'No.'

'Oh, hon, what are we going to do?'

Lisey had a practical answer for that, and no surprise there; Darla might think differently, but Lisey and Jodi had always been the practical ones. 'Lay her back down, wait for business hours, then call that place,' she said. 'Greenlawn. And hope she doesn't piss the bed again in the meantime.'

4

While they waited, they drank coffee and played cribbage, a game each of the Debusher girls had learned from Dandy long before they'd taken their first rides on the big yellow Lisbon Falls schoolbus. Every third or fourth hand, one of them would check on Amanda. She was always the same, lying on her back and staring up at the ceiling. In the first game, Darla skunked her younger sister; in the second she skipped out with a run of three in the crib, leaving Lisey stuck in the mudhole. That this should put her in a good humor even with Manda gorked out upstairs gave Lisey something to think about . . . but nothing she wanted to say right out loud. It was going to be a long day, and if Darla started it with a smile on her face, terrific. Lisey declined a third game and the two of them watched some country singer on the last segment of the *Today* show. Lisey could almost hear Scott saying, *He ain't gonna put Ole Hank out of business.* By whom he meant, of course, Hank Williams. When it came to country music, for Scott there had been Ole Hank . . . and then all the rest of them.

At five past nine, Lisey sat down in front of the telephone and got the Greenlawn number from Directory Assistance. She gave Darla a wan and nervous smile. 'Wish me luck, Darl.'

'Oh, I do. Believe me, I do.'

Lisey dialed. The phone on the other end rang exactly once. 'Hello,' a pleasant female voice said. 'This is Greenlawn

Recovery and Rehabilitation, a service of Fedders Health Corporation of America.'

'Hello, my name is—' Lisey got this far before the pleasant female voice began enumerating all the possible destinations one could reach . . . if, that was, one were possessed of a touch-tone phone. It was a recording. Lisey had been booled.

Yeah, but they've gotten so good, she thought, punching 5 for Patient Intake Information.

'Please hold while your call is processed,' the pleasant female voice told her, and was replaced by the Prozac Orchestra playing something that vaguely resembled Paul Simon's 'Homeward Bound'.

Lisey looked around to tell Darla she was on hold, but Darla had gone up to check on Amanda.

Bullshit, she thought. *She just couldn't take the susp*—

'Hello, this is Cassandra, how may I help you?'

A name of ill omen, babyluv, opined the Scott who kept house in her head.

'My name is Lisa Landon . . . Mrs Scott Landon?'

She had probably referred to herself as Mrs Scott Landon less than half a dozen times in all the years of her married life, and never once during the twenty-six months of her widowhood. It wasn't hard to understand why she had done so now. It was what Scott called 'the fame-card', and he himself had played it sparingly. Partly, he said, because doing so made him feel like a conceited asshole, and partly because he was afraid it wouldn't work; that if he murmured some version of *Don't you know who I am?* in the headwaiter's ear, the headwaiter would murmur back, *Non, Monsieur – who ze fuck air you?*

186

As Lisey spoke, recounting her sister's previous episodes of self-mutilation and semi-catatonia and this morning's great leap forward, she heard the soft clitter of computer keys. When Lisey paused, Cassandra said: 'I understand your concern, Mrs Landon, but Greenlawn is very full at the present time.'

Lisey's heart sank. She instantly pictured Amanda in a closet-sized room at Stephens Memorial in No Soapa, wearing a foodstained johnnie and looking out a barred window at the blinker-light where Route 117 crossed 19. 'Oh. I see. Um . . . are you sure? This wouldn't be Medicaid or Blue Cross or any of those things — I'd be paying cash, you see . . .' Grasping at straws. Sounding dumb. When all else fails, chuck money. 'If that makes a difference,' she finished lamely.

'It really doesn't, Mrs Landon.' She thought she detected a faint frost in Cassandra's voice now, and Lisey's heart sank even farther. 'It's a question of space and commitments. You see, we only have—'

Lisey heard a faint *bing!* then. It was very close to the sound her toaster-oven made when the Pop-Tarts or breakfast burritos were done.

'Mrs Landon, can I put you on hold?'

'If you need to, of course.'

There was a faint click and the Prozac Orchestra returned, this time with what might once have been the theme from *Shaft*. Lisey listened with a mild sense of unreality, thinking that if Isaac Hayes heard it, he would probably crawl into his bathtub with a plastic bag over his head. The time on hold lengthened until she began to suspect she'd been forgotten — God knew it had happened to her before, especially when trying to buy airline tickets or change rental car arrangements. Darla came downstairs and held her hands out in a *What's happening? Give!* gesture. Lisey shook her head, indicating both *Nothing* and *I don't know.*

At that moment the horrific holdmusic was gone and Cassandra was back. The frost was gone from her voice, and for the first time she sounded to Lisey like a human being. In fact, she sounded *familiar*, somehow. 'Mrs Landon?'

'Yes?'

'I'm sorry to have kept you waiting so long, but I had a note on my computer to get in touch with Dr Alberness if either you or your husband called. Dr Alberness is actually in his office now. May I transfer you?'

'Yes,' Lisey told her. *Now* she knew where she was, exactly where she was. She knew that before he told her anything else, Dr Alberness would tell her how sorry he was for her loss, as if Scott had died last month or last week. And she would thank him. In fact, if Dr Alberness promised to take the troublesome Amanda off their hands in spite of Greenlawn's current booked-up state, Lisey would probably be happy to get on her knees and give him a nice juicy hummer. A wild laugh threatened to surge out of her at that, and she had to clamp her lips tightly shut for a few seconds. And she knew why Cassandra had suddenly sounded so familiar: it was how people had sounded when they suddenly recognized Scott, realized they were dealing with someone who'd been on the cover of smucking *Newsweek* magazine. And if that famous person had his famous arm around someone, why *she* must be famous, too, if only by association. Or, as Scott himself had once said, by injection.

'Hello?' a pleasantly rough male voice said. 'This is Hugh Alberness. Am I speaking to Mrs Landon?'

'Yes, Doctor,' Lisey said, motioning for Darla to sit down and stop pacing circles in front of her. 'This is Lisa Landon.'

'Mrs Landon, let me begin by saying how sorry I am for your loss. Your husband signed five of his books for me, and they are among my most treasured possessions.'

'Thank you, Dr Alberness,' she said, and to Darla she made an *It's-in-the-bag* circle with her thumb and fore-finger. 'That's so very kind of you.'

5

When Darla got back from using the Pop's Café ladies' room, Lisey said she thought she had better make a visit, as well – it was twenty miles to Castle View, and often the afternoon traffic was slow. For Darla, that would just be the first leg. After packing a bag for Amanda – a chore they'd both forgotten that morning – she'd have to drive back to Greenlawn with it. Once it was delivered, a second return trip to Castle Rock. She'd be turning into her own driveway for good around eight-thirty, and only that early if luck – and traffic – were with her.

'I'd take a deep breath and hold your nose while you go,' Darla said.

'Bad?'

Darla shrugged, then yawned. 'I've been in worse.'

So had Lisey, especially during her travels with Scott. She went with her thighs tensed and her bottom hovering over the seat – the well-remembered Book Tour Crouch

– flushed, washed her hands, splashed water on her face, combed her hair, then looked at herself in the mirror. 'New woman,' she told her reflection. 'American Beauty.' She bared a great deal of expensive dental work at herself. The eyes above this gator grin, however, looked doubtful.

'Mr Landon said if I ever met you, I should ask—'

Be quiet about that, leave it be.

'I should ask you about how he fooled the nurse—'

'Only Scott never said *fooled*,' she told her reflection. *Shut up, little Lisey!*

'—how he fooled the nurse that time in Nashville.'

'Scott said *booled*. Didn't he?'

That coppery taste was in her mouth again, the taste of pennies and panic. Yes, Scott had said *booled*. Sure. Scott had said that Dr Alberness should ask Lisey (if he ever met her) how Scott booled the nurse that time in Nashville, Scott knowing perfectly well that she would get the message.

Had he been sending her messages? *Had* he, even then?

'Leave it *alone*,' she whispered at her reflection, and left the ladies' room. It would have been nice to leave that voice trapped inside, but now it always seemed to be there. For a long time it had been quiet, either sleeping or agreeing with Lisey's conscious mind that there were some things one simply did not speak about, not even among the various versions of one's self. What the nurse had said on the day after Scott had been shot, for instance. Or

(hush do hush)

what had happened in

(Hush!)

the winter of 1996.

(YOU HUSH NOW!)

And for a blue-eyed wonder that voice did ... but she sensed it watching and listening, and she was afraid.

6

Lisey exited the ladies' room just in time to see Darla hanging up the pay telephone.

'I was calling that motel across from Greenlawn,' she said. 'It looked clean, so I booked a room for tonight. I really don't want to drive all the way back to Castle View, and this way I can see Manda first thing tomorrow morning. All I'll have to do is be like the chicken and cross the road.' She looked at her younger sister with an apprehensive expression Lisey found rather surreal, given all the years she'd spent listening to Darla lay down the law, usually in a strident, take-no-prisoners tone of voice. 'Do you think that's silly?'

'I think it's a great idea.' Lisey gave Darla's hand a squeeze, and Darla's relieved smile broke her heart a little. She thought: *This is also what money does. It makes you the smart one. It makes you the boss.* 'Come on, Darl – I'll drive back, how's that?'

'Works for me,' Darla said, and followed her younger sister out into the latening day.

7

The drive back to Castle View was as slow as Lisey had feared it might be; they got behind an overloaded, waddling pulp truck, and on the hills and curves there was no place to pass. The best Lisey could do was hang back so they didn't have to eat too much of the guy's half-cooked exhaust. It gave her time to reflect on the day. At least there was that.

Speaking with Dr Alberness had been like getting to a baseball game in the bottom of the fourth inning, but that was nothing new; playing catch-up had always been part of life with Scott. She remembered the day a furniture van from Portland had shown up with a two-thousand-dollar sectional sofa. Scott had been in his study, writing with the music cranked to its usual deafening levels – she could faintly hear Steve Earle singing 'Guitar Town' in the house even with the soundproofing – and interrupting him was apt to do another two thousand dollars' worth of damage to her ears, in Lisey's opinion. The furniture guys said 'the mister' told them she'd let them know where to put the new piece of furniture. Lisey had briskly directed them to carry the current sofa – the perfectly *good* current sofa – out to the barn, and place the new sectional where it had been. The color was at least a fair match for the room, and that was a relief. She knew she and Scott had never discussed a new sofa, sectional or otherwise, just as she knew Scott would declare – oh yes, most vehemently – that they *had*. She was sure he'd discussed it with her in his head; he just sometimes forgot to vocalize those discussions. Forgetting was a skill he had honed.

His luncheon with Hugh Alberness might have been only another case in point. He might have meant to tell Lisey all about it, and if you'd asked him six months or a year later, he might well have told you he *had* told her all about it: *Lunch with Alberness? Sure, filled her in that very night.* When what he'd really done that very night was go out to his study, put on the new Dylan CD, and work on a new short story.

Or maybe this time it had been different – not Scott just forgetting (as he'd once forgotten they'd had a date, as he'd forgotten to tell her about his *extremely* smucked-up childhood), but Scott hiding clues for her to find after a death he had already foreseen; laying out what he himself would have called 'stations of the bool'.

In either case, Lisey had caught up with him before, and she got most of the blanks filled in on the phone, saying *Uh-huh* and *Oh, really!* And *You know, I forgot about that!* in all the right places.

When Amanda had tried to excise her navel in the spring of 2001 and then lapsed into a week-long state of sludge her shrink called semi-catatonia, the family had discussed the possibility of sending her to Greenlawn (or *some* mental care facility) at a long, emotional, and some-times rancorous family dinner that Lisey remembered well. She also remembered that Scott had been unusually quiet through most of the discussion, and had only picked at his food that day. When the discussion began to wind down, he said that if nobody objected, he'd pick up some pamphlets and brochures they could all look at.

'You make it sound like a vacation cruise,' Cantata had said – rather snidely, Lisey thought.

Scott had shrugged, Lisey remembered as she followed the pulp truck past the bullet-pocked sign reading CASTLE COUNTY WELCOMES YOU. 'She's away, all right,' he had said. 'It might be important for someone to show her the way home while she still wants to come.'

Canty's husband had snorted at that. The fact that Scott had made millions from his books had never kept Richard from regarding him as your basic dewy-eyed dreamer, and when Rich nominated an opinion, Canty Lawlor could be depended upon to second it. It had never occurred to Lisey to tell them that Scott knew what he was talking about, but now that she thought back, she hadn't eaten much herself that day.

In any case, Scott had brought home a number of Greenlawn brochures and folders; Lisey remembered finding them spread out on the kitchen counter. One, bearing a photograph of a large building that looked quite a bit like Tara in *Gone With the Wind*, had been titled *Mental Illness, Your Family, and You*. But she didn't remember any further discussion of Greenlawn, and really, why would she? Once Amanda began to get better, she had improved quickly. And Scott had certainly never mentioned his lunch with Dr Alberness, which had come in October of '01 – months after Amanda had resumed what in her passed for normality.

According to Dr Alberness (this Lisey got over the phone, in response to her appreciative little *Uh-huh*s and *Oh, really*s and *I'd forgotten*s), Scott had told him at this lunch of theirs that he was convinced Amanda Debusher was headed for a more serious break with reality, perhaps a permanent one, and after reading the brochures and touring the facility with the good doctor, he believed Greenlawn would be exactly the right place for her, if it happened. That Scott had extracted Dr Alberness's promise of a place for his sister-in-law when and if the time came – all in exchange for a single lunch and five signed books – didn't surprise Lisey at all. Not after the years she'd spent observing the liquorish way fame worked on some people.

She reached for the car radio, wanting some nice loud country music (there was another bad habit Scott had taught her in the last few years of his life, one she hadn't yet given up), then glanced over at Darla and saw that Darla had gone to sleep with her head resting against the passenger window. Not the right time for Shooter Jennings or Big & Rich. Sighing, Lisey dropped her hand from the radio.

8

Dr Alberness had wanted to reminisce at length about his lunch with the great Scott Landon, and Lisey had been willing to let him do so in spite of Darla's repeated hand-signals, most of which meant *Can't you hurry him up?*

Lisey probably could have, but she thought doing so might have been bad for their cause. Besides, she was curious. More, she was hungry. For what? News of Scott. In a way, listening to Dr Alberness had been like looking at those old memories hidden away in the study book-snake. She didn't know if Alberness's *entire* recollections constituted one of Scott's 'stations of the bool' – she suspected not – but she knew they raised a dry yet compelling hurt in her. Was that what remained of grief after two years? That hard and ashy sadness?

First Scott had called Alberness on the phone. Had he known in advance that the doctor was a puffickly *huh-yooge* fan, or was that just a coincidence? Lisey didn't believe it had been a coincidence, thought that was just a little, ahem, too coincidental, but if Scott had known, *how* had he known? She hadn't been able to think of a way to ask without breaking into the doctor's flood of reminiscence, and that was all right; probably it didn't matter. In any case, Alberness had been intensely flattered to receive that call (pretty much *bowled over*, as the saying was), and more than receptive both to Scott's enquiries about his sister-in-law and his suggestion that they have lunch. Would it be all right, Dr Alberness had asked, if he brought along a few of his favorite Landons for signature? More than all right, Scott had replied, he'd be pleased to do it.

Alberness had brought his favorite Landons; Scott had brought Amanda's medical records. Which led Lisey, now less than a mile from Amanda's little Cape Cod, to yet another question: how had Scott gotten hold of them? Had he charmed Amanda into handing them over? Had he charmed Jane Whitlow, the shrink with the beads? Had he charmed both of them? Lisey knew it was possible. Scott's ability to charm wasn't universal – Dashmiel, the southern-fried chickenshit, was a case in point – but many people had been susceptible. Certainly Amanda had felt it, although Lisey was sure that her sister had never fully trusted Scott (Manda *had* read all of his books, even *Empty Devils* . . . after which, Amanda said, she had slept with the lights on for an entire week). About Jane Whitlow Lisey had no idea.

How Scott had obtained the records might be another point upon which Lisey's curiosity would never be satisfied. She might have to content herself with knowing that he had, and that Dr Alberness had willingly studied them, and had concurred with Scott's opinion: Amanda Debusher was probably headed for more trouble down the line. And at some point (probably long before they'd finished their dessert), Alberness had promised his favorite writer that if the feared break came, he would find a place for Ms Debusher at Greenlawn.

'That was so wonderful of you,' Lisey had told him warmly, and now – turning in to Amanda's driveway for the second time that day – she wondered at what point in the conversation the doctor had asked Scott where he got his ideas. Had it been early or late? With the appetizers or the coffee?

'Wake up, Darla-darlin,' she said, turning off the engine. 'We're here.'

Darla sat up, looked at Amanda's house, and said: 'Oh, shit.'

Lisey burst out laughing. She couldn't help it.

9

Packing for Manda turned out to be an unexpectedly sad affair for both of them. They found her bags in the third-floor cubby that served as her attic. There were just two Samsonite suitcases, battered and still bearing **MIA** tags from the Florida trip she'd taken to see Jodotha . . . when? Seven years ago?

No, Lisey thought, *ten*. She regarded them sadly, then pulled out the larger of the two.

'Maybe we ought to take both,' Darla said doubtfully, then wiped her face. 'Whoo! Hot up here!'

'Let's just take the big one,' Lisey said. She almost added that she didn't think Amanda would be going to the Catatonics' Ball this year, then bit her tongue. One look at Darla's tired, sweaty face told her this was absolutely the

197

wrong time to try and be witty. 'We can get enough in it for a week, at least. She won't be going far. Remember what the doc said?'

Darla nodded and wiped her face again. 'Mostly in her room, at least to start with.'

Under ordinary circumstances, Greenlawn would have sent a physician out to examine Amanda *in situ*, but thanks to Scott, Alberness had cut right to the chase. After ascertaining that Dr Whitlow was gone and Amanda either could not or would not walk (and that she was incontinent), he had told Lisey he would send out a Greenlawn ambulance – unmarked, he emphasized. To most folks it looked like just another delivery van. Lisey and Darla had followed it to Greenlawn in Lisey's BMW, and both of them had been extremely grateful – Darla to Dr Alberness, Lisey to Scott. The wait while Alberness examined her, however, had seemed much longer than forty minutes, and his report had been far from encouraging. The only part of it Lisey wanted to concentrate on right now was what Darla had just mentioned: Amanda would be spending most of her first week under close observation, in her room or on the little terrace outside her room if she could be persuaded to ambulate that far. She wouldn't even be visiting the Hay Common Room at the end of the corridor unless she showed sudden and drastic improvement. 'Which I don't expect,' Dr Alberness had told them. 'It happens, but it's rare. I believe in telling the truth, ladies, and the truth is that Ms Debusher is probably in for the long haul.'

'Besides,' Lisey said, examining the bigger of the two suitcases, 'I want to buy her some new luggage. This stuff is beat to shit.'

'Let me do it,' Darla said. Her voice had gone thick and wavery. 'You do so much, Lisey. Dear little Lisey.' She took Lisey's hand, lifted it to her lips, and planted a kiss on it.

Lisey was surprised – almost shocked. She and Darla had buried their ancient quarrels, but this sort of affection was still very unlike her older sister.

'Do you really want to, Darl?'

Darla nodded vehemently, started to speak, and settled for scrubbing her face again.

'Are you okay?'

Darla began to nod, then shook her head. 'New luggage!' she cried. 'What a joke! Do you think she's ever going to need new luggage? You heard him – no response to the snap test, no response to the clap test, no response to the pin test! I know what the nurses call people like her, they call em *gorks*, and I don't give a shit what he says about therapy and wonder drugs, if she ever comes back it'll be a blue-eyed miracle!'

As the saying is, Lisey thought, and smiled . . . but only inside, where it was safe to smile. She led her tired, slightly weepy sister down the short, steep flight of attic steps and below the worst of the heat. Then, instead of telling her that where there was life there was hope, or to let a smile be her umbrella, or that it was always darkest just before the dawn, or anything else that had just lately fallen out of the dog's ass, she simply held her. Because sometimes only holding was best. That was one of the things she had taught the man whose last name she had taken for her own – that sometimes it was best to be quiet; sometimes it was best to just shut your everlasting mouth and hang on, hang on, hang on.

10

Lisey asked again if Darla didn't want company on the ride back to Greenlawn, and Darla shook her head. She had an old Michael Noonan novel on cassette tapes, she said, and this would be a good chance to dig into it. By then she had washed her face in Amanda's bathroom, reapplied her makeup, and tied her hair back. She looked good, and in Lisey's experience, a woman who looked good usually felt that way. So she gave Darla's hand a little squeeze, told her to drive carefully, and watched her out of sight. Then she made a slow tour of Amanda's house, first inside and then out, making sure everything was locked up: windows, doors, cellar bulkhead, garage. She left two of the garage windows a quarter-inch open to keep the heat from building up. This was a thing Scott had taught *her*, a thing he'd learned from his father, the redoubtable Sparky Landon . . . along with how to read (at the precocious age of two), how to sum on the little blackboard that was kept beside the stove in the kitchen, how to jump from the bench in the front hall with a cry of *Geronimo!* . . . and about blood-bools, of course.

'*Stations of the bool — like stations of the cross, I guess.*'

He says this and then he laughs. It's a nervous laugh, an I'm-looking-over-my-shoulder laugh. A child's laugh at a dirty joke.

'Yeah, exactly like that,' Lisey murmured, and shivered in spite of the late afternoon heat. The way those old memories kept bubbling to the surface in the present tense was disturbing. It was as if the past had never died; as if on some level of time's great tower, everything was still happening.

That's a bad way to think, thinking that way will get you in the bad-gunky.

'I don't doubt it,' Lisey said, and gave her own nervous laugh. She headed for her car with Amanda's key-ring – surprisingly heavy, heavier than her own, although Lisey's house was far bigger – hung over the forefinger of her right hand. She had a feeling she was *already* in the bad-gunky. Amanda in the nutbarn was just the beginning. There was also 'Zack McCool' and that detestable Incunk, Professor Woodbody. The events of the day had driven the latter two out of her mind, but that didn't mean they'd ceased to exist. She felt too tired and dispirited to take on Woodbody this evening, too tired and dispirited even to track him to his lair ... but she thought she'd better do it just the same, if only because her phone-pal 'Zack' had sounded as though he could really be dangerous.

She got into her car, put big sissa Manda-Bunny's keys into the glove-compartment, and backed down the driveway. As she did, the lowering sun cast a bright net of reflections off something behind her and up onto the roof. Startled, Lisey pressed the brake, looked over her shoulder – and saw the silver spade. *COMMENCEMENT, SHIPMAN LIBRARY.* Lisey reached back, touched the wooden handle, and felt her mind calm a bit. She looked in both directions along the blacktop, saw nothing coming, and turned toward home. Mrs Jones was sitting on her front stoop, and raised her hand in a wave. Lisey raised hers in return. Then she reached between the BMW's bucket seats again, so she could grasp the shaft of the spade.

11

If she was honest with herself, she thought as she began her short ride home, then she had to admit she was more frightened by these returning memories – by the sense that they were happening *again*, happening *now* – than she was by what might or might not have happened in bed just before sunrise. That she could dismiss (well . . . almost) as the half-waking dream of an anxious mind. But she hadn't thought of Gerd Allen Cole for ever so long, and if asked for the name of Scott's father or where he had worked, she would have said she honestly didn't remember.

'U.S. Gypsum,' she said. 'Only Sparky called it U.S. Gyppum.' And then, low and fierce, almost growling it: 'Stop, now. That's enough. You stop.'

But *could* she? That was the question. And it was an *important* question, because her late husband wasn't the only one who had squirreled away certain painful and frightening memories. She'd put up some sort of mental curtain between **LISEY NOW** and **LISEY! THE EARLY YEARS!**, and she had always thought it was strong, but this evening she just didn't know. Certainly there were holes in it, and if you looked through them, you ran the risk of seeing things in the purple haze beyond that you maybe didn't want to see. It was better not to look, just as it was better not even to glance at yourself in a mirror after dark unless all the lights in the room were on, or eat

(nightfood)

an orange or a bowl of strawberries after sundown. Some memories were all right, but others were dangerous.

LISEY'S STORY

It was best to live in the present. Because if you got hold of the wrong memory, you might—

'Might *what*?' Lisey asked herself in an angry, shaky voice, and then, immediately: 'I don't want to know.'

A PT Cruiser going the other way came out of the declining sun, and the guy behind the wheel tipped her a wave. Lisey tipped him one right back, although she couldn't think of anyone of her acquaintance who owned a PT Cruiser. It didn't matter, out here in Sticksville you always waved back; it was plain country courtesy. Her mind was elsewhere, in any case. The fact was, she did not have the luxury of refusing *all* her memories just because there were some things

(Scott in the rocker, nothing but eyes while the wind howls outside, a killer gale all the way down from Yellowknife)

she didn't feel capable of looking at. Not all of them were lost in the purple, either; some were just tucked away in her own mental booksnake, all too accessible. The business of the bools, for instance. Scott had given her the complete lowdown on bools once, hadn't he?

'Yes,' she said, lowering her visor to block the declining sun. 'In New Hampshire. A month before we got married. But I don't remember exactly where.'

It's called The Antlers.

All right, okay, big deal. The Antlers. And Scott had called it their early honeymoon, or something like that—

Frontloaded honeymoon. He calls it their frontloaded honeymoon. Says 'Come on, babyluv, pack it up and strap it on.'

'And when babyluv asked where we were going—' she murmured.

—and when Lisey asks where they're going he says 'We'll

203

know when we get there.' And they do. By then the sky is white and the radio says snow is coming, incredible as that might seem with the leaves still on the trees and only starting to turn . . .

They'd gone there to celebrate the paperback sale of *Empty Devils*, the horrible, scary book that put Scott Landon on the bestseller lists for the first time and made them rich. They were the only guests, it turned out. And there was a freak early autumn snowstorm. On Saturday they donned snowshoes and walked a trail into the woods and sat under

(the yum-yum tree)

a tree, a special tree, and he lit a cigarette and said there was something he had to tell her, something hard, and if it changed her mind about marrying him he'd be sorry . . . hell, he'd be broken-smucking-*hearted*, but—

Lisey swerved abruptly over to the side of Route 17 and stopped, scrunching up a cloud of dust behind her. The light was still bright, but its quality was changing, edging toward the silky extravagant dream-light that is the exclusive property of June evenings in New England, the summerglow adults born north of Massachusetts remember most clearly from their childhoods.

I don't want to go back to The Antlers and that weekend. Not to the snow we thought was so magical, not under the yum-yum tree where we ate the sandwiches and drank the wine, not to the bed we shared that night and the stories he told – benches and bools and lunatic fathers. I'm so afraid that all I can reach will lead me to all I dare not see. Please, no more.

Lisey became aware that she was saying this out loud in a low voice, over and over: 'No more. No more. No more.'

But she was on a bool hunt, and maybe it was already

too late to say no more. According to the thing in bed with her this morning, she'd already found the first three stations. A few more and she could claim her prize. Sometimes a candybar! Sometimes a drink, a Coke or an RC! Always a card reading **BOOL! The End!**

I left you a bool, the thing in Amanda's nightgown had said . . . and now that the sun was going down, she was once more finding it hard to believe that thing had really *been* Amanda. Or *only* Amanda.

You have a blood-bool coming.

'But first a *good* bool,' Lisey murmured. 'A few more stations and I get my prize. A drink. I'd like a double whiskey, please.' She laughed, rather wildly. 'But if the stations go behind the purple, how the hell can it be *good*? I don't *want* to go behind the purple.'

Were her *memories* stations of the bool? If so, she could count three vivid ones in the last twenty-four hours: cold-cocking the madman, kneeling with Scott on the broiling pavement, and seeing him come out of the dark with his bloody hand held out to her like an offering . . . which was exactly what he'd meant it to be.

It's a bool, Lisey! And not just any bool, it's a blood-bool!

Lying on the pavement, he'd told her his long boy – the thing with the endless piebald side – was very close. *I can't see it, but I hear it taking its meal,* he'd said.

'*I don't want to think about this stuff anymore!*' she heard herself almost scream, but her voice seemed to come from a terrible distance, across an awful gulf; suddenly the real world felt thin, like ice. Or a mirror into which one dared not look for more than a second or two.

I could call it that way. It would come.

Sitting behind the wheel of her BMW, Lisey thought of how her husband had begged for ice and how it had come – a kind of miracle – and put her hands over her face. Invention at short notice had been Scott's forte, not Lisey's, but when Dr Alberness had asked about the nurse in Nashville, Lisey had done her best, making up something about Scott holding his breath and opening his eyes – playing dead, in other words – and Alberness had laughed as though it were the funniest thing he'd ever heard. It didn't make Lisey envy the staff under the guy's command, but at least it had gotten her out of Greenlawn and eventually here, parked at the side of a country highway with old memories barking around her heels like hungry dogs and nipping at her purple curtain . . . her hateful, precious purple curtain.

'Boy, am I lost,' she said, and dropped her hands. She managed a weak laugh. 'Lost in the deepest, darkest smucking woods.'

No, I think the deepest darkest woods are still ahead – where the trees are thick and their smell is sweet and the past is still happening. Always *happening. Do you remember how you followed him that day? How you followed him through the strange October snow and into the woods?*

Of course she did. He broke trail and she followed, trying to clap her snowshoes into her perplexing young man's tracks. And this was very like that, wasn't it? Only if she was going to do it, there was something else she needed first. Another piece of the past.

Lisey dropped the gearshift into Drive, looked into her rearview mirror for oncoming traffic, then turned around and drove back the way she had come, making her BMW really scat.

12

Naresh Patel, owner of Patel's Market, was himself on duty when Lisey came in at just past five o'clock on that long, long Thursday. He was sitting behind the cash register in a lawn chair, eating a curry and watching Shania Twain gyrate on Country Music Television. He put his curry aside and actually stood up for Lisey. His tee-shirt read **I ♥ DARK SCORE LAKE**.

'I'd like a pack of Salem Lights, please,' Lisey said. 'Actually, you better make that two.'

Mr Patel had been keeping store – first as an employee in his father's New Jersey market, then as owner of his own – for nearly forty years, and he knew better than to comment on apparent teetotalers who suddenly began buying booze or apparent non-smokers who suddenly began buying cigarettes. He simply found this lady's particular poison in his well-stocked racks of the stuff, put it on the counter, and commented on the beauty of the day. He affected not to notice Mrs Landon's expression of near shock at the price of her poison. It only showed how long her pause had been between cessation and resumption. At least this one could afford her poison; Mr Patel had customers who took food out of their children's mouths to buy this stuff.

'Thank you,' she said.

'Very welcome, please come again,' Mr Patel said, and settled back to watch Darryl Worley sing 'Awful, Beautiful Life'. It was one of his favorites.

13

Lisey had parked beside the store so as not to block access to any of the gas pumps – there were fourteen, on seven spanking-clean islands – and once she was behind the wheel of her car again, she started the engine so she could roll down her window. The XM radio under the dash (how Scott would have loved all those music channels) came on at the same time, playing low. It was tuned to The 50s on 5, and Lisey wasn't exactly surprised to hear 'Sh-Boom'. Not The Chords, though; this was the cover version, recorded by a quartet Scott had insisted on calling The Four White Boys. Except when he was drunk. Then he called them The Four Cleancut Honkies.

She tore the top off one of her new packs and slipped a Salem Light between her lips for the first time in ... when was the last time she'd slipped? Five years ago? Seven? When the BMW's lighter popped, she applied it to the tip of her cigarette and took a cautious drag of mentholated smoke. She coughed it back out at once, eyes watering. She tried another drag. That one went a little better, but now her head was starting to swim. A third drag. Not coughing at all now, just feeling like she was going to faint. If she fell forward against the steering wheel, the horn would start blaring and Mr Patel would rush out to see what was wrong. Maybe he'd be in time to keep her from burning her stupid self up – was that kind of death immolation or defenestration? Scott would have known, just as he'd known who had done the black version of 'Sh-Boom' – The Chords – and who'd owned the pool hall in *The Last Picture Show* – Sam the Lion.

But Scott, The Chords, and Sam the Lion were all gone.

She butted the cigarette in the previously immaculate ashtray. She couldn't remember the name of the motel in Nashville, either, the one she'd gone back to when she'd finally left the hospital ('Yea, you returneth like a drunkard to his wine and a dog to its spew,' she heard the Scott in her head intone), only that the desk clerk had given her one of the crappy rooms in back with nothing to look at but a high board fence. It seemed to her that every dog in Nashville had been behind it, barking and barking and barking. Those dogs made the long-ago Pluto seem like a piker. She had lain in one of the twin beds knowing she'd never get to sleep, that every time she got close she'd see Blondie swiveling the muzzle of his cunting little gun toward Scott's heart, would hear Blondie saying *I got to end all this ding-dong for the freesias*, and snap wide-awake again. But eventually she *had* gone to sleep, had gotten just enough to stagger through the next day on – three hours, maybe four – and how had she managed that remarkable feat? With the help of the silver spade, that was how. She'd laid it on the floor next to the bed where she could reach down and touch it any old time she began to think she had been too late and too slow. Or that Scott would take a turn for the worse in the night. And that was something else she hadn't thought of in all the years since. Lisey reached back and touched the spade now. She lit another Salem Light with her free hand and made herself remember going in to see him the next morning, climbing up to the third-floor ICU wing in the already sweltering heat because there was a sign in front of the only two patient elevators on that side of the hospital reading **OUT OF SERVICE**. She thought about what had happened as she approached his room. It was silly, really, just one of those

14

It's one of those silly things where you scare the living hell out of someone without meaning to. Lisey's coming down the hall from the stairs at the end of the wing, and the nurse is coming out of room 319 with a tray in her hands, looking back over her shoulder into the room with a frown on her face. Lisey says hello so the nurse (who can't be a day over twenty-three and looks even younger) will know she's there. It's a mild greeting, a little-Lisey hello for sure, but the nurse gives out a tiny high-pitched scream and drops the tray. The plate and coffee cup both survive – they are tough old cafeteria birds – but the juice-glass shatters, spraying oj on the linoleum and the nurse's previously immaculate white shoes. She gives Lisey a wide-eyed deer-in-the-headlights glance, seems for a moment about to take to her heels, then grabs hold of herself and says the conventional thing: 'Oh, sorry, you startled me.' She squats, the hem of her uniform pulling up over her white-stockinged Nancy Nurse knees, and puts the plate and cup back on the tray. Then, moving with a grace that is both swift and careful, she begins plucking up the pieces of broken glass. Lisey squats and begins to help.

'Oh, ma'am, you don't have to,' the nurse says. She speaks with a deep southern twang. 'It was entirely my fault. I wasn't looking where I was going.'

'That's okay,' Lisey says. She manages to beat the

young nurse to a few shards and deposits them on the tray. Then she uses the napkin to begin blotting up the spilled juice. 'That's my husband's breakfast tray. I'd feel guilty if I didn't help.'

The nurse gives her a funny look – akin to the *You're married to HIM?* stare Lisey has more or less gotten used to – but it's not *exactly* that look. Then she drops her gaze back to the floor and begins hunting for any pieces of glass she might have missed.

'He ate, didn't he?' Lisey says, smiling.

'Yes, ma'am. He did very well, considering what he's been through. Half a cup of coffee – all he's allowed right now – a scrambled egg, some applesauce, and a cup of Jell-O. The juice he didn't finish. As you see.' She stands up with the tray. 'I'll get a hand-towel from the nurses' station and mop up the rest of that.'

The young nurse hesitates, then gives a nervous little laugh.

'Your husband's a little bit of a magician, isn't he?'

For no reason at all Lisey thinks: *SOWISA: Strap On Whenever It Seems Appropriate.* But she only smiles and says, 'He has a bag of tricks, all right. Sick or well. Which one did he play on you?' And somewhere deep down is she remembering the night of the first bool, sleepwalking to the bathroom in her Cleaves Mills apartment, saying *Scott, hurry up* as she goes? Saying it because he must be in there, he's sure not in bed with her anymore?

'I went in to see how he was doing,' the nurse says, 'and I could have sworn the bed was empty. I mean, the IV pole was there, and the bags were still hanging from it, but . . . I thought he must have pulled out the needle and gone to the bathroom. Patients do all kinds of weird stuff when they're doped up, you know.'

Lisey nods, hoping the same small expectant smile is on her face. The one that says *I have heard this story before but I'm not tired of it yet*.

'So I went into the bathroom and *that* was empty. Then, when I turned around—'

'There he was,' Lisey finishes for her. She speaks softly, still with the little smile. 'Presto change-o, abracadabra.' *And bool, the end*, she thinks.

'Yes, how did you know?'

'Well,' Lisey says, still smiling, 'Scott has a way of blending in with his surroundings.'

This should sound exquisitely stupid – the bad lie of a person without much imagination – but it doesn't. Because it's not a lie at all. She's always losing track of him in super-markets and department stores (places where he for some reason almost always goes unrecognized), and once she hunted for him for nearly half an hour in the University of Maine Library before spying him in the Periodicals Room, which she had checked twice before. When she scolded him for keeping her waiting and making her hunt for him in a place where she couldn't even raise her voice to call his name, Scott had shrugged and protested that he'd been in Periodicals all along, browsing the new poetry magazines. And the thing was, she didn't think he was even stretching the truth, let alone lying. She had just somehow . . . overlooked him.

The nurse brightens and tells her, 'That's exactly what Scott said – he just kind of blends in.' She blushes. 'He told us to call him Scott. Practically demanded it. I hope you don't mind, Mrs Landon.' From this young southern nurse, *Mrs* comes out *Miz*, but her accent doesn't grate on Lisey the way Dashmiel's did.

'Perfectly okay. He tells that to all the girls, especially the pretty ones.'

The nurse smiles and blushes harder. 'He said he saw me go by and look right at him. He said something like, "I always was one of your whiter white men, but since I lost all of that blood, I must be in the top ten."'

Lisey laughs politely, her stomach churning.

'And of course with the white sheets and the white johnny he's wearing . . .' The young nurse is starting to slow down. She *wants* to believe it, and Lisey has no doubt she *did* believe it when Scott was actually talking to her and gazing at her with his bright hazel eyes, but now she's starting to sense the absurdity which lurks just beneath what she's saying.

Lisey jumps in and helps her out. 'Also, he's got a way of being so *still*,' she says, although Scott is just about the *jumpiest* man she knows. Even when he's reading a book he's constantly shifting in his chair, gnawing at his nails (a habit he stopped for awhile after her tirade and then resumed again), scratching his arms like a junkie in need of a fix, sometimes even doing curls with the little five-pound hand-weights that are always parked under his favorite easy chair. She has only known him to be quiet in deep sleep and when he's writing and the writing's going exceptionally well. But the nurse still looks doubtful, so Lisey forges ahead, speaking in a gay tone that sounds horribly false to her own ear. 'Sometimes I swear he's like a piece of furniture. I've walked right past him myself, plenty of times.' She touches the nurse's hand. 'I'm sure that's what happened, dear.'

She's sure of no such thing, but the nurse gives her a grateful smile and the subject of Scott's absence is dropped. *Or rather we pass it*, Lisey thinks. *Like a small kidney stone.*

'He's ever so much better today,' the nurse says. 'Dr. Wendlestadt was in for early rounds, and he was absolutely *amazed.*'

Lisey bets. And she tells the nurse what Scott told her all those years ago, in her Cleaves Mills apartment. She thought back then it was just one of those things you say, but now she believes it. Oh yes, now she believes it completely.

'All the Landons are fast healers,' she says, and then goes in to see her husband.

15

He's lying there with his eyes closed and his head turned to one side, a very white man in a very white bed – that much is certainly true – but it's impossible to miss that mop of shoulder-length dark hair. The chair she sat in last night is where she left it, and she resumes her position beside his bed. She takes out her book – *Savages*, by Shirley Conran. She's removing the matchbook cover that marks her place when she feels Scott's eyes on her and looks up.

'How are you this morning, dear one?' she asks him.

He says nothing for a long time. His breath is wheezing, but no longer *screaming* as it did while he lay in the parking lot begging for ice. *He really is better*, she thinks. Then, with some effort, he moves his hand until it's over hers. He squeezes. His lips (which look dreadfully dry, she'll get a Chap Stick or Carmex for them later) part in a smile.

'Lisey,' he says. 'Little Lisey.'

He goes back to sleep with his hand still covering hers, and that's perfectly okay with Lisey. She can turn the pages of her book with one hand.

16

Lisey stirred like a woman awaking from a doze, looked out the driver's-side window of her BMW, and saw the shadow of her car had grown noticeably longer on Mr Patel's clean black pavement. There was not one butt in her ashtray, or two, but three. She looked out through the windshield and saw a face looking back at her from one of the small windows at the rear of the Market, in what had to be the storage area. It was gone before she could tell if it was Mr Patel's wife or one of his two teenage daughters, but she had time to mark the expression: curiosity or concern. Either way it was time to move on. Lisey backed out of her space, glad she had at least butted her cigarettes in her own ashtray instead of tossing them out onto that weirdly clean asphalt, and once again turned for home.

Remembering that day in the hospital — and what the nurse said — that was another station of the bool.

Yes? Yes.

Something had been in bed with her this morning, and for now she would go on believing it had been Scott. He had for some reason sent her on a bool hunt, just like the ones his big brother Paul had made for him when they

215

were a pair of unhappy boys growing up in rural Pennsylvania. Only instead of little riddles leading her from one station to the next, she was being led . . .

'You're leading me into the past,' she said in a low voice. 'But why would you do that? *Why*, when that's where the bad-gunky is?'

The one you're on is a good *bool. It goes behind the purple.*

'Scott, I don't want to go behind the purple.' Approaching the house now. 'I'll be *smucked* if I want to go behind the purple.'

But I don't think I have any choice.

If that was true, and if the next station of the bool meant reliving their weekend visit to The Antlers – Scott's frontloaded honeymoon – then she wanted Good Ma's cedar box. It was all she had of her mother now that the

(africans)

afghans were gone, and Lisey supposed it was her more humble version of the memory nook in Scott's office. It was a place where she'd stored all sorts of mementos from

(SCOTT AND LISEY! THE EARLY YEARS!)

the first decade of their marriage: photos, postcards, napkins, matchbooks, menus, drink-coasters, stupid stuff like that. How long had she collected those things? Ten years? No, not that long. Six at most. Probably less. After *Empty Devils*, the changes had come thick and fast – not just the Germany experiment but *everything*. Their married life had become something like the berserk merry-go-round (sort of a pun there, she thought – merry-go-round, marry-go-round) at the end of Alfred Hitchcock's *Strangers on a Train*. She'd quit saving things like cocktail napkins and souvenir matchbooks because there'd been too many lounges and too many restaurants in too many hotels. Pretty soon she'd quit saving everything. And Good Ma's cedar box that smelled so sweet when you opened it, where was that? *Somewhere* in the house, she was sure of it, and she meant to find it.

Maybe it'll turn out to be the next station of the bool, she thought, and then she saw her mailbox up ahead. The door was down and a clutch of letters was rubber-banded to it. Curious, Lisey pulled up next to the pole. She'd often come home to a full mailbox when Scott was alive, but since then her mail tended to be on the thin side, and more often than not addressed to OCCUPANT or MR AND MRS HOME OWNER. In truth, this current sheaf looked pretty thin: four envelopes and a postcard. Mr Simmons, the RFD 3 mailman, must have tucked a package in the box, although on fair days he was more apt to use a rubber band or two to attach them to the sturdy metal flag. Lisey glanced at the letters – bills, advertising come-ons, a postcard from Cantata – and then reached into the mailbox. She touched something soft, furry and wet. She screamed in surprise, yanked her hand back, saw the blood on her fingers, and screamed again, this time in horror. In that first moment she was positive she'd been bitten: something had climbed the cedar mailbox pole and then wormed its way inside. Maybe a rat, maybe something even worse – something rabid, like a woodchuck or a baby coon.

She wiped her hand on her blouse, breathing in audible gasps that weren't quite moans, then reluctantly raised her hand to see how many wounds there were.

And how deep. For a moment her conviction that she must have been bitten was so strong that she actually saw the marks. Then she blinked her eyes and reality reasserted itself. There were smears of blood, but no cuts or bites or breaks in the skin. Something was in her mailbox, all right, some horrible furry surprise, but its biting days were done.

Lisey opened the glove compartment and her unopened pack of cigarettes fell out. She rummaged until she came up with the little disposable flashlight that she had transferred from the glove compartment of her last car, a Lexus she had driven for four years. It had been a fine car, that Lexus. She had only traded it because she associated it with Scott, who called it Lisey's Sexy Lexus. It was surprising how much small things could hurt when someone close to you died; talk about the princess and the smucking pea. Now she only hoped there was some juice left in the flashlight.

There was. The beam shone out bright and steady and confident. Lisey shifted sideways, took a deep breath, and shone it into the mailbox. She was distantly aware that she'd folded her lips over her teeth and was pressing them together so tightly that it hurt. At first she saw only a darkish shape and a green glimmer, like light reflecting off a marble. And wetness on the corrugated metal floor of the mailbox. She supposed that was the blood she'd gotten on her fingers. She shifted farther left, settling her side all the way against the driver's door, gingerly pushing the flashlight farther into the mailbox. The darkish shape grew fur, and ears, and a nose that probably would have been pink in daylight. There was no mistaking the eyes; even dulled in death, their shape was distinctive. There was a dead cat in her mailbox.

Lisey began to laugh. It was not exactly normal laughter, but it wasn't entirely hysterical, either. There was genuine humor in it. She didn't need Scott to tell her that a slaughtered cat in the mailbox was too, too *Fatal Attraction*. That had been no Swedish-meatball movie with subtitles, and she had seen it twice. What made it funny was that Lisey didn't *own* a cat.

She let the laughter run its course, then lit a Salem Light and pulled into her driveway.

CHAPTER SIX

LISEY AND THE PROFESSOR (THIS IS WHAT IT GETS YOU)

1

Lisey felt no fear now, and her momentary lapse into amusement had been replaced by hard clean rage. She left the BMW parked in front of the locked barn doors and strode stilt-legged to the house, wondering if she would find her new friend's missive at the kitchen door or the one in front. She never doubted there would be a missive, and she was right. It was in the back, a white business-length envelope sticking out from between the screen door and the jamb. Cigarette clamped between her front teeth, Lisey tore the envelope open and unfolded a single sheet of paper. The message was typewritten.

> Mrs: I am sorry to do this as I love aminals
> but btter your Cat than You. I don't want to hurt
> You. I don't want to but you need to call
> 555-298-8188 and tell 'The Man' that you are
> donatinf those papers we talked about to the

school library by way of Him. We don't want to
let any grass grow under our feet on this Mrs,
so call him by 8 PM tonight ald he'll get in touch
with me. Let us finisg this business with no one
hut except for your poor Pet about which I am
so SORRY.

> Your freind,
> Zack

   PS: I'm not a bit mad you told me to go
'F' myself. I know you were upsert.
   Z

Lisey looked at the *Z* which was 'Zack McCool's'
final bit of communication to her and thought of Zorro,
galloping through the night with his cape billowing out
behind him. Her eyes were watering. She thought for a
moment that she was crying, then realized it was smoke.
The cigarette between her teeth had burned down to the
filter. She spat it to the brickwork of the walk and ground
it grimly beneath her heel. She looked up at the high board
fence that went all the way around their backyard . . .
though solely for the sake of symmetry, as their only neighbors were on the south side, to Lisey's left as she stood by
her kitchen door with 'Zack McCool's' infuriating, poorly
typed missive – his smucking ultimatum – in her hand. It
was the Galloways on the other side of the board fence,
and the Galloways had half a dozen cats – what were called
'barncats' in this neck of the woods. They sometimes foraged
in the Landons' yard, especially when no one was home.
Lisey had no doubt it was a Galloway barncat in her mailbox,
just as she had no doubt it had been Zack in the PT

Cruiser that had passed her not long after she finished locking up and left Amanda's house. Mr PT Cruiser had been heading east, coming almost directly out of the lowering sun, so she hadn't been able to get a good look at him. The bastard had even had the balls to tip her a wave. *Howdy, there, Missus, left you a little something in your mailbox!* And she had waved back, because that was what you did out here in Sticksville.

'You bastard,' she murmured, so angry she didn't even know which one she was cursing, Zack or the crazed Incunk who had sicced Zack on her. But since Zack had so considerately provided her with Woodbody's phone number (she had recognized the Pittsburgh area code instantly), she knew which one she intended to deal with first, and she found she was looking forward to it. But before she dealt with anyone, she had a distasteful housekeeping chore to perform.

Lisey stuffed 'Zack McCool's' letter into her back pocket, briefly touching Amanda's Little Notebook of Compulsions without even being aware of it, and yanked out her housekeys. She was still too angry to be aware of much, including the possibility of the sender's fingerprints on the letter. Nor was she thinking about calling the County Sheriff's Office, although that had certainly been on her To Do list earlier. Rage had narrowed coherent thought to something very like the beam of the little flashlight she had used to look into the mailbox, and right now that limited her to just a pair of ideas: take care of the cat, then call Woodbody and tell him to take care of 'Zack McCool'. To call him off. Or else.

2

From the cabinet under her kitchen sink she got a pair of floor-buckets, some clean rags, an old pair of Playtex rubber gloves, and a garbage bag that she tucked into the back pocket of her jeans. She squirted Top Job into one of the buckets and filled it with hot water, using the sink's hand-held spray attachment to make the soap foam up faster. Then she went outside, pausing only to get a pair of tongs out of what Scott had called the kitchen's Things Drawer – the big ones she used on the rare occasions when she decided to barbecue. She heard herself singing the kick-out line of 'Jambalaya' over and over again as she went about these small, grim chores: 'Son of a gun, we'll have big fun on the bayou!'

Big fun. No doubt.

Outside, she filled the second bucket with cold rinse from the hose-bib and then walked up the driveway, a bucket in each hand, the rags tossed over her shoulder, the long tongs sticking out of one back pocket and the Hefty bag in the other. When she got to the mailbox, she set the buckets down and wrinkled her nose. Could she smell blood, or was that only her imagination? She peered into the mailbox. Hard to see; the light was going the wrong way. *Should have brought the flash*, she thought, but she was damned if she was going to go back and get it. Not while she was strapped and ready.

Lisey probed with the tongs, stopping when they hit something that wasn't soft but wasn't quite hard, either. She opened them as wide as she could, clamped them down, and pulled. At first nothing happened. Then the cat

223

– really just a sense of weight at the end of her arm – began to move reluctantly forward.

The tongs lost their hold and clicked together. Lisey pulled them out. There was blood and a few gray hairs on the spatulate ends – what Scott had always called 'the grabbers'. She remembered telling him *grabbers* was one fish he must have found floating dead on the surface of his precious pool. That had made him laugh.

Lisey bent and peered into the mailbox. The cat had come about halfway and was easy enough to see now. It was a nondescript smoke color, a Galloway barncat for sure. She clicked the tongs together twice – for luck – and was about to reach in again when she heard a car approaching from the east. She turned with a sinking in her belly. She didn't just *think* it was Zack returning in his sporty little PT Cruiser; she knew it. He'd pull over and lean out and ask her if she wanted a little hep with that. He'd call it hep. *Missus*, he'd say, *do you want a little hep with that.* But it was some kind of SUV, and a woman behind the wheel.

You're getting paranoid, little Lisey.

Probably so. And under the circumstances, she had a right to be.

Get it done. You came out here to do it, so do it.

She reached in with the tongs again, this time looking at what she was doing, and as she opened the grabbers and positioned them around one of the unlucky barncat's stiffening paws, she thought of Dick Powell in some old black-and-white movie, carving a turkey and asking *Who wants a leg?* And yes, she could smell the thing's blood. She gagged a little, bent her head, spat between her sneakers.

Get it done.

Lisey closed the grabbers (not such a bad word after all, not once you made friends with it) and pulled. She fumbled the green garbage bag open with her other hand and in the cat tumbled, headfirst. She twirled the bag closed and knotted the neck, since stupid little Lisey had also forgotten to bring one of the yellow plastic ties. Then she resolutely began to scrub her mailbox clean of the blood and fur.

3

When she was finished with the mailbox, Lisey trudged back down the driveway with her buckets in the long evening light. Breakfast had been coffee and oatmeal, lunch little more than a scoop of tuna and mayo on a scrap of lettuce, and dead cat or no dead cat, she was starved. She decided to put off her call to Woodbody until she had some food in her belly. The thought of calling the Sheriff's Office – anyone in a blue uniform, for that matter – hadn't yet returned to her.

She washed her hands for three minutes, using very hot water and making sure any speck of blood was gone from under her nails. Then she found the Tupperware dish containing the leftover Cheeseburger Pie, scraped it onto a plate, and blasted it in the microwave. While she waited for the chime, she hunted a Pepsi out of the fridge. She remembered thinking she'd never finish the Hamburger Helper stuff once her initial lust for it had been slaked. You could add that to the bottom of the long, long list of Things in Life Lisey Has Been Wrong About, but so what?

Big diddly, as Cantata had been fond of saying in her teenage years.

'I never claimed to be the brains of the outfit,' Lisey told the empty kitchen, and the microwave bleeped as if to second that.

The reheated gloop was almost too hot to eat but Lisey gobbled it anyway, cooling her mouth with fizzy mouthfuls of cold Pepsi. As she was finishing the last bite, she remembered the low whispering sound the cat's fur had made against the tin sleeve of the mailbox, and the weird *pulling* sensation she'd felt as the body began, reluctantly, to come forward. *He must have really crammed it in there*, she thought, and Dick Powell once more came to mind, black-and-white Dick Powell, this time saying *And have some stuffing!*

She was up and rushing for the sink so fast she knocked her chair over, sure she was going to vomit everything she'd just eaten, she was going to *blow her groceries, toss her cookies, throw her heels, donate her lunch*. She hung over the sink, eyes closed, mouth open, midsection locked and straining. After a pregnant five-second pause, she produced one monstrous cola-burp that buzzed like a cicada. She leaned there a moment longer, wanting to make absolutely sure that was all. When she was, she rinsed her mouth, spat, and pulled 'Zack McCool's' letter from her jeans pocket. It was time to call Joseph Woodbody.

4

She expected to reach his office at Pitt – who'd give a looney-tune like her new friend Zack his home phone number? –

and she was prepared to leave what Scott might have called 'a *huh-yoogely* provocative message' on Woodbody's answering machine. Instead the telephone was answered on the second ring and a woman's voice, quite pleasant and perhaps lubricated by that all-important first before-dinner drink, told Lisey that she had reached the Woodbody residence and then asked who was calling. For the second time that day Lisey identified herself as Mrs Scott Landon.

'I'd like to speak to Professor Woodbody,' she said. Her voice was mild and pleasant.

'May I say what this is regarding?'

'My late husband's papers,' Lisey said, spinning her opened pack of Salem Lights on the coffee table in front of her. She realized that she once again had cigarettes and no fire. Perhaps it was a warning that she should give the habit up again, after all, before it could settle its little yellow hooks back into her brain stem. She thought of adding *I'm sure he'll want to talk to me* and didn't bother. His wife would know that.

'Just a moment, please.'

Lisey waited. She hadn't planned what she was going to say. This was in accordance with another of Landon's Rules: you only planned out what you were going to say for *disagreements*. When you were really angry – when you wanted to *tear someone a new asshole*, as the saying was – it was usually best to just rear back and let it rip.

So she sat there, mind a careful blank, spinning her pack of cigarettes. Around and around it went.

At last a smooth masculine voice she thought she remembered said, 'Hello, Mrs Landon, this is a pleasant surprise.'

SOWISA, she thought. *SOWISA, babyluv*.

'No,' Lisey said, 'it's not going to be pleasant at all.'

There was a pause. Then, cautiously: 'I beg pardon? Is this Lisa Landon? Mrs Scott L—'

'Listen to me, you son of a bitch. There's a man harassing me. I think he's a dangerous man. Yesterday he threatened to hurt me.'

'Mrs Landon—'

'In places I didn't let the boys touch at the junior high school dances was how he put it, I think. And tonight—'

'Mrs Landon, I don't—'

'*Tonight* he left a dead cat in my mailbox and a letter stuck in my door, and the letter had a telephone number on it, *this* number, so don't tell me you don't know what I'm talking about when I know you *do*!' On the last word, Lisey batted the pack of cigarettes with the side of her hand. Batted it like a badminton birdie. It flew all the way across the room, shedding Salem Lights as it went. She was breathing hard and fast, but with her mouth wide open. She didn't want Woodbody to hear her doing it and mistake her rage for fear.

Woodbody made no reply. Lisey gave him time. When he still didn't talk, she said, 'Are you there? You better be.'

She knew it was the same man who replied, but the smooth round lecture-hall tones were gone. This man sounded both younger and somehow older. 'I'm going to put you on hold, Mrs Landon, and take this in my study.'

'Where your wife can't hear, is what you mean.'

'Hold on, please.'

'It better not be long, Woodsmucky, or—'

There was a click, then silence. Lisey wished she had used the cordless phone in the kitchen; she wanted to pace around, maybe snag one of her cigarettes and light it off a stove-burner. But maybe this was better. This way she couldn't blow off any of her rage. This way she had to stay strapped so tight it hurt.

Ten seconds went by. Twenty. Thirty. She was preparing to hang up when there was another click on the line and the King of the Incunks spoke to her again in his new young-old voice. It had picked up a funny little hiccup-ping tremor. *It's his heartbeat*, she thought. It was her thought, but it could have been Scott's insight. *His heart's beating so hard I can actually hear it. I wanted to scare him? I scared him. Now why should that scare* me?

And yes, all of a sudden she *was* scared. It was like a yellow thread weaving in and out of the bright red overblanket of her rage.

'Mrs Landon, is he a man named Dooley? James or Jim Dooley? Tall and skinny, with a little bit of a hill accent? Like West Vir—'

'I don't know his name. He called himself Zack McCool on the phone, and that's the name he signed to his—'

'Fuck,' Woodbody said. Only he stretched it out – *Fuu-uuuck* – and turned it into something almost incanta-tory. This was followed by a sound that might have been a groan. In Lisey's mind, a second bright yellow thread joined the first.

'What?' she asked sharply.

'That's him,' Woodbody said. 'It has to be. The e-mail address he gave me was Zack991.'

'You told him to scare me into giving you Scott's unpublished papers, didn't you? That was the deal.'

'Mrs Landon, you don't understa—'

'I think I do. I've dealt with some fairly crazy people since Scott died, and the academics put the collectors to shame, but you make the rest of the academics look normal, Woodsmucky. That's probably why you were able to hide it at first. The really crazy people *have* to be able to do that. It's a survival skill.'

'Mrs. Landon, if you'll only let me expl—'

'I'm being threatened and you're responsible, you don't need to explain that. So listen up, and listen up good: call him off right now. I haven't given your name to the authorities yet, but I really think the police getting your name is the least of your worries. If I get one more call, one more letter, or one more dead animal from this Deep Space Cowboy, I'll go to the newspapers.' Inspiration struck. 'I'll start with the ones in Pittsburgh. They'll love it. CRAZED ACADEMIC THREATENS FAMOUS WRITER'S WIDOW. When *that* shows up on page one, a few questions from the cops in Maine will be the least of your problems. Goodbye, tenure.'

Lisey thought all of this sounded good, and it hid those yellow threads of fear – at least for the moment. Unfortunately, what Woodbody said next brought them back again, brighter than ever.

'You don't understand, Mrs Landon. I can't call him off.'

5

For a moment Lisey was too flabbergasted to speak. Then she said, 'What do you *mean*, you can't?'

'I mean I've already tried.'

'You have his e-mail address! Zack999 or whatever it was—'

'Zack991 at Sail-dot-com, for what it's worth. Might as well be triple zero. It doesn't work. It did the first couple of times I used it, but since then my e-mails just bounce back marked CANNOT DELIVER.'

He began babbling about trying again, but Lisey hardly paid attention. She was replaying her conversation with 'Zack McCool' – or Jim Dooley, if that was his real name. He'd said Woodbody was either going to telephone him or—

'Do you have some special e-mail account?' she asked, interrupting Woodbody in mid-flow. 'He said you were going to e-mail him in some special way and tell him when you'd gotten what you wanted. So where is it? Your University office? An internet café?'

'*No!*' Woodbody nearly wailed. 'Listen to me – of *course* I have an e-mail address at Pitt, but I never gave it to Dooley! It would have been insane! I have two grad students who regularly access the mail there, not to mention the English Department secretary!'

'And at home?'

'I gave him my home e-mail address, yes, but he's never used it.'

'What about the phone number you have for him?'

There was a moment of silence on the line, and when

Woodbody spoke again, he sounded honestly puzzled. This scared her worse still. She looked at the wide living room window and saw that the sky in the northeast was turning lavender. It would soon be night. She had an idea this might be a long one.

'Phone number?' Woodbody said. 'He never gave me a phone number. Just an e-mail address that worked twice, then quit. He was either lying or fantasizing.'

'Which do you think it was?'

Woodbody nearly whispered, 'I don't know.'

Lisey thought this was Woodbody's chickenshit way of trying not to admit what he really thought: that Dooley was crazy.

'Hold on a minute.' She started to put the handset down on the sofa, then thought better of it. 'You better be there when I get back, Professor.'

There was no need to use one of the stove-burners, after all. There were long decorative matches for lighting the fireplace in a brass cuspidor next to the fire-tools. She picked a Salem Light up off the floor and scraped one of the long matches alight on a hearthstone. She took one of the ceramic vases for a temporary ashtray, laying aside the flowers that had been in it and reflecting (not for the first time, either) that smoking was one of the world's nastier habits. Then she went back to the sofa, sat down, and picked up the phone. 'Tell me what happened.'

'Mrs. Landon, my wife and I have plans to go out—'

'Your plans have changed,' Lisey said. 'Start at the beginning.'

6

Well of course in the beginning were the Incunks, those pagan worshippers of original texts and unpublished manuscripts, and Professor Joseph Woodbody, who was their king, as far as Lisey was concerned. God knew how many scholarly articles he'd published concerning the works of Scott Landon, or how many of them might even now be quietly gathering dust in the booksnake above the barn. Nor did she care how badly tormented Professor Woodbody had been by the thought of the unpublished works that might also be gathering dust in Scott's study. What mattered was that Woodbody made a habit of having two or three beers two or three evenings a week on his way home from campus, always at the same bar, a place called The Place. There were plenty of college-type drinking establishments near Pitt, some of them by-the-pitcher beerdives, some of them the smart-bars where faculty and class-conscious grad students went to drink – the kind of places with spider-plants in the windows and Bright Eyes on the jukebox instead of My Chemical Romance. The Place was a workingman's bar a mile from the campus and the closest thing to rock on the jukebox was a Travis Tritt-John Mellencamp duet. Woodbody said he liked going there because it was quiet on weekday afternoons and early evenings, also because the ambience made him think of his father, who had worked in one of U.S. Steel's rolling mills. (Lisey didn't give a sweet smuck about Woodbody's father.) It was in this bar that he had met the man who called himself Jim Dooley. Dooley was another late afternoon/early evening drinker, a soft-spoken fellow who favored blue chambray work shirts and the kind of Dickies with cuffs that Woodbody's father had worn. Woodbody described Dooley as about six-one, lanky, slightly stooped, with thinning dark hair that often tumbled over his brow. He thought Dooley's eyes had been blue, but wasn't sure, although they had drunk together over a period of six weeks and had become what Woodbody described as 'sort of buddies'. They had exchanged not life stories but patchwork pieces of life stories, as men do in bars. For his part, Woodbody claimed to have told the truth. He now had reasons to doubt that Dooley had done the same. Yes, Dooley might well have drifted down to The Burg from West Virginia twelve or fourteen years ago, and probably *had* worked a series of low-paying manual-labor jobs since then. Yes, he might have done some prison time; he had that institutional look about him, always seeming to glance up into the backbar mirror as he reached for his beer, always looking back over his shoulder at least once on his way to the men's. And yes, he might really have come by the scar just above his right wrist during a brief but vicious fight in the prison laundry. Or not. Hey, maybe he had just tripped over his trike when he was a kid and landed wrong. All Woodbody knew for sure was that Dooley had read all of Scott Landon's books and was able to discuss them intelligently. And he had listened sympathetically to Woodbody's tale of woe concerning the intransigent Widow Landon, who was sitting on an intellectual treasure-trove of unpublished Landon manuscripts, a completed novel among them, according to rumor. But sympathy was really too mild a word. He had listened with growing outrage.

According to Woodbody, it was Dooley who had started calling her Yoko.

Woodbody characterized their meetings at The Place as 'occasional, bordering on regular.' Lisey parsed this intellectual bullshit and decided it meant Woodbody-Dooley bitchfests about Yoko Landon four and sometimes five afternoons a week, and that when Woodbody said 'a beer or two', he probably meant a pitcher or two. So there they were, this intellectual Oscar and Felix, getting soused just about every weekday afternoon, at first talking about how great Scott's books were and then progressing naturally to what a miserable withholding bitch his widow had turned out to be.

According to Woodbody, it was Dooley who had turned their conversations in this direction. Lisey, who knew how Woodbody sounded when he was denied what he wanted, doubted if it had taken much effort.

And at some point, Dooley had told Woodbody that he, Dooley, could persuade the widow to change her mind about those unpublished manuscripts. After all, how hard could it be to talk sense to her when the man's papers were almost certainly going to end up in the University of Pittsburgh Library with the rest of the Landon Collection anyway? He was *good* at changing people's minds, Dooley said. He had a knack for it. The King of the Incunks (looking at his new friend with a drunk's bleary shrewdness, Lisey had no doubt) asked Dooley how much he'd want for such a service. Dooley had said he wasn't looking to make a *profit*. They were talking about a service to mankind, weren't they? Prying a great treasure away from a woman who was too stupid to understand what it was she was sitting on, like a broody hen on a clutch of eggs. Well, yes, Woodbody had responded, but the workman was worthy of his hire.

Dooley considered this and said he'd keep a record of his various expenses. Then, when they got together and he transferred the papers to Woodbody, they could discuss the matter of payment. And with that, Dooley had extended his hand over the bar to his new friend, just as if they had closed a deal which actually made sense. Woodbody had taken it, feeling both delighted and contemptuous. He had gone back and forth in his mind about Dooley during the five or seven weeks he'd known him, he told Lisey. There were days when he thought Dooley was a serious hardass, a self-made jailhouse scholar whose blood-chilling stories of stickups and fights and spoonhandle knifings were all true. Then there were days (the day of the shake being one of them) when he was positive that Jim Dooley was nothing but talk, and the most dangerous crime he'd ever committed was stealing a gallon or two of paint thinner out of the Wal-Mart in Monroeville where he'd worked for six months or so in 2004. So for Woodbody it had been little more than a half-drunk joke, especially when Dooley more or less told him he was going to talk Lisey out of her dead husband's papers for the sake of Art. That, at least, was what the King of the Incunks told Lisey on that afternoon in June, but of course this was the same King of the Incunks who had sat half-drunk in a bar with a man he hardly knew, a self-confessed 'hard-time con', the two of them calling her Yoko and agreeing that Scott must have kept her around for one thing and one thing only, because what else could he have wanted her for? Woodbody said that, as far as he was concerned, the whole thing had been little more than a joke, just two guys blue-skying in a bar. It *was* true that the two guys in question had exchanged e-mail addresses, but these days everybody had an e-mail address, didn't they? The King of the Incunks had met his loyal subject just one more time following the day of the handshake. That had been two afternoons later. Dooley had limited himself to just a single beer on that occasion, telling Woodbody that he was 'in training'. After that one beer he'd slid off his barstool, saying he had an appointment 'to see a fella'. He also told Woodbody he'd probably meet him the following day, next week for sure. But Woodbody had never seen Jim Dooley again. After a couple of weeks he'd stopped looking. And the Zack991 e-mail address stopped working. In a way, he thought, losing track of Jim Dooley was a good thing. He had been drinking too much, and there was something about Dooley that was just *wrong*. (*Figured that out a little late, didn't you?* Lisey thought sourly.) Woodbody's drinking dropped back to its previous level of one or two beers a week, and without even really thinking about it, he moved to a bar a couple of blocks away. It didn't occur to him until later (*until my head cleared* was how he put it) that he was unconsciously putting distance between himself and the last place he'd seen Dooley; that he had, in fact, repented of the whole thing. If, that was, it had ever been anything other than a fantasy, just one more Jim Dooley air-castle which Joe Woodbody had helped to furnish while drinking away the waning weeks of another miserable Pittsburgh winter. And that was what he *had* believed, he finished, summing up as earnestly as a lawyer whose client faces lethal injection if he screws up. He had come to the conclusion that most of Jim Dooley's stories of banditry and survival at Brushy Mountain had been complete fabrications, and his idea of getting Mrs

Landon to give up her late husband's manuscripts was just one more. Their deal had been nothing but a child's game of What–If.

'If that's true, tell me something,' Lisey said. 'If Dooley had shown up with a truckload of Scott's stories, would that have kept you from taking them?'

'I don't know.'

That, she thought, was actually honest, and so she asked him something else. 'Do you know what you've done? What you've set in motion?'

To this Professor Woodbody said nothing, and she thought that was also honest. As honest, maybe, as he was capable of being.

7

After a pause to think, Lisey said: 'Did you give him the number where he called me? Do I have you to thank for that, too?'

'No! Absolutely not! I didn't give him *any* number, I promise you!'

Lisey believed him. 'You're going to do something for me, Professor,' she said. 'If Dooley gets in touch with you again, maybe just to tell you he's hot on the trail and things are lookin good, you're going to tell him the deal's off. Totally off.'

'I will.' The man's eagerness was almost abject. 'Believe me, I—' He was interrupted by a woman's voice – his wife's, Lisey had no doubt – asking something. There came a rustling sound as he covered the bottom part of the telephone with his hand.

Lisey didn't mind. She was adding up her situation here and not liking the total. Dooley had told her she could turn off the heat by giving Woodbody Scott's papers and unpublished manuscripts. The Professor would then call the madman, tell him everything was cool, and that would be that. Only the former King of the Incunks claimed he no longer had any way of getting in touch with Dooley, and Lisey believed him. Was it an oversight on Dooley's part? A glitch in his planning? She didn't think so. She thought that Dooley really might have some vague intention of showing up at Woodbody's office (or suburban castle) with Scott's papers . . . but before he did, he planned to first terrorize her and then hurt her in places she'd never let the boys touch at the junior high school dances. And why would he do that, after going to such great lengths to assure both the Professor and Lisey herself that there was a fail-safe system in place to keep bad things from happening if she cooperated?

Maybe because he needs to give himself permission.

That rang true. And later on – after she was dead, maybe, or so grotesquely maimed she *wished* she were dead – Jim Dooley's conscience would be able to assure itself that Lisey herself had been to blame. *I gave her every chance,* her friend 'Zack' would think. *It was nobody's fault but her own. She had to be Yoko to the bitter end.*

Okay. Okay, then. If he showed up, she'd just give him the keys to the barn and the study and tell him to take whatever he wanted. *I'll tell him to knock himself out, have a ball.*

But at this thought Lisey's lips thinned into the humorless moon-smile perhaps only her sisters and her late husband, who called it Lisey's Tornado Look, would have recognized. 'The smuck I *will*,' she muttered, and looked around for the silver spade. It wasn't there. She'd left it in the car. If she wanted it, she'd better go out and get it before it got completely dar—

'Mrs Landon?' It was the Professor, sounding more anxious than ever. She'd forgotten all about him. 'Are you still there?'

'Yeah,' she said. 'This is what it gets you, you know.'

'I beg pardon?'

'You know what I'm talking about. All the stuff you wanted so bad, the stuff you thought you had to have? This is what it gets you. How you feel right now. Plus the questions you'll have to answer when I hang up, of course.'

'Mrs Landon, I don't—'

'If the police call you, I want you to tell them everything you've told me. Which means you better answer your wife's questions first, don't you think?'

'Mrs Landon, *please*!' Woodbody sounded panicky now.

'You bought into this. You and your friend Dooley.'

'Stop calling him my *friend*!'

Lisey's Tornado Look grew stronger, the lips thinning until they showed the tops of her teeth. At the same time, her eyes narrowed until they were no more than blue sparks. It was a feral look, and it was all Debusher.

'But he *is*!' she cried. 'You're the one who drank with him, and told him your tale of woe, and laughed when he called me Yoko Landon. You were the one who set him on me, whether you said it in so many words or not, and now it turns out he's just as crazy as a shithouse rat and you can't pull him off. So *yes*, Professor, I'm going to call the County Sheriff, and *yessirree*, I'll be giving them your name, I'll be giving them anything that'll help them find your friend, because he's not *done*, you know it and so do I, because he doesn't *want* to be done, he's having a *good smucking time*, and this is what it *gets* you. You bought it, you own it! Okay? *Okay?*'

No answer. But she could hear the wet sound of breathing and knew the former King of the Incunks was trying not to cry. She hung up, snagged another ciggy off the floor, lit it. She went back to the telephone, then shook her head. She'd call the Sheriff's Office in a minute. First she wanted to get the silver spade out of the Beemer, and she wanted to do it right away, before all the light was gone and her part of the world swapped day for night.

8

The side yard – which she supposed she'd go to her grave thinking of as the dooryard – was already too dark for comfort, although Venus, the wishing-star, had yet to make her appearance in the sky. The shadows where the barn joined the toolshed were especially dark, and the BMW was parked less than twenty feet from there. Of course Dooley wasn't hiding in that well of shadows, and if he *was* on the place, he might be anywhere: leaning against the changing-hut by the pool, peering around the corner of the house where the kitchen was, crouched behind the cellar bulkhead . . .

Lisey whirled on her heels at that idea, but there was still enough light to see there was nothing on either side of the bulkhead. And the bulkhead doors themselves were locked, so she didn't have to worry about Dooley in the cellar. Unless, of course, he'd broken into the house somehow and hidden down there before she got home.

Stop it Lisey you're creeping yourself ou—

She paused with her fingers curled around the handle of the BMW's rear door. She stood that way for maybe five seconds, then let her cigarette drop from her free hand and stamped out the butt. There was someone standing in the deep angle where the barn and the toolshed met. Standing there very tall and still.

Lisey opened the Beemer's rear passenger door and snatched out the silver spade. The light inside the car stayed on when she closed the door again. She'd forgotten that, how the inside lights of cars now stayed on for a little while, the courtesy light they called it, but she found nothing courteous about the idea that Dooley could see her and she could no longer see him thanks to the way that smucking light was screwing up her vision. She stepped away from the car, holding the shaft of the spade diagonally across her breasts. The light inside the BMW finally went out. For a moment that made things worse. She could see only a world of indistinct purple shapes under the fading lavender sky, and she fully expected him to leap out at her, calling her Missus and asking why she hadn't listen as his hands closed around her throat and her breath rattled to an end.

It didn't happen and in another three seconds or so, her eyes readapted to the low light. Now she could see him again, tall and straight, grave and still, standing there in the angle of the big building and the small one. With something at his feet. Some kind of square package. It could have been a suitcase.

Good God, he doesn't think he can get all of Scott's papers in there, does he? she thought, and took another cautious step to her left, holding the silver spade so tightly that her fists throbbed. 'Zack, is that you?' Another step. Two. Three.

She heard a car coming and understood that its head-lights were going to sweep the yard, revealing him fully. When that happened, he would leap at her. She swung the silver spade back over her shoulder just as she had in August of 1988, finishing her windup as the approaching car breasted Sugar Top Hill, flooding her yard with momen-tary light and revealing the power-mower she herself had left in the angle of the barn and the shed. The shadow of its handle leaped upward on the side of the barn, then faded as the car's headlights faded. Once more the lawn-mower could have been a man with a suitcase at his feet, she supposed, although once you'd seen the truth . . .

In a horror movie, she thought, *this is where the monster would leap out of the darkness and grab me. Just as I'm starting to relax.*

Nothing leaped out to grab her, but Lisey didn't think it would hurt to take the silver spade inside with her, if only for good luck. Carrying it in one hand now, down by the collar where the shaft met the silver scoop, Lisey went to call Norris Ridgewick, the Castle County Sheriff.

CHAPTER SEVEN

LISEY AND THE LAW (OBSESSION AND THE EXHAUSTED MIND)

1

The woman who took Lisey's call identified herself as Communications Officer Soames and said she couldn't put Lisey through to Sheriff Ridgewick, because Sheriff Ridgewick had been married the week before. He and his new bride were on the island of Maui, and would be for the next ten days.

'Who *can* I talk to?' Lisey asked. She didn't like the close-to-strident sound of her voice, but she understood it. Oh God, did she. This had been one long goddam day.

'Hold on, ma'am,' CO Soames said. Then Lisey was in limbo with McGruff the Crime Dog, who was talking about Neighborhood Watch groups. Lisey thought this a considerable improvement on the Two Thousand Comatose Strings. After a minute or so of McGruff, a cop with a name Scott would have loved came on the line.

'This is Deputy Andy Clutterbuck, ma'am, how can I help you?'

For the third time that day – *third time's the charm*, Good Ma would have said, *third time pays for all* – Lisey introduced herself as Mrs Scott Landon. Then she told Deputy Clutterbuck a slightly edited version of the Zack McCool story, beginning with the call she had received the previous evening and finishing with the one she'd made tonight, the one that had netted the Jim Dooley name. Clutterbuck contented himself with uh-huhs and variations thereof until she had finished, then asked her who had given her 'Zack McCool's' other, possibly real name.

With a twinge of conscience

(tattle-tale tit all the dogs in town come to have a little bit)

that caused her a moment of bitter amusement, Lisey gave up the King of the Incunks. She did not call him Woodsmucky.

'Are you going to talk to him, Deputy Clutterbuck?'

'I think that's indicated, don't you?'

'I guess so,' Lisey said, wondering what, if anything, Castle County's acting Sheriff could get out of Woodbody that she hadn't been able to pry loose. She supposed there might be something – she'd been pretty mad. She also realized that wasn't what was bothering her. 'Will he be arrested?'

'On the basis of what you've told me? Not even close. You might have grounds for a civil action – you'd have to ask your lawyer – but in court I'm sure he'd say that as far as *he* knew, all this guy Dooley meant to do was show up on your doorstep and try a little high-pressure sales routine. He'd claim not to know anything about dead cats in mailboxes and threats of personal injury . . . and he'd be telling the truth, based on what you've just said. Right?'

Lisey agreed, rather dispiritedly, that it *was* right.

'I'm going to want the letter this stalker left,' Clutterbuck said, 'and I'm going to want the cat. What did you do with the remains?'

'We have a wooden box-thingy attached to the house,' Lisey said. She picked up a cigarette, considered it, put it back down again. 'My husband had a word for it – my husband had a word for just about *everything* – but I can't remember for the life of me what it was. Anyway, it keeps the raccoons out of the swill. I put the cat's body in a garbage bag and put the bag in the orlop.' Now that she wasn't struggling to find it, Scott's word came effortlessly to mind.

'Uh-huh, uh-huh, do you have a freezer?'

'Yes . . .' Already dreading what he was going to tell her to do next.

'I want you to put the cat in your freezer, Mrs Landon. It's perfectly okay to leave it in the bag. Someone will pick it up tomorrow and take it over to Kendall and Jepperson. They're the vets we have our county account with. They'll try to determine a cause of death—'

'It shouldn't be hard,' Lisey said. 'The mailbox was full of blood.'

'Uh-huh. Too bad you didn't take a few Polaroids before you wiped it all up.'

'Well excuse me all to hell and gone!' Lisey cried, stung.

'Calm down,' Clutterbuck said. Calmly. 'I understand that you were upset. Anybody would have been.'

Not you, Lisey thought resentfully. *You would have been as cool as . . . as a dead cat in a freezer.*

246

She said, 'That takes care of Professor Woodbody and the dead cat; now what about me?'

Clutterbuck told her he would send a deputy at once – Deputy Boeckman or Deputy Alston, whichever was closer – to take charge of the letter. Now that he thought of it, he said, the deputy who visited her could take a few Polaroid snaps of the dead cat, too. All the deputies carried Polaroid cameras in their cars. Then the deputy (and, later on, his eleven P.M. relief) would take up station on Route 19 within view of her house. Unless, of course, there was an emergency call – an accident or something of that nature. If Dooley 'checked by' (Clutterbuck's oddly delicate way of putting it), he'd see the County cruiser and move along.

Lisey hoped Clutterbuck was right about that.

Guys like this Dooley, Clutterbuck continued, were usually more show than go. If they couldn't scare someone into giving them what they wanted, they had a tendency to forget the whole deal. 'My guess is you'll never see him again.'

Lisey hoped he was right about that, too. She herself had her doubts. What she kept coming back to was the way 'Zack' had set things up. How he'd done it so he couldn't be called off, at least not by the man who had hired him.

2

Not twenty minutes after finishing her conversation with Deputy Clutterbuck (whom her tired mind now kept wanting to call either Deputy Butterhug or – perhaps

247

cross-referencing Polaroid cameras – Deputy Shutterbug), a slim man dressed in khaki and wearing a large gun on his hip showed up at her front door. He introduced himself as Deputy Dan Boeckman and told her he'd been instructed to take 'a certain letter' into safekeeping and photograph 'a certain deceased animal'. Lisey kept a straight face at that, although she had to bite down hard on the soft inner lining of her cheeks to manage the feat. Boeckman placed the letter (along with the plain white envelope) into a Baggie which Lisey provided, then asked if she had put the 'deceased animal' in the freezer. Lisey had done this as soon as she finished talking to Clutterbuck, depositing the green garbage bag in the far left corner of her big Trawlsen, where there was nothing but an elderly stack of venison steaks in hoarfrosty plastic bags, a present to her and Scott from their electrician, Smiley Flanders. Smiley had won a permit in the moose lottery of '01 or '02 – Lisey couldn't remember which – and had dropped 'a tol'able big 'un' up in the St John Valley. Where Charlie Corriveau had bagged his new bride, now that Lisey thought of it. Next to the meat, which she would almost certainly never get around to eating (except perhaps in the event of a nuclear war), was the only place for a dead Galloway barncat, and she told Deputy Boeckman to make sure he put it back there and nowhere else when he had finished his photography. He promised with perfect seriousness that he would 'comply with her request', and she once more found it necessary to bite the insides of her cheeks. Even so, that one was close. As soon as he was clumping stolidly down the basement stairs, Lisey turned herself to the wall like a naughty child with her forehead against the plaster and her hands over her mouth, laughing in whispery, wide-throated squeals.

It was as this throe passed that she began thinking again about Good Ma's cedar box (it had been Lisey's for over thirty-five years, but she had never *thought* of it as hers). Remembering the box and all the little mementos tucked away inside helped to ease the hysteria bubbling up from deep inside her. What helped even more was her growing certainty that she had put the box in the attic. Which made perfect sense, of course. The detritus of Scott's working life was out there in the barn and the study; the detritus of the life she had lived while he was working would be here, in the house she had chosen and they had both come to love.

In the attic were at least four expensive Turkish rugs she had once adored and which had at some point, for reasons she did not understand, begun to give her the creeps . . .

At least three sets of retired luggage that had taken everything two dozen airlines, many of them dinky little commuter puddle-jumper outfits, could throw at them; battered warriors that deserved medals and parades, but would have to be content with honorable attic retirement (hell, boys, it beats the town dump) . . .

The Danish-Modern living room furniture that Scott said looked pretentious, and how angry with him she'd been, mostly because she'd thought he was probably right . . .

The rolltop desk, a 'bargain' that turned out to have one short leg which had to be shimmed, only the shim was always coming out and then one day the rolltop had unrolled on her fingers and that had been *it*, buddy, up to the smucking attic with you . . .

Ashtrays on stands from their smoking days . . .

Scott's old IBM Selectric, which she had used for correspondence until it started getting hard to find the ribbons and CorrecTapes . . .

Stuff like-a *dis*, stuff like-a *dat*, stuff like-a *d'other-t'ing*. Another world, really, and yet it was all *rah-cheer*, or at least right up *dere*. And somewhere – probably behind a stack of magazines or sitting on top of the rocking chair with the unreliable split back – would be the cedar box. Thinking about it was like thinking about cold water when you were thirsty on a hot day. She didn't know just why that should be so, but it was.

By the time Deputy Boeckman came up from the cellar with his Polaroids, she was impatient for him to be gone. Perversely he hung on (*hung on like a toothache*, Dad Debusher would've said), first telling her it looked like the cat had been stabbed with some sort of tool (possibly a screwdriver), then assuring her he'd be parked right outside. It might not say TO SERVE AND PROTECT on their units (he called them units), but the thought was there every minute, and he wanted her to feel perfectly safe. Lisey said she felt so safe she was actually thinking about going to bed – it had been a long day, she'd had a family emergency to deal with as well as this stalker business, and she was utterly whipped. Deputy Boeckman finally took the hint and left after telling her one final time that she was as safe as could be, safe as houses, and there was no need for any of that sleeping-with-one-eye-open stuff. Then he clumped down her front steps as stolidly as he'd clumped down her cellar stairs, shuffling through his dead-cat photos a final time while he still had light enough to see them. A minute or two later she heard what sounded like a puffickly *huh-yooge* engine rev twice. Headlights washed across the lawn and the house, then abruptly went out. She thought of Deputy Daniel Boeckman sitting across the road with his cruiser parked prominently on the shoulder. She smiled. Then she went upstairs to the attic, with no idea that she would be lying on her bed fully dressed two hours later, exhausted and weeping.

3

The exhausted mind is obsession's easiest prey, and after half an hour of fruitless searching in the attic, where the air was hot and still, the light was poor, and the shadows seemed slyly determined to hide every nook she wanted to investigate, Lisey gave way to obsession without even realizing it. She'd had no clear reason for wanting the box in the first place, only a strong intuition that something inside, some souvenir from her early marriage, was the next station of the bool. After awhile, however, the box itself became her goal, Good Ma's cedar box. Bools be damned, if she didn't lay hands on that cedar box – a foot long, maybe nine inches wide and six deep – she'd never be able to sleep. She'd only lie there tortured by thoughts of dead cats and dead husbands and empty beds and Incunk warriors and sisters who cut themselves and fathers who cut—

(hush Lisey hush)

She'd only lie there, leave it at that.

An hour's search was enough to convince her the

cedar box wasn't in the attic, after all. But by then she was sure it was probably in the spare bedroom. It was perfectly reasonable to think it had migrated back there ... except another forty minutes (including a teetery stepladder exploration of the top shelf in the closet) convinced her the spare room was another dry hole. So the box was down cellar. *Had* to be. Very likely it had come to rest behind the stairs, where there was a bunch of cardboard boxes containing curtains, rug-remnants, old stereo components, and a few bits of sporting equipment: ice skates, a croquet set, a badminton net with a hole in it. As she hurried down the cellar stairs (not thinking at all of the dead cat now lying beside the pile of petrified moose-meat in her freezer), Lisey began to believe she had even *seen* the box down there. By then she was very tired, but only distantly aware of the fact.

It took her twenty minutes to drag all the cartons from their long-term resting place. Some were damp and split open. By the time she'd finished going through the stuff inside, her limbs were trembling with exhaustion, her clothes were sticking to her, and a nasty little headache had begun thumping at the back of her skull. She shoved back the cartons that were still holding together and left the ones that had split apart where they were. Good Ma's box was in the attic after all. Must be, had been all along. As she wasted time down here among the rusty ice skates and forgotten jigsaw puzzles, the cedar box was waiting patiently up there. Lisey could now think of half a dozen places she'd neglected to search, including the crawlspace all the way back under the eaves. That was the most likely spot. She'd probably put the box there and just forgotten all about—

The thought broke off cleanly as she realized someone was standing behind her. She could see him from the corner of her eye. Call him Jim Dooley or Zack McCool, by either name he would in the next moment drop a hand on her sweaty shoulder and call her Missus. Then she'd *really* have something to worry about.

This sensation was so real that Lisey actually heard the shuffle of Dooley's feet. She wheeled around, hands coming up to protect her face, and had just an instant to see the Hoover vacuum she herself had pulled out from under the stairs. Then she tripped over the moldering card-board carton with the old badminton net stuffed inside. She waved her arms for balance, almost caught it, lost it, had time to think *shit-a-brick*, and went down. The top of her head missed the underside of the stairs by a whisker, and that was good, because that would have been a nasty crack indeed, maybe the kind that laid you out uncon-scious. Laid you out dead, if you came down hard enough on the cement floor. Lisey managed to break her fall with her splayed hands, one knee landing safely on the springy mat of the rotted badminton net, the other suffering a harder landing on the cellar floor. Luckily, she was still wearing her jeans.

The fall was fortunate in another way, she thought fifteen minutes later as she lay on her bed, still fully dressed but with her hard crying over; she was by then down to the isolated sobs and rueful, watery gasps for breath that are strong emotion's hangover. The fall – and the scare that had preceded it, she supposed – had cleared her head. She might have gone on hunting the box for another two hours – longer, if her strength had held out. Back to the attic, back to the spare bedroom, back to the cellar. *Back to the future*, Scott would surely have added; he had a knack for cracking wise at precisely the wrong moment. Or what turned out, later on, to have been precisely the right one.

In any case she might well have gone on until dawn's early light and it would have gotten her a lot of hot air in one hand and a big pile of jack shit in the other. Lisey was now convinced the box was either in a place so obvious she'd already passed it half a dozen times or it was just *gone*, maybe stolen by one of the cleaning women who'd worked for the Landons over the years or by some workman who'd spied it and thought his wife would like a nice box like that and that Mr Landon's Missus (funny how that word got into your head) would never miss it.

Fiddle-de-dee, little Lisey, said the Scott who kept his place in her head. *Think about it tomorrow, for tomorrow is another day.*

'Yep,' Lisey said, then sat up, suddenly aware that she was a sweaty, smelly woman living inside a set of sweaty, dirty clothes. She got out of them as quickly as she could, left them in a heap by the foot of the bed, and headed for the shower. She had scraped the palms of both hands breaking her fall in the cellar, but she ignored their stinging and soaped her hair twice, letting suds run down the sides of her face. Then, after almost dozing under the hot water for five minutes or so, she resolutely turned the shower's control-lever all the way over to **C**, rinsed off under the near-freezing needle-spray, and stepped out, gasping. She used one of the big towels, and as she dropped it into the hamper she realized she felt like herself again, sane and ready to let this day go.

She went to bed, and her last thought before sleep swatted her into the black was of Deputy Boeckman standing watch. It was a comforting thought, particularly after her scare in the cellar, and she slept deeply, without dreams, until the shrill of the telephone woke her.

4

It was Cantata, calling from Boston. Of course it was. Darla had called her. Darla always called Canty when there was trouble, usually sooner rather than later. Canty wanted to know if she should come home. Lisey assured her sister that there was absolutely no reason to return from Boston early no matter how distressed Darla might have sounded. Amanda was resting comfortably, and there was really nothing Canty could do. 'You can visit, but unless there's been a big change – which Dr Alberness told us not to expect – you won't be able to tell if she even knows you're there.'

'Jesus,' Canty said. 'That's so awful, Lisa.'

'Yes. But she's with people who understand her situation – or understand how to care for people in her situation, at least. And Darla and I will be sure to keep you in the loo—'

Lisey had been pacing around the bedroom with the cordless phone. Now she stopped, staring at the notebook that had slid most of the way from the right rear pocket of her discarded blue jeans. It was Amanda's Little Notebook of Compulsions, only now Lisey was the one who felt compelled.

'Lisa?' Canty was the only one who called her that

on a regular basis and it always made her feel like the sort of woman who showed off the prizes on some TV game show or other – *Lisa, show Hank and Martha what they've won!* 'Lisa, are you still there?'

'Yeah, honey.' Eyes on the notebook. Little rings gleaming in the sun. Little steel loops. 'I said Darla and I will be sure to keep you in the loops. *Loop.*' The notebook was still curved with the shape of the buttock against which it had spent so many hours, and as she looked at it, Canty's voice seemed to be fading. Lisey heard herself saying she was sure Canty would have done all the same things if she'd been the one on the spot. She bent over and slipped the notebook the rest of the way out of the jeans pocket. She told Cantata she would call that evening, told Cantata she loved her, told Cantata goodbye and tossed the cordless phone on the bed without so much as a glance. She had eyes only for the battered little notebook, seventy-nine cents at any Walgreen's or Rexall. And why should she be so fascinated? Why, now that it was morning and she was rested? Clean and rested? With fresh sunshine pouring in, her compulsive search for the cedar box the night before seemed silly, nothing but a behavioral externalization of all the day's anxieties, but this notebook didn't seem silly, no, not at all.

And just to add to the fun, Scott's voice spoke to her, more clearly than ever. God, but that voice was clear! And strong.

I left you a note, babyluv. I left you a bool.

She thought of Scott under the yum-yum tree, Scott in the weird October snow, telling her that sometimes Paul would tease him with a hard bool . . . but never *too* hard.

256

She hadn't thought of that in years. Had pushed it away, of course, with all the other things she didn't want to think of; she'd put it behind her purple curtain. But what was so bad about this?

'He was never mean,' Scott had said. There had been tears in his eyes but none in his voice; his voice had been clear and steady. As always when he had a story to tell, he meant to be heard. 'When I was little, Paul was never mean to me and I was never mean to him. We stuck together. We had to. I loved him, Lisey. I loved him so.'

By now she had flipped past the pages of numbers – poor Amanda's numbers, all crammed madly together. She found nothing but blank pages beyond. Lisey thumbed through them faster and faster, her certainty that there was something here to find waning, then reached a page near the end with a single word printed on it:

HOLLYHOCKS

Why was that familiar? At first it wouldn't come, and then it did. *What's my prize?* she'd asked the thing in Amanda's nightgown, the thing turned away from her. *A drink*, it had said. *A Coke? An RC?* she had asked, and it had said—

'It said . . . she or he said . . . "Shut up, we want to watch the hollyhocks,"' Lisey murmured.

Yes, that was right, or almost right; close enough for government work, anyway. It meant nothing to her, and yet it almost did. She stared at the word a moment or two longer, then thumbed through to the end of the notebook. All the pages were blank. She was about to toss it aside when she saw ghostly words *behind* the last page. She flipped it up and found this printed on the bent inner surface of the notebook's back cover:

4th Station: Look Under the Bed

But before bending to look under the bed, Lisey flipped first back to the numbers at the front of the book and then to **HOLLYHOCKS**, which she had found half a dozen pages from the end, confirming what she already knew: Amanda printed her fours with a right angle and a downward slash, as they had been taught in grammar school: **4.** It was *Scott* who had made fours that looked a little like an ampersand: **4.** It had been *Scott* who looped his *o*'s together and had been in the habit of drawing a line under his jotted notes and memos. And it had always been Amanda's habit to print in tiny capitals . . . with slightly lazy round letters: C's, G's, Y's, and S's.

Lisey flipped back and forth between **HOLLYHOCKS** and *4th Station: Look Under the Bed.* She thought that if she put the two writing samples in front of Darla and Canty, they would without hesitation identify the former as Amanda's work and the latter as Scott's.

And the thing in the bed with her yesterday morning . . .

'It sounded like *both* of them,' she whispered. Her flesh was creeping. She hadn't realized flesh could actually do that. 'People would call me crazy, but it really did sound like both of them.'

Look under the bed.

At last she did as the note instructed. And the only bool she spied was an old pair of carpet slippers.

5

Lisey Landon sat in a bar of morning sun with her legs crossed at the shins and her hands resting on the balls of her knees. She had slept nude and sat that way now; the shadow of the sheers drawn across the east window lay on her slim body like the shadow of a stocking. She looked again at the note directing her to the fourth station of the bool — a short bool, a good bool, a few more and she'd get her prize.

Sometimes Paul would tease me with a hard bool . . . but never too hard.

Never too hard. With that in mind she closed the notebook with a snap and looked at the back cover. There, written in tiny dark letters below the Dennison trade name, was this:

mein gott

Lisey got to her feet and quickly began to dress.

6

The tree closes them in their own world. Beyond is the snow. And under the yum-yum tree is Scott's voice, Scott's hypnotic voice, and did she think *Empty Devils* was his horror story? *This* is his horror story, and except for his tears when he speaks of Paul and how they hung together through all the cutting and terror and blood on the floor, he tells it unfalteringly.

'We never had bool hunts when Daddy was home,' he says, 'only when he was at work.' Scott has for the most part gotten the western Pennsylvania accent out of his talk, but now it creeps in, far deeper than her own Yankee accent, and somehow childish: not *home* but *hum*, not *work* but a strange distortion that comes out *rurk*. 'Paul would always put the first one close by. It might say "5 stations of the bool" – to tell you how many clues there were – and then something like "Go look in the closet." The first one was only sometimes a riddle, but the others almost always were. I member one that said "Go where Daddy kicked the cat," and accourse that was the old well. Another one said "Go where we 'farm all' day." And after a little bit I figured out that meant the old Farmall tractor down in eastfield by the rock wall, and sure enough, there was a station of the bool right there on the seat, held down with a rock. Because a station of the bool was only a scrap of paper, you know, written on and folded over. I almost always got the riddles, but if I was stuck, Paul would give me more clues until I solved it. And at the end I'd get my prize of a Coke or an RC Cola or a candybar.'

He looks at her. Beyond him is nothing but white – a wall of white. The yum-yum tree – it is actually a willow – bends around them in a magic circle, shutting out the world.

He says: 'Sometimes when Daddy got the bad-gunky, cutting himself wasn't enough to let it out, Lisey. One day when he was like that he put me

7

up on the bench in the hall, that was what he had said next, she could remember it now (whether she wanted to or not), but before she could follow the memory deeper into the purple where it had been hidden all this time, she saw a man standing on her back porch stoop. And it *was* a man, not a lawnmower or a vacuum cleaner but an actual man. Luckily, she had time to register the fact that, although he wasn't Deputy Boeckman, he was also dressed in Castle County khaki. This saved her the embarrassment of screaming like Jamie Lee Curtis in a *Halloween* movie.

Her visitor introduced himself as Deputy Alston. He had come to fetch away the dead cat in Lisey's freezer, and also to assure her that he would be checking on her throughout the day. He asked if she had a cell phone and Lisey said she did. It was in the BMW, and she thought it might even be working. Deputy Alston suggested she keep it with her at all times, and that she program the Sheriff's Office into the speed-dial directory. He saw her expression and told her he was prepared to do that for her, if she 'was not conversant with that feature'.

Lisey, who rarely used the little cell phone at all, led Deputy Alston to her BMW. The gadget turned out to be only half-charged, but the cord was in the console compartment between the seats. Deputy Alston reached out to unplug the cigarette lighter, saw the light scattering of ashes around it, and paused.

'Go ahead,' Lisey told him. 'I thought I was going to take the habit up again, but I guess I've changed my mind.'

'Probably wise, ma'am,' Deputy Alston said, unsmiling.

STEPHEN KING

He removed the Beemer's cigarette lighter and plugged in the phone. Lisey had had no idea you could do that; when she thought of it at all, she'd always recharged the little Motorola phone in the kitchen. Two years, and she still hadn't quite gotten used to the idea that there was no man around to read the instructions and puzzle out the meanings of Fig 1 and Fig 2.

She asked Deputy Alston how long the charging-up would take.

'To full? No more than an hour, maybe less. Will you be within reach of a telephone in the meantime?'

'Yes, I've got some things to do in the barn. There's one there.'

'Fine. Once this one's charged, clip it to your belt or hang it on the waistband of your pants. Any cause for alarm, hit the 1-key and bam, you're talking to a cop.'

'Thank you.'

'Don't mention it. And as I said, I'll be checking on you. Dan Boeckman will make this his twenty again tonight unless he has to roll on a call. That'll probably happen – small towns like this, Friday nights are busy nights – but you've got your phone and your speed-dial, and he'll always return here.'

'That's fine. Have you heard anything at all about the man who's been bothering me?'

'Not boo, ma'am,' Deputy Alston said, comfortably enough . . . but of course he could *afford* to be comfortable, no one had threatened to hurt *him*, and quite likely no one would. He stood approximately six-five and probably weighed two hundred and fifty pounds. *Might go one-seventy-five, dressed n hung*, her father might have added; in

Lisbon, Dandy Debusher had been known for such witticisms.

'If Andy hears anything – Deputy Clutterbuck, I mean, he's running things until Sheriff Ridgewick gets back from his honeymoon – I'm sure he'll let you know right away. All you have to do in the meantime is take a few sensible precautions. Doors locked when you're inside, right? Especially after dark.'

'Right.'

'And keep that phone handy.'

'I will.'

He gave her a thumbs-up and smiled when she gave it right back. 'I'll just go on and get that kitty now. Bet you'll be glad to see the last of it.'

'Yes,' Lisey said, but what she really wanted to be rid of, at least for the time being, was Deputy Alston. So she could go out to the barn and check under the bed. The one that had spent the last twenty years or so sitting in a whitewashed chicken-pen. The one they had bought

(mein gott)

in Germany. In Germany where

8

everything that can go wrong does go wrong.

Lisey doesn't remember where she heard this phrase and of course it doesn't matter, but it occurs to her with increasing frequency during their nine months in Bremen: *Everything that can go wrong does go wrong.*

Everything that *can, does.*

The house on the Bergenstrasse Ring Road is drafty

in the fall, cold in the winter, and leaky when the damp and hungover excuse for a spring finally comes. Both showers are balky. The downstairs toilet is a chuckling horror. The landlord makes promises, then stops taking Scott's calls. Finally Scott hires a firm of German lawyers at a paralyzing expense – mostly, he tells Lisey, because he cannot stand to let the sonofabitching landlord get away with it, cannot stand to let him win. The sonofabitching landlord, who sometimes winks at Lisey in a knowing way when Scott isn't looking (she has never dared to tell Scott, who has no sense of humor when it comes to the sono-fabitching landlord), does not win. Under threat of legal action, he makes some repairs: the roof stops leaking and the downstairs toilet stops its horrible midnight laughter. He actually replaces the furnace. A blue-eyed miracle. Then he shows up one night, drunk, and screams at Scott in a mixture of German and English, calling Scott *the American Communist boiling-potter*, a phrase her husband treasures to the end of his days. Scott, far from sober himself (in Germany Scott and sober rarely even exchange postcards), at one point offers the sonofabitching landlord a cigarette and tells him *Goinzee on! Goinzee on, mein Führer, bitte, bitte!* That year Scott is drinking, Scott is joking, and Scott is siccing lawyers on sonofabitching landlords, but Scott isn't writing. Not writing because he's always drunk or always drunk because he's not writing? Lisey doesn't know. It's sixenze of one, half a dozene of the other. By May, when his teaching gig finally, mercifully ends, she no longer cares. By May she only wants to be someplace where conversation in the supermarket or the shops along the high street doesn't sound to her like the manimals in that movie *The*

Island of Dr Moreau. She knows that's not fair, but she also knows she hasn't been able to make a single friend in Bremen, not even among the faculty wives who speak English, and her husband is gone too much at the University. She spends too much time in the drafty house, wrapped in a shawl but still usually cold, almost always lonely and miserable, watching television programs she doesn't understand and listening to trucks rumble around the rotary up the hill. The big ones, the Peugeots, make the floors shake. The fact that Scott is also miserable, that his classes are going badly and his lectures are near-disasters, doesn't help at all. Why in God's name would it? Whoever said *misery loves company* was full of shite. *Whatever can go wrong will go wrong*, however . . . *that* guy was onto something.

When Scott *is* at home, he's in her eye a great deal more than she's used to, because he's not crawling off to the grim little room that's been designated his study to write stories. He *tries* to write them at first, but by December his efforts have become sporadic and by February he's given up entirely. The man who can write in a Motel 6 with eight lanes of traffic pounding by outside and a frat party going on upstairs has come utterly and completely unstrappinzee. But he doesn't brood about it, not that she can see. Instead of writing he spends long, hilarious, and ultimately exhausting weekends with his wife. Often she drinks with him and gets drunk with him, because other than fuck him it's all she can think of to do. There are blue hungover Mondays when Lisey is actually glad to see him going out the door, although when ten P.M. comes and he's still not back, she's always perched by the living room window that looks out on the Ring Road, waiting anxiously for the leased Audi he drives, wondering where he is and who he's drinking with. How *much* he's drinking. There are Saturdays when he persuades her to play strenuous games of hide and seek with him in the big drafty house; he says it will keep them warm, at least, and he's right about that. Or they will chase each other, racing up and downstairs or pounding along the halls in their ridiculous *lederhosen*, laughing like a pair of dopey (not to mention horny) kids, yelling out their German buzzwords: *Achtung!* and *Jawohl!* and *Ich habe Kopfschmerzen!* and – most frequently – *Mein gott!* More often than not these silly games end in sex. With booze or without it (but usually with), Scott always wants sex that winter and spring, and she believes that before they vacate the drafty house on the Bergenstrasse, they have done it in all the rooms, most of the bathrooms (including the one with the hideous laughing toilet), and even some of the closets. All that sex is one of the reasons that she never (well, *almost* never) worries that he's having an affair, in spite of the long hours he's gone, in spite of the hard drinking, in spite of the fact that he's not doing what he was *made* to do, which is to write stories.

But of course she's not doing what *she* was made to do, either, and there are times when that knowledge catches up to her. She can't say he lied to her, or even misdirected her; no, she can never say that. He only told her once, but that one time he was perfectly straight about it: there could be no kids. If she felt she had to have children – and he knew she came from a big family – then they couldn't get married. It would break his heart, but if that was how she felt, that was the way it would have to be. He had told her that under the yum-yum tree, where they'd sat enclosed in the strange October snow. She only permits herself to remember that conversation during the lonely weekday afternoons in Bremen, when the sky always seems to be white and the hour none and the trucks rumble endlessly and the bed shakes beneath her. The bed that he bought and will later insist on having shipped back to America. Often she lies there with her arm over her eyes, thinking that this was a really *terrible* idea in spite of their laughing weekends and their passionate (sometimes febrile) love-making. They have done things in that lovemaking that she wouldn't have credited even six months ago, and Lisey knows these variations have little to do with love; they're about boredom, homesickness, booze, and the blues. His drinking, always heavy, has now begun to scare her. She sees the inevitable crash coming if he doesn't pull back. And the emptiness of her womb has begun to depress her. They made a deal, yeah, sure, but under the yum-yum tree she didn't fully understand that the years pass and time has weight. He may begin to write again when they get back to America, but what will *she* do? *He never lied to me*, she thinks as she lies on the Bremen bed with her arm over her eyes, but she sees a time — and not all that distant — when this fact will no longer satisfy, and the prospect frightens her. Sometimes she wishes she had never sat under that smucking willow with Scott Landon.

Sometimes she wishes she had never met him at all.

9

'That's not true,' she whispered to the shadowy barn, but she felt the deadweight of his study above her as a denial

– all those books, all those stories, all that gone life. She didn't repent her marriage, but yes, sometimes she *did* wish she had never met her troubling and troublesome man. Had met someone else instead. A nice safe computer programmer, for instance, a fellow who made seventy thousand a year and would have given her three children. Two boys and a girl, one by now grown up and married, two still in school. But that was not the life she had found. Or the one that had found her.

Instead of turning immediately to the Bremen bed (that seemed too much, too soon), Lisey turned to her pathetic little excuse for an office, opened the door, and surveyed it. What had she meant to do in here while Scott wrote his stories upstairs? She couldn't remember, but knew what had drawn her here now: the answering machine. She looked at the red **1** glowing in the window with UNPLAYED MESSAGES printed beneath it, and wondered if she should call in Deputy Alston to listen. She decided not to. If it was Dooley, she could play it for him later.

Of course it's Dooley – who else?

She steeled herself for more threats delivered in that calm, superficially reasonable voice and pushed PLAY. A moment later a young woman named Emma was explaining the really *extraordinary* savings Lisey could enjoy by switching to MCI. Lisey killed this rapturous message in mid-flow, pushed ERASE, and thought: *So much for women's intuition.*

She left the office laughing.

10

Lisey looked at the swaddled shape of the Bremen bed with neither sorrow nor nostalgia, although she supposed she and Scott had made love in it – or fucked, anyway; she couldn't remember how much actual *love* there had been during **SCOTT AND LISEY IN GERMANY** – hundreds of times. *Hundreds?* Was that possible during a mere nine-month stretch, especially when there had been days, sometimes whole working weeks, when she didn't see him from the time he sleepwalked out the door at seven A.M. with his briefcase banging his knee to the time he shuffled back in, usually half-lit, at ten P.M. or quarter to eleven? Yes, she supposed it was, if you spent whole weekends having what Scott sometimes called 'smuckaramas'. Why would she hold any affection for this silent sheeted monstrosity, no matter how many times they had bounced on it? She had better cause to hate it, because she understood in some way that wasn't intuitive but was rather the working of subconscious logic *(Lisey's smart as the devil, as long as she doesn't think about it*, she had once overheard Scott telling someone at a party, and hadn't known whether to feel flattered or ashamed) that their marriage had almost broken in that bed. Never mind how nasty-fine the sex had been, or that he'd fucked her to effortless multiple orgasms and tossed her salad until she thought she might go out of her mind from the nerve-popping pleasure of it; never mind the place she'd found, the one she could touch before he came and sometimes he'd just shudder but sometimes he'd scream and that made her go goosebumps

269

all over, even when he was deep inside her and as hot
as . . . well, as hot as a suck-oven. She thought it was
right the goddam thing should be shrouded like an enormous corpse, because – in her memory, at least – everything that had occurred between them there had been
wrong and violent, one chokehold shake after another
on the throat of their marriage. Love? Make *love*? Maybe.
Maybe a few times. Mostly what she remembered was
one uglyfuck after another. Choke . . . and let go. Choke
. . . and let go. And every time it took longer for the
thing that was Scott-and-Lisey to breathe again. Finally
they left Germany. They took the *QE2* back to New
York from Southampton, and on the second day out she
had come back from a walk on the deck and had paused
outside their stateroom with her key in her hand, head
tilted, listening. From inside had come the slow but
steady click of his typewriter, and Lisey had smiled.

She wouldn't allow herself to believe it was all right,
but standing outside that door and hearing his resumption, she had known it *could* be. And it was. When he told
her he'd made arrangements to have what he called the
Mein Gott Bed shipped stateside, she had said nothing,
knowing they would never sleep in it or make love in it
again. If Scott had suggested they do so – *Just vunce, liddle
Leezie, for old dimes' zake!* – she would have refused. In
fact, she would have told him to go smuck himself. If
ever there was a haunted piece of furniture, it was this
one.

She approached it, dropped onto her knees, swept
back the hem of the dropcloth that covered it, and peered
beneath. And there, in that musty, enclosed space where

270

the smell of old chickenshit had come creeping back (*like a dog to its vomit*, she thought), was what she had been looking for.

There in the shadows was Good Ma Debusher's cedar box.

CHAPTER EIGHT

LISEY AND SCOTT
(UNDER THE
YUM-YUM TREE)

1

She had no more than entered her sunny kitchen with the cedar box clasped in her arms when the phone began to ring. She put the box on the table and answered with an absent hello, no longer fearing Jim Dooley's voice. If it was he, she would just tell him she had called the police and then hang up. She was currently too busy to be scared.

It was Darla, not Dooley, calling from the Greenlawn Visitors' Lounge, and Lisey wasn't exactly surprised to find that Darla had the guilts about calling Canty in Boston. And if it had been the other way around, Canty in Maine and Darla in Boston? Lisey thought it would have been about the same deal. She didn't know how much Canty and Darla still loved each other, but they still used each other the way drunks used the booze. When they were kids, Good Ma used to say that if Cantata caught the flu, Darlanna ran her fever.

Lisey tried to make all the right responses, just as she had earlier while on the phone with Canty, and for exactly the same reason: so she could get past this shite and go on with her business. She supposed she would come back to caring about her sisters later – she hoped so – but right now Darla's guilty conscience mattered as little to her as Amanda's gorked-out state. As little as Jim Dooley's current whereabouts, come to that, as long as he wasn't in the room with her, waving a knife.

No, she assured Darla, she hadn't been wrong to call Canty. Yes, she had been right to tell Canty to stay put down there in Boston. And yes indeed, Lisey would be up to visit Amanda later on that day.

'It's horrible,' Darla said, and in spite of her own preoccupation, Lisey heard the misery in Darla's voice. '*She's* horrible.' Then, immediately, in a rush: 'I don't mean that, she's not, of course she's not, but it's horrible to *see* her. She only *sits* there, Lisey. The sun was hitting the side of her face when I was in, the morning sun, and her skin looks so gray and *old* . . .'

'Take it easy, hon,' Lisey said, running the tips of her fingers over the smooth, lacquered surface of Good Ma's box. Even closed she could smell its sweetness. When she opened it, she would bend forward into that aroma and it would be like inhaling the past.

'They're feeding her through a tube,' Darla said. 'They put it in and then take it out. If she doesn't start to eat on her own, I suppose they'll just leave it in all the time.' She gave a huge, watery sniff. 'They're feeding her through a *tube* and she's already so *thin* and she won't *talk* and I spoke to a nurse who said sometimes they go on this way for *years*, sometimes they never come *back*, oh Lisey, I don't think I can *stand* it!'

Lisey smiled a little at this as her fingers moved to the hinges at the back of the box. It was a smile of relief. Here was Darla the Drama Queen, Darla the Diva, and that meant they were back on safe ground, two sisters with well-worn scripts in hand. At one end of the wire is Darla the Sensitive. Give her a hand, ladies and gentlemen. At the other end, Little Lisey, Small But Tough. Let's hear it for her.

'I'll be up this afternoon, Darla, and I'll have another talk with Dr Alberness. They'll have a clearer picture of her condition by then—'

Darla, doubtful: 'Do you really think so?'

Lisey, with no smucking idea: 'Absolutely. And what *you* need is to go home and put your feet up. Maybe take a nap.'

Darla, in tones of dramatic proclamation: 'Oh, Lisey, I could never sleep!'

Lisey didn't care if Darla ate, busted a joint, or took a shit in the begonias. She just wanted to get off the phone. 'Well, you come on back, honey, and take it easy for a little while, anyway. I have to get off the phone – I've got something in the oven.'

Darla was instantly delighted. 'Oh, Lisey! *You?*' Lisey found this extremely annoying, as if she had never cooked anything more strenuous in her life than . . . well, Hamburger Helper. 'Is it banana bread?'

'Close. Cranberry bread. I've got to go check it.'

'But you'll be coming to see Manda later, right?'

Lisey felt like screaming. Instead she said, 'Right. This afternoon.'

'Well, then . . .' Doubt was back. *Convince me*, it said. *Stay on the phone another fifteen minutes or so and convince me.* 'I guess I'll come on home.'

'Good deal. Bye, Darl.'

'And you really don't think I was wrong to call Canty?'

No! Call Bruce Springsteen! Call Hal Holbrook! Call Condi Smucking Rice! Just LEAVE ME ALONE!

'Not at all. I think it's good that you did. Keep her . . .' Lisey thought of Amanda's Little Notebook of Compulsions. 'Keep her in the loop, you know.'

'Well . . . okay. Goodbye, Lisey. I guess I'll see you later.'

'Bye, Darl.'

Click.

At last.

Lisey closed her eyes, opened the box, and inhaled the strong scent of cedar. For a moment she allowed herself to be five again, wearing a pair of Darla's hand-me-down shorts and her own scuffed but beloved Li'l Rider cowboy boots, the ones with the faded pink swoops up the sides.

Then she looked into the box to see what there was, and where it would take her.

2

On top was a foil packet, six or eight inches long, maybe four inches wide and two inches deep. Two lumps poked out of it, rounding the foil. She didn't know what it was as she lifted it out, caught a ghostly whiff of peppermint – had she been smelling it already, along with the cedar-scent of the box? – and remembered even before she unfolded one side and saw the rock-hard slice of wedding cake. Embedded in it were two plastic figures: a boy-doll in morning-coat and top-hat, a girl-doll in a white wedding dress. Lisey had meant to save this for a year and then share it with Scott on their first anniversary. Wasn't that the superstition? If so, she should have put it in the freezer. Instead, it had wound up here.

Lisey chipped off a piece of the frosting with her nail and put it in her mouth. It had almost no taste, just a ghost of sweetness and a last fading whisper of peppermint. They had been married in the Newman Chapel at the University of Maine, in a civil ceremony. All of her sisters had come, even Jodi. Lincoln, Dad Debusher's surviving brother, came up from Sabbatus to give away the bride. Scott's friends from Pitt and UMO had been there, and his literary agent had done the best-man honors. No Landon family, of course; Scott's family was dead.

Below the petrified slice of cake was a pair of wedding invitations. She and Scott had hand-written them, each doing half, and she had saved one of Scott's and one of her own. Below those was a souvenir matchbook. They had discussed having both the invitations and matchbooks printed, it was an expense they probably could have managed even though the money from the *Empty Devils* paperback sale hadn't begun to flow yet, but in the end they had decided on handmade as more intimate (not to mention funkier). She remembered buying a fifty-count box of plain paper matches at the Cleaves Mills IGA and hand-lettering them herself, using a red pen with a fine-point ball. The matchbook in her hand was quite likely the last of that tribe, and she examined it with the curiosity of an archaeologist and the ache of a lover.

Scott and Lisa Landon
November 19th, 1979
'Now we are two.'

Lisey felt tears prick her eyes. *Now we are two* had been Scott's idea, he said it was a riff on a Winnie-the-Pooh title. She remembered the one he meant at once – how many times had she pestered either Jodotha or Amanda into reading her away to the Hundred-Acre Wood? – and thought *Now we are two* was brilliant, perfect. She had kissed him for it. Now she could hardly bear to look at the matchbook with its foolishly brave motto. This was the other end of the rainbow, now she was one, and what a stupid number it was. She tucked the matchbook away in the breast pocket of her blouse and then wiped tears from her cheeks – some few had spilled after all. It seemed investigating the past was wet work.

What's happening to me?

She would have given the price of her pricey Beemer and more to know the answer to that question. She had seemed so all right! Had mourned him and gone on; had put away her weeds and gone on. For over two years now the old song seemed to be true: I get along without you very well. Then she had begun the work of cleaning out his study, and that had awakened his ghost, not in some ethery out-there spirit-world, but in *her*. She even knew when and where it had begun: at the end of the first day, in that not-quite-triangular corner Scott liked to call his

277

memory nook. That was where the literary awards hung on the wall, citations under glass: his National Book Award, his Pulitzer for fiction, his World Fantasy Award for *Empty Devils*. And what had happened?

'I broke,' Lisey said in a small, frightened voice, and sealed the foil back over the fossilized slice of wedding cake.

There was no other word for it. She *broke*. Her memory of it wasn't terribly clear, only that it started because she was thirsty. She went to get a glass of water in that stupid smucking bar alcove – stupid because Scott no longer used the booze, although his adventures with alcohol had lasted years longer than his love-affair with the smokes – and the water wouldn't come, nothing came but the maddening sound of chugging pipes blowing up blasts of air, and she could have waited for the water, it would have come eventually, but instead she turned off the faucets and went back to the doorway between the alcove and the so-called memory nook, and the overhead light was on, but it was the kind on a rheostat and dialed low. With the light like that everything looked normal – everything the same, ha-ha. You almost expected him to open the door from the outside stairway, walk in, crank the tunes, and start to write. Just like he hadn't come unstrapped forever. And what had she expected to feel? Sadness? *Nostalgia?* Really? Something as polite, as dear-dear-lady, as *nostalgia*? If so, that was a real knee-slapper, because what had come over her then, both fever-hot and freezing cold, was

3

What comes over her – practical Lisey, Lisey who always stays cool (except maybe on the day she had to swing the silver spade, and even on that day she flatters herself that she did okay), little Lisey who keeps her head when those all about her are losing theirs – what comes over her is a kind of seamless and bulging rage, a divine fury that seems to push her mind aside and take control of her body. Yet (she doesn't know if this is a paradox or not) this fury also seems to clarify her thinking, *must*, because she finally understands. Two years is a long time, but *the penny finally drops*. She *gets the picture*. She *sees the light*.

He has *kicked the bucket*, as the saying is. (Do you like it?)

He has *popped off*. (Do you love it?)

He is *eating a dirt sandwich*. (It's a big one I caught in the pool where we all go down to drink and fish.)

And when you boil it down, what's left? Why, he has jilted her. Done a runner. Put an egg in his shoe and beat it, hit the road, Jack, took the Midnight Special out of town. He lit out for the Territories. He left the woman who loved him with every cell in her body and every brain in her not-so-smart head, and all she has is this shitty . . . smucking . . . *shell*.

She breaks. Lisey breaks. As she bolts forward into his stupid smucking memory nook she seems to hear him saying *SOWISA, babyluv – Strap On Whenever It Seems Appropriate*, and then that is gone and she begins tearing his plaques and pictures and framed citations from the walls. She picks up the bust of Lovecraft the World Fantasy Award judges gave him for *Empty Devils*, that hateful book, and throws it the length of the study, screaming 'Fuck *you*, Scott, fuck *you!*' It's one of the few times she's used the word in its unvarnished form since the night he put his hand through the greenhouse glass, the night of the blood-bool. She was angry with him then but never in her life has she been so angry with him as she is now; if he were here, she might kill him all over again. She's on a full-bore rampage, tearing all that useless vanity crap off the walls until they are bare (few of the things she throws down break on the floor because of the deep-pile carpet – lucky for her, she'll think later on, when sanity returns). As she whirls around and around, a tornado now for sure, she screams his name again and again, screams *Scott* and *Scott* and *Scott*, crying for grief, crying for loss, crying for rage; crying for him to explain how he could leave her so, crying for him to come back, oh to come back. Never mind *everything the same, nothing* is the same without him, she hates him, she misses him, there's a hole in her, a wind even colder than the one that blew all the way down from Yellowknife now blows through *her*, the world is so empty and so loveless when there's no one in it to holler your name and holler you home. At the end she seizes the monitor of the computer that sits in the memory nook and something in her back gives a warning creak as she lifts it but *smuck* her back, the bare walls mock her and she is raging. She spins awkwardly with the monitor in her arms and heaves it against the wall. There is a hollow shattering noise – *POOMP!*, it sounds like – and then silence again.

No, there are crickets outside.

Lisey collapses to the littered carpet, sobbing weakly, all in. And *does* she call him back somehow? Does she call him back into her life by the very force of her angry delayed grief? Has he come like water through a long-empty pipe? She thinks the answer to that is

4

'No,' Lisey murmured. Because – crazy as it seemed – Scott seemed to have been at work placing the stations of this bool hunt for her *long before he died*. Getting in touch with Dr Alberness, for instance, who happened to have been such a puffickly *huh-yooge* fan. Somehow laying hands on Amanda's medical records and bringing them to lunch, for heaven's sake. And then the kicker: *Mr Landon said if I ever met you, I should ask you about how he fooled the nurse that time in Nashville.*

And . . . when had he put Good Ma's cedar box under the Bremen bed out in the barn? Because surely it had been Scott, she knew she had never put it there.

1996?

(hush)

In the winter of 1996, when Scott's mind had broken and she had

(YOU HUSH NOW LISEY!)

All right . . . all right, she would hush about the winter of '96 – for now – but that felt about right. And . . .

A bool hunt. But *why*? To what purpose? To allow her to face in stages something she couldn't face all at once? Maybe. *Probably*. Scott would know about such things, would surely sympathize with a mind that would want to

281

hide its most terrible memories behind curtains or squirrel them away in sweet-smelling boxes.

A good bool.

Oh Scott, what's good about this? What's good about all this pain and sorrow?

A short bool.

If so, the cedar box was either the end or close to the end, and she had an idea that if she looked much further, there would be no going back.

Baby, he sighed . . . but only in her head. There were no ghosts. Only memory. Only the voice of her dead husband. She believed that; she *knew* it. She could close the box. She could draw the curtain. She could let the past be past.

Babyluv.

He would always have his say. Even dead, he would have his say.

She sighed – it was a wretched, lonely sound to her own ears – and decided to go on. To play Pandora after all.

5

The only other thing she'd squirreled away in here from their cut-rate, non-religious (but it had held for all that, had held very well) wedding day was a photograph taken at the reception, which had been held at The Rock – Cleaves Mills's raunchiest, rowdiest, low-down-and-dirtiest rock-and-roll bar. It showed her and Scott out on the floor as they began the first dance. She was in her white lace dress, Scott in a plain black suit – *My undertaker's suit,* he'd called it – which he'd bought special for the occasion (and had worn again and again on the *Empty Devils* book-tour that winter). In the background she could see Jodotha and Amanda, both of them impossibly young and pretty, their hair up, their hands frozen in mid-clap. She was looking at Scott and he was smiling down at her, his hands on her waist, and oh God, look how long his hair had been, almost brushing his shoulders, she had forgotten that.

Lisey brushed the surface of the photograph with the tips of her fingers, slipping them across the people they'd been back at **SCOTT AND LISEY, THE BEGINNING!** and found she could even remember the name of the band from Boston (The Swinging Johnsons, pretty funny) and the song to which they had danced in front of their friends: a cover of 'Too Late to Turn Back Now,' by Cornelius Brothers and Sister Rose.

'Oh Scott,' she said. Another tear slipped down her cheek and she wiped it away absently. Then she put the photo on the sunny kitchen table and prospected deeper. Here was a thin stack of menus, bar-napkins, and matchbooks from motels in the Midwest, also a program from Indiana University in Bloomington, announcing a reading from *Empty Devils*, by Scott Linden. She remembered saving that one for the misprint, telling him it would be worth a fortune someday, and Scott replying *Don't hold your breath, babyluv*. The date on the program was March 19th, 1980 . . . so where were her souvenirs from The Antlers? Had she taken nothing? In those days she almost always took *something*, it was a kind of hobby, and she could have *sworn*—

She lifted out the 'Scott Linden' program and there

beneath it was a dark purple menu with **The Antlers** and **Rome, New Hampshire** stamped on it in gold. And she could hear Scott as clearly as if he were speaking in her ear: *When in Rome, do as the Romans do.* He'd said it that night in the dining room (empty except for them and a single waitress), ordering the Chef's Special for both of them. And again, later, in bed, as he covered her naked body with his own.

'I offered to pay for this,' she murmured, holding the menu up to her sunny, empty kitchen, 'and the guy said I could just take it. Because we were their only guests. And because of the snowstorm.'

That weird October snowstorm. They had stayed two nights instead of just the one that had been in the plan, and on the second she had remained awake long after Scott had gone to sleep. Already the cold front that had brought the unusual snow was moving out and she could hear it melting, dripping from the eaves. She had lain there in that strange bed (the first of so many strange beds she'd shared with Scott), thinking about Andrew 'Sparky' Landon, and Paul Landon, and Scott Landon – Scott the survivor. Thinking about bools. Good bools and blood-bools.

Thinking about the purple. Thinking about that, too.

At some point the clouds had broken open and the room had been flooded with windy moonlight. In that light she had at last fallen asleep. The next day, a Sunday, they had driven through countryside that was reverting back from winter to fall, and less than a month later they had been dancing to The Swinging Johnsons: 'Too Late to Turn Back Now.'

She opened the gold-stamped menu to see what the

Chef's Special had been that long-ago night, and a photo-graph fell out. Lisey remembered it at once. The owner of the place had taken it with Scott's little Nikon. The guy had scrounged up two pairs of snowshoes (his cross-country skis were still in storage up in North Conway, he said, along with his four snowmobiles), and insisted that Scott and Lisey take a hike along the trail behind the inn. *The woods are magical in the snow*, Lisey remembered him telling them, *and you'll have them all to yourselves — not a single skier or snow machine. It's the chance of a lifetime.*

He had even packed them a picnic lunch with a bottle of red wine on the house. And here they were, togged out in snowpants and parkas and the earmuffs which the guy's amiable wife had found for them (Lisey's parka comically too big, the hem drooping all the way to her knees), standing for their portrait outside a country bed-and-breakfast in what looked like a Hollywood special-effects blizzard, wearing snowshoes and grinning like a couple of cheerful nitwits. The pack Scott wore to hold their lunch and the bottle of *vino* was another loaner. Scott and Lisey, bound for the yum-yum tree, although neither had known it then. Bound for a trip down Memory Lane. Only for Scott Landon, Memory Lane was Freak Alley, and it was no wonder he didn't choose to go there often.

Still, she thought, skating the tips of her fingers over this photograph as she had over the one of their wedding-dance, *you must have known you'd have to go there at least once before I married you, like it or not. You had something to tell me, didn't you? The story that would back up your one non-negotiable condition. You must have been looking for the right spot for weeks. And when you saw that tree, that willow so drooped over with snow it made a grotto inside, you knew you'd found it and you couldn't put it off any longer. How nervous were you, I wonder? How afraid that I'd hear you out and then tell you I didn't want to marry you after all?*

Lisey thought he'd been nervous, all right. She could remember his silence in the car. Hadn't she thought even then that something was on his mind? Yes, because Scott was usually so talkative.

'But you must have known me well enough by then . . .' she began, then trailed off. The nice thing about talking to yourself was that mostly you didn't have to finish what you were saying. By October of 1979 he must have known her well enough to believe she'd stick. Hell, when she didn't tell him to take a hike after he cut his hand to ribbons on a pane of Parks Greenhouse glass, he must have believed she was in for the long haul. But had he been nervous about exposing those old memories, touching those ancient live wires? She guessed about that he'd been *more* than nervous. She guessed about that he'd been scared to smucking death.

All the same he had taken her gloved hand in one of his, pointed, and said, 'Let's eat there, Lisey – let's go under that

6

'Let's eat under that willow,' he says, and Lisey is more than willing to fall in with this plan. For one thing, she's hugely hungry. For another, her legs – especially her calves – are aching from the unaccustomed exercise involved in using the snowshoes: lift, twist, and *shake* . . . lift, twist, and *shake*. Mostly, though, she wants a rest from looking at the ceaselessly falling snow. The walk has been every bit as gorgeous as the innkeeper promised, and the quiet is something she thinks she'll remember for the rest of her life, the only sounds the crunch of their snowshoes, the sound of their breathing, and the restless tackhammer of a far-off woodpecker. Yet the steady downpour (there is really no other word) of huge flakes has started to freak her out. It's coming so thick and fast that it's messed up her ability to focus, and that's making her feel disoriented and a little dizzy. The willow sits on the edge of a clearing, its still-green fronds weighted down with thick white frosting.

Do you call them fronds? Lisey wonders, and thinks she will ask Scott over lunch. Scott will know. She never asks. Other matters intervene.

Scott approaches the willow and Lisey follows, lifting her feet and twisting them to shake off the snowshoes, walking in her fiancé's tracks. When he reaches the tree, Scott parts the snow-covered − fronds, branches, whatever they are − like a curtain, and peers inside. His blue-jeaned butt is sticking out invitingly in her direction.

'Lisey!' he says. 'This is pretty neat! Wait 'til you s—'

She raises Snowshoe A and applies it to Blue-Jeaned Butt B. Fiancé C promptly disappears into Snow-Covered Willow D (with a surprised curse). It's amusing, quite amusing indeed, and Lisey begins to giggle as she stands in the pouring snow. She is coated with it; even her eyelashes are heavy.

'Lisey?' From inside the drooping white umbrella.

'Yes, Scott?'

'Can you see me?'

'Nope,' she says.

'Come a little closer, then.'

She does, stepping in his tracks, knowing what to expect, but when his arm shoots out through the snow-covered curtain and his hand seizes her wrist, it's still a surprise and she shrieks with laughter because she's a bit more than startled; she's actually a little frightened. He pulls her forward and cold whiteness dashes across her face, blinding her for a moment. The hood of her parka is back and snow slides down her neck, freezing on her warm skin. Her earmuffs are pulled askew. She hears a muffled *flump* as heavy clots of snow fall off the tree behind her.

'Scott!' she gasps. 'Scott, you scared m—' But here she stops.

He's on his knees before her, the hood of his own parka pushed back to reveal a spill of dark hair that's almost as long as hers. He's wearing his earmuffs around his neck like headphones. The pack is beside him, leaning against the tree-trunk. He's looking at her, smiling, waiting for her to dig it. And Lisey does. She digs it bigtime. *Anybody would*, she thinks.

It's a little like being allowed in the clubhouse where her big sister Manda and her friends played at being girl pirates—

But no. It's better than that, because it doesn't smell of ancient wood and damp magazines and moldy old mouseshit. It's as if he's taken her into an entirely different world, pulled her into a secret circle, a white-roofed dome that belongs to nobody but them. It's about twenty feet across. In the center is the trunk of the willow. The grass growing out from it is still the perfect green of summer.

'Oh, Scott,' she says, and no vapor comes out of her mouth. It's *warm* in here, she realizes. The snow caught on the drooping branches has insulated the space beneath. She unzips her jacket.

'Neat, isn't it? Now listen to the quiet.'

He falls silent. So does she. At first she thinks there's no sound at all, but that's not quite right. There's one. She can hear a slow drum muffled in velvet. It's her heart. He reaches out, strips off her gloves, takes her hands. He kisses each palm, deep in the center of the cup. For a moment neither of them says anything. It's Lisey who breaks the silence; her stomach rumbles. Scott bursts into laughter, falling back against the trunk of the tree and pointing at her.

'Me too,' he says. 'I wanted to skin you out of those snowpants and screw in here, Lisey — it's warm enough — but after all that exercise, I'm too hungry.'

'Maybe later,' she says. Knowing that later she'll almost certainly be too full for screwing, but that's okay; if the snow keeps up, they'll almost certainly be spending another night here at The Antlers, and that's fine with her.

She opens the pack and lays out lunch. There are two thick chicken sandwiches (lots of mayo), salad, and two hefty slices of what proves to be raisin pie. 'Yum,' he says as she hands him one of the paper plates.

'Of course yum,' she says. 'We're under the yum-yum tree.'

He laughs. 'Under the yum-yum tree. I like it.' Then his smile fades and he looks at her solemnly. 'It's nice here, isn't it?'

'Yes, Scott. Very nice.'

He leans over the food; she leans to meet him; they kiss above the salad. 'I love you, little Lisey.'

'I love you, too.' And at that moment, hidden away from the world in this green and secret circle of silence, she has never loved him more. This is now.

7

Despite his profession of hunger, Scott eats only half his sandwich and a few bites of salad. The raisin pie he doesn't touch at all, but he drinks more than his share of the wine. Lisey eats with better appetite, but not quite as heartily as she thought she would. There's a worm of unease gnawing at her. Whatever has been on Scott's mind, the telling will be hard for him and maybe even harder for her. What makes her most uneasy is that she can't think what it might be. Some kind of trouble with the law back in the rural western Pennsylvania town where he grew up? Did he perhaps father a child? Was there maybe even some kind of teenage marriage, a quickie job that ended in a divorce or an annulment two months later? Is it Paul, the brother who died? Whatever it is, it's coming now. *Sure as rain follows thunder*, Good Ma would have said. He looks at his slice of pie, seems to think about taking a bite, then pulls out his cigarettes instead.

She remembers his saying *Families suck* and thinks, *It's the bools. He brought me here to tell me about the bools.* She isn't surprised to find the thought scares her badly.

'Lisey,' he says. 'There's something I have to explain. And if it changes your mind about marrying m—'

'Scott, I'm not sure I want to hear—'

His grin is both weary and frightened. 'I bet you're not. And I know I don't want to tell. But it's like getting a shot at the doctor's office . . . no, worse, like getting a cyst opened up or a carbuncle lanced. But some things just have to be done.' His brilliant hazel eyes are fixed on hers. 'Lisey, if we get married, we can't have kids. That's flat. I don't know how badly you want them right now, but you come from a big family and I guess it'd be natural for you to want to fill up a big house with a big family of your own someday. You need to know that if you're with me, that can't happen. And I don't want you to be facing me across a room somewhere five or ten years down the line and screaming "You never told me this was part of the deal."'

He draws on his cigarette and jets smoke from his nostrils. It rises in a blue-gray fume. He turns back to her. His face is very pale, his eyes enormous. *Like jewels*, she thinks, fascinated. For the first and only time she sees him not as handsome (which he is not, although in the right light he can be striking) but as beautiful, the way some women are beautiful. This fascinates her, and for some reason horrifies her.

'I love you too much to lie to you, Lisey. I love you with all that passes for my heart. I suspect that kind of all-out love becomes a burden to a woman in time, but it's the only kind I have to give. I think we're going to be quite a wealthy couple in terms of money, but I'll almost certainly be an emotional pauper all my life. I've got the money coming, but as for the rest I've got just enough for you, and I won't ever dirty it or dilute it with lies. Not with the words I say, not with the ones I hold back.' He sighs – a long, shuddering sound – and places the heel of the hand holding the cigarette against the center of his brow, as if his head hurts. Then he takes it away and looks at her again. 'No kids, Lisey. We can't. *I* can't.'

'Scott, are you . . . did a doctor . . .'

He's shaking his head. 'It's not physical. Listen, babyluv. It's here.' He taps his forehead, between the eyes. 'Lunacy and the Landons go together like peaches and cream, and I'm not talking about an Edgar Allan Poe story or any genteel Victorian we-keep-auntie-in-the-attic ladies' novel; I'm talking about the real-world dangerous kind that runs in the blood.'

'Scott, you're not crazy—' But she's thinking about his walking out of the dark and holding the bleeding ruins of his hand out to her, his voice full of jubilation and relief. *Crazy* relief. She's remembering her own thought as she wrapped that ruin in her blouse: that he might be in love with her, but he was also half in love with death.

'I *am*,' he says softly. 'I *am* crazy. I have delusions and visions. I write them down, that's all. I write them down and people pay me to read them.'

For a moment she's too stunned by this (or maybe it's the memory of his mangled hand, which she has deliberately put away from her, that has stunned her) to reply. He is speaking of his craft – that is always how he refers to it in his lectures, never as his *art* but as his *craft* – as delusion. And that *is* madness.

'Scott,' she says at last, 'writing's your *job*.'

'You think you understand that,' he says, 'but you don't understand the *gone* part. I hope you stay lucky that

292

way, little Lisey. And I'm not going to sit here under this tree and give you the history of the Landons, because I only know a little. I went back three generations, got scared of all the blood I was finding on the walls, and quit. I saw enough blood – some of it my own – when I was a kid. Took my Daddy's word for the rest. When I was a kid, Daddy said that the Landons – and the Landreaus before them – split into two types: gomers and bad-gunky. Bad-gunky was better, because you could let it out by cutting. You *had* to cut, if you didn't want to spend your life in the bughouse or the jailhouse. He said it was the only way.'

'Are you talking about self-mutilation, Scott?'

He shrugs, as if unsure. She is unsure, as well. She has seen him naked, after all. He has a few scars, but only a few.

'Blood-bools?' she asks.

This time he's more positive. 'Blood-bools, yeah.'

'That night when you stuck your hand through the greenhouse glass, were you letting out the bad-gunky?'

'I suppose. Sure. In a way.' He stubs his cigarette in the grass. He takes a long time, and doesn't look at her while he does it. 'It's complicated. You have to remember how terrible I felt that night, a lot of things had been piling up—'

'I should never have—'

'No,' he says, 'let me finish. I can only say this once.' She stills.

'I was drunk, I was feeling terrible, and I hadn't let it out – *it* – in a long time. I hadn't had to. Mostly because of you, Lisey.'

Lisey has a sister who went through an alarming bout

of self-mutilation in her early twenties. Amanda's past all that now – thank God – but she bears the scars, mostly high on her inner arms and thighs. 'Scott, if you've been cutting yourself, shouldn't you have scars—'

It's as if he hasn't heard her. 'Then last spring, long after I thought he'd shut up for good, I be good-goddam if he didn't start up talking to me again. "It runs in you, Scoot," I'd hear him say. "It runs in your blood just like a sweetmother. Don't it?"'

'Who, Scott? Who started talking to you?' Knowing it's either Paul or his father, and probably not Paul.

'Daddy. He says, "Scooter, if you want to be righteous, you better let that bad-gunky out. Get after it, now, don't smuckin wait.' So I did. Little . . . little . . .' He makes small cutting gestures – one on his cheek, one on his arm – to illustrate. 'Then that night, when you were mad . . .' He shrugs. 'I got after the rest. Over and done with. Over and out. And we 'us fine. We 'us *fine*. Tell you one thing, I'd bleed myself dry like a hog on a chain before I'd hurt you. Before I'd *ever* hurt you.' His face draws down in an expression of contempt she has never seen before. 'I ain't never yet been like *him*. My Daddy.' And then, almost spitting it: 'Fuckin Mister *Sparky*.'

She doesn't speak. She doesn't dare. Isn't sure she could, anyway. For the first time in months she wonders how he could cut his hand so badly and have so little scarring. Surely it isn't possible. She thinks: *His hand wasn't just cut; his hand was mangled.*

Scott, meanwhile, has lit another Herbert Tareyton with hands that are shaking just the smallest bit. 'I'll tell you a story,' he says. 'Just one story, and let it stand for all the stories of a certain man's childhood. Because stories are what I do.' He looks at the rising cigarette smoke. 'I net them from the pool. I've told you about the pool, right?'

'Yes, Scott. Where we all go down to drink.'

'Yep. And cast our nets. Sometimes the really brave fisherfolk – the Austens, the Dostoevskys, the Faulkners – even launch boats and go out to where the big ones swim, but that pool is tricky. It's bigger than it looks, it's deeper than any man can tell, and it changes its aspect, especially after dark.'

She says nothing to this. His hand slips around her neck. At some point it steals inside her unzipped parka to cup her breast. Not out of lust, she's quite sure; for comfort.

'All right,' he says. 'Story-time. Close your eyes, little Lisey.'

She closes them. For a moment all is dark as well as silent under the yum-yum tree, but she isn't afraid; there's the smell of him and the bulk of him beside her; there's the feel of his hand, currently resting on the rod of her collarbone. He could choke her easily with that hand, but she doesn't need him to tell her he'd never hurt her, at least not physically; this is just a thing Lisey knows. He will cause her pain, yes, but mostly with his mouth. His everlasting *mouth*.

'All right,' says the man she will marry in less than a month. 'This story might have four parts. Part One is called "Scooter on the Bench".

'Once upon a time there was a boy, a skinny little frightened boy named Scott, only when his Daddy got in the bad-gunky and cutting himself wasn't enough to let it out, his Daddy called him Scooter. And one day – one bad, mad day – the little boy stood up on a high place, looking down at a polished wooden plain far below, and watching as his brother's blood

8

runs slowly along the crack between two boards.

—*Jump*, his father tells him. Not for the first time, either. —*Jump, you little bastard, you sweetmother chickenkike, jump right now!*

—*Daddy, I'm afraid! It's too high!*

—*It's not and I don't give a shit if you're afraid or not, you smucking jump or I'll make you sorry and your buddy sorrier, now paratroops over the side!*

Daddy pauses a moment, looking around, eyeballs shifting the way they do when he gets in the bad-gunky, almost *ticking* from side to side, then he looks back at the three-year-old who stands trembling on the long bench in the front hall of the big old dilapidated farmhouse with its million puffing drafts. Stands there with his back pressed against the stenciled leaves on the pink wall of this farm-house far out in the country where people mind their own business.

—*You can say Geronimo if you want to, Scoot. They say sometimes that helps. If you scream it real loud when you jump out of the plane.*

So Scott does, he will take any help he can get, he screams GEROMINO! – which isn't quite right and doesn't help anyway because he still can't jump off the bench to the polished wooden floor-plain so far below.

—Ahhhh, sweet-smockin chicken-kikin Christ.

Daddy yanks Paul forward. Paul is six now, six going on seven, he is tall and his hair is a darkish blond, long in front and on the sides, he needs a haircut, needs to go see Mr Baumer at the barbershop in Martensburg, Mr Baumer with the elk's head on his wall and the faded decal in his window that shows a Merican flag and says I SERVED, but it will be awhile before they go near Martensburg and Scott knows it. They don't go to town when Daddy is in the bad-gunky and Daddy won't even go to work for awhile because this is his vacation from U.S. Gyppum.

Paul has blue eyes and Scott loves him more than anyone, more than he loves himself. This morning Paul's arms are covered with blood, criss-crossed with cuts, and now Daddy goes to his pocketknife again, the hateful pocketknife that has drunk so much of their blood, and raises it up to catch the morning sun. Daddy came downstairs yelling for them, yelling—*Bool! Bool! Get in here, you two!* If the bool's on Paul he cuts Scott and if the bool's on Scott he cuts Paul. Even in the bad-gunky Daddy understands love.

—You gonna jump you coward or am I gonna have to cut him again?

—Don't, Daddy! Scott shrieks. *—Please don't cut im no more, I'll jump!*

—Then do so! Daddy's top lip rolls back to show his teeth. His eyes roll in their sockets, they roll roll roll like he's looking for folks in the corners, and maybe he is, *prolly* he is, because sometimes they hear him talking to folks who ain't there. Sometimes Scott and his brother call them

the Bad-Gunky Folks and sometimes the Bloody Bool
People.

—*You do it, Scooter! You do it, you ole Scoot! Yell Geronimo
and then paratroops over the side! No cowardy kikes in this
family! Right now!*

—*GEROMINO!* he yells, and although his feet
tremble and his legs jerk, he still can't make himself jump.
Cowardy legs, cowardy kike legs. Daddy doesn't give him
another chance. Daddy cuts deep into Paul's arm and the
blood falls down in a sheet. Some goes on Paul's shorts
and some goes on his sneaks and most goes on the floor.
Paul grimaces but doesn't cry out. His eyes beg Scott to
make it stop, but his mouth stays shut. His mouth will not
beg.

At U.S. Gypsum (which the boys call U.S. Gyppum
because it's what their Daddy calls it) the men call Andrew
Landon Sparky or sometimes Mister Sparks. Now his face
looms over Paul's shoulder and his fluff of whitening hair
stands up as if all the lectricity he works with has gotten
inside of him and his crooked teeth show in a Halloween
grin and his eyes are empty because Daddy is gone, he's a
goner, there's nothing in his shoes but the bad-gunky, he's
no longer a man or a daddy but just a blood-bool with
eyes.

—*Stay up there this time and I'll cut off his ear*, says the
thing with their Daddy's lectric hair, the thing standing up
in their Daddy's shoes. —*Stay up there next time and I'll cut
his mothersmuckin throat, I don't give a shit. Up to you, Scooter
Scooter you ole Scoot. You say you love him but you don't love
him enough to stop me cutting him, do you? When all you have
to do is jump off a sweetmother three-foot bench! What do you*

think of that, Paul? What have you got to say to your chick-enkike little brother now?

But Paul says nothing, only looks at his brother, dark blue eyes locked on hazel ones, and this hell will go on for another twenty-five hundred days; seven endless years. *Do what you can and let the rest go* is what Paul's eyes say to Scott and it breaks his heart and when he jumps from the bench at last (to what part of him is firmly convinced will be his death) it isn't because of their father's threats but because his brother's eyes have given him permission to stay right where he is if in the end he's just too scared to do it.

To stay on the bench even if it gets Paul Landon killed.

He lands and falls on his knees in the blood on the boards and begins crying, shocked to find he is still alive, and then his father's arm is around him, his father's strong arm is lifting him up, now in love rather than in anger. His father's lips are first on his cheek and then pressed firmly against the corner of his mouth.

—*See, Scooter old Scooter you old Scoot? I knew you could do it.*

Then Daddy is saying it's over, the blood-bool is over and Scott can take care of his brother. His father tells him he's brave, one brave little sumbitch, his father says he loves him and in that moment of victory Scott doesn't even mind the blood on the floor, he loves his father too, he loves his crazy blood-bool Daddy for letting it be over this time even though he knows, even at three he knows that next time will come.

9

Scott stops, looks around, spies the wine. He doesn't bother with the glass but drinks straight from the bottle. 'It really wasn't much of a jump,' he says, and shrugs. 'Looked like a lot to a three-year-old, though.'

'Scott, my God,' Lisey says. 'How often was he like that?'

'Often enough. A lot of the times I've blocked out. That time on the bench, though, that one's stone clear. And like I said, it can stand for the rest.'

'Was it . . . was he drunk?'

'No. He almost never drank. Are you ready for Part Two of the story, Lisey?'

'If it's like Part One, I'm not sure I am.'

'Don't worry. Part Two is "Paul and the Good Bool". No, I take that back, it's "Paul and the *Best* Bool", and it was only a few days after the old man made me jump off the bench. He got called in to work, and as soon as his truck was out of sight, Paul told me to be good while he went down to Mulie's.' He stops, laughs, and shakes his head as people do when they realize they're being silly. '*Mueller's.* That's what it really was. I told you about going back to Martensburg when the bank auctioned off the home place, right? Just before I met you?'

'No, Scott.'

He looks puzzled – for a moment almost frighteningly vague. 'No?'

'No.' This isn't the time to tell him he's told her next to nothing about his childhood—

Next to nothing? Nothing at all. Until today, under the yum-yum tree.

'Well,' he says (a little doubtfully), 'I got a letter from Daddy's bank – First Rural of Pennsylvania . . . you know, like there was a *Second* Rural out there somewhere . . . and they said it was out of court after all these years and I was set for a piece of the proceeds. So I said what the smuck and went back. First time in seven years. I graduated Martensburg Township High when I was sixteen. Took a lot of tests, got a papal dispensation. Surely I told you *that.*'

'No, Scott.'

He laughs uneasily. 'Well, I did. Go, you Ravens, peck em and deck em.' He makes a cawing sound, laughs more uneasily still, then takes a big glug of wine. It's almost gone. 'The home place ended up going for seventy grand, something like that, of which I got thirty-two hundred, big smogging deal, huh? But anyway, I took a ride around our part of Martensburg before the auction and the store was still there, a mile down the road from the home place, and if you'd told me when I was a kid it was only a mile I would have said you were full of shit up to your tick-tock. It was empty, all boarded up, FOR SALE sign in front but so faded you could hardly read it. The sign on the roof was actually in better shape, and that one said MUELLER'S GENERAL STORE. Only we always called it Mulie's, see, because that 'us what Daddy called it. Like he called U.S. Steel U.S. Beg Borrow and Steal . . . and he'd call The Burg Pittsburgh Shitty . . . and . . . oh dammit, Lisey, am I crying?'

'Yes, Scott.' Her voice sounds faraway to her own ears.

He takes one of the paper napkins that came with the picnic lunch and wipes his eyes. When he puts the napkin down, he's smiling. 'Paul told me to be good when

301

he was gone to Mulie's and I did what Paul said. I always did. You know?'

She nods. You're good for the ones you love. You *want* to be good for the ones you love, because you know that your time with them will end up being too short, no matter how long it is.

'Anyway, when he came back I saw he had two bottles of RC and I knew he was going to make a good bool, and that made me happy. He told me to go in my bedroom and look at my books awhile so he could make it. It took him a long time and I knew it was going to be a *long* good bool, and I was happy about that, too. Finally he hollered to me to come out to the kitchen and look on the table.'

'Did he ever call you Scooter?' Lisey asks.

'Not him, not never. By the time I got out there t' kitchen, he was gone. He 'us hidin. But I knew he 'us watching me. There was a piece of paper on the table that said BOOL! and then it said—'

'Wait a second,' Lisey said.

Scott looks at her, eyebrows raised.

'You were three . . . he was six . . . or maybe going on seven—'

'Right—'

'But *he* could write little riddles and *you* could read them. Not only read them, figure them out.'

'Yes?' Raised eyebrows asking what the big deal is.

'Scott – did your crazy Daddy understand he was abusing a couple of smucking child prodigies?'

Scott surprises her by throwing back his head and laughing. 'That would have been the least of his concerns!'

he says. 'Just listen, Lisey. Because that was the best day I can remember having as a kid, maybe because it was such a *long* day. Probably someone at the Gypsum plant screwed up and the old man had to put in some serious overtime, I don't know, but we had the house to ourselves from eight that morning until sundown—'

'No babysitter?'

He doesn't reply, only looks at her as if she might have a screw loose.

'No neighbor-lady checking in?'

'Our nearest neighbors were four miles away. *Mulie's* was closer. That's how Daddy liked it, and believe me, that's the way people in town liked it, too.'

'All right. Tell me Part Two. "Scott and the Good Bool".'

'"*Paul* and the Good Bool. The Great Bool. The *Excellent* Bool."' His face smooths out at the memory. One to balance the horror of the bench. 'Paul had a notebook with blue-ruled lines, a Dennison notebook, and when he made stations of the bool, he'd take a sheet out and then fold it so he could tear it into strips. That made the notebook last longer, do you see?'

'Yes.'

'Only that day he must have ripped out two sheets or even *three* – Lisey, it was *such* a long bool!' In his remembered pleasure, Lisey can see the child he was. 'The strip on the table said BOOL! – the first one and the last one always said that – and then, right underneath—

10

Right underneath BOOL! it says this in Paul's big and careful capital letters:

1 FIND ME CLOSE IN SOMETHING SWEET! 16

But before considering the riddle, Scott looks at the number, savoring that **16**. Sixteen stations! He is filled with a tingling, pleasurable excitement. The best part of it is knowing Paul never teases. If he promises sixteen stations, there will be fifteen riddles. And if Scott can't get one, Paul will help. Paul will call from his hiding place in a spooky scary voice (it's a Daddyvoice, although Scott won't realize this until years later, when he is writing a spooky scary story called *Empty Devils*), giving hints until Scott *does* get it. More and more often, though, Scott doesn't need the hints. He improves swiftly at the art of solving, just as Paul improves swiftly at the art of making.

Find me close in something sweet.

Scott looks around and almost at once fixes on the big white bowl standing on the table in a mote-filled bar of morning sun. He has to stand on a chair to reach it and giggles when Paul calls out in his spooky Daddyvoice, — *Don't spill it, you mother!*

Scott lifts the lid, and on top of the sugar is another strip of paper with another message printed in his brother's careful capital letters:

**2 I'M WHERE CLIDE USED TO PLAY
WITH SPULES IN THE SUN**

Until he disappeared in the spring, Clyde was their cat and both boys loved him, but *Daddy* didn't love him because Clyde used to *waow* all the time to be let in or out and although neither of them says it out loud (and neither would *ever* dare ask Daddy), they have a good idea that something a lot bigger and a lot meaner than a fox or a fisher got Clyde. In any case, Scott knows perfectly well where Clyde used to play in the sun and hurries there now, trotting down the main hall to the back porch without giving the bloodstains under his feet or the terrible bench so much as a glance (well, maybe just one). On the back porch is a vast lumpy couch that exudes weird smells when you sit down on it. —*It smells like fried farts*, Paul said one day, and Scott laughed until he wet his pants. (If Daddy had been there, wetting his pants would have meant BIG TROUBLE, but Daddy was at work.) Scott goes to this couch now, where Clyde used to lie on his back and play with the spools of thread Paul and Scott would dangle above him, reaching up with his front paws and making a giant boxing shadow-cat on the wall. Now Scott falls on his knees and looks under the lumpy cushions one by one until he finds the third scrap of paper, the third station of the bool, and this one sends him to—

It doesn't matter where it sends him. What matters is that long suspended day. There are two boys who spend the morning ranging in and around a slumped distempered farmhouse far out in the country as the sun climbs slowly in the sky toward depthless shadowless noon. This is a simple tale of shouts and laughter and dooryard dust and socks that fall down until they puddle around dirty ankles; this is a story of boys who are too busy to pee inside and so water the briars on the south side of the house instead. It's about a little kid not that long out of his diapers collecting slips of paper from the foot of a ladder leading up to the barn loft, from under the porch stoop steps, from behind the junked-out Maytag washer in the backyard, and beneath a stone near the old dry well. (—*Don't fall in, you little booger!* says the spooky Daddyvoice, now coming from the high weeds at the edge of the bean field, which has been left fallow this year.) And finally Scott is directed this way:

15 I'M UNDERNEATH YOUR EVERY DREEM

Underneath my every dream, he thinks. *Underneath my every dream . . . where is that?*

—*Need help, you little booger?* the spooky voice intones. —*Because I'm getting hungry for my lunch.*

Scott is, too. It's afternoon, now, he's been at this for *hours*, but he asks for another minute. The spooky Daddyvoice informs him he can have thirty seconds.

Scott thinks furiously. *Underneath my every dream . . . underneath my every . . .*

He's blessedly de-quipped with ideas having to do with the subconscious mind or the id, but has already begun to think in metaphor, and the answer comes to him in a divine, happy flash. He races up the stairs as fast as his small legs will carry him, hair flying back from his tanned and grimy forehead. He goes to his bed in the room he shares with Paul, looks beneath his pillow, and sure enough, there is his bottle of RC Cola — a *tall* one! — along with a final slip of paper. The message on it is the same as always:

16 BOOL! THE END!

He lifts the bottle as he will much later hold up a certain silver spade (a hero is what he feels like), then turns around. Paul comes sauntering in the door, holding his own bottle of RC and carrying the church-key from the Things Drawer in the kitchen.

—*Not bad, Scott-O. Took you awhile, but you got there.*

Paul opens his bottle, then Scott's. They clink the longnecks together. Paul says this is 'having a host', and when you do it you have to make a wish.

—*What do you wish for, Scott?*

—*I wish the Bookmobile comes this summer. What do you wish for, Paul?*

His brother looks at him calmly. In a little while he will go downstairs and make them peanut-butter-and-jelly sandwiches, taking the step-stool from the back porch, where their fatally noisy pet once slept and played, in order to get a fresh jar of Shedd's from the top shelf in the pantry. And he says

11

But here Scott falls silent. He looks at the bottle of wine, but the bottle of wine is empty. He and Lisey have taken off their parkas and laid them aside. It has grown more than warm under the yum-yum tree; it's hot, really just short of stifling, and Lisey thinks: *We'll have to leave soon. If we don't, the snow lying on the fronds will melt enough to come crashing down on us.*

12

Sitting in her kitchen with the menu from The Antlers in her hands, Lisey thought, *I'll have to leave these memories soon, too. If I don't, something a lot heavier than snow will come crashing down on me.*

But wasn't that what Scott had wanted? What he'd planned? And wasn't this bool hunt her chance to strap it on?

Oh, but I'm scared. Because now I'm so close.

Close to what? Close to what?

'Hush,' she whispered, and shivered as if before a cold wind. One all the way down from Yellowknife, perhaps. But then, because she was two-minded, two-hearted: 'Just a little more.'

It's dangerous. Dangerous, little Lisey.

She knew it was, could already see bits of the truth shining through holes in her purple curtain. Shining like eyes. Could hear voices whispering that there were *reasons* why you didn't look into mirrors unless you really had to (especially not after dark and *never* at twilight), *reasons* to avoid fresh fruit after sunset and to fast completely between midnight and six A.M.

Reasons not to unbury the dead.

But she didn't want to leave the yum-yum tree. Not just yet.

Didn't want to leave *him*.

He had wished for the Bookmobile, even at the age of three a very Scott wish. And Paul? What was Paul's

13

'What, Scott?' she asks him. 'What was Paul's wish?'

'He said, "I wish Daddy dies at work. That he gets lectercuted and dies."'

She looks at him, mute with horror and pity.

Abruptly Scott begins stuffing things back into the pack. 'Let's get out of here before we roast,' he says. 'I thought I could tell you a lot more, Lisey, but I can't. And don't say I'm not like the old man, because that's not the point, okay? The point is that *everyone* in my family got some of it.'

'Paul, too?'

'I don't know if I can talk about Paul anymore now.'

'Okay,' she says. 'Let's go back. We'll take a nap, then build a snowman, or something.'

The look of intense gratitude he shoots her makes her feel ashamed, because really, she was *ready* for him to stop – she's taken in all she can process, at least for the time being. In a word, she's freaked. But she can't leave it completely, because she's got a good idea of how the rest of this story must go. She almost thinks she could finish it *for* him. But first she has a question.

'Scott, when your brother went after the RC Colas that morning . . . the prizes for the good bool . . .'

He's nodding, smiling. 'The *great* bool.'

'Uh-huh. When he went down to that little store . . . Mulie's . . . didn't anybody think it was weird to see a six-year-old kid come in all covered with cuts? Even if the cuts were covered with Band-Aids?'

He stops doing up the buckles on the pack and looks

at her very seriously. He's still smiling, but the flush in his cheeks has faded almost entirely; his skin looks pale, almost waxy. 'The Landons are fast healers,' he says. 'Didn't I ever tell you that?'

'Yes,' she agrees. 'You did.' And then, freaked or not, she pushes ahead a little farther. 'Seven more years,' she says.

'Seven, yes.' He looks at her, the pack between his bluejeaned knees. His eyes ask how much she wants to know. How much she *dares* to know.

'And Paul was thirteen when he died?'

'Thirteen. Yes.' His voice is calm enough, but now all the red is gone from his cheeks, although she can see sweat trickling down the skin there, and his hair is limp with it. 'Almost fourteen.'

'And your father, did he kill him with his knife?'

'No,' Scott says in that same calm voice, 'with his rifle. His .30-06. In the cellar. But Lisey, it's not what you think.'

Not in a rage, that's what she believes he's trying to tell her. Not in a rage but in cold blood. That is what she thinks under the yum-yum tree, when she still sees Part Three of her fiancé's story as 'The Murder of the Saintly Older Brother'.

14

Hush, Lisey, hush, little Lisey, she told herself in the kitchen – badly frightened now, and not only because she had been so wrong in what she'd believed about the death of Paul Landon. She was frightened because she was realizing – too late, too late – that what's done can't be undone, and what's remembered must somehow be lived with ever after.

Even if the memories are insane.

'I don't *have* to remember,' she said, bending the menu swiftly back and forth in her hands. 'I don't *have* to, I don't *have* to, I don't *have* to unbury the dead, crazy shite like that doesn't happen, it

15

'It isn't what you think.'

She will think what she thinks, however; she may love Scott Landon, but she isn't bound to the wheel of his terrible past, and she will think what she thinks. She will know what she knows.

'And you were ten when it happened? When your father—?'

'Yes.'

Just ten years old when his father killed his beloved older brother. When his father *murdered* his beloved older brother. And Part Four of this story has its own dark inevitability, doesn't it? There's no doubt in her mind. She knows what she knows. The fact that he was only ten doesn't change it. He was, after all, a prodigy in other ways.

'And did you kill *him*, Scott? Did you kill your father? You did, didn't you?'

His head is lowered. His hair hangs, obscuring his face. Then from below that dark curtain comes a single hard dry barking sob. It is followed by silence, but she can see his chest heaving, trying to unlock. Then:

'I put a pickaxe in his head while he was a-sleepun

311

and then dump him down the old dry well. It was in March, during the bad sleet-storm. I drug him outside by the feet. I tried to take him where Paul was burrit but I coont. I trite, I trite and I trite, but Lisey he woon't go. He was like the firs' shovel. So I dump him down the well. So far as I know he's still there, although when they auctioned the farm I was ... I ... Lisey ... I ... I ... I was *afraid* ... '

He reaches out for her blindly and if she hadn't been there he would have gone right on his face but she *is* there and then they are

They are

Somehow they are

16

'*No!*' Lisey snarled. She threw the menu, now so strenuously bent it was almost a tube, back into the cedar box and slammed the lid. But it was too late. She had gone too far. It was too late because

17

Somehow they're outside in the pouring snow.

She took him in her arms under the yum-yum tree, and then

(boom! bool!)

they are outside in the snow.

18

Lisey sat in her kitchen with the cedar box on the table before her, eyes closed. The sunlight pouring in the east window came through her lids and made a dark red beer soup that moved with the rhythm of her heart – a rhythm that was just now much too fast.

She thought: *All right, that one got through. But I guess I can live with just one. Just one won't kill me.*

I trite and I trite.

She opened her eyes and looked at the cedar box sitting there on the table. The box for which she had searched so diligently. And thought of something Scott's father had told him. *The Landons – and the Landreaus before them – split into two types: gomers and bad-gunky.*

The bad-gunky was – among other things – a species of homicidal mania.

And gomers? Scott had given her the lowdown on those that night. Gomers were your garden-variety cata-tonics, like her very own sister, up there in Greenlawn.

'If this is all about saving Amanda, Scott,' Lisey whis-pered, 'you can forget it. She's my sis and I love her, but not quite that much. I'd go back into that . . . that *hell* . . . for you, Scott, but not for her or anyone else.'

In the living room the telephone began to ring. Lisey jumped in her seat as if stabbed, and screamed.

CHAPTER NINE

LISEY AND THE BLACK PRINCE OF THE INCUNKS (THE DUTY OF LOVE)

1

If Lisey didn't sound like herself, Darla didn't notice. She was too guilty. Also too happy and relieved. Canty was coming back from Boston to 'help out with Mandy'. As if she could. *As if anyone can, including Hugh Alberness and the entire Greenlawn staff*, Lisey thought, listening to Darla prattle on.

You can help, Scott murmured – Scott, who would always have his say. It seemed that not even death would stop him. *You can, babyluv.*

'—entirely her own idea,' Darla was assuring.

'Uh-huh,' Lisey said. She could have pointed out that Canty would still be enjoying her time away with her husband, entirely unaware that Amanda had a problem if Darla hadn't felt the need to call her (hadn't *stuck her oar in*, as the saying was), but the last thing Lisey wanted right now was an argument. What she wanted was to put the damned cedar box back under the *mein gott* bed and see if she could forget she had ever found it in the first place. While talking to Darla, another of Scott's old maxims had occurred to her: the harder you had to work to open a package, the less you ended up caring about what was inside. She was sure you could adapt that to missing items – cedar boxes, for instance.

'Her flight gets into the Portland Jetport just a little past noon,' Darla was saying, all in a rush. 'She said she'd rent a car and I said no, that's silly, I said I'll come down and pick you up.' Here she paused, gathering herself for the final leap. 'You could meet us there, Lisey. If you wanted. We could have lunch at the Snow Squall – just us girls, like in the good old days. Then we could go up to see Amanda.'

Now which good old days would those be? Lisey thought. *The ones when you used to pull my hair, or the ones when Canty used to chase me around and call me Miss Lisa No Tits?* What she said was, 'You go on down and I'll join you if I can, Darl. I've got some things here I have to—'

'More cooking?' Now that she had confessed to guilting Cantata into coming north, Darla sounded positively roguish.

'No, this has to do with donating Scott's old papers.' And in a way, it was the truth. Because no matter how the business with Dooley/McCool turned out, she wanted Scott's study *emptied*. No more dawdling. Let the papers go to Pitt, that *was* undoubtedly where they belonged, but with the stipulation that her professor pal should have nothing to do with them. Woodsmucky could go hang.

'Oh,' Darla said, sounding suitably impressed. 'Well, in *that* case . . .'

'I'll join you if I can,' Lisey repeated. 'If not, I'll see you both this afternoon, at Greenlawn.'

That was jake with Darla. She passed on Canty's flight information, which Lisey obediently wrote down. Hell, she supposed she might even go down to Portland. At the very least it would get her out of the house – away from the phone, the cedar box, and most of the memories that now seemed poised above her head like the contents of some terrible sagging *piñata*.

And then, before she could stop it, one more fell out. She thought: *You didn't just go out from under the willow into the snow, Lisey. There was a little more to it than that. He took you—*

'NO!' she shouted, and slapped the table. The sound of herself shouting was frightening but it did the trick, lopped off the dangerous train of thought cleanly and completely. It might grow back, though – that was the trouble.

Lisey looked at the cedar box sitting on the table. It was the look a woman might give a well-loved dog that has bitten her for no particular reason. *Back under the bed with you*, she thought. *Back under the mein gott bed, and then what?*

'Bool-the-end, that's what,' she said. Then she left the house, crossing the dooryard to the barn, holding the cedar box out before her as if it contained something either breakable or highly explosive.

2

Her office door stood open. From its foot a bright rectangle of electric light lay across the barn floor. The last time Lisey had been in there, she'd left laughing. What she *didn't* remember was if she'd left the door open or shut. She *thought* the light had been off, thought she'd never turned it on in the first place. On the other hand, at one point she'd been absolutely positive that Good Ma's cedar box had been in the attic, hadn't she? Was it possible one of the deputies had gone in there for a peek and left the light on? Lisey supposed it was. She supposed anything was possible.

Clutching the cedar box to her middle almost protectively, she went to the open office door and looked in. It was empty . . . *appeared* to be empty . . . but . . .

Without the least self-consciousness, she applied one eye to the crack between the jamb and the door. 'Zack McCool' wasn't standing back there. No one was. But when she looked into the office again, she could see that the answering machine's message window was once more lit up with a bright red **1**. She went in, tucked the box under one arm, and pushed the PLAY button. There was a moment of silence, and then Jim Dooley's calm voice spoke.

'Missus, I thought we agreed on eight o'clock last night,' he said. 'Now I see cops around the place. Seems like you don't understand how serious this bi'ness is, although I sh'd think a dead cat in a mailbox would be pretty hard to misunderstand.' A pause. She looked down at the answering machine, fascinated. *I can hear him breathing*, she thought. 'I'll be seeing you, Missus,' he said.

'Smuck you,' she whispered.

'Now Missus, that ain't – *isn't* – nice,' said Jim Dooley, and for a moment she thought the answering machine had, well, answered her. Then she realized this second version of Dooley's voice was in living color, so to speak, and had come from behind her. Once again feeling like an inhabitant in one of her own dreams, Lisey Landon turned around to face him.

3

She was dismayed by his ordinariness. Even standing in the doorway of her little never-was barn office with a gun in one hand (he had what looked like a lunch-sack in the other), she wasn't sure she could have picked him out of a police line-up, assuming the other men in it were also slim, dressed in summerweight khaki workclothes, and wearing Portland Sea Dogs baseball caps. His face was narrow and unlined, the eyes bright blue – the face of a million Yankees, in other words, not to mention six or seven million hillbilly men from the mid- and deep South. He might have been six feet tall; he might have been a little under. The lick of hair which escaped the ball cap's round rim was an unremarkable sandy brown.

Lisey looked into the black eye of the pistol he held and felt the strength run out of her legs. This was no cheap hockshop .22, this was the real deal, a big automatic (she thought it was an automatic) that would make a big hole. She sat down on the edge of her desk. If the desk hadn't been there, she was pretty sure she would have gone sprawling on the floor. For a moment she was almost positive she was going to wet her pants, but she managed to hold her water. For the time being, at least.

'Take what you want,' she whispered through lips that felt Novocain-numb. 'Take all of it.'

'Come upstairs, Missus,' he said. 'We'll talk about it upstairs.'

The idea of being in Scott's study with this man filled her with horror and revulsion. 'No. Just take his papers and go. Leave me alone.'

He stared at her patiently. At first glance he looked thirty-five. Then you saw the little fans of wrinkles at the corners of his eyes and mouth and realized he was five more than that, five at least. 'Upstairs, Missus, unless you want to start this with a bullet in the foot. That'd be a painful way to talk bi'ness. There's a lot of bones and tendons in a person's foot.'

'You won't . . . you don't dare . . . the noise . . .' Her voice sounded farther away with each word. It was as if her voice were on a train, and the train was pulling out of the station; her voice was leaning out of its window to bid her a fond farewell. *Bye-bye, little Lisey, voice must leave you now, soon you'll be mute.*

'Oh, the noise wouldn't fuss me a bit,' Dooley said, looking amused. 'Your next-door neighbors are gone – off to work, I imagine – and your pet cop's off on a run.' His smile faded, yet he still managed to look amused. 'You've come all over gray. Reckon you've had quite a shock to the system. Reckon you're gonna pass clean out, Missus. Save me some trouble if you do, maybe.'

'Stop . . . stop calling me . . .' *Missus* was how she wanted to finish, but a series of wings seemed to be enfolding her, wings of darker and darker gray. Before they grew too dark and too thick to see through, she was faintly

319

aware of Dooley shoving the gun into the waistband of his pants (*Blow your balls off*, Lisey thought dreamily, *do the world a favor*) and darting forward to catch her. She didn't know if he made it. Before the issue was decided, Lisey had fainted.

4

She became aware of something wet stroking her face and at first thought a dog was licking her – Louise, maybe. Except Lou had been their Collie back in Lisbon Falls, and Lisbon Falls had been a long time ago. She and Scott had never had a dog, maybe because they'd never had kids and the two things just naturally seemed to go together like peanut butter and jelly, or peaches and cr—

Come upstairs, Missus . . . unless you want to start this with a bullet in the foot.

That brought her back fast. She opened her eyes and saw Dooley squatting before her with a damp washcloth in one hand, watching her: those bright blue eyes. She tried to pull away from them. There was a metallic rattle, then a dull thud of pain in her shoulder as something snubbed tight and stopped her. *'Ow!'*

'Don't yank and you won't hurt yourself,' Dooley said, as though this were the most reasonable thing in the world. Lisey supposed that to a nutjob like him, it probably was.

There was music playing through Scott's sound-system for the first time in Christ knew how long, maybe since April or May of 2004, the last time he was in here, writing. 'Waymore's Blues.' Not Ole Hank but someone's cover version – The Crickets, maybe. Not super-loud, not cranked the way Scott used to crank the music, but loud enough. She had a very good idea

(I am going to hurt you)

of why Mr Jim 'Zack McCool' Dooley had turned on the sound-system. She didn't

(places you didn't let the boys to touch)

want to think about that – what she wanted was to be unconscious again, actually – but she couldn't seem to help it. 'The mind is a monkey,' Scott used to say, and Lisey remembered the source of that one even now, sitting on the floor in the bar alcove with one wrist apparently hand-cuffed to a waterpipe under the sink: *Dog Soldiers*, by Robert Stone.

Go to the head of the class, little Lisey! If, that is, you can ever go anywhere, ever again.

'Ain't that just the cutest song?' Dooley said, sitting down in the alcove doorway. He crossed his legs tailor-fashion. His brown paper lunch-sack was in the diamond-shaped hole thus formed by them. The pistol lay on the floor beside his right hand. Dooley looked at her sincerely. 'Lot of truth in it, too. You did yourself a favor, you know, passin out the way you did – I tell you what.' Now she could hear the South in his voice, not all showy, like the chickenshit asshole from Nashville, but just a fact of life: *Fayvuh . . . tail yew whut.*

From his sack he took a quart mayonnaise jar with the Hellmann's label still on it. Inside, floating in a puddle of clear liquid, was a crumpled white rag.

'Chloroform,' he said, sounding as proud as Smiley Flanders had been of his moose. 'I was told how to use it by a fella claimed to know, but he also said it was easy to do things wrong. At the very best you would have awoken up with a bad headache, Missus. But I knew you wouldn't want to come up here. I had a tuition about that.'

He cocked a finger at her like a gun, smiling as he did so, and on the sound-system Dwight Yoakam began to sing 'A Thousand Miles from Nowhere'. Dooley must have found one of Scott's homemade honky-tonk CDs.

'May I have a drink of water, Mr Dooley?'

'Huh? Oh, *sure*! Mouth a little dry, is it? A person has a shock to the system, that's gonna happen ever' time.' He got up, leaving the gun where it was – probably out of her reach, even if she lunged to the limit of the hand-cuff chain . . . and to try for it and come up short would be a bad idea, indeed.

He turned on the tap. The pipes chugged and glugged. After a moment or two she heard the faucet begin to spit water. Yes, the gun was probably out of reach, but Dooley's crotch was almost directly over her head, no more than a foot away. And she had one hand free.

As if reading her mind, Dooley said: 'You could ring my chimes a damn good 'un if you wanted, I guess. But these are Doc Martens I'm wearing on my feet, and you're not wearing anything at all on your hands.' From Dooley, *at all* came out one word: *tall*. 'Be smart, Missus, and settle for a nice cool drink. This tap ain't been run much for awhile, but it's clearing out a right smart.'

'Rinse the glass before you fill it,' she said. Her voice sounded hoarse, on the verge of breaking. 'They haven't been used much, either.'

'Roger, wilco.' Just as pleasant as could be. Reminded

her of anyone from town. Reminded her of her own Dad, for that matter. Of course, Dooley also reminded her of Gerd Allen Cole, the original 51–50 Kid. For a moment she almost reached up and twisted his balls anyway, just for daring to put her in this position. For a moment she could barely restrain herself.

Then Dooley was bending down, holding out one of the heavy Waterford glasses. It was three-quarters full, and while the water hadn't run entirely clear, it looked clear enough to drink. It looked wonderful. 'Slow and easy does it,' Dooley said in a solicitous tone. 'I'll let you hold the glass, but if you throw it at me, I'm gonna have to snap your ankle. *Hit* me with it and I'll snap both of em for you, even if you don't draw blood. I mean it, all right?'

She nodded, and sipped her glass of water. On the stereo, Dwight Yoakam gave way to Ole Hank himself, asking the eternal questions: Why don't you love me like you used to do? How come you treat me like a worn-out shoe?

Dooley squatted on his hunkers, his butt almost touching the raised heels of his boots, one arm wrapped around his knees. He could have been a farmer watching a cow drink at a stream in the north forty. She judged he was on alert but not on *high* alert. He didn't expect her to throw the clunky drinking glass, and of course he was right not to expect it. Lisey didn't want her ankles snapped.

Why, I've never even taken that all-important first in-line skating lesson, she thought, *and Tuesday nights are Singles Nights at Oxford Skate Central.*

When her thirst was slaked, she held the glass out to him. Dooley took it, examined it. 'You sure you don't want them – *those* – last two swallows, Missus?' Not even close to *swallers*, and Lisey had a sudden tuition of her own: Dooley was exaggerating the good-old-boy thing. Maybe on purpose, maybe without even realizing it. When it came to language he corrected up because it would have been pretentious to correct down. Did it matter? Probably not.

'I've had enough.'

Dooley polished the last two swallows off himself, his adam's apple sliding in his skinny throat. Then he asked if she was feeling any better.

'I'll feel better when you're gone.'

'Fair enough. I won't take up much of your time.' He tucked the gun back into his waistband and got to his feet. His knees popped and Lisey thought again (marveled, really), *This is no dream. This is really happening to me*. He kicked the glass absently, and it rolled a little way onto the oyster-white wall-to-wall carpet out there in the main office. He hitched up his pants. 'Can't afford to linger in any case, Missus. Your cop'll be back, him or another, and I got an idear you got some kind of sister-twister goin on as well, isn't that so?'

Lisey made no reply.

Dooley shrugged as if to say *Have it your way* and then leaned out of the bar alcove. For Lisey it was a surreal moment, because she had seen Scott do exactly the same thing many times, one hand gripping each side of the door-less doorway, feet on the bare wood of the alcove, head and torso out in the study. But Scott would never have been caught dead in khakis; he had been a bluejeans man to the end. Also, there had been no bald spot at the back of his head. *My husband died with a full head of hair*, she thought.

'Awful nice place,' he said. 'What is it? Converted hayloft? Must be.'

She said nothing.

Dooley continued to lean out, now rocking back and forth a little, looking first left, then right. *Lord of all he surveys*, she thought.

'*Real* nice place,' he said. 'Just about what I would have expected. You got your three rooms – what I'd call rooms – and your three skylights, so there's plenty of natural light. Down home we call places all a-row like this shotgun houses or sometimes shotgun shacks, but ain't nothing shacky about this, is it?'

Lisey said nothing.

He turned to her, looking serious. 'Not that I begrudge him, Missus – or you, now that he's dead. I did some time in Brushy Mountain State Prison. Maybe the Prof told you that. And it was your husbun got me through the worst of it. I read all his books, and you know which one I liked best?'

Of course, Lisey thought. Empty Devils. *You probably read it nine times.*

But Dooley surprised her. '*The Coaster's Daughter.* And I didn't just like it, Missus, I *loved* it. I've made it my bi'ness to read that book ever' two or three years since I found it in the jailhouse library, and I could quote you whole long passages of it. You know what part I like best? Where Gene finally talks back and tells his father he's leaving whether the old man likes it or not. Do you know what he tells that miserable holy-rollin old fuck, pardon my French?'

That he has never understood the duty of love, Lisey thought, but she said nothing. Dooley didn't seem to mind; he was on a roll now, enraptured.

325

'Gene says his old man has never understood the duty of love. The *duty* of *love*! How beautiful is that? How many of us have *felt* something like that but haven't never had the words to *say* it? But your husbun did. For all of us who otherwise would have stood mute, that's what the Prof said. God must have loved your man, Missus, to give him such a tongue.'

Dooley looked up at the ceiling. The cords on his neck stood out.

'The *DUTY*! Of *LOVE*! And the ones God loves best he takes home soonest, to be with Him. Amen.' He lowered his head briefly. His wallet stuck out of his back pocket. It was on a chain. Of course it was. Men like Jim Dooley always wore their wallets on chains that were attached to their belt-loops. Now he looked up again and said: 'He deserved a nice place like this. I hope he enjoyed it, when he wasn't agonizin over his creations.'

Lisey thought of Scott at the desk he called Dumbo's Big Jumbo, sitting before his big-screen Mac and laughing at something he'd just written. Chewing either a plastic straw or his own fingernails. Sometimes singing along with the music. Making arm-farts if it was summer and hot and his shirt was off. That was how he agonized over his smucking creations. But she still said nothing. On the sound-system, Ole Hank gave way to his son. Junior was singing 'Whiskey Bent and Hell Bound'.

Dooley said: 'Giving me the old silent treatment? Well, more power to you, but it won't do you no good, Missus. You have got some correction comin. I won't try to sell you the old one about how it's gonna hurt me more than it's gonna hurt you, but I *will* say I've come to like

your spunk in the short time I've known you, and that it's
gonna – *going to* – hurt both of us. I also want to say I'll
go as easy as I can, because I don't want to break that spirit
of yours. Still – we had an agreement, and you didn't keep
to it.'

An agreement? Lisey felt a chill sweep through her
body. For the first time she got a clear picture of the breadth
and complexity of Dooley's insanity. The gray wings threatened to descend across her vision and this time she fought
them fiercely.

Dooley heard the rattle of the handcuff-chain (he
must have had the cuffs in his sack, along with the mayonnaise jar) and turned to her.

Easy, babyluv, easy, Scott murmured. *Talk to the guy –
run your everlasting mouth.*

This was advice Lisey hardly needed. As long as the
talking was going on, the correctin would remain deferred.

'Listen to me, Mr Dooley. We didn't have an agreement, you're mistaken about that—' She saw his brow begin
to furrow, his look begin to darken, and hurried on.
'Sometimes it's hard to get things together over the phone,
but I'm ready to work with you now.' She swallowed and
heard a distinct click in her throat. She was ready for more
water, a good long cool drink of it, but this didn't seem
like a good time to ask. She leaned forward, fixed his eyes
with her own, blue on blue, and spoke with all the earnest-
ness and sincerity she could muster. 'I'm saying that as far
as I'm concerned, you've made your point. And you know
what? You were just looking at the manuscripts your . . .
um . . . your colleague especially wants. Did you notice the
black file-cabinets in the central space?'

Now he was looking at her with his eyebrows hoisted and a skeptical little smile playing on his mouth ... but that might only be his dickering look. Lisey allowed herself to hope. 'Looked to me like there was a right smart of boxes downstairs, too,' he said. 'More of his books, from the look of them.'

'Those are—' What was she going to tell him? *Those are bools, not books?* She guessed that most of them were, but Dooley wouldn't understand. *They're practical jokes, Scott's version of itchy-powder and plastic vomit?* That he'd understand but likely not believe.

He was still looking at her with that skeptical smile. Not a dickering look at all. No, this was a look that said *While you're at it, why don't you go on and pull the other one, Missus?*

'There's nothing in those cartons downstairs but carbon copies and Xeroxes and blank sheets,' she said, and it sounded like a lie because it *was* a lie, and what was she supposed to say? *You're too crazy to understand the truth, Mr Dooley?* Instead she rushed on. 'The stuff Woodsmucky wants – the good stuff – is all up here. Unpublished stories ... copies of letters to other writers ... their letters back to him ...'

Dooley threw back his head and laughed. 'Woodsmucky! Missus, you got your husbun's way with words.' Then the laughter faded, and although the smile stayed on his lips, there was no more amusement in his eyes. His eyes looked like blue ice. 'So what do you think I sh'd do? Hie over to Oxford or Mechanic Falls and rent a U-Haul, then come back here to load those filing cabinets up? Say, maybe you could get one of those deputy-boys to he'p me!'

'I—'

'Shut up.' Pointing a finger at her. The smile all gone by now. 'Why, if I was to go away and then come back, you'd have a dozen State Police graybacks here waitin for me, I reckon. They'd take me in and Missus, I tell you what, I'd deserve another ten years inside just for believin such a thing.'

'But—'

'And besides, that wadnt – *wasn't* – the deal we made. The deal was that you'd call the Prof, ole Woodsmucky – girl, I *like* that – and he'd send me a e-mail the special way we have, and then *he'd* arrange about the papers. Right?'

Some part of him actually believed this. *Had* to believe it, or why would he keep on with it when it was just the two of them?

'Ma'am?' Dooley asked her. He sounded solicitous. 'Missus?'

If there was a part of him that had to go on telling lies when it was just the two of them, maybe it was because there was a part of him that needed lying to. If so, *that* was the part of Jim Dooley she needed to reach. The part that might still be sane.

'Mr Dooley, listen to me.' She pitched her voice low and kept her delivery slow. It had been the way she talked to Scott when Scott was ready to go off half-cocked over anything from a bad review to a shoddy piece of plumbing. 'Professor Woodbody has no way of getting in touch with you, and down inside somewhere, you know that. But *I* can get in touch with him. I already have. I called him last night.'

'You're lyin,' he said, but this time she wasn't and he

knew she wasn't, and for some reason it upset him. That reaction ran exactly counter to the one she wanted to provoke – she wanted to soothe him – but she thought she had to go on, hoping the sane part of Jim Dooley was in there somewhere, listening.

'I'm not,' she said. 'You left me his number and I called him.' Holding Dooley's eyes with hers. Mustering every bit of sincerity she could manage as she headed back into the Land of Fabrication. 'I promised him the manuscripts and told him to call you off and he said he *couldn't* call you off because he had no way of getting in touch with you anymore, he said his first two e-mails went through, but after that they just bounced ba—'

'One lies and the other swears to it,' Jim Dooley said, and after that things happened with a speed and a ferocity Lisey could hardly credit, although every moment of the beating and mutilation that followed remained vivid in her mind for the rest of her life, right down to the sound of his dry and rapid breathing, right down to the way his khaki shirt strained at the buttons, showing little winks of the white tee-shirt he wore beneath as he slapped her across the face, backhand and then forehand, backhand and then forehand, backhand and then forehand, backhand and then forehand again. Eight blows in all, *eight-eight-lay-them-straight* they chanted as children skip-roping in the dooryard dust, and the sound of his skin on her skin was like dry kindling snapped over a knee, and although the hand he used was ringless – there was that much to be grateful for – the fourth and fifth blows beat the blood from her lips, the sixth and seventh sent it spraying, and the last rode high enough to smash into her nose and set that gushing, as well. By then she was crying in fear and pain. Her head thumped repeatedly against the underside of the bar sink, making her ears ring. She heard herself crying out for him to stop, that he could have whatever he wanted if he would only stop. Then he *did* stop and she heard herself saying, 'I can give you the manuscript of a new novel, his last novel, it's all done, he finished it a month before he died and never got a chance to revise it, it's a real treasure, Woodsmucky'll love it.' She had time to think *That's pretty inventive, what are you going to do if he takes you up on it*, but Jim Dooley wasn't taking her up on anything. He was on his knees in front of her, panting harshly – it was hot up here already, if she'd known she was going to be taking a beating in Scott's study today she certainly would have turned on the air-conditioning first thing – and rummaging in his lunch-sack again. There were big sweat-rings spreading out from under his arms.

'Missus, I'm sorry as hell to do this, but at least it ain't your pussy,' he said, and she had time to register two things before he swept his left hand down the front of her, tearing open her blouse and popping the catch at the front of her bra so that her small breasts tumbled free. The first was that he wasn't sorry a bit. The second was that the object in his right hand had almost certainly come from her very own Things Drawer. Scott had called it *Lisey's yuppie church-key*. It was her Oxo can opener, the one with the heavy-duty rubber handgrips.

CHAPTER TEN

LISEY AND THE ARGUMENTS AGAINST INSANITY (THE GOOD BROTHER)

1

The arguments against insanity fall through with a soft shirring sound.

This line kept going through Lisey's head as she crawled from the memory nook and then slowly across the center space of her dead husband's long and rambling office, leaving an ugly trail behind her: splotches of blood from her nose, mouth, and mutilated breast.

The blood will never come out of this carpet, she thought, and the line recurred, as if in answer: *The arguments against insanity fall through with a soft shirring sound.*

There was insanity in this story, all right, but the only sound she remembered just lately wasn't whirring, purring, *or* shirring; it was the sound of her screams when Jim Dooley had attached her can opener to her left breast like a mechanical leech. She had screamed, and then she had fainted, and then he had slapped her awake to tell her one

332

more thing. After that he'd let her go back under again, but he had pinned a note to her shirt – after considerately pulling off her ruined bra and buttoning the shirt back up, that was – to make sure she wouldn't forget. She hadn't needed the note. She remembered what he'd said perfectly.

'I'd better hear from the Prof by eight tonight, or next time the hurtin will be a lot worse. And tend yourself *by* yourself, Missus, you hear me, now? Tell anyone I was here and I'll kill you.' That was what Dooley had said. To this the note pinned to her shirt had added: *Let's get this business finish, we will both be happier when it is. Signed, your good freind, 'Zack'!*

Lisey had no idea how long she was out the second time. All she knew was that when she came to, the mangled bra was in the wastebasket and the note was pinned to the right side of her shirt. The left side was soaked with blood. She had unbuttoned enough to take one quick peek, then moaned and averted her eyes. It looked worse than anything Amanda had ever done to herself, including the thing with the navel. As to the pain . . . all she could remember was something enormous and obliterating.

The handcuffs had been removed, and Dooley had even left her a glass of water. Lisey drank it greedily. When she tried to get to her feet, however, her legs were trembling too badly to hold her. So she had crawled out of the alcove on all fours, dripping blood and bloody sweat on Scott's carpet as she went (ah, but she'd never cared for that oyster-white anyway, it showed every speck of dirt), hair plastered to her forehead, tears drying on her cheeks, blood drying to a crust on her nose, lips, and chin.

At first she thought she was headed for the phone,

probably to call Deputy Buttercluck in spite of Dooley's admonitions and the failure of the Castle County Sheriff's Department to protect her on its first try. Then that line of poetry

(the arguments against insanity)

started to go through her head and she saw Good Ma's cedar box lying overturned on the carpet between the stairs going down to the barn and the desk Scott had called Dumbo's Big Jumbo. The cedar box's contents were spilled on the carpet in an untidy litter. She understood that the box and its spilled contents had been her destination all along. She especially wanted the yellow thing she could see draped over the bent purple shape of The Antlers menu.

The arguments against insanity fall through with a soft shirring sound.

From one of Scott's poems. He didn't write many, and those he *did* he almost never published – he said they weren't good, and he wrote them just for himself. But she had thought that one *very* good, even though she hadn't been entirely sure what it meant, or even what it was about. She had particularly liked that first line, because sometimes you just heard things *going,* didn't you? They fell down, level after level, leaving a hole you could look through. Or fall into, if you weren't careful.

SOWISA, babyluv. You're bound for the rabbit-hole, so strap on nice and tight.

Dooley must have brought Good Ma's box up to the study because he thought it had to do with what he wanted. Guys like Dooley and Gerd Allen Cole, aka Blondie, aka Monsieur Ding-Dong for the Freesias, thought *every-*

thing had to do with what they wanted, didn't they? Their nightmares, their phobias, their midnight inspirations. What had Dooley thought was in the cedar box? A secret list of Scott's manuscripts (perhaps in code)? God knew. In any case he'd dumped it out, seen nothing but a jumble of uninteresting rickrack (uninteresting to him, at least), and then dragged the widow Landon deeper into the study, looking for a place where he could cuff her up before she regained consciousness. The pipes under the bar sink had done quite nicely.

Lisey crawled steadily toward the scattered contents of the box, her eyes fixed on the yellow knitted square. She wondered if she would have discovered it on her own. She had an idea the answer was no; she had gotten her fill of memories. Now, however—

The arguments against insanity fall through with a soft shirring sound.

So it seemed. And if her precious purple curtain finally came down, would it make that same soft, sad sound? She wouldn't be at all surprised. It had never been much more than spun cobwebs to begin with; look at all she'd already remembered.

No more, Lisey, you don't dare, hush.

'Hush yourself,' she croaked. Her outraged breast throbbed and burned. Scott had gotten his chest-wound; now she had hers. She thought of him coming back up her lawn that night, coming out of the shadows while Pluto barked and barked and barked next door. Scott holding up what had been a hand and was now nothing but a clot of blood with things that looked vaguely like fingers sticking out of it. Scott telling her it was a blood-bool, and it was for her. Scott later soaking that sliced-up meat in a basin filled with weak tea, telling her how it was something

(Paul thought this up)

his brother had shown him how to do. Telling her all the Landons were fast healers, they had to be. This memory fell through to the one beneath, the one where she and Scott were sitting under the yum-yum tree four months later. *The blood fell down in a sheet*, Scott told her, and Lisey asked if Paul soaked his cuts in tea afterward and Scott had said no—

Hush, Lisey – he never said that. You never asked and he never said.

But she *had* asked. She had asked him all sorts of things, and Scott had answered. Not then, not under the yum-yum tree, but later on. That night, in bed. Their second night in The Antlers, after making love. How could she have forgotten?

Lisey lay for a moment on the oyster-white carpet, resting. 'Never forgot,' she said. 'It was in the purple. Behind the curtain. Big difference.' She fixed her eyes on the yellow square and began crawling again.

I'm pretty sure the tea-cure came later, Lisey. Yeah, I know it did.

Scott lying next to her, smoking, watching the smoke from his cigarette go up and up, to that place where it disappeared. The way the stripes on a barber-pole disappear. The way Scott himself sometimes disappeared.

I know, because by then I was doing fractions.

In school?

No, Lisey. He said this in a tone that said more, that said she should know better. Sparky Landon had never been that kind of Daddy. *Me n Paul, we 'us home-schooled. Daddy called public school the Donkey Corral.*

But Paul's cuts that day – the day you jumped from the bench – they were bad? Not just nicks?

A long pause while he watched the smoke rise and stack and disappear, leaving only its trail of sweetish-bitter fragrance behind. At last, flat: *Daddy cut deep.*

To that dry certainty there seemed no possible reply, so she had kept silent.

And then he'd said: *Anyway, that's not what you want to ask. Ask what you want, Lisey. Go ahead, I'll tell you. But you have to ask.*

She either couldn't remember what had come next or wasn't ready to, but now she remembered how they had left their refuge under the yum-yum tree. He had taken her in his arms beneath that white umbrella and they had been outside in the snow an instant later. And now, crawling on her hands and knees toward the overturned cedar box, memory

(insanity)

fell through

(with a soft shirring sound)

and Lisey finally allowed her mind to believe what her second heart, her secret hidden heart, had known all along. For a moment they had been neither under the yum-yum tree nor out in the snow but in *another* place. It had been warm and filled with hazy red light. It had been filled with the sound of distant calling birds and tropical smells. Some of these she knew – frangipani, jasmine, bougainvillea, mimosa, the moist breathing earth upon which they knelt like the lovers they most surely were –

but the sweetest ones were unknown to her and she ached for their names. She remembered opening her mouth to speak, and Scott putting the side of his hand

(hush)

to her mouth. She remembered thinking how strange it was that they should be dressed for winter in such a tropical place, and she saw he was afraid. Then they had been outside in the snow. That crazy downpouring October snow.

How long had they been in the between-place? Three seconds? Maybe even less. But now, crawling because she was too weak and shocked to stand, Lisey was at last willing to own up to the truth of it. By the time they made it back to The Antlers that day, she'd gotten a fair distance toward convincing herself it hadn't happened, but it had.

'Happened again, too,' she said. 'Happened that night.'

She was so smucking thirsty. Wanted another drink of water in the worst way, but of course the bar alcove was behind her, she was going the wrong way for water and she could remember Scott singing one of Ole Hank's songs as they drove back that Sunday, singing *All day I've faced the barren waste, Without a single taste of water, cool water.*

You'll get your drink, babyluv.

'Will I?' Still nothing but a crow-croak. 'A drink of water would surely help. This hurts so bad.'

To this there was no reply, and perhaps she didn't need one. She had finally reached the scatter of objects around the overturned cedar box. She reached out for the yellow square, plucked it off the purple menu, and closed it tight in her hand. She lay on her side – the one that didn't hurt – and looked at it closely: the little lines of knits and purls, those tiny locks. There was blood on her fingers and it smeared on the wool, but she hardly noticed. Good Ma had knitted dozens of afghans out of squares like this, afghans of rose and gray, afghans of blue and gold, afghans of green and burnt orange. They were Good Ma's specialty and spilled from her needles, one after the other, as she sat in front of the chattering TV at night. Lisey remembered how, as a child, she had thought such knitted blankets were called 'africans'. Their female cousins (Angletons, Darbys, Wiggenses, and Washburns as well as Debushers almost beyond counting) had all been gifted with africans when they married; each of the Debusher girls had gotten at least three. And with each african came one extra square in the same shade or pattern. Good Ma called these extra squares 'delights'. They were meant as table decorations, or to be framed and hung on the wall. Because the yellow african had been Good Ma's wedding present to Lisey and Scott, and because Scott had always loved it, Lisey had saved the accompanying delight in the cedar box. Now she lay bleeding on his carpet, holding the square, and gave up trying to forget. She thought, *Bool! The End!*, and began to cry. She understood she was incapable of coherence, but maybe that was all right; order would come later, if it was needed.

And, of course, if there was a later.

The gomers and the bad-gunky. For the Landons and the Landreaus before them, it's always been one or the other. And it always comes out.

It was really no surprise Scott had recognized Amanda for what she was – he'd known about cutting behavior firsthand. How many times had he cut himself? She didn't

339

know. You couldn't read his scars the way you could read Amanda's, because . . . well, because. The one incidence of self-mutilation she knew about for sure – the night of the greenhouse – had been spectacular, however. And he had learned about cutting from his father, who only turned his knife on his boys when his own body would not suffice to let the bad-gunky out.

Gomers and bad-gunky. Always one or the other. It always comes out.

And if Scott had missed the worst of the bad-gunky, what did that leave?

In December of 1995, the weather had turned rottenly cold. And something started going wrong with Scott. He had a number of speaking gigs planned after the turn of the year at schools in Texas, Oklahoma, New Mexico, and Arizona (what he referred to as The Scott Landon 1996 Western Yahoo Tour), but called his literary agent and had him cancel the whole deal. The booking agency screamed blue murder (no surprise there, that was three hundred thousand dollars' worth of speaking dates he was talking about flushing down the commode), but Scott held firm. He said the tour was impossible, said he was sick. He was sick, all right; as that winter sank its claws in deeper, Scott Landon had been a sick man, indeed. Lisey knew as early as November that something

2

She knows *something's* wrong with him, and it isn't bronchitis, as he's been claiming. He has no cough, and his skin's cool to the touch, so even though he won't let her take his temperature, won't even let her put one of those fever-strip thingies on his forehead, she's pretty sure he's not running a fever. The problem seems to be mental rather than physical, and that scares the hell out of her. The one time she gets up enough courage to suggest he go see Dr Bjorn, he just about *tears her head off*, accuses her of being a doctor-junkie 'like the rest of your nutbox sisters'.

And how is she supposed to respond to that? What, exactly, are the symptoms he's displaying? Would any doctor – even a sympathetic one like Rick Bjorn – take them seriously? He's stopped listening to music when he writes, that's one thing. And he's not writing much, that's another, much bigger, thing. Forward progress on his new novel – which Lisey Landon, admittedly no great book critic, happens to love – has slowed from his usual all-out sprint to a labored crawl. Bigger still . . . dear Christ, where's his sense of humor? That boisterous sense of good humor can be wearing, but its sudden absence as fall gives way to cold weather is downright spooky; it's like the moment in one of those old jungle movies where the native drums suddenly fall silent. He's drinking more, too, and later into the night. She has always gone to bed earlier than he does – usually much earlier – but she almost always knows when he turns in and what she smells on his breath when he does. She also knows what she sees in his trashcans up in his study, and as her worries grow, she makes a special point to look every two or three days. She's used to seeing beer cans, sometimes a great lot of them, Scott has always liked his beer, but in December of 1995 and early January of 1996 she also begins to see Jim Beam bottles. And Scott is suffering hangovers. For some reason this bothers her

341

more than all the rest. Sometimes he wanders the house – pale, silent, ill – until the middle of the afternoon before finally perking up. On several occasions she has heard him vomiting behind the closed bathroom door, and she knows by the speed with which the aspirin is disappearing that he's suffering bad headaches. Nothing unusual in that, you might say; drink a case of beer or a bottle of Beam between nine and midnight, you're gonna pay the price, Patrick. And maybe that's all it is, but Scott has been a heavy drinker since the night she met him in that University lounge, when he had a bottle squirreled away in his jacket pocket (he shared it with her), and he's never suffered more than the mildest of hangovers. Now when she sees the empties in his wastebasket and that only a page or two has been added to the *Outlaw's Honeymoon* manuscript on his big desk (some days there are no new pages at all), she wonders just how much more he's drinking than what she knows about.

For a little while she's able to forget her worries in the round of year-end holiday visiting and the jostle of Christmas shopping. Scott has never been much of a shopper even when things are slow and the stores are empty, but this season he throws himself into it with hectic good cheer. He's out with her every smucking day, doing battle at either the Auburn Mall or the Main Street shops in Castle Rock. He's recognized often but cheerfully refuses the frequent autograph requests from people who smell the chance for a one-of-a-kind gift, telling them that if he doesn't stick with his wife, he probably won't see her again until Easter. He may have lost his sense of humor but she never sees him lose his temper, not even when some of the folks who want autographs get pushy, and so for awhile there he seems *sort* of all right, sort of himself in spite of the drinking, the canceled tour, and his slow progress on the new book.

Christmas itself is a happy day, with lots of presents exchanged and an energetic midday tumble in the sack. Christmas dinner is at Canty and Rich's, and over dessert Rich asks Scott when he's going to produce one of the movies made from his novels. 'That's where the *big* money is,' Rich says, seemingly ignorant of the fact that of four film adaptations so far, three have bombed. Only the movie version of *Empty Devils* (which Lisey has never seen) made money.

On the way home, Scott's sense of humor swoops back in like a big old B-1 bomber and he does a killer imitation of Rich that has Lisey laughing until her belly cramps up. And when they arrive back at Sugar Top Hill, they proceed upstairs for a *second* tumble in the sack. In the afterglow Lisey finds herself thinking that if Scott is sick, maybe more people should catch what he has, the world would be a better place.

She wakes around two A.M. on Boxing Day, needing to use the bathroom, and – talk about *déjà vu* all over again – he's not in bed. But this time not *gone*. She has come to know the difference without even letting herself know what she means when she thinks

(gone)

about that thing he sometimes does, that place he sometimes goes.

She urinates with her eyes shut, listening to the wind outside the house. It sounds cold, that wind, but she doesn't

343

know what cold is. Not yet. Let another couple of weeks pass and she will. Let another couple of weeks pass and she'll know all sorts of things.

When she's done with the toilet, she peeks out the bathroom window. This looks toward the barn and Scott's study in the converted hayloft. If he was up there – and when he gets restless in the middle of the night, that is where he usually goes – she'd see the lights, perhaps even hear the happy carnival sounds of his rock-and-roll music, very faint. Tonight the barn is dark, and the only music she hears is the pitchpipe of the wind. This makes her a little uneasy; hatches thoughts in the back of her brain

(heart attack stroke)

that are too unpleasant to completely consider, yet a little too strong, given how . . . how *off* he's been lately . . . to completely dismiss. So instead of sleepwalking back to the bedroom, she goes to the bathroom's other door, the one that gives on the upstairs hall. She calls his name and gets no answer, but she sees a slim gold bar of light shining beneath the closed door at the far end. And now, very faint, she hears the sound of music coming from down there. Not rock and roll but country. It's Hank Williams. Ole Hank is singing 'Kaw-Liga'.

'Scott?' she calls again, and when there's no answer she goes down there brushing the hair out of her eyes, bare feet whispering on a carpet that will later wind up in the attic, frightened for no reason she can articulate, except it has something to do with

(gone)

things that are either finished or should be. *All done and buttoned up*, Dad Debusher might have said; that was one old Dandy caught from the pool, the one where we all go down to drink, the one where we cast our nets.

'Scott?'

She stands before the guest-room door for a moment and a horrible premonition comes to her: he's sitting dead in the rocking chair in front of the television, dead by his own hand, why has she not seen this coming, haven't all the symptoms been on display for a month or more? He has held out until Christmas, held out for her sake, but now—

'Scott?'

She turns the knob and pushes the door open and he's in the rocking chair just as she has imagined him, but very much alive, swaddled in his favorite Good Ma african, the yellow one. On the television, the sound turned low, is his favorite movie: *The Last Picture Show*. His eyes don't move from it to her.

'Scott? Are you okay?'

His eyes don't move, don't blink. She begins to be very afraid then, and in the back of her mind one of Scott's strange words

(gomer)

pops off a haunted assembly line, and she swats it back into her subconscious with a barely articulated

(Smuck it!)

curse. She steps into the room and speaks his name again. This time he *does* blink – thank God – and turns his head to look at her, and smiles. It's the Scott Landon smile she fell in love with the first time she saw it. Mostly the way it makes his eyes turn up at the corners.

'Hey, Lisey,' he says. 'What're you doing up?'

345

'I could ask you the same question,' she says. She looks for booze – a can of beer, maybe a half-finished bottle of Beam – and doesn't see any. That's good. 'It's late, don't you know, late.'

There is a long pause during which he seems to think this over very carefully. Then he says, 'The wind woke me. It was rattling one of the gutters against the side of the house and I couldn't go back to sleep.'

She starts to speak, then doesn't. When you've been married a long time – she supposes *how* long varies from marriage to marriage, with them it took about fifteen years – a kind of telepathy sets in. Right now it's telling her he has something more to say. So she stays quiet, waiting to see if she's right. At first it seems she is. He opens his mouth. Then the wind gusts outside and she hears it – a low quick rattling like the chatter of metal teeth. He cocks his head toward it . . . smiles a little . . . not a nice smile . . . the smile of someone who has a secret . . . and closes his mouth again. Instead of saying whatever it was he meant to say, he looks back at the TV screen, where Jeff Bridges – a very *young* Jeff Bridges – and his best friend are now driving to Mexico. When they get back, Sam the Lion will be dead.

'Do you think you could go to sleep now?' she asks him, and when he doesn't respond, she begins to feel afraid again. 'Scott!' she says, a little more sharply than she intended, and when he returns his eyes to her (reluctantly, Lisey fancies, although he has seen this movie at least two dozen times), she repeats her question more quietly. 'Do you think you could go back to sleep now?'

'Maybe,' he allows, and she sees something that is

both terrible and sad: he is afraid. 'If you sleep spoons with me.'

'As cold as it is tonight? Are you kidding? Come on, turn off the TV and come back to bed.'

He does, and she lies there listening to the wind and luxuriating in the man-driven warmth of him.

She begins to see her butterflies. This is what almost always happens to her when she begins to drift into sleep. She sees great red and black butterflies opening their wings in the dark. It has occurred to her that she will see them when her dying-time comes around. The thought scares her, but only a little.

'Lisey?' It's Scott, from far away. He's drifting, too. She senses that.

'Hmmmm?'

'It doesn't like me to talk.'

'What doesn't?'

'I don't know.' Very faint and far. 'Maybe it's the wind. The cold north wind. The one that comes down from . . .'

The last word might be *Canada*, probably is, but there's no way to tell for sure because by then she's lost in the land of sleep and he is too, and when they go there they never go together, and she is afraid that is also a preview of death, a place where there may be dreams but never love, never home, never a hand to hold yours when squadrons of birds flock across the burnt-orange sun at the close of the day.

3

There's a period of time – two weeks, maybe – when she goes on trying to believe that things are getting better. Later she'll ask herself how she could be so stupid, so willfully blind, how she could mistake his frantic struggle to hold onto the world (and her!) for any kind of improvement, but of course when straws are all you have, you grasp them.

There are some fat ones to grasp at. During the opening days of 1996 his drinking seems to stop entirely, except for a glass of wine with dinner on a couple of occasions, and he trundles out to his study every day. It will only be later – *later, later, percolator*, they used to chant when they were little kids building their first word-castles in the sand at the edge of the pool – that she'll realize he hasn't added a single page to the manuscript of his novel during those days, has done nothing but drink secret whiskey and eat Certs and write disjointed notes to himself. Tucked beneath the keyboard of the Mac he's currently using, she'll find one piece of paper – a sheet of stationery, actually, with **FROM THE DESK OF SCOTT LANDON** printed across the top – upon which he has scrawled *Tractor-chain say youre too late Scoot you old scoot, even now*. It's only when that cold wind, the one all the way down from Yellowknife, is booming around the house that she'll finally see the deep crescent-moon cuts in the palms of his hands. Cuts he could only have made with his own fingernails as he struggled to hold onto his life and sanity like a mountain-climber trying to hold onto a smucking ledge in a sleet-storm. It's only later that she'll find his cache of empty

Beam bottles, better than a dozen in all, and on that one at least she's able to give herself a pass, because those empties were well-hidden.

4

The first couple of days of 1996 are unseasonably warm; it is what the oldtimers call the January Thaw. But as early as January third, the weather forecasters begin warning of a big change, an awesome cold wave rolling down from the white wastes of central Canada. Mainers are told to make sure their fuel-oil tanks are topped up, that their waterpipes are insulated, and that they have plenty of 'warm space' for their animals. Temperatures are going to drop to twenty-five degrees below zero, but the temperatures are going to be the very least of it. They're going to be accompanied by gale-force winds that will drive the chill-factor to sixty or seventy below.

Lisey is frightened enough to call their general contractor after failing to raise any real concern in Scott. Gary assures her that the Landons have got the tightest house in Castle View, tells her he'll keep a close eye on Lisey's kinfolk (especially on Amanda, it almost goes without saying), and reminds her that cold weather is just a part of living in Maine. A few three-dog nights and we'll be on the way to spring, he says.

But when the subzero cold and screaming winds finally roll in on the fifth of January, it's worse than anything Lisey can remember, even casting her mind back to childhood, when every thunderbuster she rode out gleefully as a child seemed magnified into a great tempest and every

349

snow flurry was a blizzard. She keeps all the thermostats in the house turned up to seventy-five and the new furnace runs constantly, but between the sixth and ninth, the temperature inside never rises above sixty-two. The wind doesn't just hoot around the eaves, it screams like a woman being gutted an inch at a time by a madman: one with a dull knife. The snow left on the ground by the January thaw is lifted by those forty-mile-an-hour winds (the gusts kick up to sixty-five, high enough to knock down half a dozen radio towers in central Maine and New Hampshire) and blown across the fields like dancing ghosts. When they hit the storm windows, the granular particles rattle like hail.

On the second night of this extravagant Canadian cold, Lisey wakes up at two in the morning and Scott is gone from their bed once more. She finds him in the guest room, again bundled up in Good Ma's yellow african, once more watching *The Last Picture Show*. Hank Williams warbles 'Kaw-Liga'; Sam the Lion is dead. She has difficulty rousing him, but at last Lisey manages. She asks him if he's all right and Scott says yeah he is. He tells her to look out the window, tells her it's beautiful but to be careful, not to look too long. 'My Daddy said it would burn your eyes when it's that bright,' he advises.

She gasps for the beauty of it. There are great drifting theater curtains in the sky, and they change color as she watches: green goes to purple, purple to vermilion, vermilion to a queer bloody shade of red she cannot name. Russet perhaps comes close, but that isn't it, exactly; she thinks no one has ever named the shade she's seeing. When Scott twitches the back of her nightgown and tells her that's enough, she ought to stop, she's stunned to look at the digital clock built into the VCR and discover that she's been looking out the frost-framed window at the northern lights for ten minutes.

'Don't look anymore,' he says, in the nagging, dragging tones of one who speaks in his sleep. 'Come back to bed with me, little Lisey.'

She's glad enough to go, glad enough to kill that somehow awful movie, to get him out of the rocker and the chilly back room. But as she leads him up the hall by the hand, he says something that makes her skin prickle. 'The wind sounds like the tractor-chain and the tractor-chain sounds like my Daddy,' he says. 'What if he's not dead?'

'Scott, that's bullshit,' she replies, but things like that don't sound like bullshit in the middle of the night, do they? Especially when the wind screams and the sky is so full of colors it seems to be screaming back.

When she wakes up the following night the wind is still howling and this time when she goes down to the guest room the TV isn't on but he's in there watching it anyway. He's in the rocking chair and bundled up in the african, Good Ma's yellow african, but he won't answer her, won't even look at her. Scott is there, but Scott is also gone.

He's gone gomer.

5

Lisey rolled over on her back in Scott's study and looked up at the skylight directly overhead. Her breast throbbed. Without thinking about it, she pressed the yellow knitted square against it. At first the pain was even worse . . . but then there was a small measure of comfort. She looked into the skylight, panting. She could smell the sour brew of sweat, tears, and blood in which her skin was marinating. She moaned.

All the Landons are fast healers, we had to be. If it was true – and she had reason to believe it was – then she had never so much wanted to be a Landon as she did now. No more Lisa Debusher from Lisbon Falls, Mama and Daddy's afterthought, Li'l Tag-Along.

You are who you are, Scott's voice responded patiently. *You're Lisey Landon. My little Lisey.* But it was hot and she hurt so *much*, now *she* was the one who wanted ice, and voice or no voice, Scott Landon had never seemed so smucking dead.

SOWISA, babyluv, he insisted, but that voice was far. Far.

Even the phone on Dumbo's Big Jumbo, from which she could theoretically summon help, seemed far. And what seemed close? A question. A simple one, actually. How could she have found her own *sister* like that and not have remembered finding her *husband* like that during the cold-wave of 1996?

I did remember, her mind whispered to her mind as she lay looking up at the skylight with the yellow knitted square turning red against her breast. *I did. But to remember Scott in the rocker was to remember The Antlers; to remember The Antlers was to remember what happened when we went from under the yum-yum tree out into the snow; to remember that was to face the truth about his brother Paul; to face the true memory of Paul meant doubling back to that cold guest room with the northern lights filling the sky as the wind boomed down from Canada, from Manitoba, all the way from Yellowknife. Don't you see, Lisey? It was all connected, it always has been, and once you allowed yourself to make the first connection, to push over the first domino—*

'I would have gone *crazy*,' she whimpered. 'Like *them*. Like the Landons and the Landreaus and whoever else knows about this. No wonder they went nuts, to know there's a world right next door to this one . . . and the wall between is so *thin* . . .'

But not even that was the worst. The worst was the thing that had so haunted him, the mottled *thing* with the endless piebald side—

'*No!*' she shrieked at the empty study. She shrieked even though it hurt her all the way down. '*Oh, no! Stop! Make it stop! Make these things STOP!*'

But it was too late. And too true to deny any longer, no matter how great the risk of madness. There really was a place where food turned bad, sometimes outright poisonous, after dark and where that piebald thing, Scott's long boy

(I'll make how it sounds when it looks around)
might be real.

'Oh, it's real, all right,' Lisey whispered. 'I saw it.'

In the empty, haunted air of the dead man's study, she began to weep. Even now she didn't know for sure if this was true, and exactly when she had seen it if it was . . . but it *felt* true. The kind of hope-ending thing cancer patients glimpse in their bleary bedside waterglasses when all the medicine is taken and the morphine pump reads **0** and the hour is none and the pain is still in there, eating its steady way deeper into your wakeful bones. And *alive*. Alive, malevolent, and hungry. The kind of thing she was sure her husband had tried, and failed, to drink away. And laugh away. And write away. The thing she had almost seen in his empty eyes as he sat in the chilly guest room with the TV this time blank and silent. He sat in

6

He sits in the rocking chair, wrapped to his staring eyes in Good Ma's hellaciously cheery yellow african. He looks both at her and through her. He doesn't respond to her increasingly frantic repetitions of his name and she doesn't know what to do.

Call someone, she thinks, *that's what*, and hurries back down the hall to their bedroom. Canty and Rich are in Florida and will be until the middle of February, but Darla and Matt are just down the road and it's Darla's number she intends to dial, she's far past worrying about waking them up in the middle of the night, she needs to talk to someone, she needs *help*.

She doesn't get it. The bitter gale, the one that's making her cold even in her flannel nightgown with a sweater thrown on top for good measure, the one that's making the furnace in the cellar run constantly as the house creaks and groans and sometimes even *crrracks* alarmingly, that big cold wind down from Canada, has torn a line down somewhere on the View and all she hears when she picks up the phone is an idiot *mmmmm*. She diddles the phone's cutoff button a couple of times with the tip of her finger anyway, because that's what you do, but she knows it will do no good, and it doesn't. She's alone in this big old converted Victorian house on Sugar Top Hill as the skies bloom with crazy-jane curtains of color and the temperatures drop to regions of cold best left unimagined. If she tries going next door to the Galloways, she knows the chances are good she'll lose an earlobe or a finger — maybe a couple — to frostbite. She might actually freeze to death on their stoop before she can rouse them. This is the kind of cold you absolutely do not fool with.

She returns the useless phone to its cradle and hurries back down the hall to him, her slippers whispering. He is as she left him. The whining '50s-vintage country-music soundtrack of *The Last Picture Show* in the middle of the night was bad but the silence is worse, worse, worst. And just before a giant gust of wind seizes the house and threatens to push it off its foundations (she can hardly believe they haven't lost the electric, surely they will before much longer), she realizes why even the big wind is a relief: she can't hear him breathing. He doesn't look dead, there's even some color in his cheeks, but how does she know he's not?

'Honey?' she murmurs, going to him. 'Hon, can you talk to me? Can you look at me?'

He says nothing, and he doesn't look at her, but when she puts her chilly fingers against his neck, she finds that the skin there is warm and she feels the beat of his heart in the big vein or artery that lies just beneath the skin. And something else. She can feel him reaching out to her. In daylight, even cold daylight, windy daylight (like the kind that seems to pervade all the exteriors in *The Last Picture Show*, now that she thinks of it), she's sure she would scoff at that, but not now. Now she knows what she knows.

He needs help, just as much as he did on that day in Nashville, first when the madman shot him and then as he lay shivering on the hot pavement, begging for ice.

'How do I help you?' she murmurs. 'How do I help you now?'

It's Darla who answers, Darla as she was as a teenager – 'Full of young tits n mean,' Good Ma had once said, an uncharacteristic vulgarity for her, so she must have been exasperated out of all measure.

You aren't gonna help *him, why are you talkin about* helpin *him?* Darla asks, and that voice is so real Lisey can almost smell the Coty face-powder Darla was allowed to use (because of her blemishes) and hear the pop of her Dubble Bubble. And say! She's been down to the pool, and cast her net, and brought back quite a catch! *He's off his rocker, Lisey, popped his cork, lost his marbles, he's riding the rubber tricycle, and the only way you can help him is to call for the men in the white coats as soon as the phone's working again.* Lisey hears Darla's laugh – that laugh of perfect teenage contempt – deep in the center of her head as she looks down at her wide-eyed husband sitting in the rocker. *Help him!* Darla snorts. *HELP him? Cheezus pleezus.*

And yet Lisey thinks she can. Lisey thinks there's a way.

The trouble is that the way to help is possibly dangerous and not at all sure. She's honest enough to recognize that she has made some of the problems herself. She has stowed away certain memories, such as their amazing exit from beneath the yum-yum tree, and hidden unbearable truths – the truth about Paul the Saintly Brother, for instance – behind a sort of curtain in her mind. There's a certain sound

(the chuffing, dear God that low nasty grunting)

behind there, and certain sights

(the crosses the graveyard the crosses in the bloodlight)

as well. She wonders sometimes if everyone has a curtain like that in their minds, one with a *don't-think* zone behind it. They should. It's handy. Saves a lot of sleepless nights. There's all sorts of dusty old crapola behind hers; stuff like-a *dis*, stuff like-a *dat*, stuff like-a *d'other t'ing*. All in all, it's quite a maze. *Oh leedle Leezy, how you amazenzee me*, mein gott . . . and what do the kids say?

'Don't goinzee there,' Lisey mutters, but she thinks she will; she thinks if she is to have any chance of saving Scott, of bringing him back, she *must* goinzee there . . . wherever *there* is.

Oh, but it's right next door.

That's the horror of it.

'You know, don't you?' she says, beginning to weep, but it isn't Scott she's asking, Scott has gone to where the gomers go. Once upon a time, under the yum-yum tree where they sat protected from the world by the strange October snow, he had referred to his job of writing stories as a kind of madness. She had protested – she, practical Lisey, to whom everything was the same – and he had said, *You don't understand the* gone *part. I hope you stay lucky that way, little Lisey.*

But tonight while the wind booms down from Yellowknife and the sky blooms with wild colors, her luck has run out.

7

Lying on her back in her dead husband's study, holding the bloody delight against her breast, Lisey said: 'I sat down beside him and worked his hand out from under the african so I could hold it.' She swallowed. There was a click in her throat. She wanted more water but didn't trust herself to get up, not just yet. 'His hand was warm but the floor

8

The floor is cold even through the flannel of her night-gown and the flannel of her longjohns and the silk panties beneath the longies. This room, like all of them upstairs, has baseboard heat that she can feel if she stretches out the hand that isn't holding Scott's, but it's small comfort. The endlessly laboring furnace sends it up, the baseboard heaters send it out, it creeps about six inches across the floorboards . . . and then, poof! Gone. Like the stripes on the barber's pole. Like cigarette smoke when it rises. Like husbands, sometimes.

Never mind the cold floor. Never mind if your ass turns blue. If you can do something for him, do it.

But what is that something? How is she supposed to start?

The answer seems to come on the next gust of wind. *Start with the tea-cure.*

'He-never-told-me-about-that-because-I-never-asked.' This comes out of her so rapidly it could almost be one long exotic word.

If so, it's an exotic one-word lie. He answered her

358

question about the tea-cure that night at The Antlers. In bed, after love. She asked him two or three questions, but the one that mattered, the *key* question, turned out to be that first one. Simple, too. He could have answered with a plain old yes or no, but when had Scott Landon ever answered *anything* with a plain old yes or no? And it turned out to be the cork in the neck of the bottle. Why? Because it returned them to Paul. And the story of Paul was, essentially, the story of his death. And the death of Paul led to—

'No, please,' she whispers, and realizes she's squeezing his hand far too tight. Scott, of course, makes no protest. In the parlance of the Landon family, he has gone gomer. Sounded funny when you put it that way, almost like a joke on *Hee-Haw.*

Say, Buck, where's Roy?

Well, I tell yew, Minnie – Roy's gone gomer!

(Audience howls with laughter.)

But Lisey isn't laughing, and she doesn't need any of her interior voices to tell her Scott has gone to gomerland. If she wants to fetch him back, first she must follow him.

'Oh God *no*,' she moans, because what that means is already looming in the back of her mind, a large shape wrapped in many sheers. 'Oh God, oh God, do I have to?'

God doesn't answer. Nor does she need Him to. She knows what she needs to do, or at least how she needs to start: she must remember their second night at The Antlers, after love. They had been drowsing toward sleep, and she had thought *What's the harm, it's Saintly Big Brother you want to know about, not Old Devil Daddy. Go ahead and ask him.* So she did. Sitting on the floor with his hand (it's cooling

359

now) folded into hers and the wind booming outside and the sky filled with crazy color, she peers around the curtain she's put up to hide her worst, most perplexing memories and sees herself asking him about the tea-cure. Asking him

9

'After that thing on the bench, did Paul soak his cuts in tea, the way you soaked your hand that night in my apartment?'

He's lying in bed next to her, the sheet pulled up to his hips, so she can see the beginning curl of his pubic hair. He's smoking what he calls *the always fabulous post-coital cigarette*, and the only light in the room is cast down on them by the lamp on his side of the bed. In the rose-dusty glow of that lamp the smoke rises and disappears into the dark, making her wonder briefly

(was there a sound, a clap of collapsing air under the yum-yum tree when we went, when we left)

about something she's already working to put out of her mind.

Meanwhile, the silence is stretching out. She has just about decided he won't answer when he does. And his tone makes her believe it was careful thought and not reluctance that made him pause. 'I'm pretty sure the tea-cure came later, Lisey.' He thinks a little more, nods. 'Yeah, I know it did, because by then I was doing fractions. One-third plus one-fourth equals seven-twelfths, stuff like-a dat.' He grins . . . but Lisey, who is coming to know his repertoire of expressions well, thinks it is a nervous grin.

'In school?' she asks.

'No, Lisey.' His tone says she should know better than this, and when he speaks again, she can hear that somehow chilling childishness

(I trite and I trite)

creeping into his voice. 'Me n Paul, we 'us home-schooled. Daddy called public school the Donkey Corral.' On the night-table beside the lamp is an ashtray sitting on top of his copy of *Slaughterhouse-Five* (Scott takes a book with him everywhere he goes, there are absolutely no exceptions), and he flicks his cigarette into it. Outside, the wind gusts and the old inn creaks.

It suddenly seems to Lisey that perhaps this isn't such a good idea after all, that the good idea would be to just roll over and go to sleep, but she is two-hearted and her curiosity drives her on. 'And Paul's cuts that day – the day you jumped from the bench – were bad? Not just nicks? I mean, you know the way kids see things . . . any busted pipe looks like a flood . . .'

She trails off. There's a very long pause while he watches the smoke from his cigarette rise out of the lamp's beam and disappear. When he speaks again, his voice is dry and flat and certain. 'Daddy cut deep.'

She opens her mouth to say something conventional that will put an end to this discussion (all kinds of warning bells are going off in her head, now; whole banks of red lights are flashing), but before she can, he goes on.

'Anyway, that's not what you want to ask. Ask what you want, Lisey. Go ahead. I'll tell you. I'm not going to keep secrets from you – not after what happened this after-noon – but you have to ask.'

What did *happen this afternoon?* That would seem to

be the logical question, but Lisey understands this cannot be a logical discussion because it's madness they're circling, *madness*, and now she's a part of it, too. Because Scott *took* her somewhere, she *knows* it, *that was not her imagination.* If she asks what happened, he'll tell her, he's as much as said so . . . but it's not the right way in. Her post-coital drowse has departed and she's never felt more awake in her life.

'After you jumped off the bench, Scott . . .'

'Daddy gave me a kiss, a kiss 'us Daddy's prize. To show the blood-bool was over.'

'Yes, I know, you told me. After you jumped off the bench and the cutting was done, did Paul . . . did he go away somewhere to heal? Is that how come he could go to the store for bottles of dope and then run around the house making a bool hunt so soon after?'

'No.' He crushes his cigarette out in the ashtray sitting on top of the book.

She feels the oddest mixture of emotions at that simple negative: sweet relief and deep disappointment. It's like having a thunderhead in her chest. She doesn't know exactly what she was thinking, but that *no* means she doesn't have to think it any mo—

'He couldn't.' Scott speaks in that same dry, flat tone of voice. With that same certainty. 'Paul couldn't. He couldn't go.' The emphasis on the last word is slight but unmistakable. 'I had to take him.'

Scott rolls toward her and takes *her* . . . but only into his arms. His face against her neck is hot with suppressed emotion.

'There's a place. We called it Boo'ya Moon, I forget

362

why. It's mostly pretty.' *Purdy*. 'I took him when he was hurt and I took him when he was dead, but I couldn't take him when he was bad-gunky. After Daddy kilt him I took him there, to Boo'ya Moon, and burrit him away.' The dam gives way and he begins sobbing. He's able to muffle the sounds a little by closing his lips, but the force of those sobs shakes the bed, and for a little while all she can do is hold him. At some point he asks her to turn the lamp out and when she asks him why he tells her, 'Because this is the rest of it, Lisey. I think I can tell it, as long as you're holding me. But not with the light on.'

And although she is more frightened than ever – even more frightened than on the night when he came out of the dark with his hand in bloody ruins – she frees an arm long enough to turn out the bedside light, brushing his face with the breast that will later suffer Jim Dooley's madness. At first the room is dark and then the furniture reappears dimly as her eyes adjust; it even takes on a faint and hallucinatory glow that announces the moon's approach through the thinning clouds.

'You think Daddy murdered Paul, don't you? You think that's how this part of the story ends.'

'Scott, you said he did it with his rifle—'

'But it wasn't murder. They would have called it that if he'd ever been tried for it in court, but I was there and I know it wasn't.' He pauses. She thinks he'll light a fresh cigarette, but he doesn't. Outside the wind gusts and the old building groans. For a moment the furniture brightens, just a little, and then the gloom returns. 'Daddy *could* have murdered him, sure. Lots of times. I know that. There were times he *would* have, if I hadn't been there to help, but in the end that isn't how it was. You know what euthanasia means, Lisey?'

'Mercy-killing.'

'Yeah. That's what my Daddy did to Paul.'

In the room beyond the bed, the furniture once more shivers toward visibility, then once more retreats into shadow.

'It was the bad-gunky, don't you see? Paul got it just like Daddy. Only Paul got too much for Daddy to cut and let out.'

Lisey sort of understands. All those times the father cut the sons – and himself as well, she presumes – he was practicing a kind of wacky preventative medicine.

'Daddy said it mos'ly skip' two generations and then came down twice as hard. "Come down on you like that tractor-chain on your foot, Scoot," he said.'

She shakes her head. She doesn't know what he's talking about. And part of her doesn't want to.

'It was December,' Scott says, 'and there come a cold snap. First one of the winter. We lived on that farm way out in the country with open fields all around us and just the one road that went down to Mulie's Store and then to Martensburg. We were pretty much cut off from the world. Pretty much on our own hook, see?'

She does. She does see. She imagines the postman came up that road once in awhile, and of course 'Sparky' Landon would drive down it in order to get to

(U.S. Gyppum)

work, but that would have been pretty much it. No school busses, because me'n Paul, we 'us home-schooled. The school busses went to the Donkey Corral.

'Snow made it worse, and cold made it worse still –

the cold kept us inside. Still, that year wasn't so bad at first. We had a Christmas tree, at least. There were years when Daddy would get in the bad-gunky . . . or just plain broody . . . and there wouldn't be any tree or any presents.' He gives out a short, humorless laugh. 'One Christmas he must have kept us up until three in the morning, reading from the Book of Revelation, about jars being opened, and plagues, and riders on horses of various shades, and he finally threw the Bible into the kitchen and roared, *"Who writes this smogging bullshit? And who are the morons who believe it?"* When he was in a roaring mood, Lisey, he could roar like Ahab during the last days of the *Pequod.* But this particular Christmas seemed nice enough. Know what we did? We all went up to Pittsburgh together for the shopping, and Daddy even took us to a movie – Clint Eastwood playing a cop and shooting up some city. It gave me a headache, and the popcorn gave me a bellyache, but I thought it was the most wonderful goddam thing I'd ever seen. I went home and started writing a story just like it and read it to Paul that night. It probably stank to high heaven, but he said it was good.'

'He sounds like a great brother,' Lisey says carefully.

Her care is wasted. He hasn't even heard her. 'What I'm telling you is that we were all getting along, had been for months, almost like a normal family. If there is such a thing, which I doubt. But . . . *but.'*

He stops, thinking. At last, he begins again.

'Then one day not long before Christmas, I was upstairs in my room. It was cold – colder than a witch's tit – and getting ready to snow. I was on my bed, reading my history lesson, when I looked out my window and saw

Daddy coming across the yard with an armload of wood. I went down the back stairs to help him stack it in the woodbox so the stovelengths wouldn't get bark all over the floor – that always made him mad. And Paul was

10

Paul is sitting at the kitchen table when his kid brother, just ten years old and needing a haircut, comes down the back stairs with the laces of his sneakers flapping. Scott thinks he'll ask if Paul wants to go out sledding on the hill behind the barn once the wood's in. If Daddy doesn't have any more chores, that is.

Paul Landon, slim and tall and already handsome at thirteen, has a book open in front of him. The book is *Introduction to Algebra*, and Scott has no reason to believe Paul is doing anything other than solving for x until Paul turns his head to look at him. Scott is still three steps from the bottom of the stairs when Paul does that. It is only an instant before Paul lunges at his younger brother, to whom he has never so much as raised a hand in their lives together, but it is long enough to see that no, Paul wasn't just sitting there. No, Paul wasn't just reading. No, Paul wasn't studying.

Paul was *lying in wait*.

It isn't blankness he sees in his brother's eyes when Paul comes surging out of his chair hard enough to knock it skittering back against the wall, but pure bad-gunky. Those eyes are blue no more. Something has burst in the brain behind them and filled them with blood. Scarlet seeds stand in the corners.

Another child might have frozen to the spot and been

killed by the monster who an hour before had been an ordinary brother with nothing on his mind but homework or perhaps what he and Scott could get Daddy for Christmas if they pooled their money. Scott, however, is no more ordinary than Paul. Ordinary children could never have survived Sparky Landon, and it's almost certainly the experience of living with his father's madness that saves Scott now. He knows the bad-gunky when he sees it, and wastes no time on disbelief. He turns instantly and tries to flee back up the stairs. He makes only three steps before Paul grabs him by the legs.

Snarling like a dog whose yard has been invaded, Paul curls his arms around Scott's shins and yanks the younger boy's legs out from under him. Scott grabs the banister and holds on. He gives a single two-word yell – '*Daddy, help!*' – and then is quiet. Yelling wastes energy. He needs all of his to hold on.

He doesn't have enough strength to do so, of course. Paul is three years older, fifty pounds heavier, and much stronger. In addition to these things, he has run mad. If Paul pulls him free of the banister then, Scott will be badly hurt or killed in spite of his quick reaction, but instead of getting Scott, what Paul gets are Scott's corduroy pants and both sneakers, which he forgot to tie when he jumped down off his bed.

(*'If I'd tied my sneakers,' he will tell his wife much later as they lie in bed on the second floor of The Antlers in New Hampshire, 'we're most likely not here tonight. Sometimes I think that's all my life comes down to, Lisey – a pair of untied Keds, size seven.'*)

The thing that was Paul roars, stumbles backward

with a hug of pants in its arms, and trips over the chair in which a handsome young fellow sat down an hour previous to map Cartesian coordinates. One sneaker falls to the bumpy, hillocky linoleum. Scott, meanwhile, is struggling to get going again, to get up to the second-floor landing while there's still time, but his sock feet spin out from under him on the smooth stair-riser and he goes back down to one knee. His tattered underwear has been pulled partway down, he can feel a cold draft blowing on the crack of his ass, and there's time to think *Please God, I don't want to die this way, with my fanny out to the wind.* Then the brother-thing is up, bellowing and casting aside the pants. They skid across the kitchen table, leaving the algebra book but knocking the sugar-bowl to the floor – *knocking it galley-west*, their father might have said. The thing that was Paul leaps for him and Scott is bracing for its hands and the feel of its nails biting into his skin when there's a terrific wooden *thonk!* and a hoarse, furious shout: —*Leave 'im alone, you smuckin bastard! You bad-gunky* fuck!

He forgot all about Daddy. The draft on his ass was Daddy coming in with the wood. Then Paul's hands *do* grab him, the fingernails *do* bite in, and he's pulled backward, his grip on the banister broken as easily as if it were a baby's. In a moment he will feel Paul's teeth. He knows it, this is the real bad-gunky, the *deep* bad-gunky, not what happens to Daddy when Daddy sees people who aren't there or makes a blood-bool on himself or one of them (a thing he does less and less to Scott as Scott grows older), but the real deal, what Daddy meant all the times he'd just laugh and shake his head when they asked him why the Landreaus left France even though it meant leaving all their money and land behind, and they were rich, the Landreaus were rich, and he's going to bite *now*, he's going to bite me *right now*, RAH-CHEER—

He never feels Paul's teeth. He feels hot breath on the unprotected meat of his left side just above the hip, and then there's another heavy wooden *thonk!* as Daddy brings the stovelength down on Paul's head again – two-handed, with all his strength. The sound is followed by a number of loose sliding sounds as Paul's body goes slithering down to the kitchen linoleum.

Scott turns over. He's lying splayed out on the lower stairs, dressed in nothing but an old flannel shirt, his underpants, and white athletic socks with holes in the heels. One foot is almost touching the floor. He's too stunned to cry. His mouth tastes like the inside of a piggybank. That last whack sounded awful, and for an instant his powerful imagination paints the kitchen with Paul's blood. He tries to cry out, but his shocked, flattened lungs can produce only a single dismayed squawk. He blinks and sees that there's no blood, only Paul lying facedown in the sugar from the now defunct bowl, which lies bust in four big and change. *That one'll never dance the tango again*, Daddy sometimes says when something breaks, a glass or a plate, but he doesn't say it now, just stands over his unconscious son in his yellow work coat. There's snow on his shoulders and in his shaggy hair, which is starting to go gray. In one gloved hand he holds the stovelength. Behind him, scattered in the entry like pickup sticks, is the rest of his armload. The door is still open and the cold draft is still blowing in. And now Scott sees there *is* blood, just a little, trickling from Paul's left ear and down the side of his face.

—*Daddy, is he dead?*

Daddy slings the stovelength into the woodbox and brushes his long hair back. There's melting snow in the stubble on his cheeks—*No he aint. That would be too easy.* He tromps to the back door and slams it shut, cutting off the draft. His every movement expresses disgust, but Scott has seen him act so before – when he gets Official Letters about taxes or schooling or things like that – and is pretty sure that what he really is is scared.

Daddy comes back and stands over his floorbound boy. He rocks from one booted foot to the other awhile. Then he looks up at the other one.

—*Help me get him down cellar, Scoot.*

It isn't wise to question Daddy when he tells you to do a thing, but Scott is frightened. Also, he is next door to naked. He comes down to the kitchen and starts pulling his pants on. —*Why, Daddy? What are you going to do with him?*

And for a wonder, Daddy doesn't hit him. Doesn't even yell at him.

—*I'll be smucked if I know. Truss him up down there for a start while I think about it. Hurry up. He won't be out long.*

—*Is it really the bad-gunky? Like with the Landreaus? And your Uncle Theo?*

—*What do you think, Scoot? Get his head, less you want it to bump all the way down. He won't be out long I tell you, and if he starts again, you might not be so lucky. Me either. Bad-gunky's strong.*

Scott does as his father says. It's the nineteen-sixties, it's America, men will soon be walking on the moon, but here they have a boy to deal with who has seemingly gone feral in the turn of a moment. The father simply accepts the fact. After his first shocked questions, the son does, as well. When they reach the bottom of the cellar stairs, Paul begins to stir again and make thick sounds deep in his throat. Sparky Landon puts his hands around his older son's throat and begins to choke him. Scott screams in horror and tries to grab his father.

—*Daddy, no!*

Sparky Landon releases one hand from what it's been doing long enough to administer an absent backhand blow to his younger son. Scott goes reeling back and strikes the table sitting in the middle of the dirt-floored room. Standing on it is an ancient hand-crank printing press that Paul has somehow coaxed back into working. He has printed some of Scott's stories on it; they are the younger brother's first publications. The crank of this quarter-ton behemoth bites painfully into Scott's back and he crumples up, grimacing, watching as his father resumes choking.

—*Daddy, don't kill im! PLEASE DON'T KILL IM!*

—*I ain't,* Landon says without looking around, *I should, but I aint. Not yet, anyway. More fool me, but he's my own boy, my fuckin firstborn, and I won't unless I have to. Which I fear I will. Sweet Mother Machree! But not yet. Mother-fogged if I will. Only it won't do to let him wake up. You aint never seen anything like this, but I have. I got lucky upstairs because I was behind him. Down here I could chase him two hours and never catch him. He'd run up the walls and halfway across the sweet-mother ceiling. Then, when he wore me down . . .*

Landon removes his hands from Paul's throat and peers fixedly into the still white face. That little trickle of blood from Paul's ear seems to have stopped.

—There. How you like that, you mother, you mother-fuck? He's out again. But he not for long. Fetch out that coil of rope from understair. That'll do until we can get some chain out of the shed. Then I dunno. Then it depends.

—Depends on what, Daddy?

Scared. Has he ever been so scared? No. And his father is looking at him in a way that scares him even more. Because it is a *knowing* way.

—Why, I guess it depends on you, Scoot. You've made him better a lot of times . . . and why do you want to come over all cow's eyes that way? You think I didn't know? Jayzus, for a smart boy ain't you dumb! He turns his head and spits on the dirt floor. *You've made him better of a lot of things. Maybe you can make him better of this. I never heard of anyone getting better from the bad-gunky . . . not the* real *bad-gunky . . . but I never heard of anybody just like you, either, so maybe you can. Have on 'til your cheeks crack, my old man would've said. But for now just fetch out that coil of rope from understair. And step to it, you little gluefoot mother-fuck, because he's*

11

'He's stirring already,' Lisey said as she lay on the oyster-white carpet of her dead husband's study. 'He's

12

'Stirring already,' Lisey says as she sits on the cold floor of the guest room, holding her husband's hand – a hand that is warm but dreadfully lax and waxy in her own. 'Scott said

13

The arguments against insanity fall through with a soft shirring
sound;
these are the sounds of dead voices on dead records
floating down the broken shaft of memory.
When I turn to you to ask if you remember,
When I turn to you in our bed

14

In bed with him is where she hears these things; in bed
with him at The Antlers, after a day when something
happened she absolutely cannot explain. He tells her as the
clouds thin and the moon nears like an announcement and
the furniture swims to the very edge of visibility. She holds
him in the dark and listens, not wanting to believe (helpless not to), as the young man who will shortly become
her husband says, 'Daddy tole me to fetch out that coil of
rope from understair. "And you want to step to it, you little
gluefoot mother-fuck," he says, "because he's not gonna
stay out for long. And when he comes to

15

—*When he comes to he's gonna be one ugly bug.*

Ugly bug. Like *Scooter you old Scoot* and *the bad-gunky,*
ugly bug is an interior idiom of his family that will haunt
his dreams (and his speech) for the rest of his productive
but too-short life.

Scott gets the coil of rope from beneath the stairs

and brings it to Daddy. Daddy trusses Paul up with quick, dancing economy, his shadow looming and turning on the cellar's stone walls in the light of three hanging seventy-five-watt bulbs, which are controlled by a turn-switch at the top of the stairs. He ties Paul's arms so stringently behind him that the balls of his shoulders stand out even through his shirt. Scott is moved to speak again, afraid of Daddy though he is.

—Daddy, that's too tight!

Daddy shoots a glance Scott's way. It's just a quick one, but Scott sees the fear there. It scares him. More than that, it *awes* him. Before today he would have said his Daddy wasn't ascairt of nothing but the School Board and their damned Registered Mails.

—You don't know, so shut up! I aint having him get a-loose! He might not kill us before it was over if that happen, but I'd most certainly have to kill him. I know what I'm doin!

You don't, Scott thinks, watching Daddy tie Paul's legs together first at the knees, then at the ankles. Already Paul has begun to stir again, and to mutter deep in his throat. *You're only guessing.* But he understands the truth of Daddy's love for Paul. It may be ugly love, but it's true and strong. If it wasn't, Daddy wouldn't guess at all. He would have just kept hammering Paul with that stovelength until he was dead. For just a moment part of Scott's mind (a cold part) wonders if Daddy would run the same risk for *him,* for Scooter old Scoot who didn't even dare jump off a three-foot bench until his brother stood cut and bleeding before him, and then he swats the thought into darkness. It isn't *him* who got the bad-gunky.

At least, not yet.

Daddy finishes by tying Paul around the middle to one of the painted steel posts that hold up the cellar's ceiling. —*There*, he says, stepping away, panting like a man who's just roped a steer in a rodeo ring. *That'll hold him awhile. You go on out to the shed, Scott. Get the light chain that's laying just inside the door and the big heavy tractor-chain that's in the bay on the left, with the truck parts. Do you know where I mean?*

Paul has been sagging over the rope around his torso. Now he sits up so suddenly he bangs his head on the post with sickening force. It makes Scott grimace. Paul looks at him with eyes that were blue only an hour ago. He grins, and the corners of his mouth stretch up far higher than they should be able to . . . almost to the lobes of his ears, it seems.

—*Scott*, his father says.

For once in his life, Scott pays no attention. He's mesmerized by the Halloween mask that used to be his brother's face. Paul's tongue comes dancing from between his parted teeth and does a jitterbug in the dank cellar air. At the same time his crotch darkens as he pisses his pa—

There's a clout upside his head that sends Scott reeling backward and he hits the printing-press table again.

—*Don't look at him, nummie, look at me! That ugly bug'll hypnotize you like a snake does a bird! You better wake the smuck up, Scooter – that aint your brother anymore.*

Scott gapes at his father. Behind them, as if to underline Daddy's point, the thing tied to the post lets out a roar much too loud to have come from a human chest. But that's all right, because it isn't a human sound. Not even close.

—Go get those chains, Scotty. Both of em. And be quick. That tie-job aint gonna hold him. I'm gonna go upstairs and get my .30-06. If he gets a-loose before you get back with those chains—

—Daddy, please don't shoot him! Don't shoot Paul!

—Bring the chains. Then we'll see what we can figger out.

—That tractor-chain's too long! Too heavy!

—Use the wheelbarra, nummie. The big barra. Go on, now, step to it.

Scott looks over his shoulder once and sees his father backing to the foot of the stairs. He does it slowly, like a lion-tamer leaving the cage after the act is over. Below him, spotlighted in the glare of one hanging bulb, is Paul. He's whamming the back of his head so rapidly against the post that Scott thinks of a jackhammer. At the same time he's jerking from side to side. Scott can't believe Paul isn't bleeding or knocking himself unconscious, but he's not. And he sees his father is right. The ropes won't hold him. Not if he keeps up that constant assault.

He won't be able to, he thinks as his father goes one way (to get his gun out of the front closet) and Scott goes another (to yank on his boots). *He'll kill himself if he goes on like that.* But then he thinks of the roar he heard bursting out of his brother's chest – that impossible catmurder roar – and doesn't really believe it.

And as he runs coatless into the cold, he thinks he might even know what's happened to Paul. There's a place where he can go when Daddy has hurt him, and he has taken Paul there when Daddy has hurt *Paul*. Yes, plenty of times. There are good things in that place, beautiful trees and healing water, but there are also bad things. Scott tries not to go there at night, and when he does he's quiet and comes back *quick*, because the deep intuition of his child's heart tells him night is when the bad things mostly come out. Night is when they hunt.

If he can go *there*, is it so hard to believe that something – a bad-gunky something – could get inside Paul and then come over *here*? Something that saw him and marked him, or maybe just a dumb germ that crawled up his nose and stuck in his brain?

And if so, whose fault is that? Who took Paul in the first place?

In the shed, Scott throws the light chain in the wheelbarrow. That's easy, the work of only seconds. Getting the tractor-chain in there is a lot harder. The tractor-chain is puffickly *huh-yooge*, talking all the while in its clanky language, which is all steel vowels. Twice heavy loops slip through his trembling arms, the second time pinching his skin and dragging it open, bringing blood in bright rosettes. The third time he almost has it in the wheelbarrow when a twenty-pound armload of links lands crooked, on the side of the barrowbed instead of on the square, and the entire load of chainlink topples over on Scott's foot, burying it in steel and making him scream a perfect soprano choir-cry of pain.

—*Scooter, you comin before the turn of two thousand?* Daddy bawls from the house. *If you're comin, you better damn well motherfuckin* come!

Scott looks that way, eyes wide and terrified, then sets the wheelbarrow up again and bends over the big greasy heap of chain. His foot will still be bruise-gaudy a month later and he'll feel pain there all the way to the end of his life (that's one problem traveling to that other place is never able to fix), but at the time he feels nothing after the initial flare. He again begins the job of loading the links into the wheelbarrow, feeling the hot sweat go rolling down his sides and back, smelling the wild stink of it, knowing that if he hears a gunshot it will mean Paul's brains are out on the cellar floor and it's his fault. Time becomes a physical thing with weight, like dirt. Like chain. He keeps expecting Daddy to yell at him again from the house and when he still hasn't by the time Scott begins trundling the wheelbarrow back toward the yellow gleam of the kitchen lights, Scott begins to have a different fear: that Paul has gotten a-loose after all. It isn't Paul's brains lying down there on the sour-smelling dirt, it's Daddy's guts, pulled from his living stomach by the thing that was Scott's brother just this afternoon. Paul's up the stairs and hiding in the house and as soon as Scott goes inside the bool hunt will start. Only this time *he* will be the prize.

All that's his imagination, of course, his damned old imagination that runs like a wildeyed nighthorse, but when his father leaps out onto the porch it has done enough work so that for a moment Scott sees not Andrew Landon but Paul, grinning like a goblin, and he shrieks. When he raises his hands to guard his face the wheelbarrow almost tips over again. Would have, if Daddy hadn't reached out to steady it. Then he raises one of those hands to swat his son but lowers it almost at once. Later there may be swatting, but not now. Now he needs him. So instead of hitting, Daddy only spits into his right hand and rubs it against his left. Then he bends, oblivious of the cold out here on the back stoop in his underwear shirt and grabs hold of the wheelbarrow's front end.

—*I'm gonna yank it up, Scooter. You hang on those handles and steer and don't let the mother tip. I gave him another tonk – I had to – but it won't keep him out long. If we spill this load of chain, I don't think he's gonna live through the night. I won't be able to let him. You understand?*

Scott understands that his brother's life is now riding in a seriously overloaded wheelbarrow filled with chain that weighs three times what he does. For one wild moment he seriously considers simply running away into the windy dark, and as fast as he can go. Then he grabs the handles. He is unaware of the tears spilling from his eyes. He nods at his Daddy and his Daddy nods back. What passes between them is nothing but life and death.

—*On three. One . . . two . . . keep it straight now, you little whoredog . . . three!*

Sparky Landon lifts the wheelbarrow from the ground to the stoop with a cry of effort that escapes in white vapor. His underwear shirt splits open beneath one arm and a tuft of crazy ginger hair springs free. While the overloaded barrow is in the air the damned thing yaws first left and then right and the boy thinks *stay up you mother, you whoredog mothersmuck.* He corrects each tilt, crying at himself not to push too hard, not to overdo it *you stupid mother, you stupid whoredog bad-gunky mother.* And it works, but Sparky Landon wastes no time in congratulations. What Sparky Landon does is to back his way into the house, rolling the wheelbarrow after him. Scott limps behind on his ballooning foot.

In the kitchen, Daddy turns the wheelbarrow around

and trundles it straight for the cellar door, which he has closed and bolted. The wheel makes a track through the spilled sugar. Scott never forgets that.

—*Get the door, Scott.*

—*Daddy, what if he's . . . there?*

—*Then I'll knock him galley-west with this thing. If you want a shot at saving him, quit running your nonsense and open that smogging door!*

Scott pulls back the bolt and opens the door. Paul isn't there. Scott can see Paul's bloated shadow still attached to the pole, and something that has been strung up high and tight inside him relaxes a little.

—*Stand aside, son.*

Scott does. His father runs the wheelbarrow to the top of the cellar stairs. Then, with another grunt, he tips it up, braking the barrow's wheel with one foot when it tries to backroll. The chain hits the stairs with a mighty unmusical clang, splintering two of the risers and then crashing most of the way down. Daddy slings the wheelbarrow to one side and starts down himself, reaching the come-to-rest chain at the halfway mark and kicking it ahead of him the rest of the way. Scott follows and has just stepped over the first broken riser when he sees Paul lolling sideways from the post, the left side of his face now covered with blood. The corner of his mouth is twitching senselessly. One of his teeth lies on the shoulder of his shirt.

—*Wha'd you do to him?* Scott nearly screams.

—*Whacked him with a board, I had to,* his father replies, sounding oddly defensive. *He was coming around and you were still out there playin fiddly-fuck in the shed. He'll be all right. You can't hurt em much when they're bad-gunky.*

380

Scott barely hears him. Seeing Paul covered with blood that way has swept what happened in the kitchen from his mind. He tries to dart around Daddy and get to his brother, but Daddy grabs him.

—*Not unless you don't want to go on living*, Sparky Landon says, and what stops Scott isn't so much the hand on his shoulder as the terrible tenderness he hears in his father's voice. *Because he'll smell you if you get right up close. Even unconscious. Smell you and come back.*

He sees his younger son looking up at him and nods.

—*Oh yeah. He's like a wild animal now. A maneater. And if we can't find a way to hold him we'll have to kill him. Do you understand?*

Scott nods, then voices one loud sob that sounds like the bray of a donkey. With that same terrible tenderness, Daddy reaches out, wipes snot from his nose, and flicks it on the floor.

—*Then stop your whingeing and help me with these chains. We'll use that central support-pole and the table with the printing-press on it. That damn press has got to weight four, five hunnert pounds.*

—*What if those things aren't enough to hold im?*

Sparky Landon shakes his head slowly.

—*Then I dunno.*

16

Lying in bed with his wife, listening to The Antlers creak in the wind, Scott says: 'It *was* enough. For three weeks, at least, it was enough. That's where my brother Paul had his last Christmas, his last New Year's Day, the last three weeks

381

of his life – that stinking cellar.' He shakes his head slowly. She feels the movement of his hair against her skin, feels how damp it is. It's sweat. It's on his face, too, so mixed with tears she can't tell which is which.

'You can't imagine what those three weeks were like, Lisey, especially when Daddy went to work and it was just him and me, *it* and me—'

'Your father went to *work*?'

'We had to eat, didn't we? And we had to pay for the Number Two, because we couldn't heat the whole *house* with wood, although God knows we tried. Most of all, we couldn't afford to make people suspicious. Daddy explained it all to me.'

I bet he did, Lisey thinks grimly, but says nothing.

'I told Daddy to cut him and let the poison out like he always did before and Daddy said it wouldn't do any good, cutting wouldn't help a mite because the bad-gunky had gone to his brain. And I knew it had. That thing could still think, though, at least a little. When Daddy was gone, it would call my name. It would say it had made me a bool, a *good* bool, and the end was a candybar *and* an RC. Sometimes it even sounded enough like Paul so I'd go to the cellar door and put my head to the wood and listen, even though I knew it was dangerous. Daddy *said* it was dangerous, said not to listen and always stay away from the cellar when I was alone, and to stick my fingers in my ears and say prayers real loud or yell '*Smuck you mother, smuck you mother-fucker, smuck you and the horse you rode in on,*' because that and prayers both came to the same and at least they'd shut him out, but not to listen, because he said Paul was gone and there wasn't nothing in the cellar but a bool-devil from the Land of the Blood-Bools, and he said "The Devil can fascinate, Scoot, no one knows better than the Landons how the devil can fascinate. And the Landreaus before em. First he fascinates the mind and then he drinks up the heart." Mostly I did what he said but sometimes I went close and listened . . . and pretended it was Paul . . . because I loved him and wanted him back, not because I really believed . . . and I never pulled the bolt . . .'

Here there falls a long pause. His heavy hair slips restlessly against her neck and chest and at last he says in a small, reluctant child's voice: 'Well, *once* I did . . . and I dint open the door . . . I never opened that cellar door unless Daddy was home, and when Daddy was home he only screamed and made the chains rattle and sometimes hooted like a owl. And when he did that sometimes Daddy, he'd hoot back . . . it was like a joke, you know, how they hooted at each other . . . Daddy in the kitchen and the . . . you know . . . chained up in the cellar . . . and I'd be ascairt even though I knew it was a joke because it was like they were both crazy . . . crazy and talking winter-owl talk to each other . . . and I'd think, "Only one left, and that's me. Only one who ain't bad-gunky and that one not even eleven and what would they think if I went to Mulie's and told?" But it didn't do no good thinkin about Mulie's because if he 'us home he'd just chase after me and drag me back. And if he wasn't . . . if they believed me and came up to t'house with me, they'd kill my brother . . . if my brother was still in 'ere somewhere . . . and take me away . . . and put me in the Poor Home. Daddy said without him to take care of me an Paul, we'd have to go

STEPHEN KING

to the Poor Home where they put a clo'pin on your dink
if you pee in your bed . . . and the big kids . . . you have
to give the big kids blowjobs all night long . . .'

He stops, struggling, caught somewhere between
where he is and where he was. Outside The Antlers, the
wind gusts and the building groans. She wants to believe
that what he's telling her cannot be true – that it is some
rich and dreadful childhood hallucination – but she knows
it is true. Every awful word. When he resumes she can hear
him trying to regain his adult voice, his adult *self*.

'There are people in mental institutions, often people
who've suffered catastrophic frontal-lobe traumas, who
regress to animal states. I've read about it. But it's a process
that usually occurs over a course of years. This happened
to my brother *all at once*. And once it had, once he'd crossed
that line . . .'

Scott swallows. The click in his throat is as loud as a
turning light-switch.

'When I came down the cellar stairs with his food
– meat and vegetables on a pie-plate, the way you'd bring
food to a big dog like a Great Dane or a German Shepherd
– he'd rush to the end of the chains that held him to the
post, one around his neck and one around his waist, with
drool flying from the corners of his mouth and then the
whole works would snub up and he'd go flying, still howling
and barking like a bool-devil, only sort of strangled until
he got his breath back, you know?'

'Yes,' she says faintly.

'You had to put the plate on the floor – I still
remember the smell of that sour dirt when I bent over,
I'll never forget it – and then push it to where he could

get it. We had a bust' rake handle for that. It didn't do to get too close. He'd claw you, maybe pull you in. I didn't need Daddy to tell me that if he caught me, he'd eat as much of me as he could, alive and screaming. And this was the brother who made the bools. The one who loved me. Without him I never would have made it. Without him Daddy would have killed me before I made five, not because he meant to but because he was in his own bad-gunky. Me and Paul made it together. Buddy system. You know?'

Lisey nods. She knows.

'Only that January my buddy was cross-chained in the cellar – to the post and to the table with the printing-press on it – and you could measure the boundary of his world by this arc . . . this arc of turds . . . where he went to the end of his chains . . . and squatted . . . and shat.'

For a moment he puts the heels of his hands to his eyes. The cords stand out on his neck. He breathes through his mouth – long harsh shaking breaths. She doesn't think she has to ask him where he learned the trick of keeping his grief silent; that she now knows. When he's still again, she asks: 'How did your father get the chains on him in the first place? Do you remember?'

'I remember everything, Lisey, but that doesn't mean I *know* everything. Half a dozen times he put stuff in Paul's food, of that I'm positive. I think it was some kind of animal tranquilizer, but how he got it I have no idea. Paul gobbled down everything we gave him except for greens, and usually food energized him. He'd yowl and bark and leap around; he'd run to the end of his chains – trying to break them, I guess – or jump up and pound his fists on the ceiling until his knuckles bled. Maybe he was trying to break through, or maybe it was just for the joy of it. Sometimes he'd lie down in the dirt and masturbate.

'But once in awhile he'd only be active for ten or fifteen minutes and then stop. Those were the times Daddy must have give him the stuff. He'd squat down, muttering, then fall over on his side and put his hands between his legs and go to sleep. The first time he did that, Daddy put on these two leather belts he made, except I guess you'd call the one that went around Paul's neck a choker, right? They had big metal claps at the back. He loop the chains through em, the tractor-chain through the waist-belt clap, the lighter chain through the choker-belt clap at the nape of his neck. Then he used a little hand-torch to weld them claps shut. And that was how Paul was trussed. When he woke up he was wild to find himself that way. Like to shook the house down.' The flattened, nasal accents of rural Pennsylvania have crept so far into his voice that *house* becomes almost Germanic, almost *haus*. 'We stood at the top of the stairs watchin 'im, and I beg Daddy to let 'im out before he broke 'is neck or choke 'imself, but Daddy, he said he wun't choke and Daddy was right. What happen after three weeks was he started to pull table and even center-pos' – the steel center-pos' that held up the kitchen floor – but he never broke his neck and he never choke 'imself.

'The other times Daddy knock him out was to see if I could take him to Boo'ya Moon – did I tell you that's what me n Paul called it, the other place?'

'Yes, Scott.' Crying herself now. Letting the tears flow, not wanting him to see her wiping her eyes, not wanting to let him see her pitying that boy in that farmhouse.

'Daddy want to see if I could take him and make him better like the times when Daddy cut him, or like that one time Daddy poke his eye with the pliers and make it come a little way out and Paul crite and crite because he couldn't hardly see good, or once Daddy yell at *me* and say "Scoot, you little whoredog, you mother-killing mother!" for trackin in the spring muddy and push me down and crack my tailbone so I couldn't walk so well. Only after I went and had a bool . . . you know, a prize . . . my tailbone was okay again.' He nods against her. 'And Daddy, he see and give me a kiss and say, "Scott, you're one in a million. I love you, you little motherfucker." And I kiss him and say "Daddy, *you* one in a million. I love you, you big motherfucker." And he laughed.' Scott pulls back from her and even in the gloom she can see that his face has almost become a child's face. And she can see the goonybird wonder there. 'He laughed so hard he almos' fell out of his chair – I made my father *laugh!*'

She has a thousand questions and doesn't dare ask a single one. Isn't sure she *could* ask a single one.

Scott puts a hand to his face, rubs it, looks at her again. And he's back. Just like that. 'Christ, Lisey,' he says. 'I've never talked about this stuff, never, not to anyone. Are you okay with this?'

'Yes, Scott.'

'You're one hell of a brave woman, then. Have you started telling yourself it's all bullshit yet?' He's even grinning a little. It's an uncertain grin, but it's genuine enough, and she finds it dear enough to kiss: first one corner, then the other, just for balance.

'Oh, I tried,' she says. 'It didn't work.'

'Because of how we boomed out from under the yum-yum tree?'

'Is that what you call it?'

'That was Paul's name for a quick trip. Just a quick trip that got you from here to there. That was a boom.'

'Like a bool, only with an *m*.'

'That's right,' he says. 'Or like a book. A book's a bool, only with a *k*.'

17

I guess it depends on you, Scoot.

These are his father's words. They linger and do not leave.

I guess it depends on you.

But he is only ten years old and the responsibility of saving his brother's life and sanity – maybe even his soul – weighs on him and steals his sleep as Christmas and New Year's pass and cold snowy January begins.

You've made him better a lot of times, you've made him better of a lot of things.

It's true, but there's never been anything like this and Scott finds he can no longer eat unless Daddy stands beside him, hectoring him into each bite. The lowest, snuffling cry from the thing in the cellar unzips his thin sleep, but most generally that's okay, because most generally what he's leaving behind are lurid, red-painted nightmares. In many of these he finds himself alone in Boo'ya Moon after dark, sometimes in a certain graveyard near a certain pool, a wilderness of stone markers and wooden crosses, listening as the laughers cackle and smelling as the formerly sweet breeze begins to smell dirty down low, where it combs through the tangles of brush. You can come to Boo'ya Moon after dark, but it's not a good idea, and if you find yourself there once the moon has fully risen, you want to be quiet. Just as quiet as a sweetmother. But in his nightmares, Scott always forgets and is appalled to find himself singing 'Jambalaya' at the top of his voice.

Maybe you can make him better of this.

But the first time Scott tries he knows it's probably impossible. He knows as soon as he puts a tentative arm around the snoring, stinking, beshitted thing curled at the foot of the steel support post. He might as well try to strap a grand piano on his back and then do the cha-cha with it. Before, he and Paul have gone easily to that other world (which is really only *this* world turned inside-out like a pocket, he will later tell Lisey). But the snoring thing in the cellar is an anvil, a bank-safe . . . a grand piano strapped to a ten-year-old's back.

He retreats to Daddy, sure he'll be paddled and not sorry. He feels that he deserves to be paddled. Or worse. But Daddy, who sat at the foot of the stairs with a stovelength in one hand watching the whole thing, doesn't paddle or strike with his fist. What he does is brush Scott's dirty, clumpy hair away from the nape of his neck and plant a kiss there with a tenderness that makes the boy quake.

—*Aint really surprised, Scott. Bad-gunky likes it right where it is.*

—*Daddy, is Paul in there at all anymore?*

—*Dunno.* Now he's got Scott between his open spread legs so that there are green Dickies on either side of the boy. Daddy's hands are locked loosely around Scott's chest and his chin is on Scott's shoulder. Together they look at the sleeping thing curled at the foot of the post. They look at the chains. They look at the arc of turds that mark the border of its basement world. —*What do you think, Scott? What do you feel?*

He considers lying to Daddy, but only for a moment. He won't do that when the man's arms are around him, not when he feels Daddy's love coming through in the clear, like WWVA at night. Daddy's love is every bit as true as his anger and madness, if less frequently seen and even less frequently demonstrated. Scott feels nothing, and reluctantly says so.

—*Little buddy, we can't go on this way.*

—*Why not? He's eatin, at least . . .*

—*Sooner or later someone'll come and hear him down here. A smucking door-to-door salesman, one lousy Fuller Brush man, that's all it'd take.*

—*He'll be quiet. Bad-gunky'll make him be quiet.*

—*Maybe, maybe not. There's no telling what bad-gunky'll do, not really. And there's the smell. I can sprinkle lime until I'm blue in the face and that shit-stink is still gonna come up through the kitchen floor. But most of all . . . . Scooter, can't you see what he's doin to that motherless table with the printin-press on it? And the post? The sweetmother post?*

Scott looks. At first he can barely credit what he's seeing, and of course he doesn't *want* to credit what he's seeing. That big table, even with five hundred pounds of ancient hand-crank Stratton printing-press on it, has been pulled at least three feet from its original position. He can see the square marks in the hardpacked earth where it used to be. Worse still is the steel post, which butts against a flat metal flange at its top end. The white-painted flange presses in turn against the beam running directly beneath their kitchen table. Scott can see a dark right-angle tattooed on that white piece of metal and knows it's where the support post used to rest. Scott measures the post itself with his eye, trying to pick up a lean. He can't, not yet. But if the thing continues to yank on it with all its inhuman strength . . . day in and day out . . .

—*Daddy, can I try again?*

Daddy sighs. Scott cranes around to look into his hated, feared, loved face.

—*Daddy?*

—*Have on 'til your cheeks crack*, Daddy says. *Have on and good luck to you.*

18

Silence in the study over the barn, where it was hot and she was hurt and her husband was dead.

Silence in the guest room, where it's cold and her husband is *gone*.

Silence in the bedroom at The Antlers, where they lie together, Scott and Lisey, **Now we are two**.

Then the living Scott speaks for the one that's dead in 2006 and *gone* in 1996, and the arguments against insanity do more than fall through; for Lisey Landon, they finally collapse completely: everything the same.

19

Outside their bedroom at The Antlers, the wind is blowing and the clouds are thinning. Inside, Scott pauses long enough to get a drink from the glass of water he always keeps by the side of the bed. The interruption breaks the hypnotic regression that has once more begun to grip him. When he resumes, he seems to be telling instead of *living*, and she finds this an enormous relief.

'I tried twice more,' he says. *Tried*, not *trite*. 'I used to think trying that last time was how I got him killed. Right up until tonight I thought that, but talking about it – *hearing* myself talk about it – has helped more than I ever would have believed. I guess psychoanalysts have got something with that old talking-cure stuff after all, huh?'

'I don't know.' Nor does she care. 'Did your father blame you?' Thinking, *Of course he did*.

But once more she seems to have underestimated the complexity of the little triangle that existed for awhile on an isolated farmyard hill in Martensburg, Pennsylvania. Because, after hesitating a moment, Scott shakes his head.

'No. It might have helped if he'd taken me in his arms – like he did after the first time I tried – and told me it wasn't my fault, wasn't *anybody's* fault, that it was just the bad-gunky, like cancer or cerebral palsy or something, but he never did that, either. He just hauled me away with one arm . . . I hung there like a puppet whose strings had been cut . . . and afterward we just . . .' In the brightening dimness, Scott explains all his silence about his past with one terrible gesture. He puts a finger to his lips for a second – it is a pallid exclamation point below his wide eyes – and holds it there: *Shhhhh*.

Lisey thinks of how it was after Jodi got pregnant and went away, and nods her understanding. Scott gives her a grateful look.

'Three tries in all,' he resumes. 'The second was only three or four days after my first go. I tried as hard as I could, but it was just like the first time. Only by then you *could* see a lean in the post he was chained to, and there was a second arc of turds, farther out, because he'd moved the table a little more and gotten a little extra slack in that chain. Daddy was starting to be afraid he might snap one of the table-legs, even though they were metal, too.

'After my second try, I told Daddy I was pretty sure I knew what was wrong. I couldn't do it – couldn't *take* him – because he was always knocked out when I got close to him. And Daddy said, "Well what's your plan, Scooter, you want to grab him when he's awake and raving? He'd rip your smockin head off." I said I knew it. I knew more than that, Lisey – I knew that if he didn't rip my head off in the cellar, he'd rip it off on the other side, in Boo'ya Moon. So then I ast Daddy if he couldn't knock him out just a little – you know, make him woozy. Enough so I could get in close and hold him the way I was holding you, today, under the yum-yum tree.'

'Oh, Scott,' she says. She is afraid for the ten-year-old boy even though she knows it must have come out all right; knows he lived to father the young man lying beside her.

'Daddy said it was dangerous. "Playin with fire there, Scoot," he said. I knew I was, but there wasn't any other way. We couldn't keep him in the cellar much longer; even I could see that. And then Daddy – he kind of ruffled my hair and said, "What happen to the little pissant ascairt to jump off the hall bench?" I was surprised he even remembered that, because he was so far in the bad-gunky, and I was proud.'

Lisey thinks what a dismal life it must have been, where pleasing such a man could make a child proud, and reminds herself he was only ten. Ten, and alone with a monster in the cellar much of the time. The father was also a monster, but at least a rational one some of the time. A monster capable of doling out the occasional kiss.

'Then . . .' Scott looks up into the dim. For a moment the moon comes out. It dashes a pale and playful paw across his face before retreating into the clouds once more. When he resumes, she hears the child beginning to take over once more. 'Daddy – see, Daddy never ast what I saw or where I went or what I did when I went there and I don't think he ever ast Paul – I dunno if Paul even remembered too much – but he come close then. He said, "And if you take him like that, Scoot. What happens if he wakes up? Is he just gonna be suddenly all better? Because if he ain't, I won't be there to help you."

'But I thought about that, see? Thought about it and thought about it until it seem like my brains'd bust wide open.' Scott gets up on one elbow and looks at her. 'I knew it had to end as well as Daddy, maybe even better. Because of the pos'. And the table. But also because of how he was losin weight, and gettin sores on his face from not eatin the right food – we give him veg'ables, but everything except the taters and onyums he slang away from him and one of his eyes – the one Daddy hurt before – had come over all milky-white on top of the red. Also more of his teeth was fallin out and one of his elbows, it come over all crookit. He was fallin apart from being down 'ere, Lisey, and what wasn't fallin apart from no sunlight and wrong food he was beatin to death. Do you see?'

She nods.

'So I had this little idea I tole Daddy. He said, "You think you're pretty motherfucking smart for ten, don't you?" And I said no, I wasn't smart about hardly anything, and if he thought there was some other way that was safer and better, then okay. Only he didn't. He said, "*I* think you're pretty motherfucking smart for ten, tell you that. And you turned out to have some guts in you after all. Unless you back out."

'"I won't back out," I said.

'And he said, "You won't need to, Scooter, because I'll be standing right at the foot of the stairs with my sweet-mother deer-gun

20

Daddy stands at the foot of the stairs with his deer-gun, his .30-06, in his hands. Scott stands beside him, looking at the thing chained to the metal post and the printing-press table, trying not to tremble. In his righthand pocket is the slim instrument Daddy has given him, a hypodermic with a plastic cap on the needle-tip. Scott doesn't need his Daddy to tell him it's a fragile mechanism. If there's a struggle, it may break. Daddy offered to put it in a little white cardboard box that once held a fountain pen, but getting the hypo out of the box would take an extra couple of seconds – at least – and that might mean the difference between life and death if he succeeds in getting the thing chained to the post over to Boo'ya Moon. In Boo'ya Moon there will be no Daddy with a .30-06 deer-gun. In Boo'ya Moon there will just be him and the thing that slipped

395

into Paul like a hand into a stolen glove. Just the two of them on top of Sweetheart Hill.

The thing that used to be his brother lies sprawled with its back against the center-post and its legs splayed. It's naked except for Paul's undershirt. Its legs and feet are dirty. Its flanks are caked with shit. The pie-plate, licked clean even of grease, lies by one grimy hand. The extra-large hamburger that was on it disappeared down the Paul-thing's gullet in a matter of seconds, but Andrew Landon agonized over the patty's creation for almost half an hour, chucking his first effort out into the night after deciding he loaded too much of 'the stuff' into it. 'The stuff' is white pills that look almost exactly like the Tums and Rolaids Daddy sometimes takes. The one time Scott asked Daddy where they came from, Daddy said—*Why don't you shut your goddam mouth, Curious George, before I shut it for you* and when Daddy says something like that you take the hint if you've got any sense. Daddy ground the pills up with the bottom of a waterglass. He talked as he worked, maybe to himself, maybe to Scott, while below them the thing chained to the printing-press roared monotonously for its supper. —*Easy enough to figure when you want to knock him out,* Daddy said, looking from the pile of white powder to the ground meat. —*Be easier still if I wanted to kill the troublesome motherfucker, ay? But no, I don't want to do that, I just want to give* him *a chance to kill the one that's still all right, more fool am I. Well smog it and smuck it, God hates a coward.* He used the side of his pinky with surprising delicacy to separate a little line of white powder from the pile. He pinched some up, sprinkled it onto the meat like salt, kneaded it in, then pinched up a tiny bit more and kneaded that in, too. He didn't bother much with what he called *hot coozine* when it came to the thing downstairs, said it would be happy to eat its dinner raw – still warm and shaking on the bone, for that matter.

Now Scott stands beside his Daddy, hypo in pocket, watching the dangerous thing loll against its post, snoring with its upper lip pulled back. It's grizzling from the corners of its mouth. The eyes are half-open but there's no sign of its irises; Scott can see only the gleaming, glabrous whites . . . *Only the whites aint white anymore,* he thinks.

—*Go on, goddam you,* Daddy says, giving him a thump on the shoulder. *If you're gonna do it, then go on before I lose my nerve or drop with a sweet-mother heart-attack . . . or do you think he's shammin? Only pretendin to be out?*

Scott shakes his head. The thing's not trying to fool them, he would feel that – and then looks at his father wonderingly.

—*What?* Daddy asks irritably. *What's on your mind besides your smuckin hair?*

—*Are you really—?*

—*Am I really scared? That what you want to know?*

Scott nods, suddenly shy.

—*Yeah, to fuckin death. Did you think you 'us the only one? Now close your mouth and do it if you're gonna. Let's have an end to this.*

He will never understand why his father's acknowledgment of fear makes him feel braver; all he knows is that it does. He walks toward the center-post. He touches the barrel of the hypo inside his pocket one more time as he goes. He reaches the outer arc of turds and steps over it. The next step takes him over the inner ring and into what you might call the thing's den. Here the smell is intense: not the odor of shit or even hair and skin but rather of fur and pelt. The thing has a penis that is bigger than Paul's was. Paul's peach-fuzzy groin has thatched in with the thing's coarse, dense pubic hair, and the feet at the end of Paul's legs (those legs are the only things that still look the same) have a queerly turned-in look, as if the bones in his ankles are warping. *Boards left out in the rain*, Scott thinks; it's not quite nonsense.

Then his eyes return to the thing's face – to its eyes. The lids are still mostly fallen, and there's still no sign of irises, only bloody whites. The breathing is likewise unchanged; the dirty hands continue to lie limp, the palms up as if in surrender. Yet Scott knows he has entered the red zone. It will not do to hesitate now. The thing will scent him and come awake at any second. This will happen in spite of 'the stuff' Daddy put in the hamburger, and so if he can do it, if he can *take* the thing that has stolen his brother—

Scott continues forward, walking on legs he can now barely feel. Part of his mind is absolutely convinced that he's going to his death. He won't even be able to boom away, not once the Paul-thing takes hold of him. Nevertheless, he steps within range of its grasp, into the most intimate concentration of its wild stench, and puts his hands on its naked, clammy sides. He thinks

(Paul come with me now)

and

(Bool Boo'ya Boo'ya Moon sweet water the pool)

and for just one heartbreaking heartbroken moment it almost happens. There's the familiar sense of things starting to rush away; up comes the hum of insects and the delicious daytime perfume of the trees on Sweetheart Hill. Then the thing's long-nailed hands are around Scott's neck. It opens its mouth and roars the sounds and smells of Boo'ya Moon away on a draft of carrion breath. To Scott it feels like someone has just shot a flaming boulder onto the delicate forming grid of his . . . his what? It's not his mind that takes him to that other place, not precisely his *mind* . . . and there's no time to think about it further because the thing has got him, it's *got* him. Everything Daddy was afraid of has come to pass. Its mouth has come unhinged in some nightmarish fashion that confounds sanity, seeming to drop its lower jaw all the way to its

(beastbone)

breastbone, contorting the dirty face into something from which every last vestige of Paul – and humanity itself – has disappeared. This is the bad-gunky with its mask off. Scott has time to think *It's going to take my whole head in a single bite, like a lollipop.* That monstrous mouth yawns, the red eyes sparkle in the naked glow of the hanging light-bulbs, and Scott is going nowhere except to his death. The thing's head draws back far enough to bang the post, then lashes forward.

But Scott has once again forgotten about Daddy. Daddy's hand comes out of the dim, seizes the Paul-thing by the hair, and somehow wrenches the head backward. Then Daddy's other hand appears, thumb curled around the stock of his deer-gun where the stock is thinnest, fore-finger hugging the trigger. He socks the gun's muzzle into the shelf of the thing's upslanted chin.

—*Daddy, no!* Scott shrieks.

Andrew Landon pays no attention, can *afford* to pay no attention. Although he's gotten a huge handful of the thing's hair, it's ripping free of his fist just the same. Now it's bellowing, and its bellows sound dreadfully like one word.

Like *Daddy.*

—*Say hello to hell, you bad-gunky motherfucker,* Sparky Landon says, and pulls the trigger. The .30-06's discharge is deafening in the enclosed space of the cellar; it will ring in Scott's ears for two hours or more. The thing's shaggy backhair flies up, as in a sudden gust of breeze, and a large splash of crimson paints the leaning center-post. The thing's legs give a single crazy cartoon kick and go still. The hands around Scott's neck twitch momentarily tighter and then fall palms-up, *flump,* onto the dirt. Daddy's arm encircles Scott and lifts him up.

—*Are you all right, Scoot? Can you breathe?*

—*I'm okay, Daddy. Did you have to kill him?*

—*Are you brainless?*

Scott hangs limp in the circle of his father's arm, unable to believe it's happened even though he knew it might. He wishes he could faint. Wishes – a little, anyway – that he could die himself.

Daddy gives him a shake. —*He was gonna kill you, wasn't he?*

—*Y-Y-Yeah.*

—*You're fucking-A he was. Christ, Scotty, he was rippin his own sweet-mother hair out by the roots to get at you. To get at your smoggin throat!*

Scott knows this is true, but he knows something else as well.

—Lookit 'im, Daddy – lookit 'im now!

For a moment or two longer he hangs from the circle of his father's arm like a ragdoll or a puppet whose strings have been cut, then Landon slowly lowers him down and Scott knows his father is seeing what Scott wanted him to see: just a boy. Just an innocent boy who has been chained in the cellar by his lunatic father and dogsbody younger brother, then starved until he's rack-thin and covered with sores; a boy who has struggled so pitifully hard for his freedom that he actually moved the steel post and the cruelly heavy table to which he has been chained. A boy who has lived three nightmare weeks as a prisoner down here before finally being shot in the head.

—I see 'im, Daddy says, and the only thing grimmer than his voice is his face.

—Why doesn't he look like before, Daddy? Why—

—Because the bad-gunky's gone, you numbskull. And here's an irony even a badly shaken ten-year-old can appreciate, at least a bright one like Scott: now that Paul lies dead, chained to a post in the cellar with his brains blown out, Daddy has never looked or sounded saner. *And if anyone else sees him like this, I'll be for either the state prison in Waynesburg or locked in that smucking nutbarn up Reedville. That's if they don't lynch me first. We'll have to bury him, although aint it gonna be a bitch-kitty with the ground like it is, hard as arn.*

Scott says, *—I'll take him, Daddy.*

—How you gonna take him? You couldn't take him when he was alive!

He doesn't have the language to explain that now it will be no more than going there dressed in his clothes,

401

which he always does. That anvil-weight, bank-vault weight, piano-weight, is gone from the thing chained to the post; the thing chained to the post is now no more than the green husk you strip off an ear of corn. Scott just says, — *I can do it now.*

—*You're a little bag of boast and wind*, Daddy says, but he leans the deer-gun against the table with the printing-press on it. He runs a hand through his hair and sighs. For the first time he looks to Scott like a man who could get old.

—*Go on, Scott, might as well give her a try. Can't hurt.* But now that there's no actual danger, Scott is bashful.

—*Turn around, Daddy.*

—*WHAT the FUCK you say?*

There's a potential beating in Daddy's voice, but for once Scott doesn't back down. It isn't the *going* part that bothers him; he doesn't care if Daddy sees that. What he's bashful about is Daddy seeing him take his dead brother in his arms. He's going to cry. He feels it coming on already, like rain on a late spring afternoon, when the day has been hot with a foretaste of summer.

—*Please*, he says in his most placating voice. *Please, Daddy*.

For a moment Scott is quite sure that his father is going to rush across the cellar to where his surviving son stands, with his tripled shadow racing beside him on the rock walls, and backhand him – perhaps knock him spang into his big brother's dead lap. He's been backhanded plenty of times and usually even the thought of it makes him cringe, but now he stands straight between Paul's splayed legs, looking into his father's eyes. It's hard to do that, but he manages. Because they have survived a terrible passage together, and will have to keep it between themselves forever: *Shhhhhh*. So he deserves to ask, and he deserves to look in Daddy's eyes while he waits for his answer.

Daddy doesn't come at him. Instead he takes a deep breath, blows it out, and turns around. —*You'll be tellin me when to warsh the floors and scrub out the tawlit next, I guess*, he grumbles. *I'll give you a count of thirty, Scoot*

21

'I'll give you a count of thirty and then I'm turning around again,' Scott tells her. 'I'm pretty sure that's how he finished it, but I never heard because by then I was gone off the face of the earth. Paul too, right out of his chains. I took him with me as easy as ever once he was dead; maybe easier. I bet Daddy never finished counting to thirty. Hell, I bet he never even got started before he heard the clink of chains or maybe the sound of air rushing in to fill the place where we'd been and he turned around and he saw he had the cellar all to himself.' Scott has relaxed against her; the sweat on his face and arms and body is drying. He has told it, gotten the worst of it out of him, sicked it up.

'The sound,' she says. 'I wondered about that, you know. If there was a sound under the willow tree when we . . . you know . . . came back out.'

'When we boomed.'

'Yes, when we . . . that.'

'When we boomed, Lisey. Say it.'

'When we boomed.' Wondering if she's crazy. Wondering if *he* is, and if it's catching.

Now he *does* light another cigarette, and in the match-glow his face is honestly curious. 'What did you see, Lisey? Do you remember?'

Doubtfully, she says: 'There was a lot of purple, slanting down a hill . . . and I had a sense of shade, like there were trees right behind us, but it was all so *quick* . . . no more than a second or two . . .'

He laughs and gives her a one-armed hug. 'That's Sweetheart Hill you're talking about.'

'Sweetheart—?'

'Paul named it that. There's dirt all around those trees – soft, deep, I don't think it's ever winter there – and that's where I buried him. That's where I buried my brother.' He looks at her solemnly and says, 'Do you want to go see, Lisey?'

22

Lisey had been asleep on the study floor in spite of the pain—

No. She hadn't been asleep, because you *couldn't* sleep with pain like this. Not without medical help. So what had she been?

Mesmerized.

She tried the word on for size and decided it fit just about perfectly. She had slid into a kind of doubled (maybe even trebled) recall. *Total* recall. But beyond this point her memories of the cold guest bedroom where she'd found him catatonic and those of the two of them in the creaky second-floor bed at The Antlers (these memories seventeen years older but even clearer) were blotted out. *Do you*

LISEY'S STORY

want to go see, Lisey? he had asked her – yes, yes – but whatever had come next was drowned in brilliant purple light, hidden behind that curtain, and when she tried to reach for it, authority-voices from childhood (Good Ma's, Dandy's, all her big sisters') clamored in alarm. *No, Lisey! That's far enough, Lisey! Stop there, Lisey!*

Her breath caught. (Had it caught as she lay there with her love?)

Her eyes opened. (They had been wide as he took her in his arms, of that she was sure.)

Bright morning Junelight – twenty-first-century Junelight – replaced the staring, glaring purple of a billion lupin. The pain of her lacerated breast flooded back in with the light. But before Lisey could react to either the light or the panicky voices commanding her to go no farther, someone called to her from the barn below, startling her so badly that she came within a thread of screaming. If the voice had stopped short at *Missus*, she would have.

'Mrs Landon?' A brief pause. 'Are you up there?'

No trace of border South in that voice, only a flat Yankee drawl that turned the words into *Aaa you up theah*, and Lisey knew who was down theah: Deputy Alston. He'd told her he'd keep checking back, and here he was, as promised. This was her chance to tell him hell yes, she was up here, she was lying on the floor bleeding because the Black Prince of the Incunks had hurt her, Alston had to take her to No Soapa with the flashers and the siren going, she needed stitches in her breast, a lot of them, and she needed protection, needed it around the clock—

No, Lisey.

It was her own mind that sent the thought up (of

405

this she was positive) like a flare into a dark sky (well . . . *almost* positive), but it came to her in Scott's voice. As if it would gain authority that way.

And it must have worked, because 'Yes, I'm here, Deputy!' was all she called back.

'Everything fi'-by? Okay, I mean?'

'Five-by, that's affirmative,' she said, amazed to find she actually *sounded* five-by-five. Especially for a woman whose blouse was soaked in blood and whose left breast was throbbing like a . . . well, there was really no accurate simile. It was just *throbbing*.

Down below – at the very foot of the stairs, Lisey calculated – Deputy Alston laughed appreciatively. 'I just stopped on my way over to Cash Corners. They got a little house-fire over there.' *House-fiah.* 'Arson suspected.' *Aaason.* 'You be all right on your own for a couple-three hours?'

'Fine.'

'Got your cell phone?'

She did indeed have her cell phone and wished she were on it right now. If she had to keep shouting down to him, she was probably going to pass out. 'Rah-cheer!' she called back.

'Ayuh?' A little dubious. God, what if he came up and saw her? He'd be plenty dubious then, dubious to the *n*th power. But when he spoke again the voice was moving away. She could hardly believe she was glad, but she was. Now that this was begun, she wanted to finish it. 'Well, you call if you need anything. And I'll be checking back later on. If you go out, leave a note so I'll know you're all right and when to expect you back, okay?'

And Lisey, who now began to see – vaguely – a

course of events ahead of her, called back 'Check!' She'd have to begin by returning to the house. But first, before anything else, a drink of water. If she didn't get some more water, and soon, her throat might catch fiah like that house over to Cash Corners.

'I'll be coming by Patel's on my way back, Mrs Landon, would you like me to pick anything up?'

Yes! A six-pack of ice-cold Coke and a carton of Salem Lights!

'No thanks, Deputy.' If she had to talk much more, her voice would give out. Even if it didn't, he'd hear something wrong in it.

'Not even doughnuts? They have great doughnuts.' A smile in his voice.

'Dieting!' It was all she dared.

'Oh-oh, I heard *that*,' he said. 'You have a nice day, Mrs Landon.'

Please God no more, she prayed, and called back, 'You too, Deputy!'

Clump-clump-clumpety-clump, and away he went.

Lisey listened for the sound of an engine and after awhile thought she heard one starting up, but very faint. He must have parked by her mailbox and then walked the length of the driveway.

Lisey lay where she was a moment longer, gathering herself, then rose to a sitting position. Dooley had sliced diagonally across her breast and up toward the hollow of her armpit. The ragged, wandering gash had stiffened and closed up a little, but her movement tore it open again. The pain was enormous. Lisey cried out and that made matters even worse. She felt fresh blood run down her ribcage. Those dark wings began to steal over her vision again and she willed them away, repeating the same mantra over and over again until the world grew solid: *I have to finish this, I have to get behind the purple. I have to finish this, I have to get behind the purple. I have to finish this and get behind the purple.*

Yes, behind the purple. On the hillside it had been lupin; in her mind it was the heavy curtain she had constructed herself – maybe with Scott's help, certainly with his tacit approval.

I've gotten behind it before.

Had she? Yes.

And I can do it again. Get behind it or rip the goddam thing down if I have to.

Question: Had she and Scott ever spoken of Boo'ya Moon again after that night at The Antlers? Lisey thought not. They had their code words, of course, and God knew those words had floated out of the purple on occasion when she'd been unable to find him in malls and grocery stores . . . not to mention the time that nurse misplaced him in his smucking hospital bed . . . and there was the muttering reference to his long boy when he'd been lying in the parking lot after Gerd Allen Cole had shot him . . . and Kentucky . . . Bowling Green, as he lay dying . . .

Stop, Lisey! the voices chorused. *You mustn't, little Lisey!* they cried. *Mein gott, you don't darenzee!*

She had tried to put Boo'ya Moon behind her, even after the winter of '96, when—

'When I went there again.' Her voice was dry but clear in her dead husband's study. 'In the winter of 1996 I went again. I went to bring him back.'

408

There it was, and the world did not end. Men in white coats did not materialize out of the walls to carry her away. In fact she thought she even felt a little better, and maybe that wasn't so surprising. Maybe when you got right down to where the short hairs grew, truth was a bool, and all it wanted was to come out.

'Okay, it's out now – some of it, the Paul part – so can I get a smucking drink of water?'

Nothing told her no, and using the edge of Dumbo's Big Jumbo as a support, Lisey managed to pull herself to her feet. The dark wings came again, but she hung her head over, trying to keep as much blood in her miserable excuse for a brain as possible, and this time the faintness passed more quickly. She set sail for the bar alcove, walking her own backtrail of blood, taking slow steps with her feet wide apart, thinking she must look like an old lady whose walker had been stolen.

She made it, sparing only a brief look for the glass lying on the carpet. She wanted nothing more to do with that one. She got another out of the cabinet, once again using her right hand – the left was still clutching the bloody square of knitting – and drew cold water. Now the water was running again and the pipes barely chugged at all. She swung out the glass mirror over the basin, and inside was what she had been hoping for: a bottle of Scott's Excedrin. No childproof cap to slow her down, either. She winced at the vinegary smell that wafted from the bottle after she popped the cap, and checked the expiration date: **JUL 05**. *Oh well*, she thought, *a girl's gotta do what a girl's gotta do.*

'I think Shakespeare said that,' she croaked, and

swallowed three of the Excedrin. She didn't know how much good they would do her, but the water was heavenly and she drank until her belly cramped. Lisey stood clutching the lip of her dead husband's bar sink, waiting for the cramp to pass. Finally it did. That left only the pain in her beaten-up face and the much deeper throbbing in her lacerated breast. In the house she had something much stronger than Scott's head-bonkers (although certainly no fresher), Vicodin from Amanda's previous adventure in self-mutilation. Darla also had some, and Canty had Manda-Bunny's bottle of Percocet. They had all agreed without ever really even discussing it that Amanda herself couldn't be allowed access to the hard stuff; she might get feeling yucky and decide to take everything at once. Call it a Tequila Sunset.

Lisey would try for the house – and the Vicodin – soon, but not quite yet. Walking in the same careful feet-wide-apart way, a half-filled glass of water in one hand and the blood-soaked square of african in the other, Lisey made her way to the dusty booksnake and sat down there, waiting to see what three geriatric Excedrin might do for her pain. And as she waited, her thoughts turned once more to the night she had found him in the guest room – in the guest room but *gone*.

I kept thinking we were on our own. That wind, that smucking wind

23

She's listening to that killer wind scream around the house, listening to snowgrit whip against the windows, knowing they're on their own – that *she* is on her own. And as she

410

listens, her thoughts turn once more to that night in New Hampshire when the hour was none and the moon kept teasing the shadows with its inconstant light. She remembers how she opened her mouth to ask if he could really do it, could really take her, and then closed it again, knowing it to be the kind of question you only ask when you want to play for time ... and don't you only play for time when you're not on the same side?

We're on the same side, she remembers thinking. *If we're going to get married, we better be.*

But there *was* one question that needed asking, maybe because that night at The Antlers it was *her* turn to jump off the bench. 'What if it's night over there? You said there are bad things over there at night.'

He smiled at her. 'It's not, honey.'

'How do you know?'

He shook his head, still smiling. 'I just do. The way a kid's dog knows it's time to go sit by the mailbox because the schoolbus will be right along. It's almost sunset over there. It often is.'

She didn't understand that, but didn't ask – one question always led on to another, that had been her experience, and the time for questions was done. If she meant to trust him, the time for questions was done. So she had taken a deep breath and said, 'All right. It's our frontloaded honeymoon. Take me someplace that isn't New Hampshire. This time I want a good look.'

He crushed his half-smoked cigarette in the ashtray and took her lightly by her upper arms, his eyes dancing with excitement and good humor – how well she remembers the feel of his fingers on her flesh that night. 'You've got a yard of guts, little Lisey – I'll tell the world that. Hold on and let's see what happens.'

And he took me, Lisey thinks as she sits in the guest room, now holding the waxy-cool hand of the breathing man-doll in the rocker. But she feels the smile on her face – little Lisey, big smile – and wonders how long it's been there. *He took me, I know he did. But that was seventeen years ago, when we were both young and brave and he was all present and accounted for. Now he's gone.*

Except his *body* is still here. Does that mean he can no longer go physically, as he did when he was a child? As she knows he has from time to time since she herself has known him? As he did from the hospital in Nashville, for example, when the nurse couldn't find him?

It is then that Lisey feels the faint tightening of his hand on hers. It's almost imperceptible, but he is her love and she feels it. His eyes still stare off toward the blank face of the TV from above the folds of the yellow african, but yes, his hand is squeezing hers. It is a kind of *long-distance* squeeze, and why not? He's plenty far away, even if his body *is* here, and where he is, he might be squeezing with all his might.

Lisey has a sudden brilliant intuition: Scott is holding a conduit open for her. God knows what it's costing him to do it, or how long he can keep it up, but that's what he's doing. Lisey lets go of his hand and gets up on her knees, ignoring the tingling burst of pins and needles in her legs, which have almost gone to sleep, likewise ignoring another great cold gust of wind that shakes the house. She tears away enough of the african so she can slide her arms between Scott's sides and his unresisting arms, so she can

clasp her hands at the middle of his back and hug him.
She puts her urgent face in the path of his blank stare.

'Pull me,' she whispers to him, and gives his limp
body a shake. 'Pull me to where you are, Scott.'

There's nothing, and she raises her voice to a shout.

*'Pull me, goddam you! Pull me to where you are so I can
bring you home! Do it! IF YOU WANT TO COME HOME,
TAKE ME TO WHERE YOU ARE!'*

24

'And you did,' Lisey muttered. '*You* did and *I* did. I'll be
smucked if I know how this thing is supposed to work
now that you're dead and gone instead of just gomered
out in the guest room, but that's what it's all been about,
hasn't it? *All* of this.'

And she *did* have an idea of how it was supposed to
work. It was far back in her mind, just a shape behind that
curtain of hers, but it was there.

Meantime, the Excedrin had kicked in. Not a lot,
but maybe enough so she could get down to the floor of
the barn without passing out and breaking her neck. If she
could get there, she could get into the house where the
really *good* dope was stashed . . . assuming it still worked.
It *better* work, because she had things to do and places to
go. Some of them far places, indeed.

'Journey of a thousand miles begin with single step,
Lisey-san,' she said, and got up from the booksnake.

Once more walking in slow, shuffling steps, Lisey set
sail for the stairs. It took her almost three minutes to nego-
tiate them, clinging to the banister every step of the way

413

and pausing twice when she felt faint, but she made it without falling, sat for a little while on the sheeted *mein gott* bed to catch her breath, and then began the long expedition to the back door of her house.

CHAPTER ELEVEN
LISEY AND THE POOL (SHHHH – NOW YOU MUST BE STILL)

1

Lisey's greatest fear, that the late-morning heat would overcome her and she'd pass out halfway between the barn and the house, came to nothing. The sun obliged her by ducking behind a cloud, and a cap of cool breeze materialized to briefly soothe her overheated skin and flushed, swollen face. By the time she got to the back stoop, the deep laceration in her breast was pounding again, but the dark wings stayed away. There was a bad moment when she couldn't find her housekey, but eventually her fumbling fingers touched the fob – a little silver elf – beneath the wad of Kleenex she usually carried in her right front pocket, so *that* was all right. And the house was cool. Cool and silent and blessedly *hers*. Now if it would only remain hers while she tended herself. No calls, no visitors, no six-foot deputies lumbering up to the back door to check on her. Also, please God (*pretty* please) no return visit from the Black Prince of the Incunks.

She crossed the kitchen and got the white plastic basin out from under the sink. It hurt to bend, hurt a *lot*, and once more she felt the warmth of flowing blood on her skin and soaking the remains of her shredded top.

He got off on doing it – you know that, don't you?

Of course she did.

And he'll be back. No matter what you promise – no matter what you deliver – he'll be back. Do you know that, too?

Yes, she knew that, too.

Because to Jim Dooley, his deal with Woodbody and Scott's manuscripts is all just so much ding-dong for the freesias. There's a reason why he went for your boob instead of your earlobe or maybe a finger.

'Sure,' she told her empty kitchen – shady, then suddenly bright as the sun sailed out from behind a cloud. 'It's the Jim Dooley version of great sex. And next time it *will* be my pussy, if the cops don't stop him.'

You stop him, Lisey. You.

'Don't be silly, dollink,' she told the empty kitchen in her best Zsa Zsa Gabor voice. Once again using her right hand, she opened the cupboard over the toaster, took out a box of Lipton teabags, and put them into the white basin. She added the bloody square of the african from Good Ma's cedar box, although she had absolutely no idea why she was still carrying it. Then she began trudging toward the stairs.

What's silly about it? You stopped Blondie, didn't you? Maybe you didn't get the credit, but you were the one who did it.

'That was different.' She stood looking up the stairs

with the white plastic basin under her right arm, held against her hip so the box of tea and the piece of knitting wouldn't fall out. The stairs looked approximately eight miles high. Lisey thought there really ought to be clouds swirling around the top.

If it was different, why are you going upstairs?

'Because that's where the Vicodin is!' she cried to the empty house. 'The damned old feel-better pills!'

The voice said one more thing and fell silent.

'SOWISA, babyluv is right,' Lisey agreed. 'You better believe it.' And she began the long, slow trek up the stairs.

2

Halfway up the wings came back, darker than ever, and for a moment Lisey was sure she was going to black out. She was telling herself to fall forward, *onto* the stairs, rather than backward into space, when her vision cleared again. She sat down with the basin drawn across her legs and stayed that way, head hung over, until she had counted to a hundred with a *Mississippi* between each number. Then she got up again and finished her climb. The second floor was cross-drafted and even cooler than the kitchen, but by the time Lisey got there she was sweating profusely again. The sweat ran into the laceration across her breast, and soon there was a maddening salt-sting on top of the deeper ache. And she was thirsty again. Thirsty all the way down her throat and into her stomach, it seemed. That, at least, could be remedied, and the sooner the better.

She glanced into the guest room as she made her slow way by. It had been redone since 1996 – twice, actually

– but she found it was all too easy to see the black rocking chair with the University of Maine seal on the back . . . and the blank eye of the television . . . and the windows filled with frost that changed color as the lights in the sky changed . . .

Let it go, little Lisey, it's in the past.

'It's all in the *past* but none of it's *done!*' she cried irritably. 'That's the smucking *trouble!*'

To that there was no answer, but here, at long last, was the master bedroom and its adjacent bathroom – what Scott, never known for his delicacy, had been wont to call Il Grande Poopatorium. She set down the basin, dumped out the toothglass (still two brushes, now both of them hers, alas), and filled the tumbler to the brim with cold water. This she drank off greedily, then she *did* take a moment to look at herself. At her face, anyway.

What she saw was not encouraging. Her eyes were glittering blue sparks peering out of dark caves. The skin beneath them had gone a dark blackish brown. Her nose was canted to the left. Lisey didn't think it was broken, but who knew? At least she could breathe through it. Below her nose was a great crust of dried blood that had broken both right and left around her mouth, giving her a grotesque Fu Manchu mustache. *Look, Ma, I'm a biker*, she tried to say, but the words wouldn't quite come out. It was a shitty joke, anyway.

Her lips were so severely swollen they actually turned out from the inside, giving her battered face a grotesquely exaggerated come-and-kiss-me pout.

Was I thinking of going up to Greenlawn, home of the famous Hugh Alberness, in this condish? Was I really? Pretty funny – they'd get one look and then call for an ambulance to take me to a real hospital, the kind where they've got an ICU.

That isn't *what you were thinking. What you were thinking—*

But she closed that off, remembering something Scott used to say: *Ninety-eight percent of what goes on in people's heads is none of their smucking business.* Maybe it was true, maybe it wasn't, but for the time being she'd do well to take this as she had the stairs: head down and one step at a time.

Lisey had another bad moment when she couldn't find the Vicodin. She almost gave up, thinking one of the three spring-cleaning girls might have walked away with the bottle, before finding it hiding behind Scott's multi-vitamins. And, wonder of wonders, the expiration on these babies was this very month.

'Waste not, want not,' Lisey said, and washed down three of them. Then she filled the plastic basin with luke-warm water and threw in a handful of teabags. She watched the clear water begin to stain amber for a moment or two, then shrugged and dumped in the rest of the teabags. They settled to the bottom of the darkening water and she thought of a young man saying *It stings a little but it works really really good.* In another life, that had been. Now she would see for herself.

She took a clean washcloth from the rod beside the sink, dropped it into the basin, and wrung it out gently. *What are you doing, Lisey?* she asked herself . . . but the answer was obvious, wasn't it? She was still following the trail her dead husband had left her. The one that led into the past.

419

She let the tatters of her blouse slip to the bathroom floor, and, with a grimace of anticipation, applied the tea-soaked washcloth to her breast. It *did* hurt, but compared to the nettlesome sting of her own sweat, it was almost pleasant, in an astringent mouthwash-on-the-canker kind of way.

It works. It really really works, Lisey.

Once she had believed that – sort of – but once she had been twenty-two and willing to believe lots of things. What she believed in now was Scott. And Boo'ya Moon? Yes, she guessed she believed in that, too. A world that was waiting right next door, and behind the purple curtain in her mind. The question was whether or not it might be in reach for the celebrated writer's gal pal now that he was dead and she was on her own.

Lisey wrung blood and tea out of the washcloth, dipped it again, replaced it on her wounded breast. This time the sting was even less. *But it's no cure*, she thought. *Just another marker on the road into the past.* Out loud she said, 'Another bool.'

Holding the washcloth gently against her and taking the bloody square of african – Good Ma's delight – in the hand folded beneath her breast, Lisey went slowly into the bedroom and sat down on the bed, looking at the silver spade with *COMMENCEMENT, SHIPMAN LIBRARY* incised on the scoop. Yes, she really could see a small dent where she'd connected first with Blondie's gun and then with Blondie's face. She had the spade, and although the yellow african in which Scott had wrapped himself on those cold nights in 1996 was long gone, she did have this remnant, this delight.

Bool, the end.

'I *wish* it was the end,' Lisey said, and lay back with the washcloth still on her breast. The pain was funneling away, but that was just Amanda's Vicodin taking hold, doing what neither Paul's tea-cure nor Scott's out-of-date aspirin could. When the Vicodin wore off, the pain would be back. So would Jim Dooley, author of the pain. The question was, what was *she* going to do in the meantime? *Could* she do something?

The one thing you absolutely cannot *do is drift off to sleep.*

No, that would be bad.

I'd better hear from the Prof by eight tonight, or next time the hurtin will be a lot worse, Dooley had told her, and Dooley had set things up so she was in a lose-lose situation. He had also told her to tend herself and not tell anyone he'd been here. So far she'd done that, but not because she was afraid of being killed. In a way, knowing that he meant to kill her anyway gave her a leg up. She didn't have to worry anymore about trying to reason with him, at least. But if she called the Sheriff's Department . . . well . . .

'You can't go on a bool hunt when the house is full of great big clutterbugging deputies,' she said. 'Also . . .'

Also, I believe that Scott's still having his say. Or trying to.

'Honey,' she told the empty room, 'I only wish I knew what it was.'

3

She looked over at the digital clock on the bedside table and was astounded to see it was only twenty to eleven.

Already this day seemed a thousand years long, but she suspected that was because she had spent so much of it re-living the past. Memories screwed up perspective, and the most vivid ones could annihilate time completely while they held sway.

But enough about the past; what was happening right now?

Well, Lisey thought, *let's see. In the Kingdom of Pittsburgh, the former King of the Incunks is no doubt suffering the sort of terror my late husband used to call Stinky Testicle Syndrome. Deputy Alston's over in Cash Corners, inspecting a little house-fiah. Aaaason suspected, deah. Jim Dooley? Maybe laid up in the woods near here, whittling on a stick with my Oxo can opener in his pocket, waiting for the day to pass. His PT Cruiser could be tucked away in any one of a dozen deserted barns or sheds on the View, or in the Deep Cut, across the Harlow town line. Darla's probably on her way to the Portland Jetport to pick up Canty. Good Ma would say she's gone tooting. And Amanda? Oh, Amanda's gone, babyluv. Just as Scott knew she would, sooner or later. Didn't he do everything but reserve her a smucking room? Because it takes one to know one. As the saying is.*

Out loud she said: 'Am I supposed to go to Boo'ya Moon? Is that the next station of the bool? It is, isn't it? Scott, you goon, how do I do that with you dead?'

You're getting ahead of yourself again, aren't you?

Sure – carrying on about her inability to reach a place she had as yet not given herself permission to fully remember.

You've got to do a lot more than lift that curtain and peep under the hem.

'I've got to rip it down,' she said dismally. 'Don't I?'

No answer. Lisey took that for a yes. She rolled over on her side and picked up the silver spade. The inscription winked in the morning sunlight. She wrapped the bloody piece of african around the handle, then took hold of it that way.

'All right,' she said, 'I'll rip it down. He asked me if I wanted to go, and I said all right. I said Geronimo.'

Lisey paused, thinking.

'No. I didn't. I said it his way. I said *Geromino*. And what happened? What happened then?'

She closed her eyes, saw only brilliant purple, and could have cried for frustration. Instead she thought *SOWISA, babyluv: strap on when it seems appropriate*, and tightened her grip on the handle of the spade. She saw herself swinging it. She saw it glitter in the hazy August sun. And the purple parted before it, snapping back like skin after a slash, and what it let out wasn't blood but light: amazing orange light that filled her heart and mind with a terrible mixture of joy, terror, and sorrow. No wonder she had repressed this memory all these years. It was too much. Far too much. That light seemed to give the fading air of evening a silken texture, and the cry of a bird struck her ear like a pebble made of glass. A cap of breeze filled her nostrils with a hundred exotic perfumes: frangipani, bougainvillea, dusty roses, and oh dear God, night-blooming cereus. Most of all what pierced her was the memory of his skin on her skin, the beat of his blood running in counterpoint against the beat of her own, for they had been lying naked in their bed at The Antlers and now knelt naked in the purple lupin near the top of the hill, naked in the thickening shadows of the sweetheart trees. And rising above one horizon came the orange mansion of the moon, bloated and burning cold, while the sun sank below the other, boiling in a crimson house of fire. She thought that mixture of furious light would kill her with its beauty.

Lying on her widow's bed with the spade clamped in her hands, a much older Lisey cried out in joy for what was remembered and grief for what was gone. Her heart was mended even as it was broken again. Cords stood out on her neck. Her swollen lips drew down and broke open, exposing her teeth and spilling fresh blood into the gutters of her gums. Tears ran from the corners of her eyes and slipped down her cheeks to her ears, where they hung like exotic jewelry. And the only clear thought in her mind was *Oh Scott, we were never made for such beauty, we were never made for such beauty, we should have died then, oh my dear, we should have, naked and in each other's arms, like lovers in a story.*

'But we didn't,' Lisey murmured. 'He held me and said we couldn't stay long because it was getting dark and it wasn't safe after dark, even most of the sweetheart trees turned bad then. But he said there was something he wanted

4

'There's something I want to show you before we go back,' he says, and pulls her to her feet.

'Oh, Scott,' she hears herself saying, very faint and weak. 'Oh, Scott.' It seems to be the only thing she can manage. In a way this reminds her of the first time she felt an orgasm approaching, only this is drawn out and drawn out and drawn out, it's like all coming and no arrival.

He's leading her someplace. She feels high grass whispering against her thighs. Then it's gone and she realizes they're on a well-worn path cutting through the drifts of lupin. It leads into what Scott calls the sweetheart trees, and she wonders if there are people here. *If there are, how do they stand it?* Lisey wonders. She wants to look again at that ascending goblin moon, but doesn't dare.

'Be quiet under the trees,' Scott says. 'We should be okay a little longer, but better safe than sorry is a good rule to follow even on the edge of the Fairy Forest.'

Lisey doesn't think she could talk much above a whisper even if he demanded it. She's doing well to manage *Oh, Scott.*

He's standing under one of the sweetheart trees now. It looks like a palm, only its trunk is shaggy, green with what looks like fur rather than moss. 'God, I hope nothing's knocked it over,' he says. 'It was okay the last time I was here, the night you were so mad and I put my hand through that dumb greenhouse – ah, okay, there!' He pulls her off the path to the right. And near one of two outlying trees that seem to guard the place where the path slips into the woods, she sees a simple cross made of two boards. To Lisey they look like nothing more than crate-slats. There's no burial mound – if anything, the ground here is slightly sunken – but the cross is enough to tell her it's a grave. On the marker's horizontal arm is one carefully printed word: **PAUL.**

'The first time I did it in pencil,' he says. His voice is clear, but it seems to be coming from far away. 'Then I tried a ballpoint, but of course it didn't work, not on rough wood like that. Magic Marker was better, but it faded. Finally I did it in black paint, from one of Paul's old paint-by-the-numbers kits.'

She looks at the cross in the strange mixed light of the dying day and the rising night, thinking (as much as she is *able* to think), *All of it's true. What seemed to happen when we came out from under the yum-yum tree really did happen. It's happening now, only longer and clearer.*

'Lisey!' He's hectic with joy, and why the hell not? He hasn't been able to share this place with anyone since Paul's death. The few times he's come here, he's had to come alone. To mourn alone. 'There's something else – let me show you!'

Somewhere a bell rings, very faint – a bell that sounds familiar. 'Scott?'

'What?' He's kneeling in the grass. 'What, babyluv?'

'Did you hear . . . ?' But it's stopped. And surely that *was* her imagination. 'Nothing. What were you going to show me?' Thinking, *As if you haven't shown me enough.*

He's sweeping his hands through the high grass near the foot of the cross, but there seems to be nothing there and slowly his goofy, happy smile begins to fade. 'Maybe something took i—' he begins, then breaks off. His face tightens in a momentary wince, then relaxes, and he lets loose a half-hysterical laugh. 'Here it is, and damn if I didn't think I pricked myself on it, that'd be a joke on me, all right – after all these years! – but the cap's still on! Look, Lisey!'

She would have said nothing could divert her from the wonder of where she is – the red-orange sky in the east and west deepening to a weird greenish-blue over-head, the exotic mixed odors, and somewhere, yes, another faint chime of some lost bell – but what Scott is holding up to the last fading daylight does the trick. It's the hypo-dermic needle his father gave him, the one Scott was supposed to stick Paul with once the boys were over here. There are little speckles of rust on the sleeve of metal at its base, but otherwise it looks brand new.

'It was all I had to leave,' Scott says. 'I didn't have a picture. The kids who went to Donkey School used to get pictures, at least.'

'You dug the grave . . . Scott, you dug it with your bare hands?'

'I tried. And I did scoop out a little hollow – the ground here is soft – but the grass . . . pulling out the grass slowed me down . . . tough old weeds, boy . . . and then it started getting dark and the laughers started . . .'

'The laughers?'

'Like hyenas, I think, only mean. They live in the Fairy Forest.'

'The Fairy Forest – did Paul name it that?'

'No, me.' He gestures to the trees. 'Paul and I never saw the laughers up close, mostly just heard them. But we saw other things . . . *I* saw other things . . . there's this one thing . . .' Scott looks toward the rapidly darkening masses of sweetheart trees, then at the path, which fades away quickly when it enters the forest. There's no mistaking the caution in his voice when he speaks again. 'We have to go back soon.'

'But you can take us, can't you?'

'With you to help? Sure.'

'Then tell me how you buried him.'

'I can tell you that when we go back, if you—'

But the slow shake of her head silences him.

'No. I understand about why you don't want to have kids. I get that now. If you ever came to me and said, "Lisey, I've changed my mind, I want to take the chance," we could talk about it because there was Paul . . . and then there was you.'

'Lisey—'

'We could talk about it *then*. Otherwise we're never going to talk about gomers and bad-gunky and this place again, okay?' She sees the way he's looking at her and softens her tone. 'It's not about you, Scott – not everything is, you know. This happens to be about *me*. It's beautiful here . . .' She looks around. And she shivers. 'It's *too* beautiful. If I spent too much time here – or even too much time thinking about it – I think the beauty would drive me insane. So if our time is short, for once in your smucking life, *you* be short. Tell me how you buried him.'

Scott half-turns away from her. The orange light of the setting sun paints the line of his body: flange of shoulder-blade, tuck of waist, curve of buttock, the long shallow arc of one thigh. He touches the arm of the cross. In the high grass, barely visible, the glass curve of the hypo glimmers like a forgotten bit of trumpery treasure.

'I covered him with grass, then I went home. I couldn't come back for almos' a week. I was sick. I had a fever. Daddy give me o'meal in the morning and soup when he come home from work. I was ascairt of Paul's ghos, but I never seen his ghos. Then I got better and trite to come here with Daddy's shovel from the shed, but it wouldn't *go*. Just me. I thought the aminals – *animals* – would have ett'n on him – the laughers and such – but they din't yet, so I went back and trite to come over again, this time with a play-shovel I found in our old toybox in the attic. That went and that's what I dug his grave with, Lisey, a red plastic play-shovel we had for the san'box when we 'us very wee.'

The sinking sun has started to fade to pink. Lisey puts her arm around him and hugs him. Scott's arms encircle her and for a moment or two he hides his face in her hair. 'You loved him so very much,' she says.

'He was my brother' is what he replies, and it is enough.

As they stand there in the growing gloom, she sees something else, or thinks she does. Another piece of wood? That's what it looks like, another crate-slat lying just beyond the place where the path leaves the lupin-covered hill (where lavender is now turning a steadily darker purple). No, not just one – two.

Is it another cross, she wonders, one that has fallen apart?

'Scott? Is someone *else* buried here?'

'Huh?' He sounds surprised. 'No! There's a graveyard, sure, but it's not here, it's by the—' He catches sight of what she's looking at and gives a little chuckle. 'Oh, wow! That's not a cross, it's a *sign*! Paul made it right around the time of the first bool hunts, back when he could still come on his own sometimes. I forgot all about that old sign!' He pulls free of her and hurries to where it lies. Hurries a little way down the path. Hurries under the trees. Lisey isn't sure she likes that.

'Scott, it's getting dark. Don't you think we better go?'

'In a minute, babyluv, in just a minute.' He picks up one of the boards and brings it back to her. She can make out letters, but they're faint. She has to bring the slat close to her eyes before she can read what's there:

TO THE POOL

'Pool?' Lisey asks.

'Pool,' he agrees. 'Rhymes with bool, don't you know.' And actually laughs. Only that's when, somewhere deep in what he calls the Fairy Forest (where night has surely come already), the first laughers raise their voices.

Only two or three, but the sound still terrifies Lisey more than anything she has ever heard in her life. To her those things don't sound like hyenas, they sound like *people*, lunatics cast into the deepest depths of some nineteenth-century Bedlam. She grasps Scott's arm, digging into his skin with her nails, and tells him in a voice she barely recognizes as her own that she wants to go back, he has to take her back right *now*.

Dim and distant, a bell tinkles.

'Yes,' he says, tossing the signboard into the weeds. Above them a dark draft of air stirs the sweetheart trees, making them sigh and give off a perfume that's stronger than the lupin – cloying, almost sickly. 'This really isn't a safe place after dark. The pool is safe, and the beach . . . the benches . . . maybe even the graveyard, but—'

More laughers join the chorus. In a matter of moments there are dozens of them. Some of the laughter runs up a jagged scale and turns into broken-glass screams that make Lisey feel like screaming back. Then they descend again, sometimes to guttering chuckles that sound as if they're coming from mud.

'Scott, what *are* those things?' she whispers. Above his shoulder the moon is a bloated gas balloon. 'They don't sound like animals at all.'

'I don't know. They run on all fours, but sometimes they . . . never mind. I never saw them close up. Neither of us did.'

'Sometimes they what, Scott?'

'Stand up. Like people. Look around. It doesn't matter. What matters is getting back. You want to go back now, right?'

'Yes!'

'Then close your eyes and visualize our room at The Antlers. See it as well as you can. It will help me. It will give us a boost.'

She closes her eyes and for one terrible second nothing comes. Then she's able to see how the bureau and the tables flanking the bed swam out of the gloom when the moon fought clear of the clouds and this brings back the wallpaper (rambler roses) and the shape of the bedstead and the comic-opera creak of the springs each time one of them moved. Suddenly the terrifying sound of those things laughing in the

(Forest Fairy Forest)

darkling woods seems to be fading. The smells are fading, too, and part of her is sad to be leaving this place, but mostly what she feels is relief. For her body (of course) and her mind (most certainly), but most of all for her soul, her immortal smucking *soul*, because maybe people like Scott Landon can jaunt off to places like Boo'ya Moon, but such strangeness and beauty were not made for ordinary folk such as she unless it's between the covers of a book or inside the safe dark of a movie theater.

And I only saw a little, she thinks.

'Good!' he tells her, and Lisey hears both relief and surprised delight in his voice. 'Lisey, you're a champ—' *at this* is how he finishes, but even before he does, before he lets go of her and she opens her eyes, Lisey knows

5

'I knew that we were home,' she finished, and opened her eyes. The intensity of her recall was so great that for a moment she expected to see the moonshadowy stillness of the bedroom they'd shared for two nights in New Hampshire twenty-seven years ago. She had been gripping the silver spade so tightly that she had to will her fingers open, one by one. She laid the yellow delight square – blood-crusted but comforting – back on her breast.

And then what? Are you going to tell me that after that, after all that, the two of you just rolled over and went to sleep?

That was pretty much what had happened, yes. She'd been anxious to start forgetting all of it, and Scott had been more than willing. It had taken all his courage to bring his past up in the first place, and no wonder. But she *had* asked him one more question that night, she remembered, and had almost asked another the following day, when they were driving back to Maine, before realizing she didn't have to. The question she'd asked had been about something he'd said just before the laughers started up, scaring all curiosity from her mind. She'd wanted to know what Scott meant when he'd said *Back when he could still come on his own sometimes.* Meaning Paul.

Scott looked startled. 'Been long years since I've thought of that,' he said, 'but yeah, he could. It was just hard for him, the way hitting a baseball was always hard for me. So mostly he let me do it, and I think after awhile he lost the knack completely.'

The question she'd thought to ask in the car was about the pool to which the broken sign had once pointed the way. Was it the one he always spoke about in his lectures? Lisey didn't ask because the answer was, after all, self-evident. His audiences might believe the myth-pool, the language-pool (to which we all go down to drink, to swim, or perhaps to catch a little fish) was figurative; she knew better. There was a real pool. She knew then because she knew *him.* She knew now because she had been there. You reached it from Sweetheart Hill by taking the path that led into the Fairy Forest; you had to pass both the Bell Tree and the graveyard to get there.

'I went to get him,' she whispered, holding the spade. Then she said abruptly, 'Oh God I remember the *moon,*' and her body broke out so painfully in gooseflesh that she writhed on the bed.

The moon. Yes, that. A bloody orange hophead moon, so suddenly different from the northern lights and the killing cold she had just left behind her. It had been sexy summer-crazy, that moon, darkly delicious, lighting the stone cleft of valley near the pool better than she might have wished. She could see it now almost as well as then because she had cut through the purple curtain, had ripped it most righteously, but memory was only memory and Lisey had an idea hers had taken her almost as far as it could. A little more, maybe – another picture or two from her own personal booksnake – but not much, and then she would actually have to go back there, to Boo'ya Moon.

The question was, could she?

Then another question occurred to her: *What if he's one of the shrouded ones now?*

For an instant, an image struggled to come clear in Lisey's mind. She saw scores of silent figures that might have been corpses wrapped in old-fashioned winding sheets. Only they were sitting up. And she thought they were breathing.

A shudder rolled through her. It hurt her lacerated breast in spite of the Vicodin she had on board, but there was no way to stop that shudder until it had run its course. When it had, she found herself able to face practical considerations again. The foremost was whether she could get over to that other world on her own . . . because she *had* to go, shrouded ones or not.

Scott had been able to do it on his own, and had been able to take his brother Paul. As an adult he had been able to take Lisey from The Antlers. The crucial question was what had happened seventeen years later, on that cold January night in 1996.

'He wasn't entirely *gone*,' she murmured. 'He squeezed my hand.' Yes, and the thought had crossed her mind that somewhere he might have been squeezing with every ounce of his force and being, but did that mean he had taken her?

'I yelled at him, too.' Lisey actually smiled. 'Told him if he wanted to come home he had to take me to where he was . . . and I always thought he did . . .'

Bullshit, little Lisey, you never thought about it at all. Did you? Not until today, when you almost literally got your tit in the wringer and had to. So if you're thinking about it, really think about it. Did he pull you to him that night? Did he?

She was on the verge of concluding it was one of those questions, like the chicken-or-egg thing, to which there was no satisfactory answer, when she remembered his saying *Lisey, you're a champ at this!*

Say she *had* done it by herself in 1996. Even so, Scott had been *alive*, and that squeeze of his hand, feeble as it had been, was enough to tell her he was there on the other side, making a conduit for her—

'It's still there,' she said. She was gripping the handle of the shovel again. 'That way through is still there, it *must* be, because he prepared for all of this. Left me a smucking bool hunt to get me ready. Then, yesterday morning, in bed with Amanda . . . that was *you*, Scott, I know it was. You said I had a blood-bool coming . . . and a prize . . . a drink, you said . . . and you called me babyluv. So where are you now? Where are you when I need you to get me over?'

No answer but the ticking of the clock on the wall.

Close your eyes. He'd said that, too. *Visualize. See as well as you can. It will help. Lisey, you're a champ at this.*

'I better be,' she told the empty, sunny, Scottless bedroom. 'Oh honey, I just better be.'

If Scott Landon had had a fatal flaw, it might have been thinking too much, but that had never been *her* problem. If she had stopped to consider the situation on that hot day in Nashville, Scott almost certainly would have died. Instead she had simply acted, and saved his life with the shovel she now held.

I trite to come here with Daddy's shovel from the shed, but it wouldn't go.

Would the silver spade from Nashville go?

Lisey thought yes. And that was good. She wanted to keep it with her. 'Friends to the end,' she whispered, and closed her eyes.

She was summoning her memories of Boo'ya Moon, now vivid indeed, when a disturbing question broke her deepening concentration: another troublesome thought to divert her.

What time is it there, little Lisey? Oh, not the hour, I don't mean that, but is it daytime or nighttime? Scott always knew – he said he did, anyway – but you're not Scott.

No, but she remembered one of his favorite rock 'n roll tunes: 'Night Time Is the Right Time'. In Boo'ya Moon, nighttime was the *wrong* time, when smells turned rotten and food could poison you. Nighttime was when the laughers came out – things that ran on all fours but sometimes stood up like people and looked around. And there were other things, worse things.

Things like Scott's long boy.

It's very close, honey. That's what he told her as he lay under the hot Nashville sun on the day when she had been sure he was dying. *I hear it taking its meal.* She had tried to tell him she didn't know what he was talking about; he had pinched her and told her not to insult his intelligence. Or her own.

Because I'd been there. Because I'd heard the laughers and believed him when he said there were worse things waiting. And there were. I saw the thing he was talking about. I saw it in 1996, when I went to Boo'ya Moon to bring him home. Just its side, but that was enough.

'It was endless,' Lisey muttered, and was horrified to realize she really believed this to be the truth. It had been night in 1996. Night when she had gone to Scott's other world from the cold guest room. She had gone down the path, into the woods, into the Fairy Forest, and—

A motor exploded into life nearby. Lisey's eyes flew open and she nearly screamed. Then she relaxed again, little by little. It was only Herb Galloway, or maybe the Luttrell kid Herb sometimes hired, cutting the grass next door. This was entirely different from the bitterly cold night in January of '96 when she'd discovered Scott in the guest room, there and still breathing but *gone* in every other way that mattered.

She thought: *Even if I could do it, I can't do it like this — it's too noisy.*

She thought: *The world is too much with us.*

She thought: *Who wrote that?* And, as happened so frequently, that thought came trailing its painful little red caboose: *Scott would know.*

Yes, Scott would know. She thought of him in all the motel rooms, bent over a portable typewriter **(SCOTT AND LISEY, THE EARLY YEARS!)** and then later, with his face lit by the glow of his laptop. Sometimes with a cigarette smoldering in an ashtray beside him, sometimes with a drink, always with the curl of hair falling forgotten across his forehead. She thought of him lying on top of her in this bed, of chasing her full-tilt through that awful house in Bremen **(SCOTT AND LISEY IN GERMANY!)**, both of them naked and laughing, horny but not really happy, while trucks and cars rumbled around and around the traffic-circle up the street. She thought of his arms around her, all the times his arms had been around her, and the smell of him, and the sandpaper rasp his cheek made against hers, and she thought she would sell her soul, yes, her immortal smucking soul, for no more than the sound of him down the hall slamming the door and then yelling *Hey, Lisey, I'm home – everything the same?*

Hush and close your eyes.

That was her voice, but it was *almost* his, a very good imitation, so Lisey closed her eyes and felt the first warm tears, almost comforting, slip out through the screen of lashes. There was a lot they didn't tell you about death, she had discovered, and one of the biggies was how long it took the ones you loved most to die in your heart. *It's a secret,* Lisey thought, *and it should be, because who would ever want to get close to another person if they knew how hard the letting-go part was? In your heart they only die a little at a time, don't they? Like a plant when you go away on a trip and forget to ask a neighbor to poke in once in awhile with the old watering-can, and it's so* sad—

She didn't want to think about that sadness, nor did she want to think about her hurt breast, where the pain had begun to creep back. She turned her thoughts to Boo'ya Moon again, instead. She recalled how utterly amazing and wonderful it had been to go from the bitter subzero Maine night to that tropical place in the wink of a maiden's eye. The somehow sad texture of the air, and the silky aromas of frangipani and bougainvillea. She remembered the tremendous light of the setting sun and the rising moon and how, far off, that bell was ringing. That same bell.

Lisey realized that the sound of the riding mower in the Galloways' yard now seemed oddly distant. So was the blat of a passing motorcycle. Something was happening, she was almost sure of it. A spring was winding, a well was filling, a wheel was turning. Maybe the world was not too much with her, after all.

But what if you get over there and it's night? Assuming that what you feel isn't just a combination of narcotics and wishful thinking, what if you get over there and it's night, when the bad things come out? Things like Scott's long boy?

Then I'll come back here.

If you have time, you mean.

Yes, that's what I mean, if there's t—

Suddenly, shockingly, the light shining through the lids of her closed eyes changed from red to a dim purple that was almost black. It was as if a shade had been pulled. But a shade wouldn't account for the glorious mixture of smells that suddenly filled her nose: the mixed perfume of all those flowers. Nor could it account for the grass she now felt pricking her calves and naked back.

She'd made it. Gotten over. Come through.

'No,' Lisey said with her eyes still shut – but it was feeble, little more than a token protest.

You know better, Lisey, Scott's voice whispered. *And time is short. SOWISA, babyluv.*

And because she knew that voice was absolutely right – time was indeed short – Lisey opened her eyes and sat up in her talented husband's childhood refuge.

Lisey sat up in Boo'ya Moon.

6

It was neither night *nor* day, and now that she was here, she wasn't surprised. She had come just before twilight on her previous two trips; was it any wonder it was just before twilight again?

The sun, brilliant orange, stood above the horizon at the end of the seemingly endless field of lupin. Looking the other way, Lisey could see the first rising arc of the moon – one far bigger than the biggest harvest moon she had ever seen in her life.

That's not our moon, is it? How can it be?

A breeze ruffled the sweaty ends of her hair, and somewhere not too far distant, that bell tinkled. A sound she remembered, a bell she remembered.

You better hurry up, don't you think?

Yes indeed. It was safe at the pool, or so Scott had said, but the way there led through the Fairy Forest, and that was not. The distance was short, but she'd do well to hurry.

She half-ran up the slope to the trees, looking for Paul's marker. At first she didn't see it, then spotted it leaning far over to one side. She didn't have time to straighten the cross . . . but took the time, anyway, because Scott would have taken the time. She set the silver spade aside for a moment (it had indeed come with her, as had the yellow knitted square) so she could use both hands. There must be weather here, because the single painstakingly printed word – **PAUL** – had faded to little more than a ghost.

I think I straightened it last time, too, she thought. *In*

'96. And thought I'd like to look for the hypodermic needle, only there was no time.

Nor was there now. This was her third real trip to Boo'ya Moon. The first hadn't been so bad because she'd been with Scott and they'd gone no farther than the broken signpost reading **TO THE POOL** before returning to the bedroom at The Antlers. The second time, however, in 1996, she'd had to take the path into the Fairy Forest on her own. She couldn't recall what bravery she must have summoned, not knowing how far it was to the pool or what she'd find when she got there. Not that this trip didn't have its own unique set of difficulties. She was topless, her badly gored left breast was starting to throb again, and God only knew what sort of things the smell of her blood might attract. Well, it was too late to worry about that now.

And if something does come at me, she thought, picking up the spade by its short wooden handle, *one of those laughers, for instance, I'll just bop it one with Little Lisey's Trusty Maniac Swatter, Copyright 1988, Patent Pending, All Rights Reserved.*

Somewhere up ahead, that bell tinkled again. Barefoot, bare-breasted, blood-smeared, wearing nothing but a pair of old denim shorts and carrying a spade with a silver scoop in her right hand, Lisey set off toward the sound along the rapidly darkening path. The pool was up ahead, surely no more than half a mile distant. There it was safe even after dark, and she would take off the few clothes she still wore, and wash herself clean.

441

7

It grew dim very quickly once she was under the canopy of trees. Lisey felt the urge to hurry more strongly than ever, but when the wind stirred the bell again – it was very close, now, and she knew it was hung from a branch by a bit of stout cord – she stopped, struck by a complex overlay of recall. She knew the bell was hung on a piece of cord because she had seen it on her last trip here, ten years ago. But Scott had swiped it long before that, even before they were married. She knew because she had heard it in 1979. Even then it had sounded familiar, in an unpleasant way. Unpleasant because she had hated the sound of that bell long before it had come over here to Boo'ya Moon.

'And I told him,' she murmured, switching the spade to her other hand and brushing back her hair. The yellow square of delight lay over her left shoulder. Around her the sweetheart trees rustled like whispering voices. 'He didn't say much, but I guess he took it to heart.'

She set off again. The path dipped, then rose to the top of a hill where the trees were a little thinner and strong red light shone through them. Not quite sunset yet, then. Good. And here the bell hung, nodding from side to side just enough to produce the faintest chime. It had, once upon a time, sat beside the cash register of Pat's Pizza & Café in Cleaves Mills. Not the kind of bell you hit with your palm, the discreet hotel-desk species that went *ding!* once and then shut up, but a kind of miniature silver school bell with a handle that went *ding-a-ling* for as long as you wanted to keep on shaking it. And Chuckie G., the cook who was on duty most nights during the year or so Lisey had waitressed at Pat's, had *loved* that bell. Sometimes, she remembered telling Scott, she heard its annoying silver ding-a-ling in her dreams, along with Chuckie G. bawling, leather-lunged: *Order's up, Lisey! Come on, let's hustle! Hungry people!* Yes, in bed she had told Scott how much she had hated Chuckie G.'s annoying little bell, in the spring of 1979 it must have been, because not long after that the annoying little bell had disappeared. She'd never associated Scott with its disappearance, not even when she'd heard it the first time she'd been here – too many other things going on then, too much weird input – and he had never said a word about it. Then, in 1996, while searching for him, she had heard Chuckie G.'s long-lost bell again, and that time she had

(let's hustle hungry people order's up)

known it for what it was. And the whole thing had made perfect crackpot sense. Scott Landon had been the man, after all, who thought the Auburn Novelty Shop was the hardy-har capital of the universe. Why wouldn't he have thought it a fine joke to swipe the bell that so annoyed his girlfriend and bring it to Boo'ya Moon? To hang it rah-cheer beside the path for the wind to ring?

There was blood on it last time, the deep voice of memory whispered. *Blood in 1996.*

Yes, and it had frightened her, but she had pushed on, anyway . . . and the blood was gone now. The weather that had faded Paul's name from the marker's crosspiece had also washed the bell clean. And the stout length of cord upon which Scott had hung it twenty-seven years before (always assuming time was the same over here) had almost worn away – soon the bell would tumble to the path. Then the joke would be over.

And now intuition spoke to her as powerfully as it ever had in her life, not in words but in a picture. She saw herself laying the silver spade at the foot of the Bell Tree, and she did so without pause or question. Nor did she ask herself why; it looked too perfect lying there at the foot of the old, gnarled tree. Silver bell above, silver spade below. As to *why* it should be perfect . . . she might as well ask herself why Boo'ya Moon existed in the first place. She'd thought the spade had been made for *her* protection this time. Apparently not. She gave it one more look (it was all the time she could afford) and then moved on.

8

The path led her down into another fold of forest. Here the strong red light of evening had faded to dimming orange and the first of the laughers woke somewhere ahead of her in the darker reaches of the woods, its horribly human voice climbing that glass mad-ladder and making her arms break out in gooseflesh.

Hurry, babyluv.

'Yes, all right.'

Now a second laugher joined the first, and although she felt more gooseflesh ripple up her bare back, she thought she was all right. Just up ahead the path curved around a vast gray rock she remembered very well. Beyond it lay a deep rock-hollow – oh yes, deep and puffickly *huh-yooge* – and the pool. At the pool she would be safe. It was scary at the pool, but it was also safe. It—

Lisey became suddenly, queerly positive that some-

444

thing was stalking her, just waiting for the last of the light to drain away before making its move.

Its *lunge*.

Heart pounding so hard it hurt her mutilated breast, she dodged around the great gray bulk of that protruding stone. And the pool was there, lying below like a dream made real. As she looked down at that ghostly shining mirror, the last memories clicked into place, and remembering was like coming home.

9

She comes around the gray rock and forgets all about the dried smear of blood on the bell, which has so troubled her. She forgets the screaming, windy cold and brilliant northern lights she has left behind. For a moment she even forgets Scott, whom she's come here to find and bring back . . . always assuming he wants to come. She looks down at the ghostly shining mirror of the pool and forgets everything else. Because it's beautiful. And even though she's never been here before in her life, it's like coming home. Even when one of those *things* starts to laugh she isn't afraid, because this is safe ground. She doesn't need anyone to tell her that; she knows it in her bones, just as she knows Scott has been talking about this place in his lectures and writing about it in his books for years.

She also knows that this is a sad place.

It's the pool where we all go down to drink, to swim, to catch a little fish from the edge of the shore; it's also the pool where some hardy souls go out in their flimsy wooden boats after the big ones. It is the pool of life, the cup of imagination, and she has an idea that different people see different versions of it, but with two things ever in common: it's always about a mile deep in the Fairy Forest, and it's always sad. Because imagination isn't the only thing this place is about. It's also about

(giving in)

waiting. Just sitting . . . and looking out over those dreamy waters . . . and waiting. *It's coming*, you think. *It's coming soon, I know it is.* But you don't know exactly what and so the years pass.

How can you know that, Lisey?

The moon told her, she supposes; and the northern lights that burn your eyes with their cold brilliance; the sweet-dust smell of roses and frangipani on Sweetheart Hill; most of all Scott's eyes told her as he struggled just to hold on, hold on, hold on. To keep from taking the path that led to this place.

More cackling voices rise in the deeper reaches of the woods and then something roars, momentarily silencing them. Behind her, the bell tinkles, then falls still again.

I ought to hurry.

Yes, even though she senses hurry is antithetical to this place. They need to be getting back to their house on Sugar Top as soon as possible, and not because there's danger of wild beasts, of ogres and trolls and

(vurts and seemies)

other strange creatures deep in the Fairy Forest where it's always dark as a dungeon and the sun never shines, but because the longer Scott stays here, the less likely she'll ever be able to bring him back. Also . . .

Lisey thinks of how it would be to see the moon

burning like a cold stone in the still surface of the pool below − and she thinks: *I might get fascinated*.

Yes.

Old wooden steps lead down this side of the slope. Beside each one is a stone post with a word carved into it. She can read these in Boo'ya Moon, but knows they would mean nothing to her back home; nor will she be able to remember anything but the simplest: [tk] means *bread*.

The stairs end in a downsloping ramp running to her left that finally empties at ground level. Here a beach of fine white sand glimmers in the rapidly failing light. Above the beach, carved on step-backs into a rock wall, are perhaps two hundred long, curved stone benches that look down on the pool. There might be space for a thousand or even two thousand people here if they were seated side by side, but they're not. She thinks there can be no more than fifty or sixty in all and most of them are hidden in gauzy wrappings that look like shrouds. But if they're dead, how can they be sitting? Does she even want to know?

On the beach, standing scattered, are maybe two dozen more. And a few people − six or eight − are actually in the water. They wade silently. As Lisey reaches the bottom of the steps and begins making her way toward the beach, her feet treading easily along the sunken rut of a path many other feet have walked before her, she sees a woman bend over and begin to lave her face. She does this with the slow gestures of someone in a dream, and Lisey recalls that day in Nashville, how everything fell into slow motion when she realized Blondie meant to shoot her husband. That was also like a dream, but wasn't.

Then she sees Scott. He's sitting on a stone bench nine or ten rows up from the pool. He's still got Good Ma's african, only here it's not bundled around him because it's too warm. It's just drawn across his knees, with the balance puddled over his feet. She doesn't know how the african can be both here and in the house on the View at the same time and thinks: *Maybe because some things are special. The way Scott is special.* And she? Is a version of Lisey Landon still back in the house on Sugar Top Hill? She thinks not. She thinks she is not that special, not her, not little Lisey. She thinks that, for better or worse, she is entirely *here*. Or entirely *gone*, depending on which world you're talking about.

She pulls in breath, meaning to call his name, then doesn't. A powerful intuition stops her.

Shhhh, she thinks. *Shhhh, little Lisey, now*

10

Now you must be still, she thought, as she had in January of 1996.

All was as it had been then, only now she saw it a little better because she had come a little earlier; the shadows in the stone valley that cupped the pool were only beginning to gather. The water had the shape, almost, of a woman's hips. At the beach end, where the hips would nip into the waist, was an arrowhead of fine white sand. Upon it, standing far apart from one another, were four people, two men and two women, staring raptly at the pool. In the water were half a dozen more. No one was swimming. Most were in no deeper than their calves; one man was in up to his waist. Lisey wished she could have read the expression on

this man's face, but she was still too far away. Behind the
waders and the people standing on the beach – those who
hadn't yet found enough courage to get wet, Lisey was
convinced – was the sloping headland that had been carved
into dozens or maybe hundreds of stone benches. Upon
them, widely scattered, sat as many as two hundred people.
She seemed to remember only fifty or sixty, but this evening
there were definitely more. Yet for every person she could
see, there had to be at least four in those horrible

(cerements)

wrappings.

There's a graveyard, too. Do you remember?

'Yes,' Lisey whispered. Her breast was hurting badly
again, but she looked at the pool and remembered Scott's
sliced-up hand. She also remembered how quickly he had
recovered from being shot in the lung by the madman –
oh, the doctors had been amazed. There was better medicine than Vicodin for her, and not far away.

'Yes,' she said again, and began making her way along
the downsloping path, this time with only one unhappy
difference: there was no Scott Landon sitting on a bench
down there.

Just before the path ended at the beach, she saw
another path splitting off to her left and away from the
pool. Lisey was once more all but overwhelmed by memory
as she saw the moon

11

She sees the moon rising through a kind of slot in the
massive granite outcropping that cups the pool. That moon

is bloated and gigantic, just as it was when her husband-to-be brought her to Boo'ya Moon from their bedroom at The Antlers, but in the widening clearing to which that slot leads, its infected red-orange face is broken into jagged segments by the silhouettes of trees and crosses. So many crosses. Lisey is looking into what might almost be a rustic country graveyard. Like the cross Scott made for his brother Paul, these appear to be made of wood, and although some are quite large and a few are ornate, they all look hand-made and many are the worse for wear. There are rounded markers as well, and some of these might be made of stone, but in the gathering gloom, Lisey cannot tell for sure. The light of the rising moon hinders rather than helps, because everything in the graveyard is backlit.

If there's a graveyard here, *why did he bury Paul back* there? *Was it because he died with the bad-gunky?*

She doesn't know or care. What she cares about is Scott. He's sitting on one of those benches like a spectator at a badly attended sporting event, and if she intends to do something, she'd better get busy. 'Keep your string a-drawing,' Good Ma would have said – that was one she caught from the pool.

Lisey leaves the graveyard and its rude crosses behind. She walks along the beach toward the stone benches where her husband sits. The sand is firm and somehow tingly. Feeling it against her soles and heels makes her realize that her feet are bare. She's still wearing her nightgown and layers of underthings, but her slippers didn't travel. The feel of the sand is dismaying and pleasant at the same time. It's also strangely *familiar*, and as she reaches the first of the stone benches, Lisey makes the connection. As a kid she had a recurring dream in which she'd go zooming around the house on a magic carpet, invisible to everyone else. She'd awaken from those dreams exhilarated, terrified, and sweat-soaked to the roots of her hair. This sand has the same magic-carpet feel . . . as if she were to bend her knees and then shoot upward, she might fly instead of jump.

I'd swoop over that pool like a dragonfly, maybe dragging my toes in the water . . . swoop around to the place where it outflows in a brook . . . along to where the brook fattens into a river . . . swooping low . . . smelling the damp rising up from the water, breaking through the little rising mists like scarves until I finally reached the sea . . . and then on . . . yes, on and on and on . . .

Tearing herself away from this powerful vision is one of the hardest things Lisey has ever done. It's like trying to rise after days of hard work and only a few hours of heavy and beautifully restful sleep. She discovers she's no longer on the sand but sitting on a bench in the third tier up from the little beach, looking out at the water with her chin propped on her palm. And she sees that the moonlight is losing its orange glow. It has become buttery, and will soon turn to silver.

How long have I been here? she asks herself, dismayed. She has an idea it's not really been that long, somewhere between fifteen minutes and half an hour, but even that is far too long . . . although she certainly understands how this place works now, doesn't she?

Lisey feels her eyes being drawn back to the pool – the peace of the pool, where now only two or three people (one is a woman with either a large bundle or a small child in her arms) are wading in the deepening evening – and

451

forces herself to look away, up at the rock horizons that encircle this place and at the stars peeping through the darkening blue above the granite and the few trees that fringe it up there. When she begins to feel a little more like herself, Lisey stands up, turns her back on the water, and locates Scott again. It's easy. That yellow knitted african all but screams, even in the gathering dark.

She goes to him, stepping up from one level to the next, as she would at a football stadium. She detours away from one of the shrouded creatures . . . but she's close enough to see the very human shape beneath its gauzy wrappings; hollow eyesockets and one hand that peeps out.

It is a woman's hand, with chipped red polish on the nails.

When she reaches Scott, her heart is pumping hard and she feels a little out of breath, even though the climb hasn't been difficult. In the distance the laughers have begun cackling up and down the scale, sharing their endless joke. Back the way she came, faint but still audible, she hears the fitful tinkle of Chuckie G.'s bell, and she thinks, *Order's up, Lisey! Come on, let's hustle!*

'Scott?' she murmurs, but Scott doesn't look at her. Scott is looking raptly at the pool, where the faintest hazy mist – a mere exhalation – has begun to rise in the light of the rising moon. Lisey allows herself only one quick glance that way before returning her regard firmly to her husband. She's learned her lesson about looking too long at the pool. Or so she hopes. 'Scott, it's time to come home.'

Nothing. No response whatsoever. She remembers protesting that he wasn't crazy, writing stories didn't make him *crazy*, and Scott telling her *I hope you stay lucky, little*

Lisey. But she hadn't, had she? Now she knows a lot more. Paul Landon went bad-gunky and wound up raving his life away chained to a post in the cellar of an isolated farmhouse. His younger brother has married and had an undeniably brilliant career, but now the bill has come due.

Your garden-variety catatonic, she thinks, and shivers.

'Scott?' she murmurs again, almost directly into his ear. She has taken both of his hands in hers. They are cool and smooth, waxy and lax. 'Scott, if you're in there and you want to come home, squeeze my hands.'

For the longest time there's nothing but the sound of the laughing things deep in the woods, and somewhere closer by the shocking, almost womanish cry of a bird. Then Lisey feels something that is either wishful thinking or the barest twitch of his fingers against hers.

She tries to think what she should do next, but the only thing she's sure of is what she *shouldn't* do: let the night swim up around them, dazzling her with silvery moonlight from above even as it drowns her in shadows rising from below. This place is a trap. She's sure that *anyone* who stays at the pool for very long will find it impossible to leave. She understands that if you look at it for a little while, you'll be able to see anything you want to. Lost loves, dead children, missed chances – anything.

The most amazing thing about this place? That there aren't more people hanging out on the stone benches. That they aren't packed in shoulder-to-shoulder like spectators at a smucking World Cup soccer match.

She catches movement in the corner of her eye and looks up the path leading from the beach to the stairs. She sees a stout gentleman wearing white pants and a billowing

STEPHEN KING

white shirt open all the way down the front. A great red gash runs down the left side of his face. His iron-gray hair is standing up at the back of his oddly flattened-looking head. He looks around briefly, then steps from the path to the sand.

Beside her, speaking with great effort, Scott says: 'Car crash.'

Lisey's heart takes a wild spring in her chest, but she's careful not to look around or to squeeze down too tightly on his hands, although she cannot forbear a slight twitch. Striving to keep her voice even, she says: 'How do you know?'

No answer from Scott. The stout gentleman in the billowing shirt spares one more dismissive glance for the silent folk sitting on the stone benches, then turns his back on them and wades into the pool. Silver tendrils of moon-smoke rise around him, and Lisey once more has to drag her eyes away.

'Scott, how do you know?'

He shrugs. His shoulders also seem to weigh a thousand pounds – that, at least, is how it looks to her – but he manages. 'Telepathy, I suppose.'

'Will he get better now?'

There's a long pause. Just when she thinks he won't answer, he does. 'He might,' he says. 'He's . . . it's deep . . . in here.' Scott touches his own head – indicating, Lisey thinks, some sort of brain injury. 'Sometimes things just . . . go too far.'

'Then do they come and sit here? Wrap themselves in sheets?'

Nothing from Scott. What she's afraid of now is losing

what little of him she's found. She doesn't need anyone to tell her how easily it could happen; she can feel it. Every nerve in her body knows this news.

'Scott, I think you want to come back. I think it's why you hung on so hard all last December. And I think it's why you brought the african. It's hard to miss, even in the gloom.'

He looks down, as if seeing it for the first time, then actually smiles a little. 'You're always . . . saving me, Lisey,' he says.

'I don't know what you're—'

'Nashville. I was going down.' With every word he seems to gain animation. For the first time she allows herself to really hope. 'I was lost in the dark and you found me. I was hot – so hot – and you gave me ice. Do you remember?'

She remembers that other Lisa

(I spilled half the fucking Coke getting back here)

and how Scott's shivering suddenly stopped when she popped a sliver of ice onto his bloody tongue. She remembers Coke-colored water dripping out of his eyebrows. She remembers it all. 'Of course I do. Now let's get out of here.'

He shakes his head, slowly but firmly. 'It's too hard. You go on, Lisey.'

'I'm supposed to go without you?' She blinks her eyes fiercely, only realizing when she feels the sting that she has begun to cry.

'It won't be hard – do it like that time in New Hampshire.' He speaks patiently, but still very slowly, as if every word were a great weight, and he is purposely misunderstanding her. She's almost sure of it. 'Just close your eyes

. . . concentrate on the place you came from . . . *see* it . . . and that's the place you'll go back to.'

'Without *you*?' she repeats fiercely, and below them, slowly, like a man moving underwater, a guy in a red flannel shirt turns to look at them.

Scott says, 'Shhhh, Lisey – here you must be still.'

'What if I don't *want* to be? This isn't the smucking *library*, Scott!'

Deep in the Fairy Forest the laughers howl as if this is the funniest thing they've ever heard, a knee-slapper worthy of the Auburn Novelty Shop. From the pool there's a single sharp splash. Lisey glances that way and sees the stout gentleman has gone to . . . well, to somewhere else. She decides she doesn't give a good goddam if it's underwater or Dimension X; her business now is with her husband. He's right, she's always saving him, just call her the U.S. Cavalry. And it's okay, she knew that practical shit was never exactly going to be Scott's main deal when she married him, but she has a right to expect a little help, doesn't she?

His gaze has drifted back to the water. She has an idea that when night comes and the moon begins to burn there like a drowned lamp, she'll lose him for good. This frightens and infuriates her. She stands up and snatches Good Ma's african. It came from *her* side of the family, after all, and if this is to be their divorce, she will have it back – *all* of it – even if it hurts him. *Especially* if it hurts him.

Scott looks at her with an expression of sleepy surprise that makes her angrier still.

'Okay,' she says, speaking with brittle lightness. It's a

tone foreign to her and seemingly to this place, as well. Several people look around, clearly disturbed and – perhaps – irritated. Well, smuck them and the various horses (or hearses, or ambulances) they rode in on. 'You want to stay here and eat lotuses, or whatever the saying is? Fine. I'll just go on back down the path—'

And for the first time she sees a strong emotion on Scott's face. It's fear. 'Lisey, no!' he says. 'Just boom back from here! You can't use the path! It's too late, almost *night*!'

'*Shhhh!*' someone says.

Fine. She'll *shhhh*. Bundling the yellow african higher in her arms, Lisey starts back down the risers. Two benches down from the bottom she chances a glance back. Part of her is sure that he'll follow her; this is *Scott*, after all. No matter how strange this place may be, he's still her husband, still her lover. The idea of divorce has crossed her mind, but surely it is absurd, a thing for other people but not for Scott and Lisey. He will not allow her to leave alone. But when she looks over her shoulder he's just sitting there in his white tee-shirt and green long underwear bottoms, with his knees together and his hands clasped tightly as if he is cold even here, where the air is so tropical. He's not coming, and for the first time Lisey lets herself acknowledge that it may be because he *can't*. If that is so, her choices are down to a pair: stay here with him or go home without him.

No, there's a third. I can gamble. I can shoot the works, as the saying is. Bet the farm. So come on, Scott. If the path is really dangerous, get off your dead ass and keep me from taking it.

She wants to look back as she crosses the beach, but doing that would show weakness. The laughers are closer now, which means that whatever else might be lurking near the path back to Sweetheart Hill will be closer, too. It will be full dark by now under the trees, and she guesses she'll have that sense of something stalking her before she gets far; that sense of something closing in. *It's very close, honey,* Scott told her that day in Nashville as he lay on the broiling pavement, bleeding from the lung and near death. And when she tried to tell him she didn't know what he was talking about, he had told her not to insult his intelligence.

Or her own.

Never mind. I'll deal with whatever's in the woods when – if – I have to. All I know right now is that Dandy Debusher's girl Lisey has finally got it strapped all the way on. That mysterious 'it' Scott said you could never define because it changed from one jackpot to the next. This is the total deal, SOWISA, babyluv, and do you know what? It feels pretty good.

She begins making her way up the slanting path that leads to the steps and behind her

12

'He called me,' Lisey murmured.

One of the women who had been standing at the edge of the pool now stood up to her knees in that still water, looking dreamily off to the horizon. Her companion turned to Lisey, her brows drawn together in a disapproving frown. At first Lisey didn't understand, then she did. People didn't like you to talk here, that hadn't changed. She had an idea that in Boo'ya Moon, few things did.

She nodded as if the frowning woman had requested

clarification. 'My husband called my name, tried to stop me. God knows what it cost him to do that, but he did.'

The woman on the beach – her hair was blond but dark at the roots, as if it needed touching up – said, 'Be . . . quiet, please. I need . . . to think.'

Lisey nodded – fine by her, although she doubted the blond woman was doing as much thinking as she might believe – and waded into the water. She thought it would be cool, but in fact it was almost hot. The heat coursed up her legs and made her sex tingle in a way it hadn't in a long time. She waded out farther but got no deeper than her waist. She took another half a dozen steps, looked around, and saw she was at least ten yards beyond the farthest of the other waders, and remembered that good food turned bad after dark in Boo'ya Moon. Might the water also turn bad? Even if it didn't, might not dangerous things come out here as well as in the woods? Pool-sharks, so to speak? And if that was the case, might she not find herself too far out to get back before one of them decided dinner was served?

This is safe ground.

Only it *wasn't* ground, it was water, and she felt a panicky urge to flounder back to the beach before some killer U-boat with teeth took off one of her legs. Lisey fought the fear down. She had come a long way, not just once but twice, her breast hurt like hell, and by God she would get what she'd come for.

She took in a deep breath, and then, not knowing what to expect, lowered herself slowly to her knees on the sandy bottom, letting the water cover her breasts – the one that was unhurt and the one that was badly wounded. For a moment her left breast hurt more than ever; she thought the pain would tear the top of her head off. But then

13

He calls her name again, loud and panicky – *'Lisey!'*

It cuts through the dreamy silence of this place like an arrow with fire at its tip. She almost looks back because there's agony as well as panic in that cry, but something deep inside tells her she must not. If she is to have any chance at all of rescuing him, she must not look back. She has made her wager. She passes the graveyard, its crosses gleaming in the light of the rising moon, with hardly a glance and climbs the steps with her back straight and her head up, still holding Good Ma's african bundled high in her arms so she won't trip on it, and she feels a crazy exhilaration, the kind she reckons you only experience when you've put everything you own – the house the car the bank account the family dog – on one throw of the dice. Above her (and not far) is the vast gray rock marking the head of the path that leads back to Sweetheart Hill. The sky is filled with strange stars and foreign constellations. Somewhere the northern lights are burning in long curtains of color. Lisey may never see them again, but she thinks she's okay with that. She reaches the top of the steps and with no hesitation walks around the rock and that is when Scott pulls her backward against him. His familiar odor has never smelled so good to her. At the same moment, she becomes aware that something is moving on her left, moving fast, not on the path leading to the hill of lupins but just beside it.

'Shhhh, Lisey,' Scott whispers. His lips are so close

they tickle the cup of her ear. 'For your life and mine, now you must be still.'

It's Scott's long boy. She doesn't need him to tell her. For years she has sensed its presence at the back of her life, like something glimpsed in a mirror from the corner of the eye. Or, say, a nasty secret hidden in the cellar. Now the secret is out. In gaps between the trees to her left, sliding at what seems like express-train speed, is a great high river of meat. It is mostly smooth, but in places there are dark spots or craters that might be moles or even, she supposes (she does not want to suppose and cannot help it) skin cancers. Her mind starts to visualize some sort of gigantic worm, then freezes. The thing over there behind those trees is no worm, and whatever it is, it's sentient, *because she can feel it thinking*. Its thoughts aren't human, aren't in the least comprehensible, but there is a terrible fascination in their very alienness . . .

It's the bad-gunky, she thinks, cold all the way to the bone. *Its thoughts are the bad-gunky and nothing else.*

The idea is awful but also *right*. A sound escapes her, something between a squeal and a moan. It's just a little sound, but she sees or senses that the thing's endless express-train progress has suddenly slowed, that it may have heard her.

Scott knows, too. The arm around her, just below her breasts, tightens a bit more. Once again his lips move against the cup of her ear. 'If we're going home, we have to go right now,' he murmurs. He's totally with her again, totally *here*. She doesn't know if it's because he's no longer looking at the pool or because he's terrified. Maybe it's both. 'Do you understand?'

Lisey nods. Her own fear is so great it's incapacitating,

461

and any sense of exhilaration at having him back is gone. Has he lived with this all his life? If so, *how* has he lived with it? But even now, in the extremity of her terror, she supposes she knows. Two things have tied him to the earth and saved him from the long boy. His writing is one. The other has a waist he can put his arms around and an ear into which he can whisper.

'Concentrate, Lisey. Do it now. Bust your brains.'

She closes her eyes and sees the guest room of their house on Sugar Top Hill. Sees Scott sitting in the rocker. Sees herself sitting on the chilly floor beside him, holding his hand. He is gripping her hand as hard as she is gripping his. Behind them, the frost-filled panes of the window are filled with fantastic shifting light. The TV is on and *The Last Picture Show* is once more playing. The boys are in Sam the Lion's black-and-white poolroom and Hank Williams is on the juke singing 'Jambalaya'.

For a moment she feels Boo'ya Moon shimmer, but then the music in her mind – music that was for a moment so clear and happy – fades. Lisey opens her eyes. She's desperate to see home, but the big gray rock and the path leading away through the sweetheart trees are both still there. Those strange stars still blaze down, only now the laughers are silent and the harsh whispering of the bushes has stilled and even Chuckie G.'s bell has quit its fitful tinkling because the long boy has stopped to listen and the whole world seems to hold its breath and listen with it. It's over there, not fifty feet away on their left; Lisey can now actually *smell* it. It smells like old farts in turnpike rest area bathrooms, or the poison whiff of bourbon and cigarette smoke you sometimes get when you turn the key and walk into a cheap motel room, or Good Ma's pissy diapers when she was old and raving senile; it's stopped behind the nearest rank of sweetheart trees, has paused in its tunnelish run through the woods, and dear God they aren't *going*, they aren't *going back*, they are for some reason stuck here.

Scott's whisper is now so low he hardly seems to be speaking at all. If not for the faint sensation of his lips moving against the sensitive skin of her ear, she could almost believe *this* was telepathy. 'It's the african, Lisey – sometimes things will go one way but not the other. Usually things that can *double*. I don't know why, but that's it. I feel it like an anchor. Drop the african.'

Lisey opens her arms and lets it fall. The sound it makes is only the softest sigh (like the arguments against insanity falling into some ultimate basement), but the long boy hears it. She feels a shift in the rowing direction of its unknowable thoughts; feels the hideous pressure of its insane regard. One of the trees snaps with an explosive rending noise as the thing over there begins to turn, and she closes her eyes again and sees the guest room as clearly as she has ever seen anything in her life, sees it with desperate intensity, and through a perfect magnifying lens of terror.

'Now,' Scott murmurs, and the most amazing thing happens. She feels the air turn inside out. Suddenly Hank Williams is singing 'Jambalaya'. He's singing

14

He was singing because the TV was on. She could now remember this as clearly as anything in her life, and she wondered how she ever could have forgotten it.

Time to get off Memory Lane, Lisey – time to go home.

Everybody out of the pool, as the saying was. Lisey had gotten what she'd come here for, had gotten it while caught up in that last terrible memory of the long boy. Her breast still hurt, but the fierce throbbing was down to a dull ache. She had felt worse as a teenager, after spending a long hot day in a bra that was too small for her. From where she knelt chin-deep in the water she could see that the moon, now smaller and almost pure silver, had risen above all but the highest of the trees in the graveyard. And now a new fear rose to trouble her: what if the long boy came back? What if it heard her thinking about it and came back? This was supposed to be a safe place and Lisey thought it probably was – from the laughers and the other nasty things that might live in the Fairy Forest, at least – but she had an idea that the long boy might not be bound by any rules that held the other things away from here. She had an idea the long boy was . . . different. The title of some old horror story first occurred to her, then clanged in her mind like an iron bell: 'Oh Whistle and I'll Come to You, My Lad'. This was followed by the title of the only Scott Landon book she had ever hated: *Empty Devils*.

But before she could start back to the sand, before she could even get to her feet again, Lisey was struck by yet another memory, this one far more recent. It was of waking in bed with her sister Amanda just before dawn and finding that past and present had gotten all tangled together. Worse still, Lisey had come to believe that she wasn't in bed with her sister at all, but with her dead husband. And in a way, that had been true. Because although the thing in bed with her had been wearing Manda's night-gown and had spoken in Manda's voice, it had used the interior language of their marriage and phrases only Scott could have known.

You have a blood-bool coming, the thing in bed with her had said, and along had come the Black Prince of the Incunks with her own Oxo can-opener in his nasty bag of tricks.

It goes behind the purple. You've already found the first three stations. A few more and you'll get your prize.

And what prize had the thing in bed with her prom-ised? A drink. She had guessed a Coke or an RC Cola because those had been Paul's prizes, but now she knew better.

Lisey lowered her head, buried her battered face in the pool, and then, without allowing herself to think about what she was doing, took two quick swallows. The water in which she stood was almost hot, but what she took in her mouth was cool and sweet and refreshing. She could have drunk a good deal more, but some intuition told her to stop at two sips. Two was just the right number. She touched her lips and found that the swelling there was almost gone. She wasn't surprised.

Not trying to be quiet (and not bothering to be grateful, at least not yet), Lisey floundered back to the beach. It seemed to take forever. No one was wading near shore now, and the beach was empty. Lisey thought she saw the woman she'd spoken to sitting on one of the stone benches with her companion, but couldn't be sure because the moon hadn't risen quite enough. She looked a bit higher, and her gaze fixed on one of the wrapped figures a dozen or so benches up from the water. Moonlight had coated one side of this creature's gauzy head with thin silver gilt, and a queer certainty came to her: that was Scott, and he was watching her. Didn't the idea make a kind of crazy sense? Didn't it, if he had held onto enough consciousness and will to come to her in the moments before dawn, as she lay in bed with her catatonic sister? Didn't it, if he was determined to have his say just one more time?

She felt the urge to call his name, even though to do so would surely be dangerous madness. She opened her mouth and water from her wet hair ran into her eyes, stinging them. Faintly, she heard the wind tinkling Chuckie G.'s bell.

It was then that Scott spoke to her, and for the last time.

—*Lisey.*

Infinitely tender, that voice. Calling her name, calling her home.

—*Little*

15

'Lisey,' he says. 'Babyluv.'

He's in the rocking chair and she's sitting on the cold floor, but he's the one doing the shivering. Lisey has a sudden brilliant memory of Granny D saying *Afeard and shidderin in the dark* and it hits her that he's cold because now all of the african is in Boo'ya Moon. But that's not all – the whole frigging *room* is cold. It was chilly before but now it's *cold*, and the lights are out, as well.

The constant whooshy whisper of the furnace has ceased, and when she looks out the frosty window she can see only the extravagant colors of the northern lights. The Galloways' pole-light next door has gone dark. *Power outage*, she thinks, but no – the television is still on and that damned movie is still playing. The boys from Anarene, Texas, are hanging out in the pool-hall, soon they'll go to Mexico and when they come back Sam the Lion will be dead, he'll be wrapped in gauze and sitting on one of those stone benches overlooking the p—

'That's not right,' Scott says. His teeth are chattering slightly, but she can still hear the perplexity in his voice. 'I never turned the goddam movie on because I thought it would wake you up, Lisey. Also—'

She knows that's true, when she came in here this time and found him the TV was off, but right now she's got something far more important on her mind. 'Scott, will it follow us?'

'No, baby,' he says. 'It can't do that unless it gets a real good whiff of your scent or a fix on your . . .' He trails off. It's the movie he's still most concerned with, it seems. 'Also, it's never "Jambalaya" in this scene. I've watched *The Last Picture Show* fifty times, except for *Citizen Kane* it may be the greatest movie ever made, and it's never "Jambalaya" in the pool-hall scene. It's Hank Williams, sure, but it's "Kaw-Liga", the song about the Indian chief. And if the TV and the VCR are working, where's the damn lights?'

He gets up and flicks the wall-switch. There's nothing. That big cold wind from Yellowknife has finally killed their power, and power all over Castle Rock, Castle View, Harlow, Motton, Tashmore Pond, and most of western Maine. At the same instant Scott flicks the useless light-switch on, the TV goes *off*. The picture dwindles to a bright white point that glows for a moment, then disappears. The next time he tries his tape of *The Last Picture Show*, he'll discover a ten-minute stretch in the middle of it is blank, as if wiped clean by a powerful magnetic field. Neither of them will ever speak of it, but Scott and Lisey will understand that although both of them were visualizing the guest room, it was probably Lisey who hollered them home with the greatest force . . . and it was *certainly* Lisey who visualized Ole Hank singing 'Jambalaya' instead of 'Kaw-Liga'. As it was Lisey who so fiercely visualized both the VCR and the TV running when they returned that those appliances *did* run for almost a minute and a half, even though the electricity was out from one end of Castle County to the other.

He stokes up the woodstove in the kitchen with oak chunks from the woodbox and she makes them a jackleg bed – blankets and an air-mattress – on the linoleum. When they lie down, he takes her in his arms.

'I'm afraid to go to sleep,' she confesses. 'I'm afraid that when I wake up in the morning, the stove will be out and you'll be gone again.'

He shakes his head. 'I'm all right – it's past for awhile.'

She looks at him with hope and doubt. 'Is that something you know, or just something you're saying to soothe the little wife?'

'Which do *you* think?'

She thinks this isn't the ghost-Scott she's been living with since November, but it's still hard for her to believe in such miraculous changes. 'You *seem* better, but I'm leery of my own wishful thinking.'

In the stove, a knot of wood explodes and she jumps. He holds her closer. She snuggles against him almost fiercely. It's warm under the covers; warm in his arms. He is all she has ever wanted in the dark.

He says, 'This . . . this *thing* that has troubled my family . . . it comes and goes. When it passes, it's like a cramp letting go.'

'But it will come back?'

'Lisey, it might not.' The strength and surety in his voice so surprises her that she looks up to check his face. She sees no duplicity there, even of the kindly sort meant to ease a troubled wife's heart. 'And if it does, it might never come back as strongly as it did this time.'

'Did your father tell you that?'

'My father didn't know much about the *gone* part. I've felt this tug toward . . . the place where you found me . . . twice before. Once the year before I met you. That time booze and rock music got me through. The second time—'

'Germany,' she says flatly.

'Yes,' he says. 'Germany. That time you pulled me through, Lisey.'

'How close, Scott? How close was it in Bremen?'

'Close,' he says simply, and it makes her cold. If she had lost him in Germany, she would have lost him for good. *Mein gott.* 'But that was a breeze compared to this. This was a hurricane.'

There are other things she wants to ask him, but mostly she only wants to hold him and believe him when he says that maybe things will be okay. The way you want to believe the doctor, she supposes, when he says the cancer is in remission and may never come back.

469

'And you're okay.' She needs to hear him say it one more time. *Needs* to.

'Yes. Good to go, as the saying is.'

'And . . . *it*?' She doesn't need to be more specific. Scott knows what she's talking about.

'It's had my scent for a long time, and it knows the shape of my thoughts. After all these years, we're practically old friends. It could probably take me if it wanted to, but it would be an effort, and that fella's pretty lazy. Also . . . something watches out for me. Something on the bright side of the equation. There *is* a bright side, you know. You *must* know, because you're a part of it.'

'Once you told me you could call it, if you wanted to.' She says this very low.

'Yes.'

'And sometimes you want to. Don't you?'

He doesn't deny it, and outside the wind howls a long cold note along the eaves. Yet here under the blankets in front of the kitchen stove, it's warm. It's warm with him.

'Stay with me, Scott,' she says.

'I will,' he tells her. 'I will as long as

16

'I will as long as I can,' Lisey said.

She realized several things at the same time. One was that she had returned to her bedroom and her bed. Another was that the bed would have to be changed, because she had come back soaking wet, and her damp feet were coated with beach sand from another world. A third was that she was shivering even though the room wasn't particularly cold. A fourth was that she no longer had the silver spade; she had left it behind. The last was that if the seated shape had indeed been her husband, she had almost certainly seen him for the last time; her husband was now one of the shrouded things, an unburied corpse.

Lying on her wet bed in her soaking shorts, Lisey burst into tears. She had a great deal to do now, and had come back with most of the steps clear in her mind – she thought that might also have been part of her prize at the end of Scott's last bool hunt – but first she needed to finish grieving for her husband. She put an arm over her eyes and lay so for the next five minutes, sobbing until her eyes were swollen nearly shut and her throat ached. She had never thought she would want him so much or miss him so badly. It was a shock. Yet at the same time, and although there was also still some pain in her damaged breast, Lisey thought she had never felt so well, so glad to be alive, or so ready to kick ass and take down names.

As the saying was.

CHAPTER TWELVE

LISEY AT GREENLAWN
(THE HOLLYHOCKS)

1

She glanced at the clock on the nightstand as she peeled off her soaked shorts and smiled, not because there was anything intrinsically funny about ten minutes to twelve on a morning in June, but because one of Scrooge's lines from *A Christmas Carol* had occurred to her: 'The spirits have done it all in one night.' It seemed to Lisey that *something* had accomplished a great deal in her own life in a very short period of time, most of it in the last few hours.

But you have to remember that I've been living in the past, and that takes up a surprising amount of a person's time, she thought . . . and after a moment's consideration let out a great, larruping laugh that probably would have sounded insane to anyone listening down the hall.

That's okay, keep laughin, babyluv, ain't nobody here but us chickadees, she thought, going into the bathroom. That big, loose laugh started to come out of her again, then stopped suddenly when it occurred to her that *Dooley* might be here. He could be holed up in the root cellar or one of this big house's many closets; he might be sweating it out this late morning in the attic, right over her head. She didn't know much about him and would be the first to admit it, but the idea that he had gone to ground here in the house fit what she *did* know. He'd already proved he was a bold sonofabitch.

Don't worry about him now. Worry about Darla and Canty.

Good idea. Lisey could get to Greenlawn ahead of her older sisters, that wouldn't be much of a horse-race, but she couldn't afford to dawdle, either. *Keep your string a-drawing*, she thought.

But she couldn't deny herself a moment in front of the full-length mirror on the back of the bedroom door, standing with her hands at her sides, looking levelly and without prejudice at her slender, unremarkable, middle-aged body – and at her face, which Scott had once described as that of a fox in summer. It was a little puffy, nothing more. She looked like she'd slept exceptionally hard (maybe after a drink or three too many), and her lips still turned out a little, giving them a strangely sensual quality that made her feel both uneasy and a tiny bit gleeful. She hesitated, not sure what to do about that, and then found a tube of Revlon Hothouse Pink at the back of her lipstick drawer. She touched some on and nodded, a little doubtfully. If people were going to look at her lips – and she thought they might – she'd do better giving them something to look at than trying to cover up what couldn't be hidden.

The breast Dooley had operated on with such lunatic absorption was marked with an ugly scarlet ditch that circled up from beneath her armpit before petering out above her ribcage. It looked like a fairly bad cut that might have happened two or three weeks ago and was now healing well. The two shallower wounds looked like no more than the sort of red marks that resulted from wearing too-tight elastic garments. Or perhaps – if you had a lively imagination – rope burns. The difference between this and the horror she had observed upon regaining consciousness was amazing.

'All the Landons are fast healers, you sonofabitch,' Lisey said, and stepped into the shower.

2

A quick rinse was all she had time for, and her breast was still sore enough to make her decide against a bra. She put on a pair of carpenter's pants and a loose tee-shirt. She slipped a vest over the latter to keep anyone from staring at her nipples, assuming guys bothered scoping out the nipples of fifty-year-old women, that was. According to Scott, they did. She remembered his telling her, once upon a happier time, that straight men stared at pretty much anyone of a female persuasion between the ages of roughly fourteen and eighty-four; he claimed it was a simple hardwired circuit between eye and cock, that the brain had nothing to do with it.

It was noon. She went downstairs, glanced into the living room, and saw the remaining pack of cigarettes sitting on the coffee table. She had no craving for cigarettes now. She got a fresh jar of Skippy out of the pantry instead (steeling herself for Jim Dooley lurking in the corner or behind the pantry door) and the strawberry jam out of the fridge. She made herself a PB&J on white and took two delicious, gummy bites before calling Professor Woodbody. The Castle County Sheriff's Department had taken 'Zack McCool's' threatening letter, but Lisey's memory for numbers had always been good, and this one was a cinch: Pittsburgh area code at one end, eighty-one and eighty-eight at the other. She was as willing to talk to the Queen of the Incunks as the King. An answering machine, however, would be inconvenient. She could leave her message, but would have no way of being sure it would reach the right ear in time to do any good.

She need not have worried. Woodbody himself answered, and he did not sound kingly. He sounded chastened and cautious. 'Yes? Hello?'

'Hello, Professor Woodbody. This is Lisa Landon.'

'I don't want to talk to you. I've spoken to my lawyer and he says I don't have to—'

'Chill,' she said, and eyed her sandwich with longing. It wouldn't do to talk with her mouth full. On the upside, she thought this conversation was going to be brief. 'I'm not going to make any trouble for you. No trouble with the cops, no trouble with lawyers, nothing like that. If you do me one teensy favor.'

'What favor?' Woodbody sounded suspicious. Lisey couldn't blame him for that.

'There's an off-chance your friend Jim Dooley may call you today—'

'That guy's no friend of *mine*!' Woodbody bleated.

Right, Lisey thought. *And you're well on your way to persuading yourself he never was.*

'Okay, drinking buddy. Passing acquaintance. Whatever. If he calls, just tell him I've changed my mind, would you do that? Say I've regained my senses. Tell him I'll see him this evening, at eight, in my husband's study.'

'You sound like someone preparing to get herself into a great deal of trouble, Mrs Landon.'

'Hey, you'd know, wouldn't you?' The sandwich was looking better and better. Lisey's stomach rumbled. 'Professor, he probably won't call you. In which case, you're golden. If he *does* call, give him my message and you're also golden. But if he calls and you *don't* give him my message – just "She's changed her mind, she wants to see you tonight in Scott's study at eight" – and I find out . . . then, sir, oy, such a mess I'm making for you.'

'You can't. My lawyer says—'

'Don't listen to what he says. Be smart and listen to what *I'm* saying. My husband left me twenty million dollars. With that kind of money, if I decide to ass-fuck you, you'll spend the next three years shitting blood from a crouch. Got it?'

Lisey hung up before he could say anything else, tore a bite from her sandwich, got the lime Kool-Aid from the fridge, thought about a glass, then drank directly from the pitcher instead.

Yum!

3

If Dooley phoned during the next few hours, she wouldn't be around to take his call. Luckily, Lisey knew which phone he'd ring in on. She went out to her unfinished office in the barn, across from the shrouded corpse of the Bremen bed. She sat in the plain kitchen-style chair (a nice new desk-chair was one of the things she'd never gotten around to ordering), pushed the RECORD MESSAGE button on the answering machine, and spoke without thinking too much. She hadn't come back from Boo'ya Moon with a plan so much as with a clear set of steps to follow and the belief that, if she did her part, Jim Dooley would be forced to do his. *I'll whistle and you'll come to me, my lad*, she thought.

'Zack – Mr Dooley – this is Lisey. If you're hearing this, I'm visiting my sister, who's in the hospital, up in Auburn. I spoke to the Prof, and I'm *so* grateful this is going to work out. I'll be in my husband's study tonight at eight, or you can call me here at seven and arrange something else, if you're worried about the police. There may be a Sheriff's Deputy parked out front, maybe even in the bushes across the road, so be careful. I'll listen for messages.'

She was afraid that might be too much for the outgoing-message tape to handle, but it wasn't. And what would Jim Dooley make of it, if he called this number and heard it? Given his current level of craziness, Lisey couldn't begin to predict. Would he break radio silence and call the Professor in Pittsburgh? He might. Whether or not the Professor would actually pass on her message if Dooley did was also impossible to predict, and maybe it didn't matter. She didn't much care if Dooley thought she was actually ready to deal or just jacking him around. She only wanted him nervous and curious, the way she imagined a fish felt when it was looking up at a lure skipping along the surface of a lake.

She didn't dare leave a note on her door – it was all too likely Deputy Boeckman or Deputy Alston would read it long before Dooley had a chance to – and that was probably taking things a step too far, anyway. For the time being, she had done all she could.

And do you really expect him to show up at eight o'clock tonight, Lisey? To just come waltzing up the stairs to Scott's office, full of trust and belief?

She didn't expect him to come waltzing, and she didn't expect him to be full of anything but the lunacy she had already experienced, but she *did* expect him to come. He would be as careful as any feral thing, casting about for a trap or a setup, possibly sneaking in from the woods as early as mid-afternoon, but Lisey believed he would know in his heart that this wasn't some trick that she'd worked out with the Sheriff's Department or the State Police. He'd know from the eagerness to please he heard in her voice, and because after what he'd done to her, he had every reason to expect her to be one cowed cow. She played the message back twice and nodded. Yeah. On the surface she sounded like a woman who was merely eager to finish some troublesome piece of business, but she thought Dooley would hear the fright and pain just beneath. Because he expected to hear them, and because he was crazy.

Lisey thought there was something else at work here, as well. She had gotten her drink. She had gotten her *bool*, and it had made her strong in some primal way. It might not last long, but that didn't matter, because a little of that strength – a little of that primal weirdness – was now on the answering machine tape. She thought that if Dooley called, he would hear and respond to it.

4

Her cell phone was still in the BMW and now fully charged. She thought of going back to the little office in the barn and re-doing the message on the answering machine, adding the mobile number, then realized she didn't know it. *I so rarely call myself, darling*, she thought, and unloosed the big, larruping laugh again.

She drove slowly out to the end of the driveway, hoping that Deputy Alston would be there. He was, looking bigger than ever and rather primal himself. Lisey got out of her car and gave him a little salute. He did not call for backup or run screaming from the sight of her face; he merely grinned and tipped the salute right back at her.

It had certainly crossed Lisey's mind to spin a tale if she found a deputy on duty, something about 'Zack McCool' calling her up and telling her he'd decided to get his li'l ole self back to his li'l ole holler in West Virginny and forget all about the writer's widder-woman; jest too many Yankee *po*-lice around. She'd do it without the *Deliverance* accent, of course, and she thought she could be fairly convincing, especially in her current state of baptismal grace, but in the end she had decided against it. Such a story might end up putting Acting Sheriff Clusterfuck and his deputies even more on their guard – they might think Jim Dooley was trying to lull them to sleep. No, much better to leave matters as they were. Dooley had found his way to her once; he could probably do it again. If they caught him, her problems would be solved . . . although in truth, seeing Jim Dooley caught was no longer her solution of choice.

In any case, she didn't like the idea of lying to either Alston or Boeckman any more than she had to. They were cops, they were doing their best to protect her, and on top of that they were a couple of likeable lummoxes.

'How's it going, Mrs Landon?'

'Fine. I just stopped to tell you I'm going up to Auburn. My sister's in the hospital up there.'

'I'm very sorry to hear that. CMG or Kingdom?'

'Greenlawn.'

She wasn't sure he'd know it, but from the little wince that tightened his face, she guessed that he did. 'Well, that's too bad . . . but at least it's a pretty day for a drive. You just want to get back before late afternoon. Radio says there's gonna be big thunderstorms, especially here in the western.'

Lisey looked around and smiled, first at the day, which was indeed summery-gorgeous (at least so far), and then at Deputy Alston. 'I'll do my best. Thanks for the heads-up.'

'Not a problem. Say, the side of your nose looks kinda swelled. Did something bite you?'

'Mosquitoes do that to me sometimes,' Lisey said. 'There's one beside my lip, too. Can you see it?'

Alston peered at her mouth, which Dooley had beaten back and forth with his open hand not long ago. 'Nope,' he said. 'Can't say that I do.'

'Good, the Benadryl must be working. As long as it doesn't make me sleepy.'

'If it does, pull over, okay? Do yourself a favor.'

'Yes, Dad,' Lisey said, and Alston laughed. He also blushed a little.

'By the way, Mrs Landon—'

'Lisey.'

'Yes, ma'am. Lisey. Andy called. He'd like you to drop by the Sheriff's Office when it's convenient and make an official report on this business. You know, something you can sign for the record. Would you do that?'

'Yes. I'll try to stop in on my way back from Auburn.'

'Well, I'll tell you a little secret, Mrs Lan – Lisey. Both our secretaries are apt to clear out early on days when it comes on to hard rain. They live out Motton way, and those roads flood if you look at em crosseyed. Need new culverts.'

Lisey shrugged. 'We'll see,' she said. She made a show of looking at her watch. 'Whoa, look at the time! I really have to run. Help yourself to the toilet if you have to go, Deputy Alston, there's—'

'Joe. If you're Lisey, I'm Joe.'

She gave him a thumbs-up. 'Okay, Joe. There's a key to the back door under the porch step. If you feel around a little, I think you'll find it.'

'Ayuh, I'm a trained investigator,' he said with a straight face.

Lisey burst out laughing and held up her hand. Deputy Joe Alston, now grinning himself, high-fived her there in the sunshine near the mailbox where she'd found the dead Galloway barncat.

5

Driving to Auburn, she mused for a little while on how Deputy Joe Alston had looked at her as they stood talking at the end of the driveway. It had been a little while since she'd attracted a *honey, you look so good* stare from a man, but she'd gotten one today, slightly swollen nose and all. Amazing. *Amazing.*

'The Get-Beat-Up-By-Jim-Dooley Beauty Treatment,' she said, and laughed. 'I could hawk it on high-channel cable TV.'

And her mouth had the most wonderfully sweet taste. If she ever wanted another cigarette, she would be surprised. Maybe she could hawk *that* on high-channel cable, too.

6

By the time Lisey got to Greenlawn, it was twenty minutes past one. She didn't expect to see Darla's car, but still let out a sigh of relief when she had made sure it wasn't one of the dozen or so scattered around the visitors' parking lot. She liked the idea of Darla and Canty well south of here, well away from the dangerous craziness of Jim Dooley. She remembered helping Mr Silver grade potatoes when she was a little girl (well, twelve or thirteen – not so little at that) and how he'd always cautioned her to wear pants and keep her sleeves rolled up when she was around the potato grader in the back shed. *You get caught in that baby, she'll undress ya,* he'd said, and she had taken the warning to heart because she'd understood old Max Silver hadn't been talking about what his hulk of a potato-grader would do to her *clothes* but what it would do to *her.* Amanda was a part of this, had been since the day she'd shown up as Lisey was halfheartedly beginning the job of cleaning out Scott's study. Lisey accepted that. Darla and Canty, however, would be an unnecessary complication. If God was good, He would keep them at the Snow Squall, eating Lazy Lobster and drinking white wine spritzers, for a *long* time. Like until midnight.

Before she got out of her car, Lisey touched her left breast lightly with her right hand, wincing in advance at the bright lance of pain she expected. All she felt was a faint throb. *Amazing*, she thought. *It's like touching a week-old bruise. Any time you get to doubting the reality of Boo'ya Moon, Lisey, just remember what he did to your breast, not even five hours ago, and what it feels like now.*

She got out of the car, locked it with the SmartKey, then paused for a moment to look around, trying to fix the spot in her mind. She had no clear reason for doing this; nothing she could have put her finger on, even if she'd wanted to. It was just more of that step-by-step thing, almost like baking bread for the first time from a cook-book recipe, and that was fine by her.

Freshly tarred and lined, the Greenlawn visitors' parking lot reminded her strongly of the parking lot where her husband had fallen eighteen years ago, and she heard the ghostly voice of Assistant Professor Roger Dashmiel, aka the southern-fried chickenshit, saying *We'll proceed on across yondah parkin lot to Nelson Hall — which is mercifully air-conditioned.* No Nelson Hall here; Nelson Hall was in the Land of Ago, as was the man who had gone there to dig a spadeful of earth and inaugurate construction of the Shipman Library.

What she saw looming over the neatly trimmed hedges wasn't an English Department building but the smooth brick and bright glass of a twenty-first-century madhouse, the sort of clean, well-lighted place where her husband might well have finished up if something, some spore the doctors in Bowling Green had eventually elected to call pneumonia (no one wanted to put *Unknown causes* on the death certificate of a man whose demise would be reported on the front page of the *New York Times*), had not finished him first.

On this side of the hedge was an oak tree; Lisey had parked so that the BMW would be in its shade, although – yes – she could see clouds massing in the west, so maybe Deputy Joe Alston was right about those afternoon thunderstorms. The tree would make a perfectly lovely marker if it had been the only one, but it wasn't. There was a whole row of them along the hedge, to Lisey they all looked the same . . . and what the smuck did it matter, anyway?

She started for the path to the main building, but something inside – a voice that didn't seem like any of the variations of her own mental voice – nagged her back, insisting that she look at her car and its place in the parking lot again. She wondered if something wanted her to move the BMW to a different spot. If so, it wasn't making its wants known very clearly. Lisey settled for a walk-around instead, as her father had told her you should always do before setting out on a long trip. Only then you were looking for uneven tire-wear, a bust' taillight, a sagging muffler, things of that sort. Now she didn't know *what* she was looking for.

Maybe I'm just putting off seeing her. Maybe that's all it is.

But it wasn't. It was more. And it was important.

484

She observed her license plate – 5761RD, with that stupid loon – and a *very* faded bumper-sticker, a joke gift from Jodi. It read JESUS LOVES ME, THIS I KNOW; THAT IS WHY I DON'T DRIVE SLOW. Nothing else.

Not good enough, that voice nagged, and then she spied something interesting in the far corner of the parking lot, almost beneath the hedge. An empty green bottle. A beer bottle, she was almost sure. Either the maintenance crew had missed it or hadn't gotten to it yet. Lisey hurried over and picked it up, getting a certain sour agricultural whiff from the neck of the thing. On the label, slightly faded, was a snarling canine. According to the label, this bottle had once held Nordic Wolf Premium Beer. Lisey brought the bottle back to her car and set it on the pavement directly beneath the loon on her license plate.

Cream-colored BMW, not good enough.

Cream-colored BMW sitting in the shadow of an oak tree, still not good enough.

Cream-colored BMW sitting in the shadow of an oak tree with an empty Nordic Wolf beer bottle under Maine Loon license plate 5761RD and slightly to the left of the joke bumper-sticker . . . good enough.

Just barely.

And why?

Lisey didn't give a sweet smuck.

She hurried for the main building.

7

There was no trouble getting in to see Amanda, even though afternoon visiting hours did not officially commence until two, which was still half an hour away. Thanks to Dr Hugh Alberness – and Scott, of course – Lisey was something of a star at Greenlawn. Ten minutes after giving her name at the main desk (dwarfed by a gigantic New Age-y mural of children with linked hands staring raptly up into the night sky), Lisey was sitting with her sister on the little patio outside Amanda's room, sipping lackluster punch from a Dixie cup and watching a game of croquet on the rolling back lawn for which the place had no doubt been named. Somewhere out of sight, a power-mower blatted monotonously. The duty-nurse had asked Amanda if she wouldn't also like a cup of 'bug-juice', and took Amanda's silence for consent. It now sat untouched beside her on the table while Amanda, dressed in a mint-green pajama set and with a matching ribbon in her freshly washed hair, looked blankly off into the distance – not at the croquet players, Lisey thought, but through them. Her hands were clasped in her lap, but Lisey could see the ugly cut that looped around the left one, and the gleam of fresh salve. Lisey had tried three different conversation-openers and Amanda had uttered not so much as a single word in response. Which, according to the nurse, was par for the course. Amanda was currently incommunicado, not taking messages, out to lunch, on vacation, visiting the asteroid belt. All her life she had been troublesome, but this was a new high, even for her.

And Lisey, who was expecting company in her husband's study only six hours from now, didn't have time for it. She took a sip of her largely flavorless drink, wished for a Coke – *verboten* here because of the caffeine – and set it aside. She looked around to make sure they were alone, then leaned forward and plucked Amanda's hands out of her lap, trying not to wince at the slimy feel of the salve and the lumpy lines of the healing slashes just beneath. If it hurt Amanda to be held so, she didn't show it. Her face remained a smooth blank, as if she were sleeping with her eyes open.

'Amanda,' Lisey said. She tried to make eye-contact with her sister, but it was impossible. 'Amanda, listen to me, now. You wanted to help me clean up what Scott left behind, and I need you to help me do that. I need your help.'

No answer.

'There's a bad man. A crazy man. He's a little like that sonofabitch Cole in Nashville – a lot like him, actually – only I can't take care of this one on my own. You have to come back from wherever you are and help me.'

No answer. Amanda stared out at the croquet players. Through the croquet players. The power-mower blatted. The paper cups of bug-juice sat on a patio table that had no corners; in this place corners were as *verboten* as caffeine.

'Do you know what I think, Manda-Bunny? I think you're sitting on one of those stone benches with the rest of the gorked-out goners, staring at the pool. I think Scott saw you there on one of his visits and said to himself, "Oh, a cutter. I recognize cutters when I see em because my Dad was a member of the tribe. Hell, *I'm* a member of the tribe." He said to himself, "There's a lady who's going to take early retirement here, unless somebody puts a spoke in her wheel, so to speak." Does that sound about right, Manda?'

Nothing.

'I don't know if he foresaw Jim Dooley, but he foresaw you ending up in Greenlawn, just as sure as shite sticks to a blanket. Do you remember how Dandy used to say that sometimes, Manda? Just as sure as shite sticks to a blanket? And when Good Ma yelled at him, he said shite was like drat, shite wasn't swearing. Do you remember?'

More nothing from Amanda. Just a vacant, maddening gape.

Lisey thought of that cold night with Scott in the guest room, when the wind thundered and the sky burned, and put her mouth close to Amanda's ear. 'If you can hear me, squeeze my hands,' she whispered. 'Squeeze just as hard as you can.'

She waited and the seconds passed. She had almost given up when there came the faintest twitch. It could have been an involuntary muscle spasm or just imagination, but Lisey didn't think so. She thought that somewhere far away, Amanda heard her sister hollering her name. Hollering her home.

'All right,' Lisey said. Her heart was pounding so hard she felt it might choke her. 'That's good. That's a start. I'm going to come get you, Amanda. I'm going to bring you home and you're going to help me. Do you hear? *You have to help me.*'

Lisey closed her eyes and once more tightened her grip on Amanda's hands, knowing she might be hurting her sister, not caring. Amanda could complain later, when she had a voice to complain with. If she had a voice to complain with. Ah, but the world was made of if, Scott had told her that once.

Lisey summoned her will and concentration and

created the clearest version of the pool she could, seeing the rocky cup in which it lay, seeing the clean white arrowhead of beach with the stone benches stepped above it in mild curves, seeing the break in the rock and the secondary path, something like a throat, that led to the graveyard. She made the water a brilliant blue, sparkling with thousands of sunpoints, she made it the pool at midday, because she'd had her fill of Boo'ya Moon at dusk, thank you very much.

Now, she thought, and waited for the air to turn and the sounds of Greenlawn to fade. For a moment she thought those sounds *did* fade, then decided that really was her imagination. She opened her eyes and the patio was still rahcheer, with Amanda's cup of bug-juice on the round table; Amanda remained in her deep catatonic placidity, so much breathing wax within her mint-green pajamas, which closed with Velcro because buttons could be swallowed. Amanda with the matching green ribbon in her hair and the oceans in her eyes.

For a moment Lisey was assailed with terrible doubt. Perhaps the whole thing had been nothing but *her* madness – all except for Jim Dooley, that was. There were no screwed-up families like the Landons outside of V. C. Andrews novels, and no places like Boo'ya Moon outside of children's fantasy tales. She had been married to a writer who died, that was all. She had saved him once, but when he got sick in Kentucky eight years later there had been nothing she could do, because you couldn't swat a microbe with a shovel, could you?

She began to relax her hold on Amanda's hands, then tightened it again. Every bit of her strong heart and considerable will rose up in protest. *No! It was real! Boo'ya Moon is real! I was there in 1979, before I married him, I went there again in 1996, to find him when he needed finding, to bring him home when he needed bringing, and I was there again this morning. All I have to do is compare how my breast felt after Jim Dooley finished with it to what it feels like now, if I start to doubt. The reason I can't go—*

'The african,' she murmured. 'He said the african was holding us there like an anchor, he didn't know why. Are you holding us *here*, Manda? Is some scared, stubborn part of you holding us here? Holding *me* here?'

Amanda didn't answer, but Lisey thought that was *exactly* what was happening. Part of Amanda wanted Lisey to come get her and bring her back, but there was another part that wanted no rescue. That part really did want to be done with all the dirty world and the dirty world's problems. That part would be more than happy to continue taking lunch through a tube, and shooting poop into a diaper, and spending warm afternoons out here on the little patio, wearing pajamas with Velcro closures, staring at the green lawns and the croquet players. And what was Manda *really* looking at?

The pool.

The pool in the morning, the pool in the afternoon, the pool at sunset and glimmering by starshine and moonlight, with little trails of vapor rising from its surface like dreams of amnesia.

Lisey realized her mouth still tasted sweet, as it usually did only first thing in the morning, and thought: *That's from the pool. My prize. My drink. Two sips. One for me and one—*

'One for you,' she said. All at once the next step was

so beautifully clear that she wondered why she had wasted so much time. Still holding Amanda by the hands, Lisey leaned forward so that her face was in front of her sister's. Amanda's eyes remained unfocused and far-seeing beneath her straight-cut, graying bangs, as if she were looking right through Lisey. Only when Lisey slid her arms up to Amanda's elbows, first pinning her in place and then putting her mouth against her sister's mouth, did Amanda's eyes widen in belated understanding; only then did Amanda struggle, and by then it was too late. Lisey's mouth *flooded* with sweetness as her last sip from the pool reversed itself. She used her tongue to force Amanda's lips open, and as she felt the second mouthful of water she had drunk from the pool flow from her mouth to her sister's, Lisey saw the pool with a perfect daytime clarity that beggared her previous efforts at concentration and visualization, fierce and driven though they had been. She could smell frangipani and bougainvillea mingled with a deep and somehow sorrowful olive smell that she knew was the daytime aroma of the sweetheart trees. She could feel the packed hot sand beneath her feet, her bare feet because her sneakers hadn't traveled. Her sneakers hadn't but she had, she had made it, she had gotten over, she was

8

She was back in Boo'ya Moon, standing on the warm packed sand of the beach, this time with a bright sun beating down overhead and making not thousands of points of light on the water but what seemed like millions. Because *this* water was wider. For a moment Lisey looked at it, fascinated, and at the great old hulk of a sailing ship that floated there. And as she looked at it, she suddenly understood something the revenant in Amanda's bed had told her.

What's my prize? Lisey had asked, and the thing – which had somehow seemed to be both Scott and Amanda at the same time – had told her that her prize would be a drink. But when Lisey asked if that meant a Coke or an RC, the thing had said, *Be quiet. We want to watch the hollyhocks.* Lisey had assumed the thing was talking about flowers. She had forgotten there had been a very different meaning for that word, once upon a time. A magical one.

That ship out there, in all that blue and shining water was what Amanda had meant . . . for that *had* been Amanda; Scott would almost surely not have known about that wonderful childhood dreamboat.

This was no pool she was looking at; this was a harbor where only one ship rode at anchor, a ship made for brave pirate-girls who dared to go seeking treasure (and boyfriends). And their captain? Why, the brave Amanda Debusher, to be sure, for once upon a time, had not yonder sailing ship been Manda's happiest fantasy? Once upon a time before she had become so outwardly angry and so inwardly afraid?

Be quiet. We want to watch the Hollyhocks.

Oh, Amanda, Lisey thought – almost mourned. This was the pool where we all came down to drink, the very cup of imagination, and so of course everyone saw it a little bit differently. This childhood refuge was Amanda's version. The benches were the same, however, which led Lisey to surmise that they, at least, were bedrock reality.

Today she saw twenty or thirty people sitting on them, looking dreamily out at the water, and roughly the same number of shrouded forms. In daylight these latter bore a sickening resemblance to insects wrapped in silk by great spiders.

She quickly spied Amanda, a dozen or so benches up. Lisey skirted two of the silent gazers and one of the scary shrouded things in order to reach her. She sat down beside her and once more took Manda's hands, which weren't cut or even scarred over here. And, as Lisey held them, Amanda's fingers closed very slowly but definitely upon hers. A queer certainty came to Lisey then. Amanda didn't need the other sip from the pool Lisey had taken, nor did she need Lisey to coax her down to the water for a healing dip. Amanda did indeed want to come home. A large part of her had been waiting to be rescued like a sleeping princess in a fairy tale . . . or a brave pirate-girl cast into durance vile. And how many of these other unshrouded ones might be in the same situation? Lisey saw their outwardly calm faces and distant eyes, but that didn't mean some of them weren't screaming on the inside for someone to help them find their way back home.

Lisey, who could only help her sister – *maybe* – shuddered away from this idea.

'Amanda,' she said, 'we're going back now, but you have to help.'

Nothing at first. Then, very faint, very low, as if spoken out of sleep: 'Lee-sey? Did you drink . . . that shitty punch?'

Lisey laughed in spite of herself. 'A little. To be polite. Now look at me.'

'I can't. I'm watching the *Hollyhocks*. I'm going to be a pirate . . . and sail . . .' Her voice was fading now. '. . . the seven seas . . . treasure . . . the Cannibal Isles . . .'

'That was make-believe,' Lisey said. She hated the harshness she heard in her own voice; it was a little like drawing a sword to kill an infant that lay placidly on the grass, hurting no one. Because wasn't that what a child-hood dream was like? 'What you see is just this place's way of catching you. It's just . . . just a bool.'

Surprising her – surprising her and *hurting* her, Manda said: 'Scott told me you'd try to come. That if I ever needed you, you'd try to come.'

'When, Manda? When did he tell you that?'

'He loved it here,' Amanda said, and fetched a deep sigh. 'He called it Boolya Mood, or something like that. He said it was easy to love. Too easy.'

'When, Manda, *when* did he say that?' Lisey wanted to shake her.

Amanda appeared to make a tremendous effort . . . and smiled. 'The last time I cut myself. Scott made me come home. He said . . . you all wanted me.'

Now so much seemed clear to Lisey. Too late to make any difference, of course, but it was still better to know. And why had he never told his wife? Because he knew that little Lisey was terrified of Boo'ya Moon and the things – one thing in particular – that lived here? Yes. Because he sensed she would find out in time for herself? Again, yes.

Amanda had once more turned her attention to the ship floating in the harbor that was her version of Scott's pool. Lisey shook her shoulder. 'I need you to help me, Manda. There's a lunatic who wants to hurt me, and I need you to help me put a spoke in his wheel. I need you to help me *now!*'

Amanda turned to look at Lisey with an almost comical expression of wonder on her face. Below them, a woman wearing a caftan and holding a snapshot of a smiling, gap-toothed child in one hand looked back and spoke in slow, drifting remonstrance. 'Be . . . quiet . . . while . . . I think of . . . why . . . I . . . did it.'

'Mind your beeswax, Betty,' Lisey told her briskly, and then turned back to Amanda. She was relieved to see Amanda was still looking at her.

'Lisey, who . . . ?'

'A crazy man. One who showed up because of Scott's damned papers and manuscripts. Only now what he's interested in is me. He hurt me this morning and he'll hurt me again if I don't . . . if *we* don't . . .' Amanda was turning once more toward the ship riding at anchor in the harbor and Lisey took her head firmly in her hands so they were looking at each other again. 'Pay attention, Beanpole.'

'Don't call me Bean—'

'Pay attention and I won't. You know my car? My BMW?'

'Yes, but Lisey . . .'

Amanda's eyes were still trying to drift toward the water. Lisey almost turned her head back again, but some instinct told her that was a quick fix at best. If she really meant to get Amanda out of here, she had to do it with her voice, with her will, and ultimately because Amanda wanted to come.

'Manda, this guy . . . never mind just hurting, if you don't help me I think there's a chance he might kill me.'

Now Amanda looked at her with amazement and perplexity. *'Kill—?'*

'Yes. *Yes.* I promise I'll explain everything, but not here. If we stay here long, I'll end up doing nothing but gawking at the *Hollyhocks* with you.' Nor did she think this was a lie. She could feel the pull of the thing, how it wanted her to look. If she gave in, twenty years might pass like twenty minutes and at the end of them she and big sissa Manda-Bunny would still be sitting here, waiting to board a pirate ship that always beckoned but never sailed.

'Will I have to drink any of that shitty punch? Any of that . . .' Amanda's brow furrowed as she struggled for memory. Then the lines smoothed out. 'Any of that bug-juuuuuice?'

The childish way she drew the word out surprised Lisey into another laugh, and once more the woman wearing the caftan and holding the photograph looked around. Amanda gladdened Lisey's heart by giving the woman a haughty *Who* you *lookin at, bitch?* stare . . . and then flipping her the bird.

'Will I, little Lisey?'

'No more punch, no more bug-juice, I promise. For now, just think of my car. Do you know the color? Are you sure you remember?'

'Cream.' Amanda's lips thinned a little and her face took on its Just A Little Home Truth Whether You Like It Or Not expression. Lisey was absolutely delighted to see it. 'I told you when you bought it that no color shows the dirt quicker, but you wouldn't listen.'

'Do you remember the bumper-sticker?'

'A joke about Jesus, I think. Sooner or later some

pissed-off Christian is going to key it off. And probably put a few scratches in your finish for good luck.'

From above them came a man's voice, heavily disapproving: 'If you need to talk. You should go. Somewhere else.'

Lisey didn't even bother turning around, let alone shooting him the bird. 'The sticker says JESUS LOVES ME, THIS I KNOW, THAT IS WHY I DON'T DRIVE SLOW. I want you to close your eyes now, Amanda, and see my car. See it from the back, so the bumper-sticker's showing. See it in the shade of a tree. The shade's moving because it's breezy. Can you do that?'

'Ye-e-es . . . I think so . . .' Her eyes cut sideways, taking one final longing glance at the ship in the harbor. 'I guess so, if it will keep someone from hurting you . . . although I don't see what it can have to do with Scott. He's been dead over two years now . . . although . . . I think he told me something about Good Ma's yellow afghan, and I think he wanted me to tell you. Of course I never did. I forgot so much about those times . . . on purpose, I suppose.'

'What times? *What* times, Manda?'

Amanda looked at Lisey as though her baby sister were the stupidest thing going. 'All the times I *cut* myself. After the last time – when I cut my belly-button – we were here.' Amanda put a finger to her cheek, creating a temporary dimple. 'It was something about a story. *Your* story, Lisey's story. And the afghan. Only he called it the *african*. Did he say it was a boop? A beep? A boon? Maybe I only dreamed it.'

This, coming so unexpectedly out of left field, jolted

Lisey but did not derail her. If she was going to get Amanda out of here – and herself – it had to be *now*. 'Never mind all that, Manda, just close your eyes and see my car. Every damn detail you can manage. I'll do the rest.'

I hope, she thought, and when she saw Amanda close her eyes, she did the same and gripped her sister's hands tightly. Now she knew why she'd needed to see her car so clearly: so they could return to the visitors' parking lot rather than to Amanda's room in what was your basic locked ward.

She saw her cream BMW (and Amanda was right, that color had been a disaster), then left that part to her sister. She concentrated on adding 5761RD to the license plate, and the *pièce de résistance*: that Nordic Wolf beer bottle, standing on the asphalt just a bit to the left of the JESUS LOVES ME, THIS I KNOW bumper-sticker. To Lisey it looked perfect, and yet there was no change in the uniquely perfumed air of this place, and she could still hear a faint rippling sound that she realized must be slack canvas in a slight breeze. There was still the feel of the cool stone bench beneath her, and she felt a touch of panic. *What if this time I can't get back?*

Then, from what seemed to be a great distance, she heard Amanda murmur in a tone of perfect exasperation: 'Oh, booger. I forgot the fucking loon on the license plate.'

A moment later, the rippling *twack* of canvas first merged with the blat of the power-mower, then disappeared. Only now the sound of the mower was distant, because—

Lisey opened her eyes. She and Amanda were standing in the parking lot behind her BMW. Amanda was holding

Lisey's hands and her eyes were tightly closed, her brow furrowed in a frown of deep concentration. She was still wearing the mint-green pajamas with the Velcro closures, but now her feet were bare, and Lisey understood that when the duty-nurse next visited the patio where she had left Amanda Debusher and her sister Lisa Landon, she would find two empty chairs, two Dixie cups of bug-juice, one pair of slippers, and one pair of sneakers with the socks still in them.

Then – and then wouldn't be long – the nurse would raise the alarm.

In the distance, back toward Castle Rock and New Hampshire beyond, thunder rumbled. A summer storm was coming.

'Amanda!' Lisey said, and here was a new fear: what if Amanda opened her eyes and there was nothing in them but those same empty oceans?

But Amanda's eyes were perfectly aware, if slightly wild. She looked at the parking lot, the BMW, her sister, then down at herself. 'Stop holding my hands so tight, Lisey,' she said. 'They hurt like hell. Also, I need some clothes. You can see right through these stupid pajamas, and I'm not wearing any underpants, let alone a bra.'

'We'll get you some clothes,' Lisey said, and then, in a kind of belated panic, she slapped at the right front pocket of her carpenter's pants and let out a sigh of relief. Her wallet was still there. Relief was short-lived, however. Her SmartKey, which she'd put in her left front pocket – she knew she had, she always did – was gone. It hadn't traveled. It was either lying on the patio outside Amanda's room with her sneakers and socks or—

'Lisey!' Amanda cried, clutching her arm.

'What? *What!*' Lisey wheeled around, but so far as she could tell, they were still alone in the parking lot.

'I'm really awake again!' Amanda cried in a hoarse voice. There were tears standing in her eyes.

'I know it,' Lisey said. She couldn't help smiling, even with the missing key to worry about. 'It's pretty smucking wonderful.'

'I'll get my clothes,' Amanda said, and started toward the building. Lisey barely grabbed her arm. For a woman who had been catatonic only minutes ago, big sissa Manda-Bunny was now just as lively as a trout at sundown.

'Never mind your clothes,' Lisey said. 'You go back in there now and I guarantee you you'll be spending the night. Is that what you want?'

'No!'

'Good, because I need you with me. Unfortunately, we may be reduced to taking the city bus.'

Amanda nearly screamed: *'You want me to get on a bus looking like a fucking pole-dancer?'*

'Amanda, I no longer have my *car key*. It's either on your patio or one of those benches . . . do you remember the benches?'

Amanda nodded reluctantly, then said: 'Didn't you used to keep a spare key in a magnetic thingamabobby under the back bumper of your Lexus? Which, by the way, was a sane color for a northern climate?'

Lisey barely heard the gibe. Scott had given her the 'magnetic thingamabobby' as a birthday present five or six years ago, and when she traded for the Beemer, she had transferred the Beemer's spare key to the little metal box almost without thinking about it. It should still be under the back bumper. Unless it had fallen off. She dropped to one knee, felt around, and just when she was starting to despair, her fingers happened on it, riding as high and snug as ever.

'Amanda, I love you. You're a genius.'

'Not at all,' Amanda said with as much dignity as a barefoot woman in flimsy green pajamas could manage. 'Just your older sister. Now could we get in the car? Because this pavement is very warm, even in the shade.'

'You bet,' Lisey said, unlocking the car with the spare key. 'We have to get out of here, only jeez, I hate to—' She paused, gave a brief laugh, shook her head.

'What?' Amanda asked in that special tone that really demands *What now?*

'Nothing. Well . . . I was just remembering something Daddy told me after I got my license. I drove a bunch of kids back from White's Beach one day, and . . . you remember White's, don't you?' They were in the car now, and Lisey was backing out of the shady space. So far this part of the world was still quiet, and that was the way she wanted to leave it.

Amanda snorted and buckled her seatbelt, doing it carefully because of her wounded hands. 'White's! Huh! Nothing but an old gravel pit that happened to have a coldspring in the bottom!' Her look of scorn melted into an expression of longing. 'Nothing at all like the sand at Southwind.'

'Is that what you called it?' Lisey asked, curious in spite of herself. She stopped at the mouth of the parking lot and waited for a break in traffic so she could make a left onto Minot Avenue and start the journey back to Castle Rock. Traffic was heavy and she had to fight the impulse to make a right instead, just so she could get them *away* from here.

'Of course,' Amanda said, sounding rather put-out with Lisey. 'Southwind is where the *Hollyhocks* always came to pick up supplies. It's also where the pirate-girls got to see their boyfriends. Don't you remember?'

'Sort of,' Lisey said, wondering if she would hear an alarm go off behind her when they discovered Amanda was gone. Probably not. Mustn't scare the patients. She saw a small break in traffic and scooted the BMW into it, earning herself a honk from some impatient driver who actually had to slow down five miles an hour to let her in.

Amanda flipped this motorist – almost certainly a man, probably wearing a baseball cap and needing a shave – a double bird, raising her fists to shoulder height and pumping the middle fingers briskly without looking around.

'Great technique,' Lisey said. 'Someday it'll get you raped and murdered.'

Amanda rolled a sly eye in her sister's direction. 'Big talk for someone in the soup.' Then, with hardly a pause for breath: 'What did Dandy tell you when you came back from White's that day? I bet it was foolish, whatever it was.'

'He saw me get out of that old Pontiac with no sneakers or sandals on and said it was against the law to drive barefoot in the state of Maine.' Lisey glanced briefly, guiltily, down at her toes on the accelerator as she finished saying this.

Amanda made a small, rusty sound. Lisey thought she

might be crying, or trying to. Then she realized Amanda was giggling. Lisey began to smile herself, partly because just ahead she saw the Route 202 bypass that would take her around the worst of the city traffic.

'What a fool he was!' Amanda said, getting the words out around further bursts of giggles. 'What a sweet old fool! Dandy Dave Debusher! Sugar for brains! Do you know what he once told *me*?'

'No, what?'

'Spit, if you want to know.'

Lisey pushed the button that lowered her window, spat, and wiped her still slightly swollen lower lip with the heel of her hand. '*What*, Manda?'

'Said if I kissed a boy with my mouth open, I'd get pregnant.'

'Bullshit, he never!'

'It's true, and I'll tell you something else.'

'What?'

'I'm pretty sure he *believed* it!'

Then they were both laughing.

CHAPTER THIRTEEN
LISEY AND AMANDA (THE SISTER THING)

1

Now that she had Amanda, Lisey wasn't exactly sure what to do with her. Right up to Greenlawn, all the steps had seemed clear, but as they drove toward Castle Rock and the thunderheads massing over New Hampshire, *nothing* seemed clear. She had just kidnapped her supposedly catatonic sister from one of central Maine's finer nuthouses, for God's sweet sake.

Amanda, however, seemed far from nuts; any fears Lisey harbored of her slipping back into catatonia dissipated in a hurry. Amanda Debusher hadn't been this sharp in years. After listening to everything that had passed between Lisey and Jim 'Zack' Dooley, she said: 'So. Scott's manuscripts may have been the main thing when he turned up, but now he's after you, because he's your basic loony who gets hard hurting women. Like that weirdo Rader, out in Wichita.'

Lisey nodded. He hadn't raped her, but he'd gotten hard, all right. What amazed her was Amanda's succinct re-statement of her situation, even down to the Rader comparison . . . whose name Lisey wouldn't have remembered. Manda had the advantage of a little distance, of course, yet her clarity of mind was still startling.

Up ahead was a sign reading CASTLE ROCK 15. As they passed it, the sun sailed behind the building clouds. When Amanda next spoke her voice was quieter. 'You mean to do it to him before he can do it to you, don't you? Kill him and get rid of the body in that other world.' Up ahead of them, thunder rumbled. Lisey waited. *Are we doing the sister thing?* she thought. *Is that what this is?*

'Why, Lisey? Other than that I guess you can?'

'He hurt me. He *fucked* with me.' She didn't think she sounded like herself at all, but if truth was the sister thing – she thought it was – then this was it, sure. 'And let me tell you, honey: the next time he fucks with me is going to be the last time he fucks with anybody.'

Amanda sat looking straight ahead at the unrolling road with her arms folded under her scant bosom. At last she said, almost to herself, 'You always were the steel in his spine.'

Lisey looked at her, more than surprised. She was shocked. 'Say *what?*'

'Scott. And he knew it.' She lifted one of her arms and looked at the red scar there. Then she looked at Lisey. 'Kill him,' she said with chilling indifference. 'I have no problem with that.'

2

Lisey swallowed and heard a click in her throat. 'Look, Manda, I really don't have any clear idea what I'm doing.

You have to know that up front. I'm pretty much flying blind here.'

'Oh, you know what, I don't believe that,' Amanda said, almost playfully. 'You left messages saying that you'd see him at eight o'clock in Scott's study – one on your answering machine, and one with that Pittsburgh professor, in case Dooley called there. You mean to kill him and that's fine. Hey, you gave the cops their shot, didn't you?' And before Lisey could reply: 'Sure you did. And the guy waltzed right past them. Almost cut your tit off with your own can opener.'

Lisey came around a curve and found herself behind another waddling pulp-truck; it was like the day she and Darla had come back from admitting Amanda all over again. Lisey squeezed the brake, once more feeling guilty that she was driving barefoot. Old ideas died hard.

'Scott had plenty of spine,' she said.

'Yep. And he used it all getting out of his childhood alive.'

'What do you know about that?' Lisey asked.

'Nothing. He never said anything about what life was like when he was a kid. Didn't you think I noticed? Maybe Darla and Canty didn't, but I did, and he knew I did. We knew each other, Lisey – the way the only two people not drinking at a big booze-up know each other. I think that's why he cared about me. And I know something else.'

'What?'

'You better pass this truck before I strangle on his exhaust.'

'I can't see far enough.'

'You can see *plenty* far enough. Besides, God hates a

coward.' A brief pause. 'That's something else people like Scott and me know all about.'

'Manda—'

'Pass him! I'm *strangling* here!'

'I really don't think I have enough—'

'Lisey's got a *boyfriend*! Lisey and Zeke, up in a tree, K-I-S-S-I—'

'Beanpole, you're being a puke.'

Amanda, laughing: 'Kissy-kissy, facey-facey, little Lisey!'

'If something's coming the other way—'

'First comes *love*, then comes *marritch*, then comes Lisey with a—'

Without allowing herself to think about what she was doing, Lisey mashed the Beemer's accelerator with her bare foot and swung out. She was dead even with the pulp-truck's cab when *another* pulp-truck appeared over the brow of the next hill, traveling toward them.

'Oh shit, somebody pass me the bong, we're fucked now!' Amanda cried. No rusty giggles now; now she was full-out laughing. Lisey was also laughing. 'Floor it, Lisey!'

Lisey did. The BMW scooted with surprising gusto, and she nipped back into her own lane with plenty of time to spare. Darla, she reflected, would have been screaming her head off by this point.

'There,' she said to Amanda, 'are you happy?'

'Yes,' Amanda said, and put her left hand over Lisey's right one, caressing it, making it give up its death-grip on the steering wheel. 'Glad to be here, very glad you came for me. Not all of me wanted to come back, but so much of me was just . . . I don't know . . . sad to be away. And afraid that pretty soon I wouldn't even care. So thank you, Lisey.'

'Thank Scott. He knew you'd need help.'

'He knew that you would, too.' Now Amanda's tone was very gentle. 'And I bet he knew only one of your sisters would be crazy enough to give it.'

Lisey took her eyes off the road long enough to glance at Amanda. 'Did you and Scott talk about me, Amanda? Did you talk about me over there?'

'We talked. Here or there, I don't remember and I don't think it matters. We talked about how much we loved you.'

Lisey could not reply. Her heart was too full. She wanted to cry, but then she wouldn't be able to see the road. And maybe there had been enough tears, anyway. Which was not to say there wouldn't be more.

3

So they rode in silence for awhile. There was no traffic once they passed the Pigwockit Campground. The sky overhead was still blue, but the sun was now buried in the oncoming clouds, rendering the day bright but queerly shadeless. Presently Amanda spoke in an uncharacteristic tone of thoughtful curiosity. 'Would you have come for me even if you didn't need a partner in crime?'

Lisey considered this. 'I like to think so,' she finally said.

Amanda lifted the Lisey-hand closest to her and planted a kiss on it − truly it was as light as a butterfly's wing − before replacing it on the steering wheel. 'I like to think so, too,' she said. 'It's a funny place, Southwind. When you're there, it seems as real as anything in *this* world, and better than *everything* in this world. But when you're here . . .' She shrugged. Wistfully, Lisey thought. 'Then it's only a moonbeam.'

Lisey thought of lying in bed with Scott at The Antlers, watching the moon struggle to come out. Listening to his story and then going with him. *Going.*

Amanda asked, 'What did Scott call it?'

'Boo'ya Moon.'

Amanda nodded. 'I was at least close, wasn't I?'

'You were.'

'I think most kids have a place they go to when they're scared or lonely or just plain bored. They call it Never Land or the Shire, Boo'ya Moon if they've got big imaginations and make it up for themselves. Most of them forget. The talented few – like Scott – harness their dreams and turn them into horses.'

'You were pretty talented yourself. You were the one who thought up Southwind, weren't you? The girls back home played that for *years.* I wouldn't be surprised if there are girls out on the Sabbatus Road still playing a version of it.'

Amanda laughed and shook her head. 'People like me were never meant to really cross over. My imagination was just big enough to get me in trouble.'

'Manda, that's not true—'

'Yes,' Amanda said. 'It is. The looneybins are full of people like me. *Our* dreams harness *us*, and they whip us with soft whips – oh, lovely whips – and we run and we run, always in the same place . . . because the ship . . . Lisey, the sails never open and the ship never weighs its anchor . . .'

Lisey risked another look. Tears were running down Amanda's cheeks. Maybe tears didn't fall on those stone benches, but yes, here they were the smucking human condish.

'I knew I was going,' Amanda said. 'All the time we were in Scott's study . . . all the time I was writing meaningless numbers in that stupid little notebook, I *knew* . . .'

'That little notebook turned out to be the key to everything,' Lisey said, remembering that **HOLLYHOCKS** as well as **mein gott** had been printed there . . . something like a message in a bottle. Or another bool – *Lisey, here's where I am, please come find me.*

'Do you mean it?' Amanda asked.

'I do.'

'That's so funny. Scott gave me those notebooks, you know – damn near a lifetime supply. For my birthday.'

'He did?'

'Yes, the year before he died. He said they might come in handy.' She managed a smile. 'I guess one of them actually did.'

'Yes,' Lisey said, wondering if **mein gott** was written on the backs of all the others, in tiny dark letters just below the trade name. Someday, maybe, she would check. If she and Amanda got out of this alive, that was.

4

When Lisey slowed in downtown Castle Rock, preparing to turn in at the Sheriff's Office, Amanda clutched her arm and asked what in God's name she thought she was doing. She listened to her sister's reply with mounting amazement.

'And what am I supposed to do while you're making your report and filling out forms?' Amanda asked in tones etched with acid. 'Sit on the bench outside Animal Registry in these pajamas, with my tits poking out on top and my woofy showing down south? Or should I just sit out here and listen to the radio? How are you going to explain showing up barefoot? Or what if someone from Greenlawn has already called to tell the Sheriff's Department that they ought to keep an eye out for the writer's widow, she was visiting her sister up there at Crackerjack Manor and now they're both gone?'

Lisey was what her less-than-brilliant father would have called hard flummoxed. She had been so fixated on the problems of getting Manda back from Nowhere Land and coping with Jim Dooley that she had completely forgotten their current state of *dishabille*, not to mention any possible repercussions of the Great Escape. By now they were nestled in a slant-parking-space in front of the brick Sheriff's Department building, with a visiting State Police cruiser to their left and a Ford sedan with CASTLE COUNTY SHERIFF'S DEPT. painted on the side to their right, and Lisey began to feel decidedly claustrophobic. The title of a country song – 'What Was I Thinking?' – popped into her mind.

Ridiculous, of course – she wasn't a fugitive, Greenlawn wasn't a prison, and Amanda wasn't exactly a prisoner, but her bare feet . . . how was she going to explain her smucking bare feet? And—

I haven't been thinking at all, not really, I've just been following the steps. The recipe. And this is like turning a page in the cookbook and finding the next one blank.

'Also,' Amanda was continuing, 'there's Darla and Canty to think about. You did fine this morning, Lisey, I'm not criticizing, but—'

'Yes you are,' Lisey said. 'And you're right to criticize. If this isn't a mess already, it soon will be. I didn't want to go to your house too soon or stay there too long in case Dooley's keeping an eye on that, too—'

'Does he know about me?'

I got an idear you got some kind of sister-twister goin on as well, isn't that so?

'I think . . .' Lisey began, then stopped. That kind of equivocation wouldn't do. 'I *know* he does, Manda.'

'Still, he's not Karnak the Great. He can't be both places at the same time.'

'No, but I don't want the cops coming by, either. I don't want them in this at all.'

'Drive us up to the View, Lisey. You know, Pretty View.'

Pretty View was what locals called the picnic area overlooking Castle Lake and Little Kin Pond. It was the entrance to Castle Rock State Park, and there was plenty of parking, even a couple of Portosans. And at mid-afternoon, with thunderstorms rolling in, it would very likely be deserted. A good place to stop, think, take stock, and kill some time. Maybe Amanda really *was* a genius.

'Come on, get us off Main Street,' Amanda said, plucking at the neckline of her pajama top. 'I feel like a stripper in church.'

Lisey backed carefully out onto the street – now that she wanted nothing to do with the County Sheriff's Department, she was absurdly sure she was going to get into a fender-bender before she could put it behind her – and turned west. Ten minutes later she was turning in at the sign reading

CASTLE ROCK STATE PARK
PICNIC AND RESTROOM FACILITIES AVAILABLE
MAY–OCTOBER
THIS PARK CLOSES AT SUNDOWN
BARREL-PICKING PROHIBITED FOR YOUR HEALTH
BY LAW

5

Lisey's was the only car in the parking lot, and the picnic area was deserted – not even a single backpacker getting high on nature (or Montpelier Gold). Amanda walked toward one of the picnic tables. The soles of her feet were very pink, and even with the sun hidden, she was clearly nude under the green pajamas.

'Amanda, do you really think that's—'

'If someone comes I'll nip right back into the car.' Manda looked back over her shoulder and flashed a grin. 'Try it – the grass feels positively *slinky*.'

Lisey walked to the edge of the pavement on the balls of her feet, then stepped up into the green. Amanda was right, slinky was the one, the perfect fish from Scott's pool of words. And the view to the west was a straight shot to the eye and heart. Thunderheads were pouring toward them through the ragged teeth of the White Mountains, and Lisey counted seven dark spots where the high slopes had been smudged away by cauls of rain. Brilliant

513

lightnings flashed inside those stormbags and between two of them, connecting them like some fantastic fairy bridge, was a double rainbow that arched over Mount Cranmore in a frayed loophole of blue. As Lisey watched that hole closed and another, over some mountain whose name she did not know, opened, and the rainbow reappeared. Below them Castle Lake was a dirty dark gray and Little Kin Pond beyond it a dead black goose-eye. The wind was rising but it was improbably warm, and when her hair lifted from her temples, Lisey lifted her arms as though she would fly – not on a magic carpet but on the ordinary alchemy of a summer storm.

'Manda!' she said. 'I'm glad I'm alive!'

'So am I,' Amanda said seriously, and held out her hands. The wind blew back her graying hair and made it fly like a child's. Lisey closed her fingers carefully around her sister's, trying to be mindful of Amanda's cuts but aware of a rising wildness in herself all the same. Thunder cracked overhead, the warm wind blew harder, and ninety miles to the west, thunderheads streamed through the ancient mountain passes. Amanda began to dance and Lisey danced with her, their bare feet in the grass, their linked hands in the sky.

'*Yes!*' Thunder cracked and Lisey had to yell it.

'Yes, *what*?' Manda hollered back. She was laughing again.

'*Yes, I mean to kill him!*'

'*That's what I said! I'll help you!*' Amanda shouted, and then the rain began and they ran back to the car, both of them laughing and holding their hands over their heads.

6

They were under cover before the first of that afternoon's half a dozen real downpours came, and so were spared a serious soaking, which they most certainly would have gotten had they dallied; thirty seconds after the first drops fell, they could no longer see the nearest picnic table, less than twenty yards away. The rain was cold, the inside of the car warm, and the windshield fogged up at once. Lisey started the engine and turned on the defroster. Amanda snared Lisey's cell phone. 'Time to call Miss Buggy Bumpers,' she said, using a childhood name for Darla Lisey hadn't heard in years.

Lisey glanced at her watch and saw it was now after three. Not much chance of Canty and Darla (once known as Miss Buggy Bumpers, and how she'd hated it) still being at lunch. 'They're probably on the road between Portland and Auburn by now,' she said.

'Yes, they probably are,' Amanda said, speaking to Lisey as though she were a child. 'That's why I'm going to call Miss Buggy's cell.'

It's Scott's fault if I'm technologically challenged, Lisey thought of saying. *Ever since he died, I keep falling farther behind the cutting edge. Why, I haven't even gotten around to buying a DVD player yet, and everybody has those.*

What she *did* say was, 'If you call Darla Miss Buggy Bumpers, she'll probably hang up even if she realizes it's you.'

'I'd never do that.' Amanda stared out at the pelting rain. It had turned the BMW's windshield into a glass river. 'Do you know why me n Canty used to call her that, and why it was so mean of us?'

'No.'

'When she was only three or four, Darla had a little red rubber dolly. *She* was the original Miss Buggy Bumpers. Darl loved that old thing. One cold night she left Miss Buggy on a radiator and she melted. Sweet baldheaded Christ, what a stink.'

Lisey tried her best to hold back more laughter and failed. Because her throat was locked and her mouth was shut, it came out through her nose and she blew a large quantity of clear snot onto her fingers.

'Euwww, charming, high tea is served, madam,' Amanda said.

'There are Kleenex in the glove compartment,' Lisey said, blushing to the roots of her hair. 'Would you give me some?' Then she thought of Miss Buggy Bumpers melting on the radiator, and this crossed with what had been Dandy's juiciest curse – *sweet baldheaded Christ* – and she started laughing again, although she recognized the sadness hidden like a sweet-sour pearl within her hilarity, something that had to do with the neatly-put-together do-it-my-way-darling adult Darla and the ghost child still hidden just beneath, that jam-smeared and often furious kid who had always seemed to *need* something.

'Oh, just wipe it on the steering wheel,' Amanda said, now laughing again herself. She was holding the hand with the phone in it against her stomach. 'I think I'm going to pee myself.'

'If you pee in those pajamas, Amanda, they'll melt. Give me that damn box of Kleenex.'

Amanda, still laughing, opened the glove compartment and handed over the Kleenex.

'Do you think you'll be able to get her?' Lisey asked. 'In all this rain?'

'If she's got her phone turned on, I'll get her. And unless she's in a movie or something, she's always got it turned on. I talk to her almost every day – sometimes twice, if Matt's off on one of his teaching orgies. 'Cause, see, sometimes Metzie calls her and Darla tells me what she says. These days Darl's the only one in the family Metzie will talk to.'

Lisey was fascinated by this. She'd had no idea Amanda and Darla talked about Amanda's troubled daughter – certainly Darla had never said anything about it. She wished she could pursue the matter further, but supposed this wasn't the time to do so. 'What will you tell her, if you get her?'

'Just listen. I think I've got it figured out, but I'm afraid if I tell you in advance, it'll lose some of its . . . I don't know. Freshness. Believability. All I want is to get the two of them far enough away so they won't come wandering in and—'

'—get caught in Max Silver's potato grader?' Lisey asked. Over the years they'd all worked for Mr Silver: a quarter for every barrel of potatoes you picked, and you ended up scrubbing dirt out from under your nails until February.

Amanda gave her a sharp look, then smiled. 'Something like that. Darla and Canty can be annoying, but I love em, so sue me. I sure wouldn't want em getting hurt just because they turned up in the wrong place at the wrong time.'

'Me either,' Lisey said softly.

A burst of hail rattled down on the roof and windshield; then it was just hard rain again.

Amanda patted her hand. 'I know that, Little.'

Little. Not little Lisey, just Little. How long since Amanda had called her that? And she'd been the only one who ever did.

7

Amanda entered the number with some difficulty because of her hands, going wrong once and having to start over. The second time she managed it, pushed the green SEND button, and put the small Motorola phone to her ear.

The rain had let up a little. Lisey realized she could see the first picnic table again. How many seconds since Amanda had sent the call on its way? She looked from the picnic table to her sister, eyebrows raised. Amanda started to shake her head, then straightened in her bucket seat and raised her right forefinger, as if summoning a waiter in a fancy restaurant.

'Darla? . . . Can you hear me? . . . Do you know who this is? . . . *Yes!* Yes, *really!*'

Amanda stuck out her tongue and bugged her eyes, miming Darla's reaction with silent and rather cruel efficiency: a game-show contestant who has just won the bonus round.

'Yes, she's right beside m . . . Darla, slow *down*! First I couldn't talk and now I can't get a word in edgeways! I'll let you talk to Lisey in just a . . .'

Amanda listened longer this time, nodding, at the same time clipping the thumb and fingers of her right hand together in a *quack-quack-quack* gesture.

'Uh-huh, I'll tell her, Darl.' Without bothering to cover the mouthpiece of the phone – probably because she wanted Darla to hear the message being passed on – Amanda said, 'She and Canty are together, Lisey, but still at the Jetport. Canty's plane was held up by thunderstorms out of Boston. Isn't that a shame?'

Amanda gave Lisey a thumbs-up as she said this last, then returned her attention to the phone.

'I'm glad I caught you guys before you started rolling, because I'm not at Greenlawn anymore. Lisey and I are at Acadia Mental Health in Derry . . . that's right, *Derry.*'

She listened, nodding.

'Yes, I guess it *is* sort of a miracle. All I know is I heard Lisey calling and I woke up. The last thing I remember before that is you guys taking me to Stephens Memorial in No Soapa. Then I just . . . I heard Lisey calling me and it was like when you hear someone calling you out of a deep sleep . . . and the docs at Greenlawn sent me up here for all these tests on my brain that probably cost a fortune . . .'

Listening.

'Yes, hon, I *do* want to say hi to Canty, and I'm sure Lisey does, too, but they want us now and the phone won't work in the room where they do their tests. You'll drive up, won't you? I'm sure you can be in Derry by seven o'clock, eight o'clock tops . . .'

At that moment the skies opened again. This cloudburst was even fiercer than the first had been, and suddenly the car was filled with its hollow drumming sound. For the first time Amanda seemed completely at a loss. She looked at Lisey, eyes wide and full of panic. One finger

519

pointed at the roof of the car, where the sound was coming from. Her lips formed the words *She wants to know what that sound is.*

Lisey didn't hesitate. She snatched the telephone away from Amanda and put it to her own ear. The connection was bell-clear in spite of the storm (maybe even because of it, for all Lisey knew). She heard not just Darla but Canty as well, talking to each other in agitated, confused, jubilant voices; in the background she could even hear a loudspeaker announcing flight delays due to bad weather.

'Darla, it's Lisey. Amanda's back! All the way back! Isn't it wonderful?'

'Lisey, I can't believe it!'

'Seeing's believing,' Lisey said. 'Get your ass up to Acadia in Derry and see for yourself.'

'Lisey, what's that *noise*? It sounds like you're in a *shower*!'

'Hydrotherapy, right across the hall!' Lisey said, lying giddily and thinking *We'll never be able to explain this later – not in a million years.* '—They've got the door open and it's awfully noisy.'

For a moment there was no sound but the steadily downpouring rain. Then Darla said, 'If she's really all right, maybe Canty and I could go to the Snow Squall anyway. It's a long drive up to Derry and we're both famished.'

For a moment Lisey was furious with her, then could almost have punched herself in the eye for feeling that way. The longer they took, the better – wasn't that right? Yet still, the put-upon petulance she heard in Darla's voice made Lisey feel a little sick to her stomach. And that was also the sister thing, she supposed.

'Sure, why not?' she said, and made a thumb-and-forefinger circle at Amanda, who smiled back and nodded. 'We're not going anywhere, Darl.'

Except maybe to Boo'ya Moon, to get rid of a dead lunatic. If we're lucky, that is. If things break our way.

'Can you put Manda on again?' Darla still sounded peeved, as if she'd never seen that dreadful catatonic heaviness and now suspected Amanda had been faking all along. 'Canty wants to talk to her.'

'You bet,' Lisey said, and mouthed *Cantata* to Amanda as she handed the phone back.

Amanda assured Canty repeatedly that yes, she was all right, and yes, it was a miracle; no, she didn't mind a bit if Canty and Darla went through with their original plan for lunch at the Snow Squall, and no, she most definitely didn't need them to divert to Castle View and pick up anything at her house. She had everything she needed, Lisey had taken care of that.

Toward the end of the conversation the rain stopped all at once, without the slightest slackening, as if God had turned off a faucet in the sky, and Lisey was struck by a queer idea: this was how it rained in Boo'ya Moon, in quick, furious, off-and-on showers.

I've left it behind, but not very far, she thought, and realized that sweet, clean taste was still in her mouth.

As Amanda told Cantata that she loved her and then broke the connection, an improbable shaft of humid June sunlight broke through the clouds and another rainbow formed in the sky, this one closer, shining above Castle Lake. *Like a promise,* Lisey thought. *The kind you want to believe but don't quite trust.*

8

Amanda's murmuring voice called her away from her contemplation of the rainbow. Manda was asking Directory Assistance for the Greenlawn number, then writing it with the tip of her finger in the fog forming on the bottom of the Beemer's windshield.

'That'll stay there even after the windshield's completely defogged, you know,' Lisey told her when Amanda had rung off. 'It'll take Windex to get rid of it. I had a pen in the center console – why didn't you ask?'

'Because I'm catatonic,' Amanda said, and held the phone out to her.

Lisey only looked at it. 'Who am I supposed to call?'

'As if you didn't know.'

'*Amanda*—'

'It has to be you, Lisey. I have no idea who to talk to, or how you even got me in there.' She was silent for a moment, twiddling her fingers on the legs of her pajamas. The clouds had closed up again, the day was once more dark, and the rainbow might have been a dream. 'Sure I do,' she said at last. 'Only it *wasn't* you, it was Scott. He fixed it somehow. Saved me a seat.'

Lisey only nodded. She didn't trust herself to say anything.

'When? After the last time I tuned up on myself? After the last time I saw him in Southwind? What he called Boonya Moon?'

Lisey didn't bother to correct her. 'He schmoozed a doc named Hugh Alberness. Alberness agreed you were headed for trouble after looking at your records, and when you freaked this time, he examined you and admitted you. You have no memory of that? Any of it?'

'No.'

Lisey took the cell phone and looked at the number on the partially fogged windshield. 'I don't have a clue what to tell him, Manda.'

'What would *Scott* have told him, Little?'

Little. There it was again. Another shower, furious but of no more than twenty seconds' duration, beat on the roof of the car, and while it drummed, Lisey found herself thinking of all the speaking engagements she'd gone to with Scott – what he called *gigs.* With the notable exception of Nashville in 1988, it seemed to her that she always had a good time, and why not? He told them what they wanted to hear; her job was only to smile and clap in the right places. Oh, and sometimes she had to mouth *Thank you* when acknowledged. Sometimes they gave him things – souvenirs, mementos – and he gave them to her and she had to hold them. Sometimes people took pictures and sometimes there were people like Tony Eddington – Toneh – whose job was to write it up and sometimes they mentioned her and sometimes they didn't and sometimes they spelled her name right and sometimes they didn't and once she had been identified as Scott Landon's *Gal Pal* and that was okay, it was *all* okay because she didn't make a fuss, she was good at quiet, but she was *not* like the little girl in the Saki story, invention at short notice was most assuredly *not* her specialty, and—

'Listen, Amanda, if channeling Scott is what you had in mind, it's not working, I'm really clueless here. Why don't you just call Dr Alberness and tell him you're all right

. . .' As she was saying this, Lisey tried to pass the cell phone back.

Amanda raised her mutilated hands to her chest in refusal. 'It wouldn't work no matter what I said. I'm *crazy*. You, on the other hand, are not only sane, you're the famous writer's widow. So make the call, Lisey. Get Dr Alberness out of our road. And do it now.'

9

Lisey dialed, and what followed was, to begin with, almost too similar to the call she'd made on her long, long Thursday – the day she had started following the stations of the bool. It was once more Cassandra on the other end, and Lisey once more recognized the soporific music when she was put on hold, but this time Cassandra sounded both excited and relieved to hear from her. She said she was going to connect Lisey with Dr Alberness at his home.

'Don't go away, now,' she instructed Lisey before disappearing into what might have been the old Donna Summer disco tune 'Love to Love You, Baby', before undergoing a musical lobotomy. *Don't go away* had an ominous ring, but the fact that Hugh Alberness was at home . . . surely that was hopeful, wasn't it?

He could have called the cops from home as easily as from his office, you know. Or the on-call doc at Greenlawn could have done it. And what are you going to tell him when he comes on? Just what the hell are you going to tell him?

What would Scott have told him?

Scott would have told him that reality is Ralph.

And yes, that was undoubtedly true.

Lisey smiled a little at the thought, and at the memory of Scott pacing around a hotel room in . . . Lincoln? Lincoln, Nebraska? More likely Omaha, because this had been a hotel room, a nice one, maybe even part of a suite. He'd been reading the newspaper when a fax from his editor had come sliding under the door. The editor, Carson Foray, wanted further changes in the third draft of Scott's new novel. Lisey couldn't remember which novel, just that it had been one of the later ones, which he sometimes referred to as 'Landon's Throbbing Love Stories'. In any case, Carson – who had been with Scott for what old Dandy would have called *a dead coon's age* – felt that a chance meeting between two characters after twenty years or so was poorly managed. 'Plot creaks a bit here, old boy,' he'd written.

'Creak on this, old boy,' Scott had grumbled, grabbing his crotch with one hand (and had that sweetly troublesome lock of hair tumbled across his brow when he did it? of course it did). And then, before she could say anything of an ameliorative nature, he had snatched up the newspaper, rattled it to the back page, and shown her an item in a feature called *This Odd World*. It was headlined DOG FINDS HIS WAY HOME – AFTER 3 YEARS. It told the story of a Border Collie named Ralph, who had been lost while on vacation with his family in Port Charlotte, Florida. Three years later Ralph had shown up at the family manse in Eugene, Oregon. He was thin, collarless, and a little footsore, but otherwise none the worse for wear. Just came walking up the driveway, sat down on the stoop, and barked to be let in.

'What do you think Monsieur Carson Foray would

make of that if it turned up in a book of mine?' Scott had demanded, brushing the hair off his forehead (it flopped right back, of course). 'Do you think he'd shoot me a fax telling me it *creaked* a bit, *old boy*?'

Lisey, both amused by his pique and almost absurdly touched by the thought of Ralph coming back after all those years (and God knew what adventures), agreed that Carson probably would.

Scott had snatched back the paper, peered balefully for a moment at the photo of Ralph looking sporty in a new collar and a paisley bandanna, then tossed it aside. 'I'll tell you something, Lisey,' he'd said, 'novelists labor under tremendous handicaps. Reality is Ralph, showing up after three years, and no one knows why. But a novelist can't tell that story! Because it *creaks* a bit, old boy!'

Having delivered himself of this diatribe, Scott had then, to the best of her recollection, gone back and rewritten the pages in question.

The hold-music cut off. 'Mrs Landon, still there?' Cassandra asked.

'Still here,' Lisey said, feeling considerably calmer. Scott had been right. Reality was a drunk buying a lottery ticket, cashing out to the tune of seventy million dollars, and splitting it with his favorite barmaid. A little girl emerging alive from the well in Texas where she'd been trapped for six days. A college boy falling from a fifth-floor balcony in Cancún and only breaking his wrist. Reality was Ralph.

'I'm transferring you now,' Cassandra said.

There was a double click, then Hugh Alberness – a very concerned Hugh Alberness, she judged, but not a panic-stricken one – was saying, 'Mrs Landon? Where are you?'

'On the road to my sister's house. We'll be there in twenty minutes.'

'Amanda's with you?'

'Yes.' Lisey had determined to answer his questions, but no more. Part of her was quite curious as to what those questions would be.

'Mrs Landon—'

'Lisey.'

'Lisey, there are a great many concerned people at Greenlawn this afternoon, especially Dr Stein, the on-call physician, Nurse Burrell, who is in charge of the Ackley Wing, and Josh Phelan, who's head of our small but ordinarily quite able campus security team.'

Lisey decided this was both a question – *What did you do?* – and an accusation – *You scared the hell out of some folks today!* – and thought she'd better respond to it. Briefly. It would be only too easy to dig herself a hole and then fall into it.

'Yes, well. I'm sorry about that. *Very*. But Amanda wanted to leave, she was very insistent about that, and she was also very insistent about not calling anyone from Greenlawn until we were well away from there. Under the circumstances, I thought it was best to go with the flow. It was a judgment call.'

Amanda gave her a vigorous double thumbs-up, but she couldn't afford to be distracted. Dr Alberness might have been *a huh-yooge* fan of her husband's books, but Lisey had no doubt he was also excellent at getting things out of people that they didn't want or mean to tell.

527

Alberness, however, sounded excited. 'Mrs. Landon
. . . Lisey . . . is your sister responding? Is she aware and
responding?'

'Hearing is believing,' Lisey said, and handed the
phone to Amanda. Amanda looked alarmed, but took the
cell phone.

Lisey mouthed the words *Be careful*.

10

'Hello, Dr Alberness?' Amanda spoke slowly and carefully
but clearly. 'Yes, this is she.' She listened. 'Amanda Debusher,
correct.' She listened. 'My middle name is Georgette.'
Listened. 'July of 1946. Which makes me not quite sixty.'
Listened. 'I have one child, a daughter named Intermezzo.
Metzie for short.' Listened. 'George W. Bush, sad to say –
I believe the man has a God-complex at least as dangerous
as that of his stated enemies.' Listened. Shook her head
minutely. 'I . . . I really can't go into all that now, Dr
Alberness. Here's Lisey.' She handed the phone back, her
eyes begging for a good review . . . or at least a passing
grade. Lisey nodded vigorously. Amanda collapsed back
against her seat like a woman who has just run a race.

'—still there?' the phone was squawking when Lisey
put it back to her ear.

'It's Lisey, Dr Alberness.'

'Lisey, *what happened*?'

'I'll have to give you the short form, Dr—'

'Hugh. Please. Hugh.'

Lisey had been sitting bolt-upright behind the wheel.
Now she allowed herself to relax a little against the

comforting leather of the driver's seat. He had asked her to call him Hugh. They were pals again. She would still have to be careful, but it was probably going to be all right.

'I was visiting her – we were on her patio – and she just came around.'

Showed up limping and without her collar, but otherwise fine, Lisey thought, and had to clamp down on a crazy bray of laughter. On the far side of the lake, lightning flashed brilliantly. Her head felt like that.

'I've never heard of such a thing,' Hugh Alberness said. This wasn't a question, so Lisey stayed silent. 'And how did you . . . uh . . . make your exit?'

'I beg pardon?'

'How did you get past the Ackley Wing reception desk? Who buzzed you out?'

Reality is Ralph, Lisey reminded herself. Taking care to sound only a little puzzled, she said: 'No one asked us to sign out, or anything – they all looked very busy. We just walked out.'

'What about the door?'

'It was open,' Lisey said.

'I'll be—' Alberness said, and then made himself stop.

Lisey waited for more. She was quite sure there would be more.

'The nurses found a key-ring, a key-case, and a pair of slippers. Also a pair of sneakers with the socks inside them.'

For a moment Lisey was stuck on her key-ring. She hadn't realized the rest of her keys were also gone, and it would probably be better not to let Alberness know that. 'I keep a spare car key under the bumper of my car in a magnetic box. As for the ones on my ring . . .' Lisey tried for a halfway genuine laugh. She had no idea if she succeeded, but at least Amanda did not pale noticeably. 'I'd be sorry to lose those! You'll have the staff hold them for me, won't you?'

'Of course, but we need to see Miss Debusher. There are certain procedures, if you want us to release her into your custody.' Dr Alberness's voice suggested he thought this was a terrible idea, but there was no question here. It was hard, but Lisey waited. On the far side of Castle Lake, the sky had once more gone dead black. Another squall was rushing their way. Lisey wanted very much to be done with this conversation before it hit, but still she waited. She had an idea that she and Alberness had reached the critical point.

'Lisey,' he said at last, 'why *did* you and your sister leave your footwear?'

'I don't really know. Amanda was insistent that we go at once, that we go barefoot, and that I not take my keys—'

'With the keys, she may have been worried about the metal detector,' Alberness said. 'Although, given her condition, I'm surprised she even . . . never mind, go on.'

Lisey looked away from the oncoming squall, which had now blotted out the hills on the far side of Castle Lake. 'Do you remember why you wanted us to leave bare-footed, Amanda?' she asked, and tilted the phone toward her.

'No,' Amanda said loudly, then added: 'Only that I wanted to feel the grass. The slinky grass.'

'Did you get that?' Lisey asked Alberness.

'Something about feeling the grass?'

'Yes, but I'm sure that it was more. She was very insistent.'

'And you just did as she asked?'

'She's my older sister, Hugh – my *oldest* sister, actually. Also, I have to admit I was too excited at having her back on planet Earth to think very straight.'

'But I – *we* – really need to see her, and make sure this is an actual recovery.'

'If I bring her back in for examination tomorrow, would that be all right?'

Amanda was shaking her head hard enough to make her hair fly, her eyes big with alarm. Lisey began nodding her own head just as emphatically.

'That will do very well,' Alberness said. Lisey could hear the relief in his voice, real relief that made her feel bad about lying to him. Some things, however, had to be done once you had it strapped on nice and tight. 'I could come in to Greenlawn around two tomorrow afternoon and speak to both of you myself. Would that suit?'

'That would be fine.' *Assuming we're still alive tomorrow at two.*

'All right, then. Lisey, I wonder if—' Just then, directly above them, a glare-bright bolt of lightning raced beneath the clouds and struck something on the far side of the highway. Lisey heard the crack; she smelled both electricity and burning. She had never been so close to a lightning strike in her whole life. Amanda screamed, the sound almost completely lost in a monstrous roll of follow-thunder.

'What was that?' Alberness shouted. Lisey thought the connection was as good as ever, but the doctor her husband

had so assiduously cultivated on Amanda's behalf five years before suddenly seemed very far away and unimportant.

'Thunder and lightning,' she said calmly. 'We're having quite a storm here, Hugh.'

'You'd better pull over to the side of the road.'

'I've already done that, but I want to get off this phone before it gives me a shock, or something. I'll see you tomorrow—'

'The Ackley Wing—'

'Yes. At two. With Amanda. Thanks for—' Lightning flared overhead and she cringed, but this time it was more diffuse, and the thunder which followed, while loud, didn't threaten to burst her eardrums. '—for being so understanding,' she finished, and pushed the END button without saying goodbye. The rain came at once, as if it had been waiting for her to finish her call. It beat the car in a white fury. Never mind the picnic bench; Lisey could no longer see to the end of her car's hood.

Amanda clutched her shoulder, and Lisey thought of another country song, the one opining that if you worked your fingers to the bone, all you got was bony fingers. 'I'm not going back there, Lisey, I'm *not*!'

'Ow, Manda, that hurts!'

Amanda let go but didn't pull back. Her eyes blazed. 'I'm not going back there.'

'You are. Just long enough to talk to Dr Alberness.'

'No—'

'Shut up and listen to me.'

Amanda blinked and sat back, recoiling from the fury in Lisey's voice.

'Darla and I had to stick you in there, we had no

choice. You were nothing but a breathing lump of meat with drool running out one end and piss running out the other. And my husband, who knew it was going to happen, did not just take care of you in one world but in *two*. You *owe* me, big sissa Manda-Bunny. Which is why you're going to help me tonight and yourself tomorrow, and I don't want to hear any more about it except "Yes, Lisey." Have you got it?'

'Yes, Lisey,' Amanda muttered. Then, looking down at her cut hands and starting to cry again: 'But what if they make me go back to that room? What if they lock me in and make me take sponge-baths and drink bug-juice?'

'They won't. They *can't*. Your committal was purely voluntary – Darla and I did the volunteering, since you were hors-de-batty.'

Amanda snickered dolefully. 'Scott used to say that. And sometimes, when he thought someone was stuck-up, he'd say they were hors-de-snotty.'

'Yes,' Lisey said, not without a pang. 'I remember. Anyway, you're okay now. That's the point.' She took one of Amanda's hands, reminding herself to be gentle. 'You're going to go in there tomorrow and charm the socks off that doc.'

'I'll try,' Amanda said. 'But not because I owe you.'

'No?'

'Because I love you,' Amanda said with simple dignity. Then, in a very small voice: 'You'll come with, won't you?'

'You bet I will.'

'Maybe . . . maybe your boyfriend will get us and I won't have to worry about Greenlawn at all.'

'Told you not to call him my boyfriend.'

Amanda smiled wanly. 'I think I can manage to remember that, if you can drop the Manda-Bunny shit.'

Lisey burst out laughing.

'Why don't you get going, Lisey? The rain's letting up. And please turn on the heater. It's getting cold in here.'

Lisey flicked it on, backed the BMW out of its parking space, and turned toward the road. 'We'll go to your house,' she said. 'Dooley's probably not watching it if it's raining as hard there as it has been here — at least I hope not. And even if he is, what's he going to see? We go to your house, then we go to my house. Two middle-aged women. Is he going to worry about two middle-aged women?'

'Unlikely,' Amanda said. 'But I'm glad we sent Canty and Miss Buggy Bumpers off on a long trip, aren't you?'

Lisey was, even though she knew that, like Lucy Ricardo, she was going to have some 'splainin to do down the line. She pulled out onto the highway, which was now deserted. She hoped she wouldn't encounter a tree lying across the road and knew it was very possible that she would. Thunder growled overhead, sounding ill-tempered.

'I can get some clothes that actually fit me,' Amanda was saying. 'Also, I have two pounds of nice ground chuck in my freezer. It'll thaw nicely in the microwave, and I'm *very* hungry.'

'*My* microwave,' Lisey said, not taking her eyes off the road. The rain had stopped entirely for the time being, but there were more dark clouds up ahead. *Black as a stage villain's hat*, Scott would have said, and she was struck by the old sick wanting of him, that empty place that could now never be filled. That needing-place.

'Did you hear me, little Lisey?' Amanda asked, and

534

Lisey realized that her sister had been talking. Saying something about something. Twenty-four hours ago she had been afraid Manda would never speak again, and here she was, already ignoring her. But wasn't that the way the world turned?

'No,' Lisey admitted. 'Guess not. Sorry.'

'That's you, always was. Off in your own . . .' Amanda's voice trailed away, and she made a business of looking out the window.

'Always off in my own little world?' Lisey asked, smiling. 'I'm sorry.'

'Don't be.' They came around a curve and Lisey swerved to avoid a large fir branch lying in the road. She considered stopping and tossing it onto the shoulder, and decided to leave it for the next person to come along. The next person to come along would probably not have a psychopath to deal with. 'If it's Boo'ya Moon you're thinking of, it's not really my world, anyway. It seems to me that everyone who goes there has his or her own version. What were you saying?'

'Just that I have something else you might want. Unless you're already strapped, that is.'

Lisey was startled. She took her eyes off the road for a moment to look at her sister. 'What? What did you say?'

'Just a figure of speech,' Amanda said. 'I mean I have a gun.'

11

There was a long white envelope propped on the sill of Amanda's screen door, well under the porch overhang and thus safe from the rain. Lisey's first alarmed thought on seeing it was *Dooley's been here already*. But the envelope Lisey had found after discovering the dead cat in her mailbox had been blank on both sides. This one had Amanda's name printed on the front. She handed it over. Amanda looked at the printing, turned the card over to read the embossing on the back – **Hallmark** – and then spoke a single disdainful word: 'Charles.'

For a moment the name meant nothing to Lisey. Then she remembered that once upon a time, before this current craziness had begun, Amanda had had a boyfriend.

Shootin' Beans, she thought, and made a strangled noise in her throat.

'Lisey?' Amanda asked. Her eyebrows went up.

'Just thinking about Canty and Miss Buggy, charging up to Derry,' Lisey said. 'I know it's not funny, but—'

'Oh, it has its humorous elements,' Amanda said. 'Probably this does, too.' She opened the envelope and removed the card. Scanned it. 'Oh. My. God. Look. What just fell out of. The dog's ass.'

'Can I see?'

Amanda passed it over. On the front was a gap-toothed little boy, Hallmark's idea of tough but endearing (too-big sweater, patched jeans), holding out a single droopy flower. Gee, I'm Sorry! read the message below the scamp's battered sneakers. Lisey flipped it open and read this:

I know I hurt your feelin's, and I guess you're feelin' bad,
This is just a note to say you ain't the only one who's sad!
  I thought I'd send a card an' apologize to you,

'Cuz to think of you down in the dumps has made me feel
so blue!

So get out an' smell the roses! Be happy for a while!
Get that spring back in your step! Put on that cheery smile!
Today I guess I made you feel a tiny bit o' sorrow,
But I hope we'll still be friends when the sun comes out
tomorrow!

It was signed *Yours in friendship (4-Ever! Remember the Good Times!!) Charles 'Charlie' Corriveau.*

Lisey tried mightily to keep a solemn face, but couldn't. She burst out laughing. And Amanda joined her. They stood on the porch together, laughing. When it began to wind down a little, Amanda stood up straight and declaimed to her rain-soaked front yard, with the card held out before her like a choir-book.

'My darling Charles, I cannot let another moment pass, without asking you to come over here and kiss my fuckin ass.'

Lisey fell against the side of the house hard enough to rattle the nearest window, screaming with laughter, her hands against her chest. Amanda gave her a haughty smile and marched down the porch stairs. She squelched two or three steps into the yard, upended the little lawn-pixie that stood guard over the rose bushes, and fished out the spare latchkey she kept stashed beneath. But while she was bent over, she took the opportunity to rub Charlie Corriveau's card briskly over her green-clad fanny.

No longer caring if Jim Dooley might be watching from the woods, no longer thinking of Jim Dooley at all,

Lisey collapsed to a sitting position on the porch, now wheezing with laughter because she had almost no breath left. She might have laughed so hard once or twice with Scott, but maybe not. Maybe not even then.

12

There was a single message on Amanda's answering machine, and it was from Darla, not Dooley. 'Lisey!' she said exuberantly. 'I don't know what you did, but wow! We're on our way to Derry! Lisey, I love you! You're a champ!'

She heard Scott saying *Lisey, you're a champ at this!* and her laughter began to dry up.

Amanda's gun turned out to be a Pathfinder .22 revolver, and when Amanda passed it over, it felt absolutely correct in Lisey's hand, as if it had been manufactured with her in mind. Amanda had been keeping it in a shoebox on the top shelf of her bedroom closet. With only minimal fiddling, Lisey was able to swing out the cylinder.

'Jesus-please-us, Manda, this thing is *loaded*!'

As if Someone Up There was displeased with Lisey's profanity, the skies opened and more rain poured down. A moment later, the windows and gutters were rattling and pinging with hail.

'What's a woman on her own supposed to do if a raper comes in?' Amanda asked. 'Point an unloaded gun at him and shout *bang*? Lisey, hook this for me, would you?' Amanda had put on a pair of jeans. Now she presented her bony back and the hooks of her bra. 'Every time I try, my hands just about *kill* me. You should have taken *me* down for a little dip in that pool of yours.'

'I was having enough trouble getting you away from it without baptizing you in it, please and thank you,' Lisey said, doing the hooks. 'Wear the red shirt with the yellow flowers, would you? I love that one on you.'

'It shows my gut.'

'Amanda, you don't *have* a gut.'

'I do s—Why in the name of Jesus, Mary, and JoJo the Carpenter are you taking the bullets *out*?'

'So I don't shoot my own kneecap off.' Lisey put the bullets in the pocket of her jeans. 'I'll re-load it later.' Although whether she could point it at Jim Dooley and actually pull the trigger . . . she just didn't know. Maybe. If she summoned up the memory of her can-opener.

But you do mean to get rid of him. Don't you?

She certainly did. He had hurt her. That was strike one. He was dangerous. That was strike two. She could trust no one else to do it, strike three and you're out. Still, she continued to look at the Pathfinder with fascination. Scott had researched gunshot wounds for one of his novels – *Relics*, she was quite sure – and she'd made the mistake of looking into a folder filled with very ugly photographs. Until then she hadn't realized how lucky Scott himself had been that day in Nashville. If Cole's bullet had hit a rib and splintered—

'Why not take it in the shoebox?' Amanda asked, pulling on a rude tee-shirt (KISS ME WHERE IT STINKS – MEET ME IN MOTTON) instead of the button-up one Lisey liked. 'There are some extra shells in it, too. You can tape it shut while I'm getting the meat out of the freezer.'

'Where did you get it, Manda?'

'Charles gave it to me,' Amanda said. She turned away,

seized a brush from her not-so-vain vanity, peered into the mirror, and went at her hair furiously. 'Last year.'

Lisey put the gun, so much like the one Gerd Allen Cole had used on her husband, back in the shoebox and watched Amanda in the mirror.

'I slept with him two and sometimes three times a week for four years,' Amanda said. 'Which is intimate. Wouldn't you agree that's intimate?'

'Yes.'

'I also washed his undershorts for four years, and scraped the scaly stuff off his scalp once a week so it wouldn't fall on the shoulders of his dark suits and embarrass him, and I think those things are a hell of a lot more intimate than fucking. What do *you* think?'

'I think you've got a point.'

'Yeah,' Amanda said. 'Four years of that and I get a Hallmark card as severance pay. That woman he found up there in the Sin-Jin is welcome to him.'

Lisey felt like cheering. No, she didn't think Manda needed a dip in the pool.

'Let's get the meat out of the freezer and go to your house,' Amanda said. 'I'm *starving*.'

13

The sun came out as they approached Patel's Market, putting a rainbow like a fairy-gate over the road ahead. 'You know what I'd like for supper?' Amanda asked.

'No, what?'

'A big, nasty mess of Hamburger Helper. I don't suppose you've got anything like that at your house, do you?'

'I did,' Lisey said, smiling guiltily, 'but I ate it.'

'Pull in to Patel's,' Amanda said. 'I'll spring for a box.'

Lisey pulled in. Amanda had insisted on bringing her house-money from the blue pitcher where she kept it stashed in the kitchen, and she now extracted a crumpled five-spot. 'What kind do you want, Little?'

'Anything but Cheeseburger Pie,' Lisey said.

CHAPTER FOURTEEN
LISEY AND SCOTT
(BABYLUV)

1

At seven-fifteen that evening, Lisey had a premonition. It wasn't the first of her life; she'd had at least two others. One in Bowling Green, shortly after entering the hospital where her husband had been taken after collapsing at an English Department reception. And certainly she'd had one on the morning of their flight to Nashville, the morning of the shattered toothglass. The third one came as the thunderstorms were clearing out and a gorgeous gold light began to shine through the breaking clouds. She and Amanda were in Scott's study over the barn. Lisey was going through the papers in Scott's main desk, aka Dumbo's Big Jumbo. So far the most interesting thing she'd found was a packet of mildly risqué French postcards with a sticky-note on top, reading, in Scott's scrawl, *Who sent me THESE THINGS???* Sitting beside the blank-eyed computer was the shoebox with the revolver inside. The lid was still on, but Lisey had slit the tape with her fingernail. Amanda was across the way, in the alcove that held Scott's TV and component sound-system. Every now and then Amanda heard her grumbling about the haphazard way things had been shelved. Once Lisey heard her wonder aloud how Scott had ever found *anything*.

That was when the premonition came. Lisey shut the drawer she had been investigating and sat down in the high-backed office chair. She closed her eyes and just waited, as something rolled toward her. It turned out to be a song. A mental jukebox lit up and the nasal but undeniably jolly voice of Hank Williams began to sing. '*Goodbye Joe, we gotta go, me-oh-my-oh; we gotta go, pole the pirogue down the bayou . . .*'

'Lisey!' Amanda called from the alcove where Scott used to sit and listen to his music or watch movies on his VCR. When he wasn't watching them in the guest room in the middle of the night, that was. And Lisey heard the voice of the professor from the Pratt College English Department – in Bowling Green, this was, only sixty miles from Nashville. Not much more'n a long spit, Missus.

I think it would be wise if you got here as soon as possible, Professor Meade had told her over the phone. *Your husband has been taken ill. Very ill indeed, I'm afraid.*

'*My Yvonne, sweetest one, me-oh-my-oh . . .*'

'Lisey!' Amanda sounded just as bright as a new-minted penny. Would anyone believe she'd been totally zonked only eight hours ago? Nay, madam. Nay, good sir.

The spirits have done it all in one night, Lisey thought. *Yay, spirits.*

Dr Jantzen feels that surgery is warranted. Something called a thoracotomy.

And Lisey thought, *The boys came back from Mexico. They came back to Anarene. Because Anarene was home.*

Which boys, pray tell? The black-and-white boys. Jeff Bridges and Timothy Bottoms. The boys from *The Last Picture Show*.

In that movie it's always now and they are always young, she thought. *They are always young and Sam the Lion is always dead.*

'Lisey?'

She opened her eyes and there was big sissa standing in the alcove doorway, her eyes as bright as her voice, and of course in her hand she was holding the VCR box containing *The Last Picture Show* and the feeling was . . . well, coming home. The feeling was coming home, me-oh-my-oh.

And why would that be? Because drinking from the pool had its little perks and privileges? Because you sometimes brought back to this world what you picked up in that world? Picked up or swallowed? Yes, yes, and yes.

'Lisey, honey, are you all right?'

Such warm concern, such smucking *motherliness*, was so foreign to Amanda's usual nature that it made Lisey feel unreal. 'Fine,' she said. 'I was just resting my eyes.'

'Would it be all right if I watched some of this? I found it with the rest of Scott's tapes. Most of them look pretty junky, but I always meant to see this one and never got around to it. Maybe it'll take my mind off things.'

'Fine by me,' Lisey said, 'but I should warn you, I'm pretty sure there's a blank spot in the middle of it. It's an old tape.'

Amanda was studying the back of the box. 'Jeff Bridges looks like such a *kid*.'

'He does, doesn't he?' Lisey said wanly.

'And Ben Johnson's dead, of course . . .' She stopped. 'Maybe I better not. We might not hear your boyf . . . we might not hear Dooley, if he comes.'

Lisey pushed the top off the shoebox, took out the Pathfinder, and pointed it at the stairs leading down to the barn. 'I locked the door to the outside stairs,' she said, 'so that's the only way up here. And I'm watching it.'

'He could start a fire down there in the barn,' Amanda said nervously.

'He doesn't want me cooked – what fun would that be?' *Also*, Lisey thought, *there's a place I can go. As long as my mouth tastes as sweet as it does right now, there's a place I can go, and I don't think I'd have any trouble taking you with me, Manda.* Not even two helpings of Hamburger Helper and two glasses of cherry Kool-Aid had taken away that lovely sweet taste in her mouth.

'Well, if you're sure it won't be bothering you . . .'

'Do I look like I'm studying for finals? Go ahead.'

Amanda went back into the alcove. 'Sure hope this VCR still works.' She sounded like a woman who has discovered a wind-up gramophone and a stack of ancient acetate records.

Lisey looked at the many drawers of Dumbo's Big Jumbo, but going through them seemed like make-work now . . . and probably was. She had an idea that there was very little of actual interest up here. Not in the drawers, not in the filing cabinets, not hiding on the computer hard drives. Oh, maybe a little treasure for the more rabid Incunks, the collectors and the academics who maintained their positions in large part by examining the literary equivalent of navel-lint in each other's abstruse journals;

545

ambitious, overeducated goofs who had lost touch with what books and reading were actually about and could be content to go on spinning straw into footnoted fool's gold for decades on end. But all the real horses were out of the barn. The Scott Landon stuff that had pleased regular readers – people stuck on airplanes between L.A. and Sydney, people stuck in hospital waiting rooms, people idling their way through long, rainy summer vacation days, taking turns between the novel of the week and the jigsaw puzzle out on the sun-porch – all that stuff had been published. *The Secret Pearl*, published a month after his death, had been the last.

No, Lisey, a voice whispered, and at first she thought it was Scott's, and then – how crazy – she thought it was the voice of Ole Hank. But that *was* crazy, because it wasn't a man's voice at all. Was that Good Ma's voice, going whisper-whisper-whisper in her head?

I think he wanted me to tell you something. Something about a story.

Not Good Ma's voice – although Good Ma's yellow afghan had figured in it somewhere – but Amanda's. They had been sitting together on those stone benches, looking out at the good ship *Hollyhocks*, which always rode at anchor but never quite set sail. Lisey had never realized how much alike their mother and her oldest sister sounded until this memory of the benches. And—

Something about a story. Your story. Lisey's *story.*

Had Amanda actually said that? It was like a dream now and Lisey couldn't be completely sure, but she thought yes.

And the afghan. Only—

'Only he called it an african,' Lisey said in a low voice. 'He called it an african, and he called it a bool. Not a boop, not a beep, a bool.'

'Lisey?' Amanda called from the other room. 'Did you say something?'

'Just talking to myself, Manda.'

'Means you've got money in the bank,' Amanda said, and then there was only the soundtrack of the movie. Lisey seemed to remember every line of it, every scratchy snatch of music.

If you left me a story, Scott, where is it? Not up here in the study, I'd bet money on it. Not in the barn, either – nothing down there but false bools like Ike Comes Home.

But that wasn't quite true. There had been at least two true prizes in the barn: the silver spade and Good Ma's cedar box, tucked away under the Bremen bed. With the delight square in it. Was that what Amanda had been talking about?

Lisey didn't think so. There *was* a story in that box, but it was *their* story – **Scott & Lisey: Now We Are Two**. So what was *her* story? And *where* was it?

And speaking of wheres, where was the Black Prince of the Incunks?

Not on the answering machine at Amanda's; not on the answering machine here, either. Lisey had found only one message, on the recorder in the house. It had been from Deputy Alston.

'Mrs Landon, this storm has done quite a lot of damage in town, particularly at the south end. Someone – I hope me or Dan Boeckman – is gonna check back on you as soon as possible, but in the meantime I want to remind you to keep your doors locked and don't let anyone in you can't identify. That means gettin em to take off their hats or push back the hoods of their slickers even if it's pourin down cats n dogs, okay? And keep that cell phone with you at all times. Remember, in an emergency all you have to do is hit SPEED-DIAL and the 1-key. The call will go right through to the Sheriff's.'

'Great,' Amanda had commented. 'Our blood'll still be runny instead of clotted when they get here. Probably speed up their DNA tests.'

Lisey hadn't bothered replying. She had no intention of letting the Castle County Sheriff's Department handle Jim Dooley. As far as she was concerned, Jim Dooley might as well have cut his own throat with her Oxo can opener.

The light on the answering machine in her barn office had been flashing, the number 1 showing in the MESSAGES RECEIVED window, but when Lisey hit the PLAY button, there had been only three seconds of silence, one soft, indrawn breath, and a hang-up. It could have been a wrong number, people dialed wrong numbers and hung up all the time, but she knew it hadn't been.

No. It had been Dooley.

Lisey sat back in the office chair, ran a finger down the rubber grip of the .22, then picked it up and swung open the cylinder. It was easy enough to do, once you'd done it a couple of times. She loaded the chambers, then swung the cylinder closed again. It made a small but final *click*.

In the other room, Amanda laughed at something in the movie. Lisey smiled a little herself. She didn't believe Scott had exactly planned all this; he didn't even plan his books, as complex as some of them were. Plotting them, he said, would take out all the fun. He claimed that for him, writing a book was like finding a brilliantly colored string in the grass and following it to see where it might lead. Sometimes the string broke and left you with nothing. But sometimes – if you were lucky, if you were brave, if you persevered – it brought you to a treasure. And the treasure was never the money you got for the book; the treasure *was* the book. Lisey supposed the Roger Dashmiels of the world didn't believe it and the Joseph Woodbodys thought it had to be something grander – more exalted – but Lisey had lived with him, and she believed it. Writing a book was a bool hunt. What he'd never told her (but she supposed she'd always guessed it) was that if the string didn't break, it always led back to the beach. Back to the pool where we all go down to drink, to cast our nets, to swim, and sometimes to drown.

And did he know? At the end, did he know *it was the end?*

She sat up a little straighter, trying to remember if Scott has discouraged her from coming along on his trip to Pratt, a small but well-regarded liberal arts school where he'd read from *The Secret Pearl* for the first and last time. He had collapsed halfway through the reception afterward. Ninety minutes later she had been in an airplane and one of the guests at that reception – a cardiovascular surgeon dragged to Scott's reading by his wife – had been operating in an attempt to save his life, or at least preserve it long enough to get him to a bigger hospital.

Did he know? Did he purposely try to keep me away because he knew it was coming?

She didn't *exactly* believe that, but when the call came from Professor Meade, hadn't she understood that Scott had known that *something* was coming? If not the long boy, then this? Wasn't that why their financial affairs had been in such apple-pie order, all the right papers neatly executed? Wasn't that why he had been so careful to see to Amanda's future problems?

I think it would be wise if you left as soon as you give permission for the surgery, Professor Meade had said. And she had done just that, calling the air charter company they used after speaking to an anonymous voice in Bowling Green Community Hospital's main office. To the hospital functionary she identified herself as Scott Landon's wife, Lisa, and gave a Dr Jantzen permission to carry out a thoracotomy (a word she could hardly pronounce) and 'all attendant procedures'. With the charter company she'd been more assured. She wanted the fastest aircraft they had available. Was the Gulfstream faster than the Lear? Fine. Make it the Gulfstream.

In the entertainment alcove, in the black-and-white land of *The Last Picture Show*, where Anarene was home and where Jeff Bridges and Timothy Bottoms would always be boys, Ole Hank was singing about that brave Indian chief, Kaw-Liga.

Outside, the air had begun to redden – as it did when sunset approached in a certain mythical land once discovered by a pair of frightened boys from Pennsylvania.

This all happened very suddenly, Mrs Landon. I wish I had some answers for you, but I don't. Perhaps Dr Jantzen will.

But he hadn't. Dr Jantzen had performed a thoracotomy, but that had provided no answers, either.

I didn't know what that was, Lisey thought, as outside the reddening sun approached the western hills. *I didn't know what a thoracotomy was, didn't know what was happening . . . except in spite of everything I'd hidden away behind the purple, I did.*

The pilots had arranged for a limo while she was still in the air. It was after eleven when the Gulfstream landed, and after midnight when she got to that little pile of cinderblocks they called a hospital, but the day had been hot and it was still hot. When the driver opened the door she remembered feeling that she could reach out her hands, twist them, and wring water right out of the air.

And there were dogs barking, of course — what sounded like every dog in Bowling Green barking at the moon — and my God, talk about your déjà vu, *there was one old guy buffing the hallway floor and two old women sitting in the waiting room, identical twins by the look of them, eighty if they were a day, and straight ahead*

2

Straight ahead of her are two elevators painted blue-gray. A sign on an easel in front of them reads OUT OF SERVICE. Lisey closes her eyes and puts a blind hand out to brace herself against the wall, for a moment quite sure she's going to faint. And why not? It seems she has traveled not just across miles but across time, as well. This isn't Bowling Green in 2004 but Nashville in 1988. Her husband has a lung problem, all right, but of the .22-caliber variety. A madman fed him a bullet, and would have fed him several more, if Lisey hadn't been quick with the silver spade.

She waits for someone to ask if she's all right, maybe even take hold of her and steady her on her shaky pins, but there's only the *Whuzzzz* of the old janitor's floor-buffer, and somewhere far away, the soft dinging of a bell that makes her think of some other bell in some other place, a bell that sometimes rings from behind the purple curtain she has carefully drawn over certain parts of her past.

She opens her eyes and sees that the main desk is deserted. There's a light on behind the window marked INFORMATION, so Lisey's pretty sure someone's supposed to be on duty there, but he or she has stepped away, maybe to use the john. The elderly twins in the waiting room are staring down at what appear to be identical waiting-room magazines. Beyond the entrance doors, her limo idles behind its yellow running lights like some exotic deep-sea fish. On this side of the doors, a small-city hospital is dozing through the first hour of a new day, and Lisey realizes that unless she *starts up a-bellerin*, as Dandy would say, she's on her own. The feeling this engenders isn't fear or irritation or perplexity but rather deep sorrow. Later, flying back to Maine with her husband's encoffined mortal remains below her feet, she'll think: *That's when I knew he'd never be leaving that place alive. He'd come to the last of it. I had a premonition. And you know what? I think it was the sign in front of the elevators that did it. That smucking OUT OF SERVICE sign. Yeah.*

She can look for a hospital directory, or she can ask directions of the janitor buffing the floor, but Lisey does neither. She's sure she'll find Scott in this hospital's ICU if he's out of surgery, and she'll find the ICU on the third floor. This intuition is so strong she almost expects to see a homely floursack magic carpet floating at the foot of the stairs when she reaches them, a dusty square of cotton with the words PILLSBURY'S BEST FLOUR printed across it. There's no such thing, of course, and by the time she reaches the third-floor landing she's sweating and sticky and her heart is pounding hard. But the door does indeed say **BGCH INTENSIVE CARE**, and that sense of being in a waking dream where past and present have joined in an endless loop grows even stronger.

He's in room 319, Lisey thinks. She's sure of it even though she can see there have been a great many changes since the last time she came to her husband lying hurt in a hospital. The most obvious one is the television monitors outside each room; they show all sorts of red and green readouts. The only ones Lisey is completely sure of are pulse and blood-pressure. Oh, and the names, she can read those. COLVETTE- **JOHN**, DUMBARTON-**ADRIAN**, TOWSON-**RICHARD**, VANDERVEAUX-**ELIZABETH** (*Lizzie Vanderveaux, now* there's *a mouthful*, she thinks), DRAYTON-**FRANKLIN**. She's approaching 319 now, and thinks *The nurse is going to come out with Scott's tray in her hands and her back to me; I won't mean to startle her but of course I will. She'll drop the tray. The plates and the coffee cup will be all right, they're tough old cafeteria birds, but that juice glass is going to break into a million pieces.*

But it's the middle of the night instead of morning, there are no fans paddling the air overhead, and the name on the monitor above the door of room 319 is YANEZ-**THOMAS**. Yet still her sense of *déjà vu* is enough to make her peek in and see a huge beached whale of a man –

Thomas Yanez – in the single bed. Then there's a sense of awakening such as sleepwalkers may experience; she looks around with growing fright and bewilderment, thinking *What am I doing here? I'm apt to catch hell for being up here on my own.* Then she thinks, *THORACOTOMY.* She thinks *AS SOON AS YOU GIVE PERMISSION FOR THE SURGERY*, and she can almost see the word *SURGERY* pulsing in drippy blood-red letters, and instead of leaving she continues quickly down to the brighter light at the center of the corridor, where the nurses' station must be. A terrible thought begins to surface in her mind

(what if he's already)

and she shoves it away, shoves it back down.

At the central station, a nurse dressed in a uniform upon which Warner Bros. cartoon characters caper crazily is making notes on a number of charts spread out before her. Another is speaking *sotto voce* into a tiny mike pinned to the lapel of her more traditional white rayon top, apparently reading numbers off a monitor. Behind them, a lanky redhead sprawls in a folding chair with his chin on the chest of his white dress shirt. Hanging over the back of his chair is a dark suit-coat that matches his pants. His shoes are off and so is his tie – Lisey can see the end of it peeking from one pocket of his jacket. His hands are clasped loosely in his lap. She may have had a premonition that Scott won't be leaving Bowling Green Community Hospital alive, but she doesn't have the slightest inkling that she's looking at the doctor who operated on him, prolonging his life enough so they can say goodbye after their twenty-five mostly good – hell, mostly *fine* – years together; she puts the age of the sleeping male at about seventeen, and thinks he might be the son of one of the ICU nurses.

'Pardon me,' Lisey says. Both nurses jump in their chairs. This time Lisey has managed to startle two nurses instead of just one. The nurse with the little mike will have an '*Oh!*' on her tape. Lisey couldn't care less. 'My name is Lisa Landon, and I understand that my husband, Scott—'

'Mrs Landon, yes. Of course.' It's the nurse with Bugs Bunny on one breast and Elmer Fudd pointing a shotgun at him from the other while Daffy Duck looks up from the valley below. 'Dr Jantzen has been waiting to talk to you. He administered first aid at the reception.'

Lisey still can't get the sense of this, perhaps in part because there was no time to look up *thoracotomy* in the *PDR*. 'Scott . . . what, he fainted? Passed out?'

'Dr Jantzen can give you the details, I'm sure. You know he performed a parietal pleurectomy as well as a thoracotomy?'

Pleuro-*what*? It seems easier to just say yes. Meanwhile, the nurse who was dictating puts out a hand and shakes the sleeping redhead. When his eyes flutter open, Lisey can see she was wrong about his age, he's probably old enough to buy a drink in a bar, but surely no one's going to tell her he was the one who cut into her husband's chest. Are they?

'The operation,' Lisey says, with no idea which one of the trio she's speaking to. She has a clear note of desperation in her voice, doesn't like it, can do nothing about it. 'Was it a success?'

The Warner Bros. nurse hesitates for just a moment, and Lisey reads everything she fears in the eyes that suddenly

555

slip away from hers. Then they come back and the nurse says, 'This is Dr Jantzen. He's been waiting for you.'

3

After that initial blank flutter, Jantzen comes around fast. Lisey thinks it must be a doctor thing – probably also a policeman and fireman thing. *It was certainly never a writer thing. You couldn't even talk to him until he'd had his second cup of coffee.*

She realizes she's just thought of her husband in the past tense, and a wave of coldness stiffens the hair at the nape of her neck and puts goosebumps on her arms. It's followed by a sense of lightness that is both marvelous and horrible. It's as if at any moment she'll float away like a balloon with a cut string. Float away to

(hush now little Lisey hush about that)

some other place. The moon, maybe. Lisey has to dig her fingernails deep into her palms to remain steady on her feet.

Meanwhile, Jantzen is murmuring to the Warner Bros. nurse. She listens and nods. 'You won't forget to put that in writing later, yuh?'

'Before the clock on the wall says two,' Jantzen assures her.

'And you're positive this is the way you want to go?' she persists – not being argumentative about whatever the subject is, Lisey thinks, just wanting to make sure she's got it all perfectly straight.

'I am,' he tells her, then turns to Lisey and asks if she's ready to go upstairs to Alton IU. That, he says, is where her husband is. Lisey says that would be fine. 'Well,' Jantzen says with a smile that looks tired and not very genuine, 'I hope you've got your hiking boots on. It's the fifth floor.'

As they walk back to the stairs – past YANEZ-**THOMAS** and VANDERVEAUX-**ELIZABETH** – the Warner Bros. nurse is on the phone. Later Lisey will understand that the murmured conversation was Jantzen telling the nurse to call upstairs and have them take Scott off the ventilator. If, that is, he's awake enough to recognize his wife and hear her goodbye. Perhaps even to tell his own back to her, if God gives him one more puff of wind to sail through his vocal cords. Later she will understand that taking him off the vent shortened his life from hours to minutes, but that Jantzen thought this was a fair trade, since in his opinion any hours gained could offer Scott Landon no hope of recovery whatsoever. Later she will understand that they put him in the closest thing their small community hospital has to a plague unit.

Later.

4

On their slow, steady walk up the hot stairwell to the fifth floor, she learns how little Jantzen can tell her about what's wrong with Scott – how precious little he knows. The thoracotomy, he says, was no cure, but only to remove a build-up of fluid; the related procedure was to remove trapped air from Scott's pleural cavities.

'Which lung are we talking about, Dr Jantzen?' she asks him, and he terrifies her by replying: 'Both.'

5

That's when he asks her how long Scott has been sick, and whether he saw a doctor 'before his current complaint escalated'. She tells him Scott hasn't *had* a current complaint. Scott hasn't been sick. He's had a bit of a runny nose for the last ten days, and he's done some coughing and sneezing, but that's pretty much the whole deal. He hasn't even been taking Allerest, although he thinks it's allergies, and she does, too. She has some of the same symptoms, gets them each late spring and early summer.

'No deep cough?' he asks as they near the fifth-floor landing. 'No deep, dry cough, like a morning smoker's cough? Sorry about the elevators, by the way.'

'That's all right,' she says, struggling not to puff and pant. 'He *did* have a cough, as I told you, but it was very light. He used to smoke, but he hasn't in years.' She thinks. 'I guess it might have been a *little* heavier in the last couple of days, and he woke me once in the night—'

'Last night?'

'Yes, but he took a drink of water and it *stopped*.' He's opening the door to another quiet hospital hall and Lisey puts a hand on his arm to stop him. 'Listen – things like this reading he did last night? There was a time when Scott would have soldiered through half a dozen of those pups even with a temperature of a hundred and four. He would have cooked up on the applause and mainlined it to keep going. But those days ended five, maybe even seven years ago. If he'd been really sick, I'm sure he would have called Professor Meade – he's head of the English Department – and *canceled* the smuh – the damn thing.'

'Mrs Landon, by the time we admitted him, your husband was running a fever of a hundred and six.'

Now she can only look at Dr Jantzen, he of the untrustworthy adolescent face, with silent horror and what is not quite disbelief. In time, however, a picture will begin to form. There's enough testimony, combined with certain memories that will not stay completely buried, to show her all she needs to see.

Scott took a charter flight from Portland to Boston, then flew United from Boston to Kentucky. A stew on the United flight who got his autograph later told a reporter that Mr Landon had been coughing 'almost constantly' and his skin was flushed. 'When I asked if he was all right,' she told the reporter, 'he said it was just a summer cold, he'd taken a couple of aspirin and would be fine.'

Frederic Borent, the grad student who met his plane, also reported the cough, and said Scott had gotten him to swing into a Nite Owl to pick up a bottle of Nyquil. 'I think I might be getting the flu,' he told Borent. Borent said he'd really been looking forward to the reading and wondered if Scott would be able to do it. Scott said, 'You might be surprised.'

Borent was. And delighted. So was most of Scott's audience that night. According to the Bowling Green *Daily News*, he gave a reading that was 'little short of mesmerizing', only stopping a few times for the politest of small coughs, which seemed easily quelled by a sip of water from the glass beside him on the podium. Speaking to Lisey hours later, Jantzen remained amazed by Scott's vitality. And it was his amazement, coupled with a message relayed by the head of the English Department during his phone call, that caused a rift in Lisey's carefully maintained curtain of repression, at least for awhile. The last thing Scott said to Meade, after the reading and just before the reception began, was 'Call my wife, would you? Tell her she may have to fly out here. Tell her I may have eaten the wrong thing after sunset. It's kind of a joke between us.'

6

Lisey blurts out her worst fear to young Dr Jantzen without even thinking about it. 'Scott is going to die of this, isn't he?'

Jantzen hesitates, and all at once she can see that he may be young but he's no kid. 'I want you to see him,' he says after a moment that seems very long. 'And I want him to see you. He's conscious, but that may not last long. Will you come with me?'

Jantzen walks very fast. He stops at the nurses' station and the male nurse on duty looks up from the journal he's been reading – *Modern Geriatrics*. Jantzen speaks to him. The conversation is low-pitched, but the floor is very quiet, and Lisey hears the male nurse say four words very clearly. They terrify her.

'He's waiting for her,' the male nurse says.

At the far end of the corridor are two closed doors with this message written on them in bright orange:

ALTON ISOLATION UNIT
SEE NURSE BEFORE ENTERING
OBSERVE ALL PRECAUTIONS
FOR **YOUR** SAKE
FOR **THEIR** SAKE
MASK AND GLOVES MAY BE REQUIRED

To the left of the door is a sink where Jantzen washes his hands and instructs Lisey to do the same. On a gurney to the right are gauze masks, latex gloves in sealed packets, stretchy yellow shoe covers in a cardboard box with FITS ALL SIZES stamped on the side, and a neat stack of surgical greengowns.

'Isolation,' she says. 'Oh Jesus, you think my husband's got the smucking Andromeda Strain.'

Jantzen hedges. 'We think he may have some exotic pneumonia, possibly even the Bird Flu, but whatever it is, we haven't been able to identify it, and it's . . .'

He doesn't finish, doesn't seem to know how, so Lisey helps him. 'It's really doing a number on him. As the saying is.'

'Just a mask should be enough, Mrs Landon, unless you have cuts. I didn't notice while you were—'

'I don't think I have to worry about cuts and I won't need a mask.' She pushes open the lefthand door before he can object. 'If it was communicable, I'd already have it.'

Jantzen follows her into the Alton IU, slipping one of the green cloth masks over his own mouth and nose.

7

There are only four rooms at the end of the fifth-floor hallway, and only one of the TV monitors is lit; only one of the rooms is producing the beeping sounds of hospital machinery and the soft, steady rush of flowing oxygen. The name on the monitor beneath the dreadfully fast pulse – 178 – and the dreadfully low blood-pressure – 79 over 44 – is LANDON-**SCOTT**.

The door stands half-open. On it is a sign that shows an orange flame-shape with an X drawn across it. Below, in bright red letters, is this message: **NO LIGHT, NO SPARK**. She's no writer, certainly no poet, but in those words she reads all she needs to know about how things end; it is the line drawn under her marriage the way you draw a line under numbers that need adding up. *No light, no spark.*

Scott, who left her with his usual impudent cry of 'Seeya later, Lisey-gator!' and a blast of Flamin' Groovies retro-rock from the CD player of his old Ford, now lies looking at her from a face as pale as milk-water. Only his eyes are fully alive, and they're too hot. They burn like the eyes of an owl trapped in a chimney. He's on his side. The ventilator has been pushed away from the bed, but she can see the slime of phlegm on its tube and knows

(hush little Lisey)

that there are germs or microbes or both in that green crap that no one will ever be able to identify, not even with the world's best electron microscope and every database under the eye of heaven.

'Hey, Lisey . . .'

There's almost nothing to that whisper – *No more'n a puff of wind under the door*, old Dandy might have said – but she hears him and goes to him. A plastic oxygen mask hangs around his neck, hissing air. Two plastic tubes sprout from his chest, where a couple of freshly stapled incisions look like a child's drawing of a bird. The tubes jutting from his back seem almost grotesquely large in comparison to the ones in front. To Lisey's dismayed eye they look as big as radiator hoses. They're transparent, and she can see cloudy fluid and bloody bits of tissue coursing down them to some sort of suitcase-thing that stands on the bed behind him. This isn't Nashville; this is no .22 bullet; although her heart clamors against it, one look is enough to convince her mind that Scott will be dead by the time the sun comes up.

'Scott,' she says, going onto her knees beside the bed and taking his hot hand in her cold ones. 'What the smuck have you done to yourself now?'

'Lisey.' He manages to squeeze her hand a little. His breathing is a loose and screamy wheeze that she remembers all too well from the parking lot that day. She knows exactly what he will say next, and Scott doesn't disappoint. 'I'm so hot, Lisey. Ice? . . . Please?'

She glances at his table but there's nothing on it. She looks over her shoulder at the doctor who's brought her up here, now the Masked Redhaired Avenger. 'Doctor . . .' she begins, and realizes she's drawing a complete blank. 'I'm sorry, I've forgotten your name.'

'Jantzen, Mrs Landon. And that's perfectly all right.'

'Can my husband have some ice? He says he's—'

'Yes, of course. I'll get it myself.' He's gone at once. Lisey realizes he's only wanted a reason to leave them alone.

Scott squeezes her hand again. 'Going,' he says in that same barely-there whisper. 'Sorry. Love you.'

'Scott, no!' And absurdly: 'The ice! The ice is coming!'

With what must be a tremendous effort – his breath screams louder than ever – he raises his hand and strokes her cheek with one hot finger. Lisey's tears begin to fall then. She knows what she must ask him. The panicky voice that never calls her Lisey but always *little* Lisey, the secret-keeper down below, clamors again that she must not, but she thrusts it aside. Every long marriage has two hearts, one light and one dark. Here again is the dark heart of theirs.

She leans closer, into the dying heat of him. She can smell the last palest ghost of the Foamy he shaved with yesterday morning and the Tea Tree he shampooed with. She leans in until her lips touch the burning cup of his ear. She whispers: '*Go*, Scott. *Drag* yourself to that smucking pool, if that's what it takes. If the doctor comes back and finds the bed empty I'll make something up, it doesn't matter, but get to the pool and make yourself better, do it, do it for me, goddam you!'

'Can't,' he whispers, and commences a papery coughing that makes her draw back a little. She thinks it will kill him, just tear him apart, but somehow he manages to get it under control. And why? Because he means to have his say. Even here, on his deathbed, in a deserted isolation unit at one o'clock in the morning in a backwater Kentucky town, he means to have his say. 'Won't . . . work.'

'Then *I'll* go! Just help me!'

But he shakes his head. 'Lying across the path . . . to the pool. *It.*'

She knows what he's talking about at once. She glances helplessly toward one of the waterglasses, where the piebald thing can sometimes be glimpsed. There, or in a mirror, or the corner of your eye. Always late at night. Always when one is lost, or in pain, or both. Scott's old boy. Scott's *long* boy.

'Slee . . . ping.' A weird noise arises from Scott's decomposing lungs. She thinks he's choking and reaches for the call-bell, then observes the mordant shine in his feverish eyes and realizes he's either laughing or trying to. 'Sleeping on . . . the path. Side . . . high . . . sky . . .' His eyes roll up to the ceiling and she's sure he's trying to say that its side is as high as the sky.

Scott plucks at the oxygen mask on his chest but can't lift it. She does it for him, placing it over his mouth and nose. Scott takes several deep breaths, then signals for her to take the mask off again. She does, and for a little while – perhaps as long as a minute – his voice is stronger.

'Went to Boo'ya Moon from the airplane,' he says with a kind of wonder. 'Never tried anything like that. Thought I might fall, but I came out on Sweetheart Hill, like always. Went again from a stall . . . airport bathroom. Last time . . . greenroom, just before the reading. Still there. Ole Freddy. Still right there.'

Christ, he even has a name for the smucking thing.

'Couldn't get to the pool, so I ate some berries . . . they're usually all right, but . . .'

He can't finish. She gives him the mask again.

'It was too late,' she says as he breathes. 'It was too late, wasn't it? You ate them after sundown.'

He nods.

'But it was all you could think of to do.'

He nods again. Motions for her to pull the mask down again.

'But you were all right at the reading!' she says. 'That Professor Meade said you were smucking *great*!'

He's smiling. It just may be the saddest smile she's ever seen. 'Dew,' he says. 'Licked it off the leaves. The last time, when I went . . . from the greenroom. Thought it might . . .'

'You thought it might be healing. Like the pool.'

He says *yes* with his eyes. His eyes never leave her.

'And that made you better. For a little while?'

'Yeah. Little while. Now . . .' He gives a sorry little shrug and turns his head aside. This time the coughing is worse, and she observes with horror that the flow into the tubes is a thicker, richer red. He gropes out and takes her hand again. 'I was lost in the dark,' he whispers. 'You found me.'

'Scott, no—'

He nods. *Yes.*

'You saw me whole. Everything . . .' He uses his free hand to make a weak circling gesture: *Everything the same.* He is smiling a little now as he looks at her.

'Hang on, Scott! Just hang on!'

He nods as if she finally gets it. 'Hang on . . . wait for the wind to change.'

'No, Scott, the ice!' It's all she can think of to say. 'Wait for the *ice!*'

He says *baby*. He calls her *babyluv*. And then the only sound is the steady hiss of oxygen from the mask around his neck. Lisey puts her hands to her face

8

and took them away dry. She was both surprised and not surprised. Certainly she was relieved; it seemed that she might finally be finished with her grieving. She guessed she still had a lot of work to do up here in Scott's office

– she and Amanda had barely made a dent – but she thought she'd made some unexpected progress in cleaning up her own shit over these last two or three days. She touched her wounded breast and felt almost no pain at all. *This is taking self-healing to a new level*, she thought, and smiled.

In the other room Amanda cried indignantly to the TV, 'Oh, you dumbass! Leave that bitch alone, can't you see she's no good?' Lisey cocked an ear in that direction and deduced that Jacy was about to wheedle Sonny into marrying her. The movie was almost over.

She must have fast-forwarded through some of it, Lisey thought, but when she looked at the dark pressing against the skylight above her, she knew that wasn't so. She'd been sitting at Dumbo's Big Jumbo and reliving the past for over an hour and a half. *Doing a little work on herself*, as the New Agers liked to say. And what conclusions had she drawn? That her husband was dead, that was all. Dead and gone on. He wasn't waiting for her along the path in Boo'ya Moon, or sitting on one of those stone benches as she had once found him; he wasn't wrapped in one of those creepy shroud-things, either. Scott had left Boo'ya Moon behind. Like Huck, he'd lit out for the Territories.

And what had caused his final illness? His death certificate claimed pneumonia, and she had no problem with that. They could have put *Nibbled to death by ducks* on it and he'd have been just as dead – but she couldn't help wondering. Had his death been on a flower that he had picked up and smelled, or a bug that had slipped its sipper under his skin as the sun went down red in its house of thunder? Did he get it on a quick visit to Boo'ya Moon a week or a month before his final reading in Kentucky, or had it been waiting for decades, ticking like a clock? It might have been in a single grain of dirt that got under one fingernail while he was digging his brother's grave. Just a single bad bug that lay asleep as the years passed, finally waking up at his computer one day when a reluctant word finally came to him and he snapped his fingers in satisfaction. Maybe – terrible thought, but who knew? – she had even brought it back herself from one of her own visits, a lethal mite in a tiny dot of pollen he had kissed from the tip of her nose.

Oh shit, now she *was* crying.

She had seen a packet of unopened Kleenex in the top lefthand drawer of the desk. She took it out, opened it, removed a couple, and began to blot her eyes with them. In the other room, she heard Timothy Bottoms shout, 'He was *sweepin*, you sonsabitches!' and knew that time had taken another of those ungainly crow-hops forward. There was only one more scene in the movie. Sonny goes back to the coach's wife. His middle-aged lover. Then the credits roll.

On the desk, the telephone gave a brief *ting*. Lisey knew what it meant as surely as she had known what Scott meant when he made that weak twirling gesture at the end of his life, the one that meant *everything the same*.

The phone was dead, the lines either cut or torn out. Dooley was here. The Black Prince of the Incunks had come for her.

CHAPTER FIFTEEN

LISEY AND THE LONG BOY
(PAFKO AT THE WALL)

1

'Amanda, come here!'

'In a minute, Lisey, the movie's almost—'

'Amanda, right now!'

She picked up the telephone, confirmed the nothing inside it, put it back down. She knew everything. It seemed to have been there all along, like the sweet taste in her mouth. The lights would be next, and if Amanda didn't come before he doused them—

But there she was, standing between the entertainment alcove and the long main room, looking suddenly afraid and old. On the VHS tape the coach's wife would soon be throwing the coffee pot at the wall, angry because her hands were too unsteady to pour. Lisey wasn't surprised to see her own hands were trembling. She picked up the .22. Amanda saw her do it and looked more frightened than ever. Like a lady who would have preferred to be in Philadelphia, all things considered. Or catatonic. *Too late, Manda*, Lisey thought.

'Lisey, is he here?'

'Yes.'

In the distance thunder rumbled, seeming to agree.

'Lisey, how do you kn—'

'Because he's cut the phone.'

'The cell—'

'Still in the car. The lights will go next.' She reached the end of the big redwood desk – *Dumbo's Big Jumbo indeed*, she thought, *you could almost put a jet fighter down on the smucking thing* – and now it was a straight shot to where her sister was standing, maybe eight steps across the rug with the maroon smears of her own blood on it.

When she reached Amanda the lights were still on, and Lisey had a moment's doubt. Wasn't it possible, after all, that a tree-branch knocked loose by the afternoon storms had finally fallen, taking down a telephone line?

Sure, but that's not what's happening.

She tried to give Amanda the gun. Amanda didn't want to take it. It thumped to the carpet and Lisey tensed for the explosion, which would be followed by either Amanda's scream of pain or her own as one of them took a bullet in the ankle. The gun didn't go off, just stared into the distance with its single idiot eye. As Lisey bent down to get it, she heard a thud from below, as if someone had walked into something down there and knocked it over. A cardboard box filled with mostly blank pages, say – one of a stack.

When Lisey looked up at her sister again, Amanda's hands were pressed, left over right, on the scant shelf of her bosom. Her face had gone pale; her eyes were dark pools of dismay.

'I can't hold that gun,' she whispered. 'My hands . . . see?' She turned them palms out, displaying the cuts.

'Take the smucking thing,' Lisey said. 'You won't have to shoot him.'

This time Amanda closed her fingers reluctantly around the Pathfinder's rubber grip. 'Do you promise?'

'No,' Lisey said. 'But almost.'

She peered toward the stairs leading down to the barn. It was darker at that end of the study, far more ominous, especially now that Amanda had the gun. Untrustworthy Amanda, who might do anything. Including, maybe fifty percent of the time, what you asked of her.

'What's your plan?' Amanda whispered. In the other room, Ole Hank was singing again, and Lisey knew *The Last Picture Show*'s final credits were rolling.

Lisey put a finger across her lips in a *Shhh* gesture

(now you must be still)

and backed away from Amanda. One step, two steps, three steps, four. Now she was in the middle of the room, equidistant from Dumbo's Big Jumbo and the alcove doorway where Amanda held the .22 awkwardly with the barrel pointed at the bloodstained rug. Thunder rumbled. Country music played. From below: silence.

'I don't think he's down there,' Amanda whispered.

Lisey took another backward step toward the big red maple desk. She still felt entirely keyed up, was almost vibrating with tension, but the rational part of her had to admit that Amanda might be right. The telephone was out, but up here on the View you could count on losing your service at least twice a month, especially during or just after storms. That thump she'd heard when she bent to pick up the gun . . . *had* she heard a thump? Or had it just been her imagination?

'I don't think *anyone's* down th—' Amanda began, and that was when the lights went out.

2

For a few seconds – endless ones – Lisey could see nothing, and damned herself for not bringing the flashlight from the car. It would have been so *easy*. It was all she could do to stay where she was, and she had to keep Amanda where *she* was.

'Manda, don't move! Stand still until I tell you!'

'Where is he, Lisey?' Amanda was starting to cry. *'Where is he?'*

'Why, right here, Missy,' Jim Dooley said easily from the pitch blackness where the stairs were. 'And I can see you both with these goggles I got on. You look a smidge green, but I can see you fine.'

'He can't, he's lying,' Lisey said, but she felt a sinking in her middle. She hadn't counted on him having some sort of night-vision equipment.

'Oh, Missus – if I'm lyin, I'm dyin.' The voice was still coming from the stairhead, and now Lisey began to see a dim figure there. She couldn't see his paper sack of horrors, but oh Jesus she could hear it crackling. 'I see you well enough to know it's Miss Tall-N-Scrawny with the peashooter. I want you to drop that gun on the floor, Missy Tall. Right now.' His voice sharpened and cracked like the end of a whip loaded with shot. 'Mind me, now! *Drop hit!*'

It was full dark out now, and if there was a moon it either hadn't risen or was occluded, but enough ambient light came through the skylights to show Lisey that Amanda

572

was lowering the gun. Not dropping it yet, but lowering it. Lisey would have given anything to have been holding it herself, but—

But I need both hands free. So when the time comes I can grab you, you sonofabitch.

'No, Amanda, hold onto it. I don't think you'll have to shoot him. That's not the plan.'

'Drop it, Missy, *that's* the plan.'

Lisey said, 'He comes in here where he doesn't belong, he calls you mean names, then tells you to drop the gun? *Your own gun?*'

The barely-there phantom that was Lisey's sister raised the Pathfinder again. Amanda didn't point it at the black cutout hovering in the shadows by the stairs, only held it with the muzzle pointing toward the ceiling, but she *was* still holding it. And her back had straightened.

'I tole you *drop* hit!' the dim figure nearly snarled, but something in Dooley's voice told Lisey he knew that battle was lost. His damned bag rattled.

'No!' Amanda shouted. 'I won't! You . . . you get on out of here! Get out and leave my sister alone!'

'He won't,' Lisey said before the shadow at the head of the stairs could reply. 'He won't because he's crazy.'

'You want to watch out for talk like that,' Dooley said. 'You seem to be forgettin I can see you like you 'us on a stage.'

'But you *are* crazy. Just as crazy as the kid who shot my husband in Nashville. Gerd Allen Cole. Do you know about him? Sure you do, you know *everything* about Scott. We used to laugh about guys like you, Jimmy—'

'That's enough now, Missus—'

573

'We called you Deep Space Cowboys. Cole was one and you're another. Slyer and meaner – because you're older – but not much different. A Deep Space Cowboy is a Deep Space Cowboy. You *toooour* the Milky Smuckin Way.'

'You want to *stop* that talk,' Dooley said. He was snarling again, and this time, Lisey thought, not just for effect. 'I'm here on *bi'ness*.' The paper bag rattled and now she could see the shadow move. The stairs were maybe fifty feet away from the desk and in the darkest part of the long main room. But Dooley was moving toward her as if her words were reeling him in and now her eyes were fully adapted to the gloom. Another few steps and his fancy mail-order goggles would make no difference. They would be on equal footing. Visually, at least.

'Why should I? It's true.' And it was. Suddenly she knew everything she needed to know about Jim Dooley, alias Zack McCool, alias the Black Prince of the Incunks. The truth was in her mouth, like that sweet taste. It *was* that sweet taste.

'Don't provoke him, Lisey,' Amanda said in a terrified voice.

'He provokes himself. All the provocation he needs comes right out of the overheated warp-drive inside his own head. Just like Cole.'

'I ain't *nuthin* like him!' Dooley shouted.

Brilliant knowledge in every nerve-ending. *Exploding* in every nerve-ending. Dooley might have learned about Cole while reading up on his literary hero, but Lisey knew this wasn't so. And it all made such perfect, divine sense.

'You were never in Brushy Mountain. That was just

a tale you told Woodbody. Barstool talk. But you were locked up, all right. That much was true. You were in the looneybin. You were in the looneybin with Cole.'

'Shut up, Missus! You listen-a me and shut up right *now*!'

'Lisey, *stop*!' Amanda cried.

She paid no attention to either of them. 'Did you two discuss your favorite Scott Landon books ... when Cole was medicated enough to talk rationally, that is? Bet you did. He liked *Empty Devils* best, right? Sure. And you liked *The Coaster's Daughter*. Just a couple of Deep Space Cowboys talking books while they got a few repairs in their smucking guidance systems—'

'That's *enough*, I said!' Swimming out of the gloom. Swimming out of it like a diver coming up from black water into the green shallows, goggles and all. Of course divers didn't hold paper bags in front of their chests as if to shield their hearts from the blows of cruel widows who knew too much. 'I ain't goan warn you again—'

Lisey took no notice. She didn't know if Amanda was still holding the gun and no longer cared. She was delirious. 'Did you and Cole talk about Scott's books in group therapy? Sure you did. About the father stuff. And then, after they let you out, there was Woodsmucky, just like a Daddy in a Scott Landon book. One of the *good* Daddies. After they let you out of the nutbarn. After they let you out of the *scream factory*. After they let you out of the *laughing academy*, as the saying i—'

With a shriek, Dooley dropped his paper sack (it clanked) and launched himself at Lisey. She had time to think, *Yes. This is why I needed my hands free.*

Amanda also shrieked, hers overlapping his. Of the three of them only Lisey was calm, because only Lisey knew precisely what she was doing . . . if not precisely why. She made no effort to run. She opened her arms to Jim Dooley and caught him like a fever.

3

He would have knocked her to the floor and landed on top of her – Lisey had no doubt this was his intention – if not for the desk. She let his weight carry her back, smelling the sweat in his hair and on his skin. She also felt the curve of the goggles digging into her temple and heard a low, rapid clicking sound just below her left ear.

That's his teeth, she thought. *That's his teeth, trying for my neck.*

Her butt smacked against the long side of Dumbo's Big Jumbo. Amanda screamed again. There was a loud report and a brief brilliant flash of light.

'Leave her alone, motherfucker!'

Big talk but she fired into the ceiling, Lisey thought, and tightened her locked hands behind Dooley's neck as he bent her backward like a dance-partner at the end of a particularly amorous tango. She could smell gunsmoke, her ears were ringing, and she could feel his cock, heavy and almost fully erect.

'Jim,' she whispered, holding him. 'I'll give you what you want. Let me give you what you want.'

His grip loosened a little. She sensed his confusion. Then, with a feline yowl, Amanda landed on his back and Lisey was forced down again, now almost sprawling on the desk. Her spine gave a warning creak, but she could see the oval smudge of his face – enough to make out how afraid he looked. *Was he afraid of me all along?* she wondered.

Now or never, little Lisey.

She sought his eyes behind the weird circles of glass, found them, locked in on them. Amanda was still yowling like a cat on a hot griddle, and Lisey could see her fists hammering Dooley's shoulders. Both fists. So she had fired that one shot into the ceiling, then dropped the gun. Ah well, maybe it was for the best.

'Jim.' God, his weight was killing her. *'Jim.'*

His head dipped, as if drawn by the lock of her eyes and the force of her will. For a moment Lisey didn't think she would be able to reach him, even so. Then, with a final desperate lunge – *Pafko at the wall*, Scott would have said, quoting God knew who – she did. She breathed the meat and onions he'd eaten for his supper as she settled her mouth on his. She used her tongue to force his lips open, kissed harder, and so passed on her second sip of the pool. She felt the sweetness go. The world she knew wavered and then began to go with it. It happened fast. The walls turned transparent and that other world's mingled scents filled her nose: frangipani, bougainvillea, roses, night-blooming cereus.

'Geromino,' she said into his mouth, and as if it had only been waiting for that word, the solid weight of the desk beneath her turned to rain. A moment later it was gone completely. She fell; Jim Dooley fell on top of her; Amanda, still screaming, fell on top of both.

Bool, Lisey thought. *Bool, the end.*

4

She landed on a thick mat of grass that she knew so well she might have been rolling around in it her whole life. She had time to register the sweetheart trees and then the breath was driven out of her in a large and noisy *woof*. Black spots danced before her in the sunset-colored air.

She might have passed out if Dooley hadn't rolled away. Amanda he shrugged off his back as if she had been no more than a troublesome kitten. Dooley surged to his feet, staring first down the hill carpeted with purple lupin and then turning the other way, toward the sweetheart trees that formed the outrider of what Paul and Scott Landon had called the Fairy Forest. Lisey was shocked by Dooley's aspect. He looked like some weird flesh-and-hair-covered skull. After a moment she realized it was his narrowness of face combined with evening shadows, and what had happened to his goggles. The lenses hadn't made the trip to Boo'ya Moon. His eyes stared out through the holes where they had been. His mouth hung open. Spit ran between the upper and lower lips in silver strings.

'You always . . . liked . . . Scott's books,' Lisey said. She sounded like a winded runner, but her breath was returning and the black flecks in front of her eyes were disappearing. 'How do you like his *world*, Mr Dooley?'

'Where . . .' His mouth moved, but he couldn't finish.

'Boo'ya Moon, on the edge of the Fairy Forest, near the grave of Scott's brother, Paul.'

She knew that Dooley would be as dangerous to her (and to Amanda) over here as in Scott's study once such wits as he possessed came back to him, but she still allowed herself a moment to look over that long purple slope, and at the darkening sky. Once more the sun was going down in orange fire while the full moon rose opposite. She thought, as she had before, that the mixture of heat and cold silver might kill her with its feverish beauty.

Not that it was beauty she had to worry about. A sunburned hand fell on her shoulder.

'What are you doin-a me, Missus?' Dooley asked. His eyes bulged inside the empty goggles. 'You tryin to hypno-lize me? Because it won't work.'

'Not at all, Mr Dooley,' Lisey said. 'You wanted what was Scott's, didn't you? And surely this is better than any unpublished story, or even cutting a woman with her own can-opener, wouldn't you say? Look! A whole other world! A place made of imagination! Dreams spun into whole cloth! Of course it's dangerous in the forest – dangerous *everywhere* at night, and it's almost night now – but I'm confident that a brave and strapping lunatic such as your-self—'

She saw what he meant to do, saw her murder clearly in those weird socketed eyes, and cried out her sister's name . . . in alarm, yes, but also starting to laugh. In spite of everything. Laughing at *him*. Partly because he looked pretty silly with the glass gone out of his goggles, mostly because at this mortal moment the punchline of some ancient whorehouse joke had popped into her mind: *Hey, youse guys, your sign fell down!* The fact that she couldn't remember the joke itself only made it funnier.

Then her breath was gone and Lisey could no longer laugh. She could only rattle.

5

She clawed at Dooley's face with her short but far from nonexistent nails and left three bleeding gouges in one cheek, but the grip on her throat didn't loosen – if anything, it tightened down. The rattle coming from her was louder now, the sound of some primitive mechanical device with dirt in its gears. Mr Silver's potato-grader, maybe.

Amanda, where the smuck are you? she thought, and then Amanda was there. Pounding her fists on Dooley's back and shoulders had done no good. This time she fell on her knees, grasped his crotch through his jeans with her wounded hands . . . and *twisted*.

Dooley howled and thrust Lisey away. She flew into the high grass, fell on her back, and then scrambled to her feet again, gasping breath down her fiery throat. Dooley was bent over with his head down and his hands between his legs, a painful pose that brought Lisey a clear memory of a seesaw accident in the schoolyard and Darla saying matter-of-factly: 'That's just *one* of the reasons I'm glad I'm not a boy.'

Amanda charged him.

'Manda, no!' Lisey shouted, but too late. Even hurt, Dooley was miserably quick. He evaded Amanda easily, then clubbed her aside with one bony fist. He tore off the useless goggles with the other hand and threw them into the grass: he slang them forth. All pretense at sanity had left those blue eyes. He could have been the dead thing in *Empty Devils*, climbing implacably out of the well to exact its revenge.

'I dunno just where we are, but I tell you one thing, Missus: you ain't never goan home.'

'Unless you catch me, *you're* the one who's never going home,' Lisey said. Then she laughed again. She was frightened – terrified – but it felt good to laugh, perhaps because she understood that her laughter was her knife. Every peal from her burning throat drove the point deeper into his flesh.

'Don't you run 'at hee-haw sound at *me*, you bitch, don't you goddam *dare!*' Dooley roared, and ran at her.

Lisey turned to flee. She had taken no more than two running steps toward the path into the woods when she heard Dooley scream in pain. She looked over her shoulder and saw him on his knees. There was something jutting out of his upper arm, and his shirt was darkening rapidly around it. Dooley staggered to his feet and plucked at it with a curse. The jutting thing wiggled but didn't come out. Lisey saw a flash of yellow, running away from it in a line. Dooley cried out again, then seized the thing stuck in his flesh with his free hand.

Lisey understood. It came in a flash, too perfect not to be true. He had started to run after her, but Amanda had tripped him before he could do more than get started. And he had come down on Paul Landon's wooden grave-marker. The crosspiece was sticking out of his bicep like an oversized pin. Now he yanked it free and threw it aside. More blood flowed from the open wound, scarlet creeping down his shirtsleeve to the elbow. Lisey knew she had to make sure Dooley didn't turn his rage on Amanda, who was lying helplessly in the grass almost at his feet.

'Can't catch a flea, can't catch me!' Lisey chanted, drawing on playground lore she didn't even know she remembered.

Then she stuck her tongue out at Dooley, twiddling her fingers in her ears for good measure.

'You bitch! You *cunt*!' Dooley screamed, and charged.

Lisey ran. She wasn't laughing now, she was finally too afraid to laugh, but she was still wearing a terrified smile as her feet found the path and she ran into the Fairy Forest, where it was already night.

6

The marker that said **TO THE POOL** was gone, but as Lisey ran down the first stretch – the path a dim white line that seemed to float amid the darker masses of the surrounding trees – broken cackles arose from ahead of her. *Laughers*, she thought, and chanced a look back over her shoulder, thinking that if her friend Dooley heard *those* babies, he might change his mind about—

But no. Dooley was still there, visible in the stutters of fading light because he had gained on her, he was really flying along in spite of the black blood now coating his left sleeve from shoulder to wrist. Lisey tripped over a root in the path, almost lost her balance, and somehow managed to keep it, in part by reminding herself that Dooley would be on top of her five seconds after she fell. The last thing she'd feel would be his breath, the last thing she'd smell would be the curdling aroma of the surrounding trees as they changed to their more dangerous night-selves, and the last thing she'd hear would be the insane laughter of the hyena-things that lived deeper in the forest.

I can hear him panting. I can hear that because he's gaining. Even running at top speed – and I won't be able to keep this up for long – he can run a little bit faster than I can. Why doesn't that squeeze in the balls she fetched him slow him down? Why doesn't the blood-loss?

The answer to those questions was simple, the logic stark: they *were* slowing him down. Without them, she'd be caught already. Lisey was in third gear. She tried to find fourth and couldn't. Apparently she didn't *have* a fourth gear. Behind her, the harsh and rapid sound of Jim Dooley's breathing grew closer still, and she knew that in only a minute, maybe less, she would feel the first brush of his fingers on the back of her shirt.

Or in her hair.

7

The path tilted and grew steeper for a few moments; the shadows grew deeper. She thought she might finally be gaining a little bit on Dooley. She didn't dare cast a glance back to see, and she prayed that Amanda wouldn't try following them. It might be safe on Sweetheart Hill, and it might be safe at the pool, but it wasn't a bit safe in these woods. Jim Dooley was far from the worst of it, either. Now she heard the faint and dreamy ring of Chuckie G.'s bell, swiped by Scott in another lifetime and hung from a tree at the top of the next rise.

Lisey saw brighter light ahead, not reddish-orange now but just a dying pink afterglow. It stole through a thinning of the trees. The path was a bit brighter, too. She could see its gentle upslope. Beyond that next rise, she remembered, it sank again, winding through even thicker forest until it reached the big rock and the pool beyond.

Can't make it, she thought. The breath tearing in and out of her throat was hot and there was the beginning of a stitch in her side. *He'll catch me before I'm halfway up that hill.*

It was Scott's voice that responded, laughing on top, surprisingly angry beneath. *You didn't come all this way for that. Go on, babyluv* – SOWISA.

SOWISA, yes. Strapping it on had never seemed more appropriate than right now. Lisey tore up the hill, hair plastered to her skull in sweaty strings, arms pumping. She breathed in huge snatches, exhaled in harsh bursts. She wished for the sweet taste in her mouth, but she'd given her last sip of the pool to the crazy smuck behind her and now what her mouth tasted of was copper and exhaustion. She could hear him closing in again, not yelling now, saving all his breath for the chase. The cramp in her side deepened. A high, sweet singing started up first in her right ear, then in both of them. The laughers cackled closer now, as if they wanted to be in at the kill. She could smell the change in the trees, how the aroma that had been sweet had grown sharp, like the smell of the ancient henna she and Darla had found in Granny D's bathroom after she died, a poison smell, and—

That's not the trees.

All the laughers had fallen silent. Now there was only the sound of Dooley ripping breath from the air as he pounded along behind her, trying to close those last few feet of distance. And what she thought of was Scott's arms sweeping around her, Scott pulling her against his body, Scott whispering *Shhhh, Lisey. For your life and mine, now you must be still.*

She thought: *It's not lying across the path, like it was when he tried to get to the pool in '04. This time it's in its run beside the path. Like it was when I came to him during the winter of the big wind from Yellowknife.*

But just as she glimpsed the bell, still hanging from that rotting length of cord, the last light of the day shining on its curve, Jim Dooley put on a final burst of speed and Lisey actually *did* feel his fingers slipping across the back of her shirt, hunting for purchase there, anything, a bra-strap would do. She managed to hold back the scream that rose in her throat, but it was a near thing. She bolted onward, finding a little more speed of her own, speed that probably would have done her no good if Dooley hadn't tripped again, going down with a cry – '*You BITCH!*' – that Lisey thought he would live to regret.

But perhaps not for long.

8

That shy tinkle came again, from what had once been
(Order's up, Lisey! Come on, let's hustle!)
the Bell Tree and was now the Bell-and-Spade Tree. And there it was, Scott's silver spade. When she had placed it here – following a powerful intuition she now understood – the laughers had been gibbering hysterically. Now the Fairy Forest was silent except for the sounds of her own tortured respiration and Dooley's gasping spew of curses. The long boy had been sleeping – dozing, at least – and Dooley's yelling had awakened it.

Maybe this was how it was supposed to go, but that did not make it easy. It was horrible to feel the awakening whisper of not-quite-alien thoughts from her undermind. They were like restless hands feeling for loose boards or testing the closed cover of a well. She found herself considering too many terrible things that had at one time or another undermined her heart: a pair of bloody teeth she'd once found on the floor of a movie-theater bathroom, two little kids crying in each other's arms outside a convenience store, the smell of her husband as he lay on his deathbed, looking at her with his burning eyes, Granny D lying dying in the chickenyard with her foot going jerk-jerk-jerk.

Terrible thoughts. Terrible images, the kind that come back to haunt you in the middle of the night when the moon is down and the medicine's gone and the hour is none.

All the bad-gunky, in other words. Just beyond those few trees.

And *now*—

In the always perfect, never-ending moment of *now*

9

Gasping, whining, her heart nothing but bloodthunder in her ears, Lisey bends to lay hold of the silver spade. Her hands, which knew their business eighteen years ago, know it as well now, even while her head fills with images of loss, pain, and heartsick despair. Dooley's coming. She hears him. He's quit cursing but she hears the approach of his respiration. It's going to be close, closer than with Blondie, even though *this* madman doesn't have a gun, because if Dooley manages to grab hold of her before she's able to turn—

But he doesn't. Not quite. Lisey pivots like a hitter going after a fat pitch, swinging the silver spade just as hard as she can. The bowl catches a last bloom of pink light, a fading corsage, and its speeding upper edge ticks the hanging bell on its way by. The bell says a final word – *TING!* – and goes flying into the gloom, trailing its bit of rotting cord after it. Lisey sees the spade carry on forward and upward, and once more she thinks *Holy smuck! I really put a charge into this one!* Then the flat of the blade connects with Jim Dooley's onrushing face, making not a crunch – the sound she remembers from Nashville – but a kind of muffled *gonging*. Dooley shrieks in surprise and agony. He is driven sideways, off the path and into the trees, flailing with his arms, trying to keep his balance. She has a moment to see that his nose is laid radically over to one side, just as Cole's was; time to see that his mouth is gushing blood from the bottom and both corners. Then there's movement from her right, not far from where Dooley is thrashing about and trying to haul himself upward. It is *vast* movement. For a moment the dark and fearsomely sad thoughts which inhabit her mind grow even sadder and darker; Lisey thinks they will either kill her or drive her insane. Then they shift in a slightly different direction, and as they do, the thing over there just beyond the trees also shifts. There's the complicated sound of breaking foliage, the snapping and tearing of trees and underbrush. Then, and suddenly, it's *there*. Scott's long boy. And she understands that once you have seen the long boy, past and future become only dreams. Once you have seen the long boy, there is only, oh dear Jesus, there is only a single moment of *now* drawn out like an agonizing note that never ends.

10

Almost before Lisey was aware of what was happening and surely before she was ready – although the idea of ever being *ready* for such a thing was a joke – suddenly it was there. The piebald thing. The living embodiment of what Scott had been talking about when he talked about the bad-gunky.

What she saw was an enormous plated side like cracked snakeskin. It came bulging through the trees, bending some and snapping others, seeming to pass right through a couple of the biggest. That was impossible, of course, but the impression never faded. There was no smell but there was an unpleasant sound, a chuffing, somehow *gutty* sound, and then its patchwork head appeared, taller than the trees and blotting out the sky. Lisey saw an eye, dead yet aware, black as wellwater and as wide as a sink-hole, peering through the foliage. She saw an opening in the meat of its vast questing blunt head and intuited that the things it took in through that vast straw of flesh did not precisely die but lived and *screamed* . . . lived and *screamed* . . . lived and *screamed*.

She herself could not scream. She was incapable of any noise at all. She took two steps backward, steps that felt weirdly calm to her. The spade, its silver bowl once more dripping with the blood of an insane man, fell from her fingers and landed on the path. She thought, *It sees me . . . and my life will never truly be mine again. It won't* let *it be mine.*

For a moment it reared, a shapeless, endless thing with patches of hair growing in random clumps from its damp and heaving slicks of flesh, its great and dully avid eye upon her. The dying pink of the day and the waxing silver glow of moonlight lit the rest of what still lay snakelike in the shrubbery.

Then its eye turned from Lisey to the screaming, thrashing creature that was trying to back out of the little copse of trees that had entangled him, Jim Dooley with blood gushing from his broken mouth, broken nose, and one swollen eye; Jim Dooley with blood even in his hair. Dooley saw what was looking at him and screamed no more. Lisey saw him trying to cover his good eye, saw his hands fall to his sides, knew he had lost his strength, and felt a moment of pity for him in spite of everything, an instant of empathy that was gruesome in its strength and nearly unendurable in its human harmony. In that moment she might have taken it all back if it had meant only her own dying, but she thought of Amanda and tried to harden her horrified mind and heart.

The huge thing tangled in the trees poked forward almost delicately and gathered Dooley in. The flesh around the hole in its blunt snout seemed to wrinkle briefly, almost to pucker, and Lisey remembered Scott lying on the hot pavement that day in Nashville. As the low snorts and the crunching sounds began and Dooley started to voice his final, seemingly endless cries, she remembered Scott whispering, *I hear it taking its meal*. She remembered how he had pursed his lips in a tight O, and she recalled with perfect clarity how blood had burst from them when he made that indescribably nasty chuffing sound: fine ruby droplets which seemed to hang in the sweltering air.

She ran then, though she would have sworn she no

longer knew how. She bolted back along the path toward the hill of lupin, away from the place near the Bell-and-Spade Tree where the long boy was eating Jim Dooley alive. She knew it was doing her and Amanda a favor, but she knew it was a lefthanded favor at best, because if she survived this night, she would now be free of the long boy no more than Scott had been, no, not a single day since his childhood. Now it had marked her as well, made her a part of its never-ending moment, its terrible world-spanning regard. From now on she would have to be careful, especially if she happened to wake up in the middle of the night . . . and Lisey had an idea that her nights of sound sleep were over. In the small hours she would have to steer her gaze away from mirrors, and window-glass, and especially from the curved surfaces of waterglasses, God knew why. She would have to protect herself as well as she could.

If she survived this night.

It's very close, honey, Scott had whispered as he lay shivering on the hot pavement. *Very close.*

Behind her, Dooley screamed as if he would never stop. Lisey thought it would drive her mad. Or that it already had.

11

Just before she emerged from the trees, Dooley's shrieking finally did cease. She didn't see Amanda. This filled Lisey with new terror. Suppose her sister had run away to who knew which point of the compass? Or suppose she was still somewhere close at hand, but curled up in a fetal position, catatonic again and concealed by the shadows?

'Amanda? *Amanda?*'

There was an endless moment during which she heard nothing. It was followed – God, at last! – by a rustling in the high grass to Lisey's left, and Amanda stood up. Her face, pale to begin with and painted paler by the light of the rising moon, now looked like that of a wraith. Or a harpy. She came stumbling forward, arms out, and Lisey gathered her in. Amanda was shivering. The hands at the nape of Lisey's neck were locked in a chilly knot.

'Oh Lisey, I thought he'd never stop!'

'Me either.'

'And so high . . . I couldn't tell . . . they were so *high* . . . I hoped it was him, but I thought, "What if it's Little? What if it's Lisey?"' Amanda began to sob against the side of Lisey's neck.

'I'm all right, Amanda. I'm here and I'm all right.'

Amanda pulled her face away from Lisey's neck so she could look down into her younger sister's face. 'Is he dead?'

'Yes.' She would not share her intuition that Dooley might have achieved a kind of hellish immortality within the thing that had eaten him. 'Dead.'

'Then I want to go back! Can we go back?'

'Yes.'

'I don't know if I can make a picture of Scott's study in my mind . . . I'm so upset . . .' Amanda looked around fearfully. 'This isn't like Southwind at *all*.'

'No,' Lisey agreed, gathering Amanda back into her arms. 'And I know you're afraid. You just do the best you can.'

Lisey was actually not worried about getting back to

Scott's study, back to Castle View, back to the world. She thought the problem now might be *staying* there. She remembered a doctor telling her once she'd have to be especially careful of her ankle after giving it a savage sprain while ice-skating. *Because once you stretch those tendons*, he'd said, *it's ever so much easier to do it next time*.

That much easier next time, right. And it had seen her. That eye, as big as a spring sinkhole, both dead and alive, had been on her.

'Lisey, you're so brave,' Amanda said in a small voice. She took one final look at the sloping hill of lupin, gilded and strange in the growing light of the moon, then pressed her face against the side of Lisey's neck again.

'Keep talking like that and I'll have you back in Greenlawn tomorrow. Close your eyes.'

'They are.'

Lisey closed her own. For a moment she saw that blunt head that wasn't a head at all but only a maw, a straw, a funnel into blackness filled with endless swirling bad-gunky. In it she still heard Jim Dooley screaming, but the sound was now thin, and mixed with other screams. With what felt like tremendous effort, she swept the images and sounds away, replacing them with a picture of the red maple desk and the sound of Ole Hank – who else? – singing 'Jambalaya'. There was time to think of how at first she and Scott hadn't been able to come back when they so badly needed to with the long boy so close, time to think of

(it's the african Lisey I feel it like an anchor)

what he had said, time to wonder why that should make her think again of Amanda looking with such longing at the good ship *Hollyhocks* (a goodbye look if there ever was one), and then time was up. Once more she felt the air *turn*, and the moonlight was gone. She knew even with her eyes closed. There was the sense of taking a short, jolting fall. Then they were in the study and the study was dark because Dooley had killed the electricity, but still Hank Williams was singing – *My Yvonne, sweetest one, me-oh-my-oh* – because even with the power cut, Ole Hank meant to have his say.

12

'Lisey? *Lisey!*'

'Manda, you're *crushing* me, get *off*—'

'Lisey, are we back?'

Two women in the dark. Lying tangled together on the carpet.

'Kinfolk come to see Yvonne by the dozens . . .' Drifting out of the alcove.

'Yes, would you get the smuck off me, I can't *breathe*!'

'Sorry . . . Lisey, you're on my arm . . .'

'Son-of-a-gun, we'll have big fun . . . on the bayou!'

Lisey managed to roll to her right. Amanda pulled her arm free, and a moment later the weight of her body came off Lisey's midsection. Lisey gasped in a deep – and deeply satisfying – breath. As she let it out, Hank Williams quit singing in mid-phrase.

'Lisey, why is it so dark in here?'

'Because Dooley cut the power, remember?'

'He cut the *lights*,' Amanda said reasonably. 'If he'd cut the *power*, the TV wouldn't have been playing.'

Lisey could have asked Amanda why the TV had suddenly *stopped* playing, but didn't bother. Other matters needed discussing. They had *other fish to fry*, as the saying was. 'Let's go in the house.'

'I'm a hundred percent down with that,' Amanda said. Her fingers touched Lisey's elbow, groped down her forearm, and seized her hand. The sisters stood up together. Amanda added, in a confiding tone: 'No offense, Lisey, but if I ever come here again it'll be too soon.'

Lisey understood how Amanda felt, but her own feelings had changed. Scott's study *had* daunted her, no argument there. It had kept her at arm's length for two long years. But she thought the major chore which had needed doing in here was now done. She and Amanda had cleansed Scott's ghost away, kindly and – time would tell, but she was almost positive – completely.

'Come on,' she said. 'Let's go in the house. I'll make hot chocolate.'

'And maybe a little brandy to start with?' Amanda asked hopefully. 'Or don't crazy ladies get brandy?'

'Crazy ladies don't. You do.'

Holding hands, they groped toward the stairs. Lisey stopped only once, when she stepped on something. She bent over and picked up a round of glass easily an inch thick. She realized it was one of the lenses from Dooley's night-vision goggles and dropped it with a grimace of disgust.

'What?' Amanda asked.

'Nothing. I'm able to see a little. How about you?'

'A little. But don't let go of my hand.'

'I won't, honey.'

They descended the stairs to the barn together. It took longer to do it that way, but it felt a lot safer.

13

Lisey set out her smallest juice glasses and poured them each a shot of brandy from a bottle she found at the very back of the dining room drinks cabinet. She held her glass up and clinked it against Amanda's. They were standing at the kitchen counter. Every light in the room was on, even the gooseneck lamp in the corner where Lisey scribbled checks at a child's schooldesk.

'Over the teeth,' Lisey said.

'Over the gums,' Amanda said.

'Look out guts, here it comes,' they said together, and drank.

Amanda bent and blew out a gust of breath. When she straightened up, there were roses in her formerly pale cheeks, a line of red forming on her brow, and a tiny saddle of scarlet on the bridge of her nose. Tears stood in her eyes.

'Shit-a-goddam! What was *that*?'

Lisey, whose throat felt as hot as Manda's face looked, took hold of the bottle and read the label. STAR BRANDY, it said. *A PRODUCT OF ROMANIA*.

'Romanian brandy?' Amanda looked aghast. 'Ain't no such animal! Where'd you get it?'

'It was a gift to Scott. He got it for doing something – I forget what – but I think they threw in a pen set, too.'

'It's probably poison. You pour it out and I'll pray we don't die.'

'You pour it out. I'll make the hot chocolate. Swiss. *Not* from Romania.'

She began to turn away, but Amanda touched her shoulder. 'Maybe we should skip the hot chocolate and just get out of here before any of those Sheriff's deputies come back to check on you.'

'Do you think so?' Even as she asked the question, Lisey knew Amanda was right.

'Yes. Do you dare to go up in the study again?'

'Of course I do.'

'Then get my little gun. Don't forget the lights are out up there.'

Lisey opened the top of the little desk where she wrote her checks and pulled out the long-barreled flash-light she kept in there. She turned it on. The light was nice and bright.

Amanda was rinsing their glasses. 'If someone found out we were here, that wouldn't be the end of the world. But if your deputies found out we came with a gun . . . and that man just happened to disappear off the face of the earth around the same time . . .'

Lisey, who had thought only as far as getting Dooley to the Bell-and-Spade Tree (and the long boy had *never* been a part of her imaginings), realized she still had work to do and had better get busy doing it. Professor Woodbody wasn't ever going to report his old drinking buddy missing, but the man might have relatives *somewhere*, and if anybody in the world had a motive for getting rid of the Black Prince of the Incunks, it was Lisey Landon. Of course there was no body (what Scott had sometimes been pleased to refer to as the *corpus delicious*), but still, she and her sister had spent what some might construe as an extremely suspicious afternoon and evening. Plus the County Sheriff's Department knew Dooley had been harassing her; she'd told them so herself.

'I'll get his shite,' she said.

Amanda did not smile. 'Good.'

14

The flashlight cut a wide swath, and the study wasn't as spooky on her own as Lisey had feared it might be. Having stuff to do no doubt helped. She began by putting the Pathfinder back in its shoebox, then went prospecting along the floor with the light. She found both of the lenses that went with the night-vision goggles, plus half a dozen double-A batteries. She assumed these were from the gadget's power-pack. The pack must have traveled, although she couldn't remember actually seeing it; the batteries obviously hadn't. Then she picked up Dooley's terrible paper bag. Amanda had either forgotten the bag or hadn't even realized Dooley had it, but the stuff in here would look bad for her if it were found. Especially when combined with the gun. Lisey knew they could do tests on the Pathfinder that would show it had been fired recently; she wasn't dumb (and she watched *CSI*). She also knew the tests wouldn't show it had been fired only once, into the ceiling. She tried to handle the paper bag so it wouldn't clank, and it clanked anyway. She looked around for other signs of Dooley and saw none. There were bloodstains on the rug, but if *that* were ever tested, both the type and the DNA would match hers. Blood on her rug would look

very bad in combination with the stuff in the bag she now
held in her hand, but with the bag gone, they'd be all right.
Probably all right.

*Where's his car? His PT Cruiser? Because I know that
car I saw was his.*

She couldn't worry about that now. It was dark. This
was what she had to worry about, this stuff rah-cheer. And
her sisters. Darla and Canty, currently on Mr Toad's Wild
Ride way the hell and gone up to Acadia Mental Health
in Derry. So they wouldn't get caught in the Jim Dooley
version of Mr Silver's potato-grader.

But did she really have to worry about those two?
No. They'd be royally pissed, of course . . . and royally
curious . . . but in the end they'd keep quiet if she and
Amanda told them they absolutely had to, and why? Because
of the sister thing, that was why. She and Amanda would
have to be careful with them, and there would have to be
some sort of story (what kind could possibly cover this Lisey
had no idea, although she was sure Scott could have come
up with something). There had to be a story because, unlike
Amanda and Lisey, Darla and Cantata had husbands. And
husbands were all too often the back door by which secrets
escaped into the outside world.

As Lisey turned to go, her eye was caught by the
booksnake sleeping against the wall. All those quarterly
reviews and scholarly journals, all those year-end annuals,
bound reports, and copies of theses done on Scott's work.
Many containing pictures of a gone life – call it **SCOTT
AND LISEY! THE MARRIED YEARS!**

She could easily see a couple of college kids dismantling the snake and loading its component parts into card-

598

board boxes with liquor brands printed on the sides, then stacking the boxes in the back of a truck and driving them away. To Pitt? *Bite your tongue*, Lisey thought. She didn't consider herself a grudge-holding woman, but after Jim Dooley, it would be a snowy day in hell before she put any more of Scott's stuff where Woodsmucky could look at it without buying a plane ticket. No, the Fogler Library at the University of Maine would do just fine – right down the road from Cleaves Mills. She could see herself standing by and watching the final packing-up, maybe bringing out a pitcher of iced tea to the kids when the work was done. And when the tea was finished, they would set their glasses down and thank her. One of them might tell her how much he'd liked her husband's books, and the other might say they were very sorry for her loss. As if he had died two weeks ago. She'd thank them. Then she would watch them drive away with all those frozen images of her life with him locked inside their truck.

You can really let go?

She thought she could. Still, that snake drowsing along the wall drew the eye. So many shut books, sleeping deep – they drew the eye. She looked a moment longer, thinking there had once been a young woman named Lisey Debusher with a young woman's high firm breasts. Lonely? A little, yes, she had been. Scared? Sure, a bit, that went with being twenty-two. And a young man had come into her life. A young man whose hair wouldn't ever stay off his forehead. A young man with a lot to say.

'I always loved you, Scott,' she told the empty study. Or perhaps it was the sleeping books she told. 'You and your everlasting mouth. I was your gal pal. Wasn't I?'

Then, shining the flashlight's beam ahead of her, she went back down the stairs with the shoebox in one hand and Dooley's awful paper bag in the other.

15

Amanda was standing at the kitchen door when Lisey came back in.

'Good,' Amanda said. 'I was getting worried. What's in the bag?'

'You don't want to know.'

'Oh . . . kay,' Amanda said. 'Is he . . . you know, gone from up there?'

'I think so, yes.'

'I hope so.' Amanda shivered. 'He was a scary guy.'

You don't know the half of it, Lisey thought.

'Well,' Amanda said, 'I guess we better get going.'

'Going where?'

'Lisbon Falls,' Amanda said. 'The old farm.'

'*What*—' Then she stopped. It made a weird kind of sense.

'I came around at Greenlawn, just like you told that Dr Alberness, and you took me to my house so I could change my clothes. Then I got freaky and started talking about the farm. Come on, Lisey, let's go, let's blow this pop-shop before someone comes.' Amanda led her out into the dark.

Lisey, bemused, let herself be led. The old Debusher place still stood on its five acres out at the end of the Sabbatus Road in Lisbon, about sixty miles from Castle View. Willed jointly to five women (and three living husbands), it would probably stand there, rotting in high weeds and fallow fields, for years to come, unless property values rose enough to cause them to drop their differing ideas of what should be done with it. A trust fund set up by Scott Landon in the late nineteen-eighties paid the property taxes.

'Why did you want to go to the old farm?' Lisey asked as she slipped behind the BMW's wheel. 'I'm not clear on that.'

'Because *I* wasn't,' Amanda said as Lisey turned in a circle and started down the long drive. 'I just said I had to go there and see the old place if I wasn't going to, you know, slip back into the Twilight Zone, so of course you took me.'

'Of course I did,' Lisey said. She looked both ways, saw no one coming – especially no County Sheriff's Department cars, praise God – and turned left, the direction that would take her through Mechanic Falls, Poland Springs, and eventually to Gray and Lisbon beyond. 'And why did we send Darla and Canty in the wrong direction?'

'I absolutely insisted,' Amanda said. 'I was afraid if they showed up, they'd take me back to my house or your house or even to Greenlawn before I got a chance to visit with Mom and Dad and then spend some time at the home place.' For a moment Lisey had no idea what Manda was talking about – *spend time with Mom and Dad?* Then she got it. The Debusher family plot was at nearby Sabbatus Vale Cemetery. Both Good Ma and Dandy were buried there, along with Grampy and Granny D and God knew how many others.

She asked, 'But weren't you afraid *I'd* take you back?'

Amanda eyed her indulgently. 'Why would *you* take me back? You were the one who took me *out*.'

'Maybe because you started acting crazy, asking to visit a farm that's been deserted for thirty years or more?'

'Foof!' Amanda waved a dismissive hand. 'I could always wrap you around my finger, Lisey – Canty and Darla both know this.'

'Bull*shit* you could!'

Amanda only gave her a maddening smile, her complexion a rather weird green in the glow of the dashboard lights, and said nothing. Lisey opened her mouth to renew the argument, then closed it again. She thought the story would work, because it came down to a pair of easily grasped ideas: Amanda had been acting crazy (nothing new there) and Lisey had been humoring her (understandable, given the circumstances). They could work with it. As for the shoebox with the gun in it . . . and Dooley's bag . . .

'We're going to stop in Mechanic Falls,' she told Amanda. 'Where the bridge goes over the Androscoggin River. I've got a couple of things to get rid of.'

'Yes you do,' Amanda said. Then she folded her hands in her lap, put her head back against the rest, and closed her eyes.

Lisey turned on the radio, and wasn't a bit surprised to get Ole Hank singing 'Honky Tonkin'. She sang along, low. She knew every word. This did not surprise her, either. Some things you never forgot. She had come to believe that the very things the practical world dismissed as ephemera – things like songs and moonlight and kisses – were sometimes the things that lasted the longest. They might be foolish, but they defied forgetting. And that was good.

That was good.

PART 3

LISEY'S STORY

'You are the call and I am the answer,
You are the wish, and I the fulfillment,
You are the night, and I the day.
    What else? It is perfect enough.
    It is perfectly complete.
    You and I,
    What more—?
Strange, how we suffer in spite of this!'
                                —D. H. Lawrence
                        Look! We Have Come Through!

CHAPTER SIXTEEN

LISEY AND THE STORY TREE (SCOTT HAS HIS SAY)

1

Once Lisey actually got going on emptying out Scott's study, the job went faster than she ever would have believed. And she never would have believed she'd end up doing it with Darla and Canty as well as Amanda. Canty remained standoffish and suspicious for a time – it felt like a *long* time to Lisey – but Amanda was completely unfazed. 'It's an act. She'll drop it and come around. Just give her time, Lisey. Sisterhood is powerful.'

Eventually Cantata *did* come around, although Lisey had a feeling Canty never entirely rid herself of the idea that Amanda had been faking in order to Get Attention, and that she and Lisey had been Up To Something. Probably Something No Good. Darla was puzzled about Amanda's recovery, and the sisters' odd trip to the old farm in Lisbon, but she, at least, never believed Amanda had been faking.

Darla had seen her, after all.

In any case, the four sisters cleaned and emptied the

long, rambling suite over the barn during the week after the Fourth of July, hiring a couple of husky high school boys to help with the heavy lifting. The worst of said heavy lifting turned out to be Dumbo's Big Jumbo, which had to be disassembled (the component parts reminded Lisey of the Exploded Man in high school biology class, only you'd have to call this version the Exploded Desk), and then lowered with a rented winch. The high school boys bawled encouragement to each other as the pieces went down. Lisey stood by with her sisters, praying like mad that neither of the boys would lose a finger or thumb in one of the slings or pulleys. Neither did, and by the end of the week, everything in Scott's study had been taken away, marked either for donation or long-term storage while Lisey figured out what the hell to do with it.

Everything, that was, except for the booksnake. That remained, dozing in the long, empty main room – the *hot* main room, now that the air conditioners had been removed. Even with the skylights open in the daytime and a couple of fans to keep the air circulating, it was hot. And why wouldn't it be? The place was nothing but a glorified barn loft with a literary pedigree.

Then there were those ugly maroon smudges on the carpet – the oyster-white carpet that couldn't be taken up until the booksnake was gone. She'd dismissed the stains as careless slops of Wood Coat varnish when Canty asked about them, but Amanda knew better, and Lisey had an idea that Darla might have a few suspicions, as well. The carpet had to go, but the books had to go first, and Lisey wasn't quite ready to dispose of them. Just why she wasn't sure. Maybe only because they were the last of Scott's things still up here, the very last of him.

So she waited.

2

On the third day of the sisters' cleaning binge, Deputy Boeckman called to tell Lisey that an abandoned PT Cruiser with Delaware plates had been found in a gravel pit on the Stackpole Church Road, about three miles from her house. Would Lisey come down to the Sheriff's Office and take a look? They had it back in the parking lot, the deputy said, where they kept the impounds and a few 'drug-rides' (whatever they were). Lisey went with Amanda. Neither Darla nor Canty was much interested; all they knew was that a kook had been sniffing around, making a pest of himself about Scott's papers. Kooks were nothing new in their sister's life; over the years of Scott's celebrity, any number of them had been drawn to him like moths to a bug-light. The most famous, of course, had been Cole. Neither Lisey nor Amanda had said anything to give Darla and Canty the idea that this one was in Cole's class. Certainly there was no mention of the dead cat in the mailbox, and Lisey had been at some pains to impress discretion on the Sheriff's deputies, as well.

The car in Stall 7 was a PT Cruiser, no more and no less, beige in color, nondescript once you got past the slightly flamboyant body-type. It could have been the one Lisey saw as she drove home from Greenlawn on that long, long Thursday; it could have been one of several thousand others. This was what she told Deputy Boeckman, reminding him that she'd seen it coming almost directly out of the setting sun. He nodded sadly. What she knew in her heart was that it *was* the one. She could smell Dooley on it. She thought: *I am going to hurt you places you didn't let the boys to touch at the junior high dances* and had to repress a shiver.

'It's a stolen car, isn't it?' Amanda asked.

'You bet your bippy,' Boeckman said.

A deputy Lisey didn't know strolled over. He was tall, probably six and a half feet; it seemed a rule that these men should be tall. Broad-shouldered, too. He introduced himself as Deputy Andy Clutterbuck and shook Lisey's hand.

'Ah,' she said, 'the acting Sheriff.'

His smile was brilliant. 'Nope, Norris is back. He's in court this afternoon, but he's back, all right. I'm just plain old Deputy Clutterbuck again.'

'Congratulations. This is my sister, Amanda Debusher.'

Clutterbuck shook Amanda's hand. 'Pleased, Ms Debusher.' Then, to both of them: 'That car was stolen out of a shopping mall in Laurel, Maryland.' He stared at it, thumbs hooked in his belt. 'Did you know that in France, they call PT Cruisers *le car Jimmy Cagney*?'

Amanda seemed unimpressed by this information. 'Were there fingerprints?'

'Nary a one,' he said. 'Wiped clean. Plus whoever was driving it took the cover off the dome-light and broke the bulb. What do you think of that?'

'I think it sounds *beaucoup* suspicious,' Amanda said.

Clutterbuck laughed. 'Yeah. But there's a retired carpenter in Delaware who's going to be very happy to get his car back, busted dome-light and all.'

Lisey said, 'Have you found out anything about Jim Dooley?'

'That would be John Doolin, Mrs Landon. Born in Shooter's Knob, Tennessee. Moved to Nashville at age five with his family, then went to live with his aunt and uncle in Moundsville, West Virginia, when his parents and older sister were killed in a fire in the winter of 1974. Doolin was then age nine. The official cause of the deaths was down to defective Christmas tree lights, but I talked to a retired detective who worked that case. He said there was some suspicion the boy might have had something to do with it. No proof.'

Lisey saw no reason to pay close attention to the rest, because whatever he called himself, her persecutor was never coming back from the place where she had taken him. Yet she did hear Clutterbuck say that Doolin had spent a good many years in a Tennessee mental institution, and she continued to believe that he had met Gerd Allen Cole there, and caught Cole's obsession

(ding-dong for the freesias)

like a virus. Scott had had a queer saying, one Lisey had never fully understood until the business of McCool/Dooley/Doolin. Some things just have to be true, Scott said, because they have no other choice.

'In any case, you want to keep your eyes peeled for the guy,' Clutterbuck told the two women, 'and if it looks like he's still around—'

'Or takes some time off and then decides to come back,' Boeckman put in.

Clutterbuck nodded. 'Yep, that's a possibility, too. If he shows up again, I think we ought to have a meeting with your family, Mrs Landon – put them all in the picture. Do you agree?'

'If he shows up, we'll certainly do that,' Lisey said. She spoke seriously, almost solemnly, but on their way out of town, she and Amanda indulged in a bout of hysterical laughter at the idea of Jim Dooley ever showing up again.

3

An hour or two before dawn the next morning, shuffling into the bathroom with one eye open, thinking of nothing but peeing and going back to bed, Lisey thought she saw something moving in the bedroom behind her. That brought her awake in a hurry, and turning on her heels. There was nothing there. She took a hand-towel from the rod beside the sink and hung it over the medicine cabinet mirror in which she'd seen the movement, wedging the towel carefully until it would stay on its own. Then and only then did she finish her business.

She was sure Scott would have understood.

4

The summer slipped by, and one day Lisey noticed that SCHOOL SUPPLIES signs had appeared in the windows of several stores on Castle Rock's Main Street. And why not? It was suddenly half-past August. Scott's study was – except for the booksnake and the stained white carpet upon which it dozed – waiting for the next thing. (If there *was* a next thing; Lisey had begun to consider the possibility of putting the house up for sale.) Canty and Rich threw their annual

Midsummer Night's Dream party on August fourteenth. Lisey set out to get righteously smashed on Rich Lawlor's Long Island Iced Tea, a thing she hadn't done since Scott had died. She asked Rich for a double to get started, then set it down untasted on one of the caterer's tables. She thought she had seen something moving either on the surface of the glass, as if reflected there, or deep within the amber depths, as if swimming there. It was utter shite, of course, but she found her urge to get absolutely stinko was gone. In truth, she wasn't sure she *dared* to get drunk (or even high). Wasn't sure she dared let her defenses down in such a way. Because if she had attracted the long boy's attention, if it was watching her from time to time . . . or even just *thinking* about her . . . well . . .

Part of her was sure that was crap.

Part of her was positive it wasn't.

As August waned and the hottest weather of the summer rolled into New England, testing tempers and the northeast power-grid, something even more distressing began happening to Lisey . . . except, like the things she sometimes thought she *might* be glimpsing in certain reflective surfaces, she wasn't entirely sure it was happening at all.

Sometimes she'd flounder up from sleep in the mornings an hour or maybe two before her usual time, gasping and covered with sweat even with the air-conditioning on, feeling as she had when coming out of nightmares as a child: that she hadn't really escaped the grip of whatever had been after her, that it was still under the bed and would curl its cold distorted hand around her ankle or reach right up through her pillow and grab her by the neck. During these panicky wakings she would run her hands over the sheets and then up to the head of her bed before opening her eyes, wanting to be sure, absolutely sure, that she wasn't . . . well, somewhere else. *Because once you stretch those tendons,* she sometimes thought, opening her eyes and looking at her familiar bedroom with great and inexpressible relief, *it's ever so much easier to do it next time.* And she had stretched a certain set of tendons, hadn't she? Yes. First by yanking Amanda, then by yanking Dooley. She had stretched them but good.

It seemed to her that after she'd awakened half a dozen times and discovered she was right where she belonged, in the bedroom that had once been hers and Scott's and was now hers alone, matters should have improved, but they didn't. They got worse instead. She felt like a loose tooth in a sick socket. And then, on the first day of the big heatwave – a heatwave to match the cold-snap of ten years before, and the ironic balance of this, coincidental though it might have been, was not lost on her – what she feared finally happened.

5

She lay back on the couch in the living room just to rest her eyes for a few moments. The unquestionably idiotic but occasionally entertaining Jerry Springer was babbling away on the idiot box – My Mother Stole My Boyfriend, My Boyfriend Stole My Mother, something like that. Lisey reached out to pick up the remote and shut the damn thing off, or maybe she only dreamed she did, because when she opened her eyes to see where the remote was, she was lying not on the couch but on the hill of lupin in Boo'ya Moon. It was full daylight and there was no sense of danger – certainly no sense that Scott's long boy (for so she thought of it and always would, although she supposed it was her long boy now, Lisey's long boy) was near, but she was terrified nevertheless, almost to the point of screaming helplessly. Instead of doing that she closed her eyes, visualized her living room, and suddenly she could hear the 'guests' on the *Springer Show* yelling at each other and feel the oblong of the remote control in her left hand. A second later she was starting up from the couch, eyes wide and skin all a-prickle. She could almost believe she had dreamed the whole deal (it certainly made sense, given her current level of anxiety on the subject), but the vividness of what she had seen in those few seconds argued against that idea, comforting as it was. So did the smear of purple on the back of the hand holding the TV controller.

6

The next day she called the Fogler Library and spoke to Mr Bertram Partridge, the head of Special Collections. That gentleman grew steadily more excited as Lisey described the books still remaining in Scott's study. He called them 'associational volumes' and said Fogler Special Collections would be very happy to have them, 'and to work with her on the tax-credit question'. Lisey said that would be very nice, just as though she had been asking herself the tax-credit question for years. Mr Partridge said he would send 'a team of removers' out the very next day to box the volumes up and bring them the hundred and twenty miles to the University of Maine's Orono campus. Lisey reminded him that the weather was supposed to be very hot, and that Scott's study, which was no longer air-conditioned, had reverted to its former loftish nature. Perhaps, she said, Mr Partridge would like to hold his removers in abeyance until cooler weather.

'Not at all, Mrs Landon,' Partridge said, chuckling expansively, and Lisey knew he was afraid she might change her mind if given too long to think the matter over. 'I've got a couple of young folks in mind who'll be perfect for the job. You wait and see.'

7

Less than an hour after her conversation with Bertram Partridge, Lisey's phone rang while she was making herself a tuna on rye for her supper: thin commons, but all she wanted. Outside, the heat lay on the land like a blanket. All color had been bleached from the sky; it was a perfect simmering white from horizon to horizon. As she mixed the tuna and mayonnaise with a little chopped onion, she had been thinking of how she'd found Amanda on one of those benches, looking out at the *Hollyhocks*, and this was strange, because she hardly ever thought of that anymore; it was like a dream to her. She remembered Amanda's asking if she'd have to drink any of that

(bug-juuuuice)

shitty punch if she came back – her way of trying to find out, Lisey supposed, if she'd have to remain incarcerated at Greenlawn – and Lisey had promised her no

614

more punch, no more bug-juice. Amanda had agreed to return, although it had been clear she didn't really want to, that she would have been happy to continue sitting on the bench and looking out at the *Hollyhocks* until, in Good Ma's words, 'eternity was halfway over'. Just sitting there among the scary shrouded things and silent gazers, a bench or two above the woman in the caftan. The one who had murdered her child.

Lisey put her sandwich down on the counter, suddenly cold all over. She couldn't know that. There was no *way* she could know that.

But she did.

Be quiet, the woman had said. *Be quiet while I think of why I did it.*

And then Amanda had said something totally unexpected, hadn't she? Something about Scott. Although nothing Amanda said *then* could be important *now*, not with Scott dead and Jim Dooley also dead (or *wishing* he were), but still Lisey wished she could remember exactly what it might have been.

'Said she'd come back,' Lisey murmured. 'Said she'd come back if it would keep Dooley from hurting me.'

Yes, and Amanda had kept her word, God bless her, but Lisey wanted to remember something she'd said *after* that. *I don't see what it can have to do with Scott,* Amanda had said in that faintly distracted voice of hers. *He's been dead such a long time . . . although . . . I think he told me something about—*

That was when the phone rang, shattering the fragile glass of Lisey's recollection. And as she picked it up, a crazy certainty came to her: it would be Dooley. *Hello, Missus,* the Black Prince of the Incunks would say. *I'm callin from inside the belly of the beast. How y'all doin today?*

'Hello?' she said. She knew she was gripping the phone too tightly, but was helpless to do anything about it.

'Danny Boeckman here, Mrs Landon,' the voice at the other end said, and the *Mrs* was too close for comfort, but *here* came out *heah*, a comfortable Yankee pronunciation, and Deputy Boeckman sounded uncharacteristically excited, almost bubbly, and therefore boyish. 'Guess what?'

'Can't guess,' Lisey said, but another crazy idea came to her: he was going to say they drew straws down at the Sheriff's Office to see who was going to call up and ask her out on a date and he drew the short one. Except why would he sound excited about *that*?

'We found the dome-light cover!'

Lisey had no idea what he was talking about. 'I beg pardon?'

'Doolin – the guy you knew as Zack McCool and then as Jim Dooley – stole that PT Cruiser and used it while he was stalking you, Mrs Landon. We were positive of that. And he was keeping it stashed out in that old gravel pit between runs, we were positive of that, too. We just couldn't prove it, because—'

'He wiped off all his fingerprints.'

'Ayuh, and got em all. But every now n then me n Plug went out there—'

'Plug?'

'I'm sorry, Joe. Deputy Alston?'

Plug, she thought. Aware for the first time, in a clear-seeing way, that these were real men with real lives. With

616

nicknames. *Plug*, she thought. *Deputy Joe Alston, also known as Plug*.

'Mrs Landon? Are you there?'

'Yes, Dan. May I call you Dan?'

'Sure, you bet. Anyway, every now n then we went sniffin round out there to see if we couldn't find some prizes, because there was plenty of sign that he'd spent time in that pit – candy-wrappers, a couple of RC bottles, things like that.'

'RC,' she said softly, and thought: *Bool, Dan. Bool, Plug. Bool, The End.*

'Right, that was the brand he seemed to favor, but not a single print on a single cast-off bottle matched up to one of his. The only match we got was to a fella who stole a car back in the late seventies and now clerks at the Quick-E-Mart over in Oxford. The other prints we got off the bottles, we surmise those were clerk-prints, too. But yest'y noon, Mrs Landon—'

'Lisey.'

There was a pause while he considered this. Then he went on. 'Yest'y noon, Lisey, on a little track leadin out of that pit, I found the grand prize – the cover to that dome-light. He'd pulled it off and threw it into the puckies.' Boeckman's voice rose, became triumphant – became not the voice of a Deputy Sheriff but perfectly human. 'And that was the one thing he forgot to handle with gloves on or wipe off later! A big thumbprint on one side, a big fat old index-finger on the other! Where he gripped it. We got the results back by fax this morning.'

'John Doolin?'

'Ayuh. Nine points of comparison. *Nine!*' There was

a pause, and when he spoke again, some of the triumph had gone out of his voice. 'Now if we could only find the son-of-a-buck.'

'I'm sure he'll turn up in time,' she said, and cast a longing glance at her tuna sandwich. She'd lost her train of thought about Amanda, but had regained her appetite. To Lisey that seemed like a fair swap, especially on such a boogery-hot day. 'Even if he doesn't, he's stopped harassing me.'

'He's left Castle County, I'd stake my reputation on that.' A note of unmistakable pride crept into Deputy Sheriff Dan Boeckman's voice. 'Got a little too hot for him here, I guess, so he ditched his ride and left. Plug feels the same. Jim Dooley and Elvis have both left the building.'

'Plug, is that for chewing tobacco?'

'No, ma'am, not at all. In high school, he and I played the line on the Castle Hills Knights team that won the Class A State Championship. Bangor Rams was favored by three touchdowns, but we shocked em. Only team from our part of the state to win a gold football since the nineteen-fifties. And Joey, no one could stop him, not that whole season. Even with four guys hangin off him, he kept pluggin. So we called him Plug, and I still do.'

'If I called him that, do you think he'd swat me?'

Dan Boeckman laughed, delighted. 'No! He'd be tickled!'

'Okay, then. I'm Lisey, you're Dan, and he's Plug.'

'That's square-john with me.'

'And thanks for the call. That was terrific police work.'

'Thanks for saying so, ma'am. Lisey.' She could hear

the glow in his voice, and that made her feel good. 'You be in touch, now, if there's anything else we can do. Or if you hear from that lowlife again.'

'I will.'

Lisey went back to her sandwich with a smile on her face and didn't think about Amanda, or the good ship *Hollyhocks*, or Boo'ya Moon, for the rest of the day. That night, however, she awoke to the sound of distant thunder and a sense that something vast was – not *hunting* her, exactly (it wouldn't bother), but *musing* on her. The idea that she should be in such a thing's unknowable mind made her feel like crying and like screaming. At the same time. It also made her want to sit up watching movies on TCM, smoking cigarettes and drinking high-tension coffee. Or beer. Beer might be better. Beer might call back sleep. Instead of getting up, she turned off the bedside lamp and lay still. *I'll never go back to sleep*, she thought. *I'll just lie here like this until it gets light in the east. Then I can get up and make the coffee I want now.*

But three minutes after having this thought she was dozing. Ten minutes later she was sleeping deeply. Later still, when the moon rose and she dreamed of floating over a certain exotic beach of fine white sand on the PILLSBURY magic carpet, her bed was for a few moments empty and the room filled with the smells of frangipani and jasmine and night-blooming cereus, scents that were somehow longing and terrible at the same time. But then she was back and in the morning Lisey barely remembered her dream, her dream of flying, her dream of flying across the beach at the edge of the pool in Boo'ya Moon.

8

As it happened, Lisey's vision of dismantling the booksnake varied in only two respects from what she had foreseen, and these were minor variations indeed. First, one half of Mr Partridge's two-person team turned out to be a girl – a strapping twentysomething with a caramel-colored pony-tail threaded through the back of a Red Sox cap. Second, Lisey hadn't guessed how quickly the job would be done. In spite of the study's fearsome heat (not even three fans turning at top speed could do much about it), all the books were packed away in a dark blue UMO van in less than an hour. When Lisey asked the two librarians from Special Collections (who called themselves – only half-jokingly, Lisey thought – the Minions of Partridge) if they'd like iced tea, they agreed enthusiastically, and put away two large glasses each. The girl was Cory. She was the one who told Lisey how much she had liked Scott's books, espe-cially *Relics*, which she claimed to have read three times. The boy was Mike, and he was the one who said they were very sorry for her loss. Lisey thanked them both for their kindness, and meant it.

'It must make you sad, seeing it so empty,' Cory said, and tipped her glass toward the barn. The ice cubes clinked in it. Lisey was careful not to look directly at the glass, lest she see something besides ice in there.

'It is a little sad, but it's freeing, too,' she said. 'I put off the job of cleaning it out for too long. My sisters helped me. I'm glad we did it. More tea, Cory?'

'No thanks, but could I use your bathroom before we start back?'

'Of course. Through the living room, first door on the right.'

Cory excused herself. Absently – *almost* absently – Lisey moved the girl's glass behind the brown plastic iced-tea pitcher. 'Another glass, Mike?'

'No thanks,' he said. 'You'll be taking up the carpet, too, I guess.'

She laughed self-consciously. 'Yes. Pretty bad, isn't it? From Scott's one experiment in wood-staining. It was a disaster.' Thinking: *Sorry, honey.*

'Looks a little like dried blood,' Mike said, and finished his iced tea. The sun, hazy and hot, ran across the surface of his glass, and for a moment an eye seemed to peer out of it at Lisey. When he set it down, she had to restrain an urge to snatch it and hide it behind the plastic pitcher with the other one.

'Everybody says that,' she agreed.

'World's worst shaving cut,' Mike said, and laughed. They both laughed. Lisey thought hers sounded almost as natural as his. She didn't look at his glass. She didn't think about the long boy that was now *her* long boy. She thought about nothing *but* the long boy.

'Sure you won't have a little more?' she asked.

'Better not, I'm driving,' Mike said, and they had another laugh.

Cory came back and Lisey thought Mike would also ask to use the bathroom, but he didn't – guys had bigger kidneys, bigger bladders, bigger somethings, or so Scott had claimed – and Lisey was glad, because that meant only the girl gave her that funny look before they drove away with the disassembled booksnake in the back of the van. Oh, she undoubtedly told Mike what she saw in the living room and found in the bathroom, told him on the long drive north to the University of Maine at Orono, but Lisey wasn't there to hear it. The girl's look wasn't so bad, come to that, because Lisey hadn't known what it meant at the time, although she *had* patted the side of her head, thinking maybe her hair had fallen funny across her ear or was standing up or something. Then, later (after popping the iced-tea glasses into the dishwasher without so much as a look at them), she'd gone to use the bathroom herself and saw the towel hanging across the mirror in there. She remembered putting the hand-towel over the medicine cabinet mirror upstairs, remembered blinding that one perfectly well, but when had she done *this* one?

Lisey didn't know.

She went back to the living room and saw there was a sheet hung in a swag over the mirror above the mantel, as well. She should have noticed that on her way through, she imagined Cory had, it was pretty smucking obvious, but the truth was little Lisey Landon didn't spend much time studying her own reflection these days.

She did a walk-through and discovered all but two of the mirrors on the ground floor had been sheeted, toweled, or (in one case) taken down and turned to the wall; the last two survivors she now covered as well, in the spirit of in for a penny, in for a pound. As she did them, Lisey wondered exactly what the young librarian in the fashionable pink Red Sox baseball cap had thought. That the famous writer's widow was either Jewish or had adopted the Jewish custom of mourning, and that her mourning still continued? That she had decided Kurt Vonnegut was right, that mirrors weren't reflective surfaces but *leaks*, portholes to another dimension? And really, wasn't that what she *did* think?

Not portholes, windows. And do I have to care what some librarian from Moo U thinks?

Oh, probably not. But there were so many reflective surfaces in a life, weren't there? Not just mirrors. There were juice glasses to avoid glancing in first thing in the morning and wineglasses not to peer into at sundown. There were so many times when you sat behind the wheel of your car and saw your own face looking back at you from the dashboard instruments. So many long nights when the mind of something . . . *other* . . . might turn to a person, if that person could not keep her mind from turning to it. And how, exactly, did you keep from doing that? How did you not think of something? The mind was a high-kicking, kilt-wearing rebel, to quote the late Scott Landon. It could get up to . . . well, shit fire and save your matches, why not say it? It could get up to such bad-gunky.

And there was something else, too. Something even more frightening. Maybe even if it didn't come to *you*, *you* wouldn't be able to help going to *it*. Because once you stretched those smucking tendons . . . once your life in the real world started to feel like a loose tooth in a sick socket—

She'd be walking downstairs, or getting into the car, or turning on the shower, or reading a book, or opening a crossword magazine, and there would be a feeling absurdly like an oncoming sneeze or

(mein gott, babyluv, mein gott, leedle Leezy—)

an approaching orgasm and she would think, *Oh smuck, I'm not coming, I'm going, I'm going over.* The world would seem to waver and there would be that sense of a whole other world waiting to be born, one where the sweetness curdled and turned to poison after dark. A world that was just a sidestep away, no more than the flick of a hand or the turn of a hip. For a moment she would feel Castle View drop away on every side and she would be Lisey on a tightrope, Lisey walking a knife-edge. Then she'd be back again, a solid (if middle-aged and a little too thin) woman in a solid world, walking down a flight of stairs, slamming a car door, adjusting the hot water, turning the page of a book, or solving eight across: Old-style gift, four-letter word, starts with *B*, ends with *N*.

9

Two days after the dismantled booksnake went north, on what the Portland branch of the National Weather Service would record as the hottest day of the year in Maine and New Hampshire, Lisey went up to the empty study with a boombox and a compact disc titled *Hank Williams' Greatest Hits*. There would be no problem playing the CD, just as there had been no problem running the fans on the day the Minions of Partridge had been up here; all Dooley had done, it turned out, was open the electrical box downstairs and flip off the three breakers that controlled the study's power.

Lisey had no idea how hot it actually was in the study, but knew it had to be a triple-digit number. She could feel her blouse begin sticking to her body and her face dampening as soon as she was at the top of the stairs. Somewhere she had read that women don't *sweat*, they *glow*, and what a crock of shit *that* was. If she stayed up here long, she'd probably pass out with heatstroke, but she didn't intend to stay up here for long. There was a country song she sometimes heard on the radio called 'Ain't Livin' Long Like This'. She didn't know who had written that song or sang it (not Ole Hank), but she could relate to it. She couldn't spend the rest of her life afraid of her own reflection − or what she might see peeking out from behind it − and she couldn't live it afraid that she might at any moment lose her hold on reality and find herself in Boo'ya Moon.

This shite had to end.

She plugged in the boombox, then sat cross-legged on the floor before it and put in the disc. Sweat ran into her eye, stinging, and she knuckled it away. Scott had played a lot of music up here, really blasting it out. When you had a twelve-thousand-dollar stereo system and sound-proofing in the alcove where most of the speakers were, you could really let it rip. The first time he played 'Rockaway Beach' for her, she'd thought the very roof over their heads might lift off. What she was about to play would sound tinny and small by comparison, but she thought it would be enough.

Old-style gift, four letters, begins with B, *ends with* N.

Amanda, sitting on one of those benches, looking out at Southwind Harbor, sitting above the child-murdering woman in the caftan, Amanda saying 'It was something about a story. Your story, Lisey's story. And the afghan. Only he called it the african. *Did he say it was a boop? A beep? A boon?'*

No, Manda, not a boon, although that is a four-letter word, now rather old-fashioned, beginning with B *and ending with* N, *that means gift. But the word Scott used—*

625

That word had been *bool*, of course. The sweat ran down Lisey's face like tears. She let it. 'As in Bool, The End. And at the end you get a prize. Sometimes a candybar. Sometimes an RC from Mulie's. Sometimes a kiss. And sometimes . . . sometimes a story. Right, honey?'

Talking to him felt all right. Because he was still here. Even with the computers gone, and the furniture, and the fancy Swedish stereo system, and the file-cabinets full of manuscripts, and the stacks of galleys (his own and those sent to him by friends and admirers), and the booksnake . . . even with those things gone, she still felt Scott. Of course she did. Because he hadn't finished having his say. He had one more story to tell.

Lisey's story.

She thought she knew which one, because there was only one he had never finished.

She touched one of the dried bloodstains on the carpet and thought about the arguments against insanity, the ones that fell through with a soft shirring sound. She thought how it had been under the yum-yum tree: like being in another world, one of their own. She thought about the Bad-Gunky Folks, the Bloody Bool Folks. She thought about how, when Jim Dooley had seen the long boy, he had stopped screaming and his hands had fallen to his sides. Because the strength had run out of his arms. That was what looking at the bad-gunky did, when the bad-gunky was looking back at you.

'Scott,' she said. 'Honey, I'm listening.'

There was no reply . . . except Lisey replied to herself. *The name of the town was Anarene. Sam the Lion owned the pool-hall. Owned the picture show. And the restau-*

rant, where every tune on the juke seemed to be a Hank Williams tune.

Somewhere something in the empty study seemed to sigh in agreement. Possibly it was just her imagination. In any case, it was time. Lisey still didn't know exactly what she was looking for, but she thought she'd know it when she saw it – surely she'd know it when she saw it, if Scott had left it for her – and it was time to go looking. Because she wasn't living long like this. She couldn't.

She pushed PLAY and Hank Williams's tired, jolly voice began to sing.

> *'Goodbye Joe, me gotta go,*
> *Me-oh-my-oh,*
> *Me gotta go pole the pirogue*
> *Down the bayou . . .'*

SOWISA, babyluv, she thought, and closed her eyes. For a moment the music was still there but hollow and so distant, like music coming down a long corridor, or from the throat of a deep cave. Then sunshine bloomed red on the inside of her eyelids and the temperature dropped twenty or even twenty-five degrees all at a go. A cool breeze, delicious with the smell of flowers, caressed her sweaty skin and blew her sticky hair back from her temples.

Lisey opened her eyes in Boo'ya Moon.

10

She was still sitting cross-legged, but now she was on the edge of the path leading down the purple hill in one direction and under the sweetheart trees in the other. She'd been here before; it was to this exact spot that her husband had brought her before he was her husband, saying there was something he wanted to show her.

Lisey got to her feet, pushing her sweat-dampened hair away from her face, relishing the breeze. The sweetness of the mixed aromas it carried – yes, of course – but even more, the coolness of it. She guessed it was mid-afternoon, the temperature a perfect seventy-five degrees. She could hear birds singing, perfectly ordinary ones by the sound – chickadees and robins for sure, probably finches and maybe a lark for good measure – but no awful laughing things in the woods. It was too early for them, she supposed. No sense of the long boy, either, and that was the best news of all.

She faced the trees and turned on her heels in a slow half-circle. She wasn't looking for the cross, because Dooley had gotten that stuck in his arm and then thrown it aside. It was the *tree* she was looking for, the one that stood just a little forward of the two others on the left side of the path—

'No, that's wrong,' she murmured. 'They were on *either side* of the path. Like soldiers guarding the way into the woods.'

Just like that she saw them. And a third standing a little in front of the one on the left. The third was the biggest, its trunk covered with moss so dense it looked like fur. At its base the ground still looked a little sunken. That was where Scott had buried the brother he had tried so hard to save. And on one side of that sunken place, she saw something with huge hollow eyes staring at her from the high grass.

For a moment she thought it was Dooley, or Dooley's corpse, somehow reanimated and come back to stalk her, but then she remembered how, after clubbing Amanda aside, he'd stripped off the useless, lensless night-vision goggles and thrown them aside. And there they were, lying beside the good brother's grave.

It's another bool hunt, she thought as she walked toward them. *From the path to the tree; from the tree to the grave; from the grave to the goggles. Where next? Where now, babyluv?*

The next station turned out to be the grave-marker, with the horizontal crosspiece turned askew so it was like clock-hands pointing to five past seven. The top of the vertical was stained to a depth of three inches with Dooley's blood, now dried to the maroon, not-quite-varnish color of the stains on the rug in Scott's study. She could still see **PAUL** printed on the crosspiece, and as she lifted it (with real reverence) out of the grass for a closer look, she saw something else as well: the length of matted yellow yarn that had been looped repeatedly around the vertical slat of the cross, then tied firmly. Tied, Lisey had absolutely no doubt, with the same sort of knot as the one that had secured Chuckie G.'s bell to the tree in the woods. The yellow yarn – which had once come spinning off Good Ma's knitting needles as she sat watching television at the farm in Lisbon – was wrapped around the vertical just above the place where the wood was stained dark with earth. And looking at it, she remembered seeing it running into the dark just before Dooley pulled the cross out of his arm and flung it away.

It's the african, the one we dropped by the big rock above the pool. He came back later, some time later, got it, and brought

it here. Unraveled some of it, tied it to the cross, then paid out
more. And expected me to find the rest at the end of it all.

Heart pounding hard and slow in her breast, Lisey dropped the cross and began following the yellow thread away from the path and along the edge of the Fairy Forest, paying it through her hands as the high grass whispered against her thighs and the grasshoppers jumped and the lupin gave up its sweet scent. Somewhere a locust sang its hot summer song and in the woods a crow – *was* it a crow? it sounded like one, a perfectly ordinary crow – called a rusty hello, but there were no cars, no airplanes, no human voices near or far. She walked through the grass, following the line of unknitted afghan, the one in which her sleepless, frightened, failing husband had swaddled on so many cold nights ten years before. Ahead of her, one sweetheart tree stood out a bit from its fellows, spreading its branches, making a pool of inviting shade. Beneath it she saw a tall metal wastebasket and a much larger pool of yellow. The color was dull now, the wool matted and shapeless, like a large yellow wig that has been left out in the rain, or perhaps the corpse of a big old tomcat, but Lisey knew it for what it was as soon as she saw it, and her chest began to hitch. In her mind she could hear The Swinging Johnsons playing 'Too Late to Turn Back Now' and feel Scott's hand as he led her out onto the floor. She followed the line of unraveled yellow yarn under the sweetheart tree and knelt beside what little remained of her mother's wedding present to her youngest daughter and her youngest daughter's husband. She picked it up – it, and whatever lay inside it. She put her face against it. It smelled damp and moldy, an old thing, a forgotten thing, a thing that smelled now more of funerals than of weddings. That was all right. That was just as it should have been. She smelled all the years it had been here, tied to Paul's grave-marker and waiting for her, something like an anchor.

11

A little time later, when her tears had stopped, she put the package (for surely that was what it was) down where it had been and looked at it, touching the place where the yellow yarn unraveled from the shrunken body of the afghan. She marveled that the line hadn't broken, either when Dooley fell on the cross, or when he tore it out of his arm, or when he flung it away – when he slang it forth. Of course it helped that Scott had tied his string to the bottom, but it was still pretty amazing, especially when you considered how long this damned thing had been out here, exposed to the elements. It was a *blue-eyed miracle*, so to speak.

But of course sometimes lost dogs came home; sometimes old strings held and led you to the prize at the end of the bool hunt. She started to unwrap the faded, matted remains of the afghan, then looked into the wastebasket, instead. What she saw made her laugh ruefully. It was nearly full of liquor bottles. One or two looked relatively new, and she was *sure* the one on the very top was, because there had been no such thing as Mike's Hard Lemonade ten years ago. But most of the bottles were old. This was where he'd come to do his drinking in '96, but even blind drunk he'd had too much respect for Boo'ya Moon to litter it up with empty bottles. And would she find other caches if she took the time to look? Maybe. Probably. But this was the only cache that mattered to her. It told her that this was where he'd come to do the last of his life's work.

She thought she had all the answers now except for the big ones, the ones she'd actually come for – how she was supposed to live with the long boy, and how she was supposed to keep from slipping over here to where it lived, especially when it was thinking of her. Perhaps Scott had left her some answers. Even if he hadn't, he'd left her *something* . . . and it was very beautiful under this tree.

Lisey picked up the african again and felt it the way she'd once felt her Christmas presents as a girl. There was a box inside, but it didn't feel a bit like Good Ma's cedar box; it was softer than that, almost mushy, as if, even wrapped in the african and left under the tree, moisture had seeped in over the years . . . and for the first time she wondered how many years they were talking about here. The bottle of Hard Lemonade suggested not very many. And the feel of the thing suggested—

'It's a manuscript box,' she murmured. 'One of his hard cardboard manuscript boxes.' Yes. She was sure of it. Only after two years under this tree . . . or three . . . or four . . . it had turned into a *soft* cardboard box.

Lisey began to unwrap the afghan. Two turns were enough to do the job; that was all that was left. And it *was* a manuscript box, its light gray color darkened to slate by seeping moisture. Scott always put a sticker on the front of his boxes and wrote the title there. The sticker on this one had pulled loose on both sides and curled upward. She pushed it back with her fingers and saw a single word in Scott's strong, dark printing: **LISEY**. She opened the box. The pages inside were lined sheets torn from a notebook. There were perhaps thirty in all, packed tight with quick, dark strokes from one of his felt-tip pens. She wasn't surprised to see that Scott had written in the present tense, that what he had written seemed couched in occasionally childish prose, and that the story seemed to start in the middle. The last was true, she reflected, only if you didn't know how two brothers had survived their crazy father and what happened to one of them and how the other couldn't save him. The story only seemed to start in the middle if you didn't know about gomers and goners and the bad-gunky. It only started in the middle if you didn't know that

12

In February he starts looking at me funny, out of the corners of his eyes. I keep expecting him to yell at me or even whip out his old pocketknife and carve on me. He hasn't done anything like that in a long time but I think it would almost be a relief. It wouldn't let the bad-gunky out of me because there <u>isn't</u> any — I saw the real bad-gunky when Paul was chained up in the cellar, not Daddy's fantasies of it — and there's <u>nothing</u> like that in me. But there's something bad in <u>him,</u> and cutting doesn't let it out. Not this time, although he's tried plenty. I know. I've seen the bloody shirts and underpants in the wash. In the trash, too. If cutting <u>me</u> would help <u>him,</u> I'd let him, because I still love him. More than ever since it's just the two of us. More than ever since what we went through with Paul. That kind of love is a kind of doom, like the bad-gunky. 'Bad-gunky's <u>strong,</u>' he said.

633

But he won't cut.

One day I'm coming back from the shed where I sat for a little while to think about Paul — to think about all the good times we had rolling around this old place — and Daddy grabs me and he shakes. <u>'You went over there!'</u> he shouts in my face. And I can see that however sick I thought he was, it's worse. He's never been as bad as this. 'Why do you go over there? What do you do over there? Who do you talk to? <u>What are you planning?</u>'

All the time shaking me and shaking me, the world tipping up and down. Then my head hits the side of the door and I see stars and I fall down there in the doorway with the heat of the kitchen on my front and the cold of the dooryard on my back.

'No, Daddy,' I say, 'I didn't go anywhere, I was just—'

He bends over me, his hands on his knees, his face down in my face, his skin pale except for two balls of color high up on his cheeks and I see the way his eyes are going back and forth, back and forth, and I know that he and right aren't even writing letters to each other anymore. And I remember Paul saying <u>Scott you dassn't ever cross Daddy when he's not right.</u>

<u>'Don't you tell me you didn't go nowhere you lying little motherfucker, I been ALL OVER THIS MOTHER-SMOCKING HOUSE!'</u>

I think to tell him I was in the shed, but I know that will make things worse instead of better. I think of Paul saying you dassn't cross him when he's not right, when he's getting in the bad, and since I know where he thinks I was, I say yes, Daddy, yes, I went to Boo'ya Moon, but only to put flowers on Paul's grave. And it works. For then, at least. He relaxes. He even grabs my hand and pulls me up and then brushes me off, as though he sees snow or dirt or something on me. There isn't any, but maybe he does see it. Who knows.

He says: 'Is it all right, Scoot? Is his grave all right? Nothing been at it, or at him?'

'Everything's fine, Daddy,' I say.

He says, 'There are Nazis at work, Scooter, did I tell you? I must've. They worship Hitler in the basement. They have a little ceramic statue of the bastard. They think I don't know.'

I'm only ten, but I know Hitler's been one dead dog since the end of the Second World War. I also know that nobody from U.S. Gyppum is worshipping even a statue of him in the basement. I know a third thing, as well, which is never to cross Daddy when he's in the bad-gunky, and so I say, 'What will you do about it?'

He leans close to me and I think he's going to hit me this time sure, at least start shaking me again. But instead he fixes his eyes on mine (I've never seen them so big or so dark) and then he grabs hold of his ear. 'What's this, Scooter? What's it look like to you, old Scoot?'

'Your ear, Daddy,' I say.

He nods, still holding his ear and still holding my eyes with his. All these years later I still see those eyes in my dreams sometimes. 'I'm going to keep it to the ground,' he says. 'And when the time comes . . .' He cocks his finger and makes shooting motions. 'Every smucking one, Scooter. Every sweetmother Nazi in the place.' Maybe he would have done it. My father, out in a blaze of rancid glory. Maybe there would have been one of those news stories — PENNSYLVANIA RECLUSE GOES ON RAMPAGE, KILLS NINE CO-WORKERS, SELF, MOTIVE UNCLEAR — but before he can get around to it, the bad-gunky takes him a different way.

February has been clear and cold, but when March comes in, the weather changes and Daddy changes with it. As the temperatures rise and the skies cloud over and the first sleety rains start to fall, he grows morose and silent. He stops shaving, then showering, then cooking our meals. There comes a day, maybe a third of the way through the month, when I realize that the three days off work he sometimes gets because of the swing shift have stretched to four . . . then five . . . then six. Finally I ask him when he's going back. I'm scared to ask him, because now he spends most of his days either upstairs in his bedroom or downstairs lying on the sofa listening to country music on WWVA out of Wheeling, West Virginia. He hardly ever says anything to me in either place, and I see his eyes going back and forth all the time now as he looks for <u>them</u>, the Bad-Gunky Folks, the Bloody Bool Folks. So — <u>no</u>, I don't want to ask him but I have to, because if he doesn't go back to work, what will happen to us? Ten is old enough to know that with no money coming in, the world will change.

'You want to know when I'm going back to work,' he says in a thoughtful tone of voice. Lying there on the sofa with beard-stubble all over his face. Lying there in an old fisherman's sweater and a pair of Dickies and his bare feet poking out. Lying there while Red Sovine sings 'Giddyup-Go' out of the radio.

'Yes, Daddy.'

He gets up on one elbow and looks at me, and I see then that he is <u>gone</u>. Worse, that something is hiding inside him, growing, getting stronger, biding its time. 'You want to <u>know</u>. <u>When</u>. I'm. Going. <u>Back</u> to <u>work</u>.'

'I guess that's your business,' I say. 'I really just came in to ask if I should put on the coffee.'

He grabs my arm, and that night I see dark blue bruises where his fingers dug into me. Four dark blue bruises in the shape of his fingers. 'Want to <u>know</u>. <u>When</u>. I'm. Going. <u>There</u>.' He lets go and sits up. His eyes are bigger than ever, and they won't stay still. They jitter in their sockets. 'I ain't never going <u>there</u> no more, Scott. <u>That</u> place is <u>closed</u>. <u>That</u> place is all blowed up. Don't you know anything, you dumb little gluefoot motherfucker?' He looks down at the dirty living room carpet. On the radio, Red Sovine gives way to Ferlin Husky.

636

Then Daddy looks up again and he <u>is</u> Daddy, and he says something that almost breaks my heart. 'You may be dumb, Scooter, but you're brave. You're my brave boy. I'm not gonna let it hurt you.'

Then he lies back down on the couch again, and turns his face away, and tells me not to bother him any more, he wants to take a nap.

That night I wake up to the sound of sleet ticking off the window and he's sitting on the side of my bed, smiling down at me. Only it's not him smiling. There's almost nothing in his eyes but the bad-gunky. 'Daddy?' I say, and he says nothing back. I think: <u>He's going to kill me. Going to put his hands around my neck and choke me, and everything we went through, all that with Paul, it will have been for nothing</u>.

But instead he says, in a kind of strangled voice: 'Go back slee',' and gets up off the bed, and walks out in this kind of herky-jerky way, with his chin leading and his ass wagging, like he's pretending to be a drill-sergeant in a parade, or something. A few seconds later I hear this terrible meat crash and I know that he's fallen downstairs, or maybe even threw himself down, and I lie there awhile, not able to get out of bed, hoping he's dead, hoping he's not, wondering what I'll do if he is, who'll take care of me, not caring, not knowing what I hope for the most. Part of me even hopes he'll finish the job, come back and kill me, just finish the job, end the horror of living in that house. Finally I call out, 'Daddy? Are you all right?'

For a long time there's no answer. I lie there listening to the sleet, thinking <u>He's dead, he is, my Daddy's dead, I'm here alone,</u> and then he bellows out of the dark, from down below: 'Yes, all right! Shut up, you little shit! Shut up unless you want the thing in the wall to hear you and come out and eat us both alive! Or do you want it to get in you like it got into Paul?'

I don't say nothing to that, just lay there shaking.

'Answer me!' he bawls. '<u>Answer, nummie, or I'll come up there and make you sorry!</u>'

But I can't, I'm too scared to answer, my tongue is nothing but this tiny huck of dried-up beef jerky lying on the bottom of my mouth. I don't cry, either. I'm even too scared to do that. I just lie there and wait for him to come upstairs and hurt me. Or dead-dog kill me.

Then, after what seems like a very long time — at least an hour, although it couldn't have been more than a minute or two — I hear him mutter something that might have been <u>My fuckin head's bleedin</u> or <u>it won't ever stop sleetin</u>. Whatever it is, it's going away from the stairs and toward the living room, and I know he'll climb on the sofa and go to sleep there. In the morning he'll either wake up or he won't, but either way he's done with me for tonight. But I'm still scared. I'm scared because there <u>is</u> a thing. I don't think it's in the wall, but there is a thing. It got Paul, and it's probably going to get my Daddy and then there's me. I've thought about that a lot, Lisey,

13

From her place under the tree — actually sitting with her back against the tree's trunk — Lisey looked up, almost as startled as she would have been if Scott's ghost had hailed her by name. In a way she supposed that was just what had happened, and really, why should she be surprised? Of course he was talking to her, her and no one else. This was her story, Lisey's story, and even though she was a slow reader, she had already worked her way through a third of the handwritten notebook pages. She thought she'd finish long before dark. That was good. Boo'ya Moon was a sweet place, but only in the daylight.

She looked back down at his last manuscript and was again amazed that he had lived through his childhood. She noted that Scott had lapsed into the past tense only when addressing her, here in her present. She smiled at that and resumed reading, thinking if she had one wish it would be to fly to that lonely kid on her highly hypothetical flour-sack magic carpet and comfort him, if only by whispering in his ear that in time the nightmare would end. Or at least that part of it.

14

I've thought about that a lot, Lisey, and I've come to two conclusions. First, that whatever got Paul was real, and that it was a kind of possessing being that might have had some perfectly mundane basis, maybe even viral or bacteriological. Second, it was <u>not</u> the long boy. Because <u>that</u> thing isn't like <u>anything</u> we can understand. It's its own thing, and better not thought of at all. Ever.

In any case, our hero, little Scott Landon, finally goes back to sleep, and in that farmhouse out in the Pennsylvania countryside, things go on as they had been for yet a few days longer, with Daddy lying on the couch like a ripe and smelly cheese and Scott cooking the meals and washing the dishes (only he says 'warshing the dishees') and the sleet ticking off the windows and the country sounds of WWVA filling the house — Donna Fargo, Waylon Jennings, Johnny Cash, Conway Twitty, 'Country' Charlie Pride, and — of course — Ole Hank. Then one afternoon around three o'clock a brown Chevrolet sedan with U.S. GYPSUM printed on the sides comes up the long driveway, sending out fans of slush on either side. Andrew Landon spends most of his time on the living room couch now, sleeps on it at night and has been lying on it all day, and Scott would never have guessed the old man could still move as fast as he does when he hears that car, which is clearly not the postman's old Ford truck or the meter-reader's van. Daddy is up in a flash and at the window that looks out on the left side of the front porch. He's bending over with the dirty white curtain twitched a little to one side. His hair is standing up in the back and Scott, who is standing in the kitchen doorway with a plate in one hand and a dishtowel over his shoulder, can see the big puffy purple place on the side of Daddy's face where he fell down the stairs that time, and he can see how one leg of Daddy's Dickies is hoicked up almost to the knee. He can hear Dick Curless on the radio singing 'Tombstone Every Mile' and he can see the murder in Daddy's eyes and in the way his lips are pulled down so his lower teeth show. Daddy whirls from the window and the leg of his pants falls back down into place and he strides across to the closet like a crazy scissors and opens it just as the engine of the Chevrolet stops and Scott hears the car door open out there, somebody coming to death's door and not knowing it, not having the slightest sweetmother idea, and Daddy takes the .30–06 out of the closet, the very one he used to end Paul's life. Or the life of the thing inside of him. Shoes clomp up the porch steps. There are three steps, and the middle one squeaks as it has forever, world without end, amen.

'Daddy, no,' I say in a low, pleading voice as Andrew 'Sparky' Landon goes toward the closed door in his new and oddly graceful scissors walk, the rifle held up to high port in front of him. I'm still holding the plate but now my fingers feel numb and I think, _I'm going to drop it. Mothersmuck'll fall to the floor and break, and that man out there, the last sounds he's ever going to hear in his life are a breaking plate and Dick Curless on the radio singing_

<u>about the Hainesville Woods in this stinking forgotten farmhouse</u>. 'Daddy, <u>no</u>,' I say again, pleading with all my heart and trying to put that plea into my eyes.

Sparky Landon hesitates, then stands against the wall so that if the door opens (<u>when</u> the door opens), it will hide him. And a series of knuckle-raps comes on that door even as he does so. I have no trouble reading the words that form silently on my father's whisker-framed lips: <u>Then get rid of him, Scoot.</u>

I go to the door. I switch the plate I meant to dry from my right hand to my left one and open the door. I see the man standing there with terrible clarity. The U.S. Gypsum man isn't very tall — at five-feet-seven or -eight, he isn't really that much taller than I am — but he looks like the very apotheosis of authority in his black billed cap, his khaki pants with their razor-sharp creases and his khaki shirt showing beneath his heavy black car-coat, which is half-unzipped. He's wearing a black tie and carrying some sort of little case, not quite a briefcase (it will be another few years before I learn the word <u>portfolio</u>). He's kind of fat and clean-shaven, with pink and shining cheeks. There are galoshes on his feet, the kind that have zippers rather than buckles. I look at the whole picture and think that if ever there was a man who looked meant to be shot on a porch in the country, it's this man. Even the single hair curling from one of his nostrils proclaims that yes, this is the guy, all right, the very one sent to take a bullet from the scissors-man's gun. Even his name, I think, is the kind you read in the paper under a headline screaming MURDERED.

'Hello, son,' he says, 'you must be one of Sparky's boys. I'm Frank Halsey, from the plant. Head of Personnel.' And he holds out his hand.

I think I won't be able to take it, but I do. And I think I won't be able to talk, but I can do that, too. And my voice sounds normal. I'm all that stands between this man and a bullet in the heart or the head, so it better. 'Yes, sir, I am. I'm Scott.'

'Good to know you, Scott,' he says, looking past me into the living room, and I try to see what he's seeing. I tried to pick it up the day before, but God knows what kind of job I did; I'm just a smocking kid, after all. 'We've kind of been missing your father.'

<u>Well</u>, I think, <u>you're awful close to missing everything, Mr Halsey. Your job, your wife; your kids, if you get em.</u>

'He didn't call you from Philly?' I ask. I have absolutely no idea where this is coming from, or where it's going, but I'm not afraid. Not of this part. I can make shit up all day long. What I'm afraid of is that Daddy will lose control and just start blazing away through the door. Hit Halsey, maybe; hit both of us, probably.

'No, son, he sure didn't.' The sleet keeps ticking down on the porch roof, but at least he's under cover, so I don't absolutely <u>have</u> to invite him in, but what if he invites <u>himself</u> in? How can I stop him? I'm just a kid, standing here in my slippers with a plate in my hand and a dishtowel slung over my shoulder.

'Well, he's been awful worried about his sister,' I say, and think of the baseball biography I've been reading. It's on my bed upstairs. I also think of Daddy's car, which is parked around back, under the shed overhang. If Mr Halsey walked to the far end of the porch, he'd see it. 'She's got the disease that killed that famous ballplayer from the Yankees.'

'Sparky's sister's got Lou Gehrig's? Aw, shit — I mean shoot. I didn't even know he <u>had</u> a sister.'

<u>Neither did I</u>, I think.

'Son — Scott — that's a shame. Who's watching out for you boys while he's gone?'

'Mrs Cole from down the road.' Jackson Cole is the name of

the guy who wrote <u>Iron Man of the Yankees.</u> 'She comes in every day. And besides, Paul knows four different ways to make meatloaf.'

Mr Halsey chuckles. 'Four ways, huh? When's Sparky gonna be back?'

'Well, she can't walk anymore, and she breathes like this.' I take a big, whooping gasp of air. It's easy, because all at once my heart is beating like crazy. It was going slow when I was pretty sure Daddy was going to kill Mr Halsey, but now that I see a chance we might get out of it, it's going six licks to the minute.

'Aw, <u>sugar</u>,' says Mr Halsey. Now he thinks he understands everything. 'Well, that's just about the worst thing I ever heard of.' He reaches under his coat and drags out his wallet. He opens it and takes out a one-dollar bill. Then he remembers that I supposedly have a brother and takes out another one. And all at once, Lisey, the strangest thing happened. All at once I wished my father <u>would</u> kill him.

'Here, son,' he says, and <u>also</u> all at once I know, like reading his mind, that he's forgotten my name, and I hate him even more. 'Take it. One for you and one for your brother. Treat yourselves at that little store down the road.'

I don't want his smucking dollar (and Paul has no more use for his), but I take them and say thank you, sir, and he says you're welcome, son, and he ruffles my hair, and while he's doing that I glance over to my left and see one of my father's eyes peering through the crack in the door. I see the muzzle of the rifle, too. Then Mr Halsey finally goes back down the steps. I close the door and my father and I watch as he gets into his company car and starts backing down the long driveway. It comes to me that if he gets stuck he'll walk up again and ask to use the phone and end up dying anyway, but he doesn't get stuck and will kiss his wife hello that night after all, and tell her he gave two poor boys a couple of dollars to treat themselves with. I look down and see I'm still holding the two bills and I give them to my father. He tucks them away into his pants pocket without so much as a look.

'He'll be back,' Daddy says. 'Him or some other. You did a good job, Scott, but tape will only hold a wet package for so long.'

I take a hard stare at him and see that he is my Daddy. At some point while I was talking to Mr Halsey, my Daddy came back. It's the last time I'll ever really see him.

He sees me looking at him and kind of nods. Then he looks at the .30—06. 'I'm going to get rid of this,' he says. 'I'm going down, that can't be—'

'No, Daddy—'

'—can't be helped, but I'll be sweetfucked if I'll take a bunch of people like that Halsey with me, so they can put me on the six o'clock news for the gomers to drool over. They'd put you and Paul there too. Of course they would. Alive or dead, you'd be the lunatic's boys.'

'Daddy, you'll be okay,' I tell him, and try to hug him. 'You're okay right now!'

He pushes me away, kind of laughing. 'Yah, and sometimes people with malaria can quote Shakespeare,' he says. 'You stay here, Scotty, I got a chore to do. It won't take long.' He walks off down the hall, past the bench I finally jumped off of all those years ago, and into the kitchen. Head down, the deer-gun in one hand. Once he's out the kitchen door I follow him and I'm looking out the window over the sink when he crosses the backyard, coatless in the sleet, head still down, still holding the .30—06. He puts it on the icy ground only long enough to push the cover off the dry well. He needs both hands to do that because the sleet has bound the cover to the brick. Then he picks the gun up again, looks at it for a second — almost like he's saying goodbye — and slides it into the gap he's made. After that he comes back to the house with his head still down and ice-drops darkening the shoulders of his shirt. It's only then that I notice his feet are bare. I don't think he ever realizes at all.

He doesn't seem surprised to see me in the kitchen. He takes out the two dollar bills Mr Halsey gave me, looks at them, then looks at me. 'You sure you don't want these?' he asks.

I shake my head. 'Not if they were the last two dollar bills on earth.'

I can see he likes that answer. 'Good,' he says. 'But now let me tell you something, Scott. You know your nana's china breakfront in the dining room?'

'Sure.'

'If you look in the blue pitcher on the top shelf, you're going to find a roll of money. <u>My</u> money, not Halsey's — do you understand the difference?'

'Yes,' I say.

'Yeah, I bet you do. You're a lot of things, but dumb hasn't ever been one of them. If I were you, Scotty, I'd take that roll of bills — it's around seven hundred dollars — and put my act on the road. Stick five in my pocket and the rest in my boot. Ten's too young to be on the road, even for a little while, and I think the chances are probably ninety-five in a hundred somebody'll rob you of your roll even before you make it over the bridge into Pittsburgh, but if you stay here, something bad's going to happen. Do you know what I'm talking about?'

'Yes, but I can't go,' I say.

'There's a lot of things people think they can't do and then discover they can when they find themselves tight-wired,' Daddy says. He looks down at his feet, which are all pink and raw-looking. 'If you were to make it to the Burg, I believe a boy bright enough to

get rid of Mr Halsey with a story about Lou Gehrig's Disease and
a sister I don't have might be bright enough to look under the C's
in the telephone book and find Child Welfare. Or you might could
knock around a little bit and maybe find an even better situation,
if you wasn't to get separated from that roll of cash. Seven hundred
parceled out five or ten bucks at a time will last a kid awhile, if
he's smart enough not to get picked up by the cops and lucky enough
not to get robbed of any more of it than what happens to be in his
pocket.'

    I tell him again: 'I can't go.'

    'Why not?'

    But I can't explain. Some of it is having lived almost my
whole life in that farmhouse, with almost no one for company but
Daddy and Paul. What I know of other places I have gotten mostly
from three sources: the television, the radio, and my imagination.
Yes, I've been to the movies, and I've been to the Burg half a dozen
times, but always with my father and big brother. The thought of
going out into that rearing strangeness alone scares the living Jesus
out of me. And, more to the point, I love him. Not in the simple
and uncomplicated (until the last few weeks, at least) way I loved
Paul, but yes, I love him. He has cut me and hit me and called me
<u>smuck-head</u> and <u>nummie</u> and <u>gluefoot mothersmucker,</u> he has terror-
ized many of my childhood days and sent me to bed on many nights
feeling small and stupid and worthless, but those bad times have
yielded their own perverse treasures; they have turned each kiss to
gold, each of his compliments, even the most offhand, into things
to be treasured. And even at ten — because I'm his son, his blood?
maybe — I understand that his kisses and compliments are always
sincere; they are always true things. He is a monster, but the monster
is not incapable of love. That was the horror of my father, little
Lisey: he loved his boys.

'I just can't,' I say.

He thinks about this — about whether or not to press me, I suppose — and then just nods again. 'All right. But listen to me, Scott. What I did to your brother I did to save your life. Do you know that?'

'Yes, Daddy.'

'But if I were to do something to you, it would be different. It would be so bad I might go to hell for it, even if there was something else inside making me do it.' His eyes shift away from mine then, and I know he's seeing them again, <u>them,</u> and that pretty soon it won't be him I'm talking to anymore. Then he looks back at me and I see him clearly for the last time. 'You won't let me go to hell, will you?' he asks me. 'You wouldn't let your Daddy go to hell and burn there forever, mean as I've been to you some of the time?'

'No, Daddy,' I say, and I can hardly talk.

'You promise? On your brother's name?'

'On Paul's name.'

He looks away, back into the corner. 'I'm going to lie down,' he says. 'Fix yourself something to eat if you want, but don't leave this smucking kitchen all beshitted.'

That night I wake up — or something wakes me up — and I hear the sleet coming down on the house harder than ever. I hear a crash out back and know it's a tree falling over from the weight of ice on it. Maybe it was another tree falling over that woke me up, but I don't think so. I think I heard him on the stairs, even though he's trying to be quiet. There's no time to do anything but slide out of bed and hide underneath it, so that's what I do even though I know it's hopeless, under the bed is where kids <u>always</u> hide, and it'll be the first place he looks.

I see his feet come in the door. They're still bare. He never says a word, just walks over to the bed and stands beside it. I think he'll stand beside it like he did before, then maybe sit down on it, but he never. Instead I hear him make a kind of grunting sound, like he does when he's lifting something heavy, a box or something, and he goes up on the balls of his feet, and there's a whistling in the air, and then a terrific SPUH-RUNNGGG noise, and the mattress and the box-spring both bow down in the middle, and dust puffs along the floor, and the point of the pickaxe from out in the shed comes shooting through the bottom of my bed. It stops in front of my face, not an inch from my mouth. It seems like I can see every flake of rust on it, and the shiny place where it scraped on one of the bedsprings. It stays still for a second or two, then there's more grunting and a terrific pig-squealing as he tries to pull it out. He tries hard, but it's good and stuck. The point wiggles and waggles back and forth in front of my face, and then he leaves off. I see his fingers appear below the edge of the bed then, and know that he's rested his palms on the balls of his knees. He's bending down, means to look under the bed and make sure I'm there before working that pickaxe free.

I don't think. I just close my eyes and go. It's the first time since I buried Paul and it's the first time from the second floor. I have just a second to think I'll fall, but I don't care, anything's better than hiding under the bed and seeing the stranger wearing my Daddy's face look under and see me looking back, cornered; anything's better than seeing the bad-gunky stranger who owns him now.

And I do fall, but only a little, only a couple of feet, and only, I think, because I believed I would. So much about Boo'ya Moon is about simple belief; there, seeing really is believing, at least some of the time . . . and as long as you don't wander too far into the woods and get lost.

It was night there, Lisey, and I remember it well because it was the only time I went there at night on purpose.

15

'Oh, Scott,' Lisey said, wiping at her cheeks. Each time he broke from the present tense and spoke to her directly was like a blow, but sweet. 'Oh, I'm so sorry.' She checked to see how many pages were left – not many. Eight? No, ten. She bent to them again, turning each into the growing pile in her lap as she read it.

16

I leave a cold room where a thing wearing my father's skin is trying to kill me and sit up beside my brother's grave on a summer night softer than velvet. The moon rides the sky like a tarnished silver dollar, and the laughers are having a party deep in the Fairy Forest. Every now and then something else — something deeper in, I think — lets out a roar. Then the laughers are quiet for awhile, but I guess whatever amuses them is eventually more than they can bear in silence, because up they start all over again — first one, then two, then half a dozen, then the whole damn Institute of Risibility. Something too big to be a hawk or an owl sails voicelessly across the moon, some kind of night-hunting bird special to this place, I guess, special to Boo'ya Moon. I can smell all the perfumes that Paul and I loved so much, but now they smell sour and curdled and somehow bed-pissy; like if you breathed too deep of them they'd sprout claws way up in your nose and dig in there. Down Purple Hill I see drifting jellyfish globes of light. I don't know what they are, but I don't like them. I think that if they touch me, they might

649

latch on, or maybe burst and leave a itchy-sore place that would spread like poison ivy if you touched it.

It's creepy by Paul's grave. I don't want to be afraid of him, and I'm not, not really, but I keep thinking of the thing inside him, and wondering if maybe it's in him still. And if things over here that are nice in daylight turn to poison at night, maybe a sleeping bad thing, even one hibernating way down in dead and rotting flesh, could come back to life. What if it shot Paul's arms out of the ground? What if it made his dirty dead hands grab me? What if his grinning face came rising up to my own, with dirt running from the corners of his eyes like tears?

I don't want to cry, ten is too old to cry (especially if you've been through the things I have), but I'm starting to blubber, I can't help it. Then I see one sweetheart tree standing a little bit apart from all the others, with its branches spread out in what looks like a low cloud.

And to me, Lisey, that tree looked ... _kind._ I didn't know why then, but I think that now, all these years later, I do. Writing this has brought it back. The nightlights, those scary cold balloons drifting just above the ground, wouldn't go under it. And as I got closer to it, I realized that this one tree, at least, smelled as sweet — or almost as sweet — at night as it did in the daytime. That's the tree you're sitting under now, little Lisey, if you're reading this last story. And I'm very tired. I don't think I can do the rest of it the justice it deserves, although I know I must try. It's my last chance to talk to you, after all.

Let us say that there's a little boy who sits in the shelter of that tree for — well, who knows, really? Not all that long night, but until the moon (which always seems to be full here, have you noticed?) is down and he has dozed in and out of half a dozen strange and sometimes lovely dreams, at least one of which will later become the basis of a novel. Long enough for him to name that wonderful shelter the Story Tree.

And long enough for him to know that something awful — something far worse than the paltry evil which has seized his father — has turned its casual gaze toward him . . . and marked him for later notice (perhaps) . . . and then turned its obscene and unknowable mind once more away. That was the first time I sensed the fellow who has lurked behind so much of my life, Lisey, the thing that has been the darkness to your light, and who also feels — as I know you always have — that everything is the same. That is a wonderful concept, but it has its dark side. I wonder if you know? I wonder if you ever will?

17

'I know,' Lisey said. 'I do now. God help me, I do.'

She looked at the pages again. Six left. Only six, and that was good. Afternoons in Boo'ya Moon were long, but she thought that this one had finally begun to fade. It was really time to be getting back. Back to her house. Her sisters. Her *life*.

She had begun to understand how it was to be done.

18

There comes a time when I hear the laughers beginning to draw closer to the edge of the Fairy Forest, and I think their amusement has taken on a sardonic, perhaps stealthy undertone. I peer around the trunk of my sheltering tree and think I see dark shapes slipping from the darker mass of the trees at the edge of the woods. This may only be my overactive imagination, but I don't think so. I think my imagination, febrile as it is, has been exhausted by the many shocks of the long day and longer night, and that I have been reduced to seeing exactly what is there. As if to confirm this, there comes a slobbering chuckle from the high grass <u>not twenty yards from where I am crouching.</u> Once more I don't think about what I'm doing; I simply close my eyes and feel the chill of my bedroom fold itself around me once more. A moment later I'm sneezing from the disturbed dust under my bed. I rear up, face contorted in a nearly gruesome effort to sneeze as quietly as possible, and I thump my forehead on the broken box-spring. If the pick had still been sticking through I might have gashed myself badly or even put out one of my eyes, but it's gone.

I drag myself out from under my bed on my elbows and my knees, conscious that a sickly five o'clock light is soaking in through the window. It's sleeting harder than ever, by the sound, but I hardly notice. I swivel my head from my floor-level position, peering stupidly around at the shambles that used to be my bedroom. The closet door has been pulled off the top hinge and leans drunkenly into the room from the lower one. My clothes have been scattered and many of them — <u>most</u> of them, it looks like — have been torn apart, as if the thing inside of Daddy has taken out on them what it couldn't take out on the boy who should have been inside them. Far worse, it has torn my few treasured paperback books — sports biographies and science fiction novels, mostly — to shreds. Their flimsy covers lie in pieces everywhere. My bureau has been overturned, the drawers slung to the corners of the room. The hole where the pickaxe went through my bed looks as big as a moon crater, and I think: <u>That's where my belly would have been, if I'd been lying there.</u> And there's a faint sour smell. It reminds me of how Boo'ya Moon smelled at night, but it's more familiar. I try to put a name on it and can't. All I can think of is <u>bad fruit,</u> and although that's not quite right, it turns out to be very close.

I don't want to leave the room, but I know I can't stay there because eventually he'll be back. I find a pair of jeans that aren't ripped and put them on. My sneakers are gone, I don't know where, but maybe my boots will still be in the mudroom. And my coat. I'll put them on and run out into the sleet. Down the driveway, following Mr Halsey's half-frozen slushy car-tracks, to the road. Then down the road to Mulie's Store. I'll run for my life, into some future I can't even imagine. Unless, that is, he catches me first and kills me.

I have to climb over the bureau, which is blocking the door, to get into the hall. Once I'm out there I see the thing has knocked down all the pictures and knocked holes in the walls, and I know I'm looking at more of its anger at not being able to get at me.

Out here the sour fruit smell is strong enough to recognize. There was a Christmas party at U.S. Gyppum last year. Daddy went because he said it would 'look funny' if he didn't. The man who drew his name gave him a jug of homemade blackberry wine for a present. Now, Andrew Landon has got a lot of problems (and he'd probably be the first to admit it, if caught in an honest moment), but alcohol isn't one of them. He poured himself a jelly-glass of that wine before dinner one night — between Christmas and New Year's, this was, with Paul chained in the cellar — took one sip, grimaced, started to pour it down the sink, then saw me looking and held it out.

<u>You want to try this, Scott?</u> he asked. <u>See what all the shouting's about? Hey, if you like it, you can have the whole sweet-mother gallon.</u>

I'm as curious about booze as any kid, I guess, but that smell was too fruity-rancid. Maybe the stuff makes you happy like I've

653

seen on TV, but I could never lick that gone-dead fruit smell. I shook my head.

You're a wise child, Scooter ole Scoot, he said, and poured the stuff in the jelly-glass down the sink. But he must have saved the rest of the jug (or just forgot about it) because that's what I smell now, sure as God made little fishes, and strong. By the time I get to the foot of the stairs it's a stench, and now I hear something besides the steady rattle of the sleet on the boards and the tinny tick-tock of it on the windows: George Jones. It's Daddy's radio, tuned to WWVA like always, playing very soft. And I also hear snoring. The relief is so great that tears go spilling down my cheeks. The thing I've been most afraid of is that he's laid up, waiting for me to show myself. Now, listening to those long, ragged snores, I know that he's not.

Nevertheless, I'm careful. I detour through the dining room so I can come into the living room from behind the sofa. The dining room is also a shambles. Nana's breakfront has been overturned, and it looks to me like he made a pretty good effort to turn it into kindling. All the dishes are broken. So's the blue pitcher, and the money inside it has been torn to pieces. Green shreds have been flung every whichever. Some even hang from the central light fixture like New Year's Eve confetti. Apparently the thing inside Daddy has no more use for money than it does for books.

In spite of those snores, in spite of being on the couch's blind side, I peer into the living room like a soldier peering over the lip of a foxhole after an artillery barrage. It's a needless precaution. His head's hanging off one end of the couch and his hair, which he hasn't taken the scissors to since before Paul went bad, is so long it's almost touching the rug. I could have marched through there crashing a pair of cymbals and he wouldn't have stirred. Daddy isn't just asleep in the jumbled wreckage of that room; he is un-smucking-conscious.

A little further in and I see there's a cut running up one cheek, and his closed eyes have a purplish, exhausted look. His lips have slid back from his teeth, making him look like an old dog that fell asleep trying to snarl. He covers the couch with an old Navajo blanket to keep off grease and spilled food, and he's wrapped part of it over him. He must have been tired of busting things up by the time he got in here, because he's poked out the eye of the television and smashed the glass over his dead wife's studio portrait and called it good. The radio's in its usual place on the end-table and that gallon jug is on the floor beside it. I look at the jug and can't hardly believe what I'm seeing: there's not but an inch or so left. It's almost impossible for me to believe he's drunk so much — he who isn't used to drinking at all — but the stink hanging around him, so thick I can almost see it, is very persuasive.

The pickaxe leans against the head of the sofa, and there's a piece of paper stuck on the end that came down through my bed. I know it's a note he's left for me, and I don't want to read it, but I have to. He's written on three lines, but there are only eight words. Too few to ever forget.

KILL ME
THEN PUT ME WITH PAUL
PLEASE

19

Lisey, crying harder than ever, turned this page into her lap along with the others. Now there were only two left. The printing had grown loose, a little wandering, not always sticking to the lines, quite clearly tired. She knew

655

what came next – *I put a pickaxe in his head while he was a-sleepun*, he had told her under the yum-yum tree – and did she have to read the details here? Was there anything in the marriage vows about having to subject yourself to your dead husband's confession of patricide?

And yet those pages called to her, *cried* to her like some lonely thing that has lost everything but its voice. She dropped her eyes to the final pages, determined that if she must finish, she would do so as quickly as she could.

20

I don't want to, but I take up the pickaxe anyway and stand there with it in my hands, looking at him, the lord of my life, the tyrant of all my days. I have hated him often and he has never given me cause to love him enough, I know that now, but he has given me some, especially during those nightmare weeks after Paul went bad. And in that five o'clock living room with the day's first gray light creeping in and the sleet ticking like a clock and the sound of his wheezing snores below me and an ad on the radio for some discount furniture store in Wheeling, West Virginia, I will never visit, I know it comes down to a bald choice between those two, love and hate. Now I'll find out which one rules my child's heart. I can let him live and run down the road to Mulie's, run into some unknown new life, and that will condemn him to the hell he fears and in many ways deserves. <u>Richly</u> deserves. First hell on earth, the hell of a cell in some looneybin, and then maybe hell forever after, which is what he really fears. Or I can kill him and set him free. This choice is mine to make, and there is no God to help me make it, for I believe in none.

Instead I pray to my brother, who loved me until the bad-gunky stole his heart and mind. I ask him to tell me what to do, if he's there. And I get an answer — although whether it is really from Paul or just from my own imagination masquerading as Paul I suppose I'll never know. In the end, I don't see that it matters; I need an answer and I get one. In my ear, just as clearly as he ever spoke when he was alive, Paul says: 'Daddy's prize is a kiss.'

I take hold on the pickaxe then. The ad on the radio finishes and Hank Williams comes on, singing 'Why don't you love me like you used to do, How come you treat me like a worn-out shoe?' And

21

Here three lines were blank before the words took up again, this time in the past tense and addressing her directly. The rest was crammed together with almost no regard for the blue-ruled notebook lines, and Lisey was sure he had written the final passage in a single rush. She read it the same way. Turning over to the last page as she did and continuing on, continually wiping away her tears so she could see clearly enough to get the sense of what he was saying. The *mental seeing* part, she found, was hellishly easy. The little boy, barefooted, wearing perhaps his only pair of untorn jeans, raising the pickaxe over his sleeping father in the gray pre-dawn light while the radio plays, and for a moment it only hangs there in the air that reeks of black-berry wine and everything is the same. Then

22

I brought it down. Lisey, I brought it down in love — I swear — and I killed my father. I thought I might have to hit him with it again

657

but that single blow was enough and all my life it's been on my mind, all my life it's been the thought inside every thought, I get up thinking <u>I killed my father</u> and go to bed thinking it. It has moved like a ghost behind every line I ever wrote in every novel, any story: <u>I killed my father.</u> I told you that day under the yum-yum tree, and I think that gave me just enough relief to keep me from exploding completely five years or ten or fifteen down the line. But a statement isn't the same as <u>telling.</u>

Lisey, if you're reading this, I've gone on. I think my time is short, but such time as I had (and it was very good time) is all down to you. You have given me so much. Just give me this much more — your eye on these last few words, the hardest I've ever written.

No tale can tell how ugly such dying is, even if it's instantaneous. Thank God I didn't hit him a glancing blow and have to do it again; thank God there was no squealing or crawling. I hit him dead center, right where I meant to, but even mercy is ugly in the living memory; that's a lesson I learned well when I was just ten. His skull exploded. Hair and blood and brains showered up, all over that blanket he'd spread on the back of the couch. Snot flew out of his nose and his tongue fell out of his mouth. His head went over to the side and I heard soft puttering noises as the blood and brains leaked out of his head. Some of it splashed on my feet and it was warm. Hank Williams was still on the radio. One of Daddy's hands made a fist, then opened again. I smelled shit and knew he'd left a load in his pants. And I knew that was the last of him.

The pickaxe was still stick out his head.

I crep away into the corn of the room and curl up and I cried. I cried and cried. I guess maybe I slep some too, I don't kno, but there came a time when it was brighter and the sun was almost out and I think it might have been noonish. If so, I guess 7 hours or so wen by. That was when I first tried to take my Daddy to Boo'ya Moon and couldn't. I thought if I got something to eat, so I did but still I couldn't. Then I thought if I took a bath and got the blut off me, his blood, and clean up some of the mess around wehre he was but still I coulnt. I tried and tried. Off and on quite a bit. Two days, I guess. Sometime I'd look at his wrap in the blanket and make believe he was say <u>You keep on pluggin Scoot you old sumbitch, you'll make it</u> like in a story. I'd try, then I'd clean, try and clean, eet somethig and try summore. I cleen that hole house! Top to bottom! Once I went to Boo'ya by myself prove I still had the nack and I dit but I coulnt take my daddy. I trite so hard Lisey.

23

Several blank lines here. At the bottom of the last page he had written: **Some things are like an ANCHOR Lisey do you remember?**

'I do, Scott,' she murmured. 'I do. And your father was one of them, wasn't he?' Wondering how many days and nights in all. How many days and nights alone with the corpse of Andrew 'Sparky' Landon before Scott finally gave up plugging and invited the world in. Wondering how in God's name he had stood up to it without going completely insane.

There was a little more on the other side of the sheet. She flipped it over and saw that he had answered one of her questions.

Five days I tride. Finaly gave up and warped him in that blanket and put him down the dry well. The next time the sleet stoped I went to Mulie's and said 'My Daddy's took my big brother and I guess they up and left me.' They took me to the County Sheriff,

a fat old man named Gosling and he took me to the Child Welfare and I was 'on the County' as they say. So far as I know Gosling was the only cop who ever went up there to the home place, and big deal. My own Daddy once said 'Sheriff Gosling couldn't find his own ass after he took a shit.'

Below this was another space of three lines, and when the printing resumed – the last four lines of communication from her husband – she could see the effort he had made to get hold of himself, to find his adult self. He had made the effort for her, she thought. No, *knew*.

Babyluv: If <u>you</u> need an anchor to hold your place in the world – not Boo'ya Moon but the one we shared, <u>use the african.</u> You know how to get it back. Kisses – at least a thousand,

Scott

P.S. Everything the same. I love you.

24

Lisey could have sat there with his letter for a long time, but the afternoon was fleeting. The sun was still yellow, but it was now approaching the horizon and would soon begin to take on that thundering orange cast she remembered so well. She didn't want to be on the path even close to sunset, and that meant she had better get moving now. She decided to leave Scott's final manuscript here, but not under the Story Tree. She would leave it at the head of the faint hollow that marked Paul Landon's final resting-place, instead.

She walked back to the sweetheart tree with the moss-shaggy trunk, the one that looked weirdly like a palm tree, carrying the remains of the yellow afghan and the damp and mushy manuscript box. She put them down, then picked up the marker with **PAUL** printed on the horizontal arm. It was splintered and bloody and all askew, but not really broken. Lisey was able to straighten the horizontal arm and slip the marker back into its former place. When she did, she spied something lying nearby, something almost hidden in the high grass. She knew what it was even before she picked it up: the hypodermic that had never been used, now rustier than ever, its cap still on.

Playin with fire there, Scoot, his father had said when Scott had suggested that maybe they could drug Paul . . . and his father had been right.

Damn if I didn't think I pricked myself on it! Scott had said to Lisey when he had taken her to Boo'ya Moon from their bedroom at The Antlers. *That'd be a joke on me, all right – after all those years! – but the cap's still on!*

It was still on now. And the nighty-night stuff was still inside, as if all the years between hadn't existed.

Lisey kissed the dull glass of the hypodermic's barrel – why she could not have said – and put it into the box with Scott's last story. Then, bundling the wasted remains of Good Ma's wedding afghan in her arms, Lisey went to the path. She glanced briefly at the board lying in the high grass to one side of it, the words on it more faded and ghostlike than ever but still discernible, still reading **TO THE POOL**, and then passed under the trees. At first she stalked rather than walked, her gait made awkward by her fear that a certain something might be lurking nearby, that its strange and terrible mind would sense her. Then, little by little, she relaxed. The long boy was somewhere else. It

661

crossed her mind that it might not even be in Boo'ya Moon at all. If it was, it had gone deep into the forest. Lisey Landon was only a small part of its business in any case, and if what she was about to do worked, she would become a smaller part of it still, because her latest intrusions in this exotic but frightening world had been involuntary, and were about to cease. With Dooley out of her life, she couldn't think why she would ever need to come back on purpose.

Some things are like an anchor Lisey do you remember?

Lisey walked faster, and when she came to where the silver spade lay on the path, its bowl still dark with Jim Dooley's blood, she stepped over it with no more than a single absent look.

By then she was nearly running.

25

When she came back to the empty study, the top of the barn was hotter than ever but Lisey was cool enough, because for the second time she had come back soaked to the skin. This time wrapped around her middle like some strange wide belt was the remains of the yellow afghan, also sopping wet.

Use the african, Scott had written, and had told her she knew how to get it back – not to Boo'ya Moon but to *this* world. And of course she did. She'd waded into the pool with it wrapped around her, then waded out again. And then, standing on the firm white sand of that beach for what was almost certainly the last time, facing not toward the sad and silent spectators on the benches but away from them, looking at the waters above which the eternally full moon would eventually rise, she had closed her eyes and had simply – what? Wished herself back? No, it was more active than that, less wistful . . . but not without sadness, for all that.

'I hollered myself home,' she told the long and empty room – empty now of his desks and word-processors, his books and his music, empty of his life. 'That's what it was. Wasn't it, Scott?'

But there was no answer. It seemed he had finally finished having his say. And maybe that was good. Maybe that was for the best.

Now, while the african was still wet from the pool, she could go back to Boo'ya Moon with it wrapped around her, if she wanted; wrapped in such damp magic she might be able to go even further, to other worlds beyond Boo'ya Moon . . . for she had no doubt such worlds existed, and that the folks who rested on the benches eventually tired of sitting and rose from their seats and found some of them. Wrapped in the soaking african she might even be able to fly, as she had in her dreams. But she wouldn't. Scott had dreamed awake, sometimes brilliantly – but that had been his talent and his job. For Lisey Landon, one world was more than enough, although she suspected she might always harbor a bone-lonely place in her heart for that other one, where she had seen the sun setting in its house of thunder while the moon rose in its house of silver silence. But hey, what the smuck. She had a place to hang her hat and a good car to drive; she had rags for the bod and shoes for the feet. She also had four sisters, one of whom was going to need plenty of help and understanding in order to get through the years ahead. It would be best to let the african dry, to let its beautiful, lethal weight of dreams and magic evaporate, to let it become an anchor again. She would eventually scissor it into pieces and always keep one with her, a bit of anti-magic, a thing to keep her feet on the earth, a ward against wandering.

In the meantime, she wanted to dry her hair and get out of her wet clothes.

Lisey walked to the stairs, dripping dark drops on some of the places where she'd bled. The wrap of the african slipped down to her hips and became skirtlike, exotic, even a little sexy. She turned and looked back over her shoulder at the long empty room, which seemed to dream in the dusty shafts of late August sunlight. She was golden in that light herself and looked young again, although she didn't know it.

'I guess I'm done up here,' she said, feeling suddenly hesitant. 'I'll be going. Bye.'

She waited. For what, she didn't know. There was nothing. There was a sense of *something*.

She lifted a hand as if to wave, then dropped it again, as if embarrassed. She smiled a little and one tear fell down her cheek, unnoticed. 'I love you, honey. Everything the same.'

Lisey went down the stairs. For a moment her shadow stayed, and then it was gone, too.

The room sighed. Then it was silent.

Center Lovell, Maine

August 4, 2005

AUTHOR'S STATEMENT

There really *is* a pool where we – and in this case by *we* I mean the vast company of readers and writers – go down to drink and cast our nets. *Lisey's Story* references literally dozens of novels, poems, and songs in an effort to illustrate that idea. I'm not saying that to try and impress anyone with my cleverness – much here is heartfelt, very little is clever – but because I want to acknowledge some of these lovely fish, and give credit where credit is due.

I'm so hot, please give me ice: *Trunk Music*, by Michael Connelly.

Suck-oven: *Cold Dog Soup*, by Stephen Dobyns.

Sweetmother: *The Stones of Summer*, by Dow Mossman.

Pafko at the wall: *Underworld*, by Don DeLillo.

Worse things waiting: The title of a short story collection by Manley Wade Wellman.

No one loves a clown at midnight: Lon Chaney

He was sweepin, ya sonsabitches: *The Last Picture Show*, by Larry McMurtry.

Empty Devils: *The Tempest*, by William Shakespeare ('Hell is empty, and all the devils are here.')

I Ain't Livin' Long Like This was written by Rodney

665

Crowell. Besides Crowell's version, the song has been recorded by Emmylou Harris, Jerry Jeff Walker, Webb Wilder, and Ole Waylon.

And, of course, everything by Ole Hank. If there's a ghost in these pages, it's as much his as Scott Landon's.

I want to take a moment of your time to thank my wife, too. She's not Lisey Landon, nor are her sisters Lisey's sisters, but I have enjoyed watching Tabitha, Margaret, Anne, Catherine, Stephanie, and Marcella do 'the sister thing' for the last thirty years. The sister thing is never the same from day to day, but it's always interesting. For the stuff I got right, thank them. For the stuff I got wrong, cut me some slack, okay? I've got a great older brother, but I *was* sister-deprived.

Nan Graham edited this book. Quite often reviewers of novels – especially novels by people who usually sell great numbers of books – will say 'So-and-so would have benefited from actual editing.' To those tempted to say that about *Lisey's Story*, I would be happy to submit sample pages from my first-draft manuscript, complete with Nan's notes. I had first-year French essays that came back cleaner. Nan did a wonderful job, and I thank her for sending me out in public with my shirt tucked in and my hair combed. As for the few cases in which the author overruled her . . . all I can say is, 'reality is Ralph.'

Thanks to L. and R.D., who were there to read these pages in first draft.

Finally, great thanks to Burton Hatlen, of the University of Maine. Burt was the greatest English teacher I ever had. It was he who first showed me the way to the pool, which he called 'the language-pool, the myth-pool, where we all go down to drink'. That was in 1968. I have trod the path that leads there often in the years since, and I can think of no better place to spend one's days; the water is still sweet, and the fish still swim.

S.K.

I will holler you home

Don't miss BLAZE by Richard Bachman coming from Hodder and published for the first time ever in June 2007.

Turn over to read the original first chapter . . .

The opening of BLAZE was written in 1972, the author using his wife's Olivetti typewriter. After producing the first draft of BLAZE, the typewriter's next job was a tale focused on a prom-night at a high school.

Chapter 1

George was somewhere in the dark. Blaze couldn't see him, but the voice was loud and clear; rough, washpish, a little hoarse. George always sounded as if he always had a cold. He'd had an accident as a kid. He never said what, but there was a dilly of a scar on his adam's apple.

"Not that one, you goddam dummy. It's got those flower decals all over it. Get a Chevvy or a Ford. Two years old. No more, no less. Dark blue or green. Nobody remembers them."

George passed the VW with the flower decals and kept walking. The faint thump of the base reached him even here, in the beer joint's parking lot. It was Saturday night and the place was crowde The air was bitterly cold; he had hitched a ride into town, but now he had been in the open air for almost forty minutes and his ears were numb. He had forgotten his hat. He always forgot something. He had started to take his hands out of his jacket pocket and put them over his ears, but George put the kibosh on that. His ears could freeze, but not his hands. You didn't hot-wire a car with your ears. It was three above zero.

"There," George said. "Right there. On your right."

Blaze looked and saw a Saab. It didn't look like the right kind of car at all.

"For Christ's sake," George said. "Your right, dummy. Your right. That's your left."

"I'm sorry, George," Blaze said. George was right, he was being a dummy again. Right, the hand you write with. He thought of that hand and looked to the other side. There was a dark green Ford there, a '70 or a '71. Blaze couldn't tell them apart after '68 or so.

Blaze walked over to the Ford with a burlesque of casualness. He looked over his shoulder. The beer-joint, a college joint calle The Bag (stupid name; a bag, that was what you called your balls), was a walk-down. There was a band on Friday night. It would be crowded and warm inside, lots of little girls in miniskirts. It would be nice to go in someplace warm and have a beer, just look—

"What are you supposed to be doing?" George's voice prodded him harshly. "Walking on the Champa-Elesis? You couldn't fool my old blind granny. Just cut the act and do it, huh?"

"Okay, okay, I was just—"

"Yeah, I know what you was just. Keep your mind on your busines

"Okay. Sorry."

George always said that if you were a dummy you were a dummy and there was no shame in it but you had to recognize it. You didn't fool anybody, not the cops, not the judge, not the jury, not the warden, nobody. If you were a dummy, you just got in and did your business and got out. Boom. And if you got caught, you spilled everything except the guys with you. You spilled it because they were going to get it anyway. A dummy can't lie worth shit, was George's view.

Now he took his hands out of his pockets and flexed them twice. The knuckles popped audibly in the cold, still air, like the crack of ice.

"I'm going in for a beer, Blaze. Take care of it."

Blaze felt panic rise in his throat. "Hey, no. I ain't done this before. I just watched you. I—"

"Your play, Blaze. Shake it and make it."

"George—"

But George didn't answer. Blaze could hear the hard crunch of snow as he went toward the beer-joint.

"Jesus," Blaze said miserably. "Oh, Jesus Christ."

But his fingers were getting cold. At this temperature they would only be good for five or six minutes at the most, and he was wasting time.

Shake it and make it.

He went around to the driver's side and the door was unlocked. A buzz went up when he opened it, but he ignored that. If you get caught, you get caught. He pulled the hood release and pulled it. He found the second catch in front and opened it up.

There was a small penlite in his pocket and now he took it out, turned it on, and trained the light on the engine.

Find the ignition wire.

But there was so much spaghetti. Battery cables, hoses, plug-wires, gasline—

There.

He reached in and pulled it free. Now what? It was cloudy in his mind. That's what you get for being a dummy. You watch it but you can't remember it, no more than the multiplication tables. It made him think of Mrs. Kweakin and the flash cards and how he hated them. Whenever she brought them out of her desk he felt like throwing up.

BLAZE

He began to fiddle around apathetically, without much hope, when it came to him in a flash. The solenoid, that was it! But you had to bend the cover up. That was why he had the screwdriver.

He took it out, fingers getting very numb now, and pried up the cover on the solenoid. Now you had to do it a certain way or you could burn everything all out. Why the Christ couldn't George wait a little longer? Why--

The wire seemed to jerk forward involuntarily in his hand and make contact. There was a yellow spark, a hot smell, and a sudden audible tick in the cold air. Then the engine cranked over, struggling a bit in the cold. It coughed twice and then idled.

Blaze stepped back and did a clumsy, delighted jig in front of the raised hood. Then he slammed it and went around to the driver's seat.

He paused getting in. What about George? Should he go and get him or wait out here? He sat inside the car and frowned at the empty key-slot. The dome-light cast a yellow light on his hands.

Screw him. George had left him to hitch-hike in, had left him to do the dirty work, he could just thumb a ride back himself.

Blaze closed the door, dropped the gear-shift into drive, and pulled out of the parking space. Once in the lane of travel, he stepped down heavily and the Ford leaped forward, rear end fish-tailing on the hard-packed snow.

He slammed on the brakes, suddenly stiff with panic. What was he doing, what was he thinking of, go without George? Get picked up on the first corner? Blow everything? He couldn't go without George, no way.

George is dead.

No. No. That isn't right. He was just here. He went in that place for a beer.

Why don't you get off it? He's dead.

"Oh George," Blaze moaned. He was hunched over the wheel, shaking. "Don't be dead." The Ford's engine burbled and purred. The gas guage said three quarters of a tank. The exhaust rose behind it, white and frozen.

George didn't come out. George was dead and had been for over 3/4 month.

After a little bit, Blaze got hold of himself and began to drive. No one stopped him on his way out of town. By the time he

got out past the Apex town line, he was doing fifty. The car slid
the tiniest bit on some of the icy patches, but this did not bother
him. He had been driving ~~Maine roads~~ in all weather since he ~~had~~
~~ten~~ ~~~~ *16,*

Outside of town he pushed it up to sixty and let it ride there.
The high beams of the stolen Ford reached far down the road, re-
bounding brilliantly from the snowbanks on either side. Boy, there
was going to be one surprised college kid when he took his girl
out to that empty slot. The thought made Blaze smile.

He twisted the dial on the radio until he found a country music
station. By the time he reached the shack, he was singing along with
Jerry Reed at the top of his voice: "Put all the money in an let's
roll 'em again; when you're hot, you're hot!"

He had forgotten all about George.

BLAZE

Chapter 2

But he remembered the next morning.

That was the curse of being a dummy; you were always being surprised by grief, because you could never forget the little bit that managed to seep over the high, stupid wall of your skull. Like that poem Mrs. Selig had made them learn in the fifth grade: Under the spreading chestnut tree, the village smithy stands. That had been twenty-five years ago, but he could still say that poem right off. And in another twenty-five he could still see his stupid hands peeling potatoes for two and be overwhelmed afresh by the knowledge that George had turned into topsoil.

Not grief, exactly. You didn't grieve for the likes of George. But the lonliness and the hurt. The fear.

(George: "Will you change your fuckin skivvies? Or is the Hershey company givin premiums now?"

(No one to tell him now and that had a name and the name was green and it was fear.)

When he got up the morning after the car, George was in the other room. "You screwed up again, King Kong."

Blaze hissed when his feet hit the cold floor, and he fumbled his shoes on. Naked except for them, he ran and looked out the window. No car. He sighed with relief, and his breath made a little puff of vapor.

"No I didn't, George. I put it into the shed, just like you told me."

"You didn't wipe the goddam tire tracks, though, did you? Why don't you just put up a neon sign, Blaze? THIS WAY TO THE HOT CAR, ADMISSION A QUARTER. Why don't you just do that?"

"Aw, George—"

"Aw, George," George mimicked savagely. "Go out and sweep them."

"Sure, okay." He started for the door.

"Blaze?"

"What?"

"Do me a favor, okay? A little one?"

"Sure."

"Put on your pants. Frostbite of the cock is worse than VD."

Blaze felt his face burn dully. George knew how to put the needle in, all right. He could always do that. Only he'd put it in once too often, and in the wrong guy. That was how you ended up—

"George?" He cocked his head, listening. "You there, George?"

No answer.

That was how you ended up dead.

And George was dead, all right. He had been making up his voice again, in his mind. He and George had been at a floating crap game behind an empty warehouse near the Portland docks, and George had wound up dead. Simple as that.

"George?" He called. "George, don't be dead no more."

No answer.

I'm crazy for even trying to go through with this, Blaze thought. A dum-dum like me.

But he pulled on his underwear shorts (checking them carefully for stains first), then a thermal undershirt, two flannel shirts, a pair of heavy courderoy pants, his Sears workboots, then his old Army parka. He hunted for his mittens and finally found them on the shelf over the delapidated woodstove in the middle of the combination kitchen-living room. He got his checkered cap with the ear-flaps and put it on carefully. Then he went out and got the broom leaning against the door.

The morning was awesomely bright, bitter cold. He felt the moisture in his nose crackle immisidately, and a sudden gust of wind that drove powdered snow before it made his eyes wince protectively. It was all right for George to give orders and then stay inside where it was warm, drinking coffee. Like last night, him taking off to get a beer while Blaze had to figure out how to get that fucking car going. Sometimes he didn't think George was a very good friend.

He swept the sharp-treaded snow-tire tracks away with the broom, working down the short driveway. He stopped at the end and leaned on the broomhandle. The plow had gone by in the night, pushing back the snow-dunes the wind drove across these high-banked country roads, and any other tracks were gone.

Blaze tromped back to the shack, shoes squeaking against the snow, and went inside. He undressed and put on the coffee pot. Then he found a country music station on the radio and sat down in his thermal undershirt and cords. Loretta Lynn was singing that your good girl is gonna go bad. That song always made Blaze feel sad.

When the coffee was hot, he jumped up and poured two cups, one with cream. He took them to the table and hollered: "George? Here's your coffee!"

No answer.

RICHARD BACHMAN
BLAZE

With a foreword by **STEPHEN KING**

Lost for years amongst Stephen King's papers,
and published now for the first time ever, *Blaze*
is a heartstopping thriller with the power
of a noir fable.

Clay Blaisdell is one big mother, but his capers are strictly small time
until his mentor introduces him to the one big score that everyone
dreams of: kidnap. But now the brains of the operation has died – or
has he? – and Blaze is alone with a baby as hostage. The Crime of the
Century has just turned into a race against time in the white hell of
the Maine woods.

Brutal and sensitive, gripping and poignant, *Blaze* is reminiscent of
John Steinbeck's *Of Mice and Men*.

King's 'dark half' Richard Bachman published five novels in his
'lifetime', and *The Regulators* after he died of cancer of the
pseudonynm. *Blaze*, written in 1973 before *Carrie*, has been updated
by Stephen King in 2007. *The Bachman Books*, *Thinner*, *The Running
Man* and *The Regulators* are all available from Hodder.

HODDER

STEPHEN KING

CARRIE

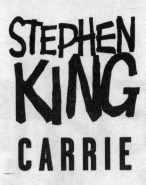

STEPHEN KING

CARRIE

Carrie White is no ordinary girl. Carrie White has a gift – the gift of telekinesis.

To be invited to Prom Night by Tommy Ross is a dream come true for Carrie – the first step towards social acceptance by her high school colleagues.

But events will take a decidedly macabre turn on that horrifying and endless night as she is forced to exercise her terrible gift on the town that mocks and loathes her . . .

'You can't help admiring King's narrative skills and his versatility as a storyteller' – *Sunday Telegraph*

'King's imagination is vast. He knows how to engage the deepest sympathies of his readers . . . one of the great storytellers of our time' – *Guardian*

HODDER

STEPHEN KING

BAG OF BONES

STEPHEN KING

BAG OF BONES

When Mike Noonan's wife dies unexpectedly, the bestselling author suffers from writer's block. Until he is drawn to his summer home, the beautiful lakeside retreat called Sara Laughs.

Here, Mike finds the once familiar town in the tyrannical grip of millionaire Max Devore. Devore is hellbent on getting custody of his deceased son's daughter and is twisting the fabric of the community to this purpose.

Three-year-old Kyra and her young mother turn to Mike for help. And Mike finds them increasingly irresistible.

But there are other more sinister forces at Sara Laughs. Kyra can feel them too . . .

'Splendid entertainment . . . Stephen King is one of those natural storytellers . . . getting hooked is easy'
– Frances Fyfield, *Express*

'An incredibly gifted writer, whose writing is so fluid you often forget that you're reading' – *Guardian*

HODDER

STEPHEN KING

MISERY

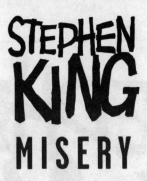

STEPHEN KING

MISERY

Misery Chastain was dead. Paul Sheldon had just killed her –
with relief, with joy. Misery had made him rich; she was the
heroine of a string of bestsellers. And now he wanted to get on
to some *real* writing.

That's when the car accident happens, and he wakes up in pain
in a strange bed. But it isn't hospital. Annie Wilkes has pulled
him from the wreck, brought him to her remote mountain
home, splinted and set his mangled legs.

The good news is that Annie was a nurse and has pain-killing
drugs. The bad news is that she has long been Paul's Number
One Fan. And when she finds out what Paul has done to
Misery, she doesn't like it. She doesn't like it at all.

And now he has to bring Misery back to life. Or else . . .

'Not since Dickens has a writer had so many readers by the
throat' – *Guardian*

'King has inspired a whole generation to read. He's made them
read good, witty prose . . . a fabulous teller of stories' – *Express*

HODDER

STEPHEN KING

THE SHINING

STEPHEN KING

THE SHINING

Danny is only five years old but in the words of old Mr Hallorann he is a 'shiner', aglow with psychic voltage.

When his father becomes caretaker of the Overlook Hotel, Danny's visions grow out of control.

As winter closes in and blizzards cut them off, the hotel seems to develop a life of its own. It is meant to be empty. So who is the lady in Room 217 and who are the masked guests going up and down in the elevator? And why do the hedges shaped like animals seem so alive?

Somewhere, somehow, there is an evil force in the hotel – and that too is beginning to shine . . .

'Obviously a masterpiece, probably the best supernatural novel in a hundred years' – Peter Straub

'As a storyteller, he is up there in the Dickens class' – *The Times*

HODDER

STEPHEN KING

KING

THE STAND

STEPHEN KING

THE STAND

After the days of the plague came the dreams.

Dark dreams that warned of the coming of the dark man. The apostate of death, his worn-down boot heels tramping the night roads. The warlord of the charnel house and Prince of Evil.

His time is at hand. His empire grows in the west and the Apocalypse looms . . .

'His work plumbs with unnerving accuracy, the hopes and fears of an entire nation' – *Observer*

'As a storyteller, he is up there in the Dickens class' – *The Times*

'A writer of excellence . . . King is one of the most fertile storytellers of the modern novel' – *The Sunday Times*

HODDER

Masterly paperbacks by Stephen King and available from Hodder

Fiction

9780340951415	Carrie
0450031063	'Salem's Lot
9780340951392	The Shining
0450042685	Night Shift
9780340951446	The Stand
0340899034	The Dead Zone
0340899042	Firestarter
0340899050	Cujo
0340899077	Different Seasons
0450058786	Cycle of the Werewolf
9780340951408	Christine
0340674458	The Talisman (With Peter Straub)
0450057690	Pet Sematary
0450411435	It
0340899085	Skeleton Crew
0340899069	The Eyes of the Dragon
9780340951439	Misery
0450488357	The Tommyknockers
045052468X	The Dark Half
0450542882	Four Past Midnight
045057458X	Needful Things
0450586235	Gerald's Game
0450588866	Dolores Claiborne
0450610098	Nightmares and Dreamscapes
0450608484	Insomnia
0340640146	Rose Madder
0340654287	Desperation
9780340951422	Bag of Bones
0340765593	The Girl who Loved Tom Gordon
034073891X	Hearts in Atlantis
0340770724	Dreamcatcher
0340770740	Everything's Eventual
0340770708	From a Buick 8
0340829753	The Dark Tower I: The Gunslinger
0340829761	The Dark Tower II: The Drawing of the Three
034082977X	The Dark Tower III: The Waste Lands
0340829778	The Dark Tower IV: Wizard and Glass
0340836156	The Dark Tower V: Wolves of the Calla
9780340836163	The Dark Tower VI: Song of Susannah
9780340836170	The Dark Tower VII: The Dark Tower

Writing as Richard Bachman

9780340952269	Thinner
9780340952283	The Running Man
9780340952252	The Bachman Books
9780340952276	The Regulators

Non-Fiction

0340820462	On Writing (A Memoir of the Craft)
0340899093	Danse Macabre

Hodder paperbacks are available at all good bookstores.